WHERE

the

WHAT IF ROAMS

and

THE MOON

is

LOUIS ARMSTRONG

a novel

ESTHER KRIVDA

Wobble Hill
·Press·

Library of Congress Control Number: 2016909151
Wobble Hill Press, Bronx, NY

ISBN: 0997589205
ISBN 9780997589207

Cover design and illustration copyright ©2016 Julie Reed

Advance Praise for *Where the What If Roams and the Moon is Louis Armstrong*

"Esther Krivda's debut novel, *Where the What If Roams and the Moon Is Louis Armstrong*, is a special kind of book, the kind of book that warrants many readings and a future CliffsNotes edition. It is a long, heady emporium of a book. Krivda herself describes it as a modern psychological fairy tale. Indeed, there are fairies in this book. But her own description almost belies, or at least over-simplifies, the ambitious nature of this marvelous and virtuosic work. This is the kind of book that scares off publishers, intimidates readers, and announces a major literary talent.

"*Where the What If Roams* alludes to both William Shakespeare's *A Midsummer Night's Dream* and Jonathan Swift's *Gulliver's Travels*. Krivda borrows from both. Dueling narrators, a self-aware author, and a rambunctious band of fairies constantly bicker and interrupt each other in the retelling of the central narrative, which revolves around a ten-year-old girl named Sophia Oomla, who, though she has trouble speaking, dreams of becoming a movie star.

"Swiftian satire is at work in the parallel stories of Sophia's parents: her mother, Sigrid, who works in the New York–like city of Goliathon as CEO of Giggle, Inc., and her father, Sigmund, who works as a Freudian psychoanalyst in the Institute, a mental hospital treating distressed movie stars, or "Artistes." The plot focuses on one pivotal week in the lives of these and supporting characters, and Krivda uses italics to break out their polyphonic inner thoughts.

"The author's technique doesn't so much produce stream-of-consciousness as it does rivers-of-consciousness. The writing is expansive, effusive, fluidly stylish, and full of quirky energy. Krivda unleashes multiple modifiers in her longer constructions, "her sparkly, coaxy, tickly, with-a-cherry-on-top voice," and shorter fragments in moments of dramatic tension: "She waited. And waited. Somebody was coming. Somebody. Was." This variety in construction, combined with an ample vocabulary and a propensity for neologisms like "CEOing," create an overall musical experience. Krivda is a verbal acrobat performing the rhythms of her imagination across the page: cartwheeling, dancing, pirouetting when needed.

"Yet her playful loquaciousness doesn't preclude moments of plaintive realism. Getting to the heart of her characters, Krivda's wording and tone shift the way a magician's cape shifts, revealing some sad and indelible reality of the human condition: "And he felt every inch of that vast, friendless space. He could have used some human companions. And a real hero. And not a room full of fancy. And a mind full of guilt."

"Though Krivda describes the novel as a "crossover" for both young readers and adults, it might be too challenging for early teen readers. But for older teens, and for adults especially, this is a fantastically important book about sorting out a cacophony of inner voices to find one's true voice. As Louis Armstrong, appearing as the Man in the Moon, reminds us toward the end of the book, "There never'll be another sound like the sound of you."

—Clarion Foreword, five out of five stars

"Debut author Krivda offers a fairy tale of sorts, about a young girl and her eccentric relatives.

The Oomlas are a tightknit, humble family. As Dr. Sigmund Oomla points out, "A rainy, foggy, snowy, hurricane could never blow away our us-time!" This "us-time" often involves Mrs. Oomla testing out her new beverage ideas on her gentle husband and her daughter, Sophia. When one of her concoctions sends the family into a fit of giggling, she knows she's hit upon a winner. Years later, the family is wealthy, though not exactly happy. In spite of the fact that they live in an enormous home and have loyal servants, the Oomlas still have personal difficulties. Sophia, for example, has a hard time speaking in school; Dr. Oomla, a psychoanalyst at the playfully named Institute for the Compassionate Care of the Extraordinary and the Always Interesting, sees his job changing and his fundamental principles challenged; and Mrs. Oomla, now a powerful, self-made CEO, feels a sting of guilt over her family's newfound wealth, as well as discontent over the pushiness of big business. Thrown into the mix are a group of fairies who narrate, comment and interject on the proceedings throughout. "Readers, as you already know, I'll be telling this story," says the narrator early on. "And so, alas, will the Fairies. I must apologize in advance for the interruptions." Krivda's book is ambitious, silly and given to episodic humor, as when Sophia feels she's been wronged by a trusted servant: "Betrayed by a person with an accent! Her favorite kind of person!" It makes for a wild romp in a fantastical world of engaging characters. ...Overall, this lengthy book manages a starkly creative style, but it's one that may be too thick for fans of lighter fairy-story fare.

A dense, wavering and eccentric adventure."

—Kirkus Reviews

To my family and to M forever …

"There is something in us that is wiser than our head."
Mr. A. Schopenhauer

"Why, oh why, don't we listen to it?"
Ms. E. Krivda, Your Author

"O, what may man within him hide ..."
Mr. W. Shakespeare

"Which we now seek ..."
Ms. E. Krivda, Your Author

• • • DRAMATIS PERSONAE • • •

PLACE – THE UNIVERSE

• • • THE HUMANS • • •

Dr. Sigmund Oomla, The Father, A Psychoanalyst
Mrs. Sigrid Oomla, The Mother, The Inventor
Sophia Oomla, The Daughter, Our Heroine
Great Aunt Hortense
Ms. Esther Krivda, Yours Truly, Me The Author
Miss Kitty, The Irish Cook And Nanny
Mr. James, The English Butler And Chauffeur
The Grandfather, Solomon Oomla
The Grandmother, Sarah Oomla
And A Cast Of Characters, Including An Old Chief, A
New Chief, Many Madcap Artistes And The Dancing Pink
Flamingos

• • • THE EMISSARIES • • •

The Fairy Mimi Meselk, aka The All-About-Me Fairy,
aka Me
The Fairy Lorraine Mafairyia Gambino, aka The Mafairyia Fairy,
aka Lorraine
The Fairy Prudence Priss Primly, aka The Rules-And-Regulations Fairy,
aka Thee
The Fairy Beatrice Nikola Om, aka The Beatnik Fairy,
aka Be
The Fairy Freesia Free, aka The Fairy From Tongue-Tied-Mountain,
aka Free
The What If, An Atomic-Sized Agitator
The Louis Armstrong Moon

·
·
·

Midsummer
Twilight

·
·
·

Dear Readers:

All I heard was a voice.

Things were looking up.

That one wasn't in my head.

You should've heard the ones in there, Readers. I'd had to. All day. They were carrying on so much, you'd've thought I'd told them to strap on megaphones and then vent away, like my soap-box was their soap-box, my mind, their mind. I was desperate to work on my novel and they were desperate for me not to and, to get their way, they were on some kind of a rampage.

Or were they just playing?

Could they be the monkeys of monkey mind? In my mind?

Were there monkey bars in there? Beats me.

Those minxes!

Or maybe desperate was right. Maybe something in my mind had a mind of its own that was of the opinion I needed - what? - a prince! No! a book contract!

Did I wonder why I had such unfriendly friends inside myself? Or why they - whoever-they-were - were desperate for me not to work on my novel? Or that I wanted to do one thing and my mind, the exact opposite? Not then. I was at its mercy then. It started out tip-toeing through my mental-tulips, making me, for one delightful hour, all dreamy but when it began slamming me the next for what I didn't have and might never have, it must've knocked out the groundskeeper. And then it just ran amok. The pining away, chirping, pecking, informing, mis-(and diss!)informing, spooking, harping I'd had to endure that day! I was a house-divided-against-itself, capable of typing 'minx-ey see, minx-ey do' over and over but not of writing a novel. I couldn't shut any of them up no matter how much I tried.

To blow the lot of them out of there I'd need some fresh air. So I went to Writers Alley to keep company with grass and trees and bushes and busts of long dead writers, all of whom never, not seldom, say any sort of word, let alone a discouraging one, to anybody.

And that's when I heard it.

"Writer darling?"

It was a stunner and it wasn't inside my head. It was coming from the other path. And I crossed over. No, I leaped over.

Why wasn't I afraid?

I should've been. I am from the Big City after all and my Mother always told me that when a man speaks to me from a bush, I should run. But she never said I shouldn't speak to a diva in a bush, especially one from the red-hot-epicenter-of-the-planet. Planet-show-off. If that voice wasn't in haute-couture clothing, I don't know what was. Its owner had to be seen to be believed. Surely, if I took a quick peek, no harm would come to me.

I know - famous last words.

"Come closer."

I did.

I saw no one.

And then the strangest thing happened.

As if by magic, I heard two completely different voices!

And I still saw no one.

But what was even odder, Readers, those new voices were coming from inside my head!

That again.

"Sophia, you can come out now. It's safe. Great Aunt Hortense has left. What did you do? Did you really spit on Great Aunt Hortense? And why wouldn't you talk to her?"

"I—"

"She said you didn't talk to her at all. Why wouldn't you talk to her?"

"Mothe—"

"Great Aunt Hortense is sometimes a little scary. Is that why you wouldn't talk?"

"I was—"

"But spitting, Sophia!"

"It wasn—"

"You know you're never supposed to do that, little princess!"

"It flew—"

"So next week, answer whatever question she asks you. I'll help you. This week, I want you to talk a lot. To talk to me a lot. To your Father. I hear you talk. But I can't always see the people you talk to - like Captain Red. This week, I want you to talk to people I can see. And you can see. That all of us can see."

"I—"

"I know you can do that. Come and talk to me."

"I—"

"No more invisible people. I'll be happy to help you with your con ver sa tion. That's when people talk to each other – back and forth – one person says something, the other listens and then says something in response to what the person just said. Like, How are you today? And the other answers, I'm fine. You'll be just brilliant at it, little princess!!"

"I—"

The voices stopped.

How dare that Mother not let her daughter finish a sentence! How could anyone be so overbearing! And how, pray tell, could a Mother not notice that as she's explaining what conversation is, of all things, to her daughter, of all people, that she left barely an ounce of space for her to converse in!

Readers, is that what you're thinking?

But you weren't there, were you? I heard that Mother's voice. I wanted to know her, talk like her. I longed for her to keep talking.

Longed?

What is this? A potboiling-melodrama? I assure you, it isn't. But what a hold that voice had on me, how could I ignore it?

I'll try to put into words what I heard.

Though I used the word ignore just now, get that I-Am-Woman voice out of your head. A voice like that speaks-up and speaks-out, like that diva voice I heard coming from that bush. There was nothing up-and-out about this voice. I tried to place it.

Was there such a thing as a Voice Museum?

Because it sure didn't come from our time. I don't know what it would've been to your ears, Readers, but to mine, it was like that voice that sang 'happy birthday mr. president' ever so long ago. But could there still be a modern woman who caressed then blew a kiss into and onto, up and down and all around each and every word? could someone still be SO girly-girl? in our age of gender-neutrality with its unwritten commandments, like, "Daughters of Eve! Be kittenish no more! Thou shalt not meow! For thou too must bring home the bacon! Go forth! And roar!"

That slip-of-a-thing! Bringing home the bacon? And would she have even known how to roar?

There I stood, speculating.

I came to.

How did that little girl feel about her Mother's voice?

Some come to! For on my next blink, I was luxuriating in what was left of it still vibrating within me! Cold comfort for our small heroine, Readers.

And then I really came to. That little voice! So stepped on! Its owner's feelings so unexpressed!

Just like mine were!

For hadn't I been dying to write my novel but been instead pounded on that entire day by all those head visitors. Well, wasn't she pounded on, too - albeit by a feather-duster, but pounded on just the same.

Hah! so much for a trip to a park to escape overbearing voices!

How did that girl feel about her Mother's voice? Did she think it better than her voice?

Wait! didn't I think the same thing? Isn't that why it took me so long to realize that the girl wasn't being heard?

And how did I feel about those monkeys from my own, as Shakespeare would say, 'vasty deep' who were undermining me? Who were these imps that lived inside me that made me feel puffed up one minute and shot down the next? Why did they want to do that? That certainly couldn't be me thinking all that. I mean, how could it be? Why would any reasonable person want to make themselves feel like a dodo one minute, and Einstein, the next? That's what I wanted to know.

So what would I like to know about her? Let's start with what I know. She sounded a little wobbly, very sweet and a bit sad. And did you notice that little girl didn't get mad and she sure didn't shut her Mother up?

Wait a minute - I didn't get mad either. I hate to get mad. Because I'm a creampuff with mush for a back-bone who prefers living in a fight-free-zone. Did she prefer the same thing? Was she just a different size creampuff?

I knew this - if I didn't stop those pests, and she didn't stop her Mother, they'd just go on interrupting, interfering, making us doubt ourselves forever.

Forever?

Okay, already! voices had been inside my head sounding off for quite a while. I hate to admit that but I didn't want any more interference! from! a! single! soul! That's what really made me long, Readers. I've wanted that for a while now. Maybe she felt haunted, too. Maybe that little girl was even trying to be her own narrator. Like I was. Maybe I'd found a kindred spirit.

Anyway, that's why I agreed to tell this story about the girl named Sophia Oomla. I was assured by that bush-diva who told me this tale that I'd watch that little girl stand up to her Mother; and because I was the one who wrote about it, I'd been known forever after as the champion of those who need to stand up for themselves.

But that bush-diva was a trickster who'd figured out that I wanted to be a champion. That I dreamed of standing up to pests. That I even had pests.

How did it know?

Because that trickster was a certain kind of trickster. Guess who that was and you're on your way to understanding just what that little girl and I were up against; and what you, dear Readers, are in for.

A kind of trickster? Remember when I heard those voices? Midsummer. Twilight. The time of year when certain creatures fly free throughout the mortal world. I'll spell it out: that voice in its haute-couture clothing belonged to a Fairy (yes, bush-diva was a Fairy); that Mother, that daughter were the mortals. The Fairy set a trap in Writers Alley for 'a writer who would, like, hear my tale, type it up all grammatical, with, like, loads of literary devices and then publish it in your, like, human world!' And as I gazed at that bust of Charles Dickens, I 'so looked the part,' I had to be it!

Incidentally, now that you know this story's source, don't be surprised if you do not understand all the events that you are about to encounter on these pages. Some of the events may actually stump you. In desperation you may even run to scientists to help you. Don't ask scientists. They'll be stumped, too. And when both you and the scientists are stumped and unable to explain every little thing, most of you will be able to live with that. But for those of you who won't, whatever you do, don't go running to the Know-It-All Society and ask them for an explanation. You'll be tempted. For one thing you won't have to run very far. They're everywhere. Just don't do it. Because faster than you can say "smarty pants," they'll rattle off an explanation. And they'll be wrong. They'll be just as stumped as the scientists but will never admit it.

And speaking of haunting! And the Know-It-All-Society! That! Fairy! was in my ear the whole time I was writing this tale. And she kept taking control of the narrative and undermining my authorial authority!! So much for being my own narrator! I - that's right, me, the creampuff - had a fight on my hands! You already know how I feel about that! That! pushy! Fairy! even wrote her own letter to you and she insists it follow this letter. En garde! the dueling letter!

Sincerely,

Esther Krivda

(me, the author)

Reader Darlings!

Bush Diva! Haugh! I'm The Fairy Mimi Meselk. But call me Mimi Me. Or just Me.

That Mother? That daughter? I magic-wanded their voices into Esther's head! There is a Father and they are the Oomlas and I am here to tell their story. Why, you wonder? Well, I'm really a Fairytarian: that's like a Humanitarian but instead of a human doing good for just humans, it's like a Fairy doing good for, like, everybody. Good? But what about evil? Don't Fairy Tales have villains in them? Who's the villain in this tale? That Mother who wouldn't let her daughter get a word in edgewise? Alas, Readers, evil has taken a beating in our modern age, what with the invention of psychology that says evildoers just Do evil but ARE not evil, they're not even devils, so that even we Fairies must watch our tongues when telling tales. But though this Fairy Tale may not contain kinglets and enchantresses and dragons, their modern equivalent - CEOs and Movie Stars and corporations - trample all over these pages (and these characters) and you just might encounter - I shan't say - the psychology-police might shut us down. Silly Author darling wanted to begin; I wanted her to write some back-story. So back-story it is and that section is called 'tick-tick-tick.' In it you'll meet the Oomlas and peek into their minds, their lives, find out what makes them ... you know ... tick. And then on to the section called 'that-week-in-February-five-years-later,' when this story really begins, when their tick-tick-ticks go ! ! !

Sincerely,
The Fairy Mimi Meselk
(Me, the Fairy)

(The nerve of that Author! Stealing my Moniker! Well then, notice if you please, I am the Capital Me)

Readers!

Just as I was to begin with Tick One - the tick that introduces Me-the-Fairy and her Emissaries-from-the-Universe pals - Me, That! Fairy! insists that she! begin instead since she! is an actual Emissary from the Universe and the expert on all things Emissary. So apparently not only must my Fairy Overseer! write her own letter to you, she! must tell you about Tick One. (You see what I mean about undermining my authorial authority?) In fact, from here on in, it'll be a tug of war between me and my Me shadow.

(Am I never to get away from these hounds?)
Beware the dueling narrators!

Sincerely,
Esther Krivda
(me, the author)

•
•
•

Tick

Tick

Tick

•
•
•

• • • TICK ONE: EMISSARIES FROM THE UNIVERSE • • •

"Reader darlings, Me, the Fairy here! Welcome to my world! My story! Parallel to your United States of America is our United States of Enchantica which is where I as well as the other Emissaries hail from. There is a pact between your U.S.A. and our U.S.E. and that pact is why I and my colleagues were in the U.S.A. to begin with, and why we knew that daughter, Sophia Oomla, and became acquainted with her family. And that pact is: five Emissaries from the Universe are placed inside the heads of all U.S.A. children until they turn eleven-years-old. Where we actually live is in a spot deep within the heads of children. That spot is called the Remarkably Small Place. In the case of Sophia, five fairies were placed inside her Remarkably Small Place. I am one of those five fairies and I am here to tell you what a time I had trying so desperately hard to save her -

"Oh - some of my associates did ... you know ... help ...

"Now about that pact - it is so hush-hush, so unwhisperable, so unbreathable, I simply must tell you about it. The U.S.E. supplies the U.S.A.'s under-eleven-year-old children with Emissaries from the Universe in exchange for the U.S.A. granting a free-fly-zone to the U.S.E. Your technology has improved so much that our Emissaries were having their flights tracked by your warp-speed-transonic-super-gizmos which filled our Emissaries with much bile and ruptured their spleens something terrible. And everyone knows, even your Government, that no one should mess with an Emissary's spleen or bile and certainly never both, and fly anyone or anything near them when they do. So when the U.S.E. offered the U.S.A. this arrangement, the U.S.A. eagerly accepted it."

Me, are you sure you should be telling the Readers this? Aren't you giving away state secrets?

"Author darling? How ever will I get caught? Emissaries do not read the books of humans; trust me on that!"

But humans do!

"Yes, and look where it's gotten you. Now where was I - There were, as I said, five of us, one hailing from Giant City in the U.S.E. - that would be Lorraine, and the rest of us from various states in the U.S.E. You'll meet them all in due course. Our mission was to make sure Sophia was happy, now and ever-after. And by the way, you humans should thank us. For you surely need us. There are just too many of you who can't seem to get over your parents. Long past your youth, so so many of you still have your Mother's and Father's pointy-fingered voices going off in your heads non-stop! I know, because I've been inside many a grown-up's head. That's why I insisted on telling you about those tick tick ticks now before the story begins so that you'll see what was percolating away inside those Oomla minds. Think of it as a sneak peek behind the curtain before their show actually begins. Because of my unique vantage point, you, our Readers, will be front row center inside actual minds."

Not so fast, Me ... did you just say inside Oomla minds? Wasn't your place in the head of their daughter?

"Of course, of course! I was in Sophia's head. Fairies just have a way of finding out things. And it's a good thing for your sakes that there are Emissaries from the Universe! Without us, how ever would you make your way through that jungle inside you? - Now, where was I, darling? Oh! Sophia. We liked to think we were her Happily-Ever-After Fairies. We were there to help her. We were her silent partners. The Fairy Dispatcher, Mr. HB, who assigned us to Sophia's Remarkably Small Place, told us we must never scare Sophia by introducing ourselves to her. So we never did. She will never know, and never find out, we were there. But we were hardly silent. We could've been heard and seen quite clearly by anyone on a walkabout inside Sophia's brain - anyone, that is, who could see inside a black-hole."

• • • TICK TWO: THE VILLAGE VAN DER SPECK • • •

Me, this part is mine.

"Darling, I agree! All things human are yours!"

Up river from That City Goliathon –

Where buildings were fifty times bigger than the tallest dinosaurs -

Where people roared and jawed up the sky even more than those buildings -

Where everyone and everything was packed together like so many sardines that had even those exemplary neighbors been citizens, they too would've turned into snapping turtles–

Lay a village that never grew tall at all - The Village Van Der Speck.

Not only didn't it have tall buildings but it didn't have very much else of what was modern either. Oh, it had electricity and cars and TV and such things as that but it didn't have the fancy stuff that made that gigantic city such a whoosh of a place - cafes where steaming, frothing cappuccino was ready in an instant or sky-high helipads where entrepreneurs from everywhere but Mars landed by the minute or building skins made not of brick but of jungle-colored neon that rippled, pulsated, shrieked and throbbed endlessly day and night -

No - those kinds of tricks hadn't made it to that village.

The city's flotsam and jetsam didn't seem to reach the de minimis village, even though that river had a tidal quirk and sometimes flowed up. But even if some of the litter would've made it that far, those villagers would've been too busy to pick up any water-logged thing that might straggle by. For the denizens of that village - excepting some crabby-contrarians; some sleepy-old-people; and some dog-tired-dogs - worked at the Institute.

• • • TICK THREE: THE INSTITUTE FOR THE COMPASSIONATE CARE OF THE EXTRAORDINARY AND THE ALWAYS INTERESTING • • •

Doctor Edwig Knitsplitter III named it that long ago when he noticed the patients stopped whatever they were doing, even if they were chatting happily, and held their head down and lowered their eyes whenever they passed the gate with the sign that read Insane Asylum. And since that Asylum was packed from its rafters to its basement with patients from Show Business, as Dr. Knitsplitter III's Asylum was a private Institute which specialized in treating people from that business - its Stars, Supporting Actors and Actresses, Directors, Producers, Writers, Studio Musicians, even the people that worked behind the scenes, below the line and beneath the footlights - those were the most dramatically bowed heads and theatrically lowered eyes a person would ever hope to see.

• • • TICK FOUR: MRS. SIGRID OOMLA • • •

Now meet the Mother who wouldn't let her daughter get a word in edgewise - Mrs. Sigrid Oomla. Sigrid could usually be found in her tiny kitchen in the Oomla's cozy cottage, rinsing some fruit or vegetable at her sink. Though she was quite lovely, with those stray hairs poking every which way from her overflowing mane, with that earth from this afternoon's garden expedition on many spots all over her person, you might've had to strain to find that loveliness. But you would've heard it instantly as she talked on the phone. Such playful pronunciations. Everyone wondered where she came from. And such diction, without it ever sounding like she had a diction lesson. Which she had not; although she had spent her early years in England which might've accounted for the tea-gowns around some of her syllables.

When she talked it was like music itself was talking. But when she sang, the world stood still to hear her. For she wrapped unforgettable melodies around her listeners. Her voice was the subject of a constant debate among the Van Der Speckians about whom out of all the lovely voiced persons in the world she sounded like. Until the poets in the village would overhear their discussion and, as they believed they were the official spokespersons for all that was angelic in the world, would say, absolutely not, those women you're naming are mere mortals and Mrs. Oomla hardly sounds like one of them. And with a sumptuosity only they could impart to description and meaning, would, on the spot, conjure up the sweetest lyrics they could dream up, breathlessly, giddily topping each other, attempting to nail the sound of it once and for all.

And, oh, the Van Der Speckians loved to hear her. And, oh, did she love to let them hear her. And, oh, did she love to hear herself. So she talked. And sang. Morning and noon and night.

• • • TICK FIVE: DR. SIGMUND OOMLA • • •

Now meet the husband and Father ... Dr. Sigmund Oomla ... on a typical morning: his 6 Feet 4 Inch, Abe Lincoln sized-frame gamboling down Main Street on his way to the Institute, thinking (thinking always thinking as he was a quiet gentleman with a contemplative nature) some variation of *'Oomla, the Institute has been slipping of late. You mustn't let it slip anymore. The Artistes really need the care and attention only you can give!'* But, as he'd make his way, he'd also regret that he'd only waved to his silent daughter, Sophia, as she sat so very solemnly eating her breakfast. And he'd wish, too, that he'd kissed his wife right smack on the lips as she stood at the stove stirring a huge pot and singing so unforgettably, so like the spring wind itself - instead of only blowing a kiss at her. Because all he usually did was pluck a piping hot scone off the table that was set with the delectable breakfast she'd prepared, wave good-bye and then sail out the back door.

But soon some variation of 'Guilt! Nothing but guilt! My family is perfectly fine. It's the Institute that isn't! I must uphold the traditions of the

Old Chief!' would kick him from behind his curtain. Yet, as he made his way, he'd begin to sing - but not like her. Pitch-perfect her! He could only add his counter-croak to nature's chorus. But croak he would. Even though music ravished his soul far more than his sublimest contemplations ever could; though it nearly hypnotized him and was just about his master; there he would be, croaking up a storm, no matter how those croaks sounded to his acutely discerning ears; and even as the wind added its whispers to his own; and even as he, the psychoanalyst, fleeced the clouds for Rorschach phantoms and inspected the earth for hidden treasures. And even as he surely tripped because he looked up and he looked down but forgot to look in front of him.

• • • TICK SIX: SOPHIA OOMLA • • •

Now meet their daughter. Sophia would have been five-years-old then.

She was usually wearing a soup-pot helmet and hidden away deep inside the inner space of a cupboard a little off, as she said (but only to herself) from the 'Talking World.' And there she'd be, transmitting life and death instructions through a ladle to Captain Red stranded up on Planet Mars.

Unlike her Mother, Sophia didn't talk and talk and talk. Only sometimes. And on those sometimes, she could talk and talk, too. But if she happened to hear herself, she surely didn't love that. And she especially didn't love if other people heard her either.

Sophia loved to hear other people's voices. But she didn't love to hear her own.

'I have a deep voice. I hate deep voices.'

But she loved her Mother's voice. And so too did her Father. Her Mother was a soprano and a virtuoso and her Mother talked exactly like what her Father, the connoisseur, loved. Being around a virtuoso and a connoisseur since she was a tiny baby had had an effect on Sophia. Her ears were just more sensitive than other children's. Her ears heard things most ears would never hear. She heard what an orange said when it was squeezed; she heard the feathers sigh in her pillow when she lay her head down on them at night. And oh! did she hear how people talked. How an old person's words hobbled and shook on creaking canes. And boy! could she hear that bad words zipped around like lit firecrackers no matter who was saying them. But when Sophia heard herself, and listened, really listened, she knew just how much she didn't sound like music or music talking. And she'd become quiet. Very quiet. And then POUFF! away from the Talking World she'd go. For a while.

• • • TICK SEVEN: THAT…THAT…STUFF… • • •

Every night Dr. Oomla would crow as he pranced about the stove, "Oomlagators! It's us-time! A rainy, foggy, snowy hurricane could never blow away our us-time!"

And every night, a rainy, foggy, snowy hurricane couldn't have stopped Mrs. Oomla from holding her experiment either. That's when Dr. Oomla and Sophia got to be that experiment's official guinea pigs; for they were the tasters of a beverage that Mrs. Oomla made fresh daily.

The concoction was something Mrs. Oomla had dreamed up and was always trying to improve. Her most secret wish, her private hope, her highly confidential scheme was that one day she'd get it just-so, and then she'd sell it and make the extra money the Oomlas so genuinely needed. At least, that's what she thought about their money situation. Though her husband was pleased with the modest salary the Institute paid him, she was not. She suspected her husband didn't care for money as much as she did. But she certainly wasn't about to come right out and ask him either. So her secret stayed her secret. She wanted to make him happy and keep him happy, for she loved him; he was her very own Robin Hood. And she knew he loved her, for as he always said, "if moonlight and river sparkles could talk, they'd sound just like you." When they strolled through the village whispering sweet nothings to each other, somebody'd always call out "there goes our perfect little lovebirds." And if her good-deed-doer husband knew that not only did she love him but that she also loved money, what would he think of her then? For how ever could Robin Hood love a fair maiden who didn't want to give away her money? Would he still whisper sweet nothings to her? And would the villagers call them the perfect little lovebirds anymore? No, no, she could never reveal her scheme to him.

So without even losing a moment of chatter time, she toiled away at it daily: boiling, straining, poaching, braising, simmering, mashing, pulping, pulverizing. It tasted something like a juice; an herb; like the extract of a root that she got from a tree in the nearby woods; like a syrup; like the essence of several exotic spices; a fermented berry; a citrus; a flower; bubbling spring water. She had never finalized the recipe because she was never quite satisfied with it, so it didn't have a name. As it simmered in a huge pot on the stove, she was always jiggering around with it, adjusting the ingredients, changing the measurements; all with an eye to improve its consistency and flavor. Effervescence was everything to her and when she realized the store-bought seltzer she added to it would never meet her high standards because she didn't care for the bounce of the bubbles, she'd even learned how to make seltzer, too.

Dr. Oomla and Sophia's job was to taste it.

At the end of the day when she finished her adjusting, the mixture would steam and brew on the back burner as it awaited its verdict. She didn't worry too much about her guinea pigs wanting to participate, since there had only been that one time when all three of them had to race to the bathroom after tasting it, the day she added the wrong kind of day-lily, the laxative kind, to the mixture.

The rule was - Mrs. Oomla went first. The guinea pigs second. But the most important rule was they all had to like it. So far that day hadn't come. Somebody always had some suggestion or complaint.

However, one night, Mrs. Oomla planned a different approach. Instead of mixing the bubbling water directly into the pot of roiling syrup and then pouring the mixture into each cup, she decided to put three tablespoons of the steaming, roiling syrup into each cup first, and then to pour her own special blend of icy chilled bubbling water on top of it. She'd never separated the cold bubbling water from the hot syrup before.

Mrs. Oomla dipped her tablespoon in the brew and measured out three tablespoons in each cup. She brought the cups over to the table, gave one to Dr. Oomla, one to Sophia and set one down for herself. Then she got a bottle of her specially bottled bubbling water, popped the cork and bent the bottle down to pour but the liquid rushed out so fast and the bubbles even faster, she had no choice but to pour into the cup closest to her.

But the bubbles grew then rushed to the top and were about to spill over its edge and Sophia couldn't follow the rule to wait for her Mother; she had to taste first. As the liquid tickled her nose, her face, her cheeks, her throat and everything it touched inside her, she began to giggle.

Mrs. Oomla poured the bubbling water into Dr. Oomla's cup. And as she did, the same thing that happened in Sophia's cup happened in his - the liquid started bubbling up so fast that he too had to drink it immediately or it would've spilled over. And Mrs. Oomla watched in amazement as her husband, Dr. Sigmund Oomla, did exactly what her five year old daughter did. Giggle.

Mrs. Oomla understood Sophia giggling, but Sigmund? Sigmund never giggled. As she reached for her cup, she wondered if there was something wrong with her concoction today and that's why they were both giggling; or maybe there was nothing wrong at all and her husband was giggling to be in cahoots with Sophia. But now that she was about to take her turn, she made up her mind, no matter how it tasted, she wouldn't be silly like them. She poured the bubbling water into her cup and, before it spilled over, she tasted it. A tidal wave of tumbling fingers wouldn't stop tickling her back teeth, her cheek walls, her tongue top, and anything else they encountered on their merry way down. What was it? - the bubbles, the syrup or both? There was nothing she could do. She had to and she did - giggle. The last thing she remembered thinking was there was nothing wrong with her concoction. Nothing at all.

Two guinea pigs. One brew master. All giggling.

Every time one of them would take a sip from their cup, the concoction seemed to reach up and do the same thing all over again, and all they could do was giggle. And they couldn't stop.

And they giggled for hours that turned out to be five minutes, til finally Sophia spoke up, "Mommy, this is delicious. I never giggled when I tasted it before. Daddy giggled. And you giggled. What is this? Giggle Pop?"

Mrs. Oomla burst out laughing. "Sophia, what a great name! I have no idea why it made us giggle. But I did do something different this time. Giggle?Pop? Did I finally get it right?"

She turned to Dr. Oomla and said, "This time I separated the seltzer from the mixture, I wonder if that's why we giggled? But I did change some of the ingredients in the syrup, too. What could have possibly done this to us?"

"You'll need more information to find out," replied Dr. Oomla. "If you wrote down exactly what you did today and what you did on other days, you'll see what you did differently this time. I hope you did because this stuff is very tasty."

"I always write down what I put in and how much. I'll study today's recipe."

Recognizing what a great moment this was for his wife's experiment, Dr. Oomla said, "My dear, it really is delicious. And I like the name too. Giggle Pop! Your experiment is finally finished."

Sophia gushed, "It's Mrs. Oomla's Giggle Pop!"

Dr. Oomla added, "Best tasting drink I've ever had. And the most fun I've ever had drinking anything. It makes you exercise the muscles in your face that you use to laugh. Your funny muscles. It's gotta be good to keep those muscles in shape since those are the muscles you use when you're happy. So it's good for you, too. Everybody needs to laugh. Everybody needs to exercise. And so do faces! And to think my beautiful wife made it AND my beautiful daughter named it!" And he leaned his 6 foot 4 inch frame over and planted kisses all around.

Sophia couldn't believe what she just heard. Her Mother had listened to every word she said AND her Mother didn't talk the whole time AND her Mother AND her Father loved the name Mrs. Oomla's Giggle Pop.

The Oomlas stayed for a little while longer, all of them feeling light-headed and unexplainably happier. Til all of them went to bed.

But that night Dr. Oomla had a nightmare. Something he never had.

The next morning, his body may have been sitting calmly with his wife and daughter at the breakfast table, but his thoughts were anything but, *'Giggle Pop - could that be why I had a nightmare? But Sigrid and Sophia both drank it and I didn't hear a peep out of either one of them all night. They weren't kept awake by the irrational imaginings of a nightmare. Since I was the only one, it couldn't have been the Giggle Pop, because if it had been the Giggle Pop, wouldn't it have bothered them too? But don't I WANT to have dreams, even if they are nightmares? I am a psychoanalyst, after all. I never have nightmares or even dreams. And isn't it odd, on the night I drink this stuff, I do have one. So why wouldn't it have been the Giggle Pop?'*

He wasn't so far-gone that he didn't know what time it was. Time to leave. This morning was Dr. Edwig Knitsplitter IV's weekly staff meeting and he mustn't be late. No one was late for that. No one dared to be.

As he rose from the table, he maintained his calm. Because he was calm, his wife and daughter were calm. And because he rose, they rose. They knew who they were - the perfect family unit. And, just like such a unit was supposed to, they floated towards the front door so harmoniously anyone who'd've seen them, would've agreed that they were in the presence of perfection.

But the wife part of the unit had not a clue that the husband part of the unit was thinking, *'Did Giggle Pop affect my mood?'* though she certainly knew he was thinking; she was used to that by now. However, when they got to the hallway, the husband stepped out of the unit. As he reached for his well worn Doctor's bag, he said something to his wife that he wouldn't have said on any other morning. He could say it because that morning the gentleman didn't weigh his words; the psychoanalyst didn't speculate about the affect those words might have on his relationship with his wife; the connoisseur didn't even worry if his words might affect the harmony in the universe; in fact, the supportive-liberated husband didn't even consider that he himself might be taken for a lord-and-master type from the era when men-were-men and not in touch with their inner dainties, or, for that matter, someone who, in this day and age, had dared to challenge his wife's sacred right, as a person, to pursue her own profession thereby gaining her very own economic power (he certainly knew what she was up to though he'd never said that to her). This morning he just let it rip.

Actually, he didn't let anything rip. The command burst out of him of its own free will, "Sigrid, I must find out what's in your Giggle Pop. Write down a list of each and every ingredient and give it to me tonight."

Though he still hadn't said what he was thinking, *'Did Giggle Pop affect my mood?'*

Readers nobody in the whole world would have felt jarred by his words. Nobody, except the Oomlas. But then the Oomlas had "Ears" with a capital "E." Mrs. Oomla's and Sophia's had popped. Plus Mrs. Oomla's insides were just topsy-turvy, though she said not a word about her condition. She just stared at him dumbstruck, as did Sophia; though both of them were thinking.

'My nice Daddy, bossy? Mr. Valentine? speaking like that? To Mommy? To anybody?'

'My husband, finding fault with ME? Checking up on me? Challenging my right to express myself as I see fit?'

Had only they known each other's thoughts, they could've been not a team, not a unit, but themselves, and each of them could've spoken their truths. Even if their truths were harsh and would sound that way to their sensitive ears. But that connoisseur, that virtuoso and their daughter simply couldn't raise their voices, they couldn't share those thoughts; their thoughts were left to scream inside them. Besides, the virtuoso simply never screamed. She couldn't imagine how thoughts such as hers would have sounded in the Oomla's morning air, especially with the connoisseur standing in that air. Such thoughts, thought she, had to be unpresentable; such thoughts would surely disturb their peace.

And if her Mother wasn't talking, Sophia certainly wasn't either. They could only stare at the Oomla who actually had disturbed the peace.

But just then Dr. Oomla said, "See you later Oomlagators!" so like his old-self, they thought that maybe he was just joking.

Little did they know what his cheer masked; a concern that had been growing second by second. *'Did Giggle Pop affect my mood?'* For Dr. Oomla was a very rare physician in this, our modern, pill-popping age. He did not like to use any artificial liquid or pills to affect the moods of his patients whatsoever at all. Of course, he fully supported the use of medication for genuine illnesses of the body; just not of the mind. He got his patients better through the teachings of his heroes, Dr. Sigmund Freud and the Old Chief of the Institute, Dr. Edwig Knitsplitter III. Period. Even the psychoanalysts at the Institute, who also were quite the exceptional lot among our modern day psychoanalysts, were not quite as devoted as he was to this principle. And he felt very alone at the Institute and missed the long dead Old Chief because of it. The Old Chief, he was sure, would've felt exactly as he did.

As he walked on that morning, all the light bulbs in all the galleries and passageways that were inside his head lit up, *'Surely it affected my mood? My mind? Or am I wrong?'* And he and his deeply held principles began to wonder.

And soon foul weather was blowing inside him.

Readers, because moods are contagious, foul weather began to blow inside Mrs. Oomla, too. And there went the Oomlagator's us-time. Going from pretty good to just barely in no time. Poor Sophia. Little did she know that her parents' minds could suddenly be attacked by snarling, snapping stuff. But then little did her parents know either. All they did know now was their thoughts felt unspeakable. And if any decent harmony-loving-citizens would've heard such stuff, like themselves, or, worse yet, another Oomlagator, they'd have to disown their own stuff. And how, ever, can a person disown themselves?

Minds?

Fairies in Sophia's?

Rainy-foggy-snowy-hurricanes inside her parents'?

Minxes in my own?

What is this - the invasion of the mind-snatchers?

Readers, let the games begin.

• • • TICK EIGHT: WHAT THE FAIRIES BELIEVE • • •

But first, before we go on to that-week-in-February-five-years-later, The Fairy Lorraine, who you haven't officially met yet, wants to tell you about this tick. I warned her you would find it preposterous and that it shouldn't even be in the tick section at all. But she wouldn't hear a word I said.

"Okay, Readers," began The Fairy Lorraine, "we Fairies believe that each of the Oomlas was, like, under a spell!"

I tried to straighten her out.

That's impossible! We humans don't have magic in our world. At least, not the kind of magic you have in the Enchanted Lands, like turning a person into a Pomeranian, for example. Humans can neither cast those kinds of spells nor be put under those kinds of spells. Unless - wait a minute - You didn't put each of them under a spell?

"That's what's impossible!" The Fairy Lorraine snapped. "Our spell casting power is stripped from us the instant we step into your lands! We can only do a few tricks here and there and That! Is! It! Anyway, we know spells! And each Oomla was under a spell! Some kind of a spell where they're, like, trying not to be, like, human, or something. I mean, we Fairies gotsta be Fairies. Fairies loves being Fairies. So why don't humans loves being humans? And hey, that dispatcher told us the Oomlas was good parents. Don't good parents have to not be so thick? Because those Oomlas had stuffing inside their heads that they don't understand even when they act like they do understand! Well, anyway, shouldn't good-parents get out from under their spells so they can, like, raise their children? Yeah! I guess not. So, what gives? Who puts you humans under spells, if we Emissaries from the Universe don't? And since youse don't have witches and wizards, how in the elf-hill do ya get outta'em?

that week in February

five years later

• • • TUESDAY, FEBRUARY 3, 5:00 AM • • •

Mrs. Oomla, splendid in a Tiffany-blue suit, did her best version of a sashay as she made her way down the staircase of her newly-built and re-splendent cottage ('cottage' as in Newport, Rhode Island) talking on her cell phone in a voice that was business speaking splendidly. She hadn't tripped on a single step in those very high-heeled, very fashionable boots of hers; nor had she ripped her splendid blue suit, or even a single article of her clothing, so far, and she was very pleased with herself. And she knew Claude, her stylist, would be, too. It was 5:00 AM and she'd had to dress in the freezing cold, after all. But she must be off to Goliathon for a breakfast meeting with a green bottling manufacturer and her helicopter (not at all green and with such an ugly carbon foot print and oh! was she achingly aware of that) was on her helipad waiting to take her there. Also waiting for her, at the bottom of the staircase, were Miss Kitty the Irish Cook and Nanny, and Mr. James the English Butler and Chauffeur; both of them hanging on her every word.

Miss Kitty wasn't exactly hanging on her every word, because she wasn't really listening to what Mrs. Oomla said. It was more how she said it. And she couldn't have stopped herself if she tried.

Miss Kitty whispered, "Oh! Mr. James, you'dda tink she was singin' songs like tose ladies on t'radio from a long long time ago 'n not talkin' business at-TALL!"

"You know, Miss Kitty, I will say this. I've been in the employ of many a distinguished personage in my day and I don't believe I've ever heard any-one converse about the capital market as if it were a musical revue! Indeed! However, Miss Kitty, as I always seem to have to remind you, we, as her em-ployees, are required to know what she, as our employer, is saying, and not to be distracted by superficialities, pleasant as those may be, because if we are distracted, we won't know what our employer has just asked us to do. And we certainly must not neglect our duties! Remember the purpose of our being here at this hour is to receive instructions and not to hear a concert."

And a blushing Miss Kitty glanced up at Mr. James and was relieved to see him smiling. And in spite of having dragged themselves out of their warm beds at 4:45 AM on this February morning so they'd be at the bottom of the stairs at 5:00 AM, they smiled.

When Mr. James, proper English Butler that he was, put his bare feet on the freezing floor that morning he demonstrated an astonishing command of the language of sailors; until he remembered Disraeli and ceased immediately. Surely Disraeli, that statesman, spoke like a statesman, no matter how inclement the weather or inopportune the moment. Benjamin Disraeli, that great debater, that model citizen, his hero, his countryman, a Prime Minister! Dead for over a century, but very much alive in Mr. James's heart.

When the bitter cold cut Miss Kitty straight to the bone, she demonstrated an astonishing command of the language of blasphemers; until she remembered she'd just been on her knees the night before praying to those very Saints she'd just blasphemed. She hastily apologized - to the Irish Saints - crossed herself and ceased immediately.

Mrs. Oomla reached the landing, and with a wave of her hand, with its French-manicure that had only a few speckles of earth crud under just a few of those nails, and a toss of her hat with its net and feather (net and feather still intact), and that voice of shimmer, they followed her like she was the pied piper. Miss Kitty trundled behind but Mr. James kept up, while Mrs. Oomla carried on as if "yield" and "net profits" and "advertising" were lyrics of a catchy tune. Her voice echoed all about the grand space and Miss Kitty and Mr. James felt like they were floating as they made their way towards the double doors of the entranceway. Mr. James reached the front doors precisely when Mrs. Oomla did but made it appear, by ducking his head behind hers, he was a step behind. Mrs. Oomla put the phone by her side and, spoke to them, changing her tune now to morning. Morning talking splendidly.

"Oh! Dear Miss Kitty, Good Morning, don't forget, hot cereal for both Dr. Oomla and Sophia. Some yogurt with slivered almonds, cranberries and cinnamon. Several different fruits too! Breakfast should be ready by 7:15. I will call you late morning and we can discuss what you should prepare for dinner this evening. Thank you, dear Miss Kitty."

Having her everyday duties sung out just to her, and stout, arthritic Miss Kitty was a mere slip of a thing again listening to Jo Stafford on the radio; a voice she still heard in her dreams. And she blushed like a sixteen year old, "Yes, mu'm, yes mu'm."

"And Mr. James, today is the day of Sophia's first meeting with the speech therapist. The school counselor and Sophia's teacher, Mr. Snoggley, are insisting Sophia see one. Remember the meeting is in the next village over, so please pick her up after school and take her there directly. The appointment is at 3:45 this afternoon. Apparently, this speech therapist is new to that village and works from her home and not from that village's after-school center. Sophia must not be late because the speech therapist's schedule is completely full and she's only fitting Sophia in for a quick fifteen minute evaluation as a favor to the school counselor. The school counselor will be handing the address and the directions to Mr. Snoggley and Sophia knows she is to give those directions to you. This is very important, Mr. James, she mustn't miss this appointment. But I know I can trust you."

"Yes, Madam. Sophia will not only not miss her appointment with the speech therapist, she will be on time for it, I assure you."

"Oh, Mr. James, I know I can count on you. Thank you. And thank you, dear Miss Kitty!"

And Mrs. Oomla walked out the door, then down the path that led to her waiting helicopter.

·∴(⋅·

("Author, darling, I really must interrupt - and Lorraine, I don't care if you hear what I say because now you can't do a thing about it!")

·∴)⋅·

• • • THE FAIRIES ARE IMPERTINENT AND WILL INTERRUPT FREQUENTLY • • •

Readers, as you already know, I'll be telling this story. And so, alas, will the Fairies.

I must apologize in advance for the interruptions. And some of their behavior. You've already met, The Fairy Mimi Meselk. You are about to officially meet The Fairy Lorraine Gambino Mafairyia.

By the way, there are three other Fairies, who I will introduce later on in the story. However, those three are not a handful and I won't have to apologize for them.

"Readers, it's Me. First off, Author darling, apologize? For Me? Without Me, your Readers wouldn't be reading this story, and you, dear Author, would not be telling it. And since I am the expert on Fairies, as I am a Fairy, I will be telling our Readers who we are and where we come from.

"Now, about our poor-little-rich women, Mrs. Oomla. Okay, okay, Lorraine, I might have been hovering a little to the left of Mrs. Oomla and flying over the top of her as she went down those stairs. And as she went down the path. And I might also have had a little to do with her still being in one piece that morning. Readers, you met Mrs. Oomla; those berry blotches! that dirt-digging! Lorraine, I had been spending a lot of time inside Mrs. Oomla kind of helping her - you know - with some of her – her - fashion decisions."

"Ya gotta be kiddin' me, Me!" screamed The Fairy Lorraine. "Ah hah! Now I get it! So that's why that rag doll who never gave an elf's patootie about clothes since I've known her started dressing like a clotheshorse! I can't believe you did that! That was, and is, and will be forever, totally and absolutely forbidden by the Dispatcher, Me! And it's in the rules agreed to in the U.S.E./U.S.A. Pact! You know, we all know, the UseUsa Pact! Every Fairy knows that us Emissaries are only allowed in the Remarkably Small Place of the child they are assigned to and are to never ever go into another person's, especially a grown up's, Remarkably Small Place.

"And not only that - to go in there and attempt to influence that person. Although! What am I thinking? Why am I having a problem believing you'd do that? Rules don't apply to you! Rule don't apply to the Great Me!"

"Alright, Lorraine! I did it! So what? I mean, that woman needed my help! Please! There she was a billionaire! walking around covered in grass stains! I mean - gross! I needed to kind of, like, go in there so I could rule over its occupant. But, like, only in that regard! I mean I just needed to let her know about hotter tastes - my much hotter tastes. Lorraine, you yourself just called her a rag doll! And rag dolls wear rags. Rags that I would've died before I'd ever, like, give to naked people. I was really there that morning just making sure that Mrs. Oomla strutted down the path, you know, the runway model way, with legs over top of feet in shoes going just so and with, you know, that attitude, exactly as I had 'subliminally suggested' she should oh so many times, and in clothes that'd've been good enough for me to wear myself, if I ever'd, like, deem to wear those graceless, boxy human fashions. And here now was Mrs. Oomla not looking boring in the slightest, like so many of those gray drones do in that gray city you color-deprived humans must work in. No! Here was our Mrs. Oomla finally looking good enough for a stroll along our Scamps Elysee - wearing her form-fitting, Tiffany-Blue suit with the skinny, hip-hugging belt; her pale dusty-beige hose; her sandy-tweeded high-heeled boots; her electric-orange hat with its gossamer blue net and its shocking-neon feather; and her silver-shirred gloved finger that hooked that purple passion coat over her shoulder oh so cat-walkingly."

"Over her shoulder? Me, it was freezin' cold outside! Ya wouldn't let her put her coat on?"

"Lorraine! And what, destroy her look! For une petite weathair? I, at least, wanted to start her out right. This is Mrs. Oomla, we're talking about, n'est-ce pas? By the time she was half way down the path, she'd ripped the net, and the feather was only slightly tilted but the rest was in place. Lorraine, ever since Mrs. Oomla invented Giggle Pop and its secret ingredient, daffeine, and then patented them, she could afford anything she wanted, including clothes that only billionaires, Trophy Wives and Rock Stars could buy. And so I had become, like, her advisor, her invisible advisor - Mrs. Oomla didn't have a clue I even existed - making sure that visions of couture plums danced in her head. Couture plums designed by the geniuses of fashion and sewn entirely by the seamstresses of the great couture houses! And tout-le-monde knows they use only the most exquisite fabrics in their clothes. Clothes that are so sumptuous they had to have their, like, pictures taken. And those pictures just had to be put in magazines. And not just any magazines, THE magazines that show THE haute couture. And I would, like, you know, simply make sure Mrs. Oomla saw those pictures and—

"Lorraine, stop looking at me like that! Since when did you become such a goody goody? Mrs. Oomla, like, boarded the helicopter but I stayed. I knew that she would be meeting with Claude her stylist as soon as she got off that helicopter, and it would be his job to keep her looking the way she must for a woman in her position. I mean I couldn't be inside Mrs. Oomla's Remarkably Small Place all the time making Mrs. Oomla stop into Birdoffs, THE store, to see what she couldn't live without before she made her way home. Without my being there, I knew she never would. But I really had to get back inside Sophia. Sophia also needed improvement. But then Sophia was not as resistant to fashion as Mrs. Oomla was. Still, I didn't have that much time left with Sophia, since all Emissaries from the Universe must remove themselves from the premises the second that child turns eleven-years-old. I mean we can visit on Sundays like human relatives do and sit around on the synapse, speaking bon-mots, eating what-nots but we must not live there anymore. Those are the Rules of Enchantment. You see, Lorraine, I did know that. And now that Sophia was ten, I didn't have a lot of time. I still had so much work to do with her. That hair! Those knee scabs! And she had not an ounce of poise! And was so ridiculously bashful! Like that dwarf, Bashful, from our nation's history books! Who remembers him? Dopey, Grumpy, certainly! But Bashful? Anyway I was tired and needed sleep. Oh! How I despised Mrs. Oomla's early hours. If Mrs. Oomla hadn't been able to afford all these clothes, I would've been sleeping with all the rest of you Fairies!"

Thank you, Me! I'm sure my Readers—

"My Readers? Our Readers, writer darling!"

Of course, our Readers. Let me go on.

"By all means, darling. By all means."

Readers, when you see the sign of the Universe - the Moon, the Stars, the Planets - separating the text and then parentheses, inside those parentheses, our Fairy friends shall be having the time of their lives, pining, opining, dissecting, inspecting, quarrelling and preachifying.. And when you see no quotation marks around the more cogent remarks, you'll know its yours truly, me the author, trying to set the record and our Fairies straight.

"Readers," said Me, "still water runs deep. And in this story, what runs between still parentheses will, too!"

Alas, Readers, it'll run shallow, too, at least when the Fairies are at it.

• • • 5:15 AM • • •

As Miss Kitty walked towards the kitchen with Mr. James, she yammered away about what Mrs. Oomla said, and not a peep about how she said it, as if how Mrs. Oomla said things hadn't just enchanted her and didn't every morning.

"SssPEEEEEch terapist! For Sophia! A terapist for Sophia t' be givin' t' speeches? Mr. James, if ye don't mind me sayin'— "

"Do pardon my interruption, Miss Kitty, and do understand that what I'm telling you is confidential, but I overheard a conversation when I was motoring Mrs. Oomla about yesterday. She was on her mobile with the school principal and from what I could ascertain, Sophia doesn't seem to like to talk up in school. So her teacher wants her to take some speech classes with a person known as a speech therapist. A speech therapist, apparently, specializes in the facilitation of oral communication."

"Glorybe t'all tesaintsin HEAVEN! In te WHOtification O whaaat? I never did me own self in all me years walkin' about upon tis grand earth 'eard a suuuch a tiiiiing!! 'N if ye don't mind me sayin' so but I be tellin' ye anyways even if ye do, my dear little Sophia may be dreamy eyed but she talks just fine. 'Nd just grand, if she's talkin' about—

"Well – ah – now - she's talkin' t' me in … ah … funny voic—

"Ah – no - 'n it's not funny at-tall. I didn't meself mean te meaning o' funny. It's – ah - more - well - she can talk jus fine, jus fine, indeed."

Miss Kitty quickly examined Mr. James's face and saw no raised eyebrows. He hadn't noticed her hesitations. And she rushed on.

"Cause I 'eard 'er with me very own ears! Cause she talks t' me, yes she does! Mr. James, she talks t' ye too, doesn't she now?"

"Miss Kitty, she does, but—"

"She does indeed! So right I am ten! 'N make no mistake about it! she can talk. When she wants to!"

"But Miss Kitty, from what I've just discovered, she doesn't seem to want to, like, for example, when her teacher asks her a question or one of her schoolmates tries to talk to her, if I understand the problem correctly, and from all that I overheard, I believe I do understand the problem correctly. And she may be able to talk to you in funny voices but ..."

Miss Kitty turned away to hide her burning cheeks.

"... she can't seem to talk to her teacher and her classmates in her own voice. And, don't forget, for someone so bright, this year, she's been getting abysmal report cards. Her teacher, who seems to be particularly strict this year, says Miss Sophia understands everything just fine; in fact, better than fine, but she just doesn't participate, and hence that's why he feels compelled to give her those low grades. And, from what I understand, it appears she's getting worse. And that, I believe, Miss Kitty, is the problem."

As Mr. James had been talking about her charge, her responsibility, Miss Kitty felt heartsick, *'Me wee Sophia!'* But she was a whole lot more than just heartsick; she was worried sick that he might find out her secret. She had every reason to worry. If he knew what she knew, she might not have a job at the Oomla's anymore. She loved her job and was not about to reveal what she knew to him, even if Mr. James had just revealed what he knew to her. So she wouldn't look at him. *'But only a guilty person won't look at somebody, 'n I certainly better not appear t' Mr. James like I'm a guilty, scheming person, even if I am. Like I'm involved in any subterfuge, even if I am!'* And she burst out gaily, "Oh, Mr. James, sir, ever since I been 'ere ye seem t' sooner or later understand all problems correctly. Mostly!"

'Mostly!!? Kitty Devine, flip! are ye now! Ye askin' for trouble? Tis problem, he better never understand correctly atall!' She'd be in the stew if he did.

"Mostly, Miss Kitty? And what do you mean by mostly?"

"Not mostly! All problems! Where would we be without ye?"

Mr. James had a good laugh and Miss Kitty did her best imitation of one. *'If Mr. James even has te slightest inkling of what I know - Well, I just pray tat I can finally 'n forever fix tis problem - which I think I've almost done - so tat he never does!'*

Mr. James took his seat at the kitchen table and pulled out his half glasses, perched them on his nose and stuck his head deep into his special newspaper that came to him from England. He was looking for articles about the debates in Parliament. Debating was his passion. And even though that newspaper was a week old by the time it reached him here in America, with week old debating news, he read that paper as if those debates had just happened a minute ago and he didn't know who won or lost. Although every time he did read it, he had to resign himself to the fact that he wouldn't be reading about the likes of a Benjamin Disraeli, or a Winston Churchill, which invariably got him thinking about what his Mother always used to say to him, "Now James, the dead aren't going to wake up and parade around for your amusement, are they now? That's what they have theatre for." And even though reading about this current crop of debaters in the newspaper was for him a consolation prize, he still wouldn't be lifting his head out of that paper til breakfast was served.

So as not to disturb Mr. James, Miss Kitty stopped her chattering. She knew it would be useless to try to talk to Mr. James when he was reading about England. She opened up the pantry doors and lifted out her pots and tried not to bang them. Even though, in her humble opinion, anyone reading about that place didn't deserve such civility. Anyone but Mr. James.

So she just banged one.

• • • 5:20 AM • • •

Usually, Mrs. Oomla didn't talk on her helicopter ride to Goliathon.

··∴Ɛ·∴·

("Ya gotta be kiddin' Lady!" interrupted The Fairy Lorraine, "Mrs. Oomla? Not tawking? Like, what is this, an alternate universe?"

"Lorraine, Author darling is correct. Every weekday morning Mrs. Oomla took this same ride and every one of those mornings, her pilot took this same route; over the country, down the river and finally over the city. And I can tell you for a fact that she was dying to chat with the pilot, Captain O'Day. But the helicopter made a lot of noise and even with the headphones and microphone each of them wore, she still would've had to shout to be heard. And darlings, our Mrs. Oomla simply didn't shout because, not only was she an Oomla, but she was a CEO and she had observed that highly polished CEOs of huge corporations do not shout! She had her image to consider, after all!"

Thank you, Me).

··∴꞉·∴·

She didn't chat non-stop, she didn't say the first thing she thought, she didn't break into song, she didn't talk freely, unforgettably; her voice may have fascinated the Van Der Speckians and she may have even been their favorite communicator, but her voice fascinated the Goliathonians for about thirty seconds; she was by no means their favorite communicator. Over the years Mrs. Oomla had come to realize that. She wasn't idle, though; this was Mrs. Oomla, after all.

But she certainly never read what she was supposed to be reading; the emails and deals and term sheets from her own corporation. That boring drivel didn't interest her at all. Whenever someone expected her to rattle off what was in that stuff, her lovely voice did what it always did: bluffed, or changed the subject. Of course, down here, in Goliath-eat-Goliath, her bluff was usually shown for what it was. Even so, she still wouldn't read that drivel. She just wasn't interested in it. Period. What she did read was article after article, whirling-dervishly, about her secret passion, as that was the only time she had during her live long day to indulge in fantasy. She'd rarely look up even to see the treetops or the water or the lights dancing beneath her.

But this was no usual day.

Because today, finally, her head felt lighter, freer. No doubt because her own personal mind-snatcher - that voice that had been going off inside her head - especially when she was up in the sky, away from the world and her responsibilities, that always seemed to get such a kick attacking her just at that moment, listing all the things she did wrong, and nothing she did right - was quiet.

·*(·

("Lady, what do you mean, that voice? Hey, Me, was that you?"

"Lorraine, darling, I merely suggest. I never attack! That certainly was not Me!")

·)*·

And to celebrate, she was looking everywhere, down below, up above, all around. And she would talk. In fact, she'd blurt, she'd even shout, even if she sounded un-CEO-like. She certainly wasn't about to read that package of material she'd received yesterday from that Occupy-the-Boardroom group that had been bombarding the CEOs throughout Goliathon. In the package were two novels: *Hard Times* by Charles Dickens that touched on the miseries that went on inside nineteenth-century factories; and *The Skyscraper Called Death* by Tove Nilsen, a book and an author she never heard of but whose plot, it suddenly occurred to her, might have something to do with what she and Giggle's board were up to this week. In the package, also, was a box of what looked like Baseball Trading Cards but were actually Rogue Trading Cards. But instead of having pictures of baseball players on one side with their stats on the other, the Rogue Cards had pictures on both sides, a CEO on one side and a third-world-worker on the other. Underneath each picture were stats - the hourly wages they received - under the Rogue CEOs' pictures, nothing under a $1,000; under the third-world-workers', nothing over a $1.00. On her card, there was no worker's picture because she had no overseas operations. Yet. When she opened the package yesterday, she certainly had noticed its unpleasantness but, now, it was getting under her skin, for it meant its makers knew what was on Giggle's agenda. For this was the day she and the board would be sitting in Giggle's very own skyscraper holding its first official meeting to determine if they would become a multinational. And if they chose to proceed, then later that week they would specify which of Giggle's back-office-operations would be outsourced, and which factories and farms to use in the third-world so they could grow and manufacture what Giggle needed there. Of course, the result of their decision would be that many Giggle employees would be terminated and their departments moved to the third-world.

All of which really meant, according to Giggle's highly confidential research, that Giggle would no longer have to pay first-world wages or follow first-world, fair-and-safe, union-approved labor-practices anymore either, thereby saving them bundles and stacks and heaps of dough!

'How much will your third-world-worker get?' snarled her mind-snatcher.

She'd shut the deck yesterday without examining her own card but she jumped now when she saw what the Occupiers had scrawled under her picture. 'How low will she go?'

'Those departments are filled with loyal employees who believe that their employer is looking out for them: wait til they find out their employer is loyal to a what and not a who. That doomsday title is wrong! When you fire those trusting souls, they won't call your skyscraper death; that's what they'll call you and the board!'

'I thought you were leaving me alone this morning!'

····C···

("Hey, Me," screamed Lorraine, "so if it isn't you, who, like, was it? Was that one of ours?"

"As I explained already, it wasn't me, and if it wasn't me, why ever would I care?")

···)···

She always hated what it had to say and she wasn't about to listen to that creep now!

And, for that matter, she certainly was in no mood to consider the Occupiers and their save-the-world, do-gooder messages either! She even liked do-gooders; she was married to one after all. And whenever she reminded the nasty one of that, he would growl that she liked money and had billions of it and that she, herself, was one of those crying-all-the-way-to-the-bank-CEOs of a heartless, soulless corporation that values profits over everything and everyone else.

'So start crying all the way to the bank like a good CEO! And always remember this, says I, thy-humble-Shadow, you'll never ever join your husband in do-gooder land!'

'Humble shadow!? Arrogant sniper!!'

·:·**C**··

("Ya know, I almost feel sorry for ole Mrs. Oomla. I don't know what I'dda done if I hadda had you, Me, in my head needling away about the House a' Dior AND the House a' Chanel but then having to listen to that mug, too! Even I ain't tough enough for that!")

··:**)**··

But today, she could not, would not think about all the wrong in the world. And all the wrong in her and what she did for a living. She ignored the voice and shoved the Occupy package out of her sight. Right now, all she wanted to do was look out the window. And chatter away.

And not have a single serious thought. What would she see?

'But the sun and the moon are not here to help me see.'

There were only the far-away lights of the city coming from way below.

'Could I see by those lights?'

'Since when do you want to see where you're going?'

'Since - oh! go away!'

There were lights, way below and far-away. From the streets. From the expressways. From the mass of buildings. Lights that rimmed those roads very edges; that shone through those buildings' windows. Lights that did help her see, even from that distance, that the buildings stood together or apart or in rows and squares. There were even lights that flashed and blinked, or were the color of jungle birds. Still all those many lights burning together were hardly enough to make that dark sky light because many small lights, even millions more, were no match for the sun or the moon. And yet she couldn't stop herself from looking at those electric lights ... the lights of the place where she spent her day.

Lines of lights on masses of massives.

The Electric Alps. That's what Sigmund called it all.

And one of the massives was her massive. Sigmund said that man had finally done the impossible: made a mountain chain. And looking down through the pre-dawn sky; at those lights that razzled even more than the hazed over stars above; at those buildings that stood taller than most anything Mother Nature made, and she saw them that way, too. Sigmund certainly had chosen not to live too near them like he had to when he was small. Though he had always told her he was in awe of it all. But if he was so in awe, why hadn't he ever come down even once and visited her when she was sitting on top of her mountain? She suspected her lovebird wasn't awed by that mountain chain, he was horrified by it. But she had never come right out and asked him either.

Though she had never told a soul - to her not only were they a mountain chain, but some of the people who lived there, at least to her countrified ways, were walking, talking Jumbotrons with very! bad! tempers! And even the ordinary, normal-sized citizens - pedestrians, men-in-suits, plain Janes - could suddenly and without warning - grow at least a foot, then ka-boom like mini-Krakatoas. Although maybe they felt they had to, to be heard and noticed in a place the size of Goliathon.

'But I am a Van Der Speckian, after all, and the Van Der Speckians' eyes can never quite get used to buildings that are taller than their tallest hills; most of which, to their eyes, are not even half as pretty. Tall is one thing, but taller than their tallest hills is quite another to a Van Der Speckian.

'But there are so many tales about giants. People are fascinated by them. Well, this is the place for them!'

The voice spoke louder, 'Well then - is this the place for you?'

This time she couldn't ignore it, 'IS this the place for me?'

'What DO I think of this place? I know what the villagers think. What Sigmund thinks. But what do I think?'

'Why are you a goliath when you're in The Village Van Der Speck?' snatched he. 'And a speck when you're in Goliathon? But then feeling a speck isn't so bad; it makes one realize just how insignificant one is.'

'Stop it! Here of all places, I shouldn't feel a speck! I am a CEO of one of these mighty corporations. All those other giants have giant corporations in them, too. And CEOs. I've met those CEOs. They don't act like specks. They don't walk around singing. They don't say the first thing they think. The way I want to. And do when I'm in my village. And neither do the professionals who work in the corporation - they don't say the first thing they think either. None of them break out into song whenever they feel like it, the way I always want to but don't anymore. I *do try to behave like them. But I know in my heart of hearts, I'm not one of them. I certainly don't talk like them. And they certainly don't talk like me. And I surely surely don't behave like those street people either. Where do I fit in here? Or do I even fit in? Is this the place for me?'*

She didn't have an answer.

The snatcher did.

Which she didn't want to hear.

So it spoke even louder.

'Famous for communicating, are you? Can you communicate with yourself? By the way, aren't you looking out the window? Don't you see where you're going? Well, is this the place for you?'

That she heard, but now that the helicopter was getting closer, she refused to wonder about something that might not lead her anywhere, or that might lead her somewhere she didn't want to go, and instead inspected the Sky Giants. She couldn't see Giggle yet, but she could make out the silhouettes of Giggle's neighbors. Giggle had a lot of them. They stood from river to river.

'Wouldn't be such a hard stretch for that sky to scratch Giggle's head - or for me either, for that matter, as I fly so high -

'Listen to me! As if the sky had arms and my arms are wings and these buildings really are alive like a forest is alive. That's no forest of trees! They don't dance about in the wind!'

As her helicopter got closer, she noticed that, with the exception of Giggle's rooftop, the rooftops of those Sky Giants, with their exposed pipes and whirring fans and little shed buildings, were not at all pleasing to gaze upon. Plus the severe straight lines on so many of the buildings pierced her eyes. She scrutinized them. And suddenly she knew what she thought about something else. Those lines and pipes and sheds. That's what she'd talk about. Because certainly talking out loud about something she understood was far less annoying than muttering silently about something she didn't understand to an invisible busybody whose sole aim was to bug her. And she would talk, even if it was awfully loud inside the helicopter, even if she'd have to shout to be heard like one of those street people and even if she didn't sound like a CEO. And even if in the process she revealed her secrets.

But her inquisitor spoke louder still, 'Go right ahead! Talk to Captain O'Day. Don't answer that question, is this the place for you. If you did, you might find what you hide from yourself. Why ever would you do that?'

Overbearing nuisance! If she talked to the pilot, she'd drown it out.

And she, the CEO, the virtuoso herself, opened her mouth so wide and blurted so loudly, that she spit into her microphone, "Captain O'Day, everybody is talking about green this and green that but look at these roofs! Look at those colorless, lifeless, dull-as-pot-metal roofs! It's hard for me to look at that unused, uninteresting, wasted space. Some of these roofs are too mechanical - "

'*Over this din, I must sound like a harpy harping!*' She hated depositing anything less than pitch-perfect sound and sense into the ears of any of her auditors, especially the auditors from this city, the city where she was a CEO. But just as long as she was louder than that voice inside her, what she said and how she said it, would have to do.

But to Captain O'Day, her words echoed through his headphones as if they had just arrived from above.

Mrs. Oomla saw Captain O'Day's smile. And she relaxed. She had succeeded. His smile was the reaction her voice had on people. She was used to that. But she also knew his smile wouldn't last. Around here, the sound of her voice falling like music-on-ears was over in no time. But today she'd talk no matter what happened. It was the only way she could take aim at her harpooner.

"Or too machine like. And some of them are worse than that. These roofs need a botanist. And an ecologist. And some green-roof engineers. How could people, who are so educated, who own skyscrapers that contain offices for our citizens, be doing only the things that show and not what really matters to green their buildings? I mean don't my neighbors want to save their city and the people in it and their buildings, too? Is that why these roofs, that the little people can't see from way below, have no greenery on them? Some beauty? Some twisty, green succulents softening those sharp straight edges, the way nature softens its edges? There's greenery on the street level but not up here. In ancient times, there were hanging gardens in the city of Babylon; legend says they were planted by Nebuchadnezzar. Wouldn't some green be beautiful and good for us? But not only could we have gardens on the roofs and the walls of the tall buildings, we could grow things inside them, the way they grow things on farms in the country. Except the farms would be in buildings in the city. They would be vertical farms."

'Oh! how perfect it would be!'

'*Stop it!*'

"Captain O'Day, I could grow everything I need to make Giggle right here in my Sky-Giant! I shouldn't have to go to South America and China to plant what I need."

"Sky Giant, ma'am?"

"Oh! - my building. The buildings. I call buildings that are so tall - giants." *'I can't believe I used that childish expression, my private joke, in front of him! Have I forgotten how quick these city people are to question what I say! But today I won't let that stop me.'* "I mean … look at them, they are big!"

"Big they are! And big they'll stay. Til they start making them even bigger!"

"Well, they shouldn't let them get so big. But no matter what size those buildings grow to be, my neighbors have got to learn about the ecological benefits of a green roof. I did it to Giggle's roof. You know some things, like buildings, are almost alive and these tall buildings should be considered as if they are giants amongst us. Look, even that sky, which never stops moving, is alive too. I bet that sky would reach down and start scratching Giggle's roof because there's something alive like itself growing on its roof."

"Ma'am, the sky is alive. Every pilot knows that. And, incidentally, that sky already reaches down and scratches everybody's heads whenever it feels like it, when it's stormy or hailing or fogging! It doesn't matter what is growing on the heads of our roofs! In fact, I can't tell you how many times that sky has personally reached down and scratched my head up here in this flying machine. And I can't say I've always liked it that much."

"Well, then maybe the sky wouldn't reach down and scratch people's heads if there were more living things growing up there on those roofs pushing it back."

"Wouldn't count on that, ma'am. Besides, if everybody greens everything, I'll be out of job. Unless they can come up with a helicopter that runs on the rainwater you collect in your rooftop barrels. Or maybe you can grow some fuel for my helicopter in that vertical farm of yours! And besides, ma'am, I spend my life looking down on the roofs of this city, and there's more green roofs than you realize. They're getting more popular."

"Well, isn't that's great! Oh, I don't really know as much as I'd like to know - like the science of it all - " *'I look like a hypocrite and sound like an idiot! I have to start looking out the window more, and get my nose out of those articles. And here I am talking about green this and green that and I'm riding in a helicopter with no other passenger than myself! I shouldn't be thinking out loud like this! Exposing what I don't know to people! I always have to be so careful whenever I talk to anybody down here. Because we're paid so much, people expect CEOs to know more than everybody! If they only knew what I don't know - and if I blurt, they'll find out!'*

And the unease she felt when she was in Goliathon returned in a rush. People in the village didn't really listen to what she said, they were usually delighted to just listen to the sound of her. But not the people here. The people here not only listened to the sound of her, they heard every word she said. She should've been used to that by now, but she wasn't. She wasn't used to people when she talked not just letting her talk; or topping her stories with their even better stories; or, worse, yet, coming up with all sorts of witty retorts and arguments and back-talk to whatever she said. And now she even had her very own back-talker inside.

Not wanting to appear defeated, or worse, unsocial, and have him think that about her, too, she continued, "I think we've got to respect all living things. And buildings and the sky're like living things. They take care of us one way or another - oh! listen to me, I'm talking too much and I sound like such a do-gooder!"

"Yes, you do ma'am, but I'd never've said you were talking too much. Listening to you is a lot nicer than listenin' to a squawky old air traffic controller."

"You are too kind."

Captain O'Day had stopped his back-talk and so had her inquisitor. She'd quit when she was ahead. She didn't want to say anything else wrong and embarrass herself again. After all, she had to remember her position. And as Aunt Hortense always reminded her – 'You are that rara avis, a woman CEO! Prepare! Perfect! Perform! Make me proud!'

And she had just blurted! CEOs don't blurt. What had gotten into her? She had a reputation to keep up. For women CEOs everywhere. She let herself relax, and an idea floated into her head, and it was wonderful. But this one she was keeping to herself.

'Maybe I really could build my own vertical farm and grow what Giggle needs in that. I studied botany after all. And then Giggle wouldn't have to go to China and South America to get what it needs. I don't have to listen to that board. They could listen to me for a change!'

The snatcher weighed in. 'Oh! That big bad board? Listen? To you? Little Flower Petal! Since when? You're the only CEO in Goliathon that gets pushed around by her board, remember? And didn't you think just an itty-bitty-bit-ago, "women are such men nowadays, they bark and growl so! But I'll never ever ever do that!"?'

She flinched, blushed, sighed and went right on dreaming.

'What would I call my vertical farm? There's always got to be a name. I've learned that from Giggle's Marketing Analysts, that multitude of the best and the brightest recruited from the top universities throughout the land; crackerjack, twenty-something-year-olds who sift through stacks and stacks of data so that they can come up with the stuff which makes them the real mastermind behind Giggle, Inc. I'm

hardly that anymore. All I ever did was invent the stuff. I set out to make a delicious drink and I succeeded. Little did I know what it contained! A substance that had never existed until I mixed up that batch. Daffeine! For so long, caffeine had been THE most popular legal stimulant and now there's another one … mine! And I own the patent on it! 'Daffeine! Get daffy! Get giddy! Not jittery! Or drunk!' And the world can't get enough of it!

'But ever since Mrs. Oomla's Giggle Pop became Giggle, Inc. and daffeine, a national sensation, I can't seem to invent anything anymore. At least, the way I like to invent, which is through my private hunches and sudden ideas and my own experiments. When they took the Mrs. Oomla off the corporation's name, it's like me and my way wasn't in it anymore. Here, my experiments have to be monitored by a team of specialists and my hunches and ideas have to be checked by a Concept Committee. Because in a corporation, committees watch over inventions; an invention would never be left to a lone, fallible person, a very human me. But then without the expertise of all of those Analysts, my little invention would never be the second biggest drink in the land. Without them, my corporation wouldn't be such a giant, and, shame on me, I wouldn't be so rich.

'Those committees of Financial and Marketing and Product Analysts, working together - always working together - came up with the idea of changing Mrs. Oomla's Giggle Pop's name into many different names so it would appeal to many different consumers. I hated the idea. I didn't want to trick people in to buying my invention. But their research showed that if Giggle were to really succeed in many markets, I couldn't just call it Giggle because the name Giggle only appealed to gullible, naïve, little-snookums, (gullible, naïve, penniless, little-snookums). And if I wanted to capture the widest possible spectrum of human beings, the cynical, large, and very unsnookum-ed humans, whose wallets just happened to be conveniently stuffed with cash and/or plastic, I'd have to find names that appealed to them, too. And after testing many names, they found just the ones.

'Who would ever think that those top-of-their-classes, clean-cut professionals - our brightest youth, our best hope for the future, gentlepersons all - could be so devious? To the mid-westerners, we call it Mrs. Oomla's Giggle Pop; (we! Hah! They!) but to the black-clad, chi-chi cynics, it's Ink; to young children, Giggle; to nine through eleven year olds, Ig; to teenagers, Suds; to LaLa Landers, JaGiGiFizz; to inner-city urbanites, GaFuzz. And they'll be in litigation in perpetuity to own those names. But Giggle, Inc., with its legion of Corporate Attorneys, wins - eventually. Because when they lose, Giggle, Inc. just sends in another flank, and when that flank loses, they send in another flank, and on and on until our plaintiff lays down before the mighty Giggle and gives up because we've worn him to a frazzle, and, to boot, after having to pay so many attorneys'

fees, he's bankrupt! And then the name is ours. I so much wanted to disown these practices but, a flankee asked me, 'Mrs. Oomla, don't you like to win? Our corporation will never run out of money or wear down to a frazzle, because a corporation can pay for armies and armies of suits that can march endlessly on and over just about everybody.'

The snatcher chimed-in, 'If you ever tell your dear Sigmund all the ruthless things that you've been a party to over these past few years, what ever would he think of you? No wonder you go to bed so early. If you were up, Ms. Chatterbox, wouldn't it all just spill out of you, and he, that protector of the downtrodden, would finally know the truth about his little songbird. His Ms. CEO!'

And she shuddered. There it was, in plain English. What she was always trying to suppress. Her inquisitor was right. It wanted her to - Own up. Fess up. Bare her soul. But she couldn't. Not today. Not now. She didn't want to think about all the wrong in the world. All the wrong she had witnessed. And not put an end to. And she shook herself loose from its claws, and stubbornly went on with her fantasy.

'So I'll have to come up with a name for my vertical farm. But I can't pick a name that requires an army of suits to wear a human down to a frazzle ... Listen to me! I'm actually worrying about being sued. Those suits have finally gotten through to me. But I am thinking like a business executive protecting my assets ...

'... or is it the corporation's assets? I think they're the corporation's assets, but if they're the corporation's assets, and I own the corporation, they're my assets. But there are all these people who work here, and then there are stockholders, too, so they're everybody's assets. I'd ask somebody but I'm sure they'd be shocked to find out that their CEO didn't know. So I don't dare ...'

'Well, maybe if you read what you're supposed to be reading, you'd know!'

'Leave me alone! Even though I'm not really sure who owns what ...'

'Got Google, Giggle?'

And she blushed even deeper and continued with her thoughts, *'when I was in a recent board meeting, I did say so so sweetly, 'Since many of my corporate colleagues are now the real brains behind Giggle's success, maybe they should share ownership of the corporation, too.' 'Hah! It was only because of all of the recent press about corporate greed that the board made a conspicuous display of considering my proposal. But when the CFO flashed his megawatt smile, at me especially, and proceeded to suit up my idea in the gray-flannel of corporate-speak and trot it around the boardroom, anyone with half an ear could've heard that that suit, with my idea in it, was marching down a shaft where no idea escapes alive!'*

"May it be noted in the minutes, our board will take our CEO's suggestion on its merits. Consequently, we shall form a Focus Group to determine if it's an ideation which could be conceptualized, made actionable and then seamlessly integrated into our remuneration platform with zero impact on our core competencies while adding value to our stock price; and if and when all of those functionalities are met with, as well as a few others, we will, of course, then give the green light to the formation of an Exploratory Committee who will then pursue any additional and necessary discoverables proactively.'

'Hah! Ideacide! Dead-words-walking!

'And then he added that all-important Weasel Clause ... ' "Of course, we must first find out if the paradigm is shifting throughout the corporate world, because if it is, so must we. And if our competitors are pursuing the same course, then action must be taken, because if they pursue the idea and we do not, we'll lose our talent. Always remember, if the grass is greener, if the dollar is dollarier, if a talent pool is poolier, talentier, our talent could become their talent, and vice versa. But, of course, if they are not, then we must not. After all, what would become of us if we did?"

'My idea was now safe inside Bone Town, Inc. Which is exactly where he, where they all, wanted it to be. He had even taken the extra added precaution of directing that walking zombie into the deepest darkest thicket of the modern corporation known as The Focus Group. Focus Groups rarely if ever get bumped into Committees.

'But I also knew behind the boards' sunny, upbeat faces, their brains were seized with apoplexy. And I know why. The boards of corporations control how much money is paid to its employees. And the boards have decided that the CEO and the Top Execs are paid just about all of that money. But now after the entire world has shamed them into thinking otherwise, those Execs are just busy trying to figure out a back door way so they'll still get, maybe not all of that money, but just about. Just about. It's like how they talk publicly about how they're going to green this and green that! But it's all talk! Talk! Talk! And more talk! And look at these un-greened buildings! They're not really doing a thing about it. It still will be the CEO and the Top Brass who gets, okay, maybe not everything but just about everything, and whatever is left over will be divided between the employees and the junior executives; okay, the employees may then receive a little more than an ounce of it, and the junior executives, a whole lot less than a ton. But no matter what they say, or do, the winner will take just about all, and they will do everything they can to keep it that way. If the employees also owned the corporation, how long would that practice last? Everyone seems to have forgotten the French Revolution, when the peasants beheaded the King for taking it all. When

will the employees start beheading the CEOs for doing the same thing as those French Kings did? And when I brought that up, I'm surprised I myself wasn't marched down shafts deep and dark!

'Oh, well, whose ever assets they are—'

'Hey … aren't you a CEO who gets everything?'

'Oh!'

'I bet you know exactly what your Sigmund thinks of CEOs—'

'He's never really told me. But then again we haven't been talking all that much lately.'

'What if your Sigmund wants to behead you?'

⋯C⋯

("Holy elfin' nork knuckles, Me! Did that little creep, that What If, go into her head too, Me, because it sure sounds like he did!" said Lorraine, "I thought he only pestered Dr. Oomla."

"He's never claimed her, but can anyone trust that nudge?"

Fairies! May I continue? I can't believe you're interrupting Mrs. Oomla at such a sensitive moment!)

⋯◖⋯

'That's ridiculous! A psychoanalyst wanting to behead someone! Hah! You think you're so smart! Well, let me inform you that a body without a head … to a psychoanalyst … that's like a picnic with no food, no soft green grass, no marshmallow clouds, no blue sky and no ants!

'I just feel guilty …

'Oh! To get away from these people! To invent something brand new all by myself and not in a committee … and to never have to listen to another Corporate Attorney or to attend another board meeting ever again! And to never, ever let Sigmund know what I've really been up to!

'Nebuchadnezzar It! That's what I'd call my vertical farm. I bet people would get a kick out of saying that. And surely I won't need legions of Corporate Attorneys to acquire the legal rights to that dead man's name.

'But what am I thinking? I have a name before I even know if the board will agree to my proposal.'

'Oh! That big bad board doesn't listen to you! You and your idea will be Nebuchadnezzaring-It right down that roof in no time!'

Her back-talker was right.

Her last meeting with that board flashed before her - that meeting! when they'd pored over the data that showed just how much money they'd save when they switched to third-world factories. And the dread returned.

She shut her eyes, lay her head on the head rest and gazed on the un-roofed, unencumbered, unlimited sky and imagined she was flying through it. And very far away from that board and today's meeting.

·∴（· ··

("Me, that's gotta be your influence!" said Lorraine, "Mortals can't fly, Me. They gotta stay right here on ole muddy earth and duke it out. That's what happens when a Fairy enters a grown-up's head and fills it with stuff. Mrs. Oomla wants to do the impossible.")

··:）∴· ·

Mrs. Oomla was dancing in the sky ...

·∴（· ··

("Yeah, Me! How is she going to feel when she finds out she ain't free?")

··:）∴· ·

... Floating in its blue dress.

'Oh! Weren't you just in green a second ago?'

'Leave me alone!'

Finally, the pilot opened the door after the rotors had subsided, but the wind was so ferocious, it all but snatched her out of the cabin. Mrs. Oomla buttoned every button on her coat. But she was still cold. *This coat won't cut this wind. I need clothes that can keep me warm. Not what I have on today.'*

"Ma'am, I hope you'll be okay getting to where you have to go! I'll pick you up at 3:30 this afternoon. Hey, if you can figure out how to keep the sky out of us pilots' hair, I'm all for it."

'He really does think I'm an idiot!' Breathe-in CEO! Bark-out CEO! And stop blushing!' "Well ... I have so many responsibilities now ... I was just think-ing out loud ... you know ... imagining ..." The wind and the cold and the dark icicled through every skimpy layer of her ensemble as she jammed everything into her briefcase, jumped out of that helicopter and, in her 3-inch heeled boots, sprinted across the s-shaped path that was cut through Giggle's planted roof. She reached the door of the structure that housed the rooftop elevator, though the wind made that door nigh impossible to open. She tugged and pulled and fell inside, free of the wind's custody. The elevator was waiting for her. She pushed the button for the lobby where Claude, her stylist, was also waiting for her.

• • • 6:00 AM • • •

After Miss Kitty had cooked the cereal til it steamed and cut up all the fruit and assembled the yogurt dish and squeezed the oranges and dripped the coffee and laid a fresh tablecloth and placed a bouquet of flowers in a jug on the kitchen table because Dr. Oomla and Sophia did not eat breakfast in the formal dining room but all of them, including Miss Kitty and Mr. James, ate in the kitchen together, and everything was just as Mrs. Oomla liked it to be, Miss Kitty snuck out of the kitchen. Mr. James didn't even look up from his newspaper. She'd heard the sound of big footsteps rushing down the back stairs; Dr. Oomla's voice calling out "Good Morning, dear Miss Kitty! Mr. James!" but she had a sinking feeling she wouldn't be hearing the sound of not-so-big ones next.

Something may not be quite right. Again.

Miss Kitty tip-toed past the library and heard the sound of paper's being shuffled about and Dr. Oomla talking to himself, "Now what did I do with that?"

'He doesn't sound his top-o'-te-mornin' self. What is he lookin' for, n' why is he runnin' down te staircase? N' another mornin', he still isn't singin'! Couldn't he at least whistle?'

But Dr. Oomla and his behavior was not what brought her out of the kitchen, so she trudged on, even though she couldn't help wondering when he'd come down those steps singing out loud and dancing like he used to. The sight of him used to make Miss Kitty laugh out loud. But for a good while now, she hadn't heard him sing out once when he came down that staircase in the morning. The only thing she'd heard was the sound of his footsteps, and those footsteps weren't dancing anymore, they were running. And even when he came home at night, he didn't play his music on that super fancy music machine that the short, roly-poly man with the shiny suit had come in and installed throughout the house. And oh how she loved the sound that system made. It made her happy when she was sad, sad when she was happy and laugh when she was tearful. And oh how she missed it now that she hadn't heard it for such a while.

She continued on, to the back of the house til she got to a door and, without making a sound, opened it and saw what she didn't want to see but feared she would. That DVD player on. A movie playing. An old movie. But this time no one was watching that movie. She crept further in and saw that the throw usually draped across the sofa arm was instead on the sofa's seat rising and falling, rising and falling, all by itself.

• • • 6:05 AM • • •

Mrs. Oomla was having her usual – le Spécialité de Claude - her hair, make-up and his once-over – and all of it done before her breakfast meeting with the green bottling manufacturer. But as the elevator door shut, and Mrs. Oomla began her long ride down to meet her stylist, she felt as she did every morning when she took this ride. Odd. Not herself. And guilty.

'I know my morning appointments with Claude are vain of me ... an extravagance even.'

So she did what she always did on her ride down. She dreamed up excuses as to why she simply must have her styling done. After all, someone might ask her why. But she knew she was kidding herself. No one in Goliathon ever would. The people of Goliathon were used to the grooming habits of its feminine creatures. And even some of its masculine ones. Why this was standard practice to the citizens of Goliathon. There was only one person who would.

Sigmund.

And it was as if he was standing right next to her on that elevator wagging his finger right in her face. And about to do what they did to the French Kings.

She knew very well Sigmund would never wag his finger right in her face or, for that matter, in the face of any living person - and he certainly would never even dream of doing what they did to the French Kings. She knew that.

But her guilt seemed to think he would and he was standing there and just about to do both of those nefarious acts to her right at this very moment. And not only that, her guilt had also shoved its way right on the elevator with her and him, and was standing up straighter and taller than the both of them ever could. And was about to push the button to a floor that would take all of them a lot lower than just the lobby. A whole lot lower. And she couldn't stop it. Or the elevator.

But the elevator did stop. It had only gone as far as the lobby. Her guilt, that figment, and that other figment, that finger-wagging, beheader Sigmund, were disappointed she was sure.

The doors opened and there stood Claude with his arms crossed and his eyes already beginning their up and down inspection of her. She felt so relieved it was no one else, that even as Claude was giving her the once over, even as he was evaluating her "Look," her guilt just melted away. Claude wasn't about to make her feel guilty. He might make her feel poorly put-together but that never made her feel guilty. Much to his consternation. She never minded Claude's gaze. She was used to it. He inspected her every morning. She knew he was taking her all in, seeing her as only he could see her and pondering what he'd need to do to her and just how he'd have to do it. What style should her hair be in to work with her ensemble? What tones should her make-up be to complement it? What else would he need to do to create her 'Look' for today? Claude, after all, was an artist of the Personal Appearance, of It, of Sparkle, of Room Presence.

Those ladies of Goliathon had told her that even though his canvas was a head of hair and a face and the body below and the ensemble that body wore and how all those parts came together to create a look, to create a "Fabulous," Claude was no less an artist than an Artist.

That's just what those ladies said out loud for all to hear; what they would only whisper to her was that Claude noticed other parts, too.

For Claude dressed every part of the person; he didn't just dress the hair. She knew that's why Claude was eyeballing her from her head to her toe. He was looking for those other parts of her that needed dressing. Beauty. Help. Parts that no other stylist in all of Goliathon would've even noticed. And even if they had, they wouldn't've had a clue how to fix. He could find what was keeping you from standing up tall, confident; from feeling beautiful. Because if those parts weren't taken care of, all his work on your "Fabulous" would flop. And those parts weren't on your outside.

Claude could see in there too. Or as Claude liked to say, "I dress outsides; I address insides!" When the insides weren't working, Claude could no longer be just a Hairdresser anymore. A Hairdresser couldn't very well blow-dry confidence into a person like a person was just an empty balloon and confidence was just so much hot air. But an all-ears, all-healing, all-forgiving Claude the Therapist certainly had his ways of getting confidence inside you. And if Claude the Therapist hadn't quite filled you up, maybe some silly remarks followed by delicious gossip delivered in slapstick by Claude the Clown might do. Or if those Claudes didn't do it, maybe Claude the Jewish Mother who hovered and butt-in-ski-ed would. And if even that Claude couldn't help, maybe a slightly more overbearing one could. And so on, til, if you still weren't quite filled up, there was always Claude, the sharp-talking Nag. And if even that Claude's sharp-talk didn't scare it into you, there was always, at the very lowest part of the far beneath bottom – Claude, the broom-riding-Witch, who, with his technique of fright and scare, could terrify the confidence right into you. Make no mistake about it - when your confidence was the thing that was making your Fabulous flop, that's when one of the Claudes: the Therapist, the Clown, the Jewish Mother, the Nag, or even the Witch, took over. And those Claudes, one of them, or all of them, or any combination in-between, simply never failed. Claude would do and did do whatever it took so that your fabulous was FABULOUS.

They didn't call him Super Claude for nothing.

Super Claude. You'll see, Sigrid, they told her.

∴⟨⟩∴

("Author darling, it's me that really deserves the credit!")

∴⟩∴

• • • THE FAIRIES ARE IMPERTINENT INDEED • • •

"I, you see, had been on quite the suggesting campaign deep inside Mrs. Oomla a few years ago to hire this Claude. I'd heard all about Him. His reputation is legendary even in the Enchanted Land."

So Me, she just improved like one, two, three?

"Miss Author Esther Whatever! Like, no! Obviously, you never saw her. And I guess my descriptions haven't been sinking in. I had so much work to do before she could even GET A LOOK!!! Like, one, two, three? Like, can you keep counting til you reach a billion? Those shoes? No makeup? Aprons? Those feet! Unpedicured! And the fingernails of a digger in dirt! I mean she was a bark scraper! Miss, like, Whatever and all of you, like, Whatevers in Reader Land, should know where we Fairies come from, that digging sort of work is for, like, gnomes and trolls and elves and muck-dwelling creatures such as that. I mean what is it with you humans and the earth? The earth is, like, covered in grime and sludge! Plus Mrs. Oomla was, like, an Apron-Wearer type person! Your Mrs. Oomla hardly dressed like she was Sigrid Oomla the inventor of Mrs. Oomla's Giggle Pop aka Giggle, Inventor of Daffeine and second only to that other, like, whatever, and was, like, a billionaire and the owner of her very own corporation. That Mrs. Oomla! That Sigrid! That one! Finally, finally, at long last, and through my hard work, she, a person with all that talent - and the kind of talent I'm referring to is the green cash kind and the real Real Estate kind - had a Look because of what I did to get it for her. I mean I'm the one who got her Claude. And I did it through a very effective and, like, really subtle and very suggestive campaign, which I, speaking of fabulous, am, like, fabulous at myself."

Me, thank you so much for making that clear. Now, may I continue?

"You, like, may not. You could if you would, like, get the story straight - but you won't without my help. In fact, without me, there'd be no story! I really need to be off on a rest cure, I mean, after those ten-years of hard servile, like, labor deep in the, like, mind-mines of the Oomlas, and the dreadful thing that Dispatcher did to me or tried to do to me ... I've had enough and really need to be taking exquisite care of myself! So if you don't mind, I'll tell this part myself. Because I want the proper screen credit – Oh! I forget this isn't a movie! Well whatever they call credit in a ... this is a book isn't it? That's right, I remember, midsummer, writer's alley. Oh, darn! Just a book? Not a glossy magazine? Oh, then there's no chance my friends will ever read it. Well ... anyway ... whatever, like, accolades you, like, get in a book, that's what I want.

"So, first off, please call this section Me and Mrs. Oomla. Don't change the order, and, like, don't even begin to give me a grammar lesson, okay? I was simply not going to let Mrs. Oomla walk out of the house every day looking like the aforementioned. So I would whisper all sorts of things inside her, and I mean I went right up into her head, into the place that makes the fantasies. First, I went to the part that makes the fantasies you can see, the part on her right side, and I would draw a picture of her in this or that, and I mean I did fashion sketches worthy of the House of Dior, but with, like, her head on the model. Then I'd fly like crazy over to the other part, the part on her left side, the part that understands stories, and I'd whisper inside her all sorts of happy talk about what would happen when she wore this or that, about how if she wore this and did her hair like that, did the works on herself from head-to-toe, all these, like, cool, like, really hot things would happen. But then every once in a while I'd throw in some sad stories, like, I'd draw the old Mrs. Oomla, in her apron and her barked up hands and spotted with, like, earth-dirt on her shoes, but I would make them look dirtier, barkier, or even worse, and let me tell you, those stories were sad, tragique even. And in no time, she was shopping in stores, the right stores, too. I mean, I can't believe it, like, took her so long.

"Of course, after that, and because of what I did, you know, she finally got style ... and then Giggle ... whatever ... really took off, and she became, like, a billionaire. And she could afford, like, everything. So, for the record, let's get this straight, in Ms-Oomla-land, there was, like, Before-Me and there was, like, After-Me, and I mean in After-Me, she was getting clothes, the right clothes. But I was still not satisfied. She was putting the clothes on a fairly good body, I mean, she wasn't pathetique! She was tall enough for those clothes, she was almost thin, (alas, she could have been thinner because, as that Duchess-lady-human-type-person, who spoke Such Immortal Words, such Perpetual Everlasting Truth for all time - and to think the most important words ever spoken by any living creature, were spoken by a human and not a fairy, oh! The Injustice! - "A woman can't be too rich or too thin." So true, so desperately true) ... and if you have, like, ears on your head, you know she has the voice of the ... like ... okay ... century, I mean, like, who doesn't know that? but as for the rest of her … well … she really needed serious styling and that hair, deep deep conditioning and highlights and her face wasn't exactly hopeless, but it needed serious moisturizing and subtly whispered make-up. I mean make-up in the hands of most women is a catastrophe. But this woman used none! Also a catastrophe and besides I never heard of such a thing … well, I mean, I've heard of it, but who wants to come face to face with the truth? Mrs. Oomla may sound beautiful but her appearance did not, like, match her voice. She shouldn't possibly have all these billions from all that Giggle whatever and, like, waste it … and so, like, then I got her Claude."

And Me sat on the top of my laptop screen giving me the eye, because I'd stopped typing. I had to. I was drowning in this flood of a story.

Now, Me, I'm not sure I understand so I need to ask you something. And it's for the sake of putting down the events in their chronological order that I ask. Did you go in before Mrs. Oomla had the billions or after she had the billions?

"Lady," hollered Lorraine, "why are ya even bothering? You know the answer. Our Readers know the answer. Me, ya went in when ya heard Mrs. Oomla had billions, so don't even try it!"

"Well then, you simply have it wrong, because it was like before. Because, as I already stated in my letter in the opening of this story, I'm really a - like – Fairytarian. Mrs. Oomla was fortunate that I was the Fairy assigned to her daughter."

Me, I'm afraid I'm with Lorraine on this one. But what exactly were you doing inside Mrs. Oomla in the first place? Didn't the Fairy Dispatcher send you inside Sophia, with very specific instructions to stay there and go in no other human's head?

And there was a loud pop and Me was gone and the only thing in her place was thin air.

And pop again! She came back immediately after I typed the above sentence. "I read that! Please type - Wafer Thin Air - because that's the only kind of air I would've ever been caught dead in." And she was gone again.

"Author Lady. You could knock me over with a flea fart!!"

And back Me came, again, "Lorraine! That's positively disgusting! Remember, the world will be reading this! I can't believe I lived for ten years in the same space with somebody who expressed, and continues to express, themselves the way you did, and still do. And apparently always will. No wonder I needed deep purges and constant moisturizing. I should send you my dry-cleaning bills!"

"Disgusting! I'll tell ya what's disgusting, Me! Never telling the rest of us what you was up too! We're here to help little humans. And to leave the big humans alone. Period. And don't tell me ya think ya helped Mrs. Oomla! What's the chance that Mrs. Oomla'd live happily-ever-after after you got through with her? Did ya happen to hear her? He?lloooo? she's imagining her husband wants to behead her. Now I ask you, is that the thought of a happy person? No! That's what happens when an Emissary-from-the-Universe-Fairy disobeys the rules and does what she wants to do instead of what she's supposed to do because she believes rules don't apply to her! Poor Mrs. Rich Oomla! I never thought I'd say that about ole motor-mouth."

Of course, Me just disappeared again.

Lorraine! And Me-wherever-you-are! I'm continuing! Now where was I?

Oh, yes, Mrs. Oomla had just stepped off the elevator and run into Claude.

• • • 6:08 AM • • •

'Oh, can Claude tell what I've just been thinking? Does it show? He always understands me. He always wants to hear what I'm thinking. He wants to hear my drama. Claude adores my drama. Or maybe Claude just adores drama. Oh! either way, I know he'll hang onto my every word.' Mrs. Oomla was dying to talk to Claude, especially since she'd been thinking so many 'career changing things.' Things she had almost confessed to Captain O'Day. And now finally she was about to pour them all out to him, because there he stood before her – Claude, who had such sympathy for her, Claude, who so understood her – until Claude's eyes landed finally on her face.

"Sigrid, darling, guilt! again! Would you stop! A woman in your position simply must be the best she can be!"

Just hearing him was enough. Maybe she wouldn't have to go into every one of her secrets right this second. It'd've required so much of her.

'That's right, why ever would you, the famous Voice, use that voice to tell anyone how you really feel!' Her sniper was back.

'I don't have to tell Claude how I feel, alright? Claude is my audience no matter what I say! He's nice to me and you're not!'

"Oh, Claude, does the guilt show? I can't seem to get rid of it the way you get rid of it for me. It's not as though I have to worry about paying for your services. And besides, I'm helping the economy. I'm spending my money.

That should make Sigmund happy, shouldn't it? He hires all these people to work at our house, just so he can spread our much-too-much money around. Well, since he's dispatching it, then so should I. I'm not hoarding my money away like some miser skinflint cheapskate who doesn't know how to live. So this is almost sort of like a charity. Except, I know it's not really benefiting needy people but ... Oh ... And besides, I just do this during the week, when Goliathonians have to look at me, so it's sort of benefiting them. Although, I guess, they don't exactly need me to look good ... although my looking good does put food on your table but ... well, anyway, I'd never do this on a weekend. Sigmund wouldn't like it. He does not appreciate me spending so much time fussing over my appearance. Oh Claude! I'll never forget when he walked into my brand new little closet in our new little cottage. He never walked in again. He never even made it past the first room. I still can't get over that! I mean a woman must be beautiful, mustn't she?"

"Sigrid, look at the sacrifices you are making to be beautiful. I mean to get up at such an hour! But what else can a woman do who is sentenced to appear in public? I mean the public - now really - a person never knows what they're going to say or do at any given moment, so a woman must be prepared and for a woman to be prepared they simply must look their best, period! Now, darling! It's just too cold to worry about such trivialities! Let's forget all about that nonsense and think about real nonsense; like, why don't we all just turn into, like, snow leopards or something! They're always ready for the cold. Oh! To be such exquisite creatures for a day, darling!"

Claude floated into the elevator, nudged the button for the executive floor with his elbow, rubbed his cashmere-lined, kid-gloved hands together, and inspected Mrs. Oomla. "A befeathered hat ... hmmmm ... with a veil ... hmmm ... a costume ... so colorful ... fit for a magical day but for le corporate culture? With its thinking-inside-the-cubicles? ... hmmm ... what say you? ... should outside-that-cubicle stick ... feathery plumes? ... veil tails? ... should day-glo phosphorescence be its only light source? Should we really look like the glitterati on a strut down a cat-walk? At this hour? Or what say you, we re-configure ourselves for the corp-walk wearing one of their many uniforms, all interchangeable, all indistinguishable but which still say loud and clear that we too are members in good standing of the vast-corporate-conspiracy?"

"Oh, Claude, is there such a thing? I was never invited to join it, thank heavens! What ever'd Sigmund've think of me then?"

'Not so fast, you know that conspiracy very well.' chimed her pest. 'You're a card carrying member.'

'Not now! I can't listen to Claude and to you!'

'C'mon! That! conspiracy!' Her pest was going nowhere, 'It's where y'all-the-corporations brag that y'all are people but won't even whisper that those others - those third-worlders - aren't. But what comes through loud and clear to we-the-pests is how you treat them-the-peasants. Everybody knows peasants are dirt poor. Which to you makes them dirt experts, right? That's gotta be why you give them your dirty work - c'mon, admit it. You're so slick you get them, in their third-world-far-aways, to build their own factories for them to do your dirty work in: for who'll ever find out that those shoddy-factories those shady-third-worlders build aren't ventilated or fireproof? Plus, wink-wink, nobody can nail you first-worlders for building dirty. So in the nighty-nighttime-stories you tell yourself, y'all're heroes, right? And look how you added to your own war-chests by saving a bundle on building materials AND payroll! AND, good for y'all, you did make them third-worlders a little less poor even as y'all made you first-worlders even more rich.

'But you should stop bragging. Because if good-little-corporations were really people, what y'all'd be proud of is your real-live-beating-heart with its loving kindness in it that give people from all worlds safe and fireproof, too. But you don't have real-live-beating-hearts, do you?'

And now Mrs. Oomla wasn't paying any attention to Claude but was examining the air above her as if the air itself was occupied, and her complexion had taken a ghostly turn.

Such pallor would never do on one of his high-visibility clients, and Claude purred, "Oh, darling, is there anything wrong? Didn't you like my vast-corporate-conspiracy-joke? I was just trying to make you laugh! Just playing around with that Occupy stuff that's permeated the Zeitgeist lately. Now don't tell me you take any of that seriously! You, of all people! Don't you know who you are? You employer of thousands! You inventor of what the world craves! You savior of the economy!"

"Claude, it's ... I just ... oh ..."

Do I really have to confess to Claude that my very own Zeitgeist has already been permeated? Tell him about my tormentor and its favorite sport? Besides, isn't Claude always sort of picking on me, too? About my appearance? Claude and my tormentor expect nothing less than perfection from me. So why would Claude be on my side if I did tell him?

'And why do I have to go into this drama now and get all sour?'

She could feel herself relaxing. Besides, Claude's flattery had done the trick; it had revived her. She'd have to be careful though; Claude put two-and-two together and always got four. He knew when she was trying to hide something.

"Oh, Claude," she twinkled, she fluttered, "you are too kind!"

It worked. She was surprised.

"Good! You do like to add a little this, a little that to whatever your home stylist's laid out for you, hoping that I won't figure out that you're the true designer of your outfits! Don't forget, your home stylist and I consult on a daily basis! So what say you, shall we re-configure, ma cherie?"

·∴(·∵·

("Hah! Lady! C'mon!" scoffed Lorraine, "We all know who the real designer of her outfits was!"

"I, Lorraine, only suggested the Tiffany-blue suit! A Fairy can only do so much, after all!"

"Wow! Look who's here. Just in time to pop another whopper, Me! Phosphorescence? Like a non-Fairy is into phosphorescence? Well, excuse me for living but somehow I find that hard to believe!")

·∵)∵·

But whatever her home stylist laid out for Mrs. Oomla was always so without ornament, so boxy, so unlike her nature friends, the feathers and flowers that arabesqued their way through life tickling things. She smiled very broadly hoping to camouflage this secret, too.

·∴(·∵·

("See, Lorraine! That feather was her idea!")

·∵)∵·

"Now, what has this unfeeling wind done to you? Darling, would you mind terribly removing that charming hat!"

She did what she was told.

"Darling, you so need me!"

• • • 6:10 AM • • •

"A magic throw!" Miss Kitty had to laugh even as her heart filled with dread. She snuck over and lifted its corner. Underneath was a mass of brown curly hair. Sophia was sound asleep.

'Well, Miss Nanny, what do ye have te say for yourself! It's te wee hours o' te mornin' 'n tere is y'r wee charge, not in her own cozy bedroom gettin' ready for school, like all te other nice ten-year-old girls in te world are presently doin', but is sprawled over te sofa sound asleep in te TeleVISion room with a movie playing! If anybody found te both of ye at tis moment … well, I just hope ye know when ye're treadin' on a minefield, Kitty Devine!'

Miss Kitty gently but urgently tugged on Miss Sophia's shoulder and whispered really low, even though all interested parties were many, many rooms away.

"Sleepin' Beauty, tis mornin'! Time for all young ones t'be'gettin' up, eatin' ter oatmeal n' goin' t'school, if tey know what's good for tem!"

Slowly, slowly Sophia turned towards the noise. She tried to open her eyes. Wouldn't open. She pulled on the blanket. Wouldn't budge. She curled herself into a round ball. *'No, no, sleep, sleep, lemme sleep, I wanna sleep. I'm so tired.'* But couldn't say any of that. So she didn't.

One look at her unresponsive responsibility and Miss Kitty knew that this time the situation was dire. *'If I don't get a move on 'n do what Mr. James hired me t' do n' serve breakfast on time with Miss Sophia sittin' in her place at te table, I'll soon be cryin' without havin' t' listen t'a note a' Dr. Oomla's music!'*

And she yanked,

'Te child won't budge!'

… then sunk low in a chair, calculating what she had yet to do;

wake the child up;

get her on her feet;

up a flight of stairs;

down a hallway;

into a bedroom;

out of Mrs. Oomla's evening gown AND the pajamas she had on underneath;

into her school clothes;

back down a flight of stairs;

into her seat at the breakfast table;

and all without Dr. Oomla and Mr. James suspecting a thing.

And as if that wasn't enough;

doing it all in no time flat.

Her arthritis told her exactly what she should do, *'Give up 'n turn Sophia over t' te authorities. Her Mother 'n Father. Mr. James.'*

But her heart bit back hard.

'Kitty Devine, it's too late for tat now. Ye're in too deep. For ten tey'd know 'Te Secret'. Sophia's Secret.

'Which is now me Secret, too!

'N besides, however would I, a 69 year old woman with arthritis, find another position as good as tis one because who ever would hire a 69 ½ year old woman with arthritis other ten tese fine people, te Oomlas? 'N, to boot, where ever would I get such wages? Tese are te highest wages tat I've ever received in me whole life. Even if tat old battle-ax

Great Aunt Hortense snoops around me fine self two-too-many-times. Dr. Oomla 'n Mrs. Oomla 'n Mr. James don't know a ting about what Miss Sophia does in te night! N' if I'm smart, tey'll never find out tat me charge Miss Sophia sneaks out of her bed 'n goes downstairs deep into te late late night 'n plays old movies on tat contraption on te TeleVISion set 'n performs along with tem as if she was te greatest little Movie Star on God's green earth as she acts all lovey doveys 'n rainstorms 'n lightnin' bolts right alongside tem. 'N I must make sure tat no one else ever finds out. Mr. James just might dismiss me to prove t' te Oomlas 'n tat bossy old Great Aunt Hortense what a conscientious representative o' te Service Profession he is. 'N speakin' of tat old know-it-all Great Aunt Hortense, who has an opinion about everyting n' everybody – well, wouldn't she be glad t' show me te good riddance! 'N she'd show it no matter how much Sophia 'n me get along. But oh if tat dear sweet sad Dr. Oomla ever got wind of what his daughter was up t' in te middle o' te night - tat his daughter is dying to be a Movie Star … A Movie Star?! Why his heart would break. Tat's te very reason tat man is a psychoanalyst … t' cure te sorrow right out o' tat pitiful lot. Why tere's not a person in tis household tat hasn't 'eard him talk about what he spends his live-long-day doing; how he has t' personally save all tem fallen, broken, weepy Movie Stars tat 'ave ended up in such a heap o' basket cases tere at his beloved Institute for tem lost people o' Show Business.

'N if he'dda ever find out tat it was I, te Nanny, whom he, te psychoanalyst, trusts with te care of his precious wee daughter! Was te very one lettin' her do te very ting he'dda never want her to do! 'N if Mr. James, who hired me because me references stated crystal clear tat I was so trustworthy, found out I was te very one aidin' n' abettin' behavior such as tat!'

And then Miss Kitty's hand started shaking even as she rose up from the chair and began tugging on Sophia's shoulder again …

'… n tat I know what Little Actress is up to!

'N

'I let it happen 'n in te middle of te night no less! On a school night! 'N tat I been keepin' it a secret!

' … Well … tis now, 'n will be forever, me mission t' make sure not a one o' tem ever finds out! I'll not be te one breakin' tat fine man's heart for anyting in tis world. Or te next one, either! Why tat'd surely break me own heart!'

Only four weeks ago she had discovered what Sophia was up to.

• • • FOUR WEEKS AGO • • •

Miss Kitty couldn't sleep. *'Is tat ye, bicarbonate, serenading about te sleep ye'll surely bring me?'* Even though it was way, way below in the pantry and she was way, way above in her bed. She knew what she had to do: travel through that dark manse to find out. So as to not disturb the slumbering household, she picked up her stout, stiff self and put it on tip-toes, which caused her arthritic, bursitic hips to needle her with pain. But tip-toe she did, down each and every step of that house's many staircases. When she reached the first floor, she even tip-toed along the back hallway, though she knew that by the time she was way down there, no one in the upper regions of that vast aerie could have ever heard her.

But when she got to the room with the TeleVISion in it, (that snooty decorator insisted that everybody call that room the Media Room but no one ever did because Mr. James called it the Telly Room and she called it the TeleVISion Room and Sophia called it Movie Land and Dr. Oomla never called it anything because he never even went into that room and neither did Mrs. Oomla) she heard the sound of the TeleVISion. Miss Kitty, thinking Mr. James must have forgotten to turn off the set, opened the door, and there to her everlasting consternation, bewilderment and astonishment was Sophia with the TeleVISion on speaking out in a voice that wasn't her own and sweeping all around the room in one of her Mother's many evening gowns and one of her many silk wraps. And even though Sophia was dusting the floor with that gown because the dress was a yard too long on her, you wouldn't have noticed by the way she was carrying on in it.

Wee quiet Sophia!

Prancing around and talking along with a movie, and doing such things all about the TeleVISion room! Where was the Sophia who, whenever company came to call, blushed? stammered? who was always putting her head down and hiding because she couldn't get a sentence out and whose Mother seemed to finish all her sentences for her? That Sophia had disappeared. And there now in her place was Actress Sophia, who knew all the words and was saying everybody's lines - the woman's lines! the man's? lines! even the lines of another female character and – *knock-me-over-with-a-clover!'* - in each of their voices! She was doing the man's voice, the woman's voice and the other character's voice, too. How could she know all the words and DO THE VOICES, TOO? Her Sophia, usually so dreamy eyed and so quiet like a wee church mouse in a wee muffler in a wee match box stuffed with wee hankies, talking like … like … an Actress! An Actress on Fire! Miss Kitty watched the Actress snap into the Actor snap into the Character. This She-He-She sure wasn't acting wee and quiet and like Sophia at all. No, wee quiet Sophia was gone. An Actress was standing there. And no wee quiet one either.

Miss Kitty became so absorbed by the story the characters were performing that she forgot she was standing on aching hips; forgot she was even looking at Miss Sophia; forgot she was supposed to be mad because her charge
was up too late; forgot she was Miss Sophia's Nanny and that tomorrow was
even a school day because Miss Kitty could only stand there realizing that
wee, quiet, stammering Sophia was making her eyes tear up because wee, quiet, stammering Sophia was an Actress and a grand one at that, simply grand!

But when one of the characters Sophia was playing turned around, the
character drained away in an instant, for Sophia had spotted Miss Kitty. And
in the next instant Sophia's face glowed fluorescent until it glowed no more
because her face, and everything attached to it, had fallen to the floor. Miss
Kitty called out, "Miss Sophia, 'r ye still with us?" as she rushed over to where
Sophia lay thinking Sophia had a heart attack until she remembered ten-
year-old girls didn't have heart attacks.

Sophia's coloring was coming back but her eyes were determinedly shut
as she whispered out from her swoon, "Oh Miss Kitty, don't tell anybody
you've caught me in my Movie Star School—"

"Movie Star School! Is tat what tis is?"

"Oh, Miss Kitty, you don't understand. And my Father wouldn't either.
So don't ever tell him! You know what I heard him say one time, Miss Kitty?
One morning, I was just about to walk into the kitchen when I heard him
tell Mr. James that Movie Stars really and truly believe that people only love
them for their outsides! But then he said they were right and it was true!
That people really do only love Movie Stars for their outsides! And that's
why they're always trying to make their outsides perfect! To make their
outsides works-of-art even! Miss Kitty, what did he mean when he said that?
That they're always trying to make their outsides works of art? What's a work
of art? Isn't that like a picture or a statue or something?"

"Miss Sophia, ye listen to me! Remove tat question from out your mouth
tis instant! First off, he wasn't talkin' t' ye so tose words weren't intended for
ye ears! N' second off! Don't even tink of ever askin' y'r poor, sad Father
what he means when he talks about Movie Stars. Ye 'n him are t' never have
a conversation about tat subject. If he had an inklin' of what ye were up to,
it'd break his heart! Why Movie Stars are what he's on tis earth t' save, 'n
here ye are struttin' around tryin' t' be one y'rself!"

"Oh! Miss Kitty, he would never want a daughter of his to be a Movie Star,
would he? Is it because some of those Movie Stars end up in his Institute?
He told Mr. James that it's too hard for anybody to be a Movie Star because
Movie Stars have to perfect! And then he said that Movie Stars were even

terrified that people won't love them anymore when people find out they aren't perfect! Which makes them sad! Sad everywhere! And then they became a mess. A mess on their insides AND their outsides! And then he said something I couldn't figure out at all. He said being a mess is okay because human beings are messy. Why is that okay, Miss Kitty?"

"Miss Sophia, it's te middle of te night 'n ye're talkin' nonsense!"

"But it's not nonsense to me. Do you think it's because when a Movie Star is messy they don't have perfect outsides anymore?"

"Miss Sophia, ye don't give up do ye? Tere is only one ting ye need t' understand! Tat ye are a child 'n ye need t' be upstairs in your bed like all te other ten-year-old children in te world!"

"But, Miss Kitty, if I were a Movie Star, I wouldn't be messy on the inside and the outside! I wouldn't be a sad Movie Star! But if I told him that I bet he'd just die! And then I'd just die Miss Kitty! I'd die dead! Very dead! And for a long time!" And she pulled on Miss Kitty's arm hard til Miss Kitty was almost on the floor with her, "Oh promise! Promise! Never tell anyone what you just saw! I know you love to tell stories, Miss Kitty, but this is our secret, isn't it?" And the look Miss Sophia gave her was so from the world of worry, a world a ten-year-old shouldn't've known a thing about, that Miss Kitty felt a chill run straight through her.

"Oh, Miss Sophia, I'll be prayin' t' me Irish Saints tat y'r sad Father 'n y'r exhausted Mother never find out what ye were up t' t'night. Especially y'r Father! What would he tink if he knew his timid daughter was actin' up a storm in te middle of te night, 'n him bein' a psychoanalyst! Why his patients are mysteries enough for him, tank you very much! He doesn't need his own daughter t' be addin' t' his perplexities. It's better tat I pray t' me saints ten tat I upset y'r Father! I'll even make a promise t' ye, 'n tis a hard one for me t' make. Tat no matter how much I love entertainin' me ladyfriends with stories, I won't mention a word about tis t' a livin' soul!"

• • • 6:45 AM • • •

'She may be smiling but I wonder, is my most prized client, my sacred-cow – shame on me! – my very own cash-cow about to cry?' If she didn't cry, Claude fretted, she wouldn't feel good all day. And if she didn't feel good, she wouldn't glow; and glow she must when he was finished with her; and cry she'd better not after he applied the make-up. Because there would go all his work. He'd have to get those tears out soon. If anyone would notice mascara

streaks rolling down one of his faces that he designed to ooze confidence as it was CEOing about town … well!

Super Claude knew what he had to do. He would not scold yet. He'd see. He'd listen first to really hear what she said. Then he'd analyze. Was it guilt? Or something else? When he had an idea, he would advise, but only when the time was right. He'd begin with compliments. Sincere compliments. Like telling her why she was so unique. But not flattery. He would mean every word he said, so that when he was finished with her, she would feel better. Of course, if he failed, there was always flattery. Desperate times called for desperate measures. Who said that? Somebody dead … or was it just somebody a few weeks ago at dinner … hmm … who cares? *'I said it and that's all that matters!'*

··*(*··

("Darlings, you see how insightful he is!"

"No, Me!" cracked Lorraine, "Like, I see why you found him. He tauks just like you!")

··*)*··

"Sigrid, darling, I simply must tell you, the other day I was telling my colleague Roberto about what you refer to as your little closet! I mean darling, THREE salon sized rooms devoted simply to clothes. What a paradise! he said. And then I told him, it has, like, every imaginable color and texture and all of it displayed and organized so artistically yet like so precisely, its arrangement could only have been done by a great master of color, like a Van Gogh or someone just like him and - oh maybe - like the neatest person who ever lived! And when I told him about the first room with the day-clothes, he couldn't get over it and then about the second room with the accessories, he was flabbergasted; and by the time I got to the third room, with just the evening and the all-black clothes, I thought he'd have a case of the vapors. I mean those rooms, Sigrid, are out of a palace! That closet is almost exactly like Birdoffs Department Store. Birdoff's? Isn't that like who designs your closet and maintains it and stocks it? I told him they only do it when Dr. Oomla is working at the Institute, and that it's a secret, that it's our little secret. Sigrid, when I went into the nitty-gritty details, Roberto almost required an oxygen tank. Those arc-shaped racks and how they sweep through the entire first room! And the clothes! To arrange them color with color, not suit with suit or dress with dress. He said, all those clothes on all those racks that curve; a picture painted by clothes! And then I said, they don't look like clothes at all – Well! listen to what he said, Sigrid, 'It's a river filled with, like, rainbow water!' Roberto is such a visionary!"

"Oh Claude, my dear Sigmund is the only person who ever entered that space who wasn't actually stunned in a good way by its color. He looked like he was going to be sick. I know Sigmund does not appreciate such vanity … such extravagance either!"

'So stop with the closet! Makes her too guilty. And I've gotta get her mind off her husband!' Quickly he added, "But look at all the people your closet puts to work. All the people who are feeding their families because you support artistic expression. Including me. Why without women like you in the world, there'd be an entire segment of the world's population that'd starve! You are doing nothing less than a service to humanity, Sigrid! And on behalf of all of them, I thank you from the bottom of my heart!"

"Thank you, Claude! You really are kind!" And a smile appeared, then vanished, "Oh, Claude, did you notice, isn't it just extra cold today? Were you cold? I'm absolutely freezing. These clothes are just not warm enough. I would love, after my morning meetings, of course, to just fly up to Birdoffs and get some warmer clothes."

Claude gave her such a look in the mirror.

"I mean I'll just wear them when I have to go home at the end of the day."

Claude shook his head.

"No, Claude, they'll be beautiful. I swear. Just warm clothes but fashionable warm clothes. Very very fashionable warm clothes."

"Now Sigrid, we all know that is probably too much to hope for. You know what all really beautiful women do in the winter, they freeze. Because we simply can no longer wear the skin of dead animals anymore." *'Good! Throw that in! She is one of those humane types.'* "But about the shopping thing, you certainly can look, because you never know. Now remember absolutely nothing too bulky. Although maybe you could make the bundled up look return, since you have become so like outrageously popular here!"

"Oh Claude, no one ever seems to look at what I'm wearing anyway, no matter how hard you try. At least, they never say anything about my clothes. As soon as I open my mouth, people in this city just want me to talk – but only, it seems, for about a minute."

"Darling, don't you understand, Tout le Goliathon knows who you are! You are Madame Daffeine! Le Giggle! La Voice!"

"But Claude what you don't understand, is how quickly their fascination ends. And besides, when they do listen, they don't care what's going on inside me. With me, it's how I sound when I say it! And they listen for about a minute to that. And then they stop listening to how I sound and start paying close attention to every word I'm saying. It's gotten to the point that La Voice doesn't even want to talk!"

"I've watched them interview you on TV and when you begin to speak they suddenly look like their brains left their craniums. Some of them even look hypnotized. You know, it really is true; it is just your voice they're interested in, even if it's just for a little while. But I'm surprised you're not used to that by now. Although, I guess, no one ever can get used to that. Everybody always says people like to feel they are liked not just for the best about them, but in spite of the worst about them. Everybody knows people get old, lose their looks, well, it's the same thing for voices too, voices crack and deepen and get shaky and lose their melody forever. I mean, I'm sure you know the day may come when you won't be able to sound the way you sound now. How many of these people would still bother with you and invite you places and want to hear you talk then?"

'Would that do it? She's simply got to cry! Before I apply the mascara!'

"HHhhhh! Oh Claude! …"

'Almost.' Claude continued. "I know, I know. Right now, Sigrid, they can't get enough. I bet people invite you here and there and everywhere just because of it, and try to make you talk the whole time."

"And when I get here and there and everywhere, there are even more people asking me questions just to get me to talk all over again! But when I do talk, believe me their captivation with my sound is over fast, because soon they're interrupting me and talking back and topping everything I say. And I can't seem to get used to it. In my village, people would just let me talk!"

'Is that what the problem is? She wants people only to listen to her? The way they did in the village? She misses her village? And she only really wants to be La Voice?' Claude knew he'd have to finesse this topic. He couldn't really lecture a very important client paying top-dollar about the importance of give-and-take in a conversation. Claude'd have to work on this problem. Cautiously. But for now, he'd try the count-your-blessings approach. "I know, but Sigrid, look at all the people you meet and the places you get to go. And isn't Giggle only using your voice to do the jingle for their commercials? And not only that! You are a CEO, and how many of us are CEOs? Now come on? Now really? Plus you invented a drink that everybody in the whole country absolutely devours—"

"Everybody but Sigmund!"

"Well, almost everybody, and didn't you tell me it doesn't agree with him? Nobody has to tell me about a sensitive, queasy stomach because I have, like, the-princess-and-the-pea of stomachs!!"

"But it's not really his stomach that bothers him, he says it makes him silly. But, Claude, I'm sure that isn't the real reason. I believe he can't stand the stuff. Though he's never come right out and said so."

"Well, he absolutely must drink it if it makes him silly! Silly psychoanalyst! Silly patients! What fun! But why don't you ask him how he feels about it. Now, darling, you can tell Claude, are you afraid what you'll find out?"

"Claude! I don't really know what I'll find out. Giggle has made me very rich and that might be what he doesn't like. I really do make a whole lot of money. More than he does. The Institute pays a pittance to all of their workers, including their psychoanalysts. Great Aunt Hortense used to wonder, 'How ever do you live on his salary?'"

"Or he just might not like Giggle. I can tell you this, Sigmund doesn't like anything artificial to alter a mind. He told me that so many psychoanalysts nowadays use drugs to alter their patients' brains. But Sigmund isn't one of them. And Sigmund won't even talk about patients' brains, he just talks about their minds. He believes that patients should alter their minds, their behavior, their thinking, their feelings, through the force of their own will and their own insight and by the one-step forward, two-steps back lessons they're learning in therapy, and not by using a drug. That's why Sigmund likes the Institute so much. The Institute lets him use his methods. And Sigmund's methods don't include drugs. To him, drugs can take control of a mind. Drugs can even put a person in a trance. And Sigmund thinks the only thing that should be in control of a person's mind is the person's mind!"

"Sigrid, I couldn't agree more!" *'Claude, you devil! Who, pray tell, is trying to control this poor woman's mind?'*

"Oh, Claude, I can't tell you the number of times he didn't come home because a distraught patient needed him, so he'd spend the night at the Institute right by that patient's side. Most of those Institute psychoanalysts would've just given that patient a drug to quiet him down and then gone home to bed. But not Sigmund. But Giggle doesn't alter minds! Daffeine is harmless. It's been tested thoroughly. If that's his reason, he's wrong!"

"Darling, your homework this evening is to ask him! Why haven't you?"

"Oh, Claude, maybe I think the truth is going to hurt. Because maybe we'll fight. Everything is always so peaceful between Sigmund and I."

"Peaceful! Hah! Darling, I don't sense peace in you. Not today. Could you - oh no! - be in a secret war? Well, a secret war is the worst kind. At least with an open war, you know you're in it. But a secret one is much more dangerous. Things are peaceful on the surface, on the tip, but lurking down below is that iceberg. That's where the trouble is. Everybody knows what happened to the Titanic. So, get down! Show each other your inner-iceberg. Before one of you gets sunk by the other's trouble. And then, whatever could I do with you? Let, as Roberto likes to say, the fur fly!"

"Claude, that's impossible! Sigmund and I never ever shout at each other, especially the Roberto-way. Besides, you don't understand, my husband likes icebergs that lurk below. To him, that's where mystery and truth and fear lie. He's always digging deep inside himself, asking himself questions, the more probing, the better. And whatever he comes up with, he just adds to his iceberg below. He doesn't bring his iceberg, his world, up out of himself and talk about it at all. He's like an inside man. And I'm like an outside one. My world is right in front of me. On the tops of things. I don't like to go deep. I prefer to glide along on surfaces, the lovelier the better. Besides, I couldn't keep things below if I tried. I may not even have an iceberg down there because if you talk about things, they're not really mysteries.

"But, Claude, come to think of it … I haven't been myself lately. I used to talk about every little thing that just popped into my head …

"Plus, it's like something has a hold on me …

"Or maybe it's someone and maybe I do have an inner iceberg after all. And I don't like it."

'Change the subject, this topic hardens her face, and will not make her cry. Note to self: Next time - though it's a ticking time bomb - must find what else has a hold on her. Besides me. But very carefully! When she explodes, it can't be all over my hard work!'

"Darling, so start popping again! Speaking of which, you know you have a real talent. You're, like, blessed. So stay on the tops of things. I mean, if you come in the way you came in here today, with your face all frowny, you'll get, like, early wrinkles, darling! And I just can't allow that to happen to you on my watch. Don't you want to do something about that? I mean aging is bad enough but premature aging, aging that you yourself could prevent is positively shameful. And I simply will not let you forget how lucky you are. For example, look what happened the one time you didn't do the jingles; the sales of Mrs. Oomla's Giggle Pop absolutely plummeted. I mean they tanked Sigrid! and the board of directors just panicked, and made you sign an exclusive contract to do the jingles for the commercials for the next ten years. And you even own the company! So smile darling!"

She didn't.

"Oh Claude, you must know that Sigmund doesn't know about that contract because I'm afraid to tell him. Me! Making even more money? I know, I have things to be thankful for, you're right, but I feel so all alone and misunderstood."

"Darling, join the club!" *'That husband again!'*

"Something is just wrong. He hasn't even been playing his music at night anymore. All three of us used to dance to that music before all this Giggle stuff happened. Now, he just stays in his library by himself, doesn't even invite me in anymore. And plus, I'm always so tired at the end of the day; I just seem to collapse into bed. The other night, it was 6:30!! But I can't help it, I have so many responsibilities. And besides I have to see you in the morning. I could never do all that you do to me, especially since so many people're looking at me. I don't know what's wrong between Sigmund and I, but something is wrong."

'Husband it is! Positive spin! Go!'

"Well, darling, somebody with his training has got to know what's wrong. He understands all sorts of things about why people do what they do. I mean, he examines the thoughts and feelings and behavior of others for a living. He simply has to know what he's thinking, and what you're thinking and why he's doing what he's doing, and why you're doing what you're doing. He's a psychoanalyst! He couldn't possibly be like the rest of us - in the grip of our deep rooted fears, so that we don't really understand why we do what we do! So ask him what's wrong!

"And about the money thing. He doesn't know about that extra salary. Your accountant isn't going to tell him. Not if he wants to stay your accountant. And don't forget, you'll be narrating the performance by Goliathon Philharmonic. Having such a distinguished group invite you to be the narrator of their performance of Peter and the Wolf is such an honor. I know you told me how much he loves music and how much he loves your voice and with your voice added to all of that, it'll be heaven for him. And look at the good you're doing with that money, the performance is already sold out and the proceeds're going to your husband's Institute."

She smiled.

"Oh, Claude, the proceeds are all going to the Institute. I'll be inviting Sigmund and Sophia and surprise both of them when I walk on to the stage. This'll be Sophia's first ever trip to Goliathon!"

"But doesn't everybody in, like, the whole universe already know you're narrating the concert? You couldn't possibly surprise them!"

"Claude, first off, Sigmund never watches television or reads any newspapers either and could care less about our metropolis. He just thinks about his patients and reads his big giant books and stays put in our village. And somehow, he's still the smartest person I know. And Sophia, she would never in a blue moon watch television, either. She couldn't possibly know about this. And she certainly doesn't read the newspaper either. She's just ten. People in our village don't really follow what's going on in Goliathon. I know that's hard for all of you here to comprehend. But that's just the way it is up there."

And then she sat up in her chair. "Oh! Sophia! I must remember—"

"How is Sophia doing? Isn't she supposed to finally be meeting with a speech therapist today?"

"Yes, Claude. I must remember to call home later today to remind Mr. James about her appointment this afternoon. But I never have to worry about Sophia. She's in such good hands. Dear Miss Kitty's and Mr. James' - they are both so dutiful. So responsible! So charming! So from a different, old-fashioned world than this world. And now Sophia is finally about to get help from an expert. I don't really understand why but she doesn't speak up in class. Her teacher says she's timid, and when she talks, she stammers and hesitates and puts her head down and doesn't always look at people and that sometimes she seems to be a million miles away. Like she's in her own world."

"Oh, I know several people like that. You know they don't seem to be part of the group but sometimes they say something and, even though it's said quietly and shyly, it can be so smart, smarter than what those talkers are saying because those quiet people are really listening and hearing and understanding more than the talkers who are only thinking of what to say next just so they can keep on talking and they're not really listening to anybody at all. So maybe she's like one of those types, you know, the really good listeners. Besides, I'm sure it's just a phase she's going through. I went through so many phases when I was growing up. I still am, darling, like the phase I'm going through now, where I simply refuse to go to Sunday brunches anymore and hiss with all those queens! Or, like, how I absolutely refuse to wear any more leopard-skin, thong underwear. It can be so chafing! You know, like that kind of phase!"

She was about to ask – Is it the spots? - But her back-talker was at it again, 'Are you that kind of talker?'

'You again, leave me alone! I am not that bad!' And she drummed his question right out of her head. *'Maybe Claude is right. Maybe Sophia is a good listener, maybe Sophia is just going through a phase. But would it pass? Oh! I hope so, but Sophia still has to do what the teacher wants her to do. I can't wait*

to hear what the speech therapist has to say about this uncommunicativeness of hers. I must call Mr. James and remind him about the appointment this morning after my breakfast meeting.' She picked up her bag and found her Agenda. She wrote in big letters, Call Home, underlining it, exclamation-pointing it, circling it. She felt better. Then she didn't. Over and over.

As Claude was fixing her hair, he'd been examining her face. He saw that the tension would leave her face, only to return again. But the lines around her eyes and her mouth were not as visible now. And she wasn't squinting up her eyes or pursing her lips together. He believed he'd gotten through to her - except for that now-you-see-it, now-you-don't, tension - and he'd done so slyly. Bringing up a client's personal failings was never easy. He could never tell a client that their failings were causing their It, their Sparkle, their Room Presence to fade. But he'd find a way; he'd keep digging in his bag of tricks til he did. But whatever he came up with, it must not offend her. But for now, she had perked up. She looked better. He hadn't lost his touch. *'Another fine day for one of my clients!'* He was Super Claude, after all.

<h2 style="text-align:center">• • • 6:50 AM • • •</h2>

As she stood besides the sleeping Sophia, Miss Kitty crimsoned, *'Didn't ye almost break y'r promise when ye was jibber-jabbering to y'r ladyfriends 'n ye found y'rself fishin' around for gossip tat would really tickle? But ye didn't! It didn't even leak out o' ye! Cause surely ten y'dda lost y'r position!*

'But so what ye kept y'r promise? Ye charge is up t' her same tricks! 'N for tat matter, ye prayers didn't work neither!!'

Suddenly she knew why.

'What was I tinkin' prayin' to me Irish Saints? Tis situation is tailor-made for te stage! It's a fascinatin' story about a stammerin' wee girl who can act like a Movie Star! 'N here I am feedin' Saints from me country such a story! Irish Saints are constitutionally unfit t' te task o' stoppin' theatrical behavior because people from me country are lovers of te stories 'n te tall tales 'n te dramatic display 'n tey wouldn't miss a grand performance for anyting. Just cause tey became Saints, tat don't mean tey changed ter nature. Which means tere probably here right now in some airy place.

'So me Saints, even toh' I know ye aren't livin' humans, ye are immortal souls, so please do what's right 'n heed te words of y'r best beseecher, Kitty Devine. Ye heard what Mr. James just told me about Miss Sophia 'n her school problems, so could ye kindly stop her performances before anyone finds out, no matter how interestin' tey are t' ye? Isn't Heaven juicy enough? Alto' it tis half a shame 'cause our little Sophia is quite te talent, isn't she now?

' 'N me, too, Miss Kitty Devine! Ye can't just rely on prayers 'n Saints. Y're gonna have t' put an end t' her fancy prancy, too! 'N be extra vigilant tat her Father never finds out what his daughter is up t' at night … IS? up to? WAS! up to, because y're puttin' a stop t' tis Movie Star School once 'n for all!

'Hah! I wager Movie Star Fool is what her Father'd call such an endeavor after what I been overhearin' him say!

' 'N one more ting, Miss Kitty Devine! Don't ye dare ask Miss Sophia what her Father would tink of what she does! Why saying such a ting t' a child who could swoon away dead like Miss Sophia would be just terrible, especially in light of what I have t' tinker together tis morning. Oh! Why hadn't I checked in her room earlier? But ten I was so sure Miss Sophia had stopped all her dramaturgicals because I had told her t' 'n Miss Sophia is such an obedient child. When she comes home from school today, won't we be havin' a good long talk!

'I'll have t' work very fast indeed because I don't want Miss Sophia t' get caught 'n I don't want t' get caught neither! 'N here I am right in te thick of it! It looks like I am in on it, too. Which I am! Dr. Oomla is a kindly man, a fair man but he is my employer after all. I know exactly how he'd feel if he knew Miss Sophia was up all hours watching old movies 'n dreamin' o' being a member of te very profession he is on tis good earth t' save! 'N doing it all on a school night!

' 'N what would Mr. James do if he finds out?

'Or Great Aunt Hortense?'

And with that horrifying thought, Miss Kitty wasted not a second more. She scooped Sophia off the sofa wishing she could run but knowing her arthritis would only let her clump. And with Sophia in her arms and as Mrs. Oomla's long, feathery gown wavered behind them, clump towards the door they did. Sophia may have been a long child in a long gown but Miss Kitty's arthritis was very thankful she was a skinny child. She opened the door, looked to the right, left. No one. Then up the back stairs. Afraid someone might overhear them, Miss Kitty didn't dare say a word to wake her. No matter how huge the house was, she just knew, if they talked even in a whisper, they'd be heard; if something could go wrong, it would. Kitty Devine knew her Murphy's Law. It was an Irish law, after all.

• • • 7:00 AM • • •

'Whose … Am I? Is somebo … but I don't feel right …

'I'm moving … I'm … picked me up. I'm so tired. Sleep. I want my bed.'

"Miss Sophia! Miss Sophia!"

'Why aren't I on my bed?'

But she'd better speak up, even if she was asleep, "I need to sleep. I have to sleep. Please, let me sleep. Please."

Then her eyes opened - Miss Kitty looked soooooooooo red and she was breathing so loud!

"Oh! Miss Kitty, are you tired too? But please, let me sleep. I just want to sleep. I don't have to go to school, do I? Can't I stay home today? I'm soooooooooooooo tired. I just want to lay down on my bed and be under my covers. I don't have to eat breakfast. I'm not hungry."

"Oh! Miss Sophia! What in all e Saints names 'r ye sayin', girl? Now ye mus' know I could never agree t' suuuuch a ting! Y'r Mother n' y'r Father would be in a world o' trouble if ye don't go t' school. 'N I'd lose me job! Miss Sophia, ye know ye're not supposed t' be watching tose old movies on tat contraption on te TeleVISion set til all hours o' te night. Tis a good ting ye Mother hasn't found out what y're up to. Have ye clear forgot about y'r Father n' wha—"

'Haugh! What am I sayin'? I shouldn't be breathin' a word about him!' Miss Kitty examined her charge for perturbments. Those particular words hadn't soaked in. Which was good. But none of her words were soaking in. *'Not good at-tall!'* So she spoke louder.

" 'N if ye start by not going t' school when ye're supposed to be goin', tey'll find out what y'r up t', won't tey now? 'N I don' have scarcely an ounce o' time left at-tall before I am to be servin' breakfast; we jes have a coupla minutes before it's 7:15, girl. Which means ye must be gettin' into y'r school clothes n' goin' downstairs so ye can take y'r seat at t' table on time so nothing looks out a' te ..."

and she fish-eyed Sophia,

" 'strordinary!"

Sophia had been listing on her bed, about to sink, head drooped down almost to her chest, feeling so tired she had a hard time hearing anything Miss Kitty said. What came through was that Miss Kitty wasn't going to let her sleep. And then something about her Father ... And then some blah-blah something else. And then Miss Kitty's fish-eye drowned in Sophia's eye but it didn't matter because by now Sophia was a cork. Because a cork can't feel. And can't be tired. And can't worry what its Father might think. But she couldn't stay a cork because she caught herself wishing and hoping. Wishing and hoping that Miss Kitty'd understand. But she knew she wouldn't.

And Sophia made up her mind on the spot to not let Miss Kitty know a thing! Her wishes! Fears! Feelings! Nothing! *'School! I have to go to school.*

Nobody at school watches old movies. They'd never understand why I do. Those people don't live and breathe every word that Movie Stars say; at least old Movie Stars! Why do I have to go to school? Those people don't know what I know. Don't love what I love. They just know about things that don't matter. Like stupid math and problem solving and music videos where nobody has a good voice and can talk. Oh, why can't I go to a Movie Star School?'

But a voice inside her said Movie Stars fight for what they believe in.

She'd try out her argument on Miss Kitty. Maybe Miss Kitty WOULD understand, maybe just a little, if she said it the right way. If she said it better. If she said it like Ginger. Ginger Rogers wouldn't just give up.

"Oh, Miss Kitty, I have to practice! I wouldda just died if I didn't watch that movie last night. It was Top Hat, the Ginger Rogers and Fred Astaire movie. She's so so soooooo ... funny ... and you know what? I could act just like her ... and talk just like her. She's so speak-up, talk-back sassy! How'll I be able to do her if I don't practice? And I COULD talk like her. Plus I had to hear both of them talk! I had to see everything she wears. I had to see them dance. Her dance. Him dance. Together. Everything. I had to! So please, please, can't I stay home today and sleep?"

"Miss Sophia, ye have a half a minute t' be gettin' out of tose clothes 'n into y'r school clothes 'n I am not movin' meself from tis spot til ye do! 'N y're not t' say another word about tat movie at-tall cause I won't listen. Now be a good girl 'n get into y'r clothes so I can get downstairs n' serve me breakfast. We can't be talkin' about tis. We don' have time!"

Sophia listened to every syllable of Miss Kitty's brogue-wrapped words. But this time, she shuddered; something that never happened when she heard an accent. And that's when she knew, *'I must really be tired!'* For ever since she could remember, Sophia was all ears, all eyes when a person with an accent was anywhere near her, silently wondering, *'How do they do that?'* silently figuring, *'Is their tongue touching the roof of their mouth or is it laying like a carpet on a floor?'* She would listen and watch and calculate and never let on to a soul what she was up to. It was her secret. (At least until Miss Kitty found her out.) For Sophia was hopelessly in love with voices and accents.

• • • INTERRUPTIONS, READERS, GET USED TO THEM • • •

"Hey, Author, Lady. Hopeless is right. Sophia was like her Father and Mother's child. She found a way to express herself in sound, too; she tauked in accents and voices. But her ears would only allow her to do that when she was all by herself. Hey Me, whadja call those two things people always say about her Mother and her Father? I can't, like, put my finger on the words. They're kinda, like, unusual?"

"You mean, they're kinda, like, big, Lorraine? Speaking English is tricky isn't it, darling? Connoisseur? Virtuoso? Are those the words you're looking for? Well, darlings, even when Sophia was a small child, she understood all too well what people meant when they said those words. With her own ears she heard the music her Father listened to; she heard the voice her Mother sang and spoke in. Having to listen to so much pitch-perfect-perfection ever since she was a tiny baby turned her ears into seekers of sweet licks, of serenades. Her ears - delicate instruments that didn't care for indelicacy. In fact, they were anti-troglodyte: meaning, if a troglodyte would've grunted around those ears, her lobes would've flapped the ears away.

But they became utterly despondent when they heard the sound of her own voice. *'I talk like a frog!'* Because that's what those snobs heard when she listened to herself. But then how else could ears feel that'd been listening to such silvery music day in, day out? Those snobs believed that her deep froggy voice would never ever ever in a million billion trillion years measure up to that kind of perfection; which might've been the real reason Sophia was so taciturn when she was out and about in the world. She didn't want her snobs to suffer. Or anyone else's, for that matter. *'Every ear on the whole entire planet'd keel over and die if they'd have to listen to me!'*

Lorraine! Me! We went over this already.

"Yeah, so what, Author Lady! Only the most important thing everybody's gotta know about Sophia, and ya, like, don't want to go over it again! Some Author you are! Readers, youse shouldda been happy ya wasn't inside Sophia when she was listening to anybody or anything! I mean the ears on her! We're tauking sensitive."

Thank you, Lorraine! I'll go on now.

"No, that's, like, not enough information, Lady! Keep going, Me!"

"Darlings, we're not exaggerating when we say that's what Sophia thought. And I'm not exaggerating when I say Sophia could be taciturn. Lorraine, by the way, do you know what taciturn means?"

"Hey, so what if I don't? I'll tell ya what I do know; Sophia clammed up when it was time to use her own voice. I mean, she could do, like, Movie Stars' when she was by herself, but she couldn't, like, do her own when she was with people! But ya know, Me, this is only part of her problem. It's not, like, her whole problem."

Lorraine, not now! Enough you two!

• • • 7:16 AM • • •

Sophia made the mistake of peeking over at the maker of those cranky syllables: Miss Kitty had plastered such a look all over her face that Sophia lugged herself off her bed and stumbled towards the dresser. When she opened her underclothes drawer and caught sight of the toad-some assortment of un-Movie-Star, completely hideous, half-johns, with their elastic that hit at her underarms and just above her knees, she groaned. Atrocities! purchased for her by Great Aunt Hortense. Since her Mother was just so busy all the time, Great Aunt Hortense had even begun to buy her underwear!

But she was too exhausted to dwell on that sorrow for her current bafflements seemed even worse. *'Why doesn't Miss Kitty understand that I just have to watch old movies? All she did was pray for me but then she didn't tell my Father or anybody when she caught me the last time, so it had to really be okay with her. Even if she did say I shouldn't watch them. Grown-ups always say you shouldn't. Shouldn't this. Shouldn't that. That's why they're grown-ups. But ever since that night, Miss Kitty's been smiling at me so extra special. That's gotta be because she appreciated me more after she saw me be a Movie Star. Grown-ups don't make any sense. I figured she liked me to be a Movie Star. So why does Miss Kitty look so mean right now? Does she hate Movie Stars all of a sudden? Miss Kitty isn't mean. I don't understand.'*

But she didn't know what to do with these bafflements. She wouldn't say them out loud; they were just her own personal, private drama and weren't real drama, like the kind she acted in her Movie Star School. That drama she spoke out loud in her many voices, when only her imaginary audience who adored her was there to hear her. But this little-ordinary-girl confusement, she'd speak inside and to herself.

And that's where it stayed. Bottled up good and tight. Til tears leaked out the side of her no matter how hard she tried to keep them in. But she wasn't about to drip wet, sloppy tears over her evening self, her Ginger feathers. And though she was all washed-up, and when she moved, everything hurt - her fingers, arms, shoulder, neck, eyelids, even her tears - ever-so-carefully, she stepped out of her Ginger dress with its swirling feathers.

She wished she could Ginger Rogers her way to school. But all she could do was lay Ginger on her bed carefully and not let even one of her tears fall on her. Because actors and their costumes always looked so good in movies, she'd concluded a while ago that members of the acting community must be required to take good care of their costumes; and since she was going to be a member of that community very soon, she'd better start now. She wouldn't have dreamed of getting dirt on her costumes the way her Mother got dirt on her clothes. Sophia had to lean against the dresser as she got one leg than the other out of her pajamas and then into her underclothes; and even as she put on her school uniform and her knee socks and her tie shoes. She might weigh tons and she just might topple over but she wasn't about to make even one crying sound. Sometimes Movie Stars don't cry out loud. She looked down at her school clothes. She wasn't a Movie Star anymore. She couldn't be. She was in her school uniform.

Sophia looked at Miss Kitty to see if Miss Kitty was looking at her and maybe noticing her falling tears but Miss Kitty wasn't paying attention to Sophia at all, she was only paying attention to Ginger now and had picked her off the bed and was shaking her gently, smoothing the material, fluffing the feathers and then scrutinizing her up close.

Sometimes Movie Stars must keep going, even when their tears are rolling. And even when there's no one watching those tears roll. And even when someone looks at that Movie Star quite crossly and even when that same someone may eventually, any second, shortly, notice those tears roll.

"Tis's a good thing for ye, I don' see a rip or a missing feather, young lady! Now Miss Sophia, ye'll have t' brush y'r teeth after breakfast n' fix y'r hair ten, too, even toh' y'r hair is extra wild tis mornin'. But we have no time t' fuss now. Jus' what were ye doin' t' make y'r hair so pouffy? Don' tell me cause I don' wanna know. Maybe ye should put one of tose clippie tings in it or wear a hair ribbon or whatever it tis tat ye should be doin' with tat hair t' make it less flouffy, so be grabbin' sometin'! We must run with te wind girl! I'll have t' be sneakin' into y'r Mother's closet 'n puttin' y'r Mother's finery away again. I'll just be prayin' for te luck of me people tat one o' y'r Mother's, as tey call temselves, Couture Curators – suuuuch fancy pantsies! If ye' ask me, jus' a simple pressin' is all anyone needs to do t' clothes but not tem! Tere in tere takin' te inventory, or steamin' te garments or wrappin' everyting in acid free paper or in crushed velvet or doin' some such ridiculous ting tat tey be doin' to y'r Mother's clothes in tat closet o' hers 'n all when I mus' be pokin' me way in ter t' return tis bit o' finery. Ye ought t' be careful snitchin' her clothes because of tose hissy ones. King Tuts, if ye be askin' me. Tey be countin' te snot out of ter own nose before tey leave in te morning! 'N if one is missin' tey'd better put it back cause how'd any of us recognize tem? Alto' why y'r Mother needs so many clothes, 'n Couture Curators for tem, I can't for te life o'me figer out! She has more clothes than te Queen herself! Oh! Listen t' me gassin' away. Sophia, we got t' dash now girl!"

Sophia took Miss Kitty's extended hand which Miss Kitty pulled back fast - Sophia's shirt was showing underneath her uniform blazer. Miss Kitty tucked it in to the skirt, took firm hold of Sophia's hand, and down the long hall and the main staircase they went. Went, that is, as fast as an elderly, stoutish, arthritic person and a barely awake 10 year old could go. They didn't stop til they reached the kitchen. It was 7:32 when they got there.

• • • 7:23 AM • • •

'Where could she be?'

Dr. Oomla had been waiting for Sophia to join him at the breakfast table but when the clock reached 7:23 and Sophia still hadn't appeared, he knew he didn't dare wind his way up and over, under then through, the outer corridors, inner chambers and long shadows of The Castle L'Oomla - the name he came up with to describe this mausoleum that Giggle Pop had built - and look for her, or he'd risk being late for the Institute.

He did eat the hearty breakfast Miss Kitty had prepared and let Mr. James regale him about a debate he'd just read about in his British newspaper. Mr. James described both sides of the argument with such persuasion, Dr. Oomla couldn't resist weighing in himself. And with Mr. James on the affirmative side, him, the negative, they debated the issue right there. But even as Dr. Oomla was making his point, even as he was keeping one eye up for Sophia, his inner eye was taking in what was going on around him and, as usual, he was thinking about what it saw. *'Our breakfasts are usually high-spirited like this. Mr. James and me acting our ages, until Sophia appears. From then on, only one of us will.'* He almost laughed out loud but Mr. James was making his rebuttal and laughing in any form, whether out loud or out the side of one's mouth, would've been bad form. Such a consideration, however, would've been tossed out if Sophia would just walk through the doorway. He would've laughed, and done just about anything to make her laugh, to make everybody laugh. Like the time he poked an upright fork into any upright fist he apprehended on the table.

And he did laugh.

'What we talk about at breakfast! I'm surprised Sophia isn't here by now; she loves our morning talks! Why isn't she here?'

And he stopped.

'Oomla, she couldn't be faking all those smiles! She always manages to overcome that natural reticence of hers and join in the fun. She couldn't be that good of an actress!'

And he went right back to laughing again.

'Miss Kitty, Mr. James, chattering away, and both Sophia and me, quiet, at first - Miss Kitty, about the old country; Mr. James, about all the great orators who ever lived; himself, withholding his comments, observing and listening only; and Sophia, not talking either, quiet, but hanging onto each and every word spoken. Until Mr. James went on about those orators, and finally, she would talk, asking the same question every morning, "Mr. James, how did that person sound when he talked? Can you talk just like him? Would you, please, oh please?"

And Mr. James would always correct her, "Oh Miss Sophia, it's not so much how they sounded but what they said. Don't ever forget, these people weren't talking for anyone's amusement; they were talking about the great issues of their day, whether they and their fellow man lived in peace or went to war." And then he would repeat solemnly, or grittily, the orator's great words; words that were enhanced considerably by his British accent.

It was their ritual.

The other part of the ritual was that Mr. James completely forgot what he just told Sophia about how the orators sounded; he'd produce such effects with his voice, sounding like a posh in one speech and a miner choking on coal dust in the other, all the while doing something with his eyebrows or his face or his elbows or his lips or his teeth, or putting on glasses or taking them off. He had entire speeches memorized. And as he spoke their ennobling words, he could make a complete character with nothing but a gesture and a voice. Sophia couldn't take her eyes off him. Dr. Oomla loved to watch Sophia watch Mr. James. She looked as if she believed Mr. James wasn't Mr. James at all but the orator himself; as if she were not sitting at a breakfast table but in a theatre looking at a great star.

Finally, Dr. Oomla would speak; he'd ask any question he could think of just to keep Mr. James orating. And when Mr. James had finished, Dr. Oomla especially loved hearing what Sophia had to say, when she spoke up only for the second time that morning. And he'd listen as she said it in her deep voice he loved so well.

'She does talk. Not at all like what they say about her in school. Why does she have such a hard time speaking up there? I know. It's like what I've always thought about her. She's a person of few words. And many thoughts. Thoughts that she doesn't often share. She can be so quiet sometimes. More than sometimes. Maybe the teacher thinks she doesn't have a thought in her head. That's what people might

think if a person doesn't talk. But look at me? I'm quiet sometimes too. More than sometimes. But I'm far from quiet on the inside. I have many thoughts. Thoughts that I don't often share. Well, she doesn't share her thoughts either! She probably just hates being called on in class when she has to speak up, and speak out. Well, I always hated being called in class too when I was young. I've never been good at public speaking. Maybe she's just like me. Maybe? She is. She's an introvert too! That's really all it is. And I'll just have to go in to that school as soon as things quiet down at the Institute and enlighten them about introverted personalities. So why isn't she here this morning? Could it have anything to do with what the teacher said to her about having to go to a speech therapist. I must find out more about what really happens to her in school. She certainly can talk at home so why not at school? I must get her side of the story. Find out what she has to say. I already know what the teacher has to say.'

But he'd never ask such a question at breakfast.

'My part is to not be serious; not to ask questions, especially serious questions. My part is to only silently wonder why she asked that question, that same question, 'Mr. James, how did that person sound when he talked?' but not to ever directly ask her why. Breakfast is the time for me and her and everybody to have fun and to forget that anyone or anywhere or anything looms over us. Like problems. Our problems. Her problems. My problems—

'Problems, Oomla? What about this? Don't you realize that breakfast is the only time during your day when you talk with everybody freely since you never seem to talk freely at the Institute! And for that matter, you don't even want to talk, or have fun, any sort of fun, when you come home at night especially after working during the week at the Institute—

'during the week?????? ... how many weekends has it been that I've been working there too?'

And finally he understood.

'No wonder my daughter is having problems. I'm not talking to her—

'Oomla! You're becoming as melodramatic as your patients!

'I'm talking to her but just not about what's going on with her at school—

'Oomla! ... You don't talk to her in the morning about such matters ...

' ... or on the weekends ...

' ... and you're certainly not talking to her at night because at night you're too defeated, deflated, depressed, to do anything but crawl into your cave and brood. Brood about the Institute—'

The Institute.

That place! And his mind began letting go. *'I can fix her problem. My sweet Sophia is just shy. How could she ever have a real and a lasting problem? Her teacher, the school, just misunderstands introverts. That's all it is.'*

And quickly his mind took a u-turn around a hair-pin turn and then catapulted down the ravine of

The REAL and the LASTING problem!

The Real and the Lasting problem which was his Quest to solve. That was The Problem. Her problem wasn't anything close to his problem. His daughter was just another misunderstood introvert. He could march into that school of hers and clear up that matter easily, when he had time. No! His problem was The Problem. And That Problem was what he had to fix; what he was trying! dying! to fix; desperately dying to fix!

But so far hadn't.

The INSTITUTE! That was the real and the lasting problem - his Quest to return the Institute to its Glory! The way it used to be under the Old Chief. Especially now. After what IV had just did.

Did yesterday!

'At my Institute!'

The Institute. Where his day was filled with so many Artistes because there were so many more of them; so much Institute because the building had grown wings; and too too many rules because IV loved rules. IV loved rules just like III, the Old Chief did. But IV's rules were nothing like the Old Chief's rules.

'The Old Chief. That crazy old codger!

'Crazy! Listen to me say that word! If the Old Chief would've heard me!'

He patted the pamphlet written by the Old Chief himself that told the story of how he'd come up with the name for the Institute.

And what a name he had come up with!

The Institute for the Compassionate Care of the Extraordinary and the Always Interesting.

Dr. Oomla could pat that pamphlet because he was wearing it. Every morning, he'd transfer it from jacket to jacket, from one breast pocket to the other so the story it told would lay close to his heart.

And what a story it told!

About the Institute and its inhabitants. About the village and its villagers.

And what it revealed about its writer!

The Old Chief, in all his contradictory glory! His head-in-the-clouds, utopian ideals but a stomach for the-down-and-the-dirty; his ego that was shockingly even more gigantic than any of the Show Business's patients he treated yet a heart miraculously even bigger than that. The Old Chief believed in the power of words, for better and for worse: to inspire, to heal, to hurt, to amuse and it showed on every one of that pamphlet's pages; and in the name he had dreamed up for the Institute, in all its sesquipedalian magniloquence. But what really cracked Dr. Oomla up when he read and reread and rereread that pamphlet was the Old Chief's sense of humor. The Old Chief laughed with everybody, at everybody, including himself; he didn't care whether they were mental or normal or who they were. He didn't even care if he revealed things about himself that were ridiculous; as long as they were comical, it was there in that pamphlet for all to know and to read. He wanted everybody, especially sick people to laugh, because he always used to say, 'people who are laughing are people who are not crying.' The Old Chief had recognized that laughter was good for patients long before the mental health community was writing articles like 'The Interposition and Effectuation of Laughter as a Mediator between Reality and Well-Being in the Mood Disordered Homo-Infirmus.' Had the Old Chief been alive when the theorists were coming up with such howlers, he would've gleefully added his own to the collection.

'I can't believe I even allowed myself to think that word crazy!' Many years ago, the Old Chief had even banned that word from being spoken in the village.

'The Institute for the Compassionate Care of the Extraordinary and the Always Interesting!'

·∴C∴·

("Lady, don't you think you ought to let the Readers actually, like, read that pamphlet."

"Author darling, Lorraine is right. They really need to learn all they can about the Old Chief, that village, that Institute, which has such a hold on our poor, brooding Dr. Oomla and which caused him, that loving husband and doting Father, to sometimes neglect to dote, to love. That even caused him, a psychoanalyst, who is supposed to understand people so much, miss what was going on with his own daughter! What was going on under his own roof! That his sweet, his shy, as he himself believes, his 'introverted' Sophia, had her own secret Midnight Movie Star School and she had it for a long time! So maybe our Dr. Oomla was not exactly correct about his Sophia. Because wouldn't you say darling that anyone who has a Midnight Movie Star may be a whole lot more than just an introvert? Unless, of course, that is how you human introverts behave."

Me, I imagine Fairy introverts and human introverts behave much the same way. Introverts keep things inside. An introvert would keep something like a Midnight Movie Star School secret.

And Lorraine, I actually agree with you about the pamphlet! Readers, what follows are the contents of the pamphlet written by the Old Chief – Dr. Knitsplitter III, that Dr. Oomla knew by heart.)

• • • HOW THE INSTITUTE GOT ITS NAME • • •
By Edwig Knitsplitter III, MD

I, Doctor Edwig Knitsplitter III, hereby take down the sign that says INSANE ASYLUM. I'll have no sign making my highly sensitive Artistes (I refuse to call them patients!) feel bad and then hanging that sign for all to read outside MY Asylum's door. I should have done this a long time ago. I, of all people, should know you don't get people BETTER by INSULTING them!

With the sign tucked under my arm, I strode back to my office and racked my brains trying to think of kinder, gentler names.

By the time I got to the veranda, it was The Institute for the Study of Behavior.

By the time I got to my office, that name was

Gutless! Witless! Wishy-Washy!

At least an insane person is a character with bona fides. Many of the greatest characters ever written for the stage are insane. Insane strides center stage. Or, at least, goes crab-wise. But no matter how they get there, center-stage is where Artistes prefer to stand. The Institute for the Study of Behavior! Where's the grandeur there? Surely those in the entertainment profession would rather be known as 'insane' than as meek, little lambs waiting to be studied. That new name hardly belongs on an Institute that takes care of those with the disposition for Show Business: its brazen provocateurs, its grandiloquent flamboyants, its shrinking violets that only grow when planted on a stage. And besides that new name would tip them off that my staff and I are studying them and their behavior. They might get complexes. And not the good kind.

So I picked up my well-worn dictionary and looked for the types of words that could describe my Artistes. I knew I should pick words from science and not from poetry and drama. But I wouldn't pick words drained of their lion's-roar either, like so many scientific words are!

In short, I'll have to find words that are worthy of those with flair; modern words that give good complexes.

In short, I confess, it wasn't.

The Institute for the Compassionate Care of the Extraordinary and the Always Interesting.

Fit-for-a-marquee!

'Extraordinary' because it gives good complexes. 'Always interesting' because it is worthy of those with flair. My Artistes would appreciate every word on that sign. My Artistes would be thrilled to stroll through the portals of an establishment with a name like that.

My Artistes'd probably be even more thrilled to star in a show with a title like that.

This new title might be so good, they actually may demand I build a marquee just so they could get their name to appear over the title. They may even start squabbling about who gets Top Billing. "Miss D now appearing at The Instit … " But just as quickly as I imagine a problem, I imagine a solution. I'll build a marquee but only if they actually do start squabbling, and, if they start squabbling about top billing, than each of them could take turns having their names appear over the title. But quickly and efficiently is how I solve any problem I encounter. The old sign will come down, the new sign will go up, a marquee if need be, and nothing will deter me from my purpose, no squabbles, no nothing.

You old Bulldog you!

However, before I told my Artistes about the Institute's name change though, I knew I would have to win over the staff. I feared my staff might say the name was a trifle long, or even worse, that it would add even more delusions to some of the already delusional Artistes, and they might try to convince me to eliminate a word or two. But I knew that the old name distressed and insulted my Artistes but that this new name, though it may flatter them, would also comfort them and I had no intention of removing even one of those important words.

So I strode around my office saying this new name - gently, persuasively, commandingly - figuring out the best way to announce this more inspiring name to my staff at the weekly staff meeting. I could see them all - the psychoanalysts and nurses and dieticians and therapists and technicians and everyone else who takes care of my Artistes – sitting around the conference table and pondering the meaning of my kindly words.

My positive, uplifting words!

I so hoped they would inspire my staff the way they inspired me that soon they would be speaking about the Institute even more respectfully than they usually do.

But how could I be sure my staff would see it the way I do?

An image popped into my head. The Statue of Liberty with its Emma Lazarus's poem! The world's favorite Colossus of Welcome with its words of Good-Will! That's how! I'd remind them what that plaque says about 'your tired, your poor … the wretched refuse.' I'll explain to them that my sign would serve the same function as that poem on the Statue of Liberty. Except my sign is more appropriate for welcoming Artistes, since movie stars are certainly not 'your tired, your poor.' Although after being run through a coupla' times by some of those maggots in Show Business, those Artistes sure could feel like 'wretched refuse!' The staff'd have to agree that my words are a Colossus of Welcome and Good-Will. And my sign will stay!

I won thanks to the colossus, alright. My colossus-sized bullying. And soon the staff set such a fine example of respect that even the people in the village couldn't help but notice - and they did the same. Til it came to pass that no one in that village would even dream of calling the Institute and its inhabitants anything other than hunky dory. No matter what the Artistes did or how they behaved.

However, everyone who came from the neighboring villages had just one word for that Institute and its inhabitants. And that word was "crazy." "Crazy" and they'd say it when a group of chorines in full tap, went tap tap tapping down the street practicing for the Institute's weekly Show. "Crazy!" and they'd say it when be-wigged, be-plumed actors went monologue-ing in full shriek down Main Street. "Crazy!" and they'd say it even when the Artistes went loping, looping and lunging by. They'd say it even if some of those very same Artistes they were saying it to were beloved Stage Actors and famous Movie Stars. They didn't care. But the shocking thing was even the people that came from Goliathon - with its endless parade of goofballs, oddballs and screwballs - would say it. In fact, those visitors had their own special nickname for our village - Dance-Dance - all because our village just so happened to be up river from Sing-Sing. (I'm not talking about Sing-Sing as in Lah-Lah. No, I'm talking about Sing-Sing as in Penitentiary.) And then they'd laugh-laugh.

I'd been pleased with my conversion of the staff and villagers. But I knew my work wasn't finished. I knew all about those people who came from the neighboring villages and from nearby Goliathon and what they said!

Those &@^^^^ visitors!

And soon after the conversion of the staff and the villagers, I made up my mind - I wasn't about to let those visitors undo my hard work either.

I'd just have to convert them too.

I'd ban the speaking of the word "crazy" in the village.

So the visitors were next. All the visitors. In fact, I decided, EVERYBODY WHO CAME TO MY VILLAGE. EVERYWHERE IN MY VILLAGE. No visitor nor villager nor staff not even the Artistes themselves would be allowed to utter the word - not walking along the walks nor shopping in the shoppes nor eating in the village's only eaterie – nowhere.

But even I, the Bulldog, knew how difficult that would be. I'd need a plan. But every time I tried to come up with one, I'd get stuck in the same fantasy.

And if those vituperaTORS viTUPerated such vituperaTIONS in front of me … no plan would be necessary … I could PERSUADE them to stop. But then I've developed … abilities … To enlighten … Special abilities … Dare I say … Freud-like abilities?? … After all, I've studied his every word for what seems like an eternity. If only I could be there when those visitors … those BLANKETY-BLANK visitors … spat out their ignominy. I could turn those foul-mouthed foreigners into poets!

And then I'd stop whatever I was doing so I could imagine myself triumphantly intervening while all my colleagues stood by in great admiration, as I used my invincible therapeutic technique that only I had mastered to its pluperfect utmost and as I solved the problems of all those wretched, fresh-mouthed visitors, once and forEVER, and that I, and only I, know how to administer, with glowing results, for each and every one of those foul-talking visitors …

And so it would go every time I tried to come up with a workable plan to ban the word "crazy" in my village. Over and over. Day after day. The same fantasy.

Until one day the responsible force within me could stand such drivel no more and rose up as a super-force, straightening me in my chair and hammering back into my head one of my own personal rules I'd forgotten - that whenever I announce official decrees to the citizens of the village and the staff and the Artistes, I, as the Institute's Chief and the most renowned of its psychoanalysts, should be the sanest person talking. After all, don't I have a reputation to uphold? Wasn't I really and truly renowned? Haven't I treated the Artistes C and C and J and B? And my Father before me, Knitsplitter II, didn't he treat the Artistes R and M and B and C? All of Show Business and certainly the villagers, surely even the people of Goliathon, indeed this great land, know the name Knitsplitter. Why the Artistes practically bow down when I pass. If Show Business had a pantheon, I would've been considered one of the wisest, most trusted people in it. After all, me, and my Father before me, had helped so many Artistes fight so many of their battles and knew so many of their secrets, and had kept them for all these years. Because no Knitsplitter had ever or would ever talk to the press about any of the Artistes, famous or infamous, we've treated for all these long years. And everybody knows how hard that is; and was, because even back then the press would pay princely sums to learn our Artistes' dirty little secrets. Wasn't that why me and my Father earned the nickname Bulldogs? The Artiste C called II, my Father, Bulldog after II bit the pants' leg off of a member of the press who was trying to find out whether an "unconfirmed report" about C was true. Well, I'm no different than II. Whenever I spot a member of the press prowling through the village hoping to get a scoop about one of my down-and-out Artistes, I'd bite the pants' leg off of him too! There isn't a member of the press who'll cross my path. They know I'd do the exact same thing my Father did. For III is a chip-off-the-old-II. For I am a Knitsplitter!

I quickly returned to my senses - realizing that if any of the Van Der Speckians would've heard what'd been going on inside my head, how rapidly they'd've concluded I was hardly the sanest person talking but was rather the personification of the very word I was trying to ban. And how they'd've hurled that word I'm trying to ban at me. Guilt must've crawled out of the primordial ooze that is my id and saved me from great embarrassment ... What was I thinking? I am hardly Freud! Why I couldn't even be God!!! I can't be everywhere.

Although I AM a Great Persuader ...

Apparently this very same super-force could stand strong for only seconds before back into the ooze it slid ...

... after all look at what I just persuaded my staff and my citizens to do ... They stopped using the word 'crazy' based on my fine example. Someone should just put me EVERYWHERE!!!!

I gazed heavenwards.

Nothing happened.

I was surprised. We Pantheon-ions aren't used to being ignored.

Okay ... okay ... I'll not be put everywhere ... I can accept that ... but if I studied and learned, if the staff, studied and learned, if the villagers studied and learned, so could the visitors study and learn. I will teach them ... WAIT ... I can't teach each and every visitor ...

... could someone else? ...

Who could always be there? Is there anyone in the village ... Would that be possible?

Until it dawned on me ...

The Village Police. They work 24 hours a day. I'll teach them ... MY WAY ... THE RIGHT WAY ... THE KNITSPLITTER WAY. My wisdom-for-the-ages! I'll make a very special plan. Special because I'll load it with my expertise - my vast experience. And it'll be MY plan.

For all people to learn by ... not just the Village Police!

My KnitsWits!

I chuckled heartily.

From then on, whenever I referred to my KnitsWits, I chuckled heartily.

From then on, whenever I referred to my KnitsWits, I chuckled alone.

I chuckled anyway.

Some Bull Dog! You, Weiner Schnitzel, you!

On that day, I, Dr. Edwig G. Knitsplitter III was ready to formulate my plan. I sat down and wrote at the top of the page "KnitsWits - The Knitsplitter's Plan for the Enlightenment of All Village Visitors" but I dropped my pen after I finished the sentence - "Whoever heard anyone say the word CRAZY would immediately call the Village Police—"

This isn't what I wanted. The Village Police dealt with the jaywalkers, the scofflaws, the cat burglars. Certainly a Visitor saying the word Crazy shouldn't be apprehended alongside that ilk. Furthermore, the people telling them to stop using the word Crazy should not be the Police either. Otherwise the Visitors might feel like common criminals. I wrote the word "Sheriff." Sheriff sounded less intimidating. I picked up my pen again and began writing ... "Henceforth, the Police in this village are to be called Sheriffs." NO ... NO ... NO ... and down the pen went again. These Sheriffs should not go walking through the village with uniforms and billy clubs scaring citizens and visitors. They couldn't wear anything like that. I want them to dress like Therapists. But no little-White-Coats. They should have beards and wear tweed. Furthermore, I want them to talk like Therapists. And since I want them to talk like Therapists, I'll train them in the ways of Therapists. Then they'll be able to enforce my plan, not forcefully like a Policeman would, but sensitively, like a Therapist would.

I was pleased until it occurred to me that the Sheriffs wouldn't really be Sheriffs anymore, so they shouldn't be called Sheriffs. They were really a cross between a Sheriff and a Therapist. I wrote the two words together, crossed out some letters in each, and put the remaining letters together and came up with SHERIPIST.

I chuckled.

And the chief of Police would be called the THERIFF.

I chuckled heartily.

And because my ideas just poured out of me, in two hours I had written a 20 page treatise. A treatise that was so learned, it could have stood on the shelves of nothing less than the Library of Congress with other such type treatises.

Now all I had to do was convince the Mayor of the village. I called up the Mayor and the Mayor agreed immediately because he had learned the hard way that I, Dr. Knitsplitter, never, ever, under any circumstance, ever took no for an answer. Rather than have me, Dr. Knitsplitter, sit out in his lobby petitioning him everyday until kingdom come came and went, he agreed quickly and got off the phone fast.

And when all of the Sheripists were trained, the Knitsplitter Plan for the Enlightenment of All Village Visitors commenced. And I was very pleased, and I said, "It's perfect. I'm perfect."

But two seconds later, I had to admit, "No, it's not! Because nothing, and no one, is perfect. Alas, even I."

If the offending word was heard, the vigilant Van Der Speckian was to call the Theriff's office, the Theriff would send for a Sheripist and pretty soon a Sheripist – a twinkly-eyed, toothy-teethed, smilely-mouthed, hirsuted human – smiling is stressed in training - would show up beside the visitor and in no time flat that unfortunate visitor would've found that this hairy-type human had placed an arm around his person and stood lecturing him in the fashion of a Dutch Uncle, punctured with frequent pokes in the ribs.

I do admit, not many people came to visit our Village.

And that is a shame because the Village Van Der Speck is a charming one - the outskirts are rimmed by a filigree of trees, and where there are no trees, leafy plants make the spaces lacey and fragrant; and once inside, there are rolling lawns filled with soft grasses; and a Main Street lined by shoppes with window boxes brimming over with flowers; and cottages that looked like they were drawn by storybook illustrators; and the best street performances from the best actors in the best costumes designed by the best costume de-signers anyone could ever hope to see; and helpful shopkeepers; and frisky puppies; and children; and smiles all around. I believe the villagers ...

Readers, the rest of the pages were missing. But stuffed inside the pam-phlet were three more items:

The first item was an old newspaper clipping of an article written by a village store owner complaining about the lack of tourists in their village.

'Despite the many charms of our village, all visitors have to do is re-member those Artistes (I'd say the 'c' word were it not banned in our village press!) and the lectures they hate from those do-gooding sheriPESTS, - and if that isn't enough, look up the hill and see looming large above them the Institute with its tolling belfry and its many gabled roofs casting its shadow down over everyone and everything - and everybody but the most loathsome of the paparazzi and the most wild-eyed of fans stay out of our village. So our visitors get fewer and fewer. Surely that is not good for a marketplace!'

And the second item was a copy of the Old Chief's Will:

"I, the ever-chuckling, ever-dreaming Dr. Edwig G. Knitsplitter III, (said 'Father') hereby make this agreement with my never-chuckling, ever-scheming son, Dr. Edwig G. Knitsplitter IV (said 'Son') and that is; even if Son will never be a chuckler and/or dreamer like Father, Father will release his considerable-but-dwindling fortune to Son if Son will just take care of Father's beloved Institute and become its Chief, Chief IV. And when Son agrees with Father, then and only then will, I, Dr. Edwig G. Knitsplitter III, hammer out the second agreement, my final agreement, the one with the Chief of All Chiefs, and that is, now that I know my beloved Institute will be taken care of, I will willingly depart this mortal Institute, the Institute for the Compassionate Care of the Extraordinary and the Always Interesting, for the Eternal Institute of the Perpetually Compassionate and the Everlastingly Interesting. Amen."

The last item in Dr. Oomla's breast pocket was a very compact notebook with 'Thoughts of Sigmund Oomla' printed on its cover. Its first two pages had just two carefully printed lines:

'Oomla, why are you fascinated with III? III is dead and buried; his son, very much alive, every inch of him, the New Chief.'

The rest of the pages were leaning-towers of hectoring:

'The New Chief? What a hoot! What a difference between The Old and The New. Between Father and Son. Between the Institute Then and the Institute Now. I can't seem to accept that I don't work at the Old Chief's Institute.

'So why am I accepting it? I see what IV's doing to it! He's dwindling its considerable fortune even further and slowly but surely undoing what his Father had done before him, because he, unlike his Father, is 75% Bull Dog, 25% Pit Bull and Zero% Weiner Schnitzel.

'What can I do about it? What would my hero do about it?

'My hero?

'DON'T YOU WANT TO BE HIM? ISN'T THAT WHY YOU WEAR HIS PAMPHLET?

'Hero? III? He's dead and this pamphlet is all I have left of him.

'OOMLA, THIS PAMPHLET IS YOUR HERO. THIS PAMPHLET IS YOUR FATHER. HAVE YOU FORGOTTEN YOUR OWN FATHER IS STILL ALIVE? WHEN DID HE STOP BEING YOUR FATHER, YOUR HERO?

'I'm definitely not my father's hero. I didn't do what he wanted me to do. But what he wanted me to do is what drove me into the mental health industry in the first place! After I saw how my Father's business, Show Business, treated people, I made up my mind I'd never go into it. I didn't do what my Father wanted me to do. I didn't do what IV did; I didn't go into my father's business. I could never have been a Theatrical Producer. And did my Father hit the roof when I told him. But, at least, I didn't wreck his business, like IV is wrecking III's. My Father should be grateful, but instead, we don't get together much anymore.

'I miss the old coot.

'Old coot? My Father? That 50% Dandie Dinmont, 50% Rat-a-Tat-Tat Terrier of troupers and divas alike, who the press can't get over, calling him the genius impresario; his theatres, THE palaces in stageland; his productions, shock-and-awe theatricals who nine times out of ten are in the red-hot epicenter of the smoke-and-mirror art; who the chattering classes call the Dapper-Dan man-about-town, that fine-wine-ing, fine-dine-ing, big-shot, big-spender; but who my Mother and a stage-full of chased-skirts describe as Shakespeare's real 'hourly promise breaker.' Until my father would sashay those skirts across the boards in one of his productions, and soon they'd be whistling a different Shakespeare, like 'all's well that ends well.' As for my Mother and I, well … he'd razzle-dazzle us too and we were full-up to the moon with him. No, there was nothing old or coot about my swell Father! The Old Chief! There's the old coot!

'The swell and the coot! How could two people be so different?

'But the Old Chief and my Father did have something in common; they could really twist an arm!

'But by the time III had IV's arm in a twist, his son was a grown-man and should have known his own limitations; which is that he didn't, and would never have any feeling for sick people, and that he should never go in to a business whose only purpose was their welfare, even if it did greatly disappoint his Father, and even when his Father began to beg and bully and bribe him to.

'Beg and bully and bribe.

'Just like your own Father tried to do you. But you don't approve of begging and bullying and bribing, do you? And you wouldn't let yourself be begged or bullied or bribed. And you were right because look at where such tactics got the Institute, and all of those pitiful Artistes who have been so dependent on that Institute for all these many years! But look where disappointing your Father has gotten you, Oomla. Your Father can't seem to make time to see you and you've been disinherited and you're sure not his hero anymore.

'And you don't have that Maestro of Wonderland in your life anymore!

'But, at least, I do what I want to do, and nobody's suffering; IV doesn't do what he wants to do, and now everybody's about to suffer.

'Hah! Nobody's suffering? When are you going to admit it, Oomla? That you're suffering. And a pamphlet isn't a Father. And your Father is your hero and, no matter what, you'd still like his approval even as old as you are. And by the way, do you honestly know what IV really wants to do? You've never opened your mouth and asked the old grouch. And, at least, the grouch didn't disappoint his Father. And 'Mister-Do-What-You-Want-To-Do' did. IV got his Father's approval - hah! Money more like it! - and you got neither, Oomla!

Boldly printed at the bottom of that page:
SO WHAT KIND OF DOG ARE YOU, OOMLA?

But then the rest of the pages were still leaning but in a whole different kind of hand, cramped and in an unsure, almost invisible line, as if not even he should read it:

'Did your Father and the Old Chief have something else in common? Did either one of them accept their sons as they really were?

'The Old Chief knew his son was a schemer; he said so right in his will.

'So how could my Father not have known who I was?

'I felt people's pain. I knew what people were thinking. I was sheveled one minute and disheveled the next. I ran away from every fight. I never stopped reading. I tripped over the tongue in my mouth and the tongue in my shoes because my tongues had minds of their own. But even when my tongues behaved, I didn't walk or talk the way a big-shot did, I skipped around and spoke in sentences that were complex and thoughtful, in a voice that no matter how much I tried, always came out clear but gentle. I listened and the big-shot talked. I observed people but didn't like people to observe, or even notice, me, and a big-shot gets noticed. A big-shot doesn't shun the spotlight and wouldn't have been relieved like I was when I moved to the Village Van Der Speck where there were no spotlights. I knew who my Father was. And he wasn't me. He loved Goliathon, tripped over nothing, spoke however he wanted and shunned not a damn thing. And, was a snappy dresser, witty, charming when he had to be, jumped smack in the middle of any fight, was in command, and expressed himself with flair. I knew I wasn't him. But I didn't want flair. All I wanted was to observe everybody and everything and then skip away so I could figure out what it all meant in the laboratory buried deep inside me. And by the time I was thirteen, I knew even then that the cloth I was cut from didn't come from any bolt found in Show Business. I knew I wasn't who he wanted and needed me to be.

'Whenever he'd say, 'Come with me so you can soak up the atmosphere of the theatre, it'll be your world one day!' I'd rush to go but not to soak up what he wanted me to soak up: what a producer did, how a theatre worked, the business of Show Business. That wasn't what fascinated me. No, when he was barking orders during rehearsals, I'd pluck myself off my plush velvet seat in those darkened houses and head back-stage to the real show where the real atmosphere was. That fake show was never what was real to me. Back stage was where I saw what the actors didn't want anyone to see; that so many of them looked different when the spotlight was off them. Some of them even seemed lost and forlorn. For days and days, I'd wonder, how could they be one way one minute and a whole other way the next.

'But when I asked my Father, 'Do you think a spotlight makes a person feel like a somebody when it's on him and a nobody when it's off him? Why is that? Nobody should feel like a nobody when nobody's looking at them, right, Pop?' But he shot back, 'Son, when you're a producer, just make sure that when that spotlight is on them, they perform the role you're paying them to perform. That's a producer's job! To make sure that the show goes on! In fact, the show going on no matter what is what Show Business is all about! Any producer worth his salt only pretends to his actors that he gives a damn about how they feel when the spotlight is off them!' But that was what I gave a damn about. I knew I was no producer. Why didn't he? Why couldn't he soak up my atmosphere? Shouldn't a Father soak up his own son's atmosphere?

'So why did the Old Chief and my Father insist IV and I take over their businesses, when it was obvious that neither one of us had the stomachs for their businesses? Why couldn't they accept us as we really were? Did our Fathers care about our true feelings and our innermost dreams? Did they even know what they were? And why should a Father pick out a child's profession anyway?

'So why do I wear III's pamphlet every day? Could I do what he did? Create a whole new way of running an Institute? I can't even save the Institute he created!

'What kind of dog are you? 50% Airedale? And Zero% Police Dog? And the remaining 50%, not even a dog but a Frizzle Chicken?

'To save the Institute, I'd have to turn into another kind of animal completely. The big-shot kind. Like my Father and III. They are bold, they take command, they impose their will, they stand and they fight. And they do it with flair - another thing III and my Father have in common. Flair, or voodoo, or whatever it is the Old Chief had, and my Father still has, makes everybody surrender. Those two could save the Institute.

'I read about daring deeds but can I do them?

'LIKE THE TIME YOU STOOD UP TO YOUR FATHER AND TOLD HIM YOU WANTED TO BE A PSYCHOANALYST AND NOT A PRODUCER. WHICH YOU DID WITH NO FLAIR, BECAUSE IF YOU HAD FLAIR, WOULDN'T YOU HAVE KEPT YOUR FATHER?

'But I'll be a leopard who can change his spots.

'YOU LOST YOUR FATHER BECAUSE YOU HAD NO FLAIR. YOU CAN NOT LOSE THE INSTITUTE. YOU CAN NOT.'

• • • 7:32 AM • • •

"Why Miss Sophia, Good Morning! We'd been wondering when we'd see you!" said Mr. James, who was all by himself at the table. "Unfortunately, Dr. Oomla had to attend to his duties and couldn't wait any longer. But he told me to tell you, Miss Sophia, and I quote, 'Have a wonderful day, Princess!' And to you, dear Miss Kitty, 'Thanks for the delicious breakfast!' "

Sophia smiled for the first time that morning. Her Father called her a princess. Her Father was nice.

'But suppose he knew what you do at night? Suppose he found out what you want to be? And that you lie! He wouldn't say nice things anymore.' And Sophia sank into her chair.

Miss Kitty was smiling - she hadn't noticed that her charge was not – Dr. Oomla wasn't there and Mr. James hadn't said a word about her not making it downstairs by 7:15 to serve breakfast; or, for that matter, that Sophia wasn't where she was supposed to be either. They didn't get caught. *'Luck-of-te-Irish!'*

Mr. James rose up, "Now please excuse me. As it is so bitter cold, I must prepare the automobile. Dr. Oomla has requested I drive Miss Sophia to school today." And he exited the kitchen.

"Miss Sophia, I'll be gettin' y'r breakfast ready."

Sophia was too tired to be hungry. But soon all her plates and bowls and glasses were filled to the top. She stared at it all but didn't dare say a word. She'd never be able to eat any of it but she'd better start moving it around her bowl. She picked up her spoon and mushed and stirred up her oatmeal. But that took such an effort, she put the spoon down. She was thirsty so she drank some milk and then some juice. She watched Miss Kitty watch her drink so that was good. But she could still feel Miss Kitty's eyes on her, so she picked up her fruit spoon and began to pick away at a blueberry. Maybe she'd put that in her mouth, it was tiny and it would be over quick. But then Miss Kitty busied herself elsewhere so Sophia instead mashed craters and poked holes in the yogurt and pushed the oatmeal high up the sides of the bowls. By the time Miss Kitty said, "Okay, Miss Sophia, time to brush y'r teeth, fix y'r hair 'n go t' school," she had drunk all her milk and juice, ate 7 blueberries and jabbed the Grand Canyon into each of her bowls.

Sophia lurched into the bathroom with Miss Kitty following close behind. Miss Kitty handed her a new toothbrush because Sophia's was upstairs in her bathroom.

"Now Miss Sophia, where might te clippie ting be for y'r hair? Remember I told ye t' grab one?"

"Oh ... I forgot. I'm sorry, Miss Kitty. I could wear a hat. It's cold today."

"Well, ye wear tat hat all day, because y'r hair needs a torough brushing. Do tey let ye wear hats in school, Miss Sophia?"

"Yes, Miss Kitty." It was a lie. *'Daddy wouldn't like that and Mother's angel voice would never tell a lie!'* And she felt her legs wobble. Then she remembered what Miss Kitty had told her about lies: that everybody has a bottle inside them filled with milk but when someone lies, they put a dark spot in their pure, white milk. So she steeled every part of herself. Lying was something she'd just have to get used to doing. She had a Midnight Movie Star School to protect. Besides, a milk bottle with a few spots that was inside her that no one could see was a small price to pay. Movie Stars only show their outsides. Because nothing, not spots on her inside milk bottle, was going to keep her out of her Movie Star School.

They tramped to the hall closet on the side of the great hallway and got their coats and scarves and hats and gloves and bundled themselves up; then slogged through the kitchen, the pantry, the mud room and out the door. The icy air stung their faces so they buried their heads deep into their scarves and lumbered towards the garage.

Sophia was so cold, her tears fell again and all she could think about was her warm, cozy bed and how she was just going to die cause she wasn't in it and was instead on her way to school. A real school. And not a Movie Star School.

Sophia dove into the back of the limousine. Usually Sophia walked to school accompanied by Miss Kitty. Dr. Oomla didn't want his daughter to be chauffeured. Dr. Oomla didn't like owning a limousine, although he really liked the driver of the limousine, Mr. James. Dr. Oomla just hated the limousine. He thought it made the Oomlas look pompous and wasteful. But since his wife needed to be in the city to run Mrs. Oomla's Giggle Pop, Inc, when she wasn't using her corporation's helicopter, she traveled back and forth from the village to the city in the limousine and his wife needed a full time car and driver. However, Dr. Oomla wanted his daughter to walk. To exercise, her legs, her ears, her eyes. To hear the music of grass, of birds. To see the dance of leaves, of branches. And to get to know the weather. Or as he'd say, as he skipped some steps and put up his collar and shivered,

Get on your get-up
and go.
And go.
Get on your get-up
and go.
See Skyclop Cyclops,
huff up their puffs
into Ghostly BrobDingNagians.
While Wizened-Domed Gnarly-Gnomes
punk up their trunks
into Bark-Beard ArborTreeMeians.
Get on your get-up
and go.
And go.
Get on your get-up
and go.

So every day Sophia, with Miss Kitty by her side, walked to school. But for some reason the North Pole was here today twisting every human, dog and tree in the Village Van Der Speck into stalactites and Dr. Oomla had insisted they take the car. Mr. James would not drive as far as the school; he would drop them off two blocks away so no one would see the Oomla's limousine.

Though Mr. James had been warming the car, the back seat was freezing, and Sophia and Miss Kitty cuddled close. Sophia's head drooped and soon she was sound asleep.

Miss Kitty was relieved; Mr. James would be wondering why they were so tardy coming down for breakfast, so tardy that they missed Dr. Oomla entirely. Now when he asked, she'd have to shush him; and he did, and she shushed. Miss Kitty knew soon enough she'd have to answer his questions, him being the major-domo of the Oomla's domo. But now that'd just have to be when they were driving back home after they dropped Miss Sophia off; after she had set her brown oxfords firmly down on the floor of the limousine. By that time she'd be ready for him. By that time, she'd've cooked up a doozy.

They reached the drop off point two blocks from the school in less than eleven minutes. Miss Kitty felt terrible having to shake Sophia awake. Mr. James was already holding the door open.

"Miss Sophia, I know ye a wee tired tis mornin', but here we are ten."

Sophia could barely pick up her head but somehow slid out of the car.

Mr. James spoke sotto voce, "Miss Kitty, in light of Miss Sophia's present somnolence," and they gazed at Sophia, her head almost to her shoulder, her eyes closed, leaning against the limousine, "I will leave it up to you to remind her to ask Mr. Irvington Snoggley, her teacher, for the driving directions to the speech therapist for her appointment this afternoon."

Miss Kitty nodded but Miss Sophia began to wobble so she steadied her, got her upright and then took hold of her arm, and off they went.

Sophia's feet walked. Right. Left. Right. Left. *'Don't feel a thing! Not cold. Not hungry. Not tired.'* But when she saw the school, it hit her. She had to go in there. And sit in her chair. At her desk. And be trapped. Til 3:00. Trapped. In school. And then she felt so tired and cold and hungry and misunderstood by everybody in the whole world and so far away from her dream, she stumbled.

Miss Kitty grabbed her arm and whispered to her, "Miss Sophia, ye'll be jus' fine, won't ye now. As te day goes on, ye'll get a second wind, ye'll see y'r friends, ye'll learn y'r lessons, ye'll listen t' te teacher. Here ye go, now." Miss Kitty knew she'd better let go of Sophia's hand before they got too near the school yard but why didn't the girl pull her hand away first? Was Sophia so tired that she didn't even realize Miss Kitty was holding her hand? Sophia would never want her school mates to see her walking into the school yard holding hands with her Nanny. Miss Kitty understood that. She was a girl herself once and knew how children loved poking fun at others. Miss Kitty felt more than a little worried now about Sophia's ability to pay attention to the teacher and learn her lessons if she didn't even notice Miss Kitty was holding her hand.

'Maybe tis'll be good for her! She'll stop watchin' old movies late into te night when she knows she'll have t' face te consequences 'n go t' school in te mornin'!'

Sophia noticed Miss Kitty's long face when she waved good bye. She looked as sad as Sophia felt. Maybe Miss Kitty really did understand that Sophia wasn't happy going where she had to go. But even if Miss Kitty did understand, she still was making her go. Her head weighed two tons and now it hurt, and her feet were great big iron boats. So slowly, slowly, Sophia lumbered over to her classmates' line in the school yard. Finally, she made it, took the last place and wouldn't pick her head up to even glance at her classmates. Only Melinda said Good Morning but Melinda said Good Morning to everybody; everybody except Milford Squeemllee because nobody said Good Morning to him since he was so shy that he turned pink when anybody talked to him and nobody liked to see a boy turn pink, even the cut-ups. Sophia did say Good Morning back to Melinda but she said it so low, Melinda didn't hear her. But that wouldn't have mattered to Melinda, Melinda was the cheerful sort and the prettiest girl in the room and believed it was her duty to greet the whole world because she believed everybody in the whole world wanted and needed to hear from her. But Sophia, at this freezing-cold moment, had both a head and a heart full-of-ache PLUS a frozen solid body AND had to swallow the bitter-pill that she, Sophia Oomla, was about to spend another day NOT in Movie Star School and that she, Sophia Oomla, was anything but cheerful and didn't want to have to talk to anybody as if she was. Shivering and praying that the Good Morning she just said was all she'd have to say to Melinda or anybody else, including Mr. Snoggley, now, or throughout the rest of the long forever day, Sophia stood behind her classmates with her head down low and her mouth shut tight.

• • • 7:35 AM • • •

Dr. Oomla—

·∴C∴·

("Not so fast, Lady!" said Lorraine. "Ya haven't even told our Readers what happened at the Institute yesterday. It's not enough that they know about the Old Chief and what the Institute means to Dr. Oomla, they also need to know what the New Chief did at the Institute the day before which really upset him. You brought up those papers that he keeps in his pocket, so they know that things at the Institute had been getting to our Dr. Oomla, but now ya gotta give them some specifics! They gotta understand why he needs to carry those papers around with him at all times!"

Lorraine, I only just got Dr. Oomla out the door!

"Well, aren't you, like, touchy! Lady, ya want to know what the dispatcher told us when he sent us in on this assignment, 'Fairies, you're lucky! Sophia's parents are loving parents. Your assignment'll be easy!' Well, us Fairies had a hard time wrapping our wings around that one, when we saw how her parents behaved! If that's what you humans call happy, us Fairies

sure don't! There is her Father complaining about his own Father not paying attention to his atmosphere! He should tawk! He wasn't paying attention to his own daughter's atmosphere! And the loving Mother was, like,
never home - which in my opinion, wasn't so bad because at least Sophia
didn't have to listen to that voice and compare herself all the time and then
come up short all the time - but still her Mother had such an impact on
Sophia since she still didn't like her own voice and here she was ten-years-
old and remember, we're, like, Sophia's Happily-Ever-After Fairies, and in
a coupla months we had to leave, like, forever. We was worried that we-the-
Fairies wouldda failed and that our charge just might not live so happily-
ever-after. Lady, the Readers need to understand what we was up against, so
they won't, like, ya know, judge us, if we don't, like, ya know, hit our target!

Do you really think I, a conscientious author, intend to deprive our
Readers of the whole entire story? If you'd just keep quiet, I'd tell it!)

·:·)·:··

Dr. Oomla could no longer stroll into the Institute at the sweet-time of 9:30
AM. Now that IV had held so many fundraisers that he could afford to add a
wing to the Institute - which he quickly filled to its tip with Artistes and every one
of those Artistes in desperate need of a psychoanalyst's services - Dr. Oomla's
schedule started at the precise hour of 8 A.M. And every twenty minutes - yes,
IV had cut the Artistes' forty-five minute appointments down to twenty - on
the dot, IV wanted Artiste out, Artiste in, back to back. IV liked his Institute
to run on schedule, like the trains in Switzerland. But running an Institute
filled with Show Business Artistes as if they were trains was ludicrous. Expecting
one Artiste to bound off the couch stage-left while another fell on stage-right
sometimes required sensitive negotiations. But IV wanted no complaints from
the Trustees or the Patrons or the board about a Doctor's non-compliance.
The Artistes may not conform but the Doctors sure better. But then again, IV
wanted no complaints from anybody about anything. Period. He may not have
wanted complaints, but he got them and IV was forever on the war path. And
everybody, especially Dr. Oomla, did everything they could to avoid him.

IV appeared to have only one interest. Holding huge fundraisers for the
Institute where he would raise large sums from wealthy patrons of the arts
and Show Business power brokers. And because the Institute and its Show
Business clientele were now famous, legendary even, they came and they
came bearing money. Huge sums of it, enormous sums of it, all of which IV
must be hoarding away to spend on the Institute, one pinched, squeezed,
red-cent at a time. And he pinched and squeezed anyone who was around
him when he spent it, too. Staff Members, in particular. But, other than

cutting their appointment time, he hadn't really pinched and squeezed the Artistes.

Until yesterday. Because at that morning staff meeting, IV removed all doubt of his intention to pinch and squeeze them too when he announced the Institute's three new rules. And Dr. Oomla and the staff were devastated. Their Institute, their lives were about to change forever. But they knew whose lives would really change, who'd really be devastated forever. The Artistes. And as IV droned on, they silently agonized: When should they tell the Artistes the news? And what, pray tell, would those over-the-buzzsaw-and-through-the-woodchipper creatures do when they heard it?

• • • THE FIRST RULE • • •

<u>The Institute's practice of Performance Therapy wherein the Artistes put on plays every week is hereby changed to putting on one play a year.</u>

IV wasn't satisfied just to state this rule and move on to the next, he wailed and snarled and brayed away on it. Or so it seemed to Dr. Oomla and his ears.

"Performance Therapy causes too much tuuuuRRmoil, too much UUUPset, too much plotting and scheming and maNIPulative behavior among some of the more mmmmercurial Artistes who are ALLLLL too often unhappy with the part they've been assigned in the weekly show. Performance Therapy may even be the sole reason some of the Artistes are staying in the Institute, feigning sssssickness just so they can be in a showwwww!"

Dr. Oomla's ears wanted nothing more than to flap away, far away, from the auditory offenses that they had to endure. But they and he went nowhere. He and they knew that every word that IV had thus spoken proclaimed nothing less than the destiny of the Artistes and the Institute. And his own. And he and they sat there obediently and took every brayed word in; though to Dr. Oomla, the brays hurt his ears and the words broke his heart.

His flesh was giving him up though; he could feel it get clammy at just the thought of even whispering this Rule to the Artistes. He looked round at his colleagues, those cool medical professionals didn't look themselves either.

"But we've always been able to handle the Artistes, Chief!" Dr. Byron, the most charismatic of the group, spoke up.

Dr. Oomla was relieved. Somebody was fighting back. Somebody who wasn't afraid of a fight. Somebody with a flair for public speaking. *I don't do grand performances. Grand performances are for The Voices of this world.'* People listened to Dr. Byron. He was funny. He wore snappy clothes. And he swaggered about like a rock star. And, to Dr. Oomla's discerning ears, Dr. Byron could command with his voice. *'Of course, it would be him, with his baritone, with his gift for gab!'* and, as if under a spell, Dr. Oomla shut his eyes, opened his ears and waited for IV's explosion.

But IV said nothing so Dr. Byron kept going, "Okay, it's true, very true that some of the Artistes swoon onto the Institute's many fainting couches when they don't get the part they've been campaigning for. And alright, some of the Artistes may even benefit from judicially issued restraining orders. And, Chief, ole pal, you may even be right that some of the Artistes feign sickness so they can stay at the Institute and be in a show. But then we get to see how truthful the Artistes are, how they handle disappointment and stress, and how they resolve their conflicts; and if they can't resolve them, we can then make those unresolvable conflicts part of the Artistes' therapies. After all, Chief, what better place for the Artistes to display their problems than under the watchful eyes of trained mental health professionals?"

IV was glaring at the wall but that didn't stop Dr. Byron, "Chief, don't forget, Performance Therapy has a 100% participation rate. It's the only therapy the Institute offers that can boast such numbers. It's the most well-attended program the Institute has ever offered!"

'Dr. Byron is no statue! Is that why IV's not exploding?'

Just then IV gazed in the direction of the conference table and muttered, "I'm not the only one who thinks this way. Mental health professionals outside the Institute are also skeptical of the benefits of our practice of Performance Therapy. They describe it as 'a dubious, possibly dangerous undertaking' and are convinced it should be tested scientifically. Such tests would show, they say, that Performance Therapy stresses all-ready over-stressed patients with too much competition; with performance anxiety; with feelings of inferiority; of superiority - feeding huge egos already huge to begin with, etcetera, etcetera!"

Swiftly, Dr. Byron responded, "Chief, we don't disagree with them. We know that Performance Therapy is not a scientifically tested treatment plan. We just know it works. After all, we're right there and see for ourselves just how engaged the Artistes are in it. We even joke that the most unscientific, most controversial of all our methods is the therapy that works the best. And it works for a simple reason. It's just folks doing what they like to do. Doing what they're good at. Because when these folks, these mental patients, are putting on a show, they aren't mental patients any more. They're Artistes. Artistes on a mission. Chief, don't forget, just weeks before, they were society's cast-outs! Who would ever think that folks like that, with mental afflictions! could be fully engaged at anything ever again? But because of the Institute's Performance Therapy, they are."

Dr. Byron waited for the staff members to show their support but they said nothing. So he said what they didn't, "Performance Therapy engages the unengageable. Lets Artistes mine what's long been buried away inside them. Lets Artistes troubles pounce across a stage for all to see. And spin their dirty secrets into performance gold. Lets the sad, the sorrowful, the useless, the crummy, rise up and release their inner demons, their inner angels so that they can at long last reveal for all to see and all to hear just who they really are! If that isn't a miracle, then what is?" And he lowered his voice to a dramatic whisper, leaned into the conference table, looked IV right square in the eye and said, "We at the Institute couldn't care less what mental health professionals have to say about the Institute's Performance Therapy. It works. Period."

"I've heard enough! The rule still stands."

Dr. Oomla felt as if he had been punched. Surely, the staff felt the same way. As he had been taking in IV's every dismissive word and Dr. Byron's every eloquent one, he was all mixed up. Daunted and envious and he didn't know what else. He tried making himself feel better, *'Performance Therapy is all but gone anyway in spite of the efforts of our-man-who-is-no-statue! What use could I, who is one, have been?'* but he didn't feel better.

And he slumped low in his chair and shut everyone out. But the Artistes would not be shut out. There, in his mind's eye, they were, and there he was, too, greeting the lost souls when they first arrived; listening to their sorrows; getting to know them and their history; checking them into the Performance Therapy Program; watching them improve, some of them even well enough to return to their profession; and thanks to Performance Therapy, with their show business chops more chop-chop than they were before.

And there, too, was the Old Chief bragging about why years ago he had started Performance Therapy:

"I know what Show Business Artistes are good at. Putting on Shows. Even when they are in all sorts of conditions. I know what talent is under the Institute's roof. Performance Therapy is the way that our Artistes recognize their strengths and use them even when they're feeling 'exhausted.' I want them to be proud of their talents and show them off. As soon as those

Artistes hear that they have to put on a show, all of a sudden, they're hunky dory because I'm right! Because I know The Rule and, more importantly, I know the Artistes know The Rule! everybody in the whole world knows The Rule because everybody in the whole world knows - "The Show Must Go On." I even had that phrase printed on signs and hung those signs in every room of the Institute. Even the bathrooms."

Now, the old phantom was winking at him, "Hopefully, no devotee of Emily Post ever had to go to the bathroom at the Institute. The graffiti in those rooms in particular, I will not repeat, here, in your mind's eye, Oomla!

"I figured all this out years ago; I knew how beneficial Performance Therapy would be for the Artistes. It's the Institute's Art, Occupational, Physical and Psycho Therapies all rolled up into one. I knew that everybody needs to exercise their talent because when they do, they feel stronger, they feel better. And I knew how much talent the Artistes have to exercise. The trick is getting those Artistes to want to exercise those talents when they're not feeling good; when they may have even forgotten they have talents. I discovered that the shows were the way. The shows are that something that make those Artistes want to get out of bed in the morning; that make their problems suddenly seem less important because the shows have a way of becoming more important than their own problems.

"I insisted that the Artistes produce and direct and write every one of the theatrical productions – they perform in them, make the costumes, design the sets, sell the tickets, run the concession and even usher. They do everything. Except be the audience because the audience are the villagers. And the Van Der Speckians flock there every Saturday night no matter what. Not, incidentally, because they're loyal to their Institute; after all most of those villagers work at the Institute and the last thing any person anywhere in the whole wide world wants to do is step even their little toe back into their place of employment on their day off and the Van Der Speckians are no different than any of those persons. They come because they want to come. They love these theatrical productions. The theatricals are better than anything anybody can see anywhere, even in Goliathon. And that's saying something, Oomla, because Goliathon is famous for its theatrical productions. But these plays are so original, far-fetched even, and are such an adventure for the audience. Those audiences never know what they're going to see. Wild horses or wild Artistes or wild Artistes on wild horses couldn't keep them away. In fact, wild Artistes are why they come, Oomla! And the Institute have been doing shows every week for years! And you're gonna keep it that way, aren't you Oomla?"

Dr. Oomla felt even more miserable.

He thought about what Performance Therapy had done for the Artistes. Himself. The villagers even. Entertainment such as that every week is probably why some of the Van Der Speckians never really took to television. Those Saturday night performances packed such a wallop that the villagers were worn out; most of them couldn't bear the thought of watching even another second of theatrics. They needed to rest up and recover.

And then a conversation he had overheard one day recently replayed inside him: he'd been at Isabella's Luncheonette downing his daily bowl of lentil soup and black bread.

"Why should we waste time watching TV?"

"TV! with its perky, plastic-people and their snappy-comebacks!"

"Yeah! And their &@^^^^ happy-talk!"

"TV! Everyone knows, after working at this Institute, that Show Business is nothing but a legal con job! But the sad thing is even the News is! Because, nine times out of ten, it's just one side making up stuff about another side! But on TV, that's legal and it's allowed to be called the News!"

"Legal con job? Try brainwashing! And they get away with it because those big corporations are so rich they can buy their own television stations and then they can put anything they want on 'em. They're the ones paying the writers for Pete's sake! And make no mistake about it, those writers are paid by the Man to write stuff that pushes some secret agenda on us poor saps out there in couch-potato land! And watch out, though the Man is dressed in corporate-clothing, he's a black-caped, silk-turbaned Svengali. And the Man makes sure that any story that's in their corporation's interest is broadcast for the whole wide world to hear, and any story that's not is either sugar-coated or doesn't see the light of day. And we-the-suckers don't even realize that our brains are being flushed right down the toilet! There oughta be a law against calling that the News. But they get away with it!"

"What about those stars! God help us! They're ravishing! They're irresistible! And what about those commercials! They're downright dangerous! They're snatching our minds! They're making us believe we're sick so we'll buy their pills. And they're coming after our wallets, our votes on election day, our hearts, our very souls!"

"TV! Hah! A million channels of escape routes that guarantee that our days of just sitting off by ourselves wondering our own-thoughts as we breathe the fresh-air in our free-thinking village are over!"

"Who needs any of that! Because we have the Institute! After those actors make mincemeat out of themselves up on that stage for the benefit of us, their loyal audience! After they utter in their own words their own truths because those words were written by them and not by teams of writers on the dole … well, you're right, all I seem to do is wonder!"

"I hate to admit this but I still watch TV, but why do I even bother? I mean, I can see some of those very same TV stars perform right here in my own village every Saturday night; but this time, they ain't plastic! They're goose-pimply! And their oozes ooze and their drips drip. I can't take my eyes off 'em!"

'I hate television for all those same reasons plus a million more of my own!'

True to himself, Dr. Oomla did not jump up from his seat at the counter and throw his two cents into the pot. Just thinking it was enough for him. He couldn't have condemned TV better himself. He never set foot in his own television room and the Artistes' scorching performances were only one reason why not.

But he'd never've allowed himself to put what he really thought about television in plain English the way they just had. After all, he made his living being a wise man, and wise men are not supposed to be prejudiced about such things. And he certainly knew he was prejudiced against television. What would his patients think if they heard him say what he really thought about their way of making a living? Television, after all, was their bread and butter.

And, to him, way too many times, the source of their problems.

And bam! fantasy over! and he was right back at that conference table. And there were his colleagues. And there was IV - trying to ban the shows altogether - but now the entire staff was putting up a fight. His ears picked up.

"If it's not broke, don't fix it."

"First, do no harm."

'Chief, you are about to fix something that isn't broke. And do harm. Fix something that benefits the Institute's Artistes. Fix it and maybe break it. And maybe harm the Artistes in the process. Losing the shows will be a terrible blow to the Artistes. There isn't an Artiste here, no matter how severe his problem is, her problem is, who doesn't come to life when it's show night, who doesn't forget himself, herself. Those shows are a source of important therapy for each and everyone of them. And for the villagers besides. But even more important than that, they love them.

'But do I say it?'

And then IV backed down. The one show a year rule stayed.

Dr. Oomla hadn't had to say a word.

And then in his mind's eye appeared the hanging judge. 'Will the prisoner Sigmund Oomla please rise? Sigmund Oomla, you are hereby sentenced to life! To a life of Hard Thinking. With no possibility of parole! You will report to the prison cell in your mind. You will never stray outside it from this moment forward. And may God have mercy on your soul. The soul that you have shared with no one! And now it's too late for it and for you!'

• • • THE SECOND RULE • • •

The Institute for the Compassionate Care of the Extraordinary and the Always Interesting is now to be called The Institute of Efficiently Applied Science.

"The Institute's name is too long! Too ridiculous! It must be changed!"

Later, when the Doctors were loitering in the staff room railing at the new name, they got so worked up that soon they were shouting at each other. Though each other was hardly who they wanted to shout at.

One member of the staff was not shouting. He was sitting in his spot in the corner. Thinking. Even after he had been sentenced to a lifetime of it.

But hanging judge be damned; sitting in a spot in the corner thinking was what Dr. Oomla did. Was what he was famous for. No matter what was going on. He knew he was famous for it. And that he might even seem detached. Or worse. He was a psychoanalyst, after all. He knew how sitting apart from a group might appear to the group he was sitting apart from. But there he would be anyway, taking great pains to appear he was reading his medical journal - though his smile hovered and floated and faded like a certain cat's would and was a dead giveaway that no medical journal was causing it to – and plugging himself into the sacred universe's constant hum, its nourishing harmony. But as it never even wheezed back, he'd snap out of it and chip into the friendly banter going on around him. Until things got too feisty and then – and this is what really made him famous - he'd slip out the door.

But Sigmund Oomla had had enough of feisty, for when he was but a child, he had wisely observed, *I live in a three-ring-circus and my own Father is the ringmaster!*

Solomon Oomla was a legit producer of considerable stature in the Show Business community of Goliathon but underneath his striped and tailored suits were the stripes for another kind of business, monkey-business. And oh! Did the ringmaster want action to follow him morning, noon and night, and everywhere he went. And oh, boy! Did it!

Sigmund's household was not only filled with an actress Mother and a producer Father, but was packed to the rafters with many dramatis personae, most of whom had plumage, which they liked to strut, often, at the same time. Which meant that in his household, feathers were all too often ruffled, or even flying. Young Sigmund very well may have been the only-child in that household but, as he wisely observed, *'I am not the only child.'* For there was his Mother, a classically-trained actress, and a tempestuous live-wire; and there were those dramatis 'peacockae' of his Father's theatres, who his Father always used to say he was 'only temporarily' housing in his vast penthouse in the skies of Goliathon; officially, for their welfare; unofficially, to keep all three of his rings filled and prancing at all time.

His Mother used to whisper to her young son that the "peacockae have big egos." And as young Sigmund again wisely observed but this time not just to himself but to his Mother, "No one ever really likes to admit that they have a big ego but they sure say someone else does. And oh brother! Can big egos make a big racket!" There were door-slammers and last-word-artists and punch-line-snappers and hissy-fitters galore. There were some velvet-tongues too, mainly his Mother's but, according to his sensitive ears, not enough of them to go around. And because these big egos were stage performers, they were used to projecting into the "house," even when they were at home and sprawled over a banister.

"Big egos," his Mother confided in him, "can be pretty entertaining." And they'd laugh over their private joke.

Sigmund had many questions about big egos; what they were and where they came from, and for that matter, why some people had big egos and some people didn't. For Sigmund was an inquisitive boy. He was sure he didn't have a big ego because he wasn't at all like the peacockae. He didn't slam doors and howl and throw fits anywhere, and never once did he dangle from a banister; he spoke only when he had something to say, and was serious about it when he did.

But he didn't know who to ask.

He couldn't ask his Mother because every once in a while he suspected she might have a big ego, too, since she sure could become hugely actressy, especially when she was doing battle with his Father; and if she knew he thought that about her, her feelings would be hurt. And Sigmund dearly loved his Mother and never wanted to hurt her feelings.

And he couldn't very well ask the peacockae because if his Mother's feelings could be hurt, he figured, so, too, could theirs.

Young Sigmund needed to find out because he had made up his mind that whenever he would speak about anyone or anything he would be correct. An authority, even. The way his Father was about everything. Or so he seemed to young Sigmund. And besides, young Sigmund was just dying to understand as much as he could about people. People fascinated him.

'If I can understand my math homework and math is hard, I can understand big egos, too! I'm going to make it my job to make sense out of something that makes no sense! But I'll have to start doing ALL my homework, and not just my math homework. I'd better start reading stacks of novels. Novels are about people and that's how I'll find out what a big ego is. And if I know things such as that, I'll be wise. And not ever get a big ego.'

Soon he was constantly reading novels and it didn't take him long to figure out that those same characters hot-dogging, hang-dogging, and show-dogging their way throughout his household had much in common with the very characters Ahab-ing and Ichabod-ing and Napolean-ing across the pages of his storybooks.

The peacockae liked to tease the serious, thoughtful, gentle boy whenever they'd catch him in the shadows supporting his head with his arm. They called him The Thinker. But he would not tease them back. In fact, his *'Okay, I get it! I'm a statue and you're action figures! But at least I'm from this planet; all of you are from the planet-hear-me-roar in a galaxy spinning in hot-air!'* stayed in his head, along with,

'These 'big egos' are really touchy, including my Mother! They need a CHAMPION! so that's who I'll be! I'll be the one who protects them! I'll be the one to save them. That'll be my mission. I'll save actors from their big egos!

'Because the peacockae're right! I am The Thinker! And The Thinker wouldn't hurt people's feelings and tell them they have big egos even if they do. That's not in his nature! The Thinker takes matters seriously and always understands what's going on. Like the way Sherlock Holmes, my hero, the great detective, understands.'

One day young Sigmund was browsing in his school library when the spine on a book caught his eye, *Sigmund and the Wonderland Within.* He figured it was about a boy Alice. But the Sigmund of the title was Sigmund Freud, the great psychoanalyst. He devoured the book in an afternoon; Sigmund Freud sure knew about people with egos. And super-egos. And from that moment on, young Sigmund's hero was Dr. Freud. Sherlock Holmes only looked for the mysteries in murders and murderers, whereas Sigmund Freud looked for mysteries in everyone. Could Sigmund Freud be the one who would turn him into the champion? Could Sigmund Freud help him understand big egos? Namely those bloviators, those happy-little basket-cases, those confused, confusing actors who lived in his home? And maybe even his Mother, too? And the Ringmaster, himself? Could he find the mystery in all of them? He wondered, *'But to uncover their mysteries, I'll have to do something that Holmes did. Hunt down clues. A murderer leaves clues and so, apparently, does a non-murderer. But the clues a non-murderer leaves aren't just things that you can find outside, like muddy boots and howling hounds. The clues a non-murdering, regular person leaves are often hidden away deep inside them. But I can't see inside people; so I'll have to do what Freud did: listen to what the person says and how he says it, note what he doesn't say, and then watch what the person actually does. Those are the kind of clues an ordinary person leaves!'*

And suddenly living in a three-ring-circus wasn't so bad. Because his home was stacked to its moonroof with actors with the heebie jeebies WITH egos! Everywhere he turned! All waiting to be studied! By him! He! had his very own laboratory! What more could a future psychoanalyst need? Secretly, he gave them nicknames which suited their dominant personality traits. There was Cyrano, the poet who was always in love; and Punch and Judy, who were also always in love; they just expressed it differently. And there were so many more. He'd race home from school, run to the banquet hall where everyone gathered at the end of the day, settle himself in his spot in a corner and, as he did his homework, listen to what they said and how they said it; watch what they did and what they didn't do. And then he'd ponder, *'Yesterday Cyrano waxed so effusively about going to that audition but here it is today and he didn't go after all. Why?'*

He developed theories about his characters but he never let anyone in on them for though he was only a schoolboy psychoanalyst, he wisely observed, *'Some of these characters are sharp-shooting elocutionists who probably won't like it if I start asking them questions and they just might outgun me! And if the Ringmaster shows up, I have this sneaking suspicion that he won't like it either. Because I think he likes his three-ring-circus filled with action no matter how crazy the people are inside the ring making the action. My Father likes chaos; though that makes no sense to me at all. I don't like it. But he's quicker on the draw than me, than everybody! 'You're not the boss of here!' he always says to whoever gets in his way. I never want him to say that to me! So I'd better keep my wise observations inside where they won't get me in trouble!'*

One day his dream wanted company, and he whispered it to his Mother, "I'm an amateur psychoanalyst! When I grow up, I'll be just like Sigmund Freud!" But his Mother gave him a look he'd never seen before, and then she pulled him close and whispered, "Whatever you do, don't tell your

Father! He wants you to take over his business and become a producer like him. And that's the only thing he wants from his only child. He believes that you, his son, must follow in his footsteps! So this must be our secret." And he never said it out loud again, though he hadn't changed his mind about his dream. He didn't want to do what his Father did for a living. He didn't want to be a producer. Because Show Business, as far as he could tell, was chaos. And he didn't want to make chaos. He wanted to control chaos. He spent his young life imagining what he might say and do to do just that. He just never told anyone.

But no matter what he did, he found he could never really ever quite control chaos. Even now that he wasn't an amateur anymore but a bona-fide psychoanalyst. His boyhood dream embarrassed him - that he could control chaos! Because the cold hard facts – in the form of his patients, the Artistes – flung their spectres at him all day long; they certainly weren't chaos-free, even after he had worked his psychoanalyst magic on them. Still, every once in a while, when he had broken through to a patient, he would catch himself mounting his high-white-horse. And then the patient would have a relapse. And back he was, alongside all the rest of the grown-ups, swallowing his bitter pill, too - roll-rock-up, rock-crash-down, roll-rock-up, rock-crash-down, over-and-over, day-in-day-out - ad-infinitum.

But at this moment, after everyone, including himself, was reeling from IV's meeting, he knew what had to be done. And then he heard that hanging judge pronounce his sentence again. And he knew what must be done, *'Control this choas! Shouldn't you at least try?'*

And he watched himself mount his high-white-horse again.

'Hah! You! In the middle of a roomful of volatile people expressing opinions vociferously! Isn't that just like the chaos of your youth!'

And he was the amateur all over again.

'You haven't become any quicker on the draw, have you? Shouldn't you steer clear of anything that resembles a shoot-out-at-the-ok-corral? Besides, when you're on a break, don't you fervently believe that you need the exact opposite of what your Father needs, a three-ring-circus?'

And though he was still in his spot in the corner and though he was mortified that he was escaping, he did, for the umpteenth time that day. But this time, to England. Where a spring day from more than a century ago awaited him. He was strolling down the street, whistling a tune and swinging his walking stick along to its beat. He came to a tall, fancily-wrought, black iron gate with a gleaming bronze name-plaque. The Society of Youth and Promise: Erudition, Athleticism, Enlightenment.

And then he understood what was really wrong with IV's rule, *Just like that! IV put an end to the gracious discourse of a bygone time!'* That's what he so loved about that old name. And, at last, he opened his mouth to tell the staff but someone began to speak inside him again, *'As if your wise observations could restore the Institute's name! Hah! Here you are in the midst of chaos, silently making wise observations, just like you did when you were a lad! Did those wise observations ever make you the boss of there? As if wise observations'll make you the boss of here! Should you really say your little fantasy out loud for all to hear?'*

·∴☾·∴

("Hey, Me," said Lorraine, "was that, like, one of ours? Was that an As If?"

"I could never find out, Lorraine!"

Not now, you two, not during Dr. Oomla's story!)

·∴☽·∴

And Dr. Oomla said not a word but, this time, he remained present in his spot in the corner.

A doctor called out, "There has to be a program or a treatment entitled Efficiently Applied Science, after all we are an accredited Psychiatric Institution; he couldn't just make up a title."

They racked their brains trying to remember if they'd ever heard of such a treatment; those with beards, and there were a lot of them, were scratching them; those without, were scratching something. They couldn't think of a one, until Dr. Byron piped in, "Hey, if he's anything like his Father, he probably did just make it up."

'The length or the ridiculousness of the name isn't IV's real reason. His real reason is concealed in the name he created. He may have constructed that name to reflect a more concise, and even a scientific, approach to handling the Artistes, but it really represents IV's only concern. The title, after all, isn't Applied Science, it's Efficiently Applied Science. The word efficiently, coming from IV, means one thing - cost cutting!'

But Dr. Oomla was not volunteering his thoughts, and the staff, not able to read his mind, carried on.

"Yeah! But his Father had a way with words! The only thing IV has a way with is swords. He's a slasher. If everybody still wore swords, IV would be Zorro!"

"Zero, you mean! Lord of the Zeros!" Dr. Byron hooted. "The only thing IV has a way with is getting those Patrons to write checks that have a long line of zeros after the first number!"

"Those poor Artistes love that old name. They drop it any chance they can."

"And they had a lot more words to drop. Not anymore! Did any of you notice how they say it with pride whenever anyone asks them where they come from and how the emphasis always seems to fall on the Extraordinary for the Stars and the Always Interesting for the Character Actors."

"And when the Thespians drop it, they make the whole name thunder out like God-himself is speaking!"

"God? To these Artistes, God doesn't mean the God in the firmament. Not at all! When they think of God, they think which actor or actress could play him. And it's usually a different actor for different people. For the Americans, it's one actor; for the Brits, another."

'Humor! That new name has no heart or humor in it at all, like the old name had! But then IV is hardly concerned with heart and humor, so we must be!' Dr. Oomla still did not volunteer his thoughts; he picked up his pen, wrote nothing and made up his mind to slip out the door, like he always did.

'Hah! If you had a tail, it would be between your legs!'

But his mind wanted only to slip into more rumination, so it and he stayed right where they were. *'The staff hasn't memorized the Old Chief's words. They don't walk around with the story of how the Institute got its name in their breast pockets. The Old Chief always used to say that coming up with that name was the best thing he ever did; and it only took him a couple of minutes. But do I say that? Because that's what has to be said. And that's why I'm still sitting in my chair in the Staff room, why I haven't left. Nobody has said what needs to be said!*

'But if you say it, wouldn't you have to be the one who confronts IV? And to do that, wouldn't The Thinker Statue have to turn into Superman? You've never shown a talent for that in all your years here on planet-here-me-roar. Besides, could I ever come up with a name even half as clever? Could I stop it from happening? As if!'

That little voice was right. What was the sense of talking if he didn't back it with action.

But nothing was stopping his colleagues, "The Artistes speak that old name with reverence because that old name really represents how most of those Artistes see themselves."

"For better or worse!"

"One of our Artistes told me that for him getting into the Institute and being around all those other Show Business personalities was as far as he was concerned, almost as good as being in a box office smash or a sleeper or getting into that Drama School."

"Speaking of that, there was a young Artiste here, an actor, not too long ago, who suffered 'exhaustion' after he couldn't get into that Drama School. But you know what he said to me, 'That's okay! I'm better off here, hanging out with my people, even if my people have turned into mental cases; they're still Show Business Mental Cases!' "

"Listen, that may not be such great praise for the Institute, our Artistes should prefer it on the outside, not here on the inside."

"Well, after IV gets through with this place, they will, trust me, they will!"

"The Old Chief must be turning over in his grave."

They stopped speaking. Each of them dreading telling the Artistes. Each of them finally realizing what Dr. Oomla had already realized; just how unfunny all of it really was.

But the Third Rule hit Dr. Oomla the hardest. Because of it, he knew he'd have no choice but to leave the Institute.

• • • THE THIRD RULE • • •

<u>If an Artiste can be helped by medication, the Artiste is to be put on medication as a first step. Medication can no longer be used as a last resort. Medication helps the Artistes return to normal appearing behavior. The use of medication will enable the Artiste to leave our care sooner thereby saving the Institute money on extended inpatient care.</u>

Because the Old Chief knew years ago that when so many of the Artistes arrived at his Institute they were already taking lots of little pills and/or drinking from big bottles to make themselves feel better, he had gotten the bright idea, that at his Institute, he'd ban any mind-altering, mood-changing, brain-fixing pills and/or liquids from any treatment programs intended for mental conditions. The Old Chief would use his own methods to get his Artistes mentally fit. Other than pills prescribed by physicians for genuine diseases of the body, the Artistes would not be swallowing a pill or a liquid to alter their mind at his Institute. Period! He wanted his Artistes to get better and feel better by using his programs. And if the Artistes didn't like it, they didn't have to stay. The most shocking thing of all was that so many of those pill-popping, bottoms-uppers did stay.

With this rule, IV had completely overruled his Father, the Old Chief. Medication! The first line of treatment! at the Institute! And not the Old Chief's programs! Of course, when the Old Chief was no more, the staff had recognized that some modern medication designed for certain psychological conditions helped the very seriously mentally ill, so they did use it on Artistes here and there who didn't respond well to the Old Chief's type of treatment.

But not Dr. Oomla.

He was dead set against the use of psychiatric medication on mental patients. At all. Which put him at odds with all the other psychoanalysts at the Institute. And possibly the entire medical community. And even the modern world. And the staff loved to tease him about that.

And something else besides.

And as they sat there in that staff room that morning, they went off on him again. He knew they would.

"So there's our very own Dr. Purity Pants. Dead set against the use of any drug or stimulant to affect mood or behavior! But what is that, you say? That the person who invented daffeine is in his own family! Daffeine! That equal-opportunity stimulant! It cracks the sane and the insane up!"

He hated when they said that to him. But above all! He hated that ... that ... stuff! And though he did indeed hate that stuff, he had to conclude after he had done exhaustive research right after that nightmare, that there was nothing harmful in his wife's invention and that he had no reason to. Yet he did. Besides, to him there was something harmful in that stuff! It harmed his sacred principle! He was dead set against using a drug or a stimulant to affect mood or behavior! His wife had violated his sacred principle! His own wife! Even now, five years later, he would steam up wondering how his wife, who he so cherished and who so cherished him, could do such a thing to him!

But he never told her how he felt.

He didn't know why he didn't tell her. He wondered, he worried: should he, shouldn't he? What would happen if he did? He even knew how ridiculous he, a psychoanalyst, was not to tell her. And still he didn't tell her. He had a harmonious home. A beautiful daughter. A lovely wife, in spite of that disgusting stuff she invented. Which had made her a billionaire! Which also thrilled-him-not. But how could he, a modern man, tell a successful woman that he didn't find her legitimate means of making a living legitimate? What kind of heart would beat in the body of someone who would? Especially, nowadays, when the universes of breadwinning women were as sacred as the universes of breadwinning men. And he, as a psychoanalyst, was the sworn protector of sacred universes. Even when he couldn't stand one of the universes he was protecting.

So no matter how the staff carried on in front of him about that stuff and even whenever they went off on him, "Hey, old pal, how's life in the

'House that Daffeine Built!' that hovel made outta, what is it, jiggle juice? But no little pills for Dr. Oomla's patients! A dose of daffeine'll doggone do em, doggone do em just fine!" he suffered in silence.

And he suffered in silence now, too, realizing, *If I want to work at the Institute, I'll have to join the modern world of psychopharmacology or psychobiology ... or whatever they call it.*

'Or leave.

'Use medication!'

And Dr. Oomla's heart wanted out of his body.

'Doesn't IV know that all these new rules won't get the Artistes to behave like normal people. As if IV cared if they did. Who would want Artistes to anyway? That's what the Old Chief would've said!'

And then the staff turned to their other favorite sport; trying to figure out - how did that Father produce this son? He's so different than his Father!"

"III would never hold fundraisers with all those wealthy patrons of the arts and all those Show Business power players!"

"III'd never have all those pictures taken of him with them so he and they can appear smiling together in all those society pages!"

"Do you think III neglected him?"

"III'd never do all that good work so that there'd be all that publicity about all the good work he does!"

"Do you think III beat him?"

"III'd never have put all that money he raised in all the Institute's many, many accounts, because III would've spent every last dime. But not IV, he puts that money in those accounts. III could have cared less if all the Trustees of the Institute and all the Members of its Board knew he spent every last dime, too. But not IV, he cares. He cares a great deal. But does all that make IV—"

"Satisfied?"

"IV is never satisfied but the Trustees and the Board are. They sure are pleased that the Institute has all this money. And they love that IV knows how to raise it. Some of those old-timers remember his Father who would spend down the Institute's accounts to the very last cent, and how they themselves had to scramble around raising money so the Institute wouldn't have to close its doors forever. They never want to go through that again. And they know that terrible things can sometimes happen in the world; earthquakes! tornados! nuclear meltdowns! terrorist attacks! whole countries bankrupted! and they know with all this money, the Institute that they so support, that so many in the mental health community respect, that the Show Business people count on as their safe harbor in times of their temporary "Exhaustion," "Rest Cure," "Rehab," etc.; that their Institute will not have to close its doors but will be open and prepared for any catastrophe!"

"And they sure don't know what IV is really up to at the Institute because no one ever tells them. We sure don't because IV would fire us if we did. And we all know there's no place for us to go that's even remotely like the Institute. An Institute where an endangered species, the nearly-extinct-Freudian, is free to roam! Why this Institute is the last of its kind. Where else could we go? And IV knows it, too. So the Board and the Trustees don't know that he has been spending a little-less and than a-little-more-less on programs for the Artistes and slowly and so so subtly cutting back on services to the Artistes. So what's the likelihood that IV ran these Rules by them? Hah! They wouldn't be pleased to know about these Rules. Not pleased at all! Because at the start of every fundraiser, thanks be to IV they always say!"

"Thanks? Thanks for nothing!"

"Yeah! IV can do what he wants. And he knows it!"

• • • YESTERDAY EVENING • • •

"Old Chief, old friend, are you turning over in your grave?"

It was the dark end of that awful day and finally Dr. Oomla was talking out loud. To a dead man.

But at the end of many a day, he'd been having business with many a thing that lived in his head, including that dead man. Sometimes he even forgot the Old Chief was dead. He wouldn't have dreamed of calling for somebody real to talk to, like the love of his life, his sleeping wife. Or his ten-year-old. Or asked Mr. James or even Miss Kitty to join him. No.

Tonight, however, he was no longer dissolved in a corner like he was at the beginning of the day but was front and center before his own fireplace.

And still he was hard to find.

The fire, the mantelpiece, the wings of his chair, the many many shelves filled with his many many books, the library vast as a ballroom, towered over him. But it was the invisible that really dwarfed him, drooped his head, steepled his hands to cover his face and slumped him so low in his chair.

The Old Chief.

Tonight he had to tell the Old Chief what happened at their beloved Institute.

He should've let it all go. After all, things at the Institute had been bad for a while. And in the evenings, he was free of it all, at least for a few hours; he should lighten up and laugh, at least for a night.

But he couldn't let it go. Especially after this news. Bad news that had really hit him hard.

"So what do you make of your son, your offspring, your namesake?"

Usually, the Old Chief answered him; what would he say tonight?

But the only voice he heard was his own, "You're locked up in yourself and by yourself, in the dark, talking to a dead man! You need comfort and joy."

And he dreamed of having somebody to talk to, somebody real, "Shouldn't I invite Sophia in?

"What am I thinking! She's sound asleep and safe in her bed for the night. But what about Mr. James? Or Miss Kitty?

"Or my wife?

"Hah! If she's even home! It's just as well. No one should witness my misery. No one should see that a man, who makes his living helping people get through their troubles, can't see a way out of his own. No! Tonight will be no different!"

He would stay by himself. Brooding. About the Institute. And IV. And the Old Chief.

"So what do you think now, Old Chief? Are you horrified about IV's love of money, and his unrelenting pursuit of the people who have it? Are you laughing at his rules? Lampooning them? Right before you break down and cry, because it's your son that came up with them, after all. And, to say the least, IV doesn't understand Artistes. And never will. In fact, wouldn't you say that medication will knock the Artiste right out of them and turn them back into patients!

"Patients!? Hah! Try drugged-out zombies!

"The Institute without Performance Therapy! Isn't that what brought those Artistes back from the depressed or lifeless or angst-ridden or hysterical wrecks they were when they got to the Institute? Or at the very least turned them into depressed or lifeless or angst-ridden or hysterical wrecks who have something to live for! Who get out of bed because they want to do something! Who have a purpose! And is what makes our Institute so unique. I ask you Old Chief, is it just because IV can't stand a little emotional turmoil at the Institute? IV has been cutting back at the Institute for a while but he hasn't exactly been treating the Artistes poorly.

"And is that about to change!

"But he's been treating us, his staff, poorly for a while. To say the very least, he doesn't appreciate us at all. He, as far as we can tell, appreciates money that appreciates. Period. Money that the Institute already has, so far as we can ascertain, in heaps and piles.

"We figured out all that about IV, Old Chief! But we don't have to figure out what he thinks of us. He told us today, without reservation, at the meeting. THAT we, HIS staff believe the only way to get HIS Institute's patients better is through thoroughly unscientific programs that come from that express-yourself, let-it-all-hang-out time of love-ins, be-ins, sit-ins. THAT professional mental health workers in our modern world should rely on modern methods, like medication, and not ridiculous, over-wrought, hysteria-promoting, psycho-drama to improve the mental health of their patients. Psycho-drama stir up pots! Medication calms pots down! THAT we, HIS staff … blah blah blah.

"So, how about that Old Chief? We followers of Sigmund Freud and his methods, and of you, Dr. Edwig Knitsplitter the III, and your methods; we, who searched high and low to find a place where we could practice what we believe and found this, your Institute, which you should realize is the last of the hold-outs, because your Institute has always believed that the reason mental patients aren't well is because their souls need attention and that the way to pay attention to souls is to let each one tell its story, its truths, first to someone it trusts, then to each other, then for all to hear.

"Those other Institutes hardly believe that, Old Chief. Those Brand-Xes don't even do the bare minimum, which is to talk to souls for even a few minutes a week. They hardly pay attention to a mental patient's soul at all because they believe that the reason mental patients are sick in the first place is because their brains are sick and that the way to get brains better is to prescribe pills to fix those brains. And you know how Brand-Xers finds out if those brains are better, Old Chief? By meeting with those brains after the owners of those brains have ingested pill after pill after pill! And you know how many times Brand-Xers meets with those brain owners? 15 minutes EVERY OTHER MONTH! Because that's how often they meet their patients and that's how long their sessions are. But when that fifteen-minute-brain-assessment-every-other-month finally arrives, those poor patients have been so pickled in drugs that the only thing they can do is droop and shuffle and drag their brains and their souls and the rest of themselves into that session; so the only thing those Brand-Xers can conclude is those patients and their brains aren't better at all. Unless Brand-Xers consider turning mental patients into zombies better! And they do, Old Chief, they do!

"So here I am, here we all are, the last-of-the-Mohicans, psychoanalysts, followers of Sigmund Freud, who firmly believe in talking to souls by interpreting their dreams and their stories; we students who burned many a midnight oil in many days now long gone in order to earn advanced degrees so we would know how to do just that; we who have practiced conversing with souls day after day, year after year; professionals who trained like thoroughbreds and work like work horses; all so we can do just that. And now here is your son changing our methods! And your methods too! What sort of person could do that to us! He's your son! And he's changing your Institute! He's changing everything around on us. On our patients. On me!"

Finally, the Old Chief answered him.

"What sort of person lets him? You talk about IV not being able to stand a little emotional turmoil at the Institute! Could that be what you're afraid of! What would happen if you stood up to him, Oomla!"

The Old Chief gave way to the hanging judge, "Too late now, Oomla!"

The judge dissolved into the one person he had stood up to.

His Father.

And there was his Father demanding that he take over the family business and become a producer like he was.

There was his Father's face when he told him he would not.

Now he hardly ever saw his Father anymore!

The ringmaster!

There were more faces. IV. His wife … The very ones he should be speaking to …

And with that, he shuddered and wouldn't allow another thought in … and, mercifully, a happier time danced into his head …

Long, long ago when he played his music on his CD player and danced about and laughed with his wife, his daughter.

Long long ago, when he'd spend evening after evening with his wife and daughter testing Mrs. Oomla's experimental drink for the first time.

Long long ago, before Mrs. Oomla's Giggle Pop was born. And the happy time danced out of his head.

Mrs. Oomla's Giggle Pop! That dreadful artificial mood-enhancing dribble. That the world couldn't get enough of!

And was the reason he barely saw his wife anymore. The very reason her unforgettable voice wasn't filling up his ears and his soul in the evenings anymore. Those evenings were long gone. Because now every evening, she was early to bed so she'd be early to rise. That is, if she even was home, because so many nights she had to be here-and-there-and-everywhere to take care of her Corporation Giggle because that was a huge and hungry entity that consumed more and more and more of her.

Long long ago … Well that's exactly when it was … long, long ago.

'Brooding and pondering about all of this is how I spend my evenings now. Shouldn't brooding and pondering lead to figuring things out and then springing into action? And not to more long lonely nights filled with more brooding and pondering!'

And he looked around … "I am sitting in splendor …

"… in a wing-backed chair in my library the size of a ballroom that has no dancers but only books."

"You no longer ask books to dance, Oomla!" said the Old Chief.

"… in front of a fire that leaps into the most intriguing shapes."

"Oomla, shapeshifters no longer intrigue you!"

"They even do their dance, Old Chief, in the grandest of all fireplaces because my dear wife's Aunt Hortense had the architect of the House-that-Daffeine-Built copy it from the grandest one in the museum. The one with the mantelpiece so high that statues six-feet-tall have to stand on either side of it balancing it with their heads and hands - on its left, Euterpe, the Goddess of Lyric Song, and on its right, Polyhymnia, the Goddess of Sacred Song."

"Oomla, you are a humble man! Why does a humble man own the grandest of anything?"

"Because, Old Chief, my dear wife insisted we let dear Aunt Hortense have her way."

"And you are a studious man! Why isn't the studious man studying?"

"Because the more he reads, Old Chief, the more he wonders, would he have been better off not reading at all?

"Did those books really have to tell me that my boyhood hero, Sigmund Freud, was not a hero? And that you, Old Chief, weren't such a hero either? And did I, the psychoanalyst, someone who should know better, someone who should be ashamed to admit, someone who would never want his colleagues to find out, really stroll into the Village's bookstore in broad daylight and buy all those self-help books? And did I then devour every last one of them and then follow their easy steps all so I could become the hero? It was an act of desperation, Old Chief! Done only after I'd pored over those many 'important' tomes by the serious thinkers that are on all those bookshelves over there. Oh, I became something, alright. The bookish frog who-craved-the-silence-in-his-library-and-not-the-chaos-of-the-world became the bookish prince who-craves-the-silence-in-his-library-and-not-the-chaos-of-the-world. Because apparently no matter what form he's in, he behaves the same. He won't even wander into his living room, let alone prance off any place else. He can't seem to get out from under the spell of ... what is it? I ask you, Old Chief, did I really have to read all those books and still find out I can't change?

"And you know what else, the more he reads, the more he sees all the things he hasn't done.

"Although those books over there, about how our culture worships stars and fame and glossy, chiseled perfection, at least, I do do something about what I've learned from them. I'm always reminding our Artistes that 'though the Showmen of Show Business may blow hot on you one day, cold the next, and then blow you off entirely, that doesn't mean you're all washed up! You're about to find out how unique you are; in fact, today's your lucky day, because you've landed here at our Institute! If you open up your heart and your mind in your therapy and participate in our programs, you'll see for yourselves that there's nobody quite like you on the whole entire planet, and that no fantasy-making-machine made you that way either. You'll see! Just stay in our programs!' "

"Programs! Hah! Going, going, gone, Oomla!"

"And will I or won't I do a thing about it? That is the question, Old Chief."

"And what is the answer, Oomla?"

"Old Chief, I'm likely to sit here in silence in this library pondering how and when and if forever! That's what I did after I read those books over there. And then I felt sick. They're the ones about those big giant pharmaceutical corporations that make those drugs that IV is now insisting we prescribe. I ask you, Old Chief, how can a lowly bookworm take on mile after mile of 100-story-tall-corporations and their billions of little-rainbow-tinted-feel-good pills, let alone all of the countless humans who fall for their little-white-libels, distortions, obfuscations, etceteras about what would happen to them when they take their pills?

"And you know how 10,000-Tall-Stories pulled off their great con-job, Old Chief? Speaking about fantasy-making-machines! Big Pharma uses all the same tricks that Show Business does when they advertise their drugs to those trusting souls out there in TV land. Show Business hires the most convincing actors who sound gee-whiz like they are speaking the plain truth and look by-golly like somebody you wish you knew. So that's what Big Pharma does, too. And pretty soon, those poor souls are duped; they start believing that those drugs they saw on TV can fix not only their sick bodies but their sorrowful minds. Worse yet, that any kind of psychic pain they feel can be fixed with a pill. A pill made by Big Pharma.

"Oh! They'll admit right there on TV that their drugs have side-effects. But are you surprised to hear that they breeze over major side effects like they're minor ones? And that they don't tell you how long they actually take to test their drugs! And what the results are of all those tests! not just the ones that show that their drugs work but the ones that show that they don't!

"And they can get away with it, Old Chief, because they have their very own voodoo box! Television. But, Old Chief, television is everybody's voodoo box! No one is safe from its spell. Big Pharma recognizes that and exploits it. Even the Artistes, who know all about Show Business tricks because they're the ones who created the tricks in the first place, aren't safe. I hear what conditions my Artistes tell me they think they have, all because they saw an ad about this or that on TV. Thank God, my little girl is not under that voodoo box's spell! At least, I did something right!

"But, Old Chief, can you just imagine what my colleagues will say to me when I start criticizing big giant pharmaceutical corporations. 'Now where is it your wife works? In a big giant corporation that sells something that makes everybody, what did you say, happy? Isn't that what a drug does, Oomla? You say, those corporations are bad, but your wife's is good? What's that? You think your wife's is bad, too, Oomla? And here we all thought you were the Village's lovebirds! So why is it bad? It wouldn't be because your wife's corporation turned giggling into a monetized commodity, would it? Or, in plain English, turned giggling into something we now have to pay for. Now, I ask you, Oomla, isn't giggling what every person on the whole entire planet has done for free since time began? Your very own lovely wife? did that? to us?' "

Dr. Oomla took a long hard look around him.

"And what about you, you shapeshifters! And you, Euterpe! And you, Polyhymnia! Can you help me fight the Corporatocracy? Fight the Corporatocracy! What am I saying! Can you just help me get up the courage to finally tell my wife what I think about her enterprise? Are any of you real? Is anybody real here? Can I talk to any of you about any of this?"

Not even the dead Old Chief answered him. And he felt every inch of that vast, friendless space. He could have used some human companions. And a real hero. And not a room full of fancy. And a mind full of guilt.

And an old dead chief. A hanging judge. And an absent Father, all of whom were making him feel even more crushed and useless.

Then tomorrow's breakfast skipped into his head ... when he would be surrounded by Sophia and Mr. James and Miss Kitty. His wife wasn't part of their breakfasts anymore ever since she started leaving every morning at 5 AM to take good care of her new family. But he still had Sophia. Mr. James. And funny dear old Miss Kitty. And at breakfast, they'd be all together. Just talking. Laughing. Smiling at each other.

But only the dark night loomed before him now. And the Old Chief spoke again.

"Are you really going to let IV get away with this?"

But now there were more voices banging to get in. The show-offs, the flirts, the air-heads. The peacockae from the original three-ring-circus. And there, too, was his own young voice, his inside voice, thinking intelligently, insightfully, and wondering should he speak up, should he speak out, because suppose he couldn't hit the target? Because to understand it all, he had learned even back then, was never enough to control it all. And then there was the voice of his sharp-shooting Father hitting the target yet again; silencing them all.

But now finally, and once and for all, didn't he know enough to control it all?

And he shuddered again.

·∴⚬∴·

("Now, Author darling," said Me, "speaking of voices inside heads, speaking of inviting anyone in, Author ... our What If ... actually, Dr. Oomla never really invited him in - he didn't even know the What If existed - it's really more that the What If would invite himself into Dr. Oom—"

"Barge is more like it, Me!" snapped Lorraine.

Barge, like what the two of you are doing to this story, Fairies! If you keep bringing up new characters, the Readers will forget their place! I've forgotten my place and I'm the author!

"Hey, Lady, WE told you the story, so we're the authors! Have you forgotten that too? And don't worry, the Fairies haven't forgotten their place; we just got Dr. Oomla out the door to the Institute. So what's the hurry? He'll get there. And about our Readers losing their place, that won't happen because we're going right out there to Readerland and giving anyone reading this story now, and in a perpe-like-tuity of nows, a magical memory. Pouff! Do youse feel your ears, like, vibrate, Readers? That's your very own magical memory at your, like, service."

"Author darling, while we are on the subject of Dr. Oomla's influences or interferences or whatever-ences … there really is something else your Readers, particularly you dabblers in psycho-babble, should keep in mind. Although I'm sure some of the wanna-bes, the armchairs, the Monday-mornings, already noticed; Dr. Oomla admitted that he wasn't his Father's hero. And that he has a hero, the Old Chief. In fact, he wants to be the Old Chief. But what about his own Father? He never said that his Father wasn't his hero. So was his Father his hero when he was a boy? And how would it make him feel that he disappointed his own Father, I mean, don't you humans believe that every boy's real hero is their own Father?"

Stop it Me! You're making my head spin! And our Readers'!

"Darling, Readers love nothing better than a good-headspinning. They simply won't be satisfied without it. Anyone who's ever told a fairy tale knows that. As I was saying, we'll really have to go into that relationship, too, in more depth right after I tell them about our What If and before we get Dr. Oomla to the Institute—

"Oh, and while I'm at it, there is one other little thing … I lie, it's really not little at all, it's big … no … it's huge because it involves Dr. Oomla and his daughter. But I really should give you some background first."

Me! You are really pushing it!

"That's right, I have something to say, so why don't you just give me my own chapter? We'll all feel so much better!"

You mean you'll feel so much better!

"Oh! Darling, you wouldn't want to make us, your benefactors, angry, would you? You wouldn't want us dropping by when you least expect us, would you? Like when you're reading from your work to the public and we start buzzing your head and only you can see us? So can't you just let us do the tattle-telling right now!"

Readers! Never negotiate with a Fairy!)

·˙꒝˙·

• • • ME'S CHAPTER • • •

"So, darlings, here I go. His entire adult life, Dr. Oomla has been help-ing those sad Artistes at the Institute restore themselves to sanity. And all of you know by now who some of those Artistes just happen to be. Movie Stars. Now, Author darling, Reader darlings, admit it, your world idolizes perfection. So I ask you, who has more of that then a Movie Star? But a Movie Star's perfection is different than other being's perfection. Those

other beings may just be perfectly smart or perfectly athletic but those at-
tributes come from that one thing, their wisdom, their agility, but Movie
Stars can make their perfection come from wherever they want it to. They
can make it radiate from their chiseled heads and even down to their supple
toes. They can don a ravishing costume, strut devil-may-care, aim their soul
out through their eyes, express a thousand attitudes with just a walk, smile
as wide as a sunset and witch or king or villain up their voices to speak
quick-wittedly, sad-heartedly, demonically. They can make themselves dazzling to behold, behear. Admit it, darlings, you humans simply adore them.
You even forget they didn't write the words they're uttering so compellingly.
You've never found anybody who sounds better and looks better and fills up
those screens you're perpetually glued to better than a Movie Star. Those
screens. Big screens in your movie palaces. Little screens in your living
rooms. Teeny tiny screens in your palms. Is that really where you prefer to
experience life? On those screens and not in the real world? Well, if you
do, you've found your doppelganger. But one with a perfect outside to rep-
resent you because nobody fills up those screens better than a charismatic,
je-ne-sais-quoi Movie Star.

"Now, imagine if you will an ordinary man, a kind soul who saved his
neighbor from his burning home but just so happens to talk like a 'dese
and dose-er and, has a big gut, a turkey neck, six greasy hairs combed over
a shiny bald head, and hairy-ape skin just about everywhere, including his
floor-scraping knuckles. How will you feel when he accepts his award for
heroism and fills up those screens looking and sounding like that? Readers,
even though you'd certainly admire his deed, you'd also just as certainly be
cringing at the sight of him, the sound of him, though you'd never admit
that's why you were cringing. You might even deny that the chump makes
you cringe. You know that good people, that kind people, that heroes, no
matter how oaf-ish they are, are the honorable members in your society.

"Now, darlings, I ask you? Is that really true? Is that really how it works
here?

"Darlings, Movie Stars are the ones in your society who have the real
stature and I know why they do; in fact, you know why they do too, because
they look best on those screens of yours! That's who has the real stature in
your society. People here in your land are happiest when they are gazing at
whoever looks the best on a screen and who looks the best on them, are the
beautiful people; but not the beautiful insides of people where their characters lay but on their outsides where their beauty is. Darlings, don't you
even have, like, some wise person who spoke about this very dilemma. What

was his name? Wasn't he like a King? King Martin Somebody? And didn't he say something like, 'where creatures will not be judged by the winning of a screen test but by the content of their character?' Do any of you really understand what he meant? And I can tell you why I say this; I fly inside your heads and hear what you're really thinking. I know who you really admire. And don't deny it, darlings! I rest my case."

"Me, everybody on the whole planet, and, like, intergalactically, and certainly in our very own homeland understands what Martin Luther King actually said and what he actually meant!

"Everybody but you, apparently! And he was NOT tawking about any dumb screen test! And ya know what else, youra fat phony! You are the most appearance obsessed Fairy in alla the Enchanted Lands!"

"Lorraine, I may be a phony, but I'm not a fat one! And darling, haven't you heard? It takes one to know one. Now getting back to our Dr. Oomla: when he's at the Institute, he sees first-hand what happens to Movie Stars in this land of yours. That so many of them need not just any Doctor's help, but a psychoanalyst's help. And he can't stop wondering, is it because Movie Stars are prized above all others? So then why do so many of them still end up in the Institute? What effect does looking so great and sounding so great on those screens of yours really have on a Movie Star? And, too, he worries about the plain folks who spend all their time gazing at those screens and falling under the spell of those Movie Stars. As you can well imagine, our Dr. Oomla doesn't have a lot of kind word for those screens of yours. So Author darling, you really need to add this, too, to what he agonizes over night after night in his library the size of a ballroom. Over and over and over he wonders just why so many of those Movie Stars end up as patients at his Institute. Could being a Movie Star in this land of yours make someone believe that they are royalty and not like everyone else? And if that's what they believe, do they think they're more important than everyone else? And doesn't everybody know what happens when someone believes they are more important than everyone else?"

"Author Lady, woujja listen to her! Yeah, Princess Me, everybody but you! Ya know what just occurred to me, HRH Me, if creatures with, like, your values are living in human heads up to the age of ten, it's no wonder. If Dr. Oomla knew where you've been living for the past ten years, he'dda never recovered."

"Just ignore her, darlings. Well, Dr. Oomla suspects that what I just said about those screens of yours, plus so so many other things that I haven't even touched on, just may be the reason those Movie Stars come crawling through the portals of the Institute so desperately seeking his help. So, now imagine this, darlings ... how do you think Dr. Oomla will feel when he finds out that his innocent, ten-year-old daughter, his only child, is one of those creatures who are mesmerized by and obsessed with Movie Stars too just like all those other possessed, obsessed creatures throughout your land! AND she met those Movie Stars on a screen that's in his very own living room! AND that his daughter wants to BE a Movie Star! AND has been spending night after night glued to that screen that's in his very own living room! AND he has never even known about it, because he's been too busy Thinker Statue-ing all alone in his very own library, just rooms away from her as she's Movie Star-ing about all alone in her very own Midnight Movie Star School!

"So now do you understand why I must get to that after I finish with those other two things. But first, as I promised, I really must begin with the What If ... Lorraine, wouldn't our pesky little friend be the first to admit he was a barger!"

"Yeah, Me, he, like, really dug being ins—"

Hold it this second the both of you! Stop hijacking the story. We are DEFINITELY NOT going into how he'll feel when he finds out his daughter wants to be a Movie Star. Presenting that to our Readers at this moment in the plot would not be logical. The only thing we ARE going into is that What If creature or I WILL QUIT and you'll have to find someone else to tell this story.

"Darling Readers, did you hear that? Darling Author expects Darling Fairies to be logical? And as I already said, darling, you wouldn't want to make us, your benefactors, angry, would you? I wasn't kidding either. Think about it, would you really want us dropping by when you least expect us? Don't you think our Readers really need to know ALL the reasons why an intelligent man might miss things that were going on right under his own nose? I mean oughtn't they to understand what was influencing him? Oughtn't they, darling, oughtn't they?"

I'll tell you what oughtn't to happen, and that is, making me, your true benefactor, angry! Tell me, how many stories have any of you published here on terra firma, because the ether doesn't count?

I didn't think so.

Since I'm the only one who has actually had a novel published, who but you, with your unpublished story, will benefit from my achievements? ...

Alright, alright ... I admit, you gave me the story, and I might benefit from publishing a book. But big deal! Because the real big deal is turning this story into a novel. So let's see you do it, because you Fairies would have to know how to do everything I know how to do; which is to turn your story into a plot that is a) logical, b) heartbreaking, c) fall-off-your-chair-funny; and that has in it d) everyone, e) everything, f) every feeling, g) every idea, h) every word - exactly where they should be and are neither too much nor too little of anyone or anything but are just enough of them all; and that, above all else, obsesses your Reader so much he can do nothing else but turn page after page, as i) his stomach churns, j) his head pounds; and even as k) he's paralyzed with fear that the hero you've created may be blown to smithereens in your pages' imaginary minefields. And remember, you'll have to put hints of the powder keg your hero is sitting on in your very first chapter because without that, Fairies, your Reader won't get hooked and then he'll go and find a book with a first chapter that does hook him. But for argument sake, let's say you do write a story that contains such a master plot. Well, don't think you're finished because after that labor has stooped your spine, then comes the next phase; and that is when silly-you realizes YOU'VE! WRITTEN! A! NOVEL! And NOVELS which contain Insights-Brilliant! Characters-Fascinating! Plots-Heartstopping! Persiflage-Galore and are not too lousy with pathos ... oh! Is it pathos galore? and are not too lousy with persiflage? ... Whatever—

"Whatever? I hope that doesn't mean you don't know, darling? I'd hate to think we've been telling this story to somebody who doesn't know her literary devices."

Me ... of cocourse, I ... know! As I was saying, novels like that are masterpieces! and you know yours has all that! because YOU! are a literary lion! So over the finish line you and your masterpiece pounce only to stumble into the office of an agent. An agent who won't even look up from his desk when he says,

How many words are in your manuscript?

How many words are in my manuscript?!???!!!!!!

And you say the harmonic, indivisible, unsubtractable number. But he doesn't even ask to read your first sentence, but demands instead that you remove the first and second word out of each group of three words so that you are left with just enough words that wouldn't challenge a chimpanzee because if you don't that devil-agent won't sling your manuscript over the publishing mountain. Well! Faster than you can say Oprah's Book Club! You shed! You shred! You splice! You dice! You are no literary lion! You are just another inkslurping-hoppytoad! who does everything Lucifer demands! But you receive your reward. Beelzebub shoots your manuscript through the printer and The Book! The Book! flies down the publishing mountain into, you hope, the hands of readers who are not on a bread-line and are only too happy to add another charge to their maxed-out credit cards. Now tell me, both of you, truthfully, are you prepared to face all of that? …

I didn't think so.

Fairies! At this point in the story, Dr. Oomla didn't understand what was what and he's a psychoanalyst, and if he didn't understand, then neither should our Readers. I'll tell the story my way, the logical way, which is to let the story unfold the way it really unfolded and not your way, which lacks logic and which throws everything at our Readers at once. And since you're the ones who found me, and I'm the professional writer, I'm the decider. I'm the one who will determine the order in which events are to be presented in this story. Take it or leave it!

"Logic is so over-rated, Ms. Decider darling! All that mental exercise!"

"Me's just kidding, Lady! Like, we'll take it, already. C'mon, Me! Give her what she wants!"

"Well, don't blame me if you baffle our discerning Readers! But do remember, Ms. Decider darling, the What If's own kind should really be the one telling the Readers about him."

"Okay, Lady, are you happy? We got a deal, just like you asked, we'll only bring up the What If now, no mention of Dr. Oomla's Father, and how Dr. Oomla'll feel when he finds out that Sophia wants to be a Movie Star. So here we go then. And notice, you unbaffled, very discerning Readers with Magical Memories, how we don't say doodalee about Dr. Oomla's Father and Sophia's Movie Star School. Right Me? So okay … when Dr. Oomla got so serious, our What If, like, ceased and desisted. He had given up on our Dr. Oomla. And when I asked the What If why, he'd say, 'Man! Dr. Oomla, like, lost his sense of humor!' "

"Darlings, the What If and Dr. Oomla have a history that went way back. I mean, Sophia had us, her five Fairies, and Dr. Oomla had his What—"

"Hey, Me! Have ya, like, forgotten? Mrs. Oomla not only had that pest, she had you! Which, remember, Readers, was absolutely forbidden by the USA/USE Rules! But, like, whatever!"

"Lorraine! Interrupting! So rude! Darlings, by now surely you are beginning to understand that forces were operating within Dr. Oomla which made him sometimes un petit distracté and he was not always paying attention to what and to whom he should be paying attention to, like, his family. Now sit back and relax and let us do the spinning."

• • • THE WHAT IF • • •

"Darlings, first, let me explain. The What If is not a Fairy but he is magical. And, oh, does he like to roam. In fact, he roams so much, he's our country's what-if-a-lo. Although where your buffalo roam and our what-if-a-lo roam are two distinctly different places. You'll see. But first let me tell you more about the What If. I know what you're thinking, a What If? Isn't that how I begin a question whenever I'm wondering about this or worrying about that? See, most of you already are quite familiar with the What If. You just didn't know there is an ACTUAL What If and that he's an eavesdropper who knows exactly when to fly inside you to persuade you to ask the question that bears his name AND that he must be at that post inside you precisely before you're about to wonder or worry. Imagine a buffalo attempting that? Now do you see? And, darlings, never forget! Though What Ifs may be as tiny as atoms, they're as mighty as atom bombs.

"Darlings, what Lorraine said about humor is true. At least, about this—"

"Watch it, Me!"

"Whatever, Lorraine! Losing your sense of humor is the only universal tragedy ever acknowledged by What Ifs. But before Dr. Oomla's troubles really began, the What If certainly hadn't given up on Dr. Oomla. In fact, our If always said that our Dr. Oomla had the kind of mind that is simply irresistible to What Ifs; it was so willing to question and wonder and ponder and flit and flop from reasoning to musing to what-iffing. In fact, our What If liked to say that he lived only to play with the contents of minds like our Dr. Oomla's. Though our What If did have one grievance. He'd never really been able to induce Dr. Oomla to jump into the deepest end of what-iffing. He'd tried so many times to lead Dr. Oomla's mind there. But even after all that flitting he got it to do, it'd always end up choosing the sensible path. Far too many times our What If had gotten Dr. Oomla down the tail end of the sensible path, out over its edge and had just about coaxed him to soar far above and beyond, but he never could. Until one night."

No! Do NOT bring up that night now!

"Author, darling, why ever not?"

Why ever not? Because that night happened five years ago! Don't you Fairy-Tale-Tellers understand what I've been trying to tell you, that only impulsive story-tellers jerk their readers from present to past to future! That's why ever not!

"Well then, darling, it's about time impulsive story-tellers ruled! And don't you remember Lorraine gave all of our Readers magical memories so they'd be able to follow us wherever we take them?

"So as I was saying … five years ago, in the pitch-black night, our Dr. Oomla was startled awake by a ferocious nightmare."

"Yeah, Me, everybody else in the human world wouldda been terrified but not our Dr. Oomla! He was, like, thrilled! But then he's a psychoanalyst sleeper! And it's no wonder! After the day he had, Dr. Oomla wasn't in full command of his mental faculties. That night, he'd tasted his wife's beverage and only that morning, he'd purchased his first CD player – which was totally out-of-character for Dr. Oomla. It meant that he'd have to put away his record player! Dr. Oomla? Putting away his record player? That'd be like asking you, Me, to throw away your front-row-pass to Fashion Week! Or for a fattee boombalattee to throw out a perfectly delectable Hot Fudge Sundae!"

"Lorraine, wouldn't you say his troubles took a turn on that day? That has to be why he had that nightmare."

"Yeah, Me, maybe it was like his inside was trying to tell him something? But with all that other wild stuff jumping around that head'a his, he couldn't hear what it was saying."

"Darlings, Dr. Oomla knew that very few people in the modern world used record players anymore, and that was fine by him. All that mattered to him was that he still could. His record player was his old friend, his tried and true, beloved relic! Which he played almost non-stop. But then he could play that relic because he mollycoddled it like a venerable elder. After all, it was the conveyor of his music. Thinking may have been a great joy to Dr. Oomla but music was his greatest joy. His most faithful friend. Plus, that CD player, this gizmo, this oddity? that? was to be the new conveyor of his greatest joy? It looked ultra-modern. Like a space-ship. And there are two things you need to know about Dr. Oomla. You already know one of them. But you may not know how old-fashioned he is. Remember, he wouldn't even watch those screens you're always watching.

"And don't forget about the other event. Which was, just before he went to bed, he tasted Mrs. Oomla's concoction. When all of them tasted it that evening, wasn't it apparent to each of them that she'd finally gotten it just right? And didn't five-year-old Sophia, without even understanding she had, give that concoction the name that was just tailor made for the marketplace? Mrs. Oomla's Giggle Pop? And maybe, just maybe, when he heard that name, it began to dawn on him his dear wife's experiment was about to become a huge hit? And maybe that left him feeling a little

... well, I am only a Fairy, and I don't do what Dr. Oomla does for a living, so I can't say with certainty, but that is when he had the nightmare. And it was a doozy!"

"You know, Me, when I, like, think about it, over these past five years, when the whole world's been, like, drinking Mrs. Oomla's Giggle Pop and giggling their patootie's off, don't it seem like the Oomlas was the only ones who wasn't?"

Alright, Me and Lorraine, enough! I'll present that right now. But I simply can't trust that you'll bring out what really needs to be brought out about Dr. Oomla. So I'll tell our Readers about Dr. Oomla and his dream; and when the What If enters, you two take over! Deal?

"Darling, like, whatever!"

Deal! And then we're going right back to the story. No more interruptions! You two should be ashamed, why Dr. Oomla just left for his day at the Institute! We've been leaving our Readers hanging! And you call yourself professionals!

"That's right, darling, we do. Because we come from the land of Fairy Tales and you don't! Ergo! The professionals are leading our Readers exactly where they'll want to be."

Professionals? Who make loop-di-loops out of a plot line that was heading straight-to-a-bull's-eye? The least you can do is remember my rule, I do Dr. Oomla and you do the What If!

• • • THE NIGHTMARE AND DR. OOMLA • • •

It was the middle of the night, five years ago and Dr. Oomla was asleep.

Asleep, until a skirt with nobody in it picked itself up and began dancing to music – exquisite, haunting music - circling Dr. Oomla where he stood in the living room, and when the music it was dancing to stopped, it didn't; but kept swirling around him, more and more rapidly, billowing over him, imprisoning him, trapping him on all sides, leaving him no choice but to watch it metamorphose into a humongous mouth, its petticoats into fangs, about to swallow him whole - and then Dr. Oomla shot up in his bed, terrified.

He was alive. In his poster bed.

And he was delighted.

Not because he was alive. Because he had a nightmare. Before he went to bed every night he prayed, "Now I lay me down to sleep I pray Oh Freud a dream to keep. Or a nightmare – even better."

'I really do pray I kick at least one dream upstairs from where it lays in my uncon-scious and grab it before it glissades into the ether. And now after night after night after night of my dreams giving me the slip, I finally have. I am like the weary-armed, bleary-eyed gambler who finally sees, after depositing coin after coin after coin and pulling on the same lever hour after incessant hour, three shining, ruby red cherries in each slot!

'Extra Extra Read All About It! Van Der Speckian Hits Jackpot!' Dr. Oomla imagined the headline that certainly ought to appear in the local newspa-per announcing his great achievement. After all such headlines always ap-peared in the paper whenever a fellow villager won anything.

'And when they find out that the lucky Van Der Speckian is a psychoanalyst from the Institute and his pay-off is a nightmare, the sound of shrieking laughter through-out the village might die down in a day or two!

'Maybe it isn't such a good idea after all!'

Even so, he could feel his smile grow. He lay back down but still couldn't shake the thought that his dream really should've been a headline.

'I, of all people, know just how worthy this story is of a headline. VAN DER SPECKIAN HITS JACKPOT! A catchy headline is the best way to introduce a dif-ficult subject.

'People'd start reading the story expecting one thing – that I'd won money, but'd be surprised to see that the story was about winning a nightmare; but since it was a NIGHTMARE - something each and everyone of them has but has a hard time understanding – that's even mysterious to them – they'd get hooked into reading the story right down to the very last word, especially the way I'd write it, because they'd've learned something about something they never understood before. They'd've learned about nightmares. Their mysterious nightmares. First, I'd tell them what a dream really is and then I'd tell them what a nightmare really is – that a dream is a whisper and a nightmare is a scream that comes from the part of a person that isn't known for speaking out loud. Or for speaking at all. That's why it should've made headlines. That's why they'd want to read about it. It's a mystery story. A mystery story where the mystery part finally talks. The part that has never talked before. THAT'S what's worthy of a headline ... Talk from a part that never talks. Talk from the unconscious. Surely that's as important a headline as one about a visitor from outer space. Because this visitor is from inner space. VISITOR FROM INNER SPACE. THAT'S the headline! The Visitor is the dream. And the Inner Space is the inner planet it comes from – the uncon-scious. Why! anyone would read a story with that headline! People are dying to learn about the unconscious ... at least, they should be - considering that each and every one of them has one.

'On top of that, my story'd finally make them see that the unconscious is mute and never speaks out loud, until it dreams. And when it does, it's ready to finally reveal its secrets and people really ought to pay attention. Yes, yes, yes - the readers'd have to know that too. Because these secrets come from the invisible, voiceless part of the person and contain information the dreamer's never heard before and needs to know. But I'll have to finish it off by telling them the really big problem with dreams. I can't leave that out. Yes … yes the big problem must be in there too … About how these messages are sent to people when they're not conscious - not conscious because they're asleep. And how that's confounded dreamers and psychoanalysts considerably. Because when the secret finally speaks, they're asleep and can't hear it. That's why there should be a headline. An Extra Extra Read All About It headline. Because a story with that headline and all these details would surely be a sensation. They'd have to read it. And then they'd understand why they ought to pay attention to their own dreams. Their own visitors. Their own Visitors from Inner Space. That's why my dream should make the newspapers.'

He twitched.

'Something is missing. And that's the truth. The whole truth. The truth about who's confounded more than anybody about dreams. Because if I tell the whole truth, I'd've had to say that the who who is confounded most of all is me. And it isn't just because I can't bear that I'm asleep when the unconscious is sending me my all important, never-before-heard secrets. That isn't the only part. The part I should put in the story would have to be about me!

'About how I - myself - Dr. Sigmund Oomla - a psychoanalyst trained in the teachings of Freud - THE Dr. Freud, who wrote a book about dreams – about dreams because he wanted everyone to know and never forgot that a dream tells a story – that I, as hard as I try, can't remember my dreams. And haven't been able to for a while. Because I'd've had to put that in the story, too; that all I can remember upon waking is often only about a second of a dream. That I can count on only one hand the times I remember a whole dream. And how sometimes I get lucky and actually hold on to a three-second movie. But how rare that is. Because most times, all I have is an image. And sometimes just a fragment of that image.

WHAT SORT OF A FREUDIAN CAN'T REMEMBER HIS DREAMS?

'That's what they'd all wonder. I know it. And then I fear the whole story'd come out. Because I'd have to be forthright, like a good psychoanalyst ought to be, like the ethical person I believe myself to be, and reveal in my newspaper story for the world to read that at the Institute when my fellow Freudians are swapping their dreams – their night-time encounters with the unconscious - which is often – far too often for me – that whenever it is my turn, I never have a whole one to tell. And then they'd all figure out pretty quickly just how deeply ashamed I am about it.

'Maybe I won't write the story after all.

'So now that I finally have a story to tell – have caught my unconscious speaking - received one of its secrets from its start to its finish - I won't be telling that story. I won't be instructing the Van Der Speckians about the importance of listening to their dreams.

'If only I could, the village people might learn something that would help them understand themselves. Just like they used to when old Dr. Knitsplitter, my true north, was the chief.'

And he remembered. Another time he should've spoken up. And didn't. And almost fell out of bed.

'I was just ten-years-old …

'my mind filled with speculations and considerations playing all about; but a mouth that'd only let out my certainties …

'just like today.

'When I became friends with Robert, another ten-year-old, who was an actor in one of my Father's shows; I'd never made friends with any of the actors in my Father's shows before. And I never did again, after Robert. When Halloween arrived, the two of us found a third so we could trick-or-treat as the Three Musketeers, if only Robert wouldn't've had to perform on Halloween night. But I was so certain if I made a well-reasoned argument to my Big-Shot Father, Robert would get the night off and one-for-all-and-all-for-one would prevail yet again. I considered so carefully what I'd say and when I knew it was right I decided that I'd even borrow my Father's voice, that authority of his, that tone he used when he was making his important pronouncements; that tone that was always ringing in my ears. But MY version of his authority squawked in odd places as it flapped its way out of me:

' "It's HalloWWWEEEEen, afTERTTTall, and we're jUSt ten! and BESIdes, Robert's UNNNNNNDerrstudy is dYINNNNG to take his place! He's never been on eVENNNNNn once for the enTIIIIRE run of the show!"

'I was humiliated. My Father's version of authority soared out of him as if he were the Judge proclaiming the verdict the world had been praying for: that a criminal would hang. "Robert is under contract! The Show Must Go On! And the son of a Producer should know that!" His locution was an execution intended to sear my ears and shut my mouth. And it succeeded. My locution was a duck on a rollercoaster! And it flopped! I flopped! Robert could not go out for Halloween!

'And my garbled reasons, my odd squeaks were rolling and pitching through my ears and I stood there agonizing - did my Father want to do what I wanted to do - push my words back down my throat so they'd stop rolling through his ears, too? But he said not a word to me, yet somehow I felt that I was right. I should've known though; my debonair Father would never've done any such thing.

'Not a whimper of protest escaped from me about his verdict. No more ducks out of my mouth! Though my mind was now exploding with brand new ideas;

about how unfair to children Show Business was. And maybe even my own Father was.

'I guess that's when I found out whose side I was on. And it wasn't the producer's side.

'Even so, I still couldn't face my friend to tell him that my Big Shot Father wouldn't let him off. And I never made friends with another actor in Father's shows again. How different the Old Chief was from my Big-Shot Father! True North v True South! No wonder I made a strategic withdrawal to this village!'

·∴*☾·∴

("Hey, Lady, like, I don't mean to be a nudge or nothing, but didn't ya, like, say ya wouldn't be going into Dr. Oomla's relationship with his Father just yet?"

Lorraine, I brought up his Father exactly when he should've been brought up, when he appeared in the story. I didn't just conjure him up out of nowhere. And I'd like to go back to Dr. Oomla's reverie, if you don't mind.)

·∴☽·∴

'The Old Chief taught the Van Der Speckians all sorts of things because he wanted his villagers to use their minds so that his village would be filled with thinkers. He even wrote an entire treatise on that very subject. But then old Dr. Knitsplitter wrote entire treatises about every subject on which he had an opinion and since he had an opinion on many subjects, he left behind a legion of treatises that, upon his demise, have been resting in peace on the Institute's library shelves for all these years until I happened upon them and am now making it my business to read and reread and reread in their entirety.'

When he'd come across a quote from the education treatise, he finally understood a road sign of the Old Chief's that was still standing, but just barely, in the village. "Welcome to The Tiny Village – Home Of The Big Thinkers." It read, 'If the village teachers teach the village children to think, then our children will grow into thinkers until our tiny village becomes quite large; not with tall buildings like tall cities are, but with big thinkers, and then our tiny village will be known as The Tiny Village With The Big Thinkers.' Old Dr. Knitsplitter believed if people read about their good reputations, and even more importantly saw other people reading about their good reputations, they might just want to keep their reputations good; all of which prompted him to put up this very sign (yet another) in the village. But this one was not about the Institute; this was about the villagers. His Thinking Villagers. And was meant to inspire all who read it. This sign still stood on the main roadway at the entrance to the village but was now so overgrown with weeds that only the top of it stuck out. And that was a good thing because the sign now read, "Welcome to The Tiny Hiney – Home Of The Big Stinkers." The handiwork of one of the Artistes no doubt. Dr. Oomla could just imagine how Old Dr. Knitsplitter would storm on about what that sign would inspire – "Fix that sign! Not for sanity's sake! For sanitation's sake!" Dr. Oomla, in his less rational moments, which he didn't like to admit he had considering his profession, would often imagine the ghost of Old Dr. Knitsplitter observing from his heavenly station the unKnitsplittery type happenings in his beloved Institute since he had passed on and his greedy son had gotten hold of it.

Dr. Oomla vowed that he'd personally dig up the weeds, paint over the sign and reprint the words so that the sign was restored to its original meaning. But as it sank into him he wasn't going to publish the story in the village's newspapers about dreams, it also sank into him that since he wouldn't, he'd never be like old Dr. Knitsplitter, unless he began teaching all its citizens the way Dr. Knitsplitter did. And teaching them about their dreams was a good place to start.

But he wasn't about to publish his nightmare story in their newspaper. He resigned himself: he wouldn't be the one to return the village to old Dr. Knitsplitter's revered tradition, it was pointless to change the sign. Unless he was willing to admit what a hard time he had getting a hold of his own dreams.

'What would my patients think of me, a psychoanalyst, who can't remember his dreams? But I should. I should. I really should. Old Dr. Knitsplitter'd be relieved. Someone finally teaching the villagers. Helping the villagers understand. The way he used to. I bet HE'D do it ... What WOULD he do? ... Have to think ... It's so late ... I'm not ... to make such decisions ... shouldn't

'... should ....

'... I'll just keep the story to myself ...

'... Why am I such a chicken? Like why didn't I speak up to my Father ... that Halloween? But I could speak up now ... the villagers ... the Artistes ... everyone could learn something.

'I'll write the story ...

'... No! It wouldn't be right for a Freudian to admit such a thing. So publicly. For all the village to know about ... I need to sleep ... but all won't be lost ... I'll fix the sign, first thing.'

But there would be one group he would tell. Would be required to tell. His fellow Freudians at the Institute. And he couldn't wait. He wished it were morning. Finally, he had a dream to tell them ... to analyze ... using Freudian principles. They'd want to know everything from its start to its finish. Everything. Hah! And would they try to trick him! He could almost hear them now; 'Why, Dr. Oomla - we know you've already told us the dream but could you repeat it to us again? Why, Dr. Oomla – you left out the part of the skirt imprisoning you? Why did you leave that part out, Dr. Oomla? Why?'

And he shot up in his bed.

'What am I doing? Wasting my time. Wishing for something that can't happen when I'm supposed to be writing down each element of the dream in my dream journal before I forget them. From its start to its finish. I hope I can remember it all. I haven't had a decent dream in years, and here I am dawdling my time away in useless fantasy! I spend my life instructing my patients to write their dreams down immediately upon waking and look at what I'm doing. Fine example I set.'

He hadn't followed his own advice. That the dreamer was to reach for the notebook and pencil that they were to keep on their bedside table and record the dream directly after it happened. That was the best way to assure they'd remember it. And that way, and most importantly, they could later study it, and wonder – why did that image appear? Could it have something to do with me? With my life? But even as he was reaching for his pencil and notebook, he was flooded with so many questions and was so distracted, that again he didn't take hold of his notebook.

'Why did this dream come through tonight? Was there anything special about this night? What does my unconscious want me to know? Freud said that dreams are wishes. What am I wishing for?

'What am I wishing for! Forget about that! First, write the dream down exactly how it unspooled and do it now!

'I might forget … the details … no matter how late it is … and how tired I am … I've got to write it down. I hope I'm not waking Sigrid.'

He looked over at Mrs. Oomla who was sound asleep on her side of the bed. She hadn't even stirred. Even when he'd shot upright in bed. Several times. But then she never did. He watched her sleep. *'She's so tired from her morning full of singing and talking to everybody and her afternoon full of singing and talking to everybody else, and her nighttime full of talking to Sophia and me, and then, when she hits her pillow, a nightcap full of extra talking that she thinks is to me, but is really to herself, and she's just too tired to realize. But what talking and singing, she does!*

'Jack Spratt could eat no fat; his wife could eat no lean.' A nursery rhyme? What was that doing in his head?

He remembered when he'd first noticed her pretty face in the group of Christmas carolers. But when she stepped forward and sang the O Holy

Night solo and her notes floated into his ears; that was it. His ears, those connoisseurs, had been waiting for that sound all their lives. No earthly soprano sounded like her! The heavens must've let go of its most musical inhabitant, the one who sings their solos. But then! Bang! He was bereft. Such a voice could only come from a professional singer or actress. The thought of a romance with another such creature and he was filled with dread. The last had left him alone night after night as she sang and acted on the stage for everybody, it seemed, but him. But then night after night after night so too had his Father and Mother left him alone, for they too were very very ambitious for the stage. He should've been used to that by now; people he needed longing for the stage. Which used to really make him curious, too, for when he was a boy, he longed only for the stage he'd built inside himself. But it also made him worry: did his parents long for that stage more than they did for him? But as they were good parents - good enough, mostly - he could never say that they did. Besides when his Father wasn't barking and his Mother wasn't anywhere near a stage and both of them were actually paying attention to people and events and him, he could never prove it. But then that was long before the estrangement with his Father, who had, to this day, not yielded an inch.

·∵C·∵

("Darling, forgive me, but since you did bring up Dr. Oomla's boyhood introversion and his later aversion to becoming a Producer, I simply must share. He, the son of that theatrical power couple, was baffled that anyone'd even want to be on the stage. It's interesting that now that he's a grown up, the only patients he treats come from Show Business and that many of them are actors. But coming from such a Show Business family, he often watched actors portraying the struggles and fears and hopes of characters in plays and was astounded that anyone'd want to do that. Way back then he forgot that the actors were not the characters they were playing. He just noticed all that turmoil those characters were presenting on the stage. And though he too was filled with struggles and fears and hopes just like those characters were, he wanted his troubles to stay inside himself because troubles were mysteries to savor and puzzle over on the inside of yourself, not displays that the whole world should watch you stagger through. The thought of him pulling even one of his troubles from out himself and setting it to strut about on a wide-open stage for just anybody to see and hear and know about, like those actors playing characters in plays did, filled him with much too much apprehension. To his young mind, displaying ones troubles in front of a live audience before one fully understood all of their possible ramifications would mean that one was revealing his confusion for everybody to hear. And to him, people who reveal their confusion are foolish. He never wanted to appear foolish to anybody. Foolish people were people who blurt out every little thing they think and feel and he did not blurt. Like characters in a play did. *'Knowledge is what I'll parade about, not foolishness!'* And there he was, a nine-year-old boy, waging a war on foolishness, a secret war. Now, darlings, I got that information from the magical creatures that lived inside Dr. Oomla's head when he was a boy! But remember, that was him then. He's grown-up now and a psychoanalyst, after all, and surely understands things differently than when he was a boy."

"Yeah, Me! Well, if he's still waging a war on foolishness, it's no wonder that What If was, like, always after him!"

Readers, our Fairy friends have taken us off our path yet again! Back to Sigmund and Sigrid's fateful first meeting.)

·∴⊃∴·

But he, the introvert and she, the caroler, were magnets that snapped together. He asked if she was a performer as if he did not dread her answer. She giggled and then spoke words he never forgot, "On a stage?! Only if you count orchids as an audience! Orchids are the only creatures I care to sing to!"

She spoke! And he heard what he never heard before. She has a speaking voice? AND a singing voice? Every utterance, a note on the Treble Clef? How could that be? Many people had beautiful singing voices but few had beautiful speaking voices, too! Though, it could hardly be called speaking. Because no person talked like that. Where did she come from? What was that slinking around her words? Whatever accent, whatever eloquence, whatever it was, was nothing less than a miracle. But when her large, round, brown eyes began to dance with his eyes, he was positively hypnotized; her eyes were dancers, too! All the talents of an actress AND SHE WASN'T AN ACTRESS! This angel was a virtuoso of sound! This angel could sing and her talk was music, too! His ears, those connoisseurs, at long last, were happy. And they warned him, never let go of that voice.

Over the years, this singing, speaking angel showed an angelic nature, as well.

And he was so confused.

Because just after a few of those years, Dr. Oomla's super sensitive ears picked up a rumbling whisper from deep inside, *'your angel, your wife, she really really really likes to talk, doesn't she?'*

And he watched her as she slept, *'But isn't she always so kind and so loving to her spellbound audience, her starry eyes shining so invitingly into their eyes?*

'... Even when she speaks to them like a mad-genius horticulturist?

'... Explaining how the world is in no uncertain terms, isn't she always using words that can only be found in the Oxford-English-Dictionary?

'... Shilling like the green-earth's savior she's desperately trying to be?

'... Saying nothing worth talking about at all, which, according to my ideas about-topics-that-are-worthy-of-conversation, is far too often?

'But doesn't all of it, every last syllable that emerges from her mouth fall on ears like so many feathers? Even the shilled and the scrappy ones? Isn't that some talent?

'Hah! Some of those same words emerging from anyone else's mouth would make few think of angels at all.

'But isn't she so genial, so gentle as she goes on, in any which way, about many many, oh so many subjects? Isn't she? Isn't she?

'Sigmund Oomla could blurt no blurt, his wife could keep none in!

'To talk eloquently is a very great art; an equally great art is to know the moment to stop.'

'A nursery rhyme? And now Mozart, too? Who else'll pop into my head? And you, Mozart, THE cognoscente-of-sound, I particularly hate when your words bound in here uninvited. You're right! So my dream angel doesn't know that moment to stop, okay? But on the subject of Mrs. Oomla, I don't care, even if you are a musical marvel! I've never ever said that to her, and I never ever will. Nobody else ever would either. For everyone knows who she is. No one, certainly not I, would even dream of saying such a thing to my, to Sophia's, to the world's harmonious angel! So there! Maestro Mozart!'

·∴（∙∵

("Wow, Author Lady? Maybe he should've! And by the way, speaking of that nightmare, that humongous mouth swallowing everybody up! I ain't no Sigmund Freud but whatsa chance that was ole wifey-poo? But our psycho-analyst didn't make the connection. And maybe she's his ears' angel, but what about the rest'a him? And didn't ya just say he said, 'never let go of that voice?' Well, don't ya get more than just a voice when ya marry? Don't you get a whole person? But our psychoanalyst didn't make that connection neither! And speaking of ears! Ja ever hear of Achilles, that guy from the, ya know, Greek Mythologies? Like, there's their Myths and our Tales, which is what you humans are supposed to read so you get all wise and stuff and stop being so stupid. Well, Dr. Oomla has an Achilles heel alright, except, in his case, it's an Achilles ear! And, while I'm at it, is Mrs. Oomla really Sophia's angel? Because maybe if Sophia hadn't seen her Father being so transported by that angel's voice so much, maybe Sophia couldda learned to like her own voice and maybe she wouldna needed no speech therapist! Howja like that?"

Lorraine, the Dr. Oomla parts are mine! And stop blaming everything on him! And stop jumping ahead of my story! Now back to—

"My story? Our story! Author Lady person!"

Okay! Our story! I'm going right back to where I was … Dr. Oomla was watching his wife sleep.)

Her talking tires her out! Tires everybody out. But how lucky we all are to hear it!' And that nursery rhyme spun round in his head again. *'The blurter and the thinker! And suppose my wife is a blurter? Don't I think too much? My thinking tires me out. I'm even too tired to tell her that I'm too tired to listen to her because I had my own day chock full of listening and thinking and talking to myself about all I just heard and thought about because that's what psychoanalysts do and then in between all of that professional listening, my very own day of listening to myself talk to myself, and when I'm not doing that, listening to my music and when I'm not doing that, listening to what's in my books, and when evening comes, even more thinking and talking to myself about all that I've just listened to and read about during the day, and when I hit my pillow, my own nightcap of summing-it-all-up-extra-thinking and extra-talking to myself about every little thing I've listened to and thought about during the day and evening and what it all might mean, that when the dark night comes for me – for both of us we are just too tired to do anything other than be ourselves – she talks to me – I talk to myself—*

'At least we're talking to the same person.'

He burst out laughing then squelched it immediately.

She still didn't stir.

He was disappointed.

If she would've, he would've had some company. He tried to remember any time when she'd woken up during the night but couldn't. She even slept through the six-alarm fire last year that had woken up the entire village. Just looking at how peacefully she was sleeping, he knew a little pen scratching'd never've awakened her.

He grabbed hold of his Dream Journal and looked inside; there were only a few pages filled out. *'How ridiculous! Finally I have the dream equivalent of a major motion picture and I'm just now writing it down! I haven't had that many dreams to record.'* Everything that had been recorded, however, had been recorded with great care, exactly as it unfolded, point by point, image by image. He could often be seen in his leisure time, reading what he had written and mulling it over.

As he opened the journal and turned its pages, he was mindful that on this night he'd at long last be adding pages and not just lines. But questions began racing through him and he forgot to pick up the pencil; in fact, they were coming at him so fast, he couldn't've answered them if he tried.

'Why did the music stop playing? Did the music not like the way the skirt was dancing? Was the skirt a person? Who? And why did the skirt keep dancing without the music? And turn into a mouth? And try to swallow me?

'Why did the music stop playing?

'Was the music not good?

'Not good …

'No … '

And the pencil dropped from his hand and the book fell to the floor and his head rolled to the side and he fell asleep. And his dream had not been written down. Not even one word.

But when thoughts as dreaded and as terrifying as the Apocalypse went thundering through him, he rose up yet again, though barely awake, and muttered them aloud,

"Suppose I don't like this new CD player. Suppose I hate it. Suppose I miss my record player. Suppose my dream is trying to tell me something. Wait a minute, didn't I drink something tonight? Could the Giggle Pop be making me feel this way? Or is it that new CD player?"

And as those fears shivered him through, the gloom of night took hold of his mind, shrouding everything else in it but those fears - his strong will and his rational mind included. Gone was his elegant will, his reliable self control; no more was he piercingly rational and clear as crystal and what-ever that was left in his mind began to boil and congeal into a muss, a mutt, a stew. And that stew raged away unchallenged inside Dr. Oomla - until fear was all that was left. And it seized control of him, charging him to get up, get out of his bed, go downstairs, and eliminate one of those disturbances – the invader that was downstairs about to ruin his music. And he must obey: he would return his record player to its place of honor in the living room once again. He stumbled through the darkness until he found the living room.

Little was he aware of what else had found his living room … or more precisely …

·:·*·(·:·

("What If had found his living room … Author darling, remember, Magical Creatures are ours … and was already cruising around it looking for action … and to tell this part, Author darling, we'll need another chapter!")

·:·)·:·

• • • THE WHAT IF AND DR. OOMLA • • •

"Darlings, here I go …

"Wasting no time, the What If zoomed over to the unsuspecting Dr. Oomla, leaned in, took a listen and heard what was going on - since he'd already heard what had been going on upstairs - and zipped inside Dr. Oomla's microscopically sized fissure and headed for his Remarkably Small Place, saying, 'WHAT IF I told you to be careful what you wish for? Because here I am Oomla! Your very own Headline! Your very own Visitor from Inner Space! If only you knew how perceptive you are!'

"Meanwhile, hardly aware that an atomic-sized agitator had just entered his person and was about to stoke his rapidly overheating furnace, Dr. Oomla groped around the dark living room looking for a lamp. He knocked into one, turned it on, but unfortunately it was the smallest lamp in the room that cast the palest of glows that could never have illumined even a drop of the darkness in that room – let alone the darkness in his head … in the night … anywhere … leaving our What If free to live up to his name …

"And it wasn't long before Dr. Oomla saw, in the lamp's dim light, through the fog and the blur, the stripped-bare, sleek-black, saucer-bowl CD player that had taken command of his living room!

"An invader!

"In his cottage!

"In his woods!

"And exactly what his fears led him to believe he saw. And he found himself saying,

" 'WHAT IF that's a space ship that has landed in my living room!

" 'A machine!

" 'Of steel!

" 'This phantom made of cold hard metal doesn't belong among my pine bookcases and the portraits of the ancestors. This isn't the kind of contraption I'm used to. It doesn't have an arm or a needle and when you lay the CD on it to play music the lid mysteriously shuts itself up so you can't see the turntable go round. You can't see what's going on inside it!'

"And though his eyes were bleary, he stared at it, and soon he found himself saying,

" 'WHAT IF it's staring back?'

"And though his eyes were bleary, he would've testified it was staring back.

"But he went up to it just the same and pushed the button and the hatch opened noiselessly. He rifled through one of the boxes on the floor and grabbed a CD not caring what kind of music it was and placed that CD on the circular pad, then pushed another button and the hatch closed. He waited. The music began.

" 'It didn't launch into space,'

"He listened.

" 'The music sounds perfect.'

"He pondered ...

" 'Too perfect.

" 'I really can't see what's going on inside: how does it make this music? Bernie, that salesman, said a laser. Why can't I see this laser the way I can see a needle. What's going on under that lid?

" 'WHAT IF it's nothing but a mini-space vehicle filled to the gills with Lilliputian-sized Martians playing teensie instruments!'

"Such absurdity dwelling even for a moment in his mind woke Dr. Oomla up.

"Exit Ear Left went the What If and exhilarated was he, because after his many, many tries over these many, many years, he finally had gotten Dr. Oomla - so coveted because he was so levelheaded - to jump over the edge and really play the game the way the What If liked it to be played.

"Dr. Oomla knew such a ridiculous hypothetical question would've yielded even louder shrieks of laughter than what he would've heard had there been a headline about a nightmare jackpot. He laughed and said it was the dimness of the light, the lateness of the hour, the sluggishness of his mind, the mysteriousness of night itself that made him susceptible to such nonsensical pondering. And he pushed all such supposing and what if-ing out of his mind. Fast. In light of his profession. And in light of his profession, he duly noted the conditions that lent themselves to producing such irrationality in himself – lack of sleep, fear of the loss of his music-playing-treasure, shock of finally having a nightmare after praying for one so long – all happening on the same night.

"Which put him in mind of his patient, Egleema Utrotly.

" 'This type of irrational thinking is not at all unlike her type of thinking. Maybe the circumstances that caused my thinking to take such a turn happen to her all the time. Scary dreams, insufficient sleep, unbeatable fears, imponderable questions. Look how quickly my rational thinking caved under these very same conditions. In only a few minutes.' "

"Me, I got this part." said Lorraine, "The What If got a whiff and hung a u-bee. Even he didn't believe it! Had he scored that big? Dr. Oomla, the logic guy, was putting himself in the same category as Egleema Utrotly? His zaniest patient? She was the What If's favorite. He didn't want to miss a word! Take it away, Me."

"Egleema Utrotly, the former Mary Hopping, was a frequent 'guest' at the Institute. Egleema/Mary may be one of the great science fiction screenwriters of your time; however, Egleema/Mary believed every word she wrote and that what she wrote was science, was provably real and was not fiction at all. And as what she wrote often scared her senseless, ergo was she the Institute's frequent guest. If only her fans knew. Mary had changed her name to Egleema since she was certain aliens were coming down specifically to hunt her down after she had given away so many of their secrets in her screenplays. She thought extraterrestrials'd never've found her with a name like Egleema Utrotly since she was convinced they wouldn't recognize the name as a human name. She was sure they'd think a name like that had to belong to one of them. She was convinced that aliens had Google up on their planets and had been using it to look up earthlings, but only certain ones. With normal, down-to-earth, names. Like Mary Hopping. And when they found an earthling's name to their liking, their favorite pastime was to descend from their planet and cast that nice, normal-named earthling out of his or her living room so they could sit in couch potato comfort and watch cooking shows.

"Egleema had told him in their session just today that aliens didn't have any comfortable chairs on their planets because they couldn't make a comfortable chair out of pointy old rocks and not a lick of cotton. Plus they were turning a sickly green from their same-old-same-old dietary choices and they thought if they cooked earth food, they would get their coloring back. They were keen on French cuisine. So their plan was to switch places with some earthlings and to then send those earthlings up into space for a couple of days while the aliens took possession of their now vacant living rooms where they would lounge around in cushy comfort watching Cooking Shows on TV, learn new tricks from the gourmet chefs, hone their cooking skills in the earthlings kitchens, and eat til they turned a ripe green. And when the space ship touched down in the earthlings' front yards in a couple of days to unload their earthling captives, the aliens, now bloated and glowing green, would lurch back to the waiting ships, leaving a gigantic, oozing, sticky mound of meringue, fondue and soufflé scraps stuck like cement on the heaped-high-to-the-ceiling-pile of dirty dishes and pots and pans all waiting for the hapless, bewildered earthlings to clean.

"Egleema had crept very close to Dr. Oomla and whispered, if she hadn't presently been in the Institute's custody, she'd be pitching the concept to cable. And then Dr. Oomla remembered, she'd told him they were coming this very night!

"So darlings! Our What If heard all that, smacked his lips, flew right back in, planted his notion, and flew back out again, laughing his atom off.

" 'WHAT IF they take me up on their space ship? I'll have to apologize for doubting her, when I see her next week … If I see her next week.'

"Later, Readers, Dr. Oomla would be embarrassed to remember that it took him a slow second until reason once again took full possession of him. But even a slow second without reason was not acceptable for a man in his profession.

" 'Such thinking for a Man of Science. A Doctor who wages war everyday on people's delusion – What am I thinking!! I'm the psychoanalyst! Not the patient! Egleema's delusion influencing me!! – Aliens in our living rooms!! Aliens in a music device! Preposterous! I need sleep.'

"And he knew he had only himself to blame.

"Because he just had to have this CD player, this gadget - a gadget, he noted, that had only been in his house for a few hours and was already causing him nightmares and anxiety.

"How would he ever get used to this apparition in his cottage?

"But as a Man of Science, he knew he must. He'd give it a chance. And as a Man of Science, at least, he could eliminate his wife's Giggle Pop as the cause of his nightmare. And he felt instant relief.

"Which soon dissipated.

"Well, Author darling, I've been a model narrator, an example to narrators everywhere. And darling Readers, now you know our What If friend."

"Ya mean fiend, Me!"

"Lorraine, what a way to talk about your own kind!"

"You use names to tawk about 'em, so why can't I? Me, youra piece a' work!"

"Lorraine, I am, aren't I? Readers, when things started to get gloomy for Dr. Oomla, and he wasn't always so amiable, so playful, soon after that, our What If simply stopped dropping in on him. Besides the What If didn't usually like to rise before noon, unless he had a sure thing. But our Dr. Oomla had seldom really ever been a sure thing, and when that morose disposition began to settle on him, what fun would it've been for our What If if he had?"

Me, the What If has gone, so so should you! Readers, I've returned. And Me, you really oughtn't to be so gleeful about Dr. Oomla! Anyone listening to you would've thought you were on the What If's side. Readers, I'm back in command and we're going back to where we left off: it's five years later and Dr. Oomla has just left for the Institute.

• • • 7:40 AM • • •

Dr. Oomla wrapped his scarf tightly around his neck and pulled the flaps from inside his hat over his ears as he raced along the shortcut to the Institute but fingers of ice slid under his coat and hat and into his boots anyway.

He had a feeling he was forgetting something. He stopped and swatted his pockets for his keys, his wallet. All there. His black bag was in his hand, he opened it, looked inside; everything that was supposed to be there was there. Nothing missing. No. Something was missing. His path was now completely covered by the immense shadow cast by The Castle L'Oomla. He trudged on. And so it seemed did the shadow. He didn't feel right. *'I'm just cold.'* He pulled up his scarf to cover his mouth, hoping his breath would warm him. It didn't. He stuck his head down to get it out of the fierce wind, and kept trudging on, on the path he knew like he knew Sigmund Freud was his hero. Today, he didn't even have to look up to fleece the clouds for Rorschach phantoms; the clouds, just like the ice, had insinuated themselves all around him.

'I won't treat the Artistes using IV's Rules. I don't want to leave my home, my village, my Artistes but IV is about to make their lives impossible. My life impossible. I don't think I can fight this man and his rules. He raises so much money. Too much money. Why won't he spend that money on the Artistes? On their programs? Doesn't he understand just how unique this Institute is! It may actually be the last of its kind. The Institute for the Compassionate Care of the Extraordinary and the Always Interesting! All who enter our Institute are taught first to make sense out of what's happened to them and then to convert what they've learned into an expression that's uniquely their own. And if that isn't extraordinary and interesting, I don't know what is. AND, it's a non-profit health organization!

'At least, we're supposed to be a non-profit. We're certainly not a for-profit corporation like my wife's corporation! Their first concern is money.

'And that's what's about to happen? at the Institute for the Compassionate Care of the Extraordinary and the Always Interesting? of all places! The main concern at our Institute has always been the welfare of our Artistes. Make no mistake about it,

the main concern of any corporation is the welfare of their money. And we're about to put money first? Profit first? Like corporations do! Will we squeeze money out of our Artistes - Artistes? Hah! The second Money Incorporated gets their mitts on them, they won't be Artistes any more! They'll be the 'mentally ill'! Well ... will we squeeze money out of Artistes the way corporations squeeze money out of their consumers? Why do I even ask? Squeeze money out of sick people? Some of whom may have no money to squeeze! And what happens to them when they can't pay? Will we still treat them? Or will we ship them off to an Institution filled with gray wards and bleak corridors where sick people in stained bathrobes pace up and down day and night? An Institution that'd never allow Artistes to let-loose, but only doles out drugs to the 'mentally ill' so that the only self they can let-loose shuffles instead of dances, mopes instead of sparkles, because that's what drugs do to people.

'But suppose we can squeeze money out of them, will our Artistes be receiving any benefit from their money? If we're slashing their programs and cutting the Institute's staff and putting them all on drugs, I don't think so.

'And since IV won't be spending that money on the Artistes and their programs, who will he spend it on? Is he keeping it for himself?

'Is IV becoming like one of those CEOs? The kind that receives a million times more money, more everything than anybody else in the corporation! And our country pretends it won't abide kings!'

And an image of his own 'queen' assaulted him right there in his tracks.

'Like my wife, the CEO, does!

'I never actually put that into words before!' He brushed it off and went on. But thugs jumped him; his mind was full of them; for there in its eye stood the shameless-swashbuckling-anglo-saxon-baronial-big-fat-phony-pile-of-ornate-doodoo that was the house, but not the home, he lived in. The Castle L'Oomla.

The House that Daffeine Built.

The Institute's staff was right.

And then there stood the cozy, music-filled, sun-dappled, timbered-bungalow he and his two beauties - his song-filled, storied-filled Sigrid and his sweet, shy, serious Sophia - used to share. Why surely Sophia chattered away back then, didn't she? Didn't she?

He stepped out of the shadow of the Castle L'Oomla only to step into an even more immense shadow - the Institute's - the Castle Gloomla, as he called it.

Back and forth. Every day, he went. Between two hills. The Castle L'Oomla on one hill. And on the other - the Institute that was so vast, with its wings, its turrets - the Castle Gloomla.

Morning - to GLOOM-La.

Night - to LOOM-La.

The Castle Gloomla, even had its own King. IV. Dr. Oomla wondered if he himself was the King of his own Castle. No. Giggle Corporation was the King of there. Nowadays only a giant Corporation could afford to manufacture a pile like that. And only Great Aunt Hortense would've insisted on that particular pile.

'Where could I go? Because I can't stay at GLOOM-La!

'Could I tell the Board and the Trustees? They sure respect IV. For one reason. For all the money he raises!

'Could I fight this man and his rules? What could I do?'

And there on a tree branch was the Old Chief cawing away, mocking him, "Don't tell me you're thinking of abandoning your usual reserve! your think-through! puzzle-out! ponder! brood! muse! over the effect each word will have on the speakee! before you, the speaker, speak it! and will actually! open!!! your mouth and express! your concerns? But won't you have to demonstrate empathy to every last person in the universe before you do?"

'Okay, Old Chief, I get it! But, I'm warning you, they'll listen politely, and not do a &@^^^^ thing about it. Because money is what those types are all about. The bottom line. Especially, nowadays when people throughout our country, the whole world are afraid that a catastrophe might strike at any moment, and money is what people believe protects them against such a catastrophe.

'But suppose I bypass the Board and the Trustees and only discuss my concerns with the Institute's Show Business contributors, might they be the ones who would care? The only ones who would care?

'But suppose they're worried, too, about a catastrophe striking at any moment and they don't care either?'

On and on he trudged, trying to answer himself and his mind-hound, the Old Chief; trying to figure out what was missing because something was, and every once in a while, patting his pockets. Trudging. Thinking. Thinking, really thinking, thinking deep, thinking deeper, searching in himself, he trudged on and on.

What was it? But no matter how deep he thought, something was missing. What was it?

'Hey, Mr. Feel-Your-Pain, Mr. Pensivity Pants, Mr. Think Tank!'

Walloped. Again.

'Do you have it in you? Do you have it in you to fight this man and his rules? The bull-dog would, but do you? So what if the Trustees and the Board and the

Show Biz people won't do a thing about what IV's doing, shouldn't you at least try to persuade them to do something, Mr. Mops Dog? But, silly me, what am I thinking? Five years ago, you wouldn't even write an article for the village newspaper describing your nightmare so you could've been like your hero, too, and teach the villagers about what their dreams mean, their nightmares mean, because you would've had to admit you have problems, too. Because then you'd have to stop deliberating, Mr. Dithers, Mr. Introspective, Mr. Navel-Gazer, and do something. Oh, and Dr. Listen, you've never even told your wife how you feel about CEOs, so how are you going to tell IV what you think about what he's doing at the Institute. You don't even really know why your daughter is having so much trouble talking in school, Dr. Fraud! You never even said a word to your Big Shot Father and stuck up for that poor actor kid who wanted to go out for Halloween! I heard you, you just admitted, didn't you, that practicing empathy on those characters won't make a bit of difference, won't get them to change their minds. You know empathy won't cut it, Oomla! And you know what comes next. Face it, you'll have to get down and dirty and fight.'

And there on the path he knew so well, he found someone he didn't know. The man, or the men, who lived inside himself who were telling the truth. Who really understood. Who knew what was going on, who knew what had to be done. Now all those inside men had to do was move outside. So he could do it. The hero's deeds. If he wanted to be like the Old Chief. And save the Artistes. Save the Institute. Save his family. And save himself.

And there on the path he knew so well, he wondered, had he found the hero, or not?

• • • 7:50 AM • • •

Dr. Oomla dragged himself through the cold and wind til he reached the bottom of the hill. He looked up and there was the Castle GLOOM-la.

As he got closer to the front gate, he noticed there were several workmen surrounding the Institute's sign. He didn't have to wonder what they were up to. There were two ladders, one at each post, with a workman standing on the top rung of each. The two workmen had loosened the Institute's sign and were beginning to tug it off its posts. Dr. Oomla came to a halt so he could watch the sad event. He wanted to stop them but didn't. He was not the King of GLOOM-La. He was not the King of this hill. As he watched, he could feel Miss Kitty's breakfast rise up in revolt.

THE INSTITUTE FOR THE COMPASSIONATE CARE OF THE EXTRAORDINARY AND THE ALWAYS INTERESTING

They were, after all, just words. But they had been put together by a wise man to mean so much to so many and had for years and years and years. Words that were humane - fanciful – grand - hopeful. He examined each word - even as the workmen were attempting to bring that sign down but were not having any luck because the wind didn't seem to want to let it go - even as the workmen managed but just barely to get hold of the sign - and even as they finally pulled it free of its posts. Those powerful words must not've wanted to let go; they knew what they stood for.

He wondered, what those words meant to the Artistes. Did they make their troubles weigh less? Did they make them laugh? Okay, maybe the Artistes who already thought of themselves as extraordinary might've been encouraged to think themselves extra-extraordinary. Is it always bad to think of yourself highly? Who, after all, aspires to be ordinary? And is flattery always bad for a person? Would all the good work those words do leave the Institute, too, when the sign was down? Would the new words of the new name on the new sign comfort them as much as the Old Chief's had? Could the words THE INSTITUTE OF EFFICIENTLY APPLIED SCIENCE help, let alone, comfort anybody?

The workmen on the ladders made many attempts to hand the sign down to the workmen on the ground for the wind kept sweeping that sign right back on its post. It took every last one of them to finally wrestle it to the ground.

'The Old Chief won't let go!'

Dr. Oomla knew the slightest dalliance would make him late but he found himself striding towards the workmen and the sign anyway.

"Good morning, Dr. Oomla, I can't believe you walked! It's so fierce today!"

'Fierce! Like the Old Chief!' But Dr. Oomla kept that to himself, "Good morning, Clyde, Good morning Sam, Joe, Mickey! No, no, this weather's good for my circulation. And it give's me time to think. Meditate. Speaking of which, the message on that sign sure could put fresh ideas in heads that needed fresh ideas put into them. Sad day for all of us to see it taken down."

Clyde said, "Yeah, I always got a kick out of this old sign but the Boss said he wanted it down first thing this morning. And down it is. Yeah, Dr. Oomla, tourists're always asking where the Institute is, because all of 'em want to have their picture taken under the sign. That sign's almost as famous as some of the nuts inside ... ooh, sorry Dr. Oomla ... I can't tell you how many times people'd call me over and ask me if I'd take their picture under the sign."

"Yeah, yeah me, too." Sam and Joe and Mickey agreed.

Clyde went on, "The tourists sure're gonna miss it. It was a joke to some but sometimes a joke's just the thing."

"You're right, Clyde, sometimes a joke is just the thing." And then Dr. Oomla hopped back on the path towards GLOOM-la, took a few steps, then ran right back to the group.

"Gentlemen, would you mind taking that old sign back to my house? You know where I live, don't you?"

"Sure, Dr. Oomla." said Clyde.

"I just hate to see it get tossed onto a pile of rubbish."

Dr. Oomla took out his wallet and handed each of them several bills. "Here's something for your trouble."

'At least, the sign will be in my care.' As soon as he said that, he felt odd but he kept walking, *'The sign will be in my care! That makes me feel funny, why?*

'Didn't I want to rescue another one of the Old Chief's signs a few years ago? Rescue? I never did anything with it. No wonder I don't feel right saying the sign will be in my care! The sign stood on the main road just before the entrance to the village, and somebody wrote over the Old Chief's words quite expressively. I wanted to repair it but I didn't even do that! It looks like I've appointed myself the Official Keeper of the Village Signs but I'm not doing such a great job. What so great about me putting me in charge of a sign, about me making myself an Official Keeper, when I didn't do a blasted thing about the first sign. I don't even know it it's still there. Is that's what going to happen with this sign too? But then again, what will I ever do with this old sign anyway?'

He'd reached the steps of the Institute and the gloom of the place set in upon him worse than before. *'Today, I have to tell the Artistes what IV has decreed.'* And as he climbed those steps, higher and higher, he felt himself sinking deeper and deeper into something he didn't like. And getting closer and closer to it. On each step.

• • • 8:00 AM • • •

When Super Claude had deducted the feather and belt and boots and stockings and veil and hat and gloves thereby de-phosphor-ing Mrs. Oomla's ensemble; had steamed and pressed that ensemble's sleekness into a crisp salute; had finished her hair; had applied her make-up to look like she wasn't wearing any at all; had coated each eyelash with mascara (that phase alone was the most delicate part of the entire head-to-toe operation requiring the steady hands of a surgeon so that each eyelash did not meet even one of its neighbors in any dreaded clump) and Mrs. Oomla was now Ms. Oomla, minimized into corporate understatement, he granted his blessing. He could now release her to join the other masqueraders - the wolves, the rats, the lambs, the skunks - for now she was a no-see-um of corporate land, too. His first order of business was to get her to her breakfast meeting with the green Bottling Manufacturer. He led her into the elevator and, just before the doors shut, ducked out; she was on her own now.

And there stood, Ms. Oomla, Super Claude-less.

Which meant that he missed the very next thing that happened to her; or more precisely, that happened to her face where all his perfectly applied make-up was. Because for some reason that Ms. Oomla didn't really understand, this morning, she didn't feel as if someone had just done magic on her, she felt as if she'd been worked over, tricked, and she was confused.

'Am I really someone who talks and doesn't listen? Why don't I ever feel right when I'm here? Did Claude really mean what he said about Sophia? About Sigmund? Was Sophia really the way he said she was? Would Sigmund think all this money I spend is really benefiting humanity? Or was Claude just saying all those things to get me to feel better so I look better and won't cry and mess up his hard work? I'm one of his prize clients, after all!'

She knew that; she was far from stupid. She was his product like Giggle was her product. Then her unease returned; that feeling she should be used to by now but wasn't. But this time she could even feel some tears falling from her eyes. And she couldn't stop them. They were crystal clear when they departed their source but were no longer when they rolled over, then through the black mascara, and then slopped on down her flawlessly made-up face.

And when the door opened and there stood the green Bottling Manufacturer before her and she stepped out to shake his hand, muddy water was streaking her perfection, streaks that would have been visible on anybody else's face but were invisible on hers because as soon as she opened her mouth and wrapped the velvet of her voice all around "Good Morning, and how are you today?" the green Bottling Manufacturer's ears opened and his eyes closed as he let her voice inside to warm him up on this frostbite morning. And she knew she could count on him staying that way for about a minute or so. At which point, his ears would close, his eyes would open and he would notice those dark streaks muddying her perfection. And then he would start blabbing away and back-talking and interrupting her like everybody else did around here.

• • • 8:30 AM • • •

Miss Kitty knew as she walked back to Mr. James and the limousine, he'd have a question for her and she'd better have an answer for him. *'A doozy. But tat'll be a cinch. All I'll have t' say when he asks me why Miss Sophia wasn't in time for breakfast was tat Miss Sophia overslept. Which won't be a lie at-tall. I just won't say where she overslept or why. Even proper English people must oversleep from time t' time. Of course, Mr. James'll understand. I'm not at-tall worried.'*

Mr. James glided out of the car, tipped his cap and opened the back door for her. Miss Kitty glided in, tipped nothing and set her feet down firmly on the floor of the car. As she oh-so-casually arranged herself, she prepared for Mr. James' question about why Miss Sophia was late for breakfast. He'd ask her about the weather first.

"A bit nippy isn't it?"

"Tis, tisn't it now."

"And I'm sure you reminded Miss Sophia to ask Mr. Snoggley for the directions to the speech therapist for her appointment this afternoon?"

'I'll lose me job!' And she sizzled with shame. *'What should I say? Not a word of what I done! Of all tings t' forget! Only te most important ting tat Mrs. Oomla entrusted us t' do today! Tis Miss Sophia 'n tat Movie Star foolishness of hers tat pushed tat speech terapist appointment clear out o' me head! But Mr. James can not find me out! He can't! Answer him. Answer him fast!'* And as nonchalant as a smoldering sinner could be, she glanced up at him. He wasn't looking at her. Maybe he hadn't noticed. Should she make up another doozy? Another! She hadn't even recited her first doozy yet.

She fussed with her hat and scarf and gloves and rustled about the back seat, stalling for time, waiting for her doozy-making-motor to kick in.

"O' Mr. James, o' course, I did." She was about to add another 'o' course!' on the tip of the doozy but felt something stop her. *'Me blessed Irish Saints!'*

"Excellent, Miss Kitty!"

And Miss Kitty changed the subject, chattering so fast she broke her own record, "Oh, Mr. James, I tought I would jus' about freeze meself into a statue I can't wait t' be gettin' back t' me nice warm kitchen can ye I'll boil over ... up ... no! ... I'll boil notin' but water for tea for us so we can have a spot for ourselves before we start with t' days' chores notin' like a nice cup o' tea t' take te bitter edge off days in North America are quite sometin' aren't tey now..."

"Do please pardon my interrupting you. Though I do agree, Miss Kitty, a cup of tea would be a wonderful reward for our efforts this morning; but

I really must inquire as to why you and Miss Sophia were so late coming down to breakfast this morning. Dr. Oomla was quite disappointed that he didn't get to see Miss Sophia. Certainly you must recall our recent discussion about how scattered the Oomla family has become, and how we might be just the ones who could remedy that situation. After all, we are the Oomlas only caretakers; they don't seem to have any relations with whom they are genuinely close. Dr. Oomla rarely sees his parents. Of course, there is Great Aunt Hortense ..."

And they rolled their eyes below ...

"And we know she's always snooping around, looking for things amiss. So Miss Kitty, one of our remedies was to make sure that Dr. Oomla spent time with his daughter in the morning. Especially since Dr. Oomla's been so ... so ... distracted every evening, and the morning is the only time he is carefree. Another remedy of ours was to make sure that the family unit itself, Father, Mother and daughter, spends more time together since we noticed they really do seem detached from each other and never are together anymore like they used to be in the old days when our employment with the Oomlas commenced. But what we didn't discuss is who pays our salaries. And they are handsome ones, indeed! So Miss Kitty, let me conclude that discussion now since it seems that what I said in our first discussion did not make a strong enough impression on you. The Oomla family must receive value for the money they are spending. And turning a scattered family into a close family would be value indeed. But they are not there yet. And it will be up to us to get them there. And if you continue to allow Miss Sophia to miss her special time with her Father, we will not ever get them there, will we? We must not lose sight of our responsibilities. We must make sure that Father and daughter spend time together. And if the morning is that time, then that's when we must make it happen. A daughter needs to receive attention from her Father when her Father is prepared to give it."

As Mr. James talked on, and on, and on, Miss Kitty watched her hands turn scarlet and was sure her face was a torch. *'I'm being cooked by te hot-place-below! Me entirety'll burst into flame any second!'* If Mr. James took one look at her, he'd know what she done. She was eternally grateful, at least, that he couldn't see inside her, where an oven was smoking whatever good that was left in her into food for the devil.

'Forgettin': One. Me promises! Two. Me duties! Three. Me charge's appointments! 'N te fourth 'n te worst of all, Lyin'!

'Miss Kitty! Will ye stop takin' inventory of te fresh batch ye just added t' y'r tally sheet! Ye need t' be spinnin' y'r doozy-making-machine!

'*But can me blessed saints ever forgive me as I'm spinnin' it, knowin' when I'm spinnin' it, I'm lyin' about a child who needs her Father 'n a Father who needs his child!*

'*But can y'r blessed saints get ye another position? Because if Mr. James or Great Aunt Hortense find ye out, ye'll be an old woman lookin' but not findin' a position because tat's what happens t' old people! Old people can't find jobs because employers don't hire tem! 'N even when old people have jobs, tey lose em because tey forget everytin'!*

'*'N now I'm one o' tem, too! An old woman who forgets!*

'*Blessed saints! don't let me old reliable doozy-making-machine shake me all about as I take it on a spin!*' As long as she could beseech her saints to forgive her shortcomings, she could live with a scold in her head that kept reminding her of them. She tipped her head in Mr. James' direction, unclamped her jaw and, when he uttered his last syllable, spoke,

"Oh, Mr. James, I intend t' help te Oomlas get close again! But our little Miss Sophia just overslept n' she was just so drowsy, I couldn't quite get her t' stand ... I mean ... t' wake up fully so we just had t' take some extra time tis morning in te TELE ... in ... te room ... in her bedroom! n' gettin' her school clothes on n' such, n' tat was just a trifle difficult on suuuch a sleepin' child but I feel jus' terrible about her missin' her breakfast with Dr. Oomla, yes, indeed, Mr. James, tis was an unfortunate circumstance tat could not be helped but it will ... I mean NOT ... it won't be happenin' in te future ... oh listen to me, Mr. James, I'm talkin' a leg off an iron pot but ye know I ..."

And as Mr. James drove home, Miss Kitty kept praying: that the leg would fall off that iron pot, and that her doozy machine would stop shaking her up so much. And Mr. James kept examining her through his rear view mirror as she did.

• • • 8:35 AM • • •

Even though Sophia's head was down, she knew who was talking. She could tell by their voices. "I'm freezing!" (girl, squeaky - Rachel Soliwitz) "That homework was too hard, Snoggley's gonna git me!" (boy, raspy - Duke Appleby) "You didn't do the homework! But it was so easy!" (boy, boy-next-door - Johnny Jones) "I did the homework but I couldn't figure it out. Hah! I bet you did it wrong, Johnny!" (boy, raspy - Duke Appleby) "Did you see her new coat?" (girl, throaty - Caitlin Mitchell) "She has so many clothes!" (girl, nose-talker - Jodi Jones, Johnny Jones's twin) "I can't believe they lost the game! He kept missing shots!" (boy, chest-boom - Skip Murphy) "He's a retard!" (boy, brat - Albert Ianucci) "Retard? Like you could do it! He's not a retard, Retard!" (boy, chest-boom - Skip Murphy)

Nobody at school ever talked about what she liked. Movies. Or if they did, the movies they talked about were the kind with androids or goons or shopaholics. They never talked about the old movies with the movie stars where all they had to do was talk with those voices and they already were so interesting, so sassy, so … so … oh! And Sophia also began to talk, but to herself, making up what Ginger would say to Fred and what Fred would say back to Ginger, Fred, Ginger, back, forth, while not saying a word to anybody, not looking at anybody. And the bell rang. THE BELL RANG! They stopped. Fred. Ginger. Everybody. The teachers were coming. Their teacher. Mr. Irvington Snoggley. Mr. Snoggley.

"Fifth Graders, your school day has begun! Straighten those lines. And we will make it a Good Day, won't we class?"

"Yes, Mr. Snoggley."

The class formed two ruler straight lines. Now it was everybody's turn to walk head down, mouths shut, into school. And not a head lifted, not an eye caught Mr. Snoggley's eye.

Sophia took her seat in the back of the room and scrunched herself up small. She felt so tired, she could barely open her books. And because her eyes kept shutting, she had to grope through her book bag with her fingers to find her homework. She managed to pull it out of her bag but it tore. She plopped it on her desk anyway and sat there as tiny as she could, eyes now really shut, hoping no one would look at her. And because she really meant no one, she'd better do what Miss Kitty did. Pray. But Miss Kitty didn't just pray to anybody, she prayed to her Irish Saints. Sophia would pray to Miss Kitty's Irish Saints, too. Miss Kitty had told her once Irish Saints were much more sympathetic to nighttime carousers. She wasn't sure what carousers were but nighttime was when she watched movies and she would probably be considered a carouser herself.

'Okay, all you Irish Saints that always help Miss Kitty, who is my Nanny, would you please make me invisible all day. I'll eat my vegetables and I won't stay up in the nighttime and watch any … and I'll really eat my vegetables.' She'd better not lie to Irish Saints, even if they were more sympathetic.

"I'd like the following people to go to the blackboard and write the solution to last night's Math Problems on the board. For Problem #1, One Million as an exponent of 10, Sophia Oomla, would you please write the answer to Problem # 1—"

'But I didn't lie! And Miss Kitty's Irish Saints didn't help me?'

⋯⋅☾⋅⋯

("Sorry, Author Lady," said Lorraine, "I'll be fast. I give all a'youse a hint about why that prayer of hers didn't work. Her not lying to any Irish Saint wouldna helped that prayer. No. The downfall of that prayer was mentioning Miss Kitty's name in it. If Sophia knew how mad those Irish Saints were at Miss Kitty, she wouldda, like, kept her name out of it entirely. Okay, keep going."

Lorraine, you mean to tell me Fairies know the saints!

"Darling, I assure you," said Me, "we Fairies do not! Lorraine thinks she's funny!"

"Yeah, and you think you're beautiful!")

⋯⋅☽⋅⋯

Sophia didn't hear another word. *'I'm standing but I have to walk on iron boats so how can I get to the blackboard? And if I get there how can I pick up the chalk if my hand is shaking?'* Half way there, she looked at her homework. *'It's not shaking like it would be if it was inside my shaking hands. Where is my homework? My homework is on my desk. I have to walk all the way back to my desk and get it! Everybody's gonna look at me.'* And she whizzed to her desk. *'Don't be slow! Or I'll feel every one of their eyes sticking on me!'* She snatched up her homework, whipped around, rushed back but tripped - because her head was down too low to see where she was going - on Marilyn Kruger's bag. MARILYN KRUGER THE TATTLETALE! But Sophia didn't say excuse me because now she was dizzy and light-headed and sick inside and she couldn't open her mouth so she pretended like it didn't happen and kept walking.

"Can't you, like, see? So ph?ia?" Marilyn said (in her girl-so-cool-she-even-put-question-marks-between-syllables voice).

"There seems to be some confusion, Miss Kruger?"

"No, Mr. Snoggley, Soph?ia, like? can't say excu?se me? because she, like, never talks? – well Sophia is, like, a speed-walking?-sleep?walker?, she's trying to, like? walk through, over and on my brand new? Paku-Pi?ku bag?"

There were just a few snickers. And Sophia didn't want to cry but she was at the blackboard and her back was turned towards the class and she knew she could. She picked up the chalk and felt the tears in her eyes and began to write the answer to Problem #1. *'But why did Marilyn say I was sleep-walking because how could she know I was tired and why did almost the whole entire class almost burst out laughing? ...*

'And I talk! I talk like a Movie Star! But I'll never be able to show them, if I'm like this. I'll just hide up here at the blackboard because no one can see my face when it's

crying because they can't see through me if my back is to the whole class. And if I write really slow, I won't have to turn around because we have to be right next to our answer when we explain it to Mr. Snoggley and to the class and when it's my turn to explain, I'll just stay the way I am, with my back towards them. Because if I turn around everybody will see that I'm talking through tears. I hope my shoulders don't start shaking.'

And then it hit her.

'What would Ginger do?

'Ginger wouldn't stand here crying, she wouldn't be afraid if she had to talk to the whole class, she'dda said her answer out loud to Mr. Snoggley! To the whole world, too! Yeah! And then she'dda sassed that Marilyn right back! She wouldn't be afraid. No! She'dda known what to do.'

Sophia looked at her uniform and then down on the floor; she was standing on feet about as good as ten-ton-nothings. And her hands were shaking! And she could feel her lips jiggling! And her tears were washing down and making a wet mess of her ripped up homework in her hand! And she was sick to her stomach! And she wasn't a Movie Star. No. She was just a kid with a bellyache who was crying.

"Class, logic requires us to begin with Problem #1. Miss Oomla, would you please explain to the class how you arrived at your solution."

Mr. Snoggley's request fell like a hard rain on Sophia, pounding on her back, knocking the very breath out of her. Until, in a blast, her breath returned. And it was loud. Everybody could hear her. And if she turned around, everybody would see her. So she concentrated on saying her answer. Just saying her answer. Because she knew the answer. And she got her mouth to open but what she said came out not anywhere near as loud as her breath, "Mr. Snog HUH Sno HUUH Snog HUUUH ley HUUUH ... I put HUHHH UHHH HUHHHHH" then her breath took over. "HUUUH UHHH HUUUH UHHHH." And she listened to herself. Ginger never sounded like that so she wouldn't let one more breath out of her mouth. But soon she felt light in her head because she wasn't letting her breath out and she was heavy everywhere else but mostly in her stomach and that heaviness was moving up fast - too fast - to where it shouldn't be, so she bolted and ran as fast as she could to the Girls Lavatory and made it in just in time for the milk, juice and seven blueberries to announce themselves all over the floor.

·∴C∴·

("Lady!" said Lorraine, "Your numbers are off by five ... five of us also announced ourselves all over that floor, too. Five suddenly very wide-awake Fairies. Five rudely-awakened, Fairies. And steamin'-mad. Steamin'!

Hoppin'! Mad! Furious! And reekin'! And covered in, like, pulverized blueberry!"

"Darlings," said Me, "unspeakable other monstrosities too! And to creatures of our delicate proportions, these monstrosities were nothing less than Godzillas. As usual you, Lorraine, were the first to inform everyone within the immediate vicinity exactly how you felt about this circumstance but your expressions are, how do I put it? too pottymouthed to be reported here and would be more suitable in, say, Tales from the Ma-fairy-ia! And then I spoke up next. My sleep ensemble! Ruined! And to make it worse, my silky tresses I just had washed and blown dry were glued to my scalp by a substance that should never be allowed near such silky tresses; and my nighttime moisturizer, by its nature thicker and more emollient, was causing every microscopic and despicable piece of debris to cling to my face and consequently I could only hope that its emollient-cy that I pay so dearly for was protecting my face or otherwise I'll be meeting the manufacturer in the Hall of Fairy Justice after I sued! But, for the record, distraught had never been presented so perfectly. But then I do do all my presentations perfectly!"

"Lady, Be and Free was cracking up. They told me later that watching the both of us carry on like that was worth it even if they had to be coated in chow to see it. Even Thee, who most certainly wasn't cracking up, was tee-hee-ing."

Thank you. I'll go on now, shall I?

"No, Lady. I think it's about time ya introduced your Readers to the rest of us Fairies.")

• • • THE REST OF THE FAIRIES • • •

"In fact," said Lorraine, "let me, like, have the honors, since it is about us. They've met Me and me, but they haven't really been, like, ya know properly introduced to Free, Thee and Be. So I'll start with Free. Free, could ya, like, ya know apparate yourself?"

There was a flash and a very demure but bony-maroney Fairy appeared. She was wearing mis-matched, brightly-colored knee-socks, one touching one knee and the other puddled around her ankle, and her wings were shivering, shaking and quaking. She looked at me, turned purple and flew into the molding on a picture frame on my studio wall. She seemed to disappear but, occasionally, I'd see a wing flutter.

"Hey, like, welcome little buddy. Don't worry Free, I'm, like, the master of ceremonies, so ya don't even have to peep! So, like, what Free said when she landed in the chow was, 'Poor poor Ophia-So! Getter sadding meselves and worriederest most by the side of the tiny minute.' Translation: 'Poor Sophia. I'm getting sadder and more worried by the second.' "

"Lorraine, darling, that was so helpful but I think it best that I do the honors. Reader darlings, some Fairy English is hard to understand. But that really depended on who was doing the talking. This lovely Fairy, The Fairy Freesia Free, hailed from the Apparitional Mountain Chain in the U.S.E., better known as The Mountain That Will Go to Mohammed. In the space of just two weeks, those mountains covered almost every inhabitable part of the U.S.E., sometimes touching down at breakfast and lifting off at lunch; hopping from backwoods to spired city to hamlet to shire. And the Fairy folks that lived on those Mountains were mixed up something terrible. Speaking of never knowing whether you were coming or going! It was pitiful. And when they ran out of sugar and had to go to a local store and ask for it - LORD HELP THEM!! There are 52 different ways to say sugar in the U.S.E. The Fairies in the hinterlands say "snow sweet" but the Fairies in Giant City call it "candy bricks." And they could never remember who said what, no matter how many magic spells they sprinkled on their thinking caps. But it did make them famous. Infamous, actually. Infamous for mangling the Fairy Language. Those poor Fairies! Every time they walked out of a fairy-goods emporium, red-faced, embarrassed, empty-handed, they left behind a group of cackling, teetering, hooting fairies. The Fairy Freesia Free was happy when she got her transfer off of that Mountain. Weren't you, Free?"

A wing fluttered.

"Yeah Me, but what about Be and Thee? And you, too, Me, because our Readers haven't really heard about you and where you come from?"

"Okay, Lorraine. Be, could you now appear?"

And in came a Fairy with long stringy hair who was dressed entirely in black. She flew onto the top border of the screen of my laptop, flopped herself flat on its edge and, as if she hadn't a care in the world, smiled then fluttered her eyes shut.

"So, here now is our Be. First off, darlings when Be fell into the hideousness, she said … tell them yourself!"

" 'Far out!' Be's head didn't even lift up when she said it.

"Be's full name is The Fairy Beatrice Nikola Om, so I'm sure all of you can guess why. Be was already awake. But then she had a hard time sleeping because of all the coffee she drank when she was hanging out in human coffeehouses because she couldn't sleep. Which had gotten her into the habit of hanging out in human coffeehouses in the first place since human coffeehouses were open all night and were the only place she ever found to hang out in when her shift inside her human was up. She had gotten into the habit of flying to these coffeehouses, rather than slipping back to the Elixir Palais in Enchantica, which didn't even serve coffee. And she dug coffee. And then she began to dig the humans that hung out drinking that coffee in those coffeehouses. Beatniks. In fact, "The Fairy Beatrice Nikola Om" wasn't her fairybirth name. She was born The Fairy Pansy Marzipanski but when she started hanging out in coffeehouses, she changed her name to Beatrice Nikola Om since Jacky Kerowacky was already taken. And to be even more authentic, she began playing bongos, writing poems, calling her cave inside her human her pad, hanging strings of colorful beads over its entrance to liven up the grayness, and greeting visitors with a 'like, Fairy-o!'

"And then there's Me! The Fairy Mimi Meselk."

"Me, like, I'll tell everyone about you. The Fairy Mimi Meselk has strong feelings about anything to do with clothes. Me was certainly the best dressed Fairy of all of us inside Sophia, even I'll, like, admit that.

"Okay, so she's, like, wearing this plain, lavender sheath that falls below the knee and has three-quarter-length sleeves. It's all form fitting and skinny-fying. Plus she's wearing gloves that go flap over the sleeves. And she's wearing a hat with a veil. It's, like, a retro-mish-mash, some Fifties, some Forties. Me wouldda been the best-dressed Fairy anywhere. Me is the daughter of the Editor of FAIRY FAIR DAILY, THE Fairy fashion bible, the absolute last word on the subject for All Fairykind – And all fashionable Fairies (and all Fairies are fashionable) – would dream about the clothes found on its pages. Mimi Meselk certainly didn't let any a' her fellow Fairies forget for one minute just WHO her Mother was. For one thing, she loved dropping her Mother's name in just about every other sentence she spoke when we was not doing our official duties, especially in just about every other sentence she spoke in front of me! It's a wonder I didn't, like, bop ya one. I still might, ya know."

"Peace, Lorraine. Darlings, though all Fairies may be fashionable, very few meet my standards. And those that do, were not in the crew I had to coexist with inside Sophia. Such DisCountesses!"

"Don't tempt me, Me!"

"Well, darlings, last but by no means least is our Thee. The one and only. Only the most responsible of us, which even I acknowledge. Thee Fairy Prudence Priss Primly (Thee for short).

And in came a Fairy who, with the rule book under her arm and her glasses, pleated skirt, white anklets and sensible shoes, looked more studious than fairyious.

"Welcome to our story." said Me. "May I introduce you?"

"Yes, you may, Me."

"Thee, you have to admit, you are all about doing your duty and making sure we did our duty. She always informed us when we weren't following the Magical Creatures Rules of Engagement. Because Thee takes rules and regulations very seriously. When she fell in, as you humans say, the drink, she said ... tell them what you said, Thee!"

" 'To be drenched in such material! So disconcerting! And Sophia has missed her Math Lesson!' "

"You see what I mean? Everything Thee says is crisp and creased just so! And did you notice, Thee was the only one who even noticed that Sophia missed her Math lesson. But to Thee, that was the real tragedy."

Thank you, Me and Lorraine. Welcome, all! Our Readers are intrigued, I'm sure. May I?

• • • 9:00 AM • • •

The hour had arrived for the very apprehensive doctors to tell their very skittish Artistes the rules. By 9:01 AM, when only a handful of Artistes knew, all was far from well and there certainly was no peace at the Institute.

At 8:58 AM, Dr. Oomla was still calculating, *'What tone should be in my voice? What words should come out of my mouth? What look should be on my face? I can't very well wear the neutral visage of the psychoanalyst! But I certainly can't go down to their level and rant or rave about the injustice of it all either.'*

The answer from within was swift, 'But you have a library full of books, a wall full of degrees and you don't know for sure?'

And all was far from well and there certainly was no peace in Dr. Oomla.

'This will not go well! Artistes' emotions are held in check by hair-triggers; if this news doesn't pull those triggers, I don't know what will! And then what will happen? Could our Artistes turn into a herd of ... of—

'elephants? from hell?'

'*What did I say? What?did?the?psychoanalyst?just?say? I am insulted so I insult? Those aren't my thoughts! Who is that inside me? Whoever you are, don't come out!*'

But he churned, '*Suppose I am right, suppose the Artistes do stampede? I've never demonstrated I have the stomach for chaos and I don't have the ears for cacophony! And if everybody falls apart, can I stay calm? Can I remain in control? But if I'm not wearing the mask of the psychoanalyst, how could I stay calm and in control?*'

'If you're not wearing the mask of the psychoanalyst, what mask will you wear?'

Did he have his very own personal crackpot? Was that who was sounding off inside him? *Just what I need!*'

As his Artiste crossed his threshold, he stuck his naked face away from her cross-examining eyes and into her chart and began flipping through his notes:

'Artiste X, the spectacularly famous movie star, (whose far and away, beyond-the-pale, out-on-a-limb - way out on a limb - over-the-top, excessive, in-the-extreme, of-a-much-too-emotional-muchness caused the movie she was starring in to shut down temporarily) has come to the Institute for some much needed, as her publicist said, 'spiritual rebirth and Tantric recentering.'

And he was appalled. What sort of medical record was that? The answer was, it wasn't. This dribble was fit for a tabloid. He noticed that the time on the entry was just last week at 1:30 in the morning. Surely, he must've been so exhausted he'd stopped thinking professionally.

But this was not 1:30 AM and, now, at this critical moment, he would not fail her or his profession: he broke the news to her very sensitively. Nevertheless, she had a full blown, panic-attack right there in Dr. Oomla's office, threatening to throw herself from the top of a turret.

His notes were accurate after all.

Though her voice crescendoed from honk to blat to hoo-ha then back down again and was seriously disturbing his ears, his precious ears—

'*She's a She-Tuba!*'

- and her much-too-emotional-muchness was jack-hammering him straight through; he remained in his chair. As he watched her he realized she wasn't watching him. How would she've ever known what he was thinking? What was going on in his gut? That her diction was making him ill? She couldn't possibly know there was an alien in his head demanding he think like her, like a mental patient.

He was there for her, in his chair for her; that's what she knew. And he realized something else. She wanted him to feel her pain.

Surely he felt it.

Except he was kidding himself. Her pain wasn't all he felt. He felt his own.

'Why is this patient getting to me? Surely other patients have behaved like this, and worse! And even if she is getting to me, so what! What sort of a psychoanalyst allows his own problems to take over during a session with a patient? A psychoanalyst who hasn't conquered his own problems, that's who!'

If Dr. Oomla believed one thing, he had conquered his problems! And he shoved away his own feelings and paid attention to hers.

She was about to lose her-stage-away-from-stage; he understood what that meant to an actor. For losing a stage, to them, is a terrible loss; for a stage, to them, is a sacred place. But a stage, to her, was much more than sacred,

"It's the only place in the entire world where I feel good about myself, Dr. Oomla!"

And now that place was being taken away from her. And she felt very very bad. But as a psychoanalyst, he also knew that her bad feeling sat on top of something inside her that felt even worse - her deep mysterious inside where her inexpressible pain, her unspeakable hurts were stored. He knew how hard it would be to get those hurts, those pains to talk to him, to talk to anybody, for they had kept quiet so long, they couldn't even talk to their owner and tell her who they were and why they were there. And whenever bad feelings sat on top of this Artiste's unspeakable, deep, inside mystery, this Artiste would blow. But then, that's what Artistes do, after all.

And his crackpot let him have it again, 'Perhaps Dr. Oomla should've been an Artiste.'

'I have a patient to take care of!'

When he was certain she wasn't about to throw herself anywhere, he began. Though how he'd begin, he actually hadn't worked out. The task was even a relief: he'd have to ignore that alien invader, the unFreud, in his head. He'd certainly not interrupt her flow with leading psychoan-alytical-type questions like - Did something like this ever happen to you before? Or Why did you use that word? – which would get her to reflect about her past and gain insight into it. He'd just let her use her theatri-cal gifts even if she was only giving into her flair for making an audience, not only feel her pain, but watch it creep and crawl along her person. Even when he knew those earth-shattering emotions she was expressing so compellingly (he never remembered being so impressed with how an Artiste expressed herself before) may not be at all how she really felt inside; even when he knew she was too scared to express what she felt because it was too scary to express. The rest of his plan, he would just have to improvise.

'IMPROVISE? YOU? SHE'S THE ONE WHO KNOWS HOW TO IMPROVISE! SHE IS THE TEACHER! WATCH HER! LEARN FROM HER!'

And he felt awful. But at least he knew what mask to wear - a pupil's.

Then he felt worse. My alien couldn't be right, could he? And he slunk even further into his chair but his alien went at him again,

'The she-tuba is turning your sacrosanct couch into her very own couch for oomp-pah-ing into her handkerchief, each and every note oozing roup and snot! Just what happened to her thespian harmo—'

What was happening to him?

But mercifully, her chaos stopped getting to him and finally her simplicity did - she felt bad and she let it out.

And he listened to her.

What was coming out of her wasn't her true feelings; and she certainly was shattering his precious eardrums and kept shattering them. She was just letting it rip, after all. She was, however, taking the first step toward her truth. Though she was gaining no deeper understanding of what the loss at the Institute really meant to her because he hadn't asked leading questions. That was just fine. Just fine. He'd get her to anchor herself to her true feelings so that she could be her authentic self on another day.

'Just who are you talking about?'

That's it, no more thinking!'

'Overthinking!'

'No more analyzing!'

'Overanalyzing!'

'That is who I am! That is how I make my living! I can't be her and she can't be me. Can't you appreciate that I am in the midst of cacophony and, look at me, I'm handling it! And I am not trying to control it! I'm almost enjoying the show! So let me be, it might even be the last time I get to see her use her special gifts here at the Institute!'

He hoped if the Old Chief, and even Freud himself would've been there, they would've given him their blessings and would not've berated him. They would've just felt bad for her, and considering how insightful they were, bad for the Institute, the Artistes. And for him, too. Surely they would've been in on his little secret: that his ears ruled him from time to time. And, no doubt, the Old Chief and Freud would've just accepted that about him and went on worrying, as he was worrying, if there was to be another day with her, or with any of the Artistes, at the Institute.

He was whistling in the dark and he knew it. And he kept right on whistling.

He even burst out laughing when for comedic effect she told him she'd be delighted to throw her main rival for the leads in the Institute's theatricals (who just so happened also to be a spectacularly famous movie star) off the turret, too.

When she saw that the serious, buttoned-up Dr. Oomla had actually burst-out-laughing at her joke, she generously offered to throw IV off as a grand finale, even though Dr. Oomla had carefully worded his statement about the Institute's new rules placing no blame on IV. But he didn't have to. Everybody knew who was behind these rules. Dr. Oomla quickly returned the neutral look to his face. Now was not the time to have anyone guess what his own feelings about IV were. But his anxiety crept right back. He willed it gone again: her feelings about IV were all he could deal with and all he would deal with.

When her time was up, Dr. Oomla was concerned she might harm someone, including herself so he thought he'd better call the Village Theriff's Office to ask for a Sheripist to escort her back to her room and stand guard over her. In all his years at the Institute, he'd never had to do anything like that before. But the line was busy. He kept speed dialing the number (which didn't please her at all and, every time she caught him, she would mutter sotto voce "Audience members should kindly refrain from cellphone use during the performance!") but the line was continuously busy. Until finally on his thirty-first try, he got through. But the precinct's operator spoke to him in such an abrupt, un-Sheripist-like manner, "Yeah, Doc, we know, we're on our way to the Institute now. Which office?" he barely could get out his answer before the operator hung up. And that's when the Artiste turned to Dr. Oomla and, on a dime, slipped out of Sheba, She-Tuba, and into 1930's-screen-goddess.

"Dr. Oomla, an actress, on a second by second basis, must be very tuned into her audience or she won't know how she's doing and I couldn't help but notice, other when you burst out laughing just now, how uptight you've been. But you must know, Dr. Oomla, you've never fooled me. I figured you out a long time ago. I've always been keenly aware that you become very uncomfortable whenever I belch fire! You are the most discriminating audi-tor I've ever had to perform for! My going off just now must've been agony for you and your ears!"

And she looked compassionately into one of his ear's, then the other, smiled ever-so-sweetly at them and then bolted over to the window, opened it, thrust her head outside and doused all below with,

"Oh oh oh Doctor Doctor Mr. MD, IV, you sir, yes, you, the quality of mercy is not - stop in the name - why-you-do-me - no Knits no …" forgetting everything she said about belching and fire.

And, as if that wasn't enough for Dr. Oomla, his inside heckler went off on him again, too, 'Didja hear that? She took a brickbat to Shakespeare! Disrespected Motown! And the sound of her would terrify a hyena! And a Dr. Oomla. And! she knows! She knows your little secret! She knows about you and your ears and your music! She's always known! And you thought that mask hid you. And now it turns out, the only one you were hiding from was you! You even believed just now she wasn't watching you. Welcome to chaos, Dr. Oomla! It's just you and, as you put it so delicately in her medical records, her much-too-emotional-muchness! What fun! But don't worry, her much too emotional muchness makes her the ridiculous one, right? There's no chance our Dr. Oomla will ever go down to her level and rant or rave about the injustice of it all, will he?'

He had heard enough, 'Stop!'"

It preferred kazooming—

'You dealt with that sound-foolery of yours in psychoanalysis years ago, right, doc?'

… and throwing its insults—

'So how could she've ever found out your dirty little secret, old pal, that you just want to live in a pitch-perfect world?'

… refusing to behave.

'You couldn't still be under that spell, could you? After all that work you've done on it in your own psychoanalysis?'

But Dr. Oomla continued to do his duty. When finally the Artiste was led away by a Sherapist, who gently pulled her from the window and then out the door, even the, by now, thoroughly rattled Dr. Oomla couldn't help but notice how that Sherapist knew exactly what to do, what to say. He was a credit to his profession. The Old Chief would have been proud. At least IV hadn't destroyed that fine tradition.

One down, 20 more to go.

• • • 9:31 AM • • •

Suddenly Sophia felt better. She wasn't breathing so loud and she could stand up straight.

The door opened. *'They'll see the mess I made!'* She didn't have time to clean or hide or anything.

"Oh, Sophia, are you okay?" (girl, voice made of sugar, more than a spoonful, a cup, maybe more.) Sophia knew that voice - before it and its owner even made their way around the partition.

Melinda Nightingale. Her again.

"As soon as I saw you run out of the room, I raised my hand and asked if I could help so Mr. Snoggley sent me in here to see how you were. I was afraid you got sick. Oh! Sophia, you did get sick. I know what I can do, my Mother always gives me some water when I throw up; first, so I can rinse my mouth, and second, so I don't get dehydrated."

Melinda took her last name seriously.

"I throw up a lot too. Don't you hate it? Let me get you some water but first I'll have to find a glass. And you know what else I can do, I can get Mr. Beadle, the janitor, he has a mop and a bucket and he can clean this up. Did you get any on yourself? Or on your uniform? If you did, I'll get water and wash it off."

And Sophia filled with relief, Melinda and Mr. Beadle were going to take care of her; she wouldn't have to clean up the mess she made because looking at it made her feel sick all over again; and she wouldn't have to talk because Melinda never stopped. And she stood there and let her. Now that she'd been sick, Mr. Snoggley couldn't make her talk to the whole class, he wouldn't do that. And now she wouldn't have to talk to anybody. And she wouldn't have to listen to herself. She'd get a rest. A good rest.

"Now I'll go find Mr. Beadle and a glass so you can have some water." And when Melinda came back, "Let me turn on the spigot and fill the glass."

⸰⸱⸴C⸱⸰

("Author, Lady," said Lorraine, "little did those two know a crowd was, like, watching them—"

Where would this story be without the scintillating details from our Fairy friends?

"Lady, sin-what? And it's too bad ya wasn't there because Melinda's Magical Creatures came out too. All of us was, like, floating around for, like, a minute. Be, do ya remember what ya said?"

Even though Be didn't even lift her head, she said, "Of course: 'Like, why are all of you surprised? Little Miss Oomla-bop, like, blows her chow, so what? What do you expect? When you live inside a ten-year old that watches movies all the time, never sleeps, eats ying food and yang food in the wrong combination, and jabbers away like a maharajah when she's all by herself and won't say doodle-li-squat when there's anybody around, and if that isn't backwards, I don't know what is. All that's just gotta build up pressure inside any chick. Especially this chick. She's got like a weak stomach or something and then she, like, explodes. That's just the way she is man! But look, her friend is smart, she's bringing water. Water is, like, the purifier.' "

"And then Free said, Lady, 'Rinse we in spigots. On are they turned by the friend LinMeDee. Get we. Wet we. Clean be. Lah Hah! FreshReFreshWe. Yes? Yes?' "

" 'Yes, excellent points Free and Be. Look, we must get to the spigots before Melinda turns them off. Come all!' that's what Thee said."

"We aimed not for the spigot itself, Lady, because that water was coming down too hard and too fast, but for the sprinkles that shot upwards, and we flew through them til each of us was soaking wet and, like, gloop-free.")

·᛫:)᛫·

Sophia filled her mouth with water and spit it out in the sink then Melinda splashed the up-chuck spots on Sophia's uniform. And for the first time that day, Sophia laughed.

"You're laughing. You must be better. Do you want to go back to the classroom now, Sophia? I'll walk with you, just in case you get sick again."

Sophia stopped laughing. "I don't want to go in there."

'I don't want the whole class to see me! I'm not ready to listen to Mr. Snoggley again! To be back at my desk again! Learning my lessons again! Being good again! Paying attention again! Besides maybe somebody might start teasing me about throwing up. And besides …'

She didn't really know why. She just didn't want to go back. But she didn't say another word to Melinda. She didn't say even one of her thoughts out loud. Melinda looked at her and waited for Sophia to say something and Sophia knew she was waiting for her to say something but she didn't want to say anything; she didn't want to hear herself talk right now and it was quiet and the quiet was quiet - which was unusual because Melinda never let quiet be quiet - until Melinda talked.

"Well, okay, but Sophia, Mr. Snoggley is not going to like that we didn't go straight back. Where could we go? We can't stand in here all day. And it's too cold to go outside; we don't have our coats and even if we did, we probably wouldn't be allowed out there anyway. I know, let's just walk back very, very slowly. That's what we should do."

Sophia didn't want to do that. She really did want to stand in there all day. Or, at least, for maybe an hour. But she knew just wanting to was not a good enough reason and wasn't as good as Melinda's reasons. So even if she could've told Melinda that she just didn't feel like going back because she just didn't want to, and all of the other even better reasons from her mile long list of reasons, like having to sit at her desk and pay attention and hear herself talk but not like a Movie Star, she didn't. She couldn't. Her reasons would sound silly after hearing Melinda's.

She knew what would happen.

They did what Melinda wanted. Melinda whispered to her the whole way down the long long corridor but Sophia was barely listening because inside herself somebody was making terrible insinuations: like that's what happened when you don't explain yourself, don't ask for what you want, don't open up and spill your dirt! See, now you have to do what she wants to do and not what you want to do! But Sophia didn't want to hear those insinuations, so she escaped, on a trip inside her head. She made up a movie, in-her-very-own-private, deep-inside-herself, film-studio, which - no matter what that stupid insinuator said - was a-never-to-be-shared-with-anyone-kind-of-a-movie, about Ginger Rogers standing at a blackboard in a feathery, flouncy gown, giggling, stepping from foot to foot, sing-songing arithmetic as she threw the chalk to her right hand, then chalked up the blackboard and twirled in her feathery skirt, then she threw the chalk to her left, chalked up the blackboard, and twirled in her feathery skirt, back and forth! Sing, Chalk, Twirl; Sing, Chalk, Twirl. Wheeew! Not dizzy! Not Ginger! No!

·⸱⸱C·⸱·

("Lady, that insinuator wasn't us. We the Fairies had our wings full, I mean we was dripping wet and freezing and flying above them two in the elfin' cold air, with our teeth clicking and clacking so loud some joker musta put a tap shoe on each and every tooth, so we had, like, no time for cogent observations. We was, like, determined to be back in our beds before Sophia put her two feet in Mr. Snoggley's classroom, even if we hadn't drip dried yet. Only one of us could stand Mr. Snoggley in particular and school in general. Thee Fairy Prudence Priss Primly. And don't say ya don't, Thee! The rest of us much preferred Sophia's after-school activities. But Thee couldn't wait to do the homework. Me was crazy about it when Sophia went into her Mother's closet, and Free, Be and I loved when Sophia watched them movies. Although I always complained there wasn't enough mafia movies, since they are, like, the best tales, besides Fairy Tales, ever told and the only thing that made me feel right at home among these humans. But right now, Me, Free, Be and I was heading back inside. We'd been up watching Sophia do her Movie Star thing last night, too, and we was, like, beat. Only Thee wasn't. Thee, you told us ya wanted to, like, accompany Sophia because somebody should. But you just like being in a classroom, admit it, Thee!")

·:·꙰·:·

Sophia and Melinda finally reached the room but Melinda pulled Sophia towards the back door, "Sophia, let's go in this way, maybe no one will see you and you won't be embarrassed!"

Ginger'd have none of that; Ginger'd never be embarrassed by a bunch of dopey ten-year-old kids. But just like that! Ginger was gone! Vanished. And it was Sophia who stood outside her classroom. Plain old Sophia. Sophia crept into the classroom the back way. But Melinda was wrong. Sophia was embarrassed; she was sure she had throw-up stuck on her, or that somebody'd tease her, or that something, she didn't know what, would happen and it wouldn't've mattered what door she entered. With her head hung low, she slunk towards her seat then into it where she could only hear him. He was still teaching Math. Since she didn't want to get in trouble for not paying attention, she did lift her head up, though an entire minute passed before she did. And the first thing she saw was that the answer she had written to Problem #1 was still on the board. All the other homework Problems were erased. He always erased each Problem once he had gone over its answer with the class. Problem #1 wouldn't be up there if he'd reviewed it. Suppose she had to go back up there and explain her answer? Would Mr. Snoggley make her do that after she was sick? But Mr. Snoggley was standing in the front of the room working on a new Math lesson, he was finished with the homework. He probably just forgot to erase it.

'So why am I so nervous just seeing it up there? Mr. Snoggley is teaching the new lesson! He isn't looking at me! And he isn't looking at the blackboard either!'

She was safe. She had to be. She was sure. Pretty sure. She hoped. But when Mr. Snoggley started to walk down her aisle, Sophia wasn't so pretty sure any more. She slunk even lower and put her head back down; maybe he wouldn't notice her since he was looking at everybody in the whole room and not at her. But when he reached her desk, he stood right next to her and continued to teach the lesson standing right there. And he didn't move. She couldn't even make a breathing sound or he'd hear her. So she didn't but in about ten seconds she felt lightheaded again and knew she couldn't do that anymore or she'd be right back in the bathroom. She'd just have to sit there like everybody else. And pray. Just not to Miss Kitty's people.

But when Mr. Snoggley finished the lesson, he didn't move. He stayed right where he was. Right next to Sophia. And then he got quiet. She could feel his eyes on her. Without even looking up, she knew Mr. Snoggley was looking down at her. She knew from experience when grown-up eyes were on her. "Miss Oomla, I'm delighted to see you! Are you feeling up to it? Do you think you could return to the blackboard and explain your answer to the class?"

She didn't look back at him. She knew what she had to do. Get her homework. Go back to the blackboard. Explain her answer to the class. The entire class. By talking. And she couldn't pray to a soul to help her. But where was her homework? She had it in her hand when she was at the blackboard. Before she got sick. She searched her desk but the truth began to sink in. It wasn't there. It was in Mr. Beadle's trash can.

And then she said in her smallest voice, her baby voice that sounded way too baby that she couldn't make grow up on its way out of her no matter how hard she tried, "Mr. SnSnoggley, my home ... wowork isn't here. I had it but it's not he ... here anymore."

"Where is it Miss Oomla?"

She hoped that only Mr. Snoggley would hear her and not the girls-with-the-attitude-who-never-spoke-baby. And on a wisp but not a prayer, she mumbled, "It's ... it's ... in ... in the gi ... gi ... girls rroom, Mr. Sss sss Snoggley!"

"Miss Oomla, you've already written the answer on the blackboard, you don't need your actual homework. Just look at what's on the blackboard. Proceed, Miss Oomla, please."

And then Mr. Snoggley leaned over and lowered his voice to a boom, "Miss Oomla, I can hardly hear you. Perhaps you are still not feeling well. I can, of course, call your parents or ... wait, don't you have a Nanny? One of them could come and pick you up. If you're not feeling well, you certainly should go home."

'Go home? Miss Kitty'd be so mad at me! She'll think I'm faking it because I don't want to be in school. And Mr. Snoggley can't call my Mother. Mother is too busy. Too important. She can't come back from where ever she is being on television or something just to pick me up from school. And Daddy is so worried all the time now. He isn't dancing around and singing like he used to. If Mr. Snoggley calls him, he'll worry more. He shouldn't have to worry extra more. Over me. I can't let Mr. Snoggley call any of them.'

She got up, walked to the blackboard, looked at what she wrote, knew what it meant, put it in her head, turned, faced the class, saw all of her classmates scrutinize her, stared right back at them and didn't even look down even when she could see that everybody in the whole entire class were examining her so thoroughly they were poking holes in her – probably because she had throw-up stuck on her. She just kept her eyes on everybody. She knew what she had to say. And it was time to say it. She opened her mouth. She could hear her words coming out. But the voice saying those words wasn't Ginger's. It was a baby girl's! A baby girl with a deep voice. She tried to make it – Older. Louder. Sassier. Soprano-ier. But couldn't. And what was worse, she couldn't tell them that that baby voice wasn't really her voice. She couldn't tell them Ginger's voice was really her voice. She couldn't even make Ginger's voice. And most of all she couldn't tell anybody what she was thinking because she'd have to use the baby girl voice to say it. And besides, even if she could've, she was in school and at the blackboard and Mr. Snoggley was there and she was supposed to be talking about Problem #1 right now and not about how she couldn't seem to talk about Problem #1 in her real voice, her Movie Star voice no matter how hard she tried. Now nobody'd understand about how sassy she could talk. How like a Movie Star.

She looked at all of her classmates. Not one of them knew anything about her. About her real voice. And now they'd never know. They'd all think she talked like a baby. A big baby.

But she couldn't just give up. She had to try. Try to get her voice like Ginger's.

Trying didn't help.

She simply couldn't make Ginger's voice like she could at night when she was watching Ginger's movie and she stopped talking. But the thought of Mr. Snoggley calling Miss Kitty or her Mother or her Father scared her more than having to listen to herself. So she went back to talking. Although to her, talking like a baby with a deep voice was hardly talking at all. But no matter how funny she sounded, she knew she must keep explaining her answer to Problem #1.

She finished but as she stood there waiting to hear what Mr. Snoggley would say, she wasn't thinking about her answer to Problem #1 at all. All she was thinking was why could she talk like a Movie Star at night and a baby girl in the morning? That was the real Problem #1. The answer to that problem, she didn't know at all. In fact, the answer to that problem was the only answer that mattered to Sophia. But since everything about the problem was a complete mystery to her, how would she ever find the answer?

.·.:*.(:·.·.

("Author, Lady, like, excuse me, but I just have to interrupt."

Lorraine, you don't have to do anything!

"Yeah I do, Lady! First off, remember, somebody was inside listening to her. Thee tell her what ya was doing."

"Ms. Author, I heard everything. I was, like, flying all around her, diving into her head, listening to her thoughts. I knew that the answer to Mr. Snoggley Problem #1 was inside Sophia's head and was the right answer. But then I could not have really changed the answer if it was the wrong answer. And, for that matter, I couldn't do anything about Sophia's own personal Problem #1 because I can't make Sophia's voice into Ginger's voice either. Only Sophia could do that. We learned our lesson on one of Great Aunt Hortense's visits. One of her more painful visits."

"Hey, Thee, one? of her more painful visits? Most a' Great Aunt Hortense's visits are painful; for one thing, she used to visit the Oomla's once a week until she upped it to just about everyday. Yick! But getting back to Sophia in this caper here, even if Thee couldda used her magic on Sophia at that blackboard, she wouldna've. Right, Thee? Thee didn't think Sophia should speak like Ginger, like a Movie Star, when she was reciting her lessons. She thought Sophia should tawk like herself. Like Sophia. Like a school girl. Because that's who Sophia was. She wasn't no Ginger. And she wasn't no baby neither, like the way she was tawking right now. She was Sophia. And nobody else.

"Lady, ya know, come to think of it, maybe now is the best time to go into the day that Sophia's tawking problem went from bad to worse. It was when her Great Aunt Hortense came to visit. I mean, for this little, church-mouse-one-minute and movie-doll-the-next to make sense to our Readers, they'll really need to know what actually happened to her on that day when she was only five-years-old. And then they'll understand why its effects lasted all these years. And why Thee couldn't help her when she was, like, up there at that blackboard. And why us Emissaries from the Universe really are not allowed to use magic to help our human children. And they'll see for themselves what happens when we do. Because that was the day all of us Fairies, including Thee, did use magic! And then, at long last, they'll find out a whole lot more about that conversation that got your attention, the one that Me magic-wanded into that bush, Author Lady, just for you. The one ya put on this book's first pages. The one between old Angel Voice herself and Sophia, where Sophia couldn't get a word in edgewise. Because that conversation happened right after Great Aunt Hortense's visit. And make no mistake about it, Lady, that Mother of hers sure had something to do with Sophia's tawking problem, too. Maybe now is the time to start looking into this, as Sophia describes it, mystery. Like, what do ya think, Lady?"

You want me to just abandon our forlorn, lost Sophia standing there at that blackboard and go back to when she was five years old? Don't you realize our Readers are at this very moment anxious to find out how she gets out of these dire straits. If she even can.

"And we'll let you tell them, Author Lady, but only after you tell them the Great Aunt Hortense part! And then this'll be, like, the last time we interrupt you. We promise, don't we?"

"Absolutely, darling! Absolutely!"

"Abso-elfin'-lutely!"

Why don't I believe you? But, Fairies, when this Great-Aunt-Hortense/ Sophia/Mother sidebar is finished, our story segues right back to Sophia – right where we left her, at the blackboard.)

·⚹⦂⟩⚹·

Alas, Readers, on to that visit from Great Aunt Hortense. Sophia was five years old. Which means our story will be out of order - Again! For which I apologize.

• • • FIVE YEARS EARLIER • • •

"The picture of persnickety, our Great Aunt Hoity – Queen of Toity! With her pince-nez on the tip of her upswept nose! Which peaks out sharply from her snapped-up head! Where her gray hair is piled like stones around her face which is up-snooted and prune-wrinkled whenever she has to talk to anyone except the President of Harvard University, and since whomever she is talking to isn't the President of Harvard University, as he has never visited our village even once, her face never, even for one second, ever deprunes or desnoots! AND she thinks being richer than everybody in the entire village means she can lord herself over everyone. But that is hardly the worst part! For the worst hard-to-take part is, EVERYONE LETS HER!"

That, Readers, was what Sophia's Father had to say about Sophia's Great Aunt Hortense, but certainly never when his wife, Sigrid, was even remotely close, as his wife was rather fond of the Lady. But then Great Aunt Hortense was both Aunt AND Mother and Father to young Sigrid as her parents had died in a tragic car accident when she was seven-years-old turning their only child (with her candyland voice) the charming, very flirty, hyper-articulate

Sigrid, into a sad orphan. But an orphan not sentenced to an orphanage: for just one day after the tragedy, Aunt Hortense, little Sigrid's only living relative, did her duty.

Rather fond of children, however, Aunt Hortense was not. Nevertheless, she adopted her niece and then raised Sigrid as if she were her own child.

Well, are you wondering – Did that Persnickety Old Prune, who was rather unfond of children, turn the charming child into a Persnickety Young Prune? And did her husband, the psychoanalyst, wonder the same thing?

As for those questions, Readers, his way of wondering about them was to mosey on up to them and instead of answering them candidly - he'd ask questions that had the answer he preferred already built in. Isn't my Sigrid well-adjusted? So lively? Articulate? With her voice so dream-girl, so from a time long gone? How ever could Persnickety have turned my Princess into a Prune? And then he'd mosey on away from it. So at least, according to his way of gathering evidence, the Persnickity Old Prune had not. Besides, hadn't he always noticed that Sigrid always treated her Aunt like she did only right and could do no wrong? So how could he have let fly a lampooning word about the Old Prune anywhere near his wife? What would his wife think if she heard it? Why it would've wounded his Sigrid in her heart. And wounding her there would've wounded him, too. There. In his own heart. For oh! did he have a heart when it came to his wife! It could admit, but just barely, that his charming wife, who-was-no-prune, was one of those 'EVERYONE LETS HER.'

However, what he and his heart could not only admit, but state crystal clearly, though only to himself, was that Great Aunt Hortense was rather fond of money. But when he could no longer deny that just about every man, woman and child on the planet was imbibing his wife's concoction and she had become an even richer woman than her Aunt, a terrible fear took possession of his heart, a fear that reared up in his head as often as the Loch Ness Monster reared up its head - which was never - a fear that if his heart would've known he had and could've named, he wouldn't have breathed it ever again to a living soul, including himself. And that was this:

HIS WIFE WAS RATHER FOND OF IT TOO!

So - Did that Persnickety Old Prune, who was rather unfond of children, turn the charming child into a Persnickety Young Prune?

Readers, would you've had the heart, the nerve to fire it at him point-blank now that you know what he fears?

Odd, you say? A psychoanalyst? Not able to speak his fears and feelings out loud? Not even able to examine himself privately, confidentially to find out what his hidden fears and deep feelings were? I say, though he spent his life examining the hidden fears and deep feelings of others, when it came to his own, especially those that involved his heart, his connoisseur ears and his charming wife, who-was-no-prune, he was as good as nothing. So if he did fear that his wife had even a smidgen of her Aunt Hortense's traits in her somewhere, it never had gotten as far as his mouth. But don't think him a poor psychoanalyst. Anyone who has ever fallen in love will understand that when it comes to love, some of us are deaf, dumb and blind; even those, like him, who have sensitive, perceptive ears that can hear music when none is playing and who can speak sensibly about the human drama that unfolds before them. And even those with x-ray vision, like psychoanalysts, who are trained to see what's buried inside the psyches of others. Just like he was trained to see.

·⸱∗☾⸱·

("Lady, tawk about us leading your Readers off track! I gotta admit that what you just said is kindda sortta interesting, but didn't you just agree to tell your Readers about Sophia and Great Aunt Hortense when Sophia was five-years-old, and that's all? Why do we have to listen to this?"

Lorraine, what I just described above is the story that comes before the story you insisted that I tell now. The back-story. A good writer knows when their Readers need to be told back-story. I'm surprised I have to tell you who comes from the land of Fairy Tales about that. Knowing when to tell back-story should be second nature to Fairies! Back-story can be told at any time within a story but, in this instance, I decided to tell it first so that when my Readers hear the facts of the actual story, they'll understand what led to those facts. I want them to see the effect Great Aunt Hortense had on Sophia's Mother and her Father before they ever see the effect Great Aunt Hortense had on Sophia. That way they'll begin to understand just who we're dealing with, just who this Great Aunt Hortense is! Here now is the story you wanted me to tell, the one about Sophia and Great Aunt Hortense. As you listen, keep that back-story in mind. You, too, Readers!)

·⸱☽∗⸱·

Five years ago, the aforementioned Great Aunt asked our Sophia a question, and instead of answering it, Sophia leaked air.

The visit had started off as any other. Sophia's Mother filling the living room with her word music, Great Aunt Hoity – Queen of Toity listening while sneering a sunless-smile and Sophia sitting silently on the sofa, when a bee flew in through an open window, lured in no doubt by the honey sweetness pouring out of Mrs. Oomla. Said bee, as bees do, bee-lined over to Mrs. Oomla but, once there, it started cartwheeling around her head. Since bees are known for bee-lining and not known for cartwheeling, said bee was behaving most unbeelike. Obviously he had become intoxicated, drawn in by Mrs. Oomla's luscious undertow. And the astonishing thing was Mrs. Oomla was hardly concerned. She had grown accustomed to bees' comporting themselves like that around her. So she oh-so-effortlessly sauntered out of the living room and headed towards the front door, where she hoped to shake out her head, lose the bee and close the door. Falling for her trap, the bee performed feats worthy of an Olympic gymnast to keep up with her as she sashayed towards the door.

Great Aunt Hortense suffered not a moment's disquietude in the presence of said bee either. But for an entirely different reason. Bees never bothered her. Not so astonishingly, bees, fearing she would sting them, were scared to death of her.

However, Mrs. Oomla's sudden indisposition did leave the burden of carrying on the conversation to Great Aunt Hortense. And as she was well informed on all of the social graces and used etiquette of only the highest tone, and knew never to allow a lull in any genial conversation, had no choice but to turn her attention to the small human sitting on the sofa who heretofore she had only ever nodded at.

She peered down from the glacier that was her face and spoke.

"Well, child, when will you be in attendance at our Village School?"

Sophia turned pink then white then her arms started trembling, all because her insides were saying, "When I'm six. When I'm six," but her mouth wouldn't budge to say it. Even though her mouth wasn't working, she could still think and couldn't help marveling. *'She spied me!!! How did she do that? Nobody can see me here. And she talked to me!'*

During Great Aunt Hortense's entire visit, Sophia had been pushing herself so far back into the sofa cushions, she believed she had disappeared and absolutely no one could see her. And there she sat with her head down looking at her two dancer fingers ice-skating back and forth on the skating rink in her kneecap. She hadn't even looked up at her Great Aunt Hortense when the bee appeared, because Sophia had learned from her years of experience with the monster that lived under her bed - *'If I don't look at the monster, the monster won't look at me.*

'Great Aunt Hortense never talked to me before. I can't talk to Great Aunt Hortense. Maybe she'll forget that she saw me! - That I'm even here! - That I'm supposed to tell her about school! - That she is waiting for me to talk! Maybe the bee will go away. Maybe Mommy will start talking again. Maybe Mommy will answer the question for me. Maybe there's a cave in the cushions and I can hide.'

There was no cave in the cushions. She just hoped wishing would put it there. But even if she couldn't hide in a cave in the cushions, she made up her mind – she still wouldn't talk to her Great Aunt Hortense even though she now knew Great Aunt Hortense could see her.

'I know, I'll just hide better and that way Great Aunt Hortense won't ever find me.'

She burrowed down even deeper, taking the parts of her that might be sticking out, like her foot and her skirt. Then the cushions clamshelled shut. And to be extra careful, she hung her head even lower just in case Great Aunt Hortense could see through cushions. Certain she was safe she waited in her bunker in the sofa for her Mother to answer the question for her. Her Mother usually did.

But the only thing she heard was nothing.

'If Mommy doesn't talk, I'm not talking because I talk like a burping frog and she doesn't and I might get the nervous shakes and she doesn't.'

The quiet stayed quiet. Nobody said anything. Sophia felt encouraged.

'Everybody must have left. I'll just peek an eye out and look.'

But Sophia thought she'd better send a scout up first. She would only let her dancer fingers leave the retreat. So off her kneecap skating rink they went, dancing oh so carefully along the cushion mountain. When they got to the ravine around her face, they drifted up to the ridge so they could push through and create a crevice for her to peer into the living room world. She lifted her head and aimed out an eye. And, dread of all dreads, there was Great Aunt Hortense glaring down at that one eye with dark eyes so commanding that Sophia's other eye surrendered then velcroed onto them, too. But Great Aunt Hortense's bunker busters weren't finished. They kept glaring until Sophia felt as if they were piercing through the Cushion Mountain, straight into her private bunker where she now sat petrified.

Great Aunt Hortense spoke again.

"Child, Child, Child, do you intend to come from behind those cushions? Is there a cat in there with you? Does he have your tongue? Are you going to answer my question? When WILL you be in attendance at the Village School? Do speak up, child, the way your Mother did when she was a child! Surely you can do that?"

Sophia listened to each and every one of those questions and went from petrified to mummified. Now she was going to have to answer those questions, too. AND SPEAK THE WAY HER MOTHER SPOKE. Her eyes stopped blinking, her breath stopped breathing, and her insides got stuck repeating over and over *'I have to speak to Great Aunt Hortense.'* At or about the seventh time of repeating it, two things finally dawned on her.

'My Mother is gone.
'I have to talk …
'ALL BY MYSELF …
'to GREAT BIG Great Aunt Hortense.
'LIKE MY MOTHER.'

Now almost every single part of her was terrified. And the unterrified part might've been able to help her out of her jam, considering it was the part of her that could think. However, it was only a smidgen of the part of her that could think. And this particular smidgen, as luck would have it - bad luck - happened to think things that were none too bright. And none too cheerful. And, true to its nature, it was very quick to point out to her that it couldn't imagine how she'd ever be able to do all this talking all by herself and like her Mother! Without her Mother.

She wondered where her Mother could be. But she knew she had to stop her wondering because she had to face the unavoidable, inescapable, ineludible fact that at this particular moment in her life she was now all by herself alone with Great Aunt Hortense and it was time for her - all by herself ALONE - to come out from behind the cushions and talk … ALL BY HERSELF ALONE … to Great Aunt Hortense

BECAUSE GREAT AUNT HORTENSE SAID SHE SHOULD.

She tried to move her leg but it wouldn't budge. She tried to scoot lower down on the cushion but couldn't. But one part of her did move. *'My arms! My underweight, underfed, under-mosquitoes that all of a sudden have become mighty, without me even trying to make them that way!'* Her arms were moving alright. But the kind of move she hated. All by themselves, without her even wanting them to. And they kept moving faster and faster until they were knocking against her bony rib-cage. She tried to get them to stop but that only made the knocking worse. Then she tried to take her eyes off of Great Aunt Hortense, since having to look at Great Aunt Hortense only made her shake more. But that was useless too. Because somehow and without saying a word, Great Aunt Hortense's eyes seemed to be ordering Sophia's eyes to stay right where they were. Right on her eyes.

THOSE EYES.

Sophia watched those eyes grow bigger and bigger. As they bore down hard on her, those eyes told her she was going to have to say something.

'Soon.'

THOSE EYES.

'Even if I'm shaking.'

THOSE EYES.

She opened her mouth, readying herself to talk but now she had a new problem. *'A set of wind-up-false-teeth must've jumped in my mouth and are making a terrible racket!'* Somehow, and she didn't know how, they were occupying the exact same spot her own teeth used to be in and were clacking up and down as if they were talking. But they weren't saying anything.

She was shaking in one place. And clacking in another.

'I have the nervous shakes.

'I can't SahSTOPpah … sha … sha … shaking if I want to.

'I'VE … TURNED … INTO … THE … NERVOUS … SHAKES … MAN.'

Like the patient her Father always talked about.

The man that never stopped shaking.

'I'M THE NERVOUS SHAKES MAN.'

Way, way down inside her, Sophia could hear herself say, the answer to all of Great Aunt Hortense's questions, especially the answer to the question about school, *'When I'm Six. When I'm Six that's when I'll go to school.'* But the answer refused to go where it should.

'Was it THOSE EYES?

'Heavy. Dark. Serious.

'Glaring down at me.

'Making my worries.

'Weigh so much?

'What is it?'

Slowly, slowly, her worries dripped.

'Why can't I put the answers where they need to be?

'In my mouth …

'On my tongue …

'Where words I talk …

'Should be …

'And I would put …

'All by myself …

'Right in Great Aunt Hortense's ear …

'I can't put them there.

'THOSE EYES …

'Just can't do that …

'Because I know …

'They wouldn't be …

'Beautiful and Perfect …

'I sound too funny …

'I shake like the Nervous Shakes Man …

'My Mother doesn't shake like the Nervous Shakes Man.
'THOSE EYES ...
'My Mother can talk to Great Aunt Hortense ...
'I can't talk to Great Aunt Hortense.
'THOSE EYES!'
Sophia's worries were about to flood over the very brim of her.
It was hopeless.
Silence reigned in the living room and Sophia was about two blinks away from being hypnotized. THOSE EYES were now so big Sophia believed Great Aunt Hortense had turned into a WHALE which finally had the effect of snapping her out of her stupor. Sophia shrunk back into her spot on the sofa certain THOSE EYES were about to swallow her. They were so strong. Stronger than her. Their force began to tug at her. She could feel them pull her off her spot. But just as they were about to suck her up and swallow her alive, at the very last second, something inside her spoke up. Something from her deep down part. Something that knew how to save her.
'YOU CAN BRAINTALK.'

                              ·∗·☾··

("Darlings, we the Fairies didn't say it."
Me, no interruptions! You promised!)

                              ··☽∗··

She said it. But this time it wasn't the none-too-bright part. This time it was the part of her that knew things. Her smart part, her bright part. The part of her that could think. It had finally, finally woken up and remembered the experiment her Father had told her about, the one with the monkey and its brain signals. Because that's when a computer had read a monkey's brain signals. Her Father said monkey's thoughts make signals in their monkey brains, and that a computer can read those signals. 'Well, I bet when I think, I make signals, too. So if a computer can see a monkey's thought signals, Great Aunt Hortense, who has eyes as big and as wide as computer screens, should be able to see inside me and read my thought signals, too!
'I can BRAINTALK!!'

                              ·∗·☾··

("We the Fairies cheered. Darling, remember, you promised, human parts: yours; Fairy parts: ours! And this is a Fairy part. Readers, at long last, we could help. Unbeknownst to Sophia, we the Fairies went to work. We would magic her braintalk by blowing on "When I'm six" the answer to Great Aunt Hortense's question, til it had the strength of a hurricane.

Sophia could feel the words reverberate all through her loud and clear. She was sure what she was feeling was her brain signals. She, of course, had no idea she was getting so much help. She thought she was doing the pushing all by herself. The words were echoing inside her and were soon so loud, all she'd have to do was blow the words up, over and out just a little bit more, and Great Aunt Hortense'd surely hear them, even the people across the river'd hear them. So up, over and out they went."

Me! Human part! My turn!)

·:):·.

Dear Reader, as you may have guessed. It didn't go so well. But you may want to see for yourself. Look carefully, it was over in less than 15 seconds.

Suddenly the little-thin-sticky Sophia, our under-mosquito, was puffing up as if an invisible baker was piping cream-filling into her, and at each new pouf, was looking more and more like a baking popover. And when she had reached a nice plump size, her shoulders began rising, then her cheeks bulged out, and when she was bung-full, she looked to make sure Great Aunt Hortense had heard her but she didn't see her so she had to turn her head just a little to find her. A turn if ever there was for the worse because it released all the air pressure inside her that had been entirely too much for such a little-thin-sticky to hold in and that had been building up with nowhere to go because when she BRAINTALKed she wasn't supposed to open her mouth. Well, it was all simply too much and her mouth burst open and out popped a -

A jet stream of hot air.

And some spit ...

Which bulls-eyed right in the middle of the left lens of Great Aunt Hortense's pince-nez, quickly coating it and then latching onto its rim, where it formed into a glutinous tear that kept expanding until it finally stopped and dangled precariously, allowing Great Aunt Hortense to make a more, shall we say, intimate acquaintance with it; but only for a moment, as it was about to begin its slow certain descent on to the collar of her freshly starched, pure-linen, hand-embroidered, immaculately-white blouse.

And finally, finally, just as the spit had started its descent, in waltzes Mrs. Oomla, head dripping wet, returned from her bee adventure. The bee hadn't taken the hint and gotten lost, so she was forced to try a different ruse. Hoping that it might behold something it would fancy more than herself, she thought she would take a stroll with it in to her garden. It might spot a flower it found more delectable than her. Surely flowers like that existed. So outdoors she went, with the bee circling her head. When she reached the banks of the river, where her garden lay, the bee wouldn't even look at the magenta snapdragons or the silvery fox gloves or any of the other enticements there. It wanted only to sputnik about her head. A drastic measure must be tried. She went down to the very edge of the river and dipped her head in. It went in with her.

And drowned.

'The poor dear!' she thought as she rushed back, all set to gush to her fan club - to Mrs. Oomla, the world and all the creatures in it were her fan club - about the unhappy end yet another besotted creature had come to on her behalf and what was she to do and this was the lot of her life and ... she danced into the living room, expecting them to cheer and they didn't even notice her return. Hadn't even glanced up. It wasn't until she looked more carefully, did she see that things were terribly amiss. There was Great Aunt Hortense, THE village dignitary, AND benefactress, the closest the village had to a ROCKEFELLER, and the only Aunt, Mother and Father she now had, looking most displeased. And if that wasn't alarming enough, there was Sophia, breathing most peculiarly, about to fall off the edge of her seat, her face flushed so red it looked like she had been smeared by a whole tube of lipstick. And on even closer examination, Great Aunt Hortense's eyes were crossed and bulging most unbecomingly ... and staring ... wait ... What was that dangling from the edge of Great Aunt Hortense's pince-nez? It looked like the continent of South America! Was it ... GOO?? Goo dangling from Great Aunt Hortense's pince-nez? Great Aunt Hortense about to be covered in GOO!!

Mrs. Oomla cried out, "Dear, dear Great Aunt Hortense, what is that dreadful substance? Stop!"

But the spit, unlike all other living creatures, wasn't listening to Mrs. Oomla. It landed a direct hit onto Great Aunt Hortense's crisply starched collar.

Sophia broke out into goose bumps knowing that the really huge gloppy thing that could fly came out of her. That was a bad thing - she was pretty sure. *'I didn't mean to do it; I didn't want to do it,'* she thought, as she watched it on its way down.

Great Aunt Hortense let out a gasp; it too could have been heard across the river. Mrs. Oomla rushed over to Great Aunt Hortense's side, expecting to have to catch her before she fainted and fell to the floor. However, Great Aunt Hortense did not faint. Nor did she fall. Instead she rose from her seat and kept rising until she seemed to stand taller than she really was. Which gave the spit the opportunity to grow with her. And keep growing. Mrs. Oomla grabbed a damask napkin from the nearby teacart, hoping to catch it before it went any further. Sophia had pried herself, and her goosebumps, off her spot on the sofa, and stood watching as the spit did its lightning quick, yo-yo string dance further and further down Great Aunt Hortense's collar. When it reached the summit of one of Great Aunt Hortense's bosoms and boinged back and forth thereon, Mrs. Oomla was just about to grab it with her napkin, but Great Aunt Hortense looked at Mrs. Oomla so forbiddingly she thought it wiser to catch up with it elsewhere. But catching up with it elsewhere proved impossible because it picked up speed on its downward trajectory until it finally came to rest on one of her highly polished, sensible oxfords.

·∴(·∴·

("And then Author Lady, at that exact moment, a really, like, brazen sunbeam came in through the window and decided to add to the drama, so it headed straight for that gooey lake and aimed its spotlight right on it front and center, which created a, like, dazzling reflection that nearly blinded them all. All they could do was stare! Nobody even peeped!")

·∴)∴·

Until Great Aunt Hortense screeches broke the silence.

"Sigrid, this child must learn far, far better manners than what she has displayed to me today. Far, far better. I am aghast. Can this child talk? I was always led to believe that Sophia was a normal child, certainly you would have told me otherwise, so there is absolutely no reason for such backwardness. What have you been teaching this child, Sigrid? Why doesn't she answer a question when a question is asked? Surely she knows to do that. You certainly could do that, and so much more, at your age."

Sophia had been slinking further and further behind her Mother until she couldn't see Great Aunt Hortense. But she could hear her. *'Great Aunt Hortense wants me to be like my Mother! But I'm not like my Mother! I can't talk like her! My mother doesn't talk like a frog! Is Great Aunt Hortense gonna make me talk! Oh! I did something really bad! I think!'* And she got an even worse case of the nervous shakes than the one she had before.

"Dear, dear Great Aunt Hortense, please tell me what happened? What is that dreadful substance? And how did it get all over you?"

"Sigrid, your daughter expectorated on me. That is what this dreadful substance is. Indeed."

"Oh Great Aunt Hortense, I can't believe it. Sophia, is this true?"

Mrs. Oomla turned to where Sophia had been standing, but by that time, Sophia had already dropped to the floor and slid under the sofa. Great Aunt Hortense could never've fit under there. She wondered what that big word was Great Aunt Hortense said. But even if she knew it, she'd never know how to do what it meant. She was just a little-girl. And little-girls don't do big-word things. She was glad she was hiding from the both of them. She didn't want to listen to anybody talking only about her and she wasn't about to answer any questions. But from where she was under the sofa, Sophia could see their shoes and she could still hear them talk about her. And her nervous shakes wouldn't let up. Hiding there wasn't the best solution; but, at least, Great Aunt Hortense couldn't see her. But even that thought didn't make her stop shaking.

"Do you think I would make up such a story for my own amusement? Yes, it is true. Entirely true. And not only that, Sigrid, as if that wasn't enough, your daughter wouldn't speak to me the entire time you left the room, wouldn't answer my questions, wouldn't come out from behind the cushions, wouldn't socialize in any way. And then, unexpectedly, quite un-expectedly – enough to give a less robust person than I heart palpitations – she puffed up like a jelly doughnut, and when she opened her mouth, it sounded like there was a wind storm blowing inside her – and her a five year old!! – and then she proceeds to EXPECTORATE on me. EXPECTORATE – ON ME!!! The very idea!! It was the most astonishing sight I have ever beheld. Sigrid, this child has developed the manners of the uncouth!"

'Oh no! I am? I did? But what will Mommy say?' Sophia inched her way under the sofa and when she could just about see the both of them, she stopped. *'Mommy looks like she saw a ghost. But she's smiling! And she's smiling at me, too. Right where I am under here! And now she's smiling at Great Aunt Hortense! The enemy!'* She peeked at Great Aunt Hortense. *'Great Aunt Hortense doesn't look half as mean anymore. Somehow Mommy made her feel good. How does Mommy do that? And she didn't even say anything!'* She watched her Mother lean down to wipe away the goo on Great Aunt Hortense's shoe. The goo that had come out of her! When her Mother's head was near the floor, their eyes locked and then her Mother winked at her.

"Now that is enough, Sigrid. Don't fuss with me anymore. I must leave immediately. There is no time for tea. I am chairing the Auxiliary Meeting for the Ladies of the Institute, and I simply must go home and change. Why I never appear anywhere if there is so much as a wrinkle in my clothes. I will certainly not appear in front of those perlustrators who live to find fault in a state of … of … dishabille! How they would talk! How they would speculate about what happened to me! Imagine what they would say. Why just thinking about it positively inflames me! Sigrid, this child must be taught to speak up to her elders in a polite manner. By all means and by any means!! And, I hasten to add, to behave in a civilized manner - I, of course, am referring to Sophia's most indelicate display.

Sigrid, I assure you I certainly understand that she is only five years old and one must make allowances for children. HOWEVER, you must start socializing children very early, when they are toddlers and she is well past those years. I will be here again next week and I expect to see a distinct improvement in your daughter. When I return your daughter is to speak to me IN A FULL SENTENCE. As for the rest of her behavior, I never expect that to happen again. Sigrid, this is elementary - you have considerable charm and charisma, so teach it to your child. Show her how to do what you do. Good day."

And she gathered her hat, handbag and gloves and swept out of the room. Mrs. Oomla caught up with her at the front door where she soothed such a warm good bye that if spoken words could glow, they would've lit a fireplace, "Dear Great Aunt Hortense, I am so sorry. Sophia and I always look so forward to your visits every week. She always asks when you're coming. Next week, she'll be just fine. Of course, Sophia can talk. You'll see. She babbles all day. She's a little timid sometimes. She was just never alone with you before. Again, I am truly sorry."

Great Aunt Hortense peered at Mrs. Oomla over the rim of her spit-slicked pince-nez, and her needle lips - sharps that ceaselessly pointed below - momentarily pointed in the other direction. Anyone who knew her would've thought her giddy. Then without saying another word, she strode out the door and down the path towards her awaiting limousine. Her chauffeur shut the car door behind her. And off they went.

Sophia was rooted under the sofa and stayed that way, even when she couldn't hear her Mother and Great Aunt Hortense talking anymore. She listened to the quiet. There were no more big words coming out of big people overpowering her. No more talk from people who were talking only about her. But still Great Aunt Hortense's words were gnawing through her and making her heavy with trouble.

'All of their words should just get out of me and fly away, far far away so my own words can came back in and fill up my head again and then there'll just be my words in my head and nobody else's!'

Sophia tried to make sense of what had happened. *'The best I can figure is that Great Aunt Hortense didn't hear what I was saying to her when I was BRAINTALKing. Even though I can hear myself when I'm BRAINTALKing! So much for what Daddy told me about monkeys and brain signals!*

'AND

'the next time Great Aunt Hortense comes back, I have to say something called a FULL SENTENCE to her!

'What is a FULL SENTENCE anyway? It has something to do with talking. Oh, how I wish I wouldn't have to! But Great Aunt Hortense is very mad and I know I'm going to have to FULL SENTENCE her.

'OR ELSE.'

When Mrs. Oomla no longer could see Great Aunt Hortense's limousine, she pirouetted from the front door and flitted towards the living room.

Readers, the conversation that takes place next is the one The Fairy Me magic-wanded from that bush, so I won't repeat it now. But let's see how Sophia felt when her Mother wouldn't let her get a word in edgewise.

Sophia's melody-seeking ears were becoming tranquilized by her Mother's comforting voice and soon Sophia was hypnotized. Remember, Readers, I felt the same way Sophia felt when I heard that voice. Now imagine if you will, the most flirtatious, breathy, hot-dish type voice you've ever heard, and read the rest of what her Mother said to Sophia, and then you may finally grasp Sophia's predicament:

"... You do it all the time without even thinking about it anyway. You just got a little scared today. Come on Sophia, let's have some of these lovely pink frosty tea cakes. We don't want them to go to waste, do we now? So why don't you get off the floor? We'll have tea together like English ladies, you and I. Come on, I'll show you how to pour tea the proper way. The way English people do. English people come from England where there is a Queen. English people have beautiful manners. They are sure to never ever spit. They wouldn't dream of it. They use instead their special manners, their high-tea manners, manners they would use should the Queen come to call. Let's pretend the Queen is here sitting with us. Come on now, little princess, I'll show you."

Sophia picked herself off the floor. Her Mother was teaching her a Queen-history lesson and Sophia loved Queens. And her Mother was promising her their very own tea-party with their very own pretend Queen in their very own house and Sophia's troubles seemed less and less bad and awfully terrible. And her Mother had called her 'little princess' and Sophia loved Princesses, too. Her Mother wasn't mad at her and her Mother was doing all the talking again, like she always did. And Sophia didn't have to talk about the wet-thing that flew out of her mouth. But it wasn't spit. Her Mother wasn't right about that. But her Mother didn't even want to talk about even that anymore. They were about to have their own tea party now. Without Great Aunt Hortense. And she wouldn't have to explain why the wet-thing-that-flew-out-of-her-mouth wasn't spit. It was safe again in the living room. It was safe again in her house. Even though her Mother said she had to talk to Great Aunt Hortense.

She didn't have to do it now. Because Great Aunt Hortense wasn't here now. Sophia forgot about every last one of her deep worries and was happy again.

⋯⋅✿⋅⋯

("'We wasn't happy.' That's what Lorraine yelped, Reader darlings."

"Hey, Me, I don't yelp! So watch it. I'll tell you what I said though, 'Aw, what she so happy about? Youse hear that. Sophia couldn't get a word in edgewise. And she didn't even get mad. She didn't even notice. With that Mother and that whipped-cream voice of hers, no wonder Sophia never gets to tawk and is shy around people. Man, somebody tawk all over me, I'da tied her tongue to her tonsils! Sweet! My foot!"

"But, darlings, our Sophia was filled with only one thought, 'Pink food! Pink food! It'll just be like eating a Fairy Skirt!' I mean the things you humans say!"

Fairies, that's it! I really wish you'd leave the story telling to the professional.

"The professional!? And you dare say that to the creatures from the land of Fairy Tales! Do you really think we don't know about back story? Who do you think invented it? Have you forgotten who told you this story? Where would you humans be without our Fairy Tales? Why our tales of pumpkins turned into carriages, scullery maids into princesses have been enthralling your little people for ages!

With you in my face, and ear, how could I have forgotten? And Readers? Were any of you under the impression the Brothers Grimm were fairies?

"Oh, and you think you're the only human we've ever visited?"

That is conveniently unprovable! And if you ARE such professionals, shouldn't you feel a sense of responsibility to our Readers, and stop your interruptions, so that I can direct their attention back to that classroom. Mr. Snoggley is about to speak.)

⋯⋅☾⋅⋯

• • • 9:40 AM • • •

"Miss Oomla, the class can hardly hear you. Your answer is correct, your reasoning is correct but how can anyone understand you if they can't hear you? So please repeat what you said and speak up this time."

Repeat what she said! Sophia didn't want to say another word. But if she didn't, Mr. Snoggley would think she was still sick and he'd call Miss Kitty or her Mother or her Father and then all of them would learn what she did at night because Miss Kitty'd have to tell them.

That thought scared her more than having to listen to herself. Because maybe they'd find out that she watched movies really a lot. A lot more than Miss Kitty knew. A whole lot more. And she didn't want them to know what she did at night. How she watched Movie Stars. Listened to Movie Stars.

But so much more than that.

For she figured out exactly how they talked so she could talk like them. She'd listen to the women's voices AND the men's voice. Did their voice make mystery? Music? Was it gangster? Girly girl? Silly? Pixie? Smoky? Cracky? Did the sound come from the nose, the throat, the head, the belly? Was there an accent? What did each person do to make that voice? And she'd figure it out and then practice doing just that til she got it right! Over and over! There was so much to listen for. And to break down, bit by bit. But she broke it down, figured it out: that to really make a voice sound right, the main trick was to know what was going on inside the mouth, where the tongue was. But even that wasn't enough; what were the lips doing? Were the lips half closed or were they wide open? Sometimes her tongue had to be in one place to get a certain kind of sound and her lips in another place to get another type of sound. And she'd practice and practice …

That was the secret she didn't want anyone to find out. That she could talk in Movie Star Voices. And that she was Sophia the Movie Star. The secret Movie Star.

She began again, "I p … pput theee …" Just like Mr. Snoggley asked. And she was louder. But she couldn't stop herself from listening to how she sounded, even now; she couldn't stop critiquing herself. *It's not sassy. It's baby! I'm no Ginger! It's hard to have to listen to me talk. But I'm always talking and listening to myself talk! But I'm never standing in front of my whole class when I am!*

A room full of people, looking at her. Staring at her. Listening to her.

But having a room full of people look at me, listen to me, is what I always dream about! But now that there is a room full of people staring at me, listening to me, I'm not speaking like a Movie Star at all! I can't. In fact, I can barely speak at all. Some Movie-Star-Voice-Talker-Expert I am! I'm only an Expert when no one was looking. So what good is being an Expert? And now my Expert ears have to listen to it all!

Doing all of that worrying and thinking and judging in her head all while standing in front of her classmates, and Mr. Snoggley, too, was making her even more nervous! *Movie Stars don't get nervous in front of people like I do.* And her voice began to wobble. "… is an expo … pppo …" And since her voice was louder, she knew, everybody else could hear her voice wobble more clearly. Which made her voice wobble more. "nnnent o … of …" But she still didn't stop, she kept talking, and listening to herself talk, and listening to herself wobble, and listening to herself think, til she had explained Problem #1 again.

···)(···

("Hey, Thee, like, tell everybody what you said!"

Don't let a little thing like your word stop you, Lorraine!

"Thanks, Lady, I won't. By now, Thee was also having a really hard time. She was, as only Thee could say it, 'cross' with Sophia."

"Thee said, 'Sophia doesn't care at all that she understands the problem and that her answer to the problem is correct, which it was. All Sophia cares about is how she sounds saying the problem. To be unhappy when she's right! In Math! All because Sophia wanted a different voice! We have work to do on this human child. A lot of work. And we don't have much time. We have to be out of Sophia before she turns eleven, and that means on the last day she is ten-years-old at the stroke of midnight and not one second later. And we have to be gone. Out. Found nowhere. Because that is The Rule. That is the agreement we made with the Fairy Dispatcher. If we left and Sophia still does not like her voice, we would have failed to make sure Sophia lived happily ever after. We would have failed Our MISSION! The very reason why we took up residence in Sophia's Remarkably Small Place in the first place. And since Sophia doesn't like her own voice, she isn't happy and if she isn't happy when she's ten, she just might not live happily ever after.' "

"See, Lady, we the Fairies sorta figure that if a child is kinda sorta happy at ten, then a person probably'd be kinda sorta happy at twenty, because, after all, the future is just like the present. Give or take. With a grain of salt. Or maybe two. Because we, like, really and truly believe even when the outsides of a person changes, when that person gets kinda older and that person is no longer a child, that person's insides still stay the same. Where it, like, really matters. Like, inside their heads. Their hearts. Usually. A happy child makes a happy person. More often than not. More than, like, less. Less than, like, more. More or less. And a child that doesn't like her own voice at ten might be, like, ya know unhappy about it her whole life. So we had to make sure Sophia did like her own voice. Before we left for, like, good. For, like, ever.

"But we had to face the facts, that we had just a few months before her eleventh birthday to make sure she did. A few months to make sure Sophia learned to like her own voice. To make sure she was happy.

Before we flew out of her head to, like, never return again. Or otherwise we the Fairies wouldda failed! Thee Fairy Prudence Priss Primly wouldda failed! And Thee Fairy Prudence Priss Primly never, like, fails. But you was really stumped at this moment, wasn't ya, Thee? For how could she, how could we, get Sophia to like her own voice? Better than a Movie Star's voice? Without performing magic? Thee flew back inside Sophia to where we was. She knew what hadda happen. We the Fairies would have to, like, make a plan. A, like, ya know serious plan. The kind of plan that didn't use magic."

Thank you so much, Lorraine and Thee. No doubt, the both of you'll be telling us more about this plan. So interruptions is what we have to look forward to! Readers, I cannot control the uncontrollable! Could you?)

··:)··

Mr. Snoggley said, "You are correct, Miss Oomla, but the way you were speaking, anyone listening to you would have thought you were wrong. You may be seated."

Sophia rushed back to her seat. This time she was careful to look where she was going so she wouldn't trip again. And now that she was looking she knew she might catch the eye of her classmates since they would be taking a gander at her, a good-long gander. They always knew when somebody was hiding something. Or was a big chicken. A big baby. And sure enough when she caught the eye of Granger Foxley, he made a face at her. A baby face. A knotted up as if he was crying baby face. His fists rubbing his eyes, baby face. He was right. She was a baby. And now everybody knew it.

And her heart tripped.

So much for being careful not to trip. And when she got back to her desk and Mr. Snoggley still hadn't moved, even when she took her seat again, her heart wouldn't budge from the very bottom of her. But when he leaned over and whispered to her -

"Miss Oomla, this afternoon you will be meeting with the speech therapist for the first time. She will work with you so you learn to speak up. I am just delighted. Your Mother is also delighted. She asked me to give you the driving directions. You are to give them to Mr. James this afternoon when he picks you up from school! He'll need them to drive you there! I have them in my desk drawer in an envelope. Please come up to my desk and get them from me before you go to lunch! And don't forget! Be sure to put them straightaway in your back pack, so you can give them to Mr. James!" -

… but the way he whispered it … like he was saving her life because her life needed saving, as if she was a hopeless person, as if he felt sorry for her, was all she needed. She couldn't even feel her heart anymore, as it now lay dead on the very floor of her.

Sophia had forgotten all about her appointment with the speech therapist. She didn't know what a speech therapist did but she bet they didn't help you speak like a Movie Star so she certainly didn't want to meet with one of them.

Finally, Mr. Snoggley walked away from her desk and back to the blackboard, continuing on with the Math lesson. But Sophia wasn't even relieved because now all she could do was sit there worrying about her new problem. Her appointment with this speech therapist. She made up her mind that the only speech help she wanted was the kind that would make her speak just like Ginger Rogers. And nobody else. And make her speak like her in front of others. Well … some others. It wouldn't be so bad if that speech therapist could teach her that. But she knew that this speech therapist, whoever it was, would never do such a thing.

Mr. Snoggley finished the Math Lesson, and started right in on the History Lesson. Sophia hid herself behind Jick Jaes, the boy who sat in front of her, the tallest boy in the class, and shut her eyes. *'Oh! I want to put my head down on top of my desk but somebody might notice, or even worse, Mr. Snoggley will and then he'll call Mother and I'll have to go home and Miss Kitty'll be really mad or Daddy'd be really really sad.'* She was so sleepy. So tired. She went a million miles away and was invisible and her school tasks and her worries just drained out of her along with all the things Mr. Snoggley was saying and had said. And would probably ever say. But why could she still hear his voice? What was he saying? Something about something she was supposed to do. What was it? *'But I can pay attention. I can stay awake. I can make it through the morning. I'm strong. Like a Movie Star. Just like a Movie St …'* And her eyes blinked open. Then they shut and she opened them and they shut and she lost the battle and fell asleep, even with her head up but not so straight, cocked to one side.

• • • 10:00 AM • • •

'That first Artiste completely threw my morning schedule!

'Hah! That's not your trouble. What got to you is her raw emotion! And you can't seem to shake it!

'Admit it, Oomla, you're rattled … through and through and now you'll have to face each Artiste for the remainder of this dreadful day and tell them the dreadful news while you're full of dread yourself!'

He'd have to continuously monitor himself so that however any of his Artistes behaved, they wouldn't make him dig up his own raw emotion, too, or otherwise, he'd be unfit to perform his duties.

Thankfully, the next Artiste did not have the same gift for expression as the Movie Star did and anything inside trying to rattle him stopped trying.

But then none of the morning Artistes had that Movie Star's gift for expression; they couldn't make scenes as dramatically as she could. These Artistes handled the news by having anxiety attacks. Still, they were some of the worst he'd ever witnessed. They'd lay there or sit there complaining about every little ache and pain, every slight, every imagining, every fear, every dream, every foreboding they ever felt, as if that were the problem, instead of the loss of the weekly theatricals, instead of what IV had done to the Institute, what IV had done to them.

And whenever he'd escort an Artiste to the door at the end of the session, there out in his waiting room was the Artiste from the session before who had joined the Artiste from the session before. None of them would leave. And soon, he, a psychoanalyst! – their psychoanalyst! had joined the ranks of them, the Artistes! his patients! and was having an anxiety attack, too. *'Mine must not show!'* However, by lunch time, Dr. Oomla's attack dial had jumped way past rattled. He felt spooked and looked spooked. His attack wasn't secret anymore; any second, he feared, he would blow, too. And he could not let that happen.

• • • 10:10 AM • • •

Mrs. Oomla never did sneak up to Birdoffs and buy warmer clothes. It's not that she didn't try. After her breakfast meeting with the bottler from the green industry, she was just about to hop into a cab, when her cell phone rang. Her panicked assistant cried, "Mrs. Oomla! The board is waiting for you!" Mrs. Oomla sprinted through the Siberian air as if it were the tropics; compared to what she was about to face, it was. *'How could I forget about the meeting with the Giggle board?'* She shot towards the elevator, her mind racing faster than her feet. *'Today starts the most important series of meetings the board'll ever hold since Giggle became a corporation! The first meeting where we'll eventually decide whether to make Giggle a multinational corporation with offices even in China! If the board had a scintilla of a suspicion ... a soupcon even'* ... and she had to laugh in spite of who she was about to face - the last time she did that day - *'That I was thinking of frippery at a time like this!'* A milestone for any corporation was the day they became a multinational.

'They'll start whispering about me all over again! Huh! Like their whispering about me ever stopped!'

As Mrs. Oomla took the elevator to the boardroom floor, those board members, jolly good fellows all, every one of them former CEOs and heads of Brain Trusts or Think Tanks or Generals or something, were in her mind's eye. But now their professional-teeth were icicling down their permafrost-edly-pleasant faces.

And she knew why; she couldn't kid herself another second.

When they got hold of her ear, they never missed the opportunity to arch up their beetled-brows, peer down their horned-rims, unlock their locked-jaws - but just barely - so they could tweedle-dee-dee plumy, chummy advice into it on how she could become just like them. Oh! If that was only all they did! For those board members really did grumble about her, their founder and CEO. She knew that. Mr. Potemkin, the official bearer of corporate news, had actually come right out and told her, "The board recognizes your talent; after all you did invent the beverage that launched this corporation. And, of course, where would we all be without that little revenue that trickles in so nicely from your other invention, daffeine?" She'd been dying to snap back - "Trickle? Surely you mean deluge! And without me, there'd be no corporation!" - but held her tongue.

And there was that time she'd never forget - when not only what he said but how he said it made her steam. She'd always believed if someone was insulting you, they should hardly be winking and smiling at you. "It was not your know-how that turned your fizzy unknown into products that appealed to a wide range of consumers, it was ours; it was not your know-how that gave each of those products its own media personality, it was ours; it was not your know-how that created each distinctive buzz for each and every one of those media personalities, it was our smart and targeted marketing. Without our know-how, there'd be no mass market to buy all that product, which means there'd be no overnight sensation, no skyscraper. Without we-the-corpora-tion, there'd have been no you-the-billionaire; in short, Mrs. Oomla's Giggle Pop'd be just another pretty little shell laying about on an enormous beach full of pretty little shells."

But what really burned her up was that she, the famous voice, lost her voice; she could not say a word in her defense because he was right. It was them who had the expertise to make her little nothing into a money-making behemoth big enough to spawn a corporation. So what she wanted to say boiled away inside her. To this day, she'd never let any of that steam that'd been building up inside her blow anywhere near him.

Mr. Potemkin never noticed the color she was turning whenever he talked to her. She always felt a little ill when she wanted to say something but didn't. "Yes, and research has showed your voice, and it is a pleasant one, does sell the product. But permit me to make a comparison - take our fine board, for instance, each member has distinguished themselves in many leadership roles throughout our community, founding and running so many successful ventures over the years. And now, if you would, let me compare them to you, who I most respectfully but most emphatically describe as lacking - lacking experience AND lacking an MBA from a first-tier Business School."

And the famous voice lost her voice again. He knew she would she was sure; she was even sure that was what he wanted. She became silent in any conversation when anyone brought up first-tier-Business-Schools. She couldn't compete in those conversations. And they knew she couldn't. She hated being reminded she had no MBA. And that she had not attended a first-tier Business School. The rule in corporations was that executives had MBAs. And went to first-tier Business Schools. *'My girlfrie - No! my women slash person slash colleagues, they have MBAs! From first-tier schools. I am the only one out of all of my power-broker, women-persons, she-hes, who doesn't!'* So whenever MBAs and first-tier-Business Schools were brought up in conversations, the famous voice never had anything to say. It might have revealed how the lack of those two credentials made its owner feel.

"Well, the board believes you might not've been able to turn those two talents of yours, that is your talent for culinary invention and your vocal abilities, into - Giggle - a huge corporation that is a publicly traded company on a Stock Exchange, employing thousands of people, all of whom work together to make a good product so that all interests can be served. And the interests I'm referring to are really just one interest and that is making money. And the all I'm referring to are the shareholders and the workers and the executives and, least of all, us, the board."

'Least of all – Hah!' Most of all, more like it.

But in their last meeting, they'd finally stopped their whispering and had come right out and said, "When will you invent anything else? Giggle has a Research & Development Department. We have plenty of research and much development, but development from our team of developers and not from you, Ms. Oomla, the one who excels at invention! Well, we very much look forward to some very interesting innovations coming from you! Or we might have to take matters into our own hands. Remember, The Street is looking at us, they want to see that our corporation has a future, and not just a past. Never forget, Ms. Oomla, that The Street is always wondering, what's next for Giggle? Ms. Oomla, innovation will drive up our stock price! A new sensation will make many more people buy our stock! Which will drive the price of our stock up! And if our stock goes up, our shareholders are happy. And remember Ms. Oomla, not only will they be happy, you and your executives will be happy too because all of your stock options will become so much more valuable. You don't want to disappoint them, do you?" And ever so pleasantly did they aim their stalactite teeth upon her.

How could she've forgotten about the meeting and those board members? But then she made it a habit to forget about them. She wasn't music to their ears. The only music to their ears came every quarter when the announcement was made that Giggle's earnings were up. And whether it was spoken in a whine or a monotone, they hardly cared; in fact, had it been said on some poor soul's last whispered or whimpered, hoarse or hacking, gulping or gasping, retching or ranting, dribbling or drooling, dying, odorific breath, the only thing they'd've been listening for was if the number went up. How that poor old soul mentioned that number, and how it smelled, wouldn't have registered in their ears, or their noses, at all; they probably wouldn't have even noticed how near the end the wretched soul was. Numbers were the only music to their ears.

As she was about to open the door and walk into the boardroom, Mrs. Oomla knew that what wowed everybody back home in the village – her sparkly, coaxy, tickly, with-a-cherry-on-top voice, her ability to talk about anything to anyone – would not help her now. Because her and her voice had to go face to face with the tone-deaf, whose talents were mathematical and not musical, and whose-sole-interest-was-the-next-super-pow-that-she'd-better-be-working-on. As she strode in to the meeting, she could just hear what they no-doubt were thinking. HER leading a multinational! At least she had seen Claude this morning and did feel beautiful. But walking into a meeting with those icemen, and beauty would do you no good. They had eyes for figures alright, just not the womanly kind.

Before the board members said a word to her, she noticed that every one of them was smiling. At her. Or rather, every single board member was flashing their professional teeth. Right at her! She hadn't ever remembered them all looking so kindly, so wholesome, so toothsome, so very very very permafrostedly-pleasant.

And she was scared, before they even said a word.

Mr. Jordan began, "Ms. Oomla you are the voice and the face of Giggle. Our research team has showed that the public likes you and trusts you. They've proven time and time again that that voice of yours has helped make Giggle a best seller! So it stands to reason that the public and the press would expect you to announce Giggle's news. And since we are about to change our status from national to multinational, Giggle has real news and you, Ms. Oomla, should be the one to broadcast our news to the press, to the world!" And then he handed her a powerpoint presentation.

"Ms. Oomla, this presentation contains the talking points we'd like you to use when you talk to the press. With this presentation, I am handing you another opportunity to put your charming voice to work for Giggle Inc. We simply ask that you commit these talking points to memory. The legal and marketing departments have labored over this language so be sure to stick to this script. Remember, Ms. Oomla, when you are talking to the press, you will be Giggle and we can't risk any misspeaking or omissions. You wouldn't want our shareholders to get nervous which, in turn, might make our stock price go down?"

And just like that, every last tooth flashed at her again. "This meeting is now adjourned! Oh! By the way, Ms. Oomla, don't miss today's Marketing meeting."

As she walked out, she was filled with so many different feelings; she didn't know how she felt. They had blatantly told her what her voice could or couldn't say! Did they think she was a parrot? A sock-puppet? But she really shouldn't complain about what they were asking her to do. They were, after all, right. She was who the public expected to hear from. And they'd made such a point of flattering her voice. She did feel flattered. But she was not comforted by the kind of flattery they'd just offered her.

She felt used by it.

And then something else hit her. And she knew how she felt about that. This was supposed to be the meeting when they decided whether or not they would become a multinational. It sure seemed to her that they had already decided they would before she even got in the room. Which means they hadn't consulted her.

This time, the steam was trying to push its way out.

But that was just the beginning of the day and one of the many, many meetings she had to attend, which now fell like a blizzard on top of her and she had no time to reflect about what had just happened and what it all meant and what would happen to all the steam that was building up inside her. So all that steam could do was roller-coaster through her as she sat through each and every one of those meetings.

She wanted to die of shame in her meeting with the Outsourcing Committee when they told her so smugly that when they went multinational, they would shut five Giggle factories in the USA where the average hourly rate was $21 an hour and move those jobs to China where the average hourly rate was a very affordable .57 cents an hour. She noticed how they grinned when they assured her that Giggle would have no fear of having to pay their Chinese employees overtime pay because there was a back room deal that had been worked out with the Chinese factory owners and the Chinese government a long time ago. "If we put our factory in a law-free-zone, we don't have to obey the laws of China. And the law we particularly don't want to obey is the one that requires us to pay those Chinese factory workers overtime pay. So as long as our factory is in that zone, we will not incur any of those pesky, budget-sucking overtime costs. And the Chinese government knows all about it; in fact, because of that deal, it's all perfectly legal. And by the way, all of our competitors' factories are in that same zone, so we'll all be doing the exact same thing. Which really is standard industry practice, Ms. Oomla." And when Mrs. Oomla remembered that packet she had received from that protest group that contained the hourly rate of the overseas workers and the novel 'Hard Times' written by Charles Dickens, that savior of exploited factory workers everywhere, AND that she had only GLANCED at it, she thought she actually should die of shame, even though, she had to admit she knew she would not die of shame BUT that if some large hand should come through that conference room window and thrown her and every last person in that meeting to a pack of wolves, it was exactly what she and the other money-grubbing, third-world-strip-miners deserved. But no such hand appeared.

She wanted to scream in the meeting with her own office staff about each of their as yet unfinished and overdue projects. But, of course, she didn't because she never screamed. Especially, since the board had given her another powerpoint presentation about that very subject entitled Finesse Drills for Those Without an MBA. Which had always struck Mrs. Oomla as a ridiculous title because someone who had Finesse would never remind anyone, let alone a CEO, that they did not have an MBA. But reminding her, apparently, was their favorite sport. Though the owner of the famous voice preferred to suffer in silence then to tell them how much their favorite sport insulted her.

One of the slides popped into her head:

"Finesse in Communication, Slide #6. When communicating, the MBA-less should always remember to be a PPP. Poised Polished Professional. Especially, when expressing themselves. Before the MBA-less makes a statement which requires emotion, the MBA-less should imagine an invisible scale that that emotion would fall upon; at the highest, most undesirable end EE, Excessively Emotional

- Sigmund had crossed that out and penciled over it Euphoniously Estranged, dim view taken; Shriekers, Frog-Marched off the Stage! –

"and at the lowest and just as undesirable other end CC, Cool Cucumbers

- Sigmund had penciled over that Cold Corpse, Cold Corpses preferred to Slimy Corpses. Slimy Corpses cannot be Frog-Marched anywhere –

"and the exact middle being PP, Poised and Polished."

- Sigmund had penciled Prince Prickslies over that.

"When the MBA-less must communicate emotionally, they are PPs, not EEs, nor CCs."

So, of course, she was that powerpoint presentation's obedient servant; she was the very image of the professional middle throughout the entire meeting. Even as she screamed inside.

And then off to yet another meeting with the Giggle attorneys who discussed her upcoming lunch where she was to speak publicly about the corporation and they wanted to make sure she said this but not that. Because if she said that, there might be legal ramifications. Or was it - say that but not this? And when she realized that again they were telling her and her famous voice what to say, this time, she almost did stop smiling professionally; she almost did open her mouth and scream. She didn't know how long she could hold out. The Marketing meeting was still hours away.

• • • 12:00 PM • • •

The noon bell rang. The History Lesson didn't wake her; the Grammar Lesson didn't wake her. Even the noon bell didn't wake her. Only Melinda did when she stood by Sophia's desk. Melinda was so close her voice tickled Sophia's ear and she woke with a start. But without even looking at Sophia, without even a glance in her direction, without even noticing that Sophia had been asleep, began to chatter away. But that's the way Melinda was; Sophia just let her talk. She wouldn't have even dreamed of asking her to be quiet. Sophia would've thought herself a very rude person if she did. Melinda was going on about every instant of her own morning. Not a word about how Sophia might be feeling or anything. How SHE had to rescue

Sophia in the bathroom this morning. And SHE had to figure out how to get the bathroom clean again. And SHE had to answer Mr. Snoggley's History question just perfectly because no one else could.

As Sophia listened, she began to think that Melinda was talking about what happened to herself this morning as if it were a movie, and not just any movie but a life or death one, as if Snidely Whiplash himself, the arch villain from the old-time Bullwinkle cartoon that Sophia had seen on the Cartoon History Show on TV, had been chasing poor Melinda and dangling her from a cliff by her ankles. And Sophia daydreamed about telling her own morning story like that too, like it was a life or death movie! And She! was Starring in It! a movie about Her! Being discovered in the TV room by Miss Kitty! About Her! Getting Sick in the School's Lavatory! About Her! Standing in front of the whole classroom and not being able to Talk! the way she Really! Talked! Like a Movie Star! Like Ginger Rogers! But only being able to talk like a Baby! A Baby! And then a miracle happened! She pictured herself! and heard herself! say all of that! like it was a life or death story! the way Melinda did when she went on and on about all the things that happened to her! She wanted to interrupt Melinda and tell her this story. Her story. Her own fascinating story. She could make it seem like old Snidely Whiplash had her in his grip, too. Snidely Whiplash! And Sophia, as tired as she was, had to smile but inside herself.

But she couldn't tell Melinda about the movie she had just made up in her head. Melinda might not understand that she was just joking. And even if she would've, she'd've laughed for about two seconds and then she would've just continued on talking. Because that's how Melinda was. Melinda talked, almost without stopping, on her outside. And Sophia talked, almost without stopping, on her inside. Sophia knew that about herself, and she knew that about Melinda. And Sophia also knew, she was the one who listened. Or had to listen. Or seemed like she was listening, anyway. Besides, somebody or other was always talking more than she did; she was used to that by now. And who would listen to Melinda if Sophia didn't? Sophia understood that, too. Maybe that's why Melinda and her were friends. And then Sophia remembered her secret, her Movie Star School. There! She got to talk! There! Oh! Did she!

Sophia and Melinda went to the cloakroom, picked up their lunch boxes and walked to the cafeteria together, Melinda talking away. But Sophia had a funny feeling.

Was she forgetting something?

What was it?

But she didn't forget her lunch box because there it was in her hand and that's all she really needed now, so she couldn't be forgetting anything. And soon the thought of eating what was inside that lunch box drove that feeling right out of her.

The only thing Sophia ever bought from the cafeteria was milk because Miss Kitty packed her lunch, and Miss Kitty packed a wonderful lunch. Sophia believed she made the best peanut butter and jelly sandwiches in the whole world. Even better than her Mother's. And her Mother's were really good. But what made Miss Kitty's the best was, besides never being soggy, she ground the peanut butter herself, preserved the jelly herself, usually blackberry, Sophia's favorite, and even made the bread herself too, usually sprouted wheat and sunflower seed, Sophia's favorite. Miss Kitty knew that peanut butter and jelly was the only sandwich Sophia would ever eat, and she'd better make it delicious or Sophia would've starved. Besides as Miss Kitty liked to always say, she made everything as if she were still living in the old country and "a hard trudge from a grocer."

Sophia finally reached her seat at the lunch table, but she was so weak after throwing up the few morsels she had managed to eat, and so achy from the crick in her neck and the grog in her head, she could barely open her Wonder-Woman lunch box. But she hardly noticed those aches and that crick when she looked inside the lunch box. For Miss Kitty had packed enough for her to make two sandwiches. She had even put in a larger bowl that was filled to the brim with cut up red grapes, green celery, yellow pineapples and snowy almonds in a honey-citrus dressing, and two gigantic oatmeal-raisin cookies and enough coins to buy three milk pints, and Sophia cheered up considerably. Miss Kitty never packed that much food before. How did she know she'd be so hungry today? She wanted to kiss Miss Kitty.

Sophia headed to the line to buy milk and then quickly returned and began eating away but Melinda hardly had time to chew, since Kathleen Ogden and Denise Twigston had joined Sophia and Melinda at their lunch table, and Melinda much preferred using her mouth for more important things, like telling Kathleen and Denise all about what happened to her and Sophia this morning.

The afternoon bell rang and Sophia, Melinda, Kathleen and Denise and the rest of the class lined up in the lunchroom waiting for Mr. Snoggley to lead them back to their classroom. Several teachers came into the lunchroom and began leading their lines of students out of the lunchroom. Then more teachers came, and led their lines to their classrooms. Til finally Sophia's class's line was the only line left. The students had already begun to wonder, "Where was Mr. Snoggley?" He'd never been late before. They waited. And waited. The lunch room clock said 1:15 as the door opened and in came Mr. Ellwood, the Principal, rushing and out of breath. All of the students were shocked to see the Principal coming towards them. Where was Mr. Snoggley?

"Now Mr. Snoggley's Grade 5, please listen, everything is fine so don't worry but Mr. Snoggley has met with an accident. A slight accident. About an hour ago, he fell and twisted his ankle. He didn't notice some branches that must have blown down in this wind …"

Calpernia Simpson, Mr. Snoggley's pet, gasped. And so did a few others. A very few others. Granger Foxley and Duke Appleby hooted. Albert Ianucci put his hand to his mouth so no one would hear him snort, but he didn't do a good job for Jay Murphy saluted Albert Ianucci's muffled snort with a snortissimo, which was soon echoed by a chorus of snorts and hoots. But when Calpernia Simpson was caught wiping tears from her face, the snorters and hooters began playing imaginary violins, and the chorus swelled into a symphony. Which made Calpernia hiss right back at them, "It's a good thing for all of you Mr. Snoggley isn't here!"

Melinda couldn't stop recounting the shock of it all to Sophia while Sophia just stood there thinking her own thoughts which Sophia didn't volunteer to share and Melinda didn't think to ask about.

"Now class, settle down. Gentlemen! Enough! Mr. Snoggley will be fine …"

Just a few loud sighs of relief along with even more low boos were piped up until Mr. Ellwood glowered at the boo-ers, silencing them immediately.

"He should be back on his feet in no time. And while he is recuperating, you'll be taught by Ms. Brandy French."

The entire class cheered. Including Sophia. Everybody loved Ms. French. She was the Floating Substitute Teacher. She was exotic yet kind and strict was a word that wasn't in her vocabulary.

"When you've settled down, we'll return to your classroom where Ms. French is waiting for you."

They settled down as if Mr. Snoggley himself had asked them to and then they filed back to their classroom without even a whimper of complaint.

The rest of the day was like a dream for Sophia. Actually, for Sophia, it was a dream. When she took her seat again after lunch, her head soon fell back down to her desk even while she was determined to keep it up. But when

Ms. French saw that Sophia had her head on her desk, she did something Mr. Snoggley would never have done, "Oh Sophia, aren't you feeling well?"

"I'm just a little tired, Ms. French."

"Then, by all means, take a rest. I hope you feel better."

• • • 12:00 PM • • •

Finally, it was time for Mrs. Oomla's luncheon. As this lunch was with a group of high school girls who had invited her to speak to them about what it was like to be a woman CEO of a huge corporation, and was to be televised and unpleasant emotions are unbecoming and not to appear on the visage of any Poised Polished Professional, Mrs. Oomla pushed out the turmoil roiling through her. After lunch, it was off to Giggle Research for a half hour to hear that their competitor was causing Giggle's sales to lag in LaLa Land. And by the time she actually made it to the Giggle Marketing meeting, she was so filled up with concerns about those factory workers and ideas about how to motivate her own staff to finish their unfinished projects and ditherings about whether it was this or it was that and frets that she might've said the wrong that/this to such young impressionable women and said them on television and worries that when the board found out about those lagging sales they'd jump all over her, that her twisting mess of feelings had now morphed into a kind of dread. And then, at last, the time had come to find out why Mr. Jordan had wanted her at the Marketing meeting.

And there stood the dazzler from the Marketing team - body-of-buff, blazer-of-blue with the boy-hair and the chiclet-teeth who surely was the aw-shucks winner, the captain, the one who everyone wanted to know and to be - announcing that they'd come up with two new products.

"Research has showed that these products'll be the overnight sensation the Street Analysts, the board members, the shareholders all've been waiting for. The first product'll be sold to the Goliathon consumer only, as they are the most sophisticated. The bottle'll be designed by a renowned architect and will have a silver-matte finish; the label, lettered with a calligrapher's hand. And because the bottle'll be manufactured by a green manufacturer, it'll appeal to Goliathon's ecologically-minded consumer. The beverage will still be Giggle but the color would be changed to clear. And, oh, by the way, some daffeine'll be removed thereby eliminating that bothersome 'giggle fit' issue which have limited our beverage from being served in that much coveted market, the Goliathon corporate function. With this little tweaking, we're assured that our beverage can stand neck to neck with all the other soft drinks at corporate functions all around town."

And like a surfer who'd just carved the Banzai Pipeline, he flashed a smile and his boy-hair caught the sun as did his pearly-whites, and then he wink-twink-twinkled his ice-blue-eyes at each attendee, setting hearts ajingle-jangle, as he knew he would, and Mrs. Oomla had to force herself to actually listen to what he was saying. "Now, for our next new product, we have teamed up with the Bull News Network where we'll advertise it exclusively on their All News! All Night! All Bull! Cable network program. And for that beverage, the daffeine will be added at quadruple strength. Apparently, the Bull execs could care less if drinking our Giggle causes their viewers to do just that; they are convinced that consuming our Giggle will ensure that their viewers stay glued to their shows thus ensuring that their viewers will receive the hidden messages they are transmitting. I must say to all of you Giggle Execs, marketing our product as a mind-control tool is something we've never considered before. And I assure you we will monitor the results of this Bull News Network venture to see if this concept actually does succeed. And, oh, by the way, the price would be quadrupled too. And, dog-gone, we'll cut the quantity of each portion in half."

And the bedazzled Mrs. Oomla sat just as the other compliant, polished, professionals did – conveying congeniality and collegiality, ever-so-pleasant-ly - but now that twisted feeling inside her was shrieking.

• • • 12:00 PM • • •

'Surely the Artistes'll have vamoosed by now!'

But there they were. Slouched and slumped and sheeplike. And thankfully no longer hammering away at Dr. Oomla and his ears anymore. He was done in himself after his own morning so he invited the lot of them to eat with him; something IV did not approve of but had not forbidden. As Dr. Oomla walked to the Institute's cafeteria surrounded by his Artistes, he noticed his colleagues were surrounded by theirs, too. Apparently, his Artistes weren't the only ones who were suffering. In all his years at the Institute, he never remembered anything like that ever happening before.

Dr. Oomla and his group got their food and sat together at a table; soon the tables were filled with his colleagues and their groups. And all around him, all he heard, all anyone could hear, was, "How could our Institute be our Institute without our theatricals?" "What'll we do with ourselves every week?" and "Who could do this to us?" The answer to the last question was always the same.

IV.

Til finally one of the Artistes who had been standing by the window, hollered, "Hey, there he goes! IV's driving away. He's afraid of us. He knows we're gonna get him. Let's do it before he gets away!"

And then every one of those Artistes ran over or hobbled or walker-walked but one way or another they got themselves to the cafeteria's windows to eyeball the villain who dared to shut down their means of self-expression! And they put a hex on him with their eyes. Spirals of double whammies – and there was a lot of Artistes so that was a lot of whammies – skewered him they were sure. But that was hardly enough. They'll! show! IV! that! their! self-expression-could-still-runneth-over! even without Performance Therapy! And like they were auditioning for a hopping-corpses-movie, they howled and hooted and hissed.

As these particular howlers were Show Business's long passed-over or its long in-demand but even longer in short-fuses, one might have assumed they wouldn't've nailed it on the first try. But nail it they did. In spite of this being their desperate hour, and their stage was but a cafeteria. After their howling subsided, their insults, salty language, barbs, invectives, vituperations, and curses that they enunciated, pronounced, orated, bloviated, grandiloquented, harangued and spittooned out of those windows were surely worthy of an Oscar, enhanced, no doubt, by all the time those Artistes had spent in the Institute's Performance Therapy diving into their very own deepest and darkest. Because when these sad people dived, they brought up dark deeds and contemptible crimes that had been perpetrated against them: crimes that had long gone unpunished. Performance Therapy had taught them to, finally, and at long last, punish those crimes: out-loud, for-all-to-hear.

And they could do it no matter where they were. They didn't care that their laments were thoroughly unsuitable for a public airing. Their mission was to spontaneously combust that air, with IV in it. Though IV wasn't smithereened, they did scald his air. And they held their heads high for being a credit to the art of the Bronx Cheer – the x-rated Bronx Cheer; an Oratorio of Blasphemia through and through, fit only for the reeking, sulfurous stage of the devil's own Palace for Spectacle and Sport, Carnegie Hell. IV may shut Performance Therapy down but he'd never shut them down.

As children may be present on these pages, their words cannot be repeated here because I, as the Author of this work, should not germinate foul seeds into fertile heads. Suffice it to say that the words boomeranging throughout that cafeteria so resoundingly that high-noon meant that no one eating in there had to spice up their food for a month.

Alas, Readers, that was not the end of that. The mood in the cafeteria grew dim and dark and depressing, til the psychoanalysts had become profoundly concerned. Without any of them even signaling to each other what they should do, they began to patrol the room, each of them speaking to a group, pleading with them to use their heads, to not forget the principles that they had been learning at the Institute. And most of the Artistes did calm down and returned to their tables and took their seats. But there were a few who wouldn't, who continued to roam around that cafeteria, stalking and leering and taunting. The psychoanalysts rapidly turned their attention to these apostates but they could not get through to them. Until finally the apostates turned away from the psychoanalysts and leaped up on the tables denouncing IV.

But then their ringleader turned towards the psychoanalysts and began to denounce them. "Why didn't you stop IV? What's wrong with all of you? Why can't you stand up to him? You say you're bothered by it too. Well! Do something about it!"

As the ringleader spoke, some of the Artistes who had taken their seats, stood back up again and glared at the psychoanalysts; those who remained seated glared, too. And the psychoanalysts, without even realizing they were, moved closer and closer, til they stood together in the cafeteria.

Dr. Oomla, however, was not among them. He was way in the back and off to the side. Ever since those very first curses had been hurled every which way throughout the cafeteria, that's where he found himself, and that's where he stayed, treating only those Artistes he'd come across way back there. In spite of his best intentions. For without even realizing they were, his ears had steered him there, away from the deafening ugliness.

And from where he and his afflicted ears were way in the back and off to the side, he examined as many Artistes as he could find. Their demeanor had changed from meek and fearful to an outraged-fangs-out, fist-pumping-menace.

Their shouting had fallen on his ears like a jack-hammer and gave his head an ache that kept banging away inside him. Dr. Oomla held his head up as best he could and examined his fellow psychoanalysts. They didn't look themselves either. It was no wonder; they were surrounded by mental patients who looked like they wanted to hurt somebody, anybody. Plus he and his fellow psychoanalysts were outnumbered; there were so few of them and so many Artistes. So many Artistes, burning mad, in misery, and ready to pounce.

The psychoanalysts weren't used to their Artistes from their Institute, the Institute for the Compassionate Care of the Extraordinary and the Always Interesting, acting that way; of course, they didn't look themselves. Things there had been so peaceful for such a while, he figured they, like him, mustn't be sure what to do. There hadn't been wounded beings who were also looking for a rumble at their peaceful Institute for a long long time, they didn't know what to do or how to treat them. They were out of practice. Still Dr. Oomla was surprised that not one of his colleagues had said a word in response to the ringleader; though the protocol among the psychoanalysts was that Dr. Simon, as the most senior member of the staff, spoke for the group.

'Dr. Simon is letting that upstart's statements go unanswered.'

But his colleagues were vulnerable themselves. He felt the way they did, and no-doubt looked the way they did, too. And he, in spite of his better judgment, which kept warning him not to show his fear to a circling mob, glanced at the Artistes, even as he knew his fear was showing. The Artistes were quiet now and seemed to be waiting to hear what the doctors, any of them, would say.

Which only made the silence from his fellow psychoanalysts even more shocking.

And yet still no word from Dr. Simon. He tried to find Dr. Simon in the group; but his colleagues had moved so close together, he could not.

Dr. Oomla soon felt as if every pair of eyes in the cafeteria were on him. But he was too overcome to see for himself.

'Surely, the Thinker Statue is imagining things! Why would they be looking at me, of all people?' The only thing he could see was that he really was sticking out. He really was far away from his colleagues. Then he noticed: he wasn't the only one really far away from his group. For there was the ringleader circling the psychoanalysts, thrusting his face right up in a face, then another, as he made his way around; a fist shut tight, as if he had something hard and sharp and lethal in it, as over and over and over he said in a menacing drone, as if in a trance, "Do something about it!" its velocity and pitch rising on each revolution of the phrase.

And then more Artistes joined the ringleader and were now circling the psychoanalysts and they too were chanting, "Do something about it!" One Artiste pushed another Artiste and a scuffle broke out and soon the scufflers were rolling around the floor, as the chant of "Do something about it!" grew louder and louder.

'Dr. Simon is letting that go unanswered because he's surrounded, we're surrounded, by ranting, cackling, hysterical, fist-wielding, mental patients.'

And then the ringleader began circling Dr. Oomla right where he stood, way in the back and off to the side. And then more Artistes joined the ringleader, and they were circling Dr. Oomla, too; all of them, red-faced and sweating, some of them so close, he could feel their hot breath on his neck, could smell their lunches, their unbrushed teeth, the pits of their arms, their other body cavities; and their fists were closed, too, as if they had something in them. And the ringleader grunted in Dr. Oomla's aching ear, "Hey, Thinker Statue, think something about that!"

Dr. Oomla had long ago realized that everyone at the Institute knew his nickname, but no Artiste had ever brickbatted him with it before. But, even worse for Dr. Oomla, his connoisseur ears were by now in agony; gross, coarse, boorish, vulgar loutishness was reverberating every which way throughout him. And he could feel himself panicking.

Dr. Oomla turned again towards the group and finally found Dr. Simon. Dr. Simon's mouth was shut tight. And then Dr. Oomla looked again at the upstarts circling him. They were inching ever closer. And again he turned towards his colleagues; they looked paralyzed and were struck dumb. And so, too, was he.

'What if for once you shut off your bloody &@^^^^ ears? What if you slug that creep, Dr. Oomla?'

·· ··(···

("Yoh, Me, was that our guy?"
"Lorraine, it sounds like him!")

··:)···

And every mouth in the room opened when the Thinker Statue opened his and spoke, "We will, we promise you. We mean every word we are saying to you. We agree with you and we will speak to IV, and above all, to the board. IV, AND the board, will know how we feel, how you feel, how important this form of therapy, those theatrical exercises are to all of you. And to all of us on the staff. We see how it helps all of you. And then we will remind IV AND THE BOARD, that the Van Der Speckians feel the same way, that they support you too because they pack your performances to the rafters every Saturday night, even if it's sleeting or hailing, never missing a performance yet!"

No one was more surprised than him. Had the Thinker Statue finally and at long last morphed into an Action Figure? Had his ears, his music-seeking, harmony-hunters, for once, lost control of him? But he knew the answer to that question; they hadn't, for Dr. Oomla had heard himself. He had been strident and boorish just like the cackling mob. And there was nothing he, or his connoisseur ears, could do about it. He had to say what he said because no one else was saying it. And now he felt every eye in the cafeteria on him. Dr. Oomla imagined what they were thinking, because he was thinking the same thing,

Dr. Oomla? Music man? Shrieking right along with the best of them! Dr. Oomla? Out of all of us? the one? who spoke? The Thinker Statue? Surrounded by a harsh ugly mob, no less AND he didn't hesitate, didn't ponder, didn't weigh the possibilities of what he could say, might say, should say before he opened his mouth! —

'... Did something happen to me today?

'... That first patient? She spoke her mind and her neurosis, she didn't care. She said whatever she wanted to say. No one censored her. Saying nothing would have been a disaster for the patients, and for the psychoanalysts, too, who, after all, are in here by themselves, unprotected and undefended and who must've momentarily forgotten, or didn't know how, or were afraid, to do their duty. Psychoanalysts are only human after all.

'But so too are the Artistes.

'The Artistes are more bold, more expressive, and far better fighters then we just showed ourselves to be. Why is that?

'Dr. Simon was afraid to say the wrong thing, so rather than say the wrong thing, he says nothing. The way I always do. But the Artistes aren't afraid to say the wrong thing. They aren't afraid to say anything!'

But he had said the right thing. He could tell by the way his colleagues were looking at him, and by the way the Artistes were, too.

But suppose he had said the wrong thing?

Would the Artistes have behaved even worse?

Just then a few of the Artistes began to applaud, then a few more, then a few more. The ringleader and the circling mob had, by now, stopped circling and were lingering on the sidelines. Dr. Oomla noticed though that not everybody was clapping. No. Some hands were not. Especially among that group, the sideline group. Then one of them picked up a piece of food and threw it against the wall. And there was a low mumble that spread throughout the room. And somebody said "Don't!" But somebody else took another piece of food and threw that against the wall. And the mumble got louder, and a few more bits of food were thrown against the wall. And the psychoanalysts moved closer together again.

And this time Dr. Oomla was with them. For now suddenly his outburst was stuck in his throat. And the noise in the room had crescendoed dramatically and was pounding away on his ears again. And the ache in his head was back to strangling him. And they, his ears, his sacred, secret chamber for the world's acoustical marvels, had just had to soak up his own raucousness, his own stridency when he spoke up just now. And they were indignant; how could their owner make them listen to that? He wanted no more of the heat from the spotlight. He didn't like being front and center; he didn't like having to worry that every word was being examined and weighed; he didn't like fretting that if he did indeed say the wrong thing that it might set the Artistes off even more than they already were. His colleagues may not have been wrong to keep their mouths shut, after all. He and they weren't free like the Artistes were to just say anything that popped into their heads. They were psychoanalysts. Their job required that they speak judiciously because they were supposed to know what things meant, what people were really all about. They were supposed to be wise. What had he done? He would never be free to say the wrong thing. Besides, no matter what, he knew that whatever he did say, his sacred chamber would have reverberated through and through with it. And he was ashamed to admit his ears and his head might not be able to take it.

Mercifully, Dr. Simon took over, "What do we want to do? What do all of us want to do? We all know the answer to that question. We want to reinstate the weekly theatrical exercises. How does throwing food get those weekly theatrical exercises reinstated? All of the staff who are in this room here with you now – we have not abandoned you. We support you. We want to keep supporting you but help us do that by sticking to this problem, and solving this problem. And that problem is – what can we all do to keep the theatrical exercises running at the Institute every week, the way they've been for years? So don't make two problems for yourself when you only have one, throwing food does nothing to help the first problem. Ask yourself, what can I do to keep our theatrical exercises going at the Institute?"

Dr. Oomla found that, though his ears were begging for calm, for peace; though they were filled to bursting with madhouse howlings and might bleed through a thousand tourniquets; though his throat was thickly coated, and he'd buried himself in the dead center of the group, his mouth had more to say, "Ask yourself, how does throwing food keep the theatricals open? Think, think, think - what is the answer to that question!"

And the ringleader spoke up, "Oh, listen to what the Thinker Statue wants us to do - think, think, think! I say throw, throw, throw!"

But this time an Artiste shouted over the ringleader, "The answer is it doesn't keep the theatricals open, Dr. Oomla!"

Dr. Oomla ignored the ringleader's taunts and the agony in his own ears, "You're right, it doesn't. Throwing food creates another problem. Let's work together. Let's— "

But just as the agitators lowered their volumes, just as some of the Artistes actually sat back down, the doors of the cafeteria were kicked open and in marched about 20 or more of what were definitely police officers in uniforms that looked more like riot gear. They wore thick padded vests, helmets with visors that were down and that completely covered their faces; no guns, but long thin sticks that were in both of their hands and carried across their chests.

But on closer look, those visors didn't completely cover their faces, for poking out of those visors were beards.

Dr. Oomla couldn't believe it – This wasn't the police! No! These characters were the Sheripists!

The Sheripists in policemen uniforms! Sheep in wolf's clothing! Turncoats! Or had IV been slowly turning them into wolves even as they wore their sheeps' clothing? When? And where did these uniforms come from? Did IV order those? Why? Had IV been anticipating trouble? What would the Old Chief say? Dr. Oomla couldn't even imagine. At the sight of those usually gentle creatures transformed into an invading army whose twinkly-eyes were now invisible behind dark shields and whose tweed-jackets were gone but in their places were impenetrable riot gear and pandemonium broke out among the Artistes.

Some of the TurnWolfs stood in front of the doors, barring the exits; others moved over to the windows, barring them. One of them had very quickly grouped the psychoanalysts together and ordered - Yes ordered! - them to stay where they were, saying that they, and not the psychoanalysts, were in charge now and they would handle this problem.

And now all Dr. Oomla and his colleagues could do was watch.

When every exit was secured, one of the SheriPests had yelled, "The cafeteria is in lock-down."

Their cafeteria in lock-down! Never before had any force invaded the Institute and locked them in. Some of the Artistes were crouching under the tables. Some of them were crying, some shouting "Leave us alone!" or "Get out of here!" or "Go away!," many still defiantly throwing food and some just wordless but not noiseless as they screamed screams and yelled yells. Some could only sit there or stand there, and say nothing at all but the looks on their faces told anyone who cared to look at them exactly how they felt - that they were scared, petrified. Some faces had gone blank with no expression at all.

Dr. Oomla had never known there to be a riot at the Institute so he knew these SheriPests had no experience with such events. He watched as each of them did something different. Some were speaking sensitively to the Artistes, the way they were trained to, but some were speaking to the Artistes in much gruffer voices than Dr. Oomla had ever heard them use before. They were not exactly talking tough but they were certainly not talking or acting the way the Old Chief had ever intended them to act.

But in a few minutes it was over, the Artistes had given up. The TurnPests had prevailed.

And there the Artistes were, around the cafeteria tables, or underneath them, looking pitiful, traumatized, some of them with tears rolling down their faces, some of them shaking. IV and his pest-machine had shut them down. Gone was their self-expression. Nothing runneth-over from them now. Even after all that time they had spent in Performance Therapy. And it was quiet, but not peaceful, though no one said a word. No one dared to mouth off; they were too afraid.

And finally, Dr. Oomla refused to think, ignored his ears and, though he and the psychoanalysts were as bedraggled as the Artistes were and as covered with food and worse, when the Pests let them go, they began walking around that cafeteria saying anything they could think of to the now broken, eerily submissive, utterly humiliated Artistes, even as ketchup, mustard and crumbs dripped and plopped from their hair, from everybody's hair. They would just wipe them off and keep going.

• • • 3:00 PM • • •

The bell rang at the end of the day but Sophia, sound asleep at her desk, didn't hear it; her classmates, so merry after spending an afternoon with Ms. French, didn't even notice. Including Calpernia Simpson, the nosiest of all who didn't miss a trick, was now too busy trying out for the role of Ms. French's pet to pay attention to anything, or anyone, else. Sophia didn't even wake up when all of her classmates were gone and the classroom was suddenly quiet. She didn't wake up until Ms. French had returned to the classroom to straighten up, and saw the deep-sleeping Sophia a full fifteen minutes later. Ms. French shook her gently.

"Oh Sophia, I'm so sorry, I don't see how I could've missed you. How're you feeling?"

"I was just a little extra tired today."

"Doesn't your Nanny pick you up after school, Sophia? I think she should know how tired you are. Her name is Miss Kitty isn't it?"

And Sophia got scared all over again. Miss Kitty was about to find out that she fell asleep at her desk. And that the teacher caught her sleeping. All because she was too tired. All because she watched Movie Stars. At night. And then Mr. James'd find out. And her Mother and her Father too! Everybody'd know. The whole world'd know. Great Aunt Hortense! Her classmates! Melinda! Grange! Denise! Albert! She wouldn't be able to go to school ever again.

"Oh, Sophia, you look like you're about to cry. Don't be afraid. Miss Kitty won't be mad. She's a sweetheart. She'll just make sure you go to bed extra early tonight."

Sophia couldn't say even one of the million words that were screaming inside her.

"Let's gather your things. Be sure to button your coat up tightly and put your scarf on, it's freezing outside. I'll walk with you and we'll find Miss Kitty together."

Sophia wound her entirety in coat, scarf, gloves; down went her hat over her eyes, her face; so nothing showed; so Ms. French, no one, could see her tears. Now she was in trouble with Ms. French, the nice teacher! And she was about to get in trouble with Miss Kitty and her Mother and her Father, too, and even probably Mr. James!

Sophia dragged herself down the hallway beside Ms. French. Just as they reached the front door, the door opened with such force from the outside, that both of them had to jump out of the way or be trampled by a giant for sure. But it was only Miss Kitty.

Who was huffing and puffing so loudly with a face as big and as red as a coca-cola sign, she really was a giant.

"Oh! Sophia! Mr. James 'n I have been in t' car waitin' n' waitin' fer ye! Where have ye been? We were so worried! Ye have tat appointment with tat terapist of t' speech talkin'!"

And Sophia screamed again inside herself, *'The speech therapist! I forgot. I have to go there. But I don't want to! I just want to go home!'*

"Oh! Ms. French? Tat's ye now, I didn't quite recognize ye with ye scarf n' hat n' such. Now where might Mr. Snoggley be? I'm afraid we're in an awful rush!"

"Miss Kitty, Mr. Snoggley had a slight accident, but he'll be fine. It happened at lunch time so I stepped in to teach the class this afternoon."

"Oh! Ms. French would he've been givin' ye t' address 'n te directions t'en?"

"The directions, Miss Kitty?"

Every last drop of red in that sign drained out of her and Miss Kitty stood before them, shriveled and shaking, "Sophia is to be takin' t' speech talkin' lessons tis afternoon on t' dot of 3:45 n' Mr. James n' I were to be drivin' her tere n' tis almost near tat time now. We must be on time or we'll miss t' lesson n' without tat address 'n tose directions, we won't know where it tis we're t' be drivin' t'. Do ye have te directions ten, Ms. French?"

Sophia remembered what she couldn't remember before. *The directions! I was supposed to get the directions from Mr. Snoggley before lunch!*' She had forgotten something when she was walking with Melinda to the cafeteria! What Mr. Snoggley said to her at her desk this morning! And the answer flew out of her. "They're in his desk drawer!"

They ran straight back to Mr. Snoggley's desk. Ms. French reached it first and tried the top drawer. Locked. The next drawer. Locked. Every drawer. All locked tight. Each and every one of them.

"Mr. Snoggley must lock everything up before he goes to lunch! Why does he do that?" said Ms French.

And Miss Kitty felt like crying. It was all her fault because she hadn't reminded Sophia to get the directions when she dropped her off this morning.

Sophia looked at Miss Kitty's misty eyes and knew how she felt. Sophia's eyes leaked in sympathy even as her mind boiled. *'I knew something wasn't right. Maybe when a person falls asleep, things really do just fall right out of their heads!'*

Miss Kitty looked at Sophia through her watery eyes and spoke but as she was trying not to drip, her words could only trickle, "Now, Sophia, didn't … wasn't be … did he … Mr. Sn … Sno … Snogg … g … ley … say anyting t' ye about tis?"

Sophia was too scared to say a word. She knew what she was supposed to do:

Tell the truth.

She knew what she wasn't ever supposed to do:

Tell a lie.

So she didn't say anything.

"Miss Sophia ... we are waitin' aren't we now? Did Mr. Snoggley say anyting t' ye about getting te directions?"

"Miss Kitty ... I ... he ... it was lunchtime ... and I ... he ... was ... and I was going to get the directions ..." and Sophia's voice got very small ... "but I had to eat my lunch."

That was a lie!

But she could only listen to herself shout the truth on her inside stage -

'I didn't get the directions because I forgot all about the directions!

'The speech therapist lesson!

'That Mr. Snoggley told me to get the directions before I went to lunch!

'I fell asleep at my desk and everything fell out of my head! But I didn't tell you that just now, Miss Kitty. I lied!'

- because that was where Sophia, the Leading Lady of her very own Movie, its tragedienne, comedienne, and all the supporting characters in between, the Actor/Actress herself! locked away all her very own monologues. That was where her personal drama scorched and ripped and ruled. She couldn't imagine, even now, at this life and death moment, that she could open her mouth and use her voices, her accents, her characters to express herself.

'Suppose somebody interrupts me? Or won't let me finish because they don't have the time to hear me out? And besides, even if I did say what I felt, I'd have to use my own voice to say it! And suppose I can't stand that voice! Or suppose I do use my own voice, and when I hear it, I can't get my thoughts out? No! Keeping all of that worry inside is what I do and is what everyone is used to me doing, because maybe they want to be the star, or maybe they don't want me to be the star. Oh! I don't know but as long as I have my Midnight Movie Star School, I don't care!'

But she did care. Leaving this monologue unspoken was causing flames to shoot out of her; she could feel them. She dropped her head low; she didn't want Miss Kitty and Ms. French to notice that she had turned into a fiery torch. Anyway, why ever would a liar hold her head up? But even though her head was hidden she could still feel Miss Kitty's eyes sear right through her which made her even hotter, and soon Sophia felt like she was inside a pot that was boiling over; which got her thinking about a movie she saw about cannibals in the jungle who cooked people in big pots. And now she knew exactly what that would feel like! And when she was the World's Greatest Actress and had to act like she was being cooked alive in a big pot, she would know exactly what to do. But, at this very second, she wasn't about to lift her face and show Miss Kitty and Ms. French what she had just learned, because if she did, both of them would know by her smoking, steaming face, that she wasn't the World's Greatest Actress, or that she was great at all but that she was the worst, the World's Worst Liar.

"Miss Sophia, ye won't look at me which don't give me too much confidence in what ye ' are sayin' 'n ye are not exactly answering me question either are ye now girl? N' I have to say, I'm most surprised, because I don't ever remember ye lyin' to me before ..."

The words may have marched out of Miss Kitty easily but they crashed into Sophia hard, who now was certain Miss Kitty knew who she was. The World's Worst Liar. And now even probably Ms. French knew it, too! The nice teacher! Sophia felt awful. Worse than she had ever remembered feeling in her whole ten-year-old life.

"So I'll be asking it again. Did Mr. Snoggley say anyting to ye about getting t' directions?"

Sophia was so ashamed. And her life as the World's Worst Liar was over. She didn't want to ever feel like this again. Her Father and her Mother and Miss Kitty and Mr. James may not love her anymore if they knew she told lies. She wanted to feel like she was good again. To be good again. Even if she had to admit she forgot to ask Mr. Snoggley for the directions. Even if she had to admit she fell asleep in school and that she stayed up very late watching Movie Stars. And even if everybody in the whole world found out her secret. Her very private secret that she had kept to herself for a long time - that she wanted to be the World's Greatest Actress. A Movie Star! And that she already was. Except nobody but her knew it. In fact, not only didn't they know that, a lot of those very same people thought she couldn't talk too good.

Sophia lifted her head just when a beam of afternoon light shot in from the window pane. But this light wasn't at all mischievous; this light was strong, strong enough to light up the real and the true.

·∴(··

("Author Lady, Thee bent it that way! I'm sorry, Thee, I know you made me swear I'd never tell anyone but we're, like, all gathered here to tell Sophia's story as it really happened, so, like, I'm off the hook, right?"

"Lorraine, a promise is sacred! And you've shown that I, of all the Fairies, broke a rule! The Readers will think I'm a hypocrite." gasped Thee.

"Hypocrite? Dah?? Like, who ain't a hypocrite?"

Lorraine, enough! And by the way, I thought you said the Fairies wouldn't do any more magic?)

·:)··

Readers, that light caught Sophia in the heart of her and was so strong, she almost couldn't see. But she didn't put her head back down, she spoke, even as that light stabbed her right in the eye, and even though her un-Movie-Star twangs crash landed on her eardrums.

"Miss Kitty, I forgot. I was supposed to ask Mr. Snoggley for the directions before I went to lunch but I forgot."

Miss Kitty took full advantage of the spotlight; she made her eyes as hard as she could and then stared into Sophia's wide, jitter-bugging eyes. "Sophia, first, ye're not truthful, ten ye are truthful. So he did tell ye! Well, ye told te truth! I'm not so sure ye wanted t' but I'm glad ye did!" And Miss Kitty, who had been so rushed and hurried since she entered the school, slowed down and for a long moment, turned the hard off in her eyes and regarded Sophia and Sophia felt as if she was the Princess of Truth and Goodness. But in the next blink, Miss Kitty was all rush and hurry again, blurting out to Ms. French, "Ms French, we need t' get te address 'n te directions ten. Do ye have any idea about how we might get te keys—"

Mr. James had raced into the classroom and the sight of him caused Miss Kitty to just about jump a foot, forget what she was saying, and, in an instant, flush red yet again. And all she could do was listen to her heart pound.

When Sophia got an eyeful of Mr. James, Miss Kitty wasn't the only one listening to her heart pound! What would he think about her and her Movie Stars now that she had to tell the truth? All the time? To everybody? Telling the truth all the time to everybody would mean she'd have to tell him about her being out of her bed when she was supposed to be in it! When Miss Kitty told her to be! When her Father and her Mother thought she was!

She could hear hers loud and clear!

But, she noticed, her heart was less loud when she began to wonder if telling the whole, entire truth plus every little thing to Mr. James about what she really did at night was absolutely necessary. Maybe he wouldn't have to know all of that. Maybe she'd just tell Miss Kitty but not Mr. James.

But suppose he asked her? Would she lie to him?

People aren't supposed to lie! And suppose she lied to him and he found out?

But suppose she told him the truth and he told everybody; then she wouldn't be allowed to watch movies ever again!

But now her heart was pounding differently, it was loud like a super-hero's heart. She knew why. That kind of pounding was making her eyes open so wide they had no choice but to take in everyone in the room even though they didn't want to. And everybody's image mixed up with everything she had just thought about, while her heart continued to beat like a super-hero. Like a Super! Hero! And there she stood digesting it all. Could she? Would she? Do what was right? Or do what was wrong?

A Super-Hero always tells the truth.

But would he ever tell a lie? Every once in a while?

Miss Kitty couldn't very well look away from Mr. James and avoid his gaze, so she returned it but then she found herself scanning him from head to toe and she saw just how impeccably groomed he was; how perfect he looked; with his bowler hat in his gloved hand; his top coat brushed thoroughly and not a speck on it; his shoe leather polished, as were the heels and even the soles of those shoes, because she had seen him at the task many the time - so much the picture of the perfect Butler and the English Gentleman. And here she stood, a failure at the task she was supposed to perform! She had no driving directions, was out-of-breath, felt a little shaky, and without even having to look, knew running in the wind did her hair not a bit of good. And now he was about to find out she had fibbed to him and that she hadn't reminded Sophia about getting the directions from Mr. Snoggley. She didn't think anybody in the Oomla household ever fibbed to Mr. James.

Or got caught at it when they did. And she wasn't about to be the first.

"Good Afternoon ... Please do pardon the interruption ... oh, I see I am addressing Ms. French and not Mr. Snoggley ... Good Afternoon, Ms. French, Miss Sophia, and of course, Miss Kitty! I take it Mr. Snoggley isn't here at the moment. But I was hoping, Miss Kitty, that you would have received the directions by now. We are already unforgivably late even if we leave now but we must proceed anyway, and take the chance that this speech therapist might be able to see Miss Sophia anyway."

"Well, Mr. James, I'm afraid Mr. Snoggley's desk is locked which is where the directions are. Miss Kitty and I have tried every drawer and not one of them will budge. And I'm afraid, Mr. Snoggley is probably still in the hospital having his ankle looked after."

"Oh, I see. So Mr. Snoggley hasn't been here then and, I take it, has sustained an injury. I do hope he's soon on the mend. Well, might you, Ms. French, have any idea about the name and address of this speech therapist?"

"No, I'm afraid, I don't and everybody has left for the day, and the Principal is not answering his cellphone. And Mr. Snoggley is, I'm sure, unreachable to call and ask."

Mr. James appeared not to be bothered, though he was, he certainly was. But as he was an outstanding representative of the Service

Profession, Species Butler, and familiar with each and every punctilio said profession required: one being to keep his emotion in reserve no matter the circumstance, his true feelings were, at this moment, where they should be, not on display but roaming around safe from view, in his internal pasture, imperceptible to most human eyes. Especially, the two pairs of very human eyes who were scouring him with what they wished, hoped and prayed were eagle eyes. Miss Kitty, for any sign he suspected she hadn't told the truth, and Sophia, for any sign he knew what she really did at night: both of them worrying, was he going to interrogate them and find out their secrets? But even an eagle couldn't have spotted just how bothered he was. And certainly Sophia and Miss Kitty, after they had just about gamma-rayed his countenance and demeanor, still hadn't a clue what he was thinking.

Mr. James, in his level tone, carried on, "Since we have no address and driving directions, we can't very well drive there can we? I shall speak to Madame and I'm sure she'll ring up and have the appointment rescheduled. Thank you, Ms. French. Please send our best wishes for a speedy recovery to Mr. Snoggley. Shall we be on our way then, Miss Kitty? Miss Sophia?"

Ms. French walked with them down the long corridor towards the school's front door, no one saying a word. Miss Kitty was immensely relieved and couldn't help remembering what her dear Sainted Mother always used to say to her when she was a jabbering away Little Miss Kitty - and just after her dear Sainted Mother had poked her - 'Te less said te better.'

And Sophia, who was just as relieved, also remembered what Miss Kitty had told her her dear Sainted Mother always said to her, 'Ye say te less! Ye say te better! ... or someting like tat.'

And in the safety of Sophia and Miss Kitty's minds - the castles for their dreams, the playgrounds for their imaginations, the treasure chests for their knowledge, the fortresses for their secrets as well as the dungeons for their delusions - they shared another thought that was the same; but this time their thoughts matched each other letter for letter, word for word, *'Maybe Mr. James won't say another word about this. And if he doesn't say another word, I won't either.'*

• • • 3:05 PM • • •

When Mrs. Oomla joined her next meeting she was screaming 'No!' so loudly inside her, she had a hard time hearing Giggle's CyberSecurity Officer. But when he explained that they needed her to record the announcement that CyberSecurity was adding an extra layer of cybersecurity to Giggle's technology and that they intended to play her announcement to all employees nationwide over the company's voicemail system, suddenly he came in loud and clear.

"Tests have shown that people who hear you speak, on television, on radio, who hear even your formal pronouncements, believe what you say and would like to friend you. Research, however, has shown they are really responding to your voice. Since Cyber's added precautions might make our employees feel like they're being spied on, we want them to feel good about it. So our message must be crafted carefully and, above all, spoken sincerely. With charm. When you transmit our message, they will welcome it even though you are telling them that we can now monitor all their social media accounts. Your voice will completely demilitarize their response. Your charm will guarantee that we in CyberSecurity will not have to disarm a soul."

My voice is about to be used as a tool in a corporate plot! I should show them what my voice can do. I should scream.

'Oh, should I really scream at security officers?'

She should not, she decided.

And then in the next meeting, she was joined by a phalanx of assistants, one of whom handed her her list-of-received-calls. She looked at her watch and screamed *'No!'* yet again inside her. Now she had 25 minutes to return 45 phone calls and she had to be back on the helicopter at 3:30.

• • • 3:30 PM • • •

Sophia and Ms. French and Miss Kitty and Mr. James stood together in the hallway by the school's front door.

Together! Sophia did not want to be! With! Anyone! And as soon Mr. James said "A very good afternoon, Ms. French" and opened the door, Sophia bolted. She wanted out and got out. She had to be far away from any questions that those two might think to ask her. But the air out there bit her hard and she was startled still and then utterly mesmerized when Miss Kitty's and Mr. James's icy-dagger-breath spliced and diced each other. Until she remembered why she had to run and all of a sudden sword-fighting air was nothing but a big nothing. Just before she made her getaway, she watched a trace of her breath twist with theirs. *'That's all those two will get out of me today! Now beat-it! Miss Kitty and Mr. James walk like old people. They'll never catch up.'*

Mr. James was unruffled by the cold. He had a duty to perform: to marshal his remaining charge to the waiting limousine.

And marshaled was Miss Kitty.

Though she, too, wished she could run down that path like Sophia and get away from Mr. James. But she knew that even if she could have, soon enough, she'd have to face his questions. Mr. James was a fair and decent gentleman but he was a principled and a just one, too, who expected people to tell him the truth. "I will be truthful with you and I expect you will be truthful with me." Those were the words he said to Miss Kitty the day he hired her. Those were the words that made his gentlemanly eyes turn forbidding. And when she saw that look in his eyes, Miss Kitty knew he meant what he said. From that day on, she prayed she'd never have to look into his forbidding eyes ever-ever-again.

And as long as he never found out how old she really was, she wouldn't.

But that was then.

'It had only ever been tat wee ting before.

'But now I've sometin' else to hide.

'Sometin' else?'

She counted.

'Lying about te directions.

'Not tellin' a soul about Sophia's movie watchin' in te middle of te night.'

No. She had a list. And maybe Mr. James might never find out, but her Irish Saints were all-knowing. They were Saints, after all. *'What do ye tink o' y'r Miss Kitty now?'*

So she made sure that no one, including her Saints, would've ever suspected she was anything less than a Saint herself, as she chattered away about any little thing she could think to say about anything but the truth as they made their way towards the limousine. *'Tis not really a true lie, tis it now?'*

The limousine was parked at the end of the path so the back door would swing open exactly into the path's center. If Mr. James had had a measuring stick, he couldn't have gotten it closer. But that, Miss Kitty realized, was just how Mr. James did everything.

Sophia had reached the car long before the old pokes did. She opened the back door and scrambled into the seat, scooching down low so that she could not be seen from the front seat. Finally, she was safe. But the air from the open door went right through her and turned the back seat into an icehouse. She shivered and her boney bones shook. Which gave her a good excuse to pull her scarf over her head and her coat all around her. *'I'm an igloo of me!'* And she shut her eyes and leaned to the side til her head rested against the cushioned door panel. *'It looks like I'm sleeping. Nobody'll ask me anything, and if I'm not talking, I won't tell anybody anything by mistake.'*

By and by the pokes arrived. Miss Kitty got in beside her and Mr. James closed the back door gently and then glided into the driver's seat. Sophia noticed that Miss Kitty was no longer quiet as she was when all of them were walking down the corridor with Ms. French because now Miss Kitty was chatting chatting chit chit chatting. Mr. James, of course, wasn't. He never chit chatted when he was chauffeuring. At this moment, as her Father would say, Mr. James was Attentive. Sophia knew that meant listening and watching. When Mr. James was in his chauffeur's seat, he really did seem to watch everything and everyone around him; and even though it was impossible, because his eyes stayed on the road ahead, he even watched those behind him. Sophia was pretty sure he was looking at her now but she wasn't going to lower her scarf and find out.

"Oh, now tis'nit suuuch a crying shame after all because Sophia'll be just fine tank you very much," Miss Kitty continued her chatter as if her life depended on it, " 'n we'll soon get te address of tat speech-talkin'-person 'n Mrs. Oomla will understand tat sometimes tings just happen 'n ..."

Underneath all her talk, Miss Kitty was feeling queer saying what she was saying. She wasn't at all sure if Mrs. Oomla would understand that sometimes things just happen but maybe her saying so would make it so and she went on sprinkling sugar over her words and sharpshooting them all about the limousine.

"... Twas just a misunderstanding, a wee misunderstanding tat will all be straightened out, we'll all see. We'll get te address 'n everyting will be just hunkery-dorkerey again ..."

Mr. James turned the keys in the ignition and the limousine began its stately roll. Miss Kitty said, "Off we go! Te Castle L'OOMla!" Dr. Oomla's nickname had stuck and now the entire household called it that; except, of course, in front of Mrs. Oomla. And as if Miss Kitty was off on a merry journey – and for somebody who forgot to remind Miss Sophia about her speech therapist appointment and for lying and saying she had, and maybe was just about to face a firing squad for saying that very thing – which, in Miss Kitty's case wouldn't be a squad but a person - Mr. James - and wouldn't be a firing from a gun but from an employer – the Oomlas - Miss Kitty kept up her prattle to drown out those very fears that were grumbling around inside her because maybe, after all, if she stayed on the sunny side and said the right thing, it might just be Mr. James' turn to forget - and merry they soon would all be. She even turned to the lumpy pile of knee socks and wool coat and curly hair that was Sophia and gave her a pat. Sophia lifted her mittened hand and willowed a wave in Miss Kitty's directions.

As the car took off, Sophia, from inside her dugout of scarf and coat, began to worry. *'Ms. French did say Miss Kitty ought to know how tired I am. But I didn't hear Ms. French say anything to Miss Kitty or Mr. James about me falling asleep in school. But suppose she did and then one of them comes right out and asks me if it's true. And then they start asking even more questions. Or maybe Ms. French'll just call up the house later and tell Miss Kitty all about it. No! She probably did speak to Miss Kitty and I just didn't notice. But I was with Miss Kitty and Ms. French the whole time, and nobody was whispering. I would've seen them if they were ...'* And even as the limousine rolled its passengers towards home, her thoughts were rolling to, over and over in her head.

Until another thought rolled right over them ... an entirely different thought ...

'I saw a movie one time and this girl was so strong and she stood up and told everybody what she thought and she didn't care what anybody had to say about what she just said ...

'So that's what I'll do. And this is what I'll say, all by myself loud and clear and in a strong voice:

'If Harry Potter can go to Wizard School, I can go to Movie Star School.

'Because I, Sophia Oomla, believe in watching movies ...

'Because movies are better than school ...

'I shouldn't have to go to real school ...

'I should go to Movie Star School!

'That's what I should say to everybody ... to all those people in my class who think I can't talk so good ... Melinda. Marilyn. Granger. Mr. Snoggley too! Because I know different. And then I'd say it to Mr. James. And maybe even my Mother. I absolutely don't want to have to talk about school things ... and if I have to talk about school things, I'll talk about school things in one of my many Movie Star voices – because if I have to talk about those types of things, I should talk about them in a VOICE ... so they sound better and because they sound better, they'd be much more interesting for everybody to listen to. And besides, I shouldn't be in any old school. After all, I'm not going to be a Math person or any old History, Spelling or Geography type person. And I definitely don't need a speech therapist who'll just probably make me talk up real smart in a school voice about Math and Spelling. Movie Stars don't talk about Spelling in school voices ... they don't even have school voices, unless, of course, they're playing a character who's in school ... No, they mostly talk about taking trains at midnight. And they walk all around in the fog, and say lovely things, forlorn things, in sad voices and then they run to catch those midnight trains, saying even more words so passionately and then they cry.

But when they run to catch trains, they run ... just so ... They don't go clop clop clop. And besides, that old speech therapist probably wouldn't even like my Movie Star voices.'

But then something very peculiar happened. She suddenly saw her very own self, in her very own school uniform, that for some reason suddenly was sharp-looking, almost glittery, or? was it made out of satin like those old dresses in the old movies? Or was it just her school uniform and it wasn't really shiny at all and it was just her that was shining? And, oh, her hair was fixed astonishingly right. And she looked actually ... not the way she always thought she looked when she saw herself in the mirror ... she looked pretty. And she was happy. Happy was glowing from her.

She was herself.

Not a Movie Star.

Although her eyes were giving off something like sparks. Or were they gleams? In her real eyes! The shine was coming from! Plain-old-her! If a camera had come in for a close-up, her regular eyes would be just like a Movie Star's eyes.

And somehow this very new and very pretty image was projected onto her own inside movie screen.

("Darling, we'll take over this part. You'd better give us another chapter. It'll be like you and the Readers are right there as it's happening."

Readers, never, ever work with Fairies.)

• • • YET ANOTHER FAIRY CHAPTER • • •

"Hey, Author Lady, I'll, like, set the scene:

"The image was so blindingly bright, youdda thought it wouldda woke us all up. It didn't. Did not wake me up. Although, Thee and Free was already awake.

"Thee, after Sophia's not-so-successful turn at the blackboard, had gone back into Sophia to tell us her brand new plan: that we had to get Sophia to stop speaking in movie star voices! and! to get her to learn to like her own voice! before! it was, like, too late! and! we had to, like, leave! Sophia Forever! and! that time was, like, running out!

"But she'd only succeeded in waking up Free. When Sophia began to burn so bright, Be, Me and me was, like, still sleeping. But the brightness did finally wake up Be and Me. I, they tell me, wouldn't budge."

{Readers, I, as the Author of this story, don't understand enough about the brain to fully comprehend myself, let alone explain to you in a plausible manner, exactly how Sophia's image was appearing on her inside's movie screen or that she, or anyone else, even has a movie screen inside themselves. So, dear Reader, you'll just have to take my words, each and every one of them, and the meanings they intend, such as they are written and even as some of them may make no sense, and believe them anyway. Here, and, for that matter, throughout the story.}

"So Author, darling, Reader darlings ..."

And then Me snapped her wand, and I was transported from my studio to Sophia's Remarkably Small Place. Remarkable, alright, not only for its size, but it was cozy, well-lit and very homey. There was a center living area very charmingly decorated with cushy furniture, glowing landscape pictures on the walls and, on the floor, a plush carpet ornamented with arabesques and curlicues. As the carpet wasn't touching the floor but was hovering over top of it, Readers, I'm sure you know what that was. All around the edge of the room were five alcoves which contained the Fairies' bedrooms. Each bedroom was decorated in the distinct personality of its occupants: Thee's, ruler straight, pin neat; Me's, like a page from an ultra-modern dwell-type magazine; Lorraine's, like a princess palace with gilded, carved cherubs dripping everywhere: Be's, a spare, bare, beaded poet's pad; and Free's, like a cyclone hit it. And there, in the center of the center room was, just as they described, the image of Sophia on something that I, too, would have to describe as a movie screen. Considering all of that was inside someone's noodle, remarkable, indeed!

And then I watched Be and Me jump up from their beds.

Me gasped, "What is this blinding light?"

Thee, Be, Free and Me ran to the edge of the bright spot, and regarded it with awe and wonder.

"Fine tis the day in hers brains toot-day ... whatsis whosis couldsis Sophia be and movie star not be? Dream is?"

"Oh Free," said Thee, "you never said a wiser thing, just look at her! But 'dream is,' is right. Would that our work was done! If it was really her in the real world, we would have succeeded brilliantly. What could have happened to Sophia to produce this miracle? Have I been so busy explaining my new plan to you, Free, that I lost track of Sophia's thoughts? I am shocked by these latest, unexpected, out-of-character imaginings of Sophia's—

"Why is Sophia thinking of herself in her school uniform, and not in the costume of a movie star? What could Sophia've been up to? Whatever it was, it had to have happened when I stopped paying attention to her. Is that it? Wait a minute," said Me, "could Sophia have actually heard me whispering about this very thing? Can Sophia hear me?????"

"It's just a fantasy, Me, like dig it, it's cool." said Be. It's just on her mind's movie screen. Like her own mind is making it like she, herself, Sophia Oomla, is the movie star. And, like, she doesn't have to be Ginger Rogers anymore! It's her instead of, like, some other cat. Nice change. But it's, like, I'm always pondering, why does she have to be all beautiful and perfect to be alright? This is, like, the first time she looks like an ordinary ten-year-old girl and she's finally cool about it."

Me said, "I must need glasses – but if I do, I know just the op-gician! - Her uniform, that sack, looks almost chic for a change ... I'm actually coveting one and am even figuring out just who from the Salon-du-Fairies-de-Faree, might be able to whip one up for me. And that, darlings, is the first time I've ever wanted one of those! Why! Sophia's dishy. Almost. And Be, I mean, ordinary? What girl wants to look ordinary? A girl has to start young. It's very competitive out there. That's why the Dispatcher put me here; I'm the one who knows how to dress. In fact, I could teach all young things everything they need to know. I should—" And I gave each Fairy an intense-once-over. "Shouldn't I?"

Thee said, "Me, Be is sort of saying what I've been trying to tell all of you. And which is why I was trying to wake all of you up. But you were sleeping late again. And by the way, we're going to have to put an end to this sleeping late SOME of you like to do during the day. And don't try to tell me you need beauty sleep. Some of you are out entirely too late at night. I know that for a fact. We have to start getting up a lot earlier if WE are to do the job WE are REQUIRED to do."

And then Thee flew up so she could: glare down at them; arch up her eyebrows at them; wag her finger at them; frown at them; then fly right back down to continue lecturing them, "Alright, now, this morning when all of you decided to go back to bed after Sophia and Melinda left the Girls Lavatory, I went back into the classroom. Sophia was certain, because she had gotten sick, Mr. Snoggley would not ask her to explain her answer to Problem # 1—"

"Hey cut the racket, I'm trying to sleep. And turn those elfing lights off!" Lorraine finally woke up.

"But Lorraine, those lights are coming from Sophia, don't you want to see what she's been dreaming about? Look!" said Thee.

"What in the ELF is that?"

Me said, "So look who's just galoomphed herself out of her bed and stomped over to where we've already been standing staring!"

"Hey! I don't galoomph anywhere and I can tawk for myself! So will you look at Sophia! And will you look at me! I just got woke up by inconsiderate noise and blinding lights, and all I can say is, 'Don't she look cute!' "

"Lorraine," said Thee, "this is very important! listen! so you know what's going on! And stop elfspheming! As I was saying … when Sophia had to go back up to that blackboard again and be in front of her class again, and see all her classmates staring at her, she wouldn't speak up loud enough. And she even knew the answer. I could hear her insides saying it. What was stopping her from saying it out loud for all to hear was what she was saying inside herself at the exact same moment – she was telling herself over and over – 'Talk like Ginger Rogers.' And when she couldn't, she kept saying, 'Why can't I?' Well, it's no wonder she has such a hard time talking. There're two parts of her talking at the same time – one saying the answer, the other saying, 'Talk like Ginger Rogers when you say it!' Not only does she have to know the answer to the math problem, which is hard enough, she has to say the answer, making sure her real voice doesn't say it but her pretend voice does. And all at the same time."

"Yeah, Thee, and all while a buncha' rat meanies and an old dried up Mr. Prune, are staring her down." said Lorraine.

"Yes, Lorraine. Can you imagine that? We Fairies couldn't even do that without magic to help us." said Thee.

"Sophia's an elfing elf-wit!" added Lorraine.

"Lorraine, no name calling and stop elfspheming!"

"Okay already, Thee!' snapped Lorraine, "but I can't believe she wants to sound like that actress that came from, like, the cave men days. Or at least everybody's Great-Grandmothers' time. Nobody'd've even known who she was tawking like, that is, if she wouldda ever even finally let them hear her tawk like Ginger Rogers. Nobody knows Ginger Rogers voice no more. And besides Ginger Rogers was famous for dancing not tawking. What gives with this kid?"

Thee said, "I know, Lorraine, I know. And the terrible thing is she even knew the answer. We all know for a fact she can talk. And do a whole lot more than talk. We've all heard her do her movie star voices. But she only wants to talk in movie star voices. I'm afraid, we may even be a little to blame, because we haven't exactly been discouraging her from watching all those old movies because, the truth is, we really love those old movies, too."

"We should be ashamed," said Lorraine, "we are downcast and wretched."

Thee said, "But no more, Fairies! No more losing ourselves in her movies! For Sophia has to learn to like her real self and her own voice, even if it's a little deep, and we must help her. It's just like Be says, she's gotta learn to accept herself. Let's start now. As she's laying there in the back seat and imagining herself in her school uniform and not in movie star clothes, let's all start whispering things in her ear right this second, good things, nice things, kind things, so she feels even better about being herself - so at the exact moment when she's being herself, she'll feel good. We can do this. It's not magic. It's legal!"

And Lorraine began to stretch and fly-in-place ready for a work-out. "We are upcast now."

Until there was a splat sound. And it was loud. Everybody stared at Lorraine.

"Hey, who you looking at? Cut it out cause that ain't me! I'm not, like, uncouth."

"But, now that we were paying closer attention, we could hear that the noise wasn't coming from Lorraine. No ... it couldn't be ...," said Me, "Look! There's Sophia right in the middle of that movie screen! That noise is coming from Sophia up there!"

"Ooh ... shooh ... oooh ... de ... dah ... dah ... be ... doo ... ooh ... bop."

Up there on Sophia's brain's movie screen, she was shooing and scatting and scooby-ing the strangest bunch of sounds that weren't exactly music and weren't exactly words and were deep and low and well - just plain peculiar ... but kind of catchy ... and sort of funny ... very funny. And then they couldn't believe what they were looking at – because now Sophia was dancing the beat of the scat she was singing – and she was only in her school uniform!

"Hey, it sounds just like my old neighborhood. That is so cool! How's she, like, doing that? I love it!"

And Thee said, "Does everybody understand? It's not really her in the real world who's doing that. It's her on her own movie screen that's inside her head."

"Hey, Thee, I know! It's like we're in a drive-in movie! And Sophia, up there on that screen, is like the movie and we're like the drive-in-ees - oh, she's like a drive-in-ee, too, watching herself up there on her own private drive-in movie screen. She's watching her and we're watching her. I love drive-in movies. If youse wouldda woken me up I mightta elfin' seen the beginning, too!"

"Lorraine, what do you think I've been trying to do?"

"Like, what's that? That's even stranger! Is that, like, the real Sophia laughing but quietly so the attentive Mr. James and the chattering Miss Kitty won't hear her? I can't believe it! Sophia is doing all that inside-scatting while her outside-self, the one in the back seat, is, like, laughing!"

"She's, like, cracking herself up!" said Be.

"Be, I believe you are correct. What we are witnessing is what she's actually thinking and what's she's actually doing, at the same time. But we should be used to that, we experience that all the time. But what's so amazing is that this time, she's thinking she's herself. We've seen her think one thing and do another all day long. But it's been such a long time, when she was actually thinking she was herself, instead of a movie star. Maybe, she's finally accepting herself. Although I have to say I'm surprised, I've never heard her sound like that before. They're not the kind of sounds she's always trying to make or wishing she could make."

"Yeah Thee! She's always trying to sound sort of well … like a girl … like a high-pitched, sweet-tawking, girly-girl. And she's got that low, deep, raspy voice – really neat – sortta like my voice. Ya know, making that kind of high voice gotta be kind of hard on her. It'd kill me if I had to go around tawking like that." Lorraine squeaked her voice right on up the register but stopped fast. "Ick, I'd hate to have to sound like that."

"Well, I'm not sure if this will work, but let's start the whispering campaign."

They took off, flew past the movie screen and POOF! the be-bopping, uniform-wearing, happy Sophia disappeared off that screen. The bright lights went out. And then they couldn't see all that good because they were seeing stars but not the movie-kind and they had to come in for a quick landing.

"Ouch is mine eyes. Sting is they burned. Movie gone is it lost? No for it ever?"

"Well, Free," said Thee, "let's wish Fairy wishes that it's not. But remember that Sophia came up with this new image by herself. Unless she heard me whisper that she's gotta learn to like herself. Look, I don't really know what she was thinking right before she came up with this picture of herself in her school uniform because, after all, I was busy talking to Free and not tuned into Sophia. Whatever it was, it must have been good, because it got her to picture herself as she really is and not somebody else. But what about that voice? We never heard her talk in that kind of voice before. If you could call that talking. It was more like singing. But it wasn't. It was an entirely different voice. A unique voice. Not like any movie star I've ever heard her do. And then she started to really laugh because she was happy. Now pay attention! We must do something so this happy Sophia, this uni-form-wearing Sophia, this un-movie star Sophia comes back! I don't know what we can do or how we can do it but it can't be magic. But whatever it is we do do, we've got to get her to like her real self and to like it all the time, and we must do it soon before all of us have to leave her forever."

And Me, Be, Lorraine and Free's wings began to droop and their eyes wouldn't meet Thee's eyes.

"Well, you were looking at me with hope, Fairies, until I reached that part. The bad news part. The part about having to leave Sophia forever. Some of us make it a habit of avoiding bad news. Some of us seem to forget that we were put inside Sophia on a mission – and that our mission was that Sophia should live Happily Ever After – and that we have to be out of her on the last second before she turns eleven years old whether we accomplish our mission or not; and in order to accomplish this mission, we have a job to do; and if we don't do our jobs and do them correctly, we might fail. And, if we fail, Sophia might not live Happily Ever After."

"We, like, have work to do," said Lorraine.

And then Be, Me and Lorraine looked at each other. Lorraine contin-ued, "Okay, Thee! Like, we feel guilty. But we really like to sleep. When we should be, like, ya know working!"

"But all-after, only humans … are we she them you."

"Free, like, Sophia is the human, we're the FAIRIES! Sometimes Free! Ya really get on my last nerve!" snapped Lorraine.

Thee continued, "So we, after all, can do far better than they! This should not be a problem for us."

"Oh for elfsakes! We're Fairies, we can do anything! Itsa piece a' cake!!"

"Cake? Lorraine, some of us are not on a first name basis with cake the way you are."

Lorraine flew up and began to scissor kick the air around Me but Be began to talk wise and Lorraine never wanted to miss what Be said so she stopped and listened to her, "Well, let me, like, help you out Me. Cake is sweet, just the way Sophia will feel when we get Sophia to be cool just being Sophia! And then we'll watch Sophia jaunty on down her path, talkin' away to everybody. And then finally our too-rich-and-too-thin friend, Me'll learn what cake tastes like because maybe she'll finally find out what it means to be all sweet inside."

And then Me cracked her wand and I was back in my studio with the Fairies.

"Author Lady, don't you just love that Be?"

• • • 3:37 PM • • •

As Mrs. Oomla returned each call on her list, her pest was crooning away -

"♪ Is it the CEO or merely the mock?

When is a Showdog? The reeeal? McCoy? ♪"

'Oh! Now you're Frank Sinatra?'

She had to do the impossible: listen to each party and not hear whatever that pest was warbling. *'Trying to drown everybody out so I'll hear what you're saying, are you? Okay! I'll drown you out!'*

But the pest had gotten to her anyway, for as she talked to each person, she fretted, *'I sound like the real McCoy, don't I? I am the real McCoy, aren't I?'* And she made sure that that crisp CEO salute she had so perfected was in every word she spoke. When she had just three more calls to return, the pest gave up. The CEO had won. And she could relax.

'The board can never say I don't return phone calls, and I don't communicate like a Polished Professional. In fact, me and my voice are soldiers in Giggle's army.'

And then off to the roof so she could hop back on the helicopter that was to take her away from this place, that was to take her home.

But her pest was at it again. This time he was screaming 'No!' again. Why was he screaming if she was finally getting away from it all? And he kept on screaming, even as she sped towards that helicopter. But she ignored its 'No! No! No!' again and again and willed her poise, her polish, her professional demeanor to return; especially now that she had to run past phalanx after phalanx of cubes, each filled with a Giggle citizen talking-the-talk: "going forward," "circling back," "net-net," "win-win," "takeaway." Until she passed one phalanx in particular of cube after cube, each filled with precisely one head that was attached to precisely one shirt, and each head popped up and greeted her with something that contained the words "hey" and "lunch-and-learn" in it.

And she had had it; she would've liked nothing better than to join forces with that pest so that she and it could do something most unCEOlike, unladylike even, to those shirts with those heads and their tongues that allowed carbon-copy words to march all over them.

Such a rare expression of solidarity coming from his host encouraged the pest and he broke into song again -

"♪ We are only Copy-Cat-Tongues,

stuck in Cardy-Board-Mouths. ♪

♪ And when we munches, we learns learns learns

what we must all repeat! ♪"

'We?!??

'He's right! I am one, too. Haven't I, The Voice, on my own phone calls, just been letting those exact same words march all over my own tongue? So wouldn't I be obligated to do the same thing to myself?

'Besides even if I did do it to them, I'd only be playing whack-a-mole since more "lunch-and-learns" will keep coming at me as I walk on down the line. And isn't that something the Red-Queen would do? CEOs shouldn't even think of behaving like that! Aren't we in enough trouble already?

'But let's say, for argument's sake, I do tie just one of their tongues to their Adam's apple, a disgruntled employee would no doubt catch me in-flagrante-delicto, shoot a cellphone video of me in mid-delicto and email it to some Occupy group, who would then stick a 'The sport of CEOs' label on it and gleefully post it on their rogues gallery website for our further vilification - oh, and would the board have something to say to me about that! "What have you done to our brand?"'

And though she felt like the howler in the Screamer painting, she talked-Lunch-and-Learn right back at them. And, of course, she didn't howl. *'I am them and they are me and we are all nothing but soldiers in Giggle's army.'*

"Good Afternoon, Ma'am. How was your day? Did you figure out a way to keep the sky out of this old pilot's hair?"

As she crawled into the helicopter, her instrument, her golden tongue was dragging. Down-for-the-count. How could a CEO salute come from that? "Aaaaugh! Ah ... yuuuh ... Cap ... O' ..." Where now was her own language, her graceful flow? And? was? she? grunting? Whatever that was, was downright prehistoric. It wasn't even a sentence fragment! But what should she say? Should she tell him that Mrs. Oomla's Giggle Pop, aka Giggle, aka the Corporation, obliterated her entire day, trampled all over her private, sacred space and swallowed her dreams whole. A brand new venture! Look what was happening to her old-venture. What was it she'd been dreaming about this morning? She remembered one thing. Sneaking up to Birdoffs to shop for warmer clothes. Well, at least she had kept so busy all day, she forgot she was cold and needed warmer clothes.

The only thing she knew she hadn't forgotten from her morning was her promise to call home and speak to Mr. James about Sophia's afternoon appointment with the speech therapist. Mr. James had assured her that Miss Kitty and he were -

"quite prepared to take Sophia to her speech therapist this afternoon, and that Mrs. Oomla has absolutely nothing to worry about."

'At least something went right today!'

Mrs. Oomla sat back in her seat, mute and pensive; the star-talker, the poised-polished-professional, gone, vanished; her phlegm rising and so were her feelings. Feelings that she hadn't given voice to all day. But she wasn't so far gone that she didn't know Captain O'Day was waiting for the star-talker to finish her sentence. She even noticed him observing her surreptitiously through his pilot's mirror. She just couldn't. She couldn't wrap even her very talented voice around all the words she would need to describe *'this very real day filled with so many annoying issues!'* She wouldn't've even been able to describe that early morning ride through her mind's sky filled with the ridiculous, the improbable to herself, let alone him. And she remained lost in thought, til something else occurred to her that hadn't ever occurred to her before,

'If I dared to act on even one of my pipe dreams, look at all of the people that'd be affected. Everything I do now affects so many people. It's not just my family and myself anymore. How can I put all of this and that and everything else together in a sentence that'd make sense to Captain O'Day? To anyone? To even myself? I'll just let that answer float away with all its blanks still in it. People do that all the time. Sigmund doesn't finish his sentences when he's lost in thought. Sophia sometimes can't get even one of her thoughts out of her and into a sentence. Well, if other people can do it, so can I! I don't have to tell Captain O'Day everything. I don't even have to tell myself everything!'

She felt herself relaxing for the first time that day.

'But I can still pretend.

'To invent again. To bring something into the world that hasn't been there before. To dig in the earth again. To grow. To plant. To wear my apron again. To have the earth under my fingernails again. And to never let a corporation anywhere near one of my whimsies, or my tongue, again.

'And, Oh! To not belong to the Species CEO anymore. To not be hated by half the world or envied by the other half. And not to have to Develop Product for a Concept Committee; or to add value to a stock price; or to worry about laid-off factory workers; or for that matter, exploited factory workers in countries I've never even been to. And to never have to hear about CyberSecurity and to record their messages ever again.

And Oh! to get my voice back. To use it the way I used to, to say whatever I think. Whatever I please. Whenever I want. To be the star-talker again. To sparkle! To enchant! To scintillate! To talk without a script! To speak without fear of saying the wrong thing!'

And again she relaxed.

"You hadn't even used your voice to speak up and say the right thing to that Marketing Bedeviler! Extra daffeine in Giggle! Mind-control!"

Him again!

And he was spot-on.

And it hit her all of the other times she hadn't spoken up. About the laid-off factory workers. About the exploited ones. To those board Members! She had said absolutely nothing to them.

At last the scare and the dread and the No! she had been suppressing rose up within her. And then she remembered the presentation that board wanted her to memorize and she was livid.

'They want, as they themselves said, 'you and your pretty voice!' to announce Giggle's news. Of course, they do; they need a pretty voice to disguise their schemes. I should've known the other day that board was up to no good when they inquired of me so civic-mindedly if I might beseech the Mayor on behalf of all Goliathon's children to keep schools open til six o'clock to, as they suggested I say to him, 'ensure that our children receive a thorough education,' but just now, on that very last call, a fellow CEO divulged the real reason:

"Corporate managements throughout Goliathon have been complaining about women employees leaving work early to pick up their children from school. Mrs. Oomla, you're the only CEO in this town that can ask the Mayor this question. We talk like eagle-scouts and yet the Occupiers and their press twist it around to make it sound like we're running rough-shod over others to get what we want but you and your ruby-slipper-voice dazzles everybody and nobody'll complain, not even the Occupiers. You'll get us what we want! Ask the Mayor, Mrs. Oomla, ask the Mayor!"

'On behalf of all Goliathon's children, my foot! On behalf of all corporate managements! The board knows darn well what Research has shown – people who hear me think I'm sweet. And trustworthy. When Mrs. Oomla talks, you can believe her. Ergo, if I ask, the Mayor will surely consider my proposal. Hah! My proposal? That board! Those CEOs! think I would use my voice! to rob children of their free-time, play-time, fun-time? What'll that board want me to do next? Run for mayor so that my ruby-slipper-voice'll make all their wishes come true?

'Those weasels! Even in this age of the slick-con-job when the world knows what they're up to, their weasel brains are still at it. I can just hear them,'

"Weasel-deedee, weasel-deedan, if Ms. Oomla can't do it, nobody can!"

'Our poor citizens! Putty in the hands of weasels! Paying low wages to foreign workers doesn't seem so bad when a pretty voice tells you about it! Adding extra daffeine to a drink to control a mind seems innocent enough when a pretty voice tells you it's been added! Of course, the board wants me to put their words into my mouth. My voice is the best thing that ever happened to that board and their schemes.

'Though, no doubt about it, adding extra daffeine would make those Bull News Network viewers giggle and giggle non-stop. Good! Bull News exists solely to protect the wealthy few and their corporations. When corporations break the law and the regulators catch them; when they underpay their workers and the unions find out; when they overpay their CEOs and the press reports it, Bull News is a master at twisting those sneaky, shameful acts around to make the corporations into the good guys and the regulators and the unions and the press into the bad guys. I can just hear Bull News, "Don't forget you out there in TV land, those corporations may be your LAST OPPORTUNITY for employment, and if we punish your ONLY opportunity, WHAT WILL BE LEFT FOR YOU?"

'Extra daffeine! Hah! It'd serve anyone who watches that network right! Those gullible fools! Hah! After Giggle gets through with them, they'll be daffy, gullible fools!

'How delicious! But how wrong. You can think it! You can laugh at it! But it's wrong to do it! That board is using me for my voice!

'And what exactly do they want my voice to say?'

But she wasn't about to open that presentation to find out.

'Polished Poised Professional! I communicate like a Polished Professional, all right! I have a copy-cat-tongue, all right! Me and my voice are soldiers in Giggle's army, all right! The nerve of that board reminding me to be a Polished Poised Professional! Them and their presentations! That's how they control me and my mind and my voice. Because they know when I speak 'Corporate-Clone,' an entire nation buys product.

'Help! I've been voice-jacked!

'I am a slave of a powerpoint presentation! I am the slave of this board!

'I am their slick con job! I am weasel-dee-dumb!

'Why? Why do I let them do this to me?'

She could only stare into the distance not saying a word out loud, but thinking many. And then she rooted through her briefcase and took out the copy of Charles Dickens 'Hard Times.' And the helicopter took off.

• • • 3:50 PM • • •

As Ms. French was packing up, she realized she hadn't told Miss Kitty that Sophia had fallen asleep in class. She looked for the Oomla's phone number in Sophia's school records and jotted it down in her lesson plan book. When she reached home, she would call Miss Kitty and tell her.

• • • 4:00 PM • • •

Sophia, in her backseat huddle, realized, *'How much I love watching myself! Hearing myself. Even if it's just in my head. I spoke truths, real truths, important truths, truths about who I really am, and said those truths to Mr. James. Melinda Nightingale. Marilyn Kruger. Granger Foxley. AND Mr. Snoggley. And to that stupid speech therapist who I haven't even met. And to Mother, too. And when I fin- ished all that truth telling, I crowed music and strutted, not Ginger-Rogers-style, but Sophia-style, while sometimes making unmusical sounds that reverberated all around my head, and were very interesting to figure out how to make and took real effort on my part to produce. Sometimes I used my deep chest, or my low throat, or my nose, or even my tongue that touched the roof of my mouth or that sometimes would even lay flat.'*

And then it dawned on her; she! wasn't imitating anybody! Even if she hadn't really done a thing and it only really happened in her head.

'In this movie, I'm me and I'm the star! and the director and the writer and the dancer and the choreographer and the composer and the costume designer. And the sound-effects person too!'

And then Sophia felt the limousine go bump a million times and the only Sophia left was the one sitting next to Miss Kitty, the one with the scarf over her head, the one who may have laughed a very muffled laugh but who had not made a single one of her sounds-unique-and-be-bopping audible for anyone but her own ears. The one who hadn't moved at all or danced a step; the one who wanted to be alone right now, but who really really wasn't. And that Sophia, without even having to lift her scarf knew Mr. James, Miss Kitty and her were riding over the cobblestones in the driveway of her house. She was finally finally home after her long, oh-so-very-long, too-long of-a-long-long-day.

'My warm-as-a-tea-cozy, comfy wee bed. That's what Miss Kitty always calls it when she tucks me in it at night - even though she shouldn't anymore because I'm so much older now - but I can hear that bed call me. I'm so close to it now. At last.'

And no sooner than she thought it, did she feel funny inside. She didn't feel sick. She wasn't going to throw-up like she did this morning, but she didn't feel right in her arms and stomach, the places in her that usually didn't feel good whenever she was worried or nervous. Suppose she wouldn't get to her bed after all? From under her scarf, she listened. Miss Kitty had stopped her chattering. Mr. James was still being Attentive. Sophia knew those things without having to pull her scarf away from her eyes. Oh, how she wanted to keep that scarf around her head now that she was home, so everybody would leave her alone there, too, just like they had during the ride. Miss Kitty and Mr. James had thought she was asleep and hadn't talked to her or asked her even one question but she knew that was all about to change as soon as she took her scarf off her head.

'I'll be safe til I get to the kitchen but when Miss Kitty is making my hot chocolate and their tea - that's when Mr. James'll start! His questions'll be very very polite because he's a Mr. Manners, but they'll be just the questions I don't want to answer. Questions about those stupid directions. And then it'll come out that Mr. Snoggley really did remind me about getting the directions! Besides, I did tell Miss Kitty what really happened, and probably she told Mr. James what really happened. And then I'll have to tell him the real reason I didn't get the directions from Mr. Snoggley at lunchtime when I was supposed to, because then I would've had the directions before Mr. Snoggley fell. Oh, why did he have to fall? But oh! because Mr. Snoggley wasn't there, Ms. French let me sleep the whole afternoon! And everybody in the class was so happy for a change. And besides if Mr. Snoggley hadn't fallen, I'd'hadda go to that stupid speech therapist.

'But I better face it ... one way or another, Mr. James'll find out that I fell asleep in class. And then he'll want to know why I'm so tired ... because he knows if I got enough sleep, I wouldn't be tired and then he'll figure out that I'm up doing something ...

'like watching movies at night ...

'or maybe Miss Kitty tells him right then and there that she's seen me watch them ...

'no ... she wouldn't tell him because then she'd get in trouble for not telling him in the first place but somehow he figures out anyway that I'm up at night and then he just figures out all the rest by himself - that I'm up watching movies because Mr. James is just so ...'

"Well then here we are, Miss Kitty, Miss Sophia." Mr. James exited the limousine and swiftly opened the door on Miss Kitty's side. Miss Kitty angled herself with great care towards the open back door, then maneuvered first one leg out, took a rest, than the other, took a rest, got one of her feet on the ground, took a rest, than the other, took a deep breath, and then with one hand on the door's inside arm handle and the other on Mr. James's arm, hoisted herself up from the seat. And on the path stood she.

From under her scarf, Sophia had been listening to the rustle of Miss Kitty's clothing and the sound of her breathing. Sophia was happy Miss Kitty had to take her good old sweet time to get out of the backs of cars since Miss Kitty had bursitis and arthritis in her hip joints. But Sophia knew that Miss Kitty's commotion would eventually stop and then it would be her turn to get out of the car. Soon she heard silence. Mr. James and Miss Kitty were waiting. She, with the scarf still hiding her head, felt the bones in her arms turn to toothpicks as she squeaked down the seat.

"Now, Miss Sophia, if ye don't remove tat scarf off y'r head, ye be tripping y'r fine self."

Sophia stopped and somehow those toothpicks pried that scarf off her head that had conveniently cemented itself there. Just as that scarf fell away, the brilliant winter sun caught her uncovered eye and just about blinded her right there on the car seat and she couldn't see to move another inch, so she didn't. In the next second, she heard another commotion but until the sun got out of her eyes she wouldn't be able to see the commotion, although she sure knew the voice making it.

It was Maria the housekeeper's voice; it was calling out, "Mistera Jamesa, Missesa Kitty, theresa phona calla for either a you froma Missesa Frencha froma Misses Sophia's schoola."

It was all over. And while sun rays stabbed Sophia's eyes, those words - those accented words - double punched her. Betrayed by a person with an accent! Her favorite kind of person! *'No more midnight movies. No more Movie Stars. No more voices. No more talking like a foreigner. No more watching everything about Movie Stars, how they walk and talk and dress. No more practicing so I can walk and talk and dress just like them. No more what I really love the most in the whole entire world. They'll never let me do that again. Children should be in bed sound asleep at midnight, they'll say. Children have to go to school. Children shouldn't be grown ups. Children can't be Movie Stars. Children are just children.'*

And Sophia's eyes filled with tears.

····C··

("Darlings, our eyes were filling with tears, too. When we heard Maria the housekeeper announce that Ms. French wanted to speak to Mr. James or Miss Kitty, we could put two and two together, too. Let me take you back again, Author darling, so you can see for yourself!"

"Loves her movies her. Sad her sad we."

"I'm not so sure, Free!" Said Thee. "We love her movies too! But listen, everybody, she doesn't know what'll happen. She's only imagining what they might say. Mr. James and Miss Kitty may not say what she thinks they'll say.

She's coming up with all this stuff and drawing conclusions before anything has actually happened. She should really just wait and see what does happen. And we should, too. She has such an imagination. Like, for example - I don't remember Mr. James or Miss Kitty or certainly her Father or even her Mother ever saying anything about what children should or shouldn't do. Where does she get this stuff?"

"But hers is afraid - hers is - to best her lost friend. Have who her if friend lost is best?"

"Free, she has us."

"Not of the earth, we. Enchanted we. Not real we, Thee!"

"Not real we is right, Free!" Be said. "I mean we're Fairy real but not Human real. And getting back to what you were saying, Thee – like, you're, like, surprised? She's only been watching these movies, movie after movie after movie since she was, like, seven-years-old. So a lot of what she thinks comes from those movies she watches. Movies've become like her family, because her Mother and Father have here lately and for some time been too preoccupied with their careers to spend quality time with her anymore! And besides, movies, in order to hold an audience's attention, are all-or-nothing, life-or-death. Movies have taught her to, like, exaggerate."

"Hey! First off, this is life-or-death!" Lorraine said, "If I don't get to see my Mafia movies, I don't know what I'll do."

"Lorraine!" Thee screaked, "You were not put inside Sophia to think about yourself!"

Me quickly added, "Yes, Lorraine, you should put Sophia first like I do!"

Everybody burst out laughing. Everybody but Me.

And then I was back in the studio again; Lorraine was the first to speak, "I wouldda've busted ya up, Me, if Sophia hadn't been in such a predicament. Each of us Fairies even had a snappy comeback - including Free - however for once everybody told me they held them inside. See, Me, we spared ya! We remembered our promise to the Fairy Dispatcher to keep the inside of Sophia a peaceable kingdom. Actually, I'll level with youse, my snappy comeback wasn't all that snappy but if it hadda been, ya wouldda heard it.")

·:)·:·

"Miss Kitty, perhaps she's found the speech therapist's address. If you don't mind, I'll take the call. And if both of you could please wait here? If she has found the address, we will have to motor off straight away."

Sophia could hear shoes clicking and then the sun stepped out of her eyes and she could plainly see that those clicking shoes belonged to Mr. James, and he, in those shoes, was hurrying up the path, heading in the direction that would end her Movie Star watching career all together. And Sophia used her sore eyes to watch Mr. James throttle on up the path. And those sore eyes got sorer and sorrier.

Sophia picked what was left of her up, got out of the back seat and slumped over to Miss Kitty. But even as bent low as she was, she was alive with ideas. *'I'm scheming, like characters do in Movies when they're in a jam - I have to find out what Mr. James knows!'* Sophia looked at Miss Kitty and saw that she was shivering. *'Probably she's too cold to talk. But even so, I've got to ask her:*

'Did you tell Mr. James ...

'that Mr. Snoggley did remind me to get the directions?

'Did you tell Mr. James ...

'that I forgot to ask Mr. Snoggley for them?

'Does Mr. James know the truth?

'Because if Mr. James knows the truth, I can't say that Mr. Snoggley never said a word!'

And Sophia felt good suddenly and her head picked up until the next second it fell even lower.

'But I can't ask Miss Kitty that. It looks like I'm trying to be sneaky or seeing how much I can get away with.

'Listen to me ... even thinking this way, shows just what I've become.' But her heart climbed to the very top of her and yelled, *'But I've got to see my Movies. My Movie Stars.'*

But her brains climbed even higher, *'Suppose Ms. French isn't calling because she's found the directions. Suppose she's calling to tell Mr. James and Miss Kitty about me falling asleep in class, because that's what Ms. French said she was gonna do.'* And Sophia worried this telephone call might be even worse for her than she thought. And she got so scared, she couldn't think another thought and pushed everything out of her head.

And there was silence in her but no peace so she tried cheering herself up. *'Maybe Ms. French forgot she was supposed to tell them about me falling asleep in class. Look ... I forgot to ask Mr. Snoggley so maybe teachers forget sometimes too ... Nah! Teachers forget nothing ... But just in case Ms. French did forget, I should ask Miss Kitty, just to be sure I know whether or not she told Mr. James. If I know, I won't say the wrong thing. And that way Mr. James won't catch me in a lie.'*

And Sophia got ready to ask Miss Kitty. She shut her eyes and prepared herself. And she thought what she would say and she was ready and about to say it. But then she thought she'd better think again because maybe she ought to say it another way. So she got ready again and was about to say it but No! she thought she should say it the first way. But then she had to re-member what the first way was. And she thought she remembered and got ready again.

But before she said anything, she thought she'd better peek at Miss Kitty to see if she could tell what Miss Kitty was thinking. Miss Kitty was still shivering, her teeth were chattering, she still wasn't her usual self, talking away as she always did. All Sophia could really see was that she was breathing out waves of white smoky air and Sophia wasn't sure if Miss Kitty was even thinking because, first off, she wasn't talking because her teeth were still too busy chattering. Because sometimes you had to hear what people are talking about to know what people are thinking. Sort of. But not all the time. Because sometimes people are really thinking the exact opposite of what they're saying.

Sophia looked at those waves of white.

And all of what Sophia thought she was more than likely about to say blew out of her, too. And Miss Kitty and Sophia stood by the limousine blow-ing white smoke.

Sophia remembered a Movie where a Movie Star stood somewhere out-side blowing white smoke, too. But the Movie Star was turning the smoke into rings. *'I got no idea how to do that but if I wouldda I'dda done that right now, too!'*

··*·(··

("Lady, ja notice, she's starting to tawk like me? I was, like, so proud!")

··:)··

But Miss Kitty was indeed thinking as she breathed out her wavy white smoke. Her thoughts had a lot of prayer mixed up in them, *'Suppose Mr. James asks me if I really did remind Sophia about her appointment with te speech terapist tis mornin'. 'N tere I am scoldin' Miss Sophia about not telling te truth! Ah, my Blessed Irish Saints will all be desertin' me now, I'm sure, 'n I'll be left on tis good earth wit'out a one o' em t' pray to 'n protect me. But if all o' ye Blessed Irish Saints restin' away up tere in te Clouded Emerald Isle would just hear me out: I can't be tellin' Mr. James every little ting can I now? Tat if I did tell him right 'n truthfully, te very next minute, I'll be losin' me position, ten out on to te street I'd be. So if ye would just stand by me tis one time 'n pray along with me tat I not be gettin' caught in tis wee lie, just in case, I have to be tellin' it t' Mr. James. After all, we are from Ireland, te land of te best yarn-spinners tat ever was! 'N aren't even ye, ye Irish Saints, good blarney-stone kissers each 'n every one o' ye? Because after all ye got y'rselves into Heaven 'n I can't believe ye never made up one story in y'r whole lives before ye did!*

So everyone o' ye should just help me say a good one, just tis once, t' Mr. James, who is notin' but an ole English man!'

⋯⋅☾⋅⋯

("Lady, Thee says, 'Sophia should be asking Miss Kitty before it's too late!'

"And Be says, 'Thee, she sure should. I, like, can't believe it. She can't even ask a simple question.'

"So I says, 'Hey, Be and Thee, this ain't so bad. This could actually be considered strategy because she has time to watch the action first.'

"So Thee says, 'Lorraine, this could hardly be described as action. You heard what she was thinking, she's afraid to speak her mind.'

"So I says, 'Hey, Thee and Be, so she's not tawking and she's blowing smoke instead, so what? Trust me, sometimes it's better to blow smoke. I should know. I wished I'dda done that many a time!' ")

⋯⋅☽⋅⋯

Sophia and Miss Kitty watched the front door open and there stood Mr. James in the doorway beckoning them to come in. Sophia and Miss Kitty jumped. Miss Kitty's teeth stopped their clattering and talk she could and talk she did: "Miss Sophia, shall we be goin' up te path?"

Now that Miss Kitty had come back to life and wasn't so mysterious, Sophia would finally be able to ask her the question. But Miss Kitty spoke before she could.

"Sophia, Ms. French, I'm sure, did not find te directions because if she would've, Mr. James would've come down te path in a big hurry!"

But then Sophia couldn't get her mouth to work because something in there was just awful. And then something in her feet was making it hard to walk up the path beside Miss Kitty. She knew it was her sad heavy heart which now would never return to its proud and rightful home. But still she tried and kept trying to get her mouth to work as she walked up that path. But she knew from the Movies she watched that it was just too hard for anybody to walk and talk at the same time as they made their way towards their doom; and with every 1000 pound footstep she found out that she was no different than all those other people she had seen in all those Movies as they crawled their way towards their THE ENDS, and she stopped trying.

Miss Kitty tugged at Sophia hurrying her as best she could and they managed to reach the front door where Mr. James stood waiting for them. Sophia couldn't even lift her head to look at him. They stepped into the hallway.

"Miss Kitty, I just spoke with Ms. French. Unfortunately, she was not calling because she had found the directions, she was calling to tell us that Sop—"

And then the unmistakable sound of a helicopter could be heard everywhere and Mr. James left that sentence hanging in the air.

'Madam!'

'Te Mistress!'

'Mommy!'

And Mr. James and Miss Kitty and Sophia, who were not even ready to face each other, knew they were not at all ready to face her. And they braced themselves as they stood in the hallway and waited for her to walk through the door. Mr. James preparing himself to tell the truth; Miss Kitty, to tell a lie, and Sophia to not say anything at all.

And as they all stood together in the entranceway, fully braced and waiting, they heard another unmistakable sound, the sound of a car passing over the cobblestones of the driveway, its wheels pouncing on each cobblestone like cat feet, its engine purring as only the most refined of engines would. And then one car door opening and then another and then footsteps coming up the path, each step like a judge's hammer. And without saying a word, they remembered what day it was. Tuesday!

'Lady Pince-nez!'

'Tat Old Hen!'

'Great Aunt Hortense!'

And none of them could believe they had forgotten that today, Tuesday, of all days, just had to fall on the day of Great Aunt Hortense's official weekly visit, too.

● ● ● 4:15 PM ● ● ●

Actually, Mr. James hadn't really forgotten about Lady Pince-nez's impending visit but as he was driving Miss Kitty and Miss Sophia back from school, he had only momentarily allowed Dame PruneHilda to sink to the bottom of his mind because he was one by one pouring over top of her all the facts he knew so far about the missed appointment, and even as Miss Kitty's constant prattle kept pouring over all of that. And so far what had kept Her Pickleship titanicked-below was:

What Miss Kitty had said about the appointment.

What Miss Kitty had said about Miss Sophia.

What Ms. French had said about Mr. Snoggley.

And there was he swimming around in all of that trying to put together all of these she saids and I saids and he fells and understand how they worked together and if there were contradictions and what those contradictions were and how the whole mess had led up to this missed appointment, and him not fulfilling his duty; it's no wonder he momentarily forgot Lady Snotquat steeping below. After all, he would have to give a full report to his employer that covered the facts and was accurate, very accurate, about why Sophia had not been driven to the speech therapist at the appointed time; about why Sophia had not received the directions from Mr. Snoggley; about why, above all, he had not kept his word to Mrs. Oomla, his employer. Not completing a duty was as serious to him as committing a crime was to anybody else. And as he awaited the front door to open and Mrs. Oomla and Lady PomPuss to step through the entranceway, he knew he did not have all the facts and would not be able to give a full and accurate report at this time. But he would. Rule Britainia, he would. He had just questioned Ms. French. He still had to question Miss Kitty. And Miss Sophia. And he would. He certainly would. He was not looking forward to these next few moments, when he had to appear unprepared in front of, of all people, Her Royal Pruneness, the Supreme Sourpuss of the Oomla household. He had left Great Britain certain he would not find the arrogance of entitled personages and hadn't until he had met this one. This one indeed. At least those in England had their titles to make them entitled but Americans had no titles and no ancestry - well, they might have had ancestry but not the type that impressed British people. He may have just been a Butler but he was an English Butler, after all, and HRH Pretension, for all her airs, was just a déclassé American. He would be true to his training; he would not appear obvious; he would at no time forget his place; he wouldn't gloat when he won; in fact, he wouldn't appear to have won at all. But he would prevail. He was An English Butler. Amen. Amen indeed.

● ● ● 4:30 PM ● ● ●

Without even realizing they were, Sophia, Miss Kitty and Mr. James moved closer to each other as they turned their eyes toward the front door. Miss Kitty and Sophia were shivering even before the door opened. And when it did, soon even Mr. James was shivering; for the air that entered that hallway, Sophia was dead certain, came from a meat-locker or from the open mouths of 10,000 polar-bears or from the coldest place that ever was. Yet no one could keep their beady eyeballs off Mrs. Oomla and Great Aunt Hortense as they strode inside. Mrs. Oomla was smiling barely any sunshine, at all. And somewhere in the visage of Great Aunt Hortense, the great continent of Antarctica itself must be drifting, for what was that north in her eyes? south in her lips? west in one crinkled cheek? east in the other? And Sophia never felt more strangled by the cold in her life. And she was glad, for surely she was about to freeze up like a statue. *'Oh, let me! Statues can't talk and tell their secrets.'*

Mrs. Oomla's vague smile faded when she caught sight of them. She looked squarely at Mr. James, then Miss Kitty and finally Sophia. And as she did, each turned the color of shame. Mrs. Oomla spoke not shrilly, not sharply but not at all like singing, "I'm so surprised to see all of you here. I was so sure you would still be at the speech therapist's. It's 4:30 and Sophia's appointment was for 3:45. Surely she couldn't be finished so soon and back already?"

And then she turned to Great Aunt Hortense, spinning her voice back to silk, "Dear Aunt Hortense, Sophia had an appointment with a speech therapist today. We hope you are pleased. We've finally taken measures as you've always said we should."

"Taken measures? taken measures? at this late hour of her life! Now that she is ten years old! and the die has already been cast! the habit formed! Mark my words, Sigrid, she may never grow out of it. When she's older, she may barely be heard when she speaks then, too!"

·∴☾∵·

("Lady, Free says, 'Hers is back, hers is! No me stands her! No me likes how speaks her about PoShia our!'"

"Then I says, 'Elf Toads! That old battle-ax! Just what we need!'

"Then Thee says, 'How can she speak about Sophia like that with Sophia standing right there!'

"Then I says, 'Thee, you couldna been righter. All a youse, listen up, we gotta do something! We can't let her get away with this!'

"But Thee says right back, 'No magic! We're not allowed!! You know that, Lorraine! The Fairy Dispatcher said that if we ever use magic again, he'll see that we are dismissed from Sophia before she turns eleven. And that would be a disgrace for all of us, for our families too. And terrible for Sophia! We just have to believe that Sophia will do and say the right thing and think the right thing. We simply have to believe in her. She can do it. Come on now, say it all together, 'Sophia, you can talk, you can talk just fine.'

"But Lady, not one of us believed that Thee was right. That Sophia wouldda really been able to speak now in front of, like, all these people, especially in front of Great Aunt Hortense and defend herself but we did know that Thee was right about one thing, the Fairy Dispatcher. So we, like, formed a circle and touched our wings and says, 'Sophia, you can tawk, you can tawk, you can tawk …' over and over again.")

.·:)·:·.

Sophia could just about feel her heart as it lay low somewhere inside. *'Barely be heard when she talks! She's talking about me! I hate Great Aunt Hortense. I just can't talk when big people are looking at me. Some big people. But not all big people. I can talk to Daddy, for instance. Besides, I can talk better than anybody. But just not when they're looking at me. But I can talk. I'll show her.'*

And she thought she should open her mouth and say something right then and there because, after all, last night she was talking along with Ginger Rogers, the Movie Star, just fine; in fact, she was talking just like her. So she could really really talk and she would show her right here and now. But her mouth wouldn't open at all. *'All these people make me nervous. And besides, if I would really talk the way I was talking last night, Great Aunt Hortense would hate it and I'd get in worse trouble. I could never talk like that in front of Great Aunt Hortense. Great Aunt Hortense would never appreciate my true talent!*

'True talent? If it were a true talent, I wouldn't be too scared to show her what I can do! But, admit it, I'm just too scared to talk to somebody who is so certain about everything, and so bossy, let alone do my fancy characters for her. I'm never as certain as she is. Or ever that bossy!'

She stood there listening to her insides. She could even hear something saying she could talk, but it was only whispering low, because there was another part of her, 'the fraidy-cat' part of her, that was screaming, screaming out just like a baby does, and wasn't saying words at all.

And there was even another part of her that knew everything that was going on, and knew exactly what to do. She just couldn't do it.

And there was something else. Something she'd seen people in the Movies feel. Despair! She felt Despair! and it was even louder. Louder than all the other parts.

Sophia had been thinking so much she hadn't looked at anybody. When, at last, she did, she'd wished she hadn't. Everybody was looking at her. Really looking. Although she only got as far as her Mother and Miss Kitty and Mr. James. She didn't dare look at Great Aunt Hortense.

But Sophia knew Great Aunt Hortense was looking at her, too. She just knew it.

·∴(·∙

("Lady, I gotta a lot to say, we all gotta lot to say. So, like, give us another chapter. And we'll take youse back again! It's just easier that way!")

·∴)∵·

• • • THE FAIRIES GET YET ANOTHER CHAPTER • • •

And there I was back inside Sophia's Remarkably Small Place. Lorraine was talking.

"Hey, why doesn't that Mother of hers say something to that old Battle Ax and defend her daughter. Her Mother shouldn't let nobody speak that way about her daughter when her daughter's standing right there listening to every word!"

Me said, "Her Mother doesn't say anything because I heard this from the Fairies that used to live in her Mother's head when she was a little girl: apparently, when Sigrid was a little girl she wouldn't have dreamed of ever saying a word of sass to her Aunt Hortense."

Thee said, "Me, you never told us this before."

Me said, "Thee, you know, I don't really like to gossip."

"Elfelant poop, you don't!"

Thee snapped, "Lorraine, such language! It's an insult to all of Fairyhood for Fairies to Elfspheme - to malign the lesser creatures, it's bad enough the poor things can't fly!"

"Thee, okay, okay, it just comes outta me sometimes. But I couldna' let Me get away with that!"

Be said, "So, like, what else did they, like, say, Me?"

"Be, I'll just tell you."

But every Fairy, including Thee, flew as fast as their wings could airy them and hovered over top of Me so they wouldn't miss a word. And just in case Sophia did take their suggestion and talked, each of them tuned their other ear into Sophia so they wouldn't miss that either.

{Don't try this at home, Readers; listening to one thing with one ear, and something completely different with the other. Fairies have pointy ears. Those points act like the points on a compass; they can aim them any place they want – NE with the left and SW with the right.}

"Darlings, how delightful. Being surrounded by my peers hanging on my every word – the way I should be. I, after all, unlike Sophia, can tell a story ...

"So those Fairies told me that Sigrid's family was too much in awe of Aunt Hortense, aka Hortense Von Hoot. Hortense Von Hoot was - and still is - the Expert of Everything. And she insisted they do things her way, because her way was the best way, the right way, the perfect way. She, who never had a child of her own, could, of course, never stop interfering with the raising of any child put in her path, especially her niece, Sigrid, the only niece she ever had. And if Aunt Hortense wasn't an expert about something, she had an opinion about it any way. And she certainly had an opinion about everything having to do with the raising of little Sigrid; how to teach her manners, how to feed her, what to feed her, how she should walk, talk, even what she should do when doing bathroom type things. Aunt Hortense could explain the finer points of doing everything. And unfortunately, there were one too many times when Sigrid's Mother found out Aunt Hortense was right. And then when her Mother and Father died so suddenly leaving Aunt Hortense as her legal guardian, poor little Sigrid ended up doing things the Aunt Hortense way, because it was just too hard for poor, little, breathy, flirty-voiced Sigrid to go up against somebody who was often times right. And, oh, by the way, Aunt Hortense just so happens to be some sort of investing genius and had turned a modest amount of money into a vast fortune. And, of course, she paid for Sigrid's education, insisting she go to, as Aunt Hortense liked to say "the finest schools with the finest people speaking refinely on subjects suitable to such refinement" even when all Sigrid ever wanted to do was to go to the local school with her friends, her real friends, her neighbors and wear her garden clothes – and not her garden-party clothes - her garden-digging ones."

Be said, "Like, Me!', I just gotta interrupt. I see you're, like, tossing your mane and rolling your eyes and making a really grumpy face when you mentioned digging, which is baffling. Me, did you make that face cause Sigrid preferred clothes she could get dirty rather than fancy clothes like you? Or is it ... no, I find this hard to believe ... you couldn't have been on Great Aunt Hortense's side in this story, could you? Especially the part about the 'the finest refinement' like doodoo? No, no, that couldn't be it. It was just you being you, the daughter of Enchantica's own FairiAna du Wintour. You don't like dirt on your clothes or on anyone else's, even if the dirt was there for a good reason. Because even you couldn't be on Great Aunt Hortenses's side, right? But, I do want to congratulate you, Me, for talking about someone other than yourself! And for so long!"

"Very funny, Be; now where was I, darlings? There was nothing Aunt Hortense had to do to improve Sigrid's voice. She was often overheard bragging about Sigrid's voice to the ladies. Although she would correct Sigrid if she pronounced even one word incorrectly or she sounded like less than a melody. It's shocking but Aunt Hortense could make Sigrid worry sometimes that her voice may sometimes not be perfect enough. But in spite of that, it was still very hard for Sigrid to resist Aunt Hortense. Sigrid loved going down to the garden, no matter what she was wearing, and crawling around on her hands and knees and digging up plants that she called specimens. Aunt Hortense paid for all sorts of lessons for Sigrid. For example, when she heard that Sigrid loved orchids, she paid for private lessons at a horticulture garden about the cultivation and care of orchids. She even built a greenhouse for her. But even though Sigrid didn't really like some things about her Aunt Hortense, she felt she ought to like them.

"The truth is, Sigrid was all mixed up and didn't know what she felt about Aunt Hortense. That's what the Fairies who told me all this said.

"But when you put all of that together: Aunt Hortense's belief her way was the only way to do most everything plus persuading others that her way was the only way to do most everything plus keenly bearing down on any individual if they disagreed that her way was the only way to do most everything plus her deep deep pockets … imagine if each of you had to face that day in and day out. Sigrid's Fairies said that Aunt Hortense would've probably been a snob even if she didn't have all that money. And now, Sigrid, with her Giggle Pop, is even richer than her Aunt Hortense. Which incidentally, hasn't stopped Great Aunt Hortense one bit from putting her two cents in about all sorts of issues, including Sophia's speech problems. The Fairies said that Great Aunt Hortense was the kind of snob who is just so convinced that their way is the superior way that they can make almost anyone who ever has to deal with them feel inferior if they don't do things their way. So that was what made Aunt Hortense … made? Listen to me! Makes! such a snob because make no mistake about it - Great Aunt Hortense is still a snob. And since she's older now, she's become very set in those ways – the ways of a snob.

"And, even though I made this point already, I'll make it again - Aunt Hortense had just entirely too much money. And she dispensed it for snobbish reasons. She knew how to do things, where to go to school, what to eat and what fork to use when you ate it - and whatever you do, don't pick up the wrong fork in front of her - and she was all too anxious to let you know she knew."

And Me beckoned for everyone to fly even closer. "I want to make something very clear, I didn't say 'entirely too much money!' Those Fairies that told me the story said that, because you know my philosophy about money. As far as I'm concerned, a person could never have 'entirely too much money.' I never heard of such a thing. Couture, we all know, is expensive. And human Couture is just outrageously so. That's just how THOSE Fairies described Aunt Hortense to me. I like money but I, unlike Great Aunt Hortense, am not at all snobby. For one thing, I'm not at all snobby about my own talents for dressing. And, never forget, I don't tell any of you how to dress. I mean, I may want Sophia to dress a certain way but that's why the Dispatcher put me here."

And POOF! Back in my studio was I.

Me flew to my ear and whispered so that only I could hear, "Author darling. I was always so worried that my Colleagues might find out that I broke the Fairy Dispatcher's rule and lived in Mrs. Oomla's head ever-so-briefly just so I might make some minor suggestions when Mrs. Oomla was having her closet constructed. And her house. And her grounds. And – oops – whenever Mrs. Oomla had to go somewhere - which was every day. But which really was just an idge of a minute. I mean, I can finally relax now that we are setting the record straight. So Author darling, watch as I pick up the conversation again ever-so-nonchalantly, and oh-so-cleverly turn my Cover-Girl face into an open-book."

And Me returned to her usual spot and continued, "When I'm not on assignment and just gliding, like, whatevering about the Enchanted Lands, I'm not at all snobby about my dreamy wardrobe, even though all of you know I really could be."

"See, Lady! As usual, Me ended the speech tawking about herself. Sooner or later we knew she would. But we didn't raise any stink about Me's 'all-about-me' conclusion. In fact, we all began to applaud. For us, Me's speech had been better than any of hers, ever. Me'd been able to tawk about someone else for more than a minute. A few minutes even. What a gas! And even now, in Sophia's absolutely direst of circumstances, we just had to stop and let her know."

"Oh! Author darling, I never remembered them applauding me before. I wished they wouldn't stop!"

"But Lady, even as we'd been, like, listening to Me, we'd never stopped straining our other ears to hear whether Sophia had gotten our, like, message. And finally our ears heard someone. But it sure wasn't Sophia. It was Mr. James who was the first to break the ice that had settled over that hallway."

• • • 4:45 PM • • •

Mr. James was mindful that not only Mrs. Oomla was listening to his every word but so too was Great Aunt Pretense. He must display a command of the situation and do it so that neither one of them, especially Great Aunt Intense, would find any fault with #1) how he conducted himself throughout the incident and, above all, with #2) his reason for not meeting his responsibilities. What he was about to say demanded nothing less than his utmost. So he ratcheted his brow to hauteur, used his Mother Tongue as it should be used, with that pronunciation that makes the English so very English, as if he were Disraeli himself, but more House of Lords than House of Commons, and began,

"Do let me explain, Mrs. Oomla. Mr. Snoggley had a rather bad fall during the luncheon recess; he injured his ankle and, unfortunately, was not able to return to Sophia's class. From what I have been able to ascertain after speaking to Ms. French on the telephone just now, he couldn't walk at all and had to be carried by several persons to the automobile that then took him to Hospital. Ms. French carried on, teaching Sophia's class this afternoon. Under the circumstances, Ms. French and Mr. Snoggley had no time to confer about any pressing school matters, including the matter of Sophia's speech therapist. Which means that Ms. French was not informed by anyone about Sophia's appointment with the speech therapist. Indeed, Ms. French confirms these facts. I can't stress enough to both of you how seriously I took this responsibility and how disappointed I am that I was unable to complete it."

"I see. Oh! Mr. James, I can't tell you how disappointed I am, too!" said Mrs. Oomla.

As Mr. James had been saying all those words in the voice of England, Sophia had been looking at her Mother and had taken a few peeks at Miss Kitty, too. *'Mommy doesn't look right. Is Mommy going to be sick the way I got sick this morning? Or maybe she's just going to cry, because she looks so sad. And Miss Kitty keeps putting her head down lower then low and even lower still on just about every word he said.'*

And Sophia felt terrible for her Mother. For Miss Kitty. Until she remembered why. Her Mother looked that way, Miss Kitty's head was down, all because of something she didn't do. Sophia wanted to run away. Up to her bedroom. Up a tree. Up. Down. Anywhere. Sophia didn't want to know what her Mother would say next. Or do next. And if she stayed, she'd find out. Sophia looked at Miss Kitty again and her head was now so low it was pitiful to behold. Maybe Miss Kitty wanted to run away just like she did. Sophia glanced at Mr. James; he looked the way he always looked. And for a quick second, she felt like she was watching people in a movie. She forgot which one. And people cried in that movie.

This was like that.

Not good at all, and wasn't ever going to be. This was trouble. She was in trouble. That's why she hadn't looked at Great Aunt Hortense, and didn't dare. Besides, she already knew how Great Aunt Hortense would look. Bossy. But Sophia couldn't wouldn't shouldn't move and didn't. Didn't dare. Sophia just stayed glued to her spot in the entranceway, her eyes, on the action, just like she would've if this'd been a Movie she'd been watching where she sat glued to the sofa, her eyes on the screen. But on this screen was no wonderful movie; she dreaded finding out what'd happen on it. But she was stuck and couldn't move. She could only watch and listen.

"Miss Kitty, do you have anything further to add?" said Mrs. Oomla.

Fifty pounds of trouble! That's how her Mother voice marched into her. *'I'm next! What will Mommy ask me? What will I say back?'* and she put her head down just like Miss Kitty had; she couldn't take the action anymore. Maybe she'd drop through the floor and really really land in China.

"Now Missus Oomla, I ah … know for ah a fact … ah … tat Mr. … Ja … James has stated ever … ah … y … ah … ting just … ah … accord … ing t' exactly how everyting really did happen, exactlyright! Tefactsyestated! Occurredliketat! Yes, oh yes, yes, oh yes, Missus Oomla."

'Miss Kitty doesn't sound like Miss Kitty at all. She's too slow! too fast! too shushed! too loud! I can hardly understand her. And she doesn't sound like she means what she just said at all. She didn't speak up the way Mr. James just did. She sounds like she means the exact opposite of what she just said. Like Mr. James didn't really know how everything happened. Miss Kitty won't be able to keep our secret!'

And Sophia didn't dare sneak even one peek at Miss Kitty.

"I'm so sorry, Miss Kitty, I couldn't quite hear you. What did you say?"

"Oh, I'm just a wee bit nervnous, you know, such excitement with everyting happening tis morning … Oh! I mean since tis afternoon 'n … ah … goin' t' pick Miss Sophia up after school 'n … ah … ten hearing … ah all tis ah … about … ah … poor Mr. Snoggley gettin' into an accident 'n …"

"Miss Kitty, you said 'with everything happening this morning?' Did anything happen this morning?"

'This morning! No! No! Is Miss Kitty gonna tell my Mother and Mr. James about my Movies! And Great Aunt Hortense too!! No! Please, please Miss Kitty's Irish Saints, don't let her tell them! Don't let her tell them where she found me this morning!' But Sophia knew now from experience that prayers wouldn't be enough. She'd have to be brave and pick up her head and get Miss Kitty's attention, even if Great Aunt Hortense was standing there. *'Nobody will notice. Because they're all looking at Miss Kitty right now, so now is the best*

time. And I'll be sneaky, really sneaky. And when I get Miss Kitty's attention, I'll shake my head 'no!' but just a little bit so that no one will see me, but enough so that Miss Kitty will know not to say a word.'

✧☙✿

("Author, Lady, ya gotta hear what we did, cause we knew she could do this. Thee didn't like it but Be got up right into Sophia's ear and whispered, 'Not too much and not too obvious or they'll see what you're doing.' "

"Darling, even though Sophia was scared, she picked up that bowed-low-head of hers not too much and not too obvious. And you and me and our Readers all know why. Because Sophia! Must! Have! Heard! Be! And Miss Kitty looked at her and Sophia was thrilled. Her prayers had worked!

"But Prayers! Irish Saints! had nothing to do with this miracle! So Miss Kitty's and her eyes met! and they looked at each other! and Sophia started to shake her head 'no!' but out of the corner of her eye … well … Be, was the first to see because she had flown outside.")

✧☙✿

'They're looking at me! They saw me shake my head at Miss Kitty! Mommy and Mr. James saw! Great Aunt Hortense saw! I wasn't sneaky enough. And not only that, they're looking at Miss Kitty, too. Then back at me. They saw Miss Kitty look at me. They saw us look at each other! That's why they're looking back and forth at us. I can see what they're thinking! Feeling! It's there on their faces. They're thinking –'SOMETHING MUST HAVE HAPPENED BETWEEN SOPHIA AND MISS KITTY BECAUSE WHY WAS MISS KITTY LOOKING AT SOPHIA? AND SOPHIA LOOKING AT MISS KITTY? WHY? WHY? WHY? -

'Because this is just like a silent movie where people's faces show what's what! And they know something did happen and it's not like what Miss Kitty said at all.'

"Now … Missus … I ah know that I just missusspoke meself no … misspoke meself … ah I … No … No … no … ting not a ting did rightly happen in te … in tis morning. No! Missus. I just meant t' say tis afternoon. I'm as I ah said just a wee ah bit nervious … nervnous … nervous not nervious at-tall."

✧☙✿

("Lady, like, not one of them says a word back to Miss Kitty. Out loud, that is. But our Sophia, as you just heard, knew when those people was thinking and what those people was thinking. She was, after all, thinkings most reliable customer.")

✧☙✿

'Miss Kitty sounds like she's not telling the truth. Even if she's not telling the truth, she shouldn't sound like she's not. She's not like Movie ladies when they lie.

Miss Kitty speaks like ladies who don't know how to lie. When I have to lie, I won't ever say lies like that. I'll say lies the way the Movie ladies do. No one will ever know when I lie! And it's all because of how they sound and how they look when they say it.'

And still no one said anything.

⋯⋯ℂ⋯⋯

("Author, Lady, you better believe someone inside Sophia was saying plenty. Thee. 'This is just terrible! Awful! We can't have her learning how to lie like a Movie Star on our watch!'

"Then Be says, 'Oh, would it be better if she told a lie like the way a Nun would tell a lie, like, above-suspicion and all-exemplary sounding?'

"Then Thee says, 'Be, nuns are not known for telling lies and Movie Stars tell lies one right after another, to the press, to their fans, to themselves. She shouldn't lie! Period! That's just a wrongful, shameful thing for her to want to learn!'

"Then Be says, 'Thee, she's just trying to, like, protect what she loves doing. Watching movies and imitating Movie Stars are her, like, favorite things in the whole world, she loves doing that more than anything else. Don't you understand that's the only reason she would lie?'

"So then Thee says, 'No, Be, what she needs to learn is to stand up and tell people who she really is no matter what the consequences are. And even if she is afraid. So I guess I'll just have to do this without your help, Be. Although, what do you say Fairies? Don't we have to stop this? If it's the last thing we do, we can not have her learn how to lie like a Movie Star, can we?'

"And then, Lady, Thee's eyes fell on mine. I knew I'd have to run for cover. I was dyin' to duck my head down but thought I'd better not. Look, everybody, I've always found being a good liar comes in handy most times. I got no trouble telling lies, which I really call Fairy Tales, because after all what am I but a Fairy and what is a lie but a make-believe and what is a make-believe but a Tale? So what am I, who am I but a Fairy telling Fairy Tales? But what could I do? Disagree with Thee? So I says out loud like I meant it, 'Yeah, oh yeah Thee, yeah, Thee, you're right we can't. No, we can't,' displaying my down-pat technique that Sophia so hoped to acquire and that she so wished Miss Kitty had.")

⋯⋯☽⋯⋯

"Miss Kitty, is there anything else you wish to tell me?"

"Sophia, is there anything you wish to tell me?" Said her Mother like so many floating rose-petals.

But like so many sticks and stones were those words to Sophia; and her ears stopped listening, her thoughts stopped thinking.

"Oh, Missssuuus Oomla, I don't really have a ting more t' say. I was just a bit confused, tat's all. Everyting is just fine, except of course tat our Miss Sophia didn't get t' go t' her speech terapist, after all. Which was so disappointin'! Tat's all. Please pardon me silly stutterin' mouth."

"You are sure you have nothing further to say to us, Miss Kitty? Sophia …?" Sophia didn't like to hear her Mother speak that way at all, and Sophia began to feel even more scared.

Mrs. Oomla looked down at her daughter but she had to bend to really see her because Sophia's hair half hid her face.

Sophia's eyes met her Mother's, but she could only look her prayer into her Mother's eyes - please please don't say anything else like that and please please leave me alone.

Quickly, Mrs. Oomla straightened herself and turned her attention back to Miss Kitty, but this time her Mother was speaking the right way, and Sophia felt much better as soon as she heard her. "Oh, Miss Kitty, we all could use some refreshment. It's just so cold. Perhaps you'll prepare some hot beverages to warm us up, some tea, and hot chocolate, all piping hot, for our very welcome guest and for all of us, and if you would be so kind, would you also assemble some treats. We're all shivering, and there is only one place to go in this house, when it's this cold outside. Aunt Hortense, let's go to the conservatory, we will have our tea in there; that's where the sun streams in, it's the warmest place in the house.

"Sophia, please accompany Miss Kitty. And, Miss Kitty, please see that Sophia assists you. Then Sophia, after you've helped Miss Kitty and had some hot chocolate and a healthful snack, please start your homework immediately."

·∴☾∴·

("Lady, it's about time Motor Mouth protected her daughter from that grouch. Ya know, sometimes I wonder about that Mother of hers. Maybe her Mother just doesn't understand Sophia. My Mother didn't understand me. And I don't like to see nobody not being understood. It reminds me when I was, like, a Fairyling.")

·∴☽∴·

'Hah! I don't have to visit with Great Aunt Hortense today! And Mommy didn't ask any more questions. And Miss Kitty didn't tell on me! Nobody knows anything. I'm safe. My secret is safe.'

And Sophia hopped the bullet-train out of there.

• • • 5:00 PM • • •

Sophia slammed into the kitchen even before swifty ole Mr. James but certainly before pokey ole Miss Kitty. She peeled off then flung her gloves, scarf, coat and hat on to the table. Then she sat at that table and examined the wooly mound of soft that beckoned her to escape from things-hard and people-difficult. And right smack down on the mound her head plopped.

Mr. James arrived with his hat in his hand and his overcoat, scarf and gloves folded symmetrically over his arm. And from her own twisted heap, she watched him go over to the garment closet and hang up each of his pieces with grave care. Sophia picked up her head and stared down at her wrinkled-crinkled, sorry-sack-of-stuff.

"Miss Sophia, perhaps you would like to bring your things over and we can hang them up together."

But Sophia was burning to pick through the mound and find her coat, her scarf, her hat, her gloves and fold them over her arm with just as much care as he did; for she was burning to be Mr. James, and not in-the-here-and-the-now as her own self. Then, too, she was burning all-over to run everywhere, because after all, she had finally escaped the awful glare of the spotlight that had been shining on her; the spotlight that came from all those eyes staring down at her as she stood in the hallway of the Castle L'Oomla awaiting her sentence. And she shuddered in fear again.

But she didn't dare mess up the very precise arrangement she had just made over her arm. So she picked up one foot carefully, then the other, and in a kind of trance – but watching her every step – went over to the closet. After they had finished, Mr. James picked up his newspaper, sat down, opened it and, just before he buried his head in it, said, "Well, Miss Sophia, something steaming hot is what we all need. And when Great Aunt Hortense and your Mother are served and all of us have had our refreshment, perhaps Miss Kitty and you and I can discuss the events of the day."

'Oh No! He wants to talk about that stupid speech therapist? again?' And Sophia felt another bad feeling creep inside her but this time she didn't let it stay; she pushed it away. Not one of them had found her secret out just now. She was okay! Great Aunt Hortense. Mr. James. Her Mother. Nobody! *'Mr. James doesn't know what I do at night. Miss Kitty didn't squeal. My Mother doesn't know either and that's all that matters. So how could Great Aunt*

Hortense find out? Or Mr. James? Mr. James couldn't want to talk to me about that, so who cares what he wants to talk about!'

Finally, Miss Kitty trundled into the kitchen and hung up her own things in the closet but as she walked away, her hat, that she had placed on its own special hook, fell to the floor. She turned around to look at it lying there all alone, "Oh! Now what made ye jump from ye cozy perch with its grand view of te kitchen? Ye can hardly see what's goin' on from down tere can ye? But maybe ye just have a mind o' ye own like te youngsterish sprite tat wears ye?" Miss Kitty picked up her hat, blew on it hard and put it right back on its hook. Then she went to work, pulling kettles and saucepans and tins and serving spoons out of their cupboards.

"Miss Sophia, please get y'r sweet self over t' te butler's pantry 'n wheel in te teacart."

As if she were just made the star in her very own Movie, Sophia tore herself away from the kitchen which prompted Miss Kitty to call after her, "N don't ye be doin' any cartwheels y'rself with tat precious antique in y'r hands as ye're wheelin' it on its journey here, tank ye very much Missy! It has survived well over a hundred years 'n I'm sure it would be down 'n dumpish t' be finally meetin' its maker with a flibbertigibbet wrapped around its handle instead of te Duke of Dandee!"

"Whatssa flibdery-jibbit? And who's the Duke of Dandee?"

"Tat's any missy who endangers old tings, like rickety tea carts 'n cranky old cooks. 'N te Duke of Dandee would be te one t' be behind te wheel a' such a splendid cart because after all he himself surely is one splendid fellow in his tails 'n a topper."

'I'm not a flibdery-jibbit but I am surely the Duke of Dandee.'

Sophia, who was now officially free from all worries, had returned to her favorite thing in the world - the land of fascinating figures. "I'm the Duke of Dandee," she said in her Mr. James voice. The Duke took the long way so he would have more space to dandee through. And through the front pantry, the back pantry and then into the butler's closet, he went, where the cart in all its polished wooden splendor sat patiently, expectantly waiting another expedition into the farthest reaches of Oomla-land, which the Duke would be happy to provide. He bowed low and straightened high and, sticking his pinkies out, gripped the handle. And because perambulate is what Mr. James called walking about, the Duke said, "Shall we perambulate, venerable relic? Guests have arrived and your services are required."

When Sophia had left the kitchen, Mr. James had gotten up from his seat at the table and soft-shoed over to the doorway that led into the front pantry, leaned around its edge, saw that Sophia was not nearby, and then, still on soft-shoe, went over to Miss Kitty who was standing at the sink. As their eyes crossed, he said distinctly yet discreetly,

"Now Miss Kitty, in all candor, I did not get a thoroughly confident feeling when Mrs. Oomla asked you if you had anything to add to my account. For example, I know you said you didn't mean to say 'this morning' and that you corrected yourself and told Mrs. Oomla that you meant to say 'this afternoon.' However, I also remember that you and Sophia were very late coming down for breakfast. And since that did happen 'this morning,' I would appreciate your telling me what happened - what actually happened - this morning to cause such a delay. I am, after all, your supervisor, and really must know."

"Oh, Mr. James, it's just like what I told you tis morning ..." And Miss Kitty had to remember what exactly she did tell Mr. James this morning so early, but she couldn't for all the tea in Anywhere. So she'd just have to phlumph up to a lush plush whatever she said, "Oh, Sophia was just a little extra tired tis morning. Ye should know Mr. James, starting around ten, which is creepin' up t' tose teen years, because now tose youngsters have two numbers in ter age 'n not just one anymore, 'n youngsters, ye know, get a little harder to rouse up in te mornin', 'specially a mornin' such as tis one. So cold, I had a terrible time gettin' up from me warm cozy meself. 'N don't even ye, as disciplined as an Admiral in Her Majesty's Service have t' admit tat ye own self did too ..."

And then the wobbly wooden wheels of the cart could be heard squawking and screeching and careering their way over each wooden floor board. As the cacophony got closer and closer to Miss Kitty and Mr. James where they stood by the sink in the kitchen - that blessed cacophony – Miss Kitty was very relieved to stop her phlumphing. But called out, as if she wasn't, "Miss Sophia, now please be watchin' tat Nineteenth Century antique tat's older tan all of us put together." And by the time that remark was out of her mouth, Mr. James had quietly returned to his seat at the table, and buried his head in his newspaper.

'Good,' Miss Kitty thought, 'I have more time t' prepare meself for any such other type question he might feel te need te inquire about.'

However, just as Sophia and the tea cart were about to make their grand entrance into the kitchen, Mr. James leaped from the table and hooted, "Blast! I'm afraid I've left the car parked directly in front of the house where Great Aunt Hortense's car should be. No doubt, her driver has parked behind us. And that can't be! - our car stationed where their car should be!

- when Great Aunt Hortense is visiting!   Their car should always be at the very edge of the main footpath so that when her door is open, Great Aunt Hortense can step out of the car and onto that footpath's direct center. I must move our car so her driver can pull her car into place; that way, at the very least, when she's ready to leave, her car will be where it should be. Please do excuse me." And he dashed to the garment closet, then into his things and was gone.

The Duke thought better of making his entrance into the kitchen *'so crash-boomily! so un-Duke-ily! how un-Dandee-ly!'* and slowed himself and the teacart up considerably. *'After all, I'm about to appear in front of my subjects! How will they know that I am the Duke of Dandee, Wheeler of the Royal Cart, disguised as I am in a silly school uniform, if I don't at least enter with dignity?'* He pulled himself as straight as a Palace Guard and grandeed into the kitchen. He noticed that one of his subjects had mysteriously disappeared; he would investigate later. The Duke stopped his teacart on the invisible dime directly beside Miss Kitty, who was arranging delicacies on a three tiered plate.

"Here I am at your service, Madam Kitty, and as you so commanded, here indeed is the teacart. Indeed," said the Duke, in a voice deep and booming, with much gravitas, for the Duke was hardly a frivolous fellow.

"Indeed, y'rself. 'N who might I have te pleasure of addressin'?"

"The Duke of Dandee!"

Miss Kitty laughed so much the crumpet in her hand kerplopped to the floor. "Now, Miss Sophia … I mean, Your Dukeness, would ye kindly go over t' y'r spot at te table 'n sit y'rself down, or Great Aunt Hortense won't have a bite t' eat."

The kerplop neither amused nor irritated the Duke. He just waited patiently for Miss Kitty to finish speaking and when she had, he said, "My pleasure, Madam!" Then the Duke bowed low and withdrew, walking backwards to the table, never smiling once or even grinning.

···**(**···

("Laughter!" said Be.

"Better than cry laugh is!" said Free.

"A crying day that ends in a laughing day is the best day." said Thee.)

···**)**···

Miss Kitty was still laughing, and the more she laughed, the more the Duke didn't. Which only made Miss Kitty laugh more and she couldn't stop herself even as she loaded the teacart with the linen napkins, the teapot, the creamer, the sugar bowl, the dishes, the silverware, the 3 tiered plate piled high, smoothed her hair, wiped her hands on her apron, went over to a drawer, pulled out a fresh apron, removed the old, put on the new and began to roll that teacart with its luscious burden of delectables towards its destination. And just before she reached the door, she called out, still laughing, "Well, Duke, wish me luck 'n meanwhile, help y'rself t' te hot chocolate tat's in te pot in te table. N look about, ye'll see tere are several tempting morsels fit for a grand personage such as y'rself."

With his subjects all gone, the Duke was alone and, in a blink, he was gone too, and Sophia sat down at the table. She reached for the pot of hot chocolate, and poured the steaming rich liquid into her mug. As the smoke rose, it filled up her nose ... and got in her eyes and it smelled wonderful and she was warm, finally, warm ... and she felt so light ... and so very tired ... and her eyes drooped ... she would eat ... yes, she would eat ... and she reached for a butterscotch crumpet because no grown-ups were there telling her not to eat sweets but it never reached her plate because Sophia's eyes were closed and her head was down, then dropped, then flat on the table, and she was asleep, sound asleep because she was tired. Dead tired.

• • • 5:30 PM • • •

After Mr. James had garaged the limousine, he returned to the front driveway so he could continue his conversation with Luther, Great-Aunt-Hoot-Aunt's chauffeur. Luther was another lad from England. They often played cards together on their nights off, and every time they played, without fail, they would reminisce about Britain, Great Britain. By the time those nights came to a close, when one or the other was pocketing the pennies they had won, Great Britain was Great no more. It was Greatest! Britain.

Mr. James had a habit of calling Luther's employer names. Every time he thought of the old Hoot, he came up with a new one. Of course, no one knew it because he never said the names out loud. After all, he was a professional and employers were off limits as subjects to discuss idly. Or jokingly. Especially jokingly. So no matter how suitable, how hilarious the name was, they were his little secret. In fact, no living soul had ever heard him utter a one.

But he yearned to let them, as the expression goes, rip, whenever he was around Luther. For, after spending his working, waking hours over-ing and under-ing, hither-ing and thither-ing Aunt Hortopolis, Luther could be downright gloomy. Poor poor Luther, being dragged from pillar to post by The Lady OverLordy! Mr. James hoped if he made him laugh, he might cheer him up. Or at least de-gloom him. But Mr. James knew he must maintain a professional tone at all times, even with his peers, and not discuss his employer, or any employer. All Butler/Chauffeurs knew that. And though it killed him, he had never slipped and was determined he never would.

And he wasn't about to now either, even though he knew he had to attend to unfinished business. But where was the harm in an all-purpose chat-up? And with boasts and bavardage, he degloomed Luther again.

He would get to the bottom of that missed appointment.

Or he would not be able to hold his head high in front of HRH Hootle-Toot, again.

He couldn't let Her! have anything on Him!

Why, there would be no peace in the Oomla kingdom.

Or in him. Especially in him.

He shook Luther's hand, bid him adieu, and then placed himself in the direct center of the footpath, ready to dash again, but found he couldn't dash anywhere. He could only tarry. He was even keen to whistle his own music before he had to face theirs but it was just too cold outside and he couldn't get his lips working properly. And then, too, the limey-kick of box-wood from the procession of carved, stone urns that lined both sides of that grand walkway was blowing all around, transporting him to a time lost and long ago when his Mother and Father, for oh so many years, were the devoted caretakers of a grand-estate and he used to tarry through its gardens. Mrs. Oomla's were as grand and as tasteful as those.

Although ever since Great PeckSnout had taken it upon herself to not only SniffSnuff HerOldeCarCass around THE OldeCarCastle AND the grounds AND the gardens, too, she'd been making the gardeners so nervous that they now trimmed and weeded and raked so efficiently that the place had taken on an unearthly kind of perfection.

·∴(·∴

("Unearthly!?" said Lorraine, "Me! don't tell me ya was messing around there, too?!"

"You think I would go anywhere near fertilizer!!" said Me.

Enough! you two.)

·∴)∴·

Mr. James had to admit that though he was indeed a practitioner of order, this kind of order made even him anxious. He looked forward to the day when Mrs. Oomla would be back in charge of Castle L'Oomla.

But that glorious boxwood - though trimmed to a suffocating perfection - still worked its magic on him for as he wended his way past planter after planter - each packed to its proper measure - and towards the front doorway and his duty, it was as if his Mother and Father were there beside him and it was not a time lost and long ago at all. How they had done everything within their power to instill their thick-and-thin, hell-or-high-water, do-and-die attitude in him. They had even given him the Christian name James even though his surname was already James but they wanted him and the world to know who he would be someday. The quintessential Butler/Chauffeur. James J. James. Though the James family had been in the service profession for generations, they wanted something more for him. No one in the James Family had ever climbed as high as that on the service profession ladder. They always told him, "Son, we've given you this name not just for the sake of merriment amongst one and all who'll say your name but, more importantly, so that everyone will know who you are. And most important of all: you will know who you are. A Butler/Chauffeur. Remember, a Butler/Chauffeur is Dignified. Discreet. Reliable. Son, that's what a Mr. James should be. So if you really want to be a Butler/Chauffeur, it'll be up to you to make sure you are all of these noble things. Remember, the Butler/Chauffeur holds the pivotal position in the households of distinguished families – only persons with fine character and an excellent work ethic need apply."

Through their lessons, their examples, their words, their deeds, how they had worked on their young son's character. They didn't have to work too hard: their dream for him was truly his dream for himself for he very much wanted to be a Butler/Chauffeur, too. And when he was accepted in the finest Butler School in all of England, how they had scrimped and saved to send him there.

He would honor his parents' memory. He would do the right thing for this distinguished family. Rule Britannia! He was ready for whatever - whatever? whoever! – he had to face. And like an arrow towards its prey, he made straight for the conservatory to see how Horror-Tale's visit was proceeding. *'Speaking of names, speaking of merriment, it's jolly good my parents can't hear what's goes on inside me – that would be the real horror tale! But there must be somewhere where I can lighten up. Besides, by keeping it all inside, I am discreet, just as they always wanted me to be.'*

He knocked on the conservatory's wide-open French-doors. He couldn't see either Madams through the lush, towering foliage and the masses of blossoming orchids, but lilting over top of the sweet birds twittering away in the adjacent aviary, was Mrs. Oomla's even sweeter piccolo. And below that, of course, was HootTube-ulous's unmistakable under-hoots.

"Mrs. Oomla, James here. Pardon the interruption, I wanted to see if you needed anything."

"Oh, Mr. James, please come in. My dear Aunt Hortense and I were just talking about the situation - the speech therapist situation, I mean. Perhaps you would have a moment to join our conversation? We hope you know, we don't blame you about the missed appointment. We understand that things can go wrong as they obviously did today. But I am not comfortable and neither is Aunt Hortense with everything that Miss Kitty said. She seemed to be hiding something. Did you get that feeling as well?"

"I do understand your concern. I intend to speak to Miss Kitty on the matter. I had just started to, actually, but Miss Sophia came back to the kitchen, and I had to stop. You see, I wanted to hold this conversation with Miss Kitty first alone. And when Miss Kitty and I have talked and she has answered each of my questions to my satisfaction, then I will speak to both Miss Sophia and Miss Kitty together."

"Now, Sigrid, one must apply the strictest standards to employees who are not truthful with their employers. I would never tolerate such behavior in my staff. And furthermore, it is a bad example to set for all who witness such behavior. I am certain she lied. And we all were witnesses. And remember Miss Kitty said this lie in front of you, her employer; and Mr. James, her direct supervisor; and me, a close relative and an elder of the village; and Sophia, a child! To lie in front of a child! Why surely that child will see with her own eyes and hear with her own ears that a grown-up just told a lie. A child must see consequences when a grown-up tells a lie. What lesson will a child learn when that child witnesses a grown-up lying and sees that the grown-up has suffered not a thing for telling this lie? The child will learn the wrong lesson! The child will learn that nothing happens to people who tell lies. And that is not the lesson any relation of mine should ever learn! A child must see that grown-ups admit their mistakes and must never see grown-ups who won't. For how else will the child learn the correct lesson? The ethical lesson.

"After all, Sigrid? Mr. James? Where would the world be if the people in it were not ethical? Suppose a banker said he had reported all of the day's deposits when he knew he hadn't? Suppose a pilot swore he talked to air traffic control when he knew he hadn't? Suppose a bridge engineer claimed he had inspected the bridge when he knew he hadn't?

"Do both of you understand that chaos! danger! surely awaits those whose paths cross the path of an unethical person? Can't you see how Sophia might come to think it is alright for her to lie if she sees grown-ups lie? I firmly believe that any child who observes such behavior when they are young is in danger of behaving the same way when they grow-up. A child must see that if a person does wrong and admits it and owns up to it, that the person will be forgiven. After all, humans make mistakes. But to lie about a mistake. To cover it up. Why I wouldn't have that in my household. I could not accept it. Nor should you."

'Great Aunt Brimstone!' Oh! how Mr. James wanted to exclaim, but, of course, he did not. *'What dangers await those who cross the path of Miss Kitty!? Miss Kitty ... an unethical person!? ... '* But that thought joined all the other unspoken thoughts lined up inside him.

Mrs. Oomla seemed to have lost her voice because her mouth was open but wasn't saying anything. Until out trickled, like a leak from the saddest pipe on the organ, "Aunt Hortense, none of us are really 100% sure yet whether Miss Kitty has actually lied. So let me ask you, Mr. James, do you think something didn't seem right when Miss Kitty was speaking? I do admit, she usually doesn't stammer and turn all red and hesitate so."

Mr. James must show Great Aunt High Test he could handle this situation. He would opine like Disraeli, and because he, like his hero, hailed from the land of pomp and streaming colors, he'd outfit each and every one of his words in a full-dress-uniform. "Mrs. Oomla and Madam, I am not at all ready to say that Miss Kitty was lying. However, I do believe something was not quite right with what she said. But I, like you, am not sure precisely what that would be. But I assure you, I assure both of you, I will get to the bottom of it."

"Thank you, Mr. James. You will let me know, I'm sure."

Mr. James hoped that every saluted syllable he'd just uttered, hadn't ruffled a single frond or petal growing in the conservatory; and, further, after listening to him, that Aunt HorseTiCulture and Mrs. Oomla would feel confident in him as a supervisor, as someone who could take care of Miss Kitty, Sophia, the missed appointment ... everything. "Do understand that tonight is Miss Kitty's night off, and I expect Miss Kitty is now tending to Miss Sophia before she goes off duty at 5:45 and it's just about that time now. So I may not be able to find out until tomorrow, but I assure both of you, I will."

"Oh, yes, by all means, let's not bother Miss Kitty on her night off. She certainly deserves that, after all, we are fair minded people and she works so hard for all of us—"

At that, Great Aunt Hortense, rolled her eyes to the heavens and huffed.

"… now, Aunt Hortense, after all—"

"That wouldn't be how I would handle this situation! I would want to know a lot sooner than that. I, for one, would not like to have a liar under my roof for even one night. However, if you insist—"

This time Mrs. Oomla's voice was neither the saddest pipe nor the sassiest one but the perfect blend to enter Aunt Hortense's ears for, after her years of experience with her Aunt's auditory chamber, she knew just what size crescendo was allowed to enter there, "Yes, I do insist. Aunt Hortense, we must give Miss Kitty the benefit of the doubt. She has made such a contribution to our household, she's such a good cook and she has such a warm spirit and is a kind-hearted old soul plus Sophia loves her so. And please do remember, Aunt Hortense, a person is considered innocent until proven otherwise. So shall we say when I return home from the office tomorrow, Mr. James and I shall meet again."

"Now, Sigrid, I really must insist that I be here as well."

"Dear Aunt Hortense, that really won't be necessary. Mr. James and I will be able to handle this without your fine guidance."

"I'm afraid, both of you will be too soft on this individual. I've seen quite enough in this household. After all, look how long it has taken you to address Sophia's speech issues, Sigrid! Why I've noticed a certain laxness in this household for years that I've never spoken to you about."

'*Too soft! I am Miss Kitty's direct supervisor. I am not soft on her or any one of my employees. I may be fair but fair is not soft. How dare that … that …*' But Mr. James wouldn't use that name, even inside himself; it would have been unfit to inhabit the mind of a service professional. Though just this once, he found himself wishing he could say out loud what he would only let percolate inside him. But he knew that if he did that he too would be seeking other employment just as Old Aunt Ug wanted Miss Kitty to do.

"Dear Aunt Hortense, I must beg to differ, I believe I run my household very well."

"Running your household well, Sigrid, when your daughter is being neglected! While you have been off during the day making this sensationalistic invention of yours a household name all throughout America, and, I understand, are now trying to make a household name throughout the world, your daughter can't get a simple sentence out of her mouth when it is her turn to speak up in class. Or to speak to me for that matter. Her Great Aunt! Or to speak to adults. And I ask you, how many children are fortunate enough to have a Great Aunt that is still living? And incidentally, it's not only her teacher who says that about her but I have also heard that said by the villagers themselves, even members of my various committees have whispered this to me. You really must know these things, Sigrid, what your neighbors are saying, what members of the community are saying about your daughter. Sigrid, your daughter has a problem. And it's time you took care of it."

"Why, Sophia is not being neglected at all. I ... Miss Kitty ... we ... all ... I ..." And then Sigrid's eyes filled with tears and she couldn't go on. *'I thought Aunt Hortense was proud of me and my accomplishments! She should be pleased I'm doing exactly what she always wanted me to do. No! Insisted I do. And now she's acting like I'm doing wrong! I can't seem to please her no matter what I do!'* And Sigrid could no longer contain the feeling that had been accumulating within her another second and she began to sob.

'Ah, to do a rondelet of fisticuffs onto Old Hortensaurus's jaw!' But Mr. James knew what was required of him and did it; he kept his hands by his side and his eyes averted. That he had to be around when family members had a row was the part of his job he did not like. However, ever since he had joined the peaceful Oomla household, he hadn't witnessed even one of them and had almost forgotten what they were. But from his experience in other less tranquil households he knew that he had to wait on his spot til he was given further instructions or was dismissed.

Neither had occurred yet. He was relieved; he wouldn't have wanted to walk away from Mrs. Oomla when she was so obviously distressed. He had never seen her cry before, and without even thinking whether it was the proper thing to do, he pulled out his fresh white handkerchief and offered it to her.

Mrs. Oomla accepted it gratefully and, with the song just about crushed out of her, she blubbered, "Oh, thank you, Mr. James, I'm so sorry, I just had a difficult day. And I'm so disappointed that Sophia had to miss her appointment. You will all please excuse me. I get up at such an early hour and my job is sometimes very stressful."

"Now, Sigrid, I dislike to see you cry. And I know the things I have said upset you. But I, after all, am the bearer of bad news and such persons are seldom ever greeted with a posey of forget-me-nots, are they now Mr. James?"

Mr. James would have preferred to sing the Irish National Anthem before he would answer a direct question from Hortle-Ax when the answer required him to agree with her, but he did his duty, "You are correct, Madam."

'You are correct! Did I just say You are correct? Listen to me! After she just insinuated that I am incapable of handling my duties! I have to stand here and speak to her like this and act like she didn't just insult me! Like nothing is wrong!

Act like I agree with everything she said! After this Miss Kitty affair is sorted out, I must speak to Mrs. Oomla and correct, for the record, Great Aunt Hobgoblin's characterization of me. But before I do, I will show Great Aunt HiggyFiggy! I will show both of them that I am a strong supervisor. She called me soft! She should never mistake fairness with softness when she talks about me! And she won't ever again!'

And his legs carried him out of the conservatory and it wasn't until he was back in the kitchen that he realized he had walked out of that conservatory without being dismissed by his employer. His legs hadn't waited for their orders. His legs had had enough. And so, he realized, had the rest of him.

• • • 6:00 PM • • •

But there was no one in the kitchen. Where was Sophia? Mr. James wondered. Where was Miss Kitty? In a pantry? But it was so quiet everywhere. Surely he would have heard some noise, coming from somewhere, especially if Miss Kitty was around. Those two were seldom this quiet. Finally he did hear footsteps coming towards the kitchen, but not from any of the pantries; they were coming from the main house instead. Heavy, slow, soft-soled. Not fast, not a child's. Not a woman's high heels either. *It's Miss Kitty, but she's by herself. Why isn't Miss Sophia with her?'*

"There you are, Miss Kitty. I wondered what happened to you and Miss Sophia. Where might Miss Sophia be?"

And placing every single word on a steamroller, she answered him, "NowMr.JameswhenI had come back intotekitchen, te wee one'shead was downon tetable, FLAT OUT, 'n she was DEAD ASLEEP!"

She gulped and tore on, "Since I've begun working here for te Oomla's I had never seen her do te likes a tat before! O'course I know tattat WAS NO GOOD. So I ups'nSHAKES her 'n WAKESher 'n SHE couldbarely BUDGE! Barely open her EYES!"

"Now, Miss Ki—"

But Miss Kitty wasn't to be interrupted, "Mr. JamesIknowwhat you're tinkin' butshewouldn't BUDGE! 'N Iknowwhatyou tink o' tat: so tat'swhyIhad te do sometin'! Te SEE YOUR CHARGE DEAD to te WHOLE WIDE WORLD! FLAT OUT ASLEEP on te table? So finally I do get her te wake UP by shakin'her'nfinally SHE OPENS HER EYES 'n allshecould-saywas, 'I'm so tired, please, please can I go to sleep?' 'N t'look at her, ye would've tought she'd had never slept a dayinherwholelife. So I said, c'monnowMissy, I'mtakin' ye upstairs to y'r own bed where yecanfallasleep in a PROPER—"

"Miss Kit—"

Though losing steam and out of breath, she charged on, "Mr. James, oh now, I know, you'rewonderin'about tat, but wouldn't ye have tought te same ting? Now wouldn't ye now—"

"Miss Ki—"

"Oh, Mr. James, Mr. James, ye don't even have t' tell me tat ye agree with me! Tat it was time she justwenttobed. Ye 'n I both know it's irregular like t'go t' bed right after school 'n without herdoin'her lessons but shecouldn't have satUPRIGHT in a chair t' evenhold A PENCIL in her hand. 'N I don't want her to get sick, bein' as it's so COLD outside already. 'N I know you wouldn't want tat either. 'N we all know tat's what happens t' people who don't get enough sleep. Tey starts t' get run down 'n ten te next ting ye know, tey've got te grippe 'n te chilblains. Or even worse tan tat. 'N if she gets run down, without enough sleep, tats whatwill happen. Tink of how many appointments she'd be missin' ten. So I wanted her t' take a good long rest. 'N tat's exactly what I had her do; in fact, tat's where I just come from. I took her upstairs 'n put her in her bed, in her pajamas, 'n in a half minute, she was sound asleep.

"Mr. James, any second I meself must be goin'. Me niece, Margaret Finnegan, te actress is coming. Do ye believe, Mr. James, from tat show she was in down tere in tat city, Mrs. Oomla's city, te grand one, she earned enough money from her wages 'n was able t' buy herself her very own car? Ah, now it's second, maybe even tird hand, but she's sittin' her fanny down on four wheels 'n it gets her around just fine. 'N she's able t' get up here without havin' t' take te ferry all te time. She's comin' to pick me up. Isn't tat just grand? I don't know where she's takin' me ... but anywhere is just fine with me ... even if it's just a spin."

Outside in the back courtyard could be heard the tinniest toot toot of a car horn and the wheezing final gasps of an engine, and Miss Kitty took off for the garment closet, got her coat and hat and ran out of that kitchen as if she never even heard of arthritis.

'I AM too soft! And Big Hurt herself will make sure I know that! The truth hurts. But this time, the truth shall not Hurt'ense me! But how? I couldn't get a word in edgewise with Miss Kitty. Here I am, Miss Kitty's direct Supervisor, trying to speak to her, and there she is, my employee, and she's not letting me speak. Would someone have ever dared do that to a statesman? I can't imagine Disraeli ever letting that happen to him. People may have dared - surely he would have stopped them.

And that's what I should have done to Miss Kitty. Stop her. But I didn't. That's not how a Direct Supervisor should behave and that's not how she should behave towards me. I couldn't get even a half a word out!! She was deliberately talking that way so I wouldn't be able to ask her anything! She's hiding something. She made such a point of telling me how tired Miss Sophia is. Why I wonder is Miss Sophia so tired all the time? I see her go to bed myself by 7:30 or 8 every night. Why is any person tired all the time? A person is tired all the time if that person doesn't get enough sleep. If Miss Sophia is going to bed every night by 7:30 or 8:00 every night, she shouldn't be tired ... so maybe that's it. We thinks she's in bed, but she's not sleeping. She's not sleeping when everybody thinks she's sleeping. Could she be up to something? What could that be?'

• • • 6:30 PM • • •

When Dr. Oomla finally got a break, he immediately called home. Mr. James, just as immediately, picked up the call; however, he and Mrs. Oomla had already heard about the trouble at the Institute. News traveled fast in that village, especially the Institute's news since so many of the village's residents worked there. Dr. Oomla told Mr. James that he would be staying at the Institute that night. He couldn't leave his Artistes when they needed him so much. Mr. James only had time to say "Yes, Dr. Oomla, I will certainly tell Mrs. Oomla," before Dr. Oomla had hung up and gone straight back to work.

• • • 6:35 PM • • •

Miss Kitty knew if her hip doctor would've seen her scramble out of that kitchen and across the courtyard and then practically pole vault herself into niece Margaret's car, he would've given her the name of another kind of Doctor; the Dr. Oomla kind. But she had escaped Mr. James and his questions. *'Tat's providential, surely!'* Though, as she maneuvered herself into her seat in niece Margaret's car, her hips were making sure she knew exactly how they felt about their exertions. "Now niece Margaret, before I say a word o' greetin' t' ye, I have t' talk t' me two old hips! Now listen both o' ye, I'm going out because I need t' have some fun 'n so do te both o' ye, if ye ask me, so stop y'r carryin'-on! Besides, as both o' ye very well know, I can't very well be leavin' ye behind!"

"Well, Aunt Kitty, you better tell'em good because in honor of my new car - and a fine one it tis - we won't be shivering anymore on that ferry

– you and me are driving down to the city to have a proper Irish dinner in a proper Irish establishment. And you better warn those two old things they might want to rest up because there will be dancing. And singing too, and they're not to be stopping you from doing either, thank you very much!"

"Now did ye hear y'r niece Margaret ye two? 'N if ye know what's good for ye, ye'll listen!" And Miss Kitty made up her mind no matter what their answer was, she would have a good time tonight. And she might even dance a jig or two. Or six. And so would they, no matter how much they complained.

Miss Kitty and her niece Margaret Finnegan had Shepherd's Pie in Finnegan's Pub, one of Goliathon's many such fine Irish establishments. "Oh! Now what do you think of that, Aunt Kitty, they named a pub after me here in America?" At Finnegan's Pub, there were always musicians playing some Irish songs and everybody who came in were soon singing or dancing or both and nobody cared if you did either badly or even if you danced with its swinging door. Niece Margaret had to keep getting up from her seat to dance with all of the young lads that were lining up to dance with her. Which pleased Miss Kitty immensely. Oh, how she hoped niece Margaret would find a decent one and get married and have babies so that she wouldn't have to work so hard on that stage anymore! Singing til she had a sore throat! Dancing til she had swollen feet! Or, worse yet, starving because she wasn't on a stage at-tall since she couldn't find work and had no prospects neither! But niece Margaret loved every roller-coaster second of it, and couldn't be talked out of it no matter how many times her Aunt Kitty tried.

When one of niece Margaret's lads said to Miss Kitty, "Well, now we can't have any foot that trod on the blessed sod of Ireland not christening the floorboards of the finest Irish pub in this fair city, can we now?" Miss Kitty got up and danced with him, ignoring every kick and prick and needle that her hip was shooting in to her. And Miss Kitty danced the jig so rightly, the whole pub stopped dancing just to watch her. After those pub-goers saw Miss Kitty jig, somebody or another would ask her to show them just exactly how she did what she did and she showed'em and all the while her hips kept warning her to stop. All too soon, it was nine o'clock, time for Miss Kitty and niece Margaret to pile into the tin lizzie and drive back to the village. The entire ride back, they couldn't stop either laughing or singing their hearts out to the Irish songs pindling out of the tin lizzie's radio. And there Miss Kitty sat, singing and laughing, riding back towards that village, every worry and fret and ponderosity about Mr. James and the missed appointment and her forgetting to remind Sophia about the appointment and her lying and saying that she did – in fact, all of what she went through that day felt to her like they were at least three counties away, even as she knew she was getting closer to them on every mile. But her hip joints weren't fooled. No, they were adding a low lament the whole way back that she was doing her best to ignore.

Eventually, they came to the sign that said the village was just a mile away. But when they turned onto the road, they soon saw something wasn't right. Abruptly they stopped their singing and laughing. A line of cars had come to a complete stand still at the entrance to the village gate. When they got even closer, they saw that the gate was shut, the entrance road to it blocked by several barricades and in front of the barricades, were several police cars with their top lights spinning and flashing. Miss Kitty never remembered seeing the gate shut before or, for that matter, those types of police cars in the village either; the Theriffs and the Sheripists didn't drive the fancy cars with the bells-and-whistles.

The tin lizzie took the last place in the line. Niece Margaret turned off the engine because she saw that all the cars had theirs off, too. But that meant the heater wasn't on and soon their teeth were doing the jig. Miss Kitty managed to get her mouth to say between its clicking and knocking, "Now tis is downright ridiculous for a person t' be out on sssssuch a night on a dark dark road in te bitter cold 'n not t' know why. A person is liable t' catch ter death." And Miss Kitty opened up the door, telling niece Margaret to stay put and protect her tin lizzie and that she alone would go up there to find out what was wrong. Miss Kitty picked herself up as best she could on hips that were screaming at her for not bringing their cane and hobbled onto that road. As she crept past the parked cars, she looked for the officer in charge. But when she made it to the gate, she saw that the officer standing there was really Mr. Pierson, one of the Theriffs. He just wasn't dressed up in his usual Theriff clothes but was wearing something that made him look like a uniformed police officer.

"Now Mr. Pierson, how do ye'do? I wish I could be sayin' tis a fine evening but I cannot. If ye wouldn't mind lettin' me on te secret – what, my fine lad, is te hold up? I n' everybody else in tis line'll be catchin' ter death soon if we can't be gettin' out of tis terrible cold."

"Oh! Miss Kitty, it's you! Good evening, good evening. There was trouble in the Institute. Some of the inmates have escaped and we had to close off the road. We don't want any of our citizens driving through the village and meeting up with 'em. We don't know what they'd do and we can't take any chances. So Miss Kitty, each car will have their own police escort back to their destination. We've already begun. I can only spare three police cars to do the escorting, so that means we can only escort three cars at a time. It shouldn't be long for you now. So Miss Kitty, why don't you - and isn't that your niece, the actress, in the car - and how is she doing? - still acting and dancing down in Goliathon is she? - my wife and I saw her dance in a show and she was so charming and talented – well, why don't the both of you wait inside the gatehouse to keep warm? Any minute it'll be your turn."

Miss Kitty couldn't believe what she was listening to. Inmates? Why did he call the Artistes inmates? Everybody knew you call the people that lived in the Institute, Artistes and that you called the people that live in the prison down the river, that Sing-Sing place, inmates. But you don't call the residence of Dance-Dance, inmates, their feelings would be hurt something terrible. And what about Dr. Oomla? Was he alright? Were these inmates going to hurt anybody? She had always thought of those Artistes as harmless creatures. And what were these poor creatures going to do out on such a cold cold night? Surely they would catch their death, too. Miss Kitty waved at niece Margaret to join her and the both of them waited in the Gatehouse for their turn, their high spirits all but drained out of them.

• • • 11:30 PM • • •

Sophia felt her stomach rattling through all the nothing inside it looking very hard for something that wasn't there. And then she woke up. Flooding through her window was the hugest brightest moon that was pulling the sleep out of her; as if there really was a Man in the Moon who could pull sleep from anybody he had a mind to pull it from. She wanted to tell him something and she mooned-up her eyes and pushed back, until she realized. "I know why you're doing that, Mr. Moon! You must know I'm hungry and you have cheese so I won't be hungry. Oh! If only you could give me cheese, I could stay right here and not be bitten by the cold, or anyone else, if I must get up to find food. Oh! How I wish you would talk back to me."

⸱⸱⸱☾⸱⸱

(And Free laughed, Lady. Free was the only one of us who hadn't gone to sleep yet and was lying peacefully on Sophia's ear lobe gazing up at her best friend the moon. "'Love moon the man, me do too, PhoSia – no – PoShia

– no! Wish talk. Wish friend. Moon friend, SOPHIA! I right got her name finally-ly!' ")

·⸱🌙⸱·

"A bucket 'a bones, that's what I am!"

Sophia remembered Miss Kitty taking her up to bed when Great Aunt Hortense and her Mother were having their hot hot drinks on that cold cold day out in the Orchid Orphanage – what her Father called her Mother's glass plant house - and then putting her in her pajamas, piling her up with covers and tucking her in. But that was the very last thing she remembered. Because here it was – and Sophia looked at her Rapunzel Rapunzel Let Down Your Hair alarm clock – 11:30 at night, a half an hour before Rapunzel let down her hair because she let down her hair every time it was 12. "Miss Kitty or Mommy better not ever find out how many times I'm up at midnight to see Rapunzel do that."

Sophia had never remembered feeling so hungry. She might really have to get bitten by the cold, or worse, for how ever would she be able to wait til breakfast time to eat? That was hours and hours away. She needed to eat something good. Something delicious. Now. But to get something good to eat, she would have to go to the kitchen and that was way down there and she was way up here. "To get there, I'll have to go all the way down all of those steps and all the way through the long and dark and freezing cold corridor caves before I even get to the steps. But I've already done that so many times before when I have to watch my movies in the middle of the night and I have to go from my bedroom on the second floor to the TV room on the first floor since there is absolutely no other way to get there since I still can't fly."

·⸱🌙⸱·

(So Free says, Lady, " 'Oh, is sad so, no she can fly. Humans little poor. Is better much so to fly.' " Lorraine continued, "Free really wished that we was with her because every time Sophia wanted to fly, all of us'd feel such piteous sorrow for Sophia. And all the other poor poor humans. But we know humans'll never be able to really fly. The only flying humans'd ever be able to do is in those elephantine contraptions of yours. And the contraptions have all the fun!")

·⸱🌙⸱·

"But I can tip-toe through the dark when I absolutely have to and I haven't died yet. I've taken myself through every glop of gloom in this gigantic Castle L'Oomla that is so spooky at midnight. There are so many shadows and noises and creeks and groans and whishes and rrrs.

And all of the walls filled with all of the paintings of people with all of their eyes that are watching me sneak by on my tip-toes because I bet our pictures are just like those Harry Potter pictures, too." She had stolen a flashlight from Mr. Dougherty's tool box, their Mr. Fix-it man, and taught herself to walk while holding it in her shaking hand even as its beam shook where ever she aimed it. But she would only shine it through the darkness in the corridors and down each and every step and never ever would she shine it up on to any of the walls. She was terrified of finding out that those painted-personages had jumped out of their pictures and were standing in the shadows waiting til she tip-toed by so they could capture her and throw her into their picture lands. But she also knew that if she ran down that corridor, somebody in the house would be sure to hear her so she never ran, even though that's what she was dying to do. She'd only let herself walk on her tip-toes right down the direct middle of the hall, but as fast as she could and, when she got to the steps, she'd put the flashlight in one hand and hold onto the banister with the other.

But what she'd never taught herself to do is not be scared to death when she did it. The only time she stopped being scared to death was when she had actually made it inside the room where all her magic happened. Her Movie Star School. That's where her friends were. That was the land of her dreams. And wishes. And big big hopes. As soon as she made it through all the spookiness, she somehow forgot how scared to death she'd just been.

It was her Magic Room.

If she didn't think she could do something, in there she thought she could do it. If she didn't think she could say something, in there she thought she could say it. And most importantly, in there, she could say it, in there, she could do it. If she didn't like her voice, in there she loved it. It was always like that in there. If she wanted to talk one way or another, she could talk one way or another. Or as many ways as she could think of. In there. She always sounded just right. In there. But that's because she was in there.

Sophia said to the moon, "I can do this. I can get to the kitchen. I already know how. If I don't, I'll starve to death. And I'll be lying dead here in my bed - soon. Just like what happens to starving people in the Movies. Just like that poor beautiful lady who was starving and sad and lying in her bed and there was a man right beside her who loved her, too, but he could only watch her lie on her bed and listen to her sing the saddest saddest song to him and when the song was over, she died just like that. And maybe I'll die just like that, too. Maybe even by tomorrow morning. And I won't be able to get up to go to school."

And that didn't seem so bad. For a minute. "No, because if I die, I won't ever become a Movie Star. And I won't get to talk to my Daddy ever again.

And no one at school or anywhere will ever hear me talk as beautifully as my Mother talks. No one will ever know that I can talk just like that, too. And I won't see Miss Kitty anymore and Mr. James won't talk to me about England."

She knew what she had to do. She didn't want to die. "I must go downstairs and get something to eat."

Sophia, as fast as she could, put one foot on the rug, then the other, and stood up. She had on her warmest pajamas but she still felt cold. She ran to her closet, and because the moon was so bright, she could find her slippers and her robe immediately. "I know! I know! When I get to the kitchen, I'll get all the food and take it into my Movie Star School, and I'll watch a movie and eat it all up in there." And in that radiant moonlight, she easily saw her flashlight's special hiding place. She had found a place for Mr. Dougherty's flashlight that no one would've ever found. Especially Maria, who dusted every crevice and crack of the Castle L'Oomla and knew where everything belonged everywhere throughout the whole entire place. Maria knew exactly what should be here and what should be there and what shouldn't be anywhere. And she would tell you too real quick if a something was where a something shouldn't be. Sophia had to be very careful of Maria. She didn't want to get caught stealing stuff. It was bad enough she took things from her Mother's closet but stealing from Mr. Dougherty, a person who wasn't even a family member! She knew she was not ever supposed to do something as bad as that! She sure was glad that Maria didn't have to dust her Mother's closet, the place that Sophia was always "borrowing" stuff from. No, only those people that came from that department store were allowed in there. And they never noticed what was there or what wasn't, and neither did her Mother either because her Mother didn't really like clothes. She liked plants, especially plants that grew flowers on them, and clothes sure couldn't do that. Sophia had figured that out a long time ago. Her Mother was only happy when she was in her Orchid Orphanage. Because that's when Sophia heard her Mother singing. Sophia's mother never sang when she was in her clothes closets. And besides her Mother always forgot she was wearing fancy clothes because she was always digging away in her Orchid Orphanage in those fancy clothes and her fancy clothes were always getting dirt all over them because Sophia would see those dirty clothes in a separate pile because that's where those department store people would put them. And that pile was always pretty big. But if Maria's job had been to take care of that closet, Maria would've noticed every little thing missing. And would've found what was missing from it too. Sophia knew she had to put that flashlight in a place that Maria would never dust. So she hid it in one of her shoeboxes. Maria only dusted the tops of shoeboxes. She'd never dust inside a shoebox. That's what Sophia hoped. And so far her hoping had worked because Maria hadn't dusted inside that shoebox and hadn't found Mr. Dougherty's flashlight.

But just as she put her hand on that shoebox, she pulled it away as if it'd bit her. The flashlight wasn't there! The flashlight was in the TV Room. She had left it there because last night at the end of the movie, she had fallen asleep on the sofa. She hadn't snuck back to her room with the flashlight guiding her way as she usually did. She hadn't put the flashlight back at all! Miss Kitty had found her early this morning sound asleep and carried her up to her room because Sophia was so dead tired. Of course, Sophia forgot all about the flashlight; she couldn't even walk that morning, how could she've ever remembered to pick up the flashlight? And now the flashlight was prob-ably lying on the floor around the sofa. "Unless Maria found it. Because Maria finds everything. And if she did find it, probably Mr. Dougherty already has it back in his tool box. And then I'll have to steal it back from him again."

·∴(∙·

("Author Lady, I heard 'steal' and woke up and told Free, 'I'm in! Sophia gotta steal, that's, like, my specialty!'

"Free says to me, 'Raine Lor, no! Lor Lor! Oh! Poshia! No! Sophia! Sophia gotfor the lightflash! In Star Room of the Movie floor!' ")

·∴)∙·

"... Unless Maria gave it to Mr. James. And then Mr. James will be won-dering how Mr. Dougherty's flashlight ended up in the TV room! I can't go downstairs without my flashlight. It's too scary. It's too dark.

·∴(∙·

("And I says, 'Yes, you can Kid! What's her problem, I travel around all the time – dark – light – whatsa difference? What is it with these humans! Different creatures are out at night then during the day! That's all ya gotta know. Ya just have to figure out where they are and who they are and if they want trouble! Is that so hard Free? It's, like, common-sense! This kid's gotta get tough Free!' "

"And Free says, " 'Is Trouble Trouble is, Lor Lor, no me like like!' ")

·∴)∙·

Sophia was struck again by all the moonlight streaming through the win-dows. She hadn't had to turn her bedside light on to find her slippers in her usually dark closet. Maybe she could get to the kitchen after all. "My room isn't the only room with windows in it. And the moon's light will reach far and brighten up the dark places. It's everywhere outside. The only dark place will be the long corridor cave with all the picture people. But I'll just have to tip-toe faster than I've ever tip-toed in my whole entire life. Like that Mother in the Movie who walked through the darkest night to save her baby who would've died if she didn't. Except that Mother walked! She! didn't have to Tip!Toe! Tip-toeing is harder. But Movie Stars are always doing hard things!"

Sophia ran to her bedroom door, opened it and peered out. Darkness. The moon's light did not go as far as there. And the most scared feeling she had ever felt filled her up. And then something inside her screamed Don't go! Don't go! Go back to bed!

("Author Lady, Free and me had been listening and watching and feeling every feeling Sophia felt. Neither of us had screamed that scream. We knew who the screamer was. It was Sophia's own self. Free agreed with the screamer and didn't want Sophia to go either. But I didn't agree one bit plus I thought that screamer was a yellow-bellied-chicken. Our itchkens ain't so chicken!")

But Sophia was starving and she didn't want to die.

And she opened the door. It was dark out there in the Castle L'Oomla and she'd have to face it. And she tipped her toe onto the floor, and then tipped and toed herself along the corridor where the picture people were. Who were watching her through that gloom, through that dark. She made it past two doors. Just three more to go before she reached the grand staircase where the big windows were, where the moon and his light were waiting for her.

And then she did something she never did. She ran. On her slippered feet. Her every footfall, a thud. Which echoed in her ears. In the picture people's ears. And throughout that gloomy corridor. Thudding. Running. She got to the next door. Thudding. Running. The next. Thudding. Running. The last. Turn, and there the staircase would be. She turned … and tripped over the edge of the hallway carpet and fell flat on her face, a huge thud. Which the whole world heard. Probably. She lay splat on the floor, wanting to punch the carpet so much but she knew the carpet wouldn't feel a thing but her hand would …

("Author Lady, don't worry, I smacked it a coupla whacks! And she's wrong! The carpet wailed!")

… and she also knew she had to get up but she lay there anyway.

But she didn't want to die at the top of the stairs and have everybody find her there, dead and with a black and blue mark on her forehead; she'd look so clumsy and not like a Movie Star who would never have been caught dead in fleecy pajamas or with a black and blue mark on her fabulous face. And she got up and ran. Down the stairs; through each and every room even as she heard her own foot-thunder, til she made it to the kitchen.

Though she stopped running when she got there, she did everything as fast as she could. She knew what she wanted. Peanut butter and jelly and bread. She even turned on all the lights in the kitchen to help her find the food faster, AND, to make sure that no picture people had followed her. She saw that those kitchen lights streaming out all those kitchen windows had cascaded into the moonlit courtyard turning that courtyard into a glowing, glistering spectacle that could have been seen for miles. But Sophia was too starving to care.

And because she was a starving person who didn't want to die, she made it her life and death business to put into both hands whatever a person absolutely had to have to make many peanut butter and jelly sandwiches. One jelly jar - one spoon, one hand; one peanut butter jar - one knife, the other; one bread loaf, underneath an arm, one plate, underneath the other. With her teeth she turned off each and every light. Then she walked carefully back through each and every room, past the grand staircase and then down the back corridor that thankfully wasn't so dark because it had help from the moon.

At long last she reached the door to the Movie Star School. She stepped inside. And her stomach knew it wouldn't starve, that it no longer had to swallow air and crunch bone to stay alive, and her heart could finally finally slow down and do its dance. Though the rest of her felt like crying and did because she had made it and made it alive into her land of dreams.

As her tears rolled down both of her cheeks, she put down the delicacies on the low table in front of the long curvy sofa and put *Rats in the Gutter* into the DVD player, a movie about people who lived in Goliathon, that city Sophia had never been to but her Mother went to every day. These rats sure talked in dirty-dirt voices …

·∴·ℭ·∴·

("Author Lady, Sophia was tawking about my people! Incidentally, Lady, it was I who was there with her on this caper. Free, when she knew Sophia was safe, had finally fallen asleep.")

·∴·ℭ·∴·

But this time Sophia was really only examining the food in front of her, and soon she was a very happy child eating a peanut butter and jelly sandwich with an eye to making another.

• • • WEDNESDAY, FEBRUARY 4, 12:25 AM • • •

Was when Miss Kitty and niece Margaret finally reached the Castle L'Oomla, after they had followed the Police Car assigned them. Miss Kitty kept her eyes peeled as they drove through the village, scouring the roadside looking for any signs of any such inmates, but she was very disappointed. She hadn't seen a soul. She was hoping to, at least, give one of them her coat and scarf and gloves, and so, too, was niece Margaret.

Rather than drive all the way back to the city, niece Margaret was spending the night in one of the many spare bedrooms in the Castle L'Oomla. She would drive back to the city in the morning. Miss Kitty brought her to the room and was about to go to her own room to finally lay down her aching bones, but she got a queer feeling and didn't dare ignore it. Not after all that happened that day. So even though the time was fast approaching for her to be at the bottom of the grand staircase to meet Mr. James and Mrs. Oomla, she knew what she had to do. She must go downstairs to make sure everything, and everyone, was in its proper place. Surely Sophia was too tired to get up tonight to watch movies! But she'd better check to make sure. Miss Kitty had come to the conclusion late in the day that she'd better watch this child far more than she had been.

'After all, I'm te only one here who knows what she does. 'N it'll be up t' me t' put a stop t' it before te both of us are gettin' ourselves in t' trouble!' She took herself down the back stairway to Sophia's bedroom, one hip-aching-step at time, to make sure Sophia Oomla was in Sophia Oomla's bed.

Miss Kitty opened the door to Miss Sophia's bedroom. The moonlight flooding that room revealed in an instant and with great clarity that Sophia's bed was empty. Miss Kitty's heart jumped, sank, drowned, rose, over and over again, as she tried to race down those backstairs to the first floor, but could only limp as quietly as she could because she certainly 'as te Good Lord sits above us all,' did not want to wake up Mr. James. And besides, that was all her old hips would let her do.

Miss Kitty opened the door to the Television Room just a crack so as not to startle its occupant, if indeed, it had an occupant, and peeked inside. It, indeed, did. For there was Sophia watching an old movie. But Sophia was not acting and prancing all over the room this time; no, she was sitting on the sofa, quiet as a wee mouse, with peanut butter and jelly all over her face; although the wee mouse sure was wolfing down in a few gulps that peanut butter and jelly sandwich! Of course, she was hungry.

She hadn't had a speck of dinner and nothing when she came home from school, and when Miss Kitty had cleared the breakfast dishes after she had returned from taking Sophia to school, she noticed she'd had barely nothing at breakfast either.

Miss Kitty inched into the room, and keeping her voice down as low as she could, she said, "Oh! Miss Sophia! Look where ye're! Exactly where ye're not supposed t' be!"

But as careful as Miss Kitty had been, Sophia was so taken aback, that her sandwich fell out of her hands and plopped all over the sofa, spreading jelly and peanut butter in clumps and blobs on the sofa's Imported French Silk Upholstery. "Oh no! Maria better not see this or she'll kill me! But Miss Kitty, I was starving!"

Miss Kitty wobbled over to the sofa to help clean up the mess but saw no napkin, no nothing to wipe the sofa with. Sophia was scraping the peanut butter off the sofa as fast as she could with the knife that she kept licking clean, even as she kept talking, "I'm not really watching Movies. The Movie is just keeping me company while I eat."

"Keeping ye company when ye eat! Oh child! Ye shouldn't be doing tis atall! I should've put a stop t' tis a while ago when I first saw ye! 'N look at ye now up at tis late hour again. Tis has got t' stop, Miss Sophia!"

⋯⋅C⋅⋯

("Author Lady, I was actually watching the movie and I was steaming. 'Elfing Elf Plops! Yakky-do busts in here yakking-doing, just when the guys are about to pull the trigger! I can't hear a word they's saying!' I had no choice but to fly off Sophia's ear, which technically the Fairy Dispatcher does not approve of, since we're supposed to stay on the premises at all time, unless we are on a break or on official business. 'Why doesn't she stroll in here when Sophia's watching those dancing movies? If Miss Kitty knew about me, and knew about how much I loved these movies, I know she wouldda shut her yap up! It's like the real thing, with gangsters and everything. Wow! These creeps are just like my uncles!' ")

⋯⋅Ɔ⋅⋯

Miss Kitty had to use the hem of her woolen skirt to remove the jelly. Together they worked until they got every blob of jelly and peanut butter off that sofa. But try as they might, they couldn't remove the stains that the peanut butter and the jelly had left on that rare fabric that Great Aunt Hortense herself had hand-picked at some Parisian decorating establishment. She knew she'd have to come back and give the sofa a thorough and proper cleaning before Maria, or God forbid, Great Aunt Hortense found the stains.

"Miss Sophia, ye have t' go t' school every day. 'N ye can't do both! Go t' school early in te morning 'n ten watch movies late into te night! Can ye now missy?"

"Oh! Miss Kitty …"

But that's all Sophia could get out of her mouth. And down her head went. As usual. She wanted to say so much but didn't. But this time, she was sick of herself. She! who never! said what she really! thought! *I hate being so afraid, but can I tell Miss Kitty the truth? Can I tell her what I want more than anything else in the whole world? Can I trust her? Can I tell her my secret? I've never told it to another living breathing soul. And that's so hard. To never tell anybody what you really care about. If I don't tell her, than I'll never know if Miss Kitty would understand. But if I do tell her, how do I know she'd really understand enough to let me have my very own Movie Star School? Somebody's got to know that watching Movies and Movie Stars teaches me everything I need to know! That it's better than anything I've ever learned in school. I can't tell Daddy, because I don't think Daddy has ever watched a Movie in his whole life, so how can he know what's so wonderful about them. I've never seen Mother watch Movies either. Besides she never has much time. And when she does have time, she just likes to watch orchids grow. Miss Kitty is the only one who could understand. She's even seen me act! I think she likes what I do.'*

Still not able to speak, still not ready to look at Miss Kitty, she sat there. As usual. And then something inside her just snapped. She heard herself think the exact opposite of what she just thought. *I will tell her. Trust her. But I can't just say it any old way. This is the most important thing I've ever had to say! I must say it with my entire heart and my whole soul! I can't tell her like a ten-year-old child would. No, I have to tell her the way a Movie Star would, with as much passion, as much feeling, as much voice as I've ever heard every Movie Star I've ever watched use to speak every word they've ever said in each and every one of all the Movies I've ever ever watched!"*

And she opened her mouth and could feel quivers and starts bumbling all around inside her, ready to come blubbering, blundering out of her but even that wouldn't stop her. No, because her words were ready, and she could even feel tears begin to fall and she was so happy even though she was so sad because she would deliver her lines with Real Tears, not Fake Tears, the way a good actress does! Real Tears! She could feel them! There they were, about to roll down her face and then finally she lifted her head and looked up because now they were rolling down her face. She wanted Miss Kitty to see them! And, oh, Miss Kitty did see them. Miss Kitty! was gazing! at Her Real! Tears!

'But Miss Kitty looks stern! Wait! I see Miss Kitty watching my Real Tears fall and Miss Kitty's look is changing. But – what does her look mean? Is Miss Kitty …

grouchy? But she hasn't heard what I have to say!' And Sophia looked at Miss Kitty and Miss Kitty looked at Sophia, and Sophia blurted,

"Oh, Miss Kitty, I hate Real School!"

······C······

("Author Lady, as I was flying in place in front of the TV watching the movie, even over all that gangster noise - the hysterics, the gun pops, the last gasps o' the dead guys, 'Swell joint ya got here. Too bad, cause it's mine now. Bang bang bang! So long sucka!' I couldn't believe my own ears, 'Did Sophia just say what I think she just said? ... or was my ears, like, deceiving me? You know, I'm pretty sure I heard her say it, I just can't believe I heard her say it. And Elf Dorp! I'm the only Fairy who did!' So I zipped back inside. Telling anybody her secret was big news and if my associates hadn't heard her tell it, I wanted, at least, to be inside Sophia. I mean I needed to know what she was thinking after she said it so I could make my report to them about that part of the equation. After all, this was history being made, Sophia History, and the Fairies would want some of the facts and I'd better make sure I had, at least, that.")

······)······

Sophia had said what she really believed! To an alive person! She even forgot to use one of her voices when she said it, and that was okay. She looked to see if Miss Kitty understood her, especially because an Actress had to know if what she said had affected her audience. She searched Miss Kitty's face to see if she'd gotten through to her, scouring every inch of it. Miss Kitty seemed ... What did the look on Miss Kitty's face mean? She couldn't figure it out.

······C······

(" 'Oh, for Elf-sakes, just ask her! What's the hold-up!' ")

······)······

Sophia went on wondering. *'Will she help me go to Movie Star School or not? Maybe what I just said to her didn't count because I was only wearing fleece pajamas. Movie Stars don't ever tell their secrets in fleece pajamas. Movie Stars always have special clothes on when they do that.'*

······C······

(Readers - Unprintable Elfspheme!

"Okay, Lady, I get it. Your Readers. But you heard what she was thinking! Ya see for yourself, she didn't just come out and ask Miss Kitty to help her! And what's wrong with fleece pajamas! I mean, the way she thinks! It's pathetic! But ya know what's really pathetic? Here we are inside Sophia and we can't straighten her out. Why was we there if we couldn't really do her any good? We couldn't even use magic to kindda sortta help her ask Miss

Kitty. Why in a elf's patootie did the Fairy Dispatcher put us there in the first place?")

·∙∶⟩∶∙·

Miss Kitty was dying to say the only school any child needed was a real school but one look at the tears rolling over the peanut butter and jelly on Sophia's face, and she kept that inside.

Sophia was aquiver; where would she get the nerve to say -

"Movie Star School is the only school I need! That's Real School!"

Astoundingly, it come out of Sophia anyway!

'Not tat again!'

Astoundingly, that stayed inside Miss Kitty.

"Oh, I see, Miss Sophia, your Movie Star School."

Miss Kitty didn't say no! Sophia wanted to kiss her. "You already know where it is! Right here in this room! So I won't have to travel far at all! That's what I'm doing in here every night!"

"Every night! Ye're in here every night?"

"Well— "

"Oh, no! It's worse tan I tought! Don't ye dare be tellin' a soul about tat."

"You're scaring me!"

"I tought ye just came down here every once in a while. Not every night! Y'r Mother 'n y'r Father 'n Mr. James would be none t' pleased about tat!"

"You must never tell anybody then. This is our secret. I don't want anyone but you to know this, Miss Kitty!"

"I certainly won't say a word about tis ye can rest assured. Let's talk about it some other time after ye have had a good night's sleep. Right now I just want to know one ting - are ye hungry still or can ye go back t' bed?"

"Oh, Miss Kitty, I'm about to die, the hunger pains are so strong! I just started to eat that sandwich and then it fell out of my hands! Couldn't I have another one, please so I don't fall in a faint on my way to my bed chamber?"

And Miss Kitty had to laugh even though that was the last thing she wanted to do. "Bed chamber? Where do ye learn suuuch language? 'N besides, child, if ye could do all tat, I might even pay a pretty penny just t' see it! But I don't want tat t' happen t' te real Miss Sophia Oomla. Te passing out, tat is, from hunger 'n starvation, considering tat I am te cook in tis household! What would tat say about me fine home cookin'?"

Miss Kitty managed to plunk her hips onto the sofa next to Sophia and then, quite ably, began assembling a sandwich for her. Sophia sank back and watched the expert at work. But just as Miss Kitty handed Sophia the sandwich, there was the sound of the door opening very very slowly behind them. And Miss Kitty's heart jumped and sank and jumped again, for she was having a heart attack she was sure,

"Oh te Good Lord save us all, it's one of te escaped inmates tat's broken into te house!" Miss Kitty knew she should've whispered, but was sure she hadn't.

And they turned round to see a brilliant red face that soon began to speak, "Now I see why Miss Sophia is always so tired!"

The voice, clipped, understated.

That was no escaped inmate.

That was Mr. James.

• • • EARLY MORNING, MISS KITTY • • •

Everything happened so fast, Miss Kitty felt like she had been pushed inside a rocket-ship and was about to become the first old lady launched to the moon. She imagined the news flash on the radio. 'Will tat saintly, elderly Irish cook, who never hurt nobody, land safely?' But her joke was not making her laugh. And as for the rocket-ship, niece Margaret's old tin lizzie was hardly rocket-propelling them down the Castle L'Oomla's driveway. Miss Kitty and niece Margaret traveled in putts and puffs and gasps, trailing a cloud of dark fumes behind them that enshrouded the Castle's allee of trees.

"Aunt Kitty, I don't know about this new little contraption of mine: either she's just too cold or she knows she's not supposed to drive my Aunt Kitty away from her home."

'Away from me home!' Aunt Kitty couldn't get niece Margaret's words out of her mind as she looked back at the Castle L'Oomla. *'Tat fantastic palace of a place! Tat I love every inch of! Tat I am so proud to be a part of!*

'Am? Was!'

'Away from me home.'

And when that old tin lizzie had finally sputtered out of the village gates, and they were on their way to the city, Miss Kitty thought, *'Here I am at te age of 72 by meself again on tis vast planet. Not allowed t' be where I want t' be. I might as well be a million miles away. A million miles away from te people I've come t' love 'n te only life I've known for tese past four years! Tat news flash is no joke, Kitty Devine! Ye might as well be on te moon!'*

She remembered feeling this way long ago when she left her Ireland, her sad Mother standing on the dock waving good bye to her as she stood on the boat bound for America. And oh, how Miss Kitty wanted to hold onto her Mother's hand but couldn't, so for dear life, she had taken hold of that boat's wooden railing. And oh, how she wanted to hold onto something now; so she took hold of the hem of niece Margaret's soft woolen coat that had fallen on the seat beside her. She could only thank the Good Lord that niece Margaret had been with her this morning and was with her now on what she feared may be her last ride down the driveway and away from the Castle L'Oomla.

Niece Margaret was taking Miss Kitty to where she lived in the big city and there Miss Kitty would have to sit til she heard from the Oomlas one way or the other. And if it was not one way and it was the other, she would be forced to find other employment. Oh! How she wanted to be forgiven and come back to work for the Oomla's and Sophia. What would Sophia do without her? And what would she do without Sophia?

'T' be suspended! From te Oomla Household. Til Dr. 'n Mrs. Oomla have te time t' review te circumstances of me case. Someting tat has never happened t' me in any position I ever held in all me 73 years.'

Oh, she had met Mr. James just as he had requested. Mrs. Oomla had just left. And then a little after 5 AM, he had told her he wanted to meet with her in his office. So her and her, by now, howling hips hobbled behind Mr. James as he marched to his office. And as he snapped into his desk chair, Miss Kitty lowered herself down by way of the handrails, inch by excruciating inch, onto the visitor chair.

And she sized him up and he her so seriously, she knew she was in hot water. And in no uncertain terms and pronouncing every syllable of every word like the true Butler of the Manor he was, he said: that there were contradictions in her statements.

And

Mrs. Oomla did not have,

and

he did not have,

and

Great Aunt Hortense did not have confidence in the answers she gave to their questions yesterday.

That all of them, in spite of what she said to the contrary, felt that she had something to do with Sophia's missed appointment.

And then he went on to her second offense.

Having to listen to him speak English so properly and him being so proper anyway, Miss Kitty remembered why her countrymen wanted to punch his countrymen right in the nose. Or should. But she was awfully glad he hadn't asked her a question about that first offense. She would've hated to lie to him again.

And as far as the second offense; which was finding her and Sophia watching the Television and making a sandwich for Sophia in the Television Room after midnight and on a school night, he said, now he knew why Sophia was always so tired, and then he did ask her questions. And Miss Kitty told him everything she knew. Almost everything. She wasn't going to lie. But she wasn't going to tell him the whole truth neither. Not the truth about anything Sophia said to keep secret: about Sophia wanting to go to Movie Star School, and that Sophia thought of the Television Room as a Movie Star School, and, above all, not what she herself had just found out: that Sophia came down to the Television Room! Every! Night! and watched movies in her Movie Star School! Every! Night!

She told him about the two times other than last night that she had found Sophia watching movies. That was, as far as Miss Kitty was concerned, enough for him and all the Oomlas to know.

And then he said, "You never told me! and you never told Mrs. Oomla! and you never told Dr. Oomla! what Miss Sophia was doing!" And Miss Kitty said, "But tat was only two times tat I found her!" which was not a lie, "Sophia is a child after all! 'n I spoke t' her about tat many many times. I was tryin' t' make sure she didn't do tat any more. Ye see tat after me night off when I returned home, I had gone in t' her room t' check t' make sure she was asleep 'n had only gone downstairs when I didn't find her tere in her bed. Mr. James, te child was hungry now, what was I supposed t' do?"

And says he, "I will be discussing all of this with the Oomlas after all the excitement at the Institute has died down for Dr. Oomla; and all of the meetings making Giggle Corporation a multinational are over for Mrs. Oomla."

And then the telephone rang, and she heard Mr. James saying "Yes, thank you for calling. No, Mrs. Oomla has already left for the day. And so I take it to understand that the village school is closed today. So the inmates still hadn't been found yet. Thank you."

Miss Kitty was to leave the Oomla household. Mr. James asked her where she would go and Miss Kitty said with niece Margaret and Mr. James took down niece Margaret's phone number and told Miss Kitty that he would be in touch with her as soon as the Oomlas and himself had discussed the circumstances of her case and they had made a decision about her future with the Oomlas.

'Her Case!' Here she was now A Case! and not Miss Kitty anymore; and there they would be discussing their Miss Kitty like that, and even planning her future.

But she couldn't picture such a conversation at all. Could that nice Dr. Oomla turn so cold all of a sudden, just like that, or, for that matter, could Mrs. Oomla? And then Miss Kitty remembered what Mr. James had been saying on the phone, that the schools were closed; what would Miss Sophia do all day and just exactly who would be minding her! Mr. James? And she couldn't picture that either! Maria? Heaven forbid! And how soon would Maria find those peanut butter and jelly stains? And poor Sophia when she did.

• • • EARLY MORNING, MR. JAMES • • •

Mr. James watched Miss Kitty wrest herself out of her chair and plod her way out of his office one slow foot at a time. He had never seen her walk with so much difficulty before. Or her head bent so low. If she felt his eyes on her she didn't let on nor did she say one word in parting. *'She is not at all pleased with me.'* He wanted to call after her, ask her if her arthritis was acting up more than usual this morning but he knew what that would make him. Soft. Besides, he knew what he should be thinking, *'I am not pleased with her!'* And he set that thought up high in his mind where principles belonged, opened his desk drawer and pulled out a sharp pencil and a spotless piece of paper. He would make a list of all the things he had to tell Mrs. Oomla about the Miss Kitty incident; what to say and how to say it and the order in which it should be said. And he'd do it soon for he had to make the breakfast today.

And down went his writing implement.

There would be no delicious food this morning. And he was hungry. He always loved how Mrs. Oomla wanted tables set, and Miss Kitty set them just like that, just as beautifully, just as appetizingly, nary a one without flowers. And such food! The best food he'd ever had in any of the households he'd ever served. Including England.

There was to be no conversation, either. No debates with Dr. Oomla. The highlight of his day. No wide-eyed admiration coming from Miss Sophia when he talked about the great British debaters. No questions from her for him to answer. No. Not this morning. There was no Miss Kitty to make that breakfast.

And for a good reason! He WAS getting soft. This morning he must take care of everything. Because this morning was completely different. For one thing, Dr. Oomla was still not back from the Institute. No doubt Dr. Oomla had his hands full and would not be able to focus on the homefront, at least this morning, and maybe not for the whole day. And that left everything to him.

But How? How? How? would the Oomlas feel about the action he'd taken vis à vis their 'dear Miss Kitty'?

He was wavering again.

Enough! He was Miss Kitty's direct supervisor and, as such, would be held accountable for her behavior. And with her employers not here, and in crisis of their own, it was up to him to run the Oomla household. And by making this decision, hadn't he taken care of it? Put simply: how could he, Mr. James, run the household with an employee who was not trustworthy? How indeed? He would inform Mrs. Oomla that the village school was closed, and then on to the more delicate part of the affair.

And at last, his high regard for rules and regulations took their rightful place alongside his principles and he began assaulting the blinding white paper with his implement:

1. That dear Miss Kitty was involved with Miss Sophia and a certain peanut butter and jelly sandwich in the television room at midnight and which I myself witnessed;

2. That dear Miss Kitty admitted to me there were two other occasions when she had found Miss Sophia up at midnight watching movies;

3. That dear Miss Kitty never told me, her direct supervisor, or Mrs. Oomla or Dr. Oomla about those two other occasions when she had found Miss Sophia up at midnight watching movies;

4. That dear Miss Kitty surely knew that these nights were school nights;

5. That dear Miss Kitty surely noticed her charge was tired all the time;

6. That dear Miss Kitty surely should have reasoned that watching movies at midnight on school nights made her charge tired and might be why her charge was required to seek the services of a speech therapist;

7. That dear Miss Kitty has surely neglected her duties and her responsibilities to you, her employer; to me, her supervisor; and, above all, to Miss Sophia, her charge.

And for these aforementioned reasons, I suspended Miss Kitty without consulting either you or Dr. Oomla.

Every entry he made increased his alarm. He WAS justified in how he handled Dear Miss Kitty. What person, when they heard such dereliction, wouldn't understand his actions? He HAD done the right thing. *'Dear Miss Kitty indeed!'* How Great-Aunt Saint-Aunt will grind each of Miss Kitty's transgression down to a thorn and drive them into Mrs. Oomla's side.

And he twitched. What about his dereliction? For all of it had happened under his watch! What would Great-Aunt Holy-Pope have to say about him if ever she got hold of his list? And woe to him! if she had. How, with relish! she would have driven HIS transgressions into Mrs. Oomla's side, too, turning him into the villain as well.

But he was no driver of thorns!

But then compared to Great-Aunt Slay-Aunt's, the true thorn-driver, what sharp implement had he?

His very civilized tongue? vs Great-Aunt Snake-Aunt's?

And he twitched and so too did his anxiety.

But then he remembered: he had a list! He, too, had a sharp implement.

When he went over His List with Mrs. Oomla, he would not use it as Great-Aunt Sneer-Snot would, Sharply and with Sting, but would speak Discreetly and Sensitively about dear Miss Kitty, so that Mrs. Oomla knew how Respectful he was of dear Miss Kitty and how Strong a Supervisor he was nevertheless. For surely, after hearing what she had done, the Oomlas couldn't possibly want Sophia taken care of by an employee whom they couldn't trust. Mrs. Oomla would certainly understand his reasons.

' *"If reasons were as plenty as blackberries, I would give no man a reason on compulsion!"'*

Old faithful. Shakespeare. *'Actually, James J. James, you're not atall sure, are you? Have you become a pulpitarian, too, who talks in rules and regulations ... like Great Aunt Horangutan? Isn't one per household enough?*

' *"Our doubts are traitors."* *You also said that Shakespeare! And here I am doubting myself. I acted decisively. That is how a strong supervisor behaves. Where would the world be without rules and regulations? There is Saint NoSaint's way with rules and regulations and then there is the right way with rules and regulations. Great HorseSense! Shall learn from me.*

'But can I really make that sort of Oomla's style of breakfast? And who will companion Sophia all day since she will not be in school? By solving this crisis, haven't I created another one? Horse-sense? If I had horse-sense, I'd have suspended her after breakfast!'

Til Maria arrived, everything was now on his shoulders. Maria would do but he wasn't so sure for how long. Maria had only proven herself as a tireless fighter in the war on dust bunnies. Never had he seen anyone attack dirt and dust with such energy and conviction. But dust bunnies you can push around; children, you cannot.

Perhaps Maria pushed dust around with just a little too much conviction. Maria, he feared, was only a temporary solution.

Mr. James was just about to dial Mrs. Oomla at 7:00 AM when the phone rang again and again it was the village school. The schools were to be closed not just for today but until further notice. Even more inmates had escaped than they realized and four of them had been found hiding in the school and they didn't want children walking anywhere in the village at all. "Please make sure that your child is supervised at all times!" the school official had said, before she got off the phone. Mr. James had to steady his hand when he dialed Mrs. Oomla.

Mrs. Oomla answered her phone on the first ring. "Oh, Mr. James, is everything alright? It's so unusual for you to call me. Is my husband back yet? I haven't been able to reach him, and I've tried both of his numbers and the Institute's switchboard as well."

"Mrs. Oomla, I'm calling actually with news of some urgency but not however about Dr. Oomla. But here is a comforting thought about why you can't reach him, perhaps his mobile needs recharging. After all, he has been at the Institute all night, and he keeps his charger here in his home office. I shall drive up there this morning as soon as I can get away. I'll bring some fresh clothes and the charger, too. And now, if I might proceed— "

"Oh, Mr. James, Dr. Oomla will appreciate that. And what is your news?"

He made a mental note to stick to the order in his list. That way Mrs. Oomla would hear his sound reasoning and would, most certainly, arrive at his same conclusion.

He hadn't even finished telling her about the school situation, when Mrs. Oomla did something he never heard her do before: she Auugghhhhhh-ed! "Mr. James, where is Sophia now? Please make sure that dear Miss Kitty stays with her all day."

And Mr. James tailored his answer precisely, "Well, Mrs. Oomla, Miss Sophia is up in her bedroom." hoping that she wouldn't notice that he hadn't mentioned Miss Kitty.

"Yes, but send dear Miss Kitty up there to check. Is dear Miss Kitty finishing breakfast now?"

"No, she is not finishing breakfast now ..." If only he could just proceed to his list ... "Miss Kitty and Miss Sophia, the both of them together, were up extremely late last night, in the Television Room, and Miss Kitty was making a sandwich for Miss Sophia, with evidence that she had made other sandwiches." His plan was working.

"Mr. James, I don't understand - eating in the Television Room? Miss Kitty and Sophia?"

Now on to item number two, "Apparently Miss Kitty has discovered Sophia watching movies twice before in the Television Ro—"

"But the most important thing, Mr. James, is to make sure that Sophia is safe now … let me speak to Miss Kitty and let's take care of first things first."

"Well … as I am explaining—" *'I am off my list!'*

"But with all that you just told me about the escapees, you must make sure Sophia is okay … Perhaps you could call dear Miss Kitty and while we are talking, she can go upstairs and check!"

"Well … as I am expla …" His list was doomed! All of his careful planning! He had no choice, "Mrs. Oomla, Miss Kitty is not here. I've suspended her."

"You've what?" *'She's bellowed again! Not atall going as planned! Not atall!'*

"Mrs. Oomla, I've suspended her because she was up last night with Miss Sophia watching movies after midnight and making sandwiches for her! And because Miss Kitty has discovered Miss Sophia watching movies on two other occasions before and she never—"

"Mr. James, if dear Miss Kitty isn't there, who will watch Sophia right now? You have enough to do. I don't understand all of this, I'm afraid … watching movies … making sandwiches—"

"Mrs. Oomla, Miss Sophia is always tired. For example, when I was driving her to school yesterday morning, she fell asleep. When I was driving her home from school yesterday afternoon, she fell asleep. Now we know why. She watches movies at night and Miss Kitty knew it and never told us, that is what I've been trying to explain! This could be affecting her ability to speak clearly when she is called on in school, the reason Mr. Snoggley thought she may need a speech therapist. She is too tired when she's in school to talk clearly."

"Ohhhhhhh, Mr. James … " and she stopped and was very silent and so was he, until she burst out, "What sort of a Mother doesn't know what her daughter is up to at midnight? Movies! How could I have not known! And why didn't Miss Kitty tell us? And why didn't Sophia tell her Mother? Sophia, up so late watching movies? Sophia, tired all the time? I'm tired all the time? Sigmund shut away in his library? What has happened to us? And Miss Kitty was watching movies with her? And neither of them told us! Movies! And that is the reason you suspended dear Miss Kitty? But then are movies such a bad thing for a child to watch … although movies aren't such a good thing either for a child who is only ten years old … of course, it just depends on the movie. How did she ever discover movies?

And why didn't she tell us she did? Why Sigmund and I seldom watch movies! Although considering who Sigmund's patients are, it's not surprising we don't. I must speak to Sophia. But what will all of us do without dear Miss Kitty? Are you sure you had to suspend Miss Kitty? But then suspending doesn't really mean firing, does it? Ah ... but the need for a speech therapist ... yes ... if someone is tired in school ... no wonder Mr. Snoggley wanted Sophia to see a speech therapist ... Oh, this day is impossible ... I cannot leave the city at all or the entire board will have my head. I simply cannot leave. And, of course, this has to be the one day that my daughter really needs me. Let me think ... I need to find someone to watch Sophia now that the schools are closed indefinitely. I will call you as soon as I can think better and sort all of this out. Please make sure Sophia is in her room. And Mr. James, can you please make the breakfast the way dear Miss Kitty would?"

Shakespeare hooted, *'Thy head stands so tickle on thy shoulders!' Cookery? From our Mr. James? 'I had rather live with cheese and garlic in a windmill!'*

And for good reason. For Mr. James never met an East Indies spice that he wouldn't sprinkle liberally on every dish he cooked until it reeked and he reeked and the kitchen reeked and all the other eaters reeked as well. The Bard was right. And he said sheepishly, "I will do my best."

But should Great-Aunt Sniff-Aunt somehow be down-wind of his cuisine and remind Mrs. Oomla that he could not do everything, he must remind Mrs. Oomla that neither could her dear Miss Kitty, "And please don't forget that yesterday, Miss Kitty, did not appear to be telling the truth. You and Great Aunt Hortense and I all spoke about that later in the conservatory. And now we know why. Miss Kitty was hiding something from us. From her employer. From her direct supervisor. I will not stand for an employee who is not forthright. I am responsible for my employee's actions, Mrs. Oomla. And in a household that I run, dishonesty is a serious offense."

"Mr. James, lying, of course, is never acceptable, I agree with you. And Sophia's not being able to speak up in school is of great concern. All of us will have to talk later. Where is Miss Kitty now?"

"She has left for Goliathon with her niece Margaret."

"Oh, good! She has a place to stay. Dear Miss Kitty. But why didn't she tell us? I don't understand. We must all talk about this later. I'll call very soon."

He, of course, had been forthright. Unlike dear Miss Kitty. Great Aunt FrankNSting could never say that about him. And didn't Shakespeare say, *'... to be honest, as this world goes, is to be one man picked out of ten thousand ...'*

'But does that mean we will have to go through 9,999 new nannies before we find the honest one? But there is no doubt about it, to find a cook as good as Miss Kitty, we'll go through 99,999, at least!'

As he went up the grand staircase to wake Sophia, he examined his time-piece. It was barely past 7. He had had quite a morning. He was just about done in. Already. And famished! And he was sweating. And something was out of place on the top of his head ... was he ... the English Butler frazzled? And that's when his good friend Shakespeare whispered in his ear yet again, ' *"Why, thou full dish of fool ... "* '

"Master Will, I get it! I should have suspended her after breakfast! Now will you leave me alone!"

Master Will would not, ' *"Those that do teach young babes do it with gentle means and easy tasks."*

And then some other random wise guy sunk his teeth in, too, *'Now is hardly the time to ask the young babe about movies and television rooms, Mr. James!'"*

And to appease the pests, Mr. James added hastily, "Nor to tell her I suspended her Nanny!"

and Sophia was sent to Goliathon

• • • WEDNESDAY, FEBRUARY 4, 6:30 PM • • •

Sophia sat in the back of the limousine and wasn't slouching; even though going where that limousine was taking her was the last place she wanted to go. She was even looking out the window, though it was nighttime and dark and there were only speeding cars to examine. But Mr. James had just said they were only a few minutes away from crossing the bridge and that soon she would see the biggest, tallest buildings and the most people she would ever see in her whole entire life. And for the first time since she was told she had to go, she finally admitted she was excited.

Because Sophia was on her way to the place she had only ever seen in the Movies and in her dreams. She was on her way to Goliathon.

·∴ᴄ··

("Darling, as soon as we heard where she must go, we were ecstatic! And here now was our Sophia stepping into the limousine with Mr. James at the wheel and we, too, were on our way to Goliathon. And every single one of us was dangling on Sophia's ear looking out that window right along with her. Be knew the best coffeehouses and I, of course, the best shops, and we couldn't have been more excited. Although, to be honest, Thee and Free were not at all sure they would even like Goliathon.

" 'We'll have to change our routine!' "

" 'Big it's so it's!' "

"Author, Lady, I was the happiest I'd been since I was roped into this assignment. 'Hey, the kid's finally going places! We're going places, it's, like, about time!' ")

··ᴐ∴·

'Goliathon!' Sophia thought, 'The Big Fruit! The Greatest Way! The Square of All Time Where Soldiers Kiss Nurses Smack on their Mouths! The Grandest of Stations where Beautiful Spies Really Catch Midnight Trains! The Building Empire *that only King Kong can climb! Where Men Wear Hats. And Women Wear Veils. And Dogs Wear Coats.'*

·∴☾∴·

("Free says, 'Putting-on-the-dog coats?' "

"Hah-hah, very funny Free! It'll be just like back home, all the little fuppies in their leaf wraps!")

·∴☾∴·

'Where the City Never Sleeps ... Or ... the Buildings Never Sleep ... NEVER Sleeps? How could that be?' Sophia would have a look around in the middle of the night to find out for herself. If she wasn't too scared. The Smiles! The Lights. The Tapping Feet! And now *'My Tapping Tootsies will tap tap tap to Toot Toot Shor's too!'* If they and she weren't too too terrified.

For she was going to stay with her Grandfather and her Grandmother, her Father's Mother and Father.

Without Miss Kitty.

Without her Father.

Without her Mother.

With relatives she didn't remember.

And Mr. James was only taking her there and not staying with her there.

And ... most horrifying of all ...she couldn't watch Movies there, because her Father's relatives didn't even have a television set or a DVD player, BECAUSE THEY DIDN'T LIKE MOVIES!

Her Mother was on her case already now that she knew.

And there she would be, by herself, without her Movie Stars, without her Movie Star School.

But Sophia was doing everything in her power to be as brave as any Movie Star she'd ever seen would be when they were scared to death - when they had to do what they didn't want to do - when they had to do what their Mothers told them to do. But then Beautiful Movie Stars' Mothers didn't usually tell them what to do. And her Mother hadn't even given her a choice. And Sophia hadn't even been able to say one word of protest about it. At least, that's what she was telling herself happened when she and her Mother were on the phone talking this morning and she should've been telling her Mother how she felt about what her Mother wanted her to do but couldn't/wouldn't/didn't; and now all she could feel was how huge the car was and how small she felt inside it.

'Tiny! I might as well be a baby. Babies can't talk! I didn't say how I feel! That's not what Movie Stars do! Movie Stars talk! They say how they feel! In fact, they are famous for saying how they feel. In fact, that's why they ARE famous

because they say how they feel with their whole heart and their whole soul like no-body else can and for everybody in the whole wide world to hear and to know and to appreciate. That's what I should've done! And that's exactly what I didn't do. And now I'm stuck going to a place that I'm not at all sure I'll like. Or even want to go to.

'Maybe if I would've said something, I wouldn't have even had to go.
'When will I say how I feel the way a Movie Star does?
'Because I didn't say how I feel:
'I almost had to go a speech therapist!
'I may never get back into my Movie Star School ever again!
'I have to be with people who don't even like Movies!
'When will I speak up? When? When?'

···☾··

("I says, 'Now you're tawking. Now you're tawking!'

"But Be says, 'No, Lorraine, that's the problem. She isn't talking. She's thinking!'")

··☽··

'But Movie Stars make the best of whatever they have to do, and look their very best when they do it, and since I am just like Them, then I will make the best of what I do, too.'

And that's when she stopped slouching and sat up straighter in the back of that limousine and tossed her head the way Movie Stars do and racked her Movie Star memory for anything she could remember seeing in the Movies about this place she had to go to. And that's when the kissing soldiers and the fancy ladies and the swell gentlemen in fine clothes tap danced into her head.

'Maybe it won't be so bad after all. There are railroad stations filled with spies and parks filled with prancing dogs wearing hats ... Maybe ... Maybe ...'

···☾··

("Prancing hats wear dogs here, too?" said Free.

"I don't think so, Free!" said Thee, "Not here! Not in this land!"

"Oh, Thee, hope so me! I see that like! I see that laugh!")

··☽··

Sophia looked at all of those cars speeding past them and she made up her mind, if Movie Stars have to go to a place where they don't know anyone and no one knew them - they're brave and they go. And they wouldn't cry. So she'd be brave, and wouldn't cry either.

'Or maybe, I'm wrong! Maybe they would've put up a big fight with whoever was sending them where they didn't want to go. Or, at the very least, they would've told

that person how they felt about being sent to a place they didn't want to go to than what I told my Mother this morning!'

·∴(⸱·

("Author Lady, I says, 'Would youse listen to her! Some spunk, finally!' ")

·⸱)∴·

'After all, I'm being sent away from the things I love most – My Movie Star School! And my Movies. And I have to be there all by myself. With people I may not like. Or who may not like me. And who don't like Movies.

'WHO DON'T LIKE MOVIES!

'When a Movie Star feels this much sadness about all that's happening to her that Movie Star would cry. They'd cry a lot.' She could feel her own tears fall. *'But Movie Stars don't cry like babies.'* So she made her tears roll quietly; not the way a baby's would.

All morning and even after lunch, Sophia had been helping Maria with the dusting and cleaning. What a day she had had. It was a day like no other. Mr. James woke her up! Not Miss Kitty! And he told her there would be no school! Because some patients were missing from the Institute! And just like that he handed her a phone and her Mother was on the line and she told her that Miss Kitty was in Goliathon with her niece Margaret taking care of some things, like her arthritis and that Miss Kitty couldn't be with her for a few days.

"Am I to be all alone? And I don't have to go to school?" But Sophia hadn't actually said that out loud. She screamed it inside.

"Mr. James told me that you watch Movies late at night. Why didn't you ever tell me? We will talk about your Movie watching and your staying up so late but only when you come back because you, Sophia, are going to Goliathon! Mr. James will drive you there but he won't be staying there with you."

'Mother is singing the Song of Sad; so sadly sad, like perfect Sad!' Sophia tried to gather each and every one of her own thoughts about what she just heard; but couldn't. She was distracted by her Mother and she stopped listening to herself. And she filled up almost to the top of her with the sound of her Mother; as if her Mother was the Star in the Movie SAD and only her Mother was allowed in that movie, and she herself was not. Because somehow her Mother's feelings seemed so much more real, so much more important than her own.

·∴(⸱·

("Author Lady, ya hear how much work we still had to do on that kid?")

·⸱)∴·

And Sophia said nothing. She had not expressed herself. She did not say how sad she felt that Miss Kitty wasn't there, how happy that there would be no school. Her Mother didn't know what she was feeling because she'd said nothing. Her Mother'd said many things, her Mother'd expressed herself. Sophia knew what her Mother was feeling; her Mother didn't know how she was feeling. But then her Mother hadn't asked her how she felt either. But maybe that was only because of what her Father had told her once – that your Mother Talks Out, and you and I Talk In.

'I'm an In-y trying to be an Out-y.'

·∴☾∴·

("Hey, Me, do you remember what Be said when Sophia thought that? She said that was the smartest thing Sophia ever thought!"

"Lorraine, darling! Remember? Of course, I don't remember. Whatever did that have to do with the shops in Goliathon?")

·∴☽∴·

And Sophia imagined what Miss In-y should've said to Mrs. Out-y. That she loved Movies! And Movie Stars! Next, she imagined what Miss In-y should've said to Mr. James. That he'd found out her secret. And he had Told! Her! Mother! He ratted on her!

And now there would be no more Movies and no more Movie Star School! And at last she allowed in what she'd been keeping out - because late last night when she was in her bed, she was just too tired to fully comprehend - that she had been caught by Mr. James.

But In-y Sophia had said one thing out loud to her Out-y Mother and she was proud.

"I'm going all by myself? Without Miss Kitty?"

And it WAS loud. But then in answer to her, her Mother said even more surprising things. Many surprising things. In fact, everything she said was about to change everything about Sophia's life so much, that she made sure her ear caught every last drop that Niagara-ed out of her Mother's mouth.

"Oh, Sophia, let me explain. You are going to stay with your Father's relatives down in Goliathon while the schools are closed because Miss Kitty is having a problem and the school is having a problem and Daddy is having a problem and I'm having a problem, and when your Father and I and you are all together again and there are no more problems that's when we will all talk about you staying up late to watch movies and keeping it secret. And, I'm afraid, you won't be able to stay up late there because your Father's relatives don't like movies at all and they don't even have one television set in their vast house. You'll be there with your Grandfather and your Grandmother, and your Great Uncle and your Great Aunt ..."

"Huuaughh ... my Great Au ...!" That came out with a bang.

"Sophia, don't worry, not a person in that house is anything like your Great Aunt Hortense. For one thing, everyone in that house works in Show Business. And I assure you every person in that house is the exact opposite of your Great Aunt Hortense, you'll soon find that out. Remember these are your Father's Mother and Father, and his relatives, and not mine, and there'll be oh so many other people there too. Great Aunt Hortense - when they made her they threw away the mold, so don't worry. And there are some people who might even be sad they did, and I'm one of them, because sometimes a person can be very strict and even a little difficult and you can still love them. But at your Grandfather's there'll be many many oh so many guests. Your Grandfather and Grandmother have visited us from time to time, but not for a while, because your Grandmother hasn't been feeling well, and your Father and his Father ... well ... so you do know them, Sophia. Do you remember them?"

"I don't think I—"

"Oh, and there you'll have lots of company, because they live in the biggest house in the biggest city in a house like no other house you or anyone in the whole world has ever seen and it's always filled with people. It's like Grand Central Station in the sky. The house sits on the roof of one of those skyscraper buildings. Your Grandfather's building has 57 floors, and his house is perched on the top of all those floors; and it's no little house either, it's big and tall as a house can be! People in cities, Sophia, don't live in houses, they live in apartments in tall buildings and the apartments that are on the highest floor of a tall building are called the Penthouses, Sophia. And that's where your Grandfather used to live. But being in a Penthouse cooped your Grandfather up.

He would complain about it all the time saying he got a Pent and not a House and if he had to live on the top of a building, he wanted a House and not a Pent. And whatever you do, Sophia, don't ask him what a 'Pent' is, he doesn't take to that question too kindly. Well, he bought the entire roof to that skyscraper and all the penthouses underneath that roof and built a house like the House of Seven Gables on it, Sophia, with a porch and a garden and everything. And they've lived there ever since. And, Sophia, wait til you see it, it's a real house with its own roof and a wide porch and turrets and gables and it even has its own garden and several winding paths and the tallest wrought iron fence around the whole thing, complete with a swinging creaky wrought iron gate. And the only thing that's different about it is, when I say that fence is tall, I'm not kidding: that fence that surrounds your Grandfather's house is the tallest fence a person has ever seen. Now, as I said, Sophia, your Grandfather and everybody else in that whole entire house works in Show Business. Yes, just like your Father's Institute except these people think they're sane. Your Grandfather is sensible, he didn't want anybody falling off that roof and down 57 floors and since he believes those who work in Show Business are seldom as sensible as himself and since those were the characters who would be coming to call - ergo that fence.

"Now remember what I'm about to tell you. And whatever you do, don't forget it, Sophia: your Grandfather does not like the movie business! He only likes live Shows or Plays or Musicals or Revues, because your Grandfather is a Producer of Shows and Plays and Musicals and Revues and just about any sort of spectacle that can be shown live and on a stage. He owns 4 theatres. And movies are bad for his theatre business. Because if people are spending money on movie tickets, they're not spending money on theatre tickets. And if so-and-so is starring in a movie, than so-and-so is not starring in one of his shows. And, oh, Sophia make no mistake about it! he doesn't like movies at all. He likes to see actors on a stage, but ... oh, don't worry, he'll tell you all about it. He tells everybody all about it. So whatever you do, don't tell him you like movies. He'll lose his temper if you talk about movies."

'I don't like him - you can't say this to him-you can't say that to him! AND he doesn't like movies AND he thinks actors aren't sensible! Everybody knows in our village, you can't say actors aren't sensible. Why my Father would never say actors aren't sensible even when they're not sensible!'

As Sophia had been listening to her Mother say all of what she just said, she'd filled up again with the sound of her Mother. Her Mother was happy one minute, sad the next, then excited, then slightly cross, then back to happy again. Sophia wasn't sure how her Mother really felt. Or maybe her Mother felt all of those feelings. And if Miss In-y opened up and told her Mother how she really felt: that she didn't want to go, that she wanted to stay home, that she didn't want to be away from her Movie Star School, she wasn't sure how her Mother would take it. She wasn't even sure if she could've even said all of what she felt since she usually never did.

⋯∗☾⋯

("Author, Lady and youse out there in Reader Land! Ya hear that?")

⋯☽∗⋯

'How everyone'd be surprised if I did!'

⋯∗☾⋯

("So I screams, Author Lady, 'Surprise them kid! We, like, can't stand the suspense!' ")

⋯☽∗⋯

"So while the schools are closed and your Father is saving the Artistes and I'm saving Giggle and Miss Kitty is ... well ... oh, Sophia, I think you'll love your Grandparents' place. I love that place. You'll have a great time. It's the liveliest place you'll ever see. There's never a dull moment there, make no mistake about it. I'll call you when it's time for Mr. James to take you to Goliathon."

'How could she be right? My Grandfather doesn't like Movies at all! How could I ever stand such a person? So how could I ever have a good time at his house? I wish I didn't have to go to such a person's house. And I wish Miss Kitty was here now! And I wish everything was the same. I even wish I could go to school. Going to school and seeing Mr. Snoggley would be better than this.'

Her Mother's call came just after Maria had gone into the TV Room aka Movie Star School to clean and found the peanut butter and jelly stains. And Mr. Dougherty's flashlight. But Maria was so upset about the stains, she forgot to wonder why Mr. Dougherty's flashlight was in the TV Room. She just put it on her cart. First, Maria had cried about the stains and then she had yelled in her own language which Sophia knew was Italian. Maria, with her accent, sounded both ridiculous and magnificent but Sophia didn't dare laugh because Maria would've guessed that Sophia was laughing at her and she would've been scared to death to laugh at Maria. Because of Maria's Evil Eye. Miss Kitty told her that Maria looked at dirt and dust and grime with the Evil Eye. Since there was only one peanut butter and jelly fiend in The Castle L'Oomla - Maria knew who put that peanut butter and jelly stain there.

Was Maria looking at her with that kind of eye?

Slippery, slyly, Sophia cocked her own eye to see. She never saw her do that even once. Certainly, Maria would do it now. But neither of Maria's eyes were doing anything different. But then Sophia figured if Maria did look at her with the Evil Eye, it would serve her right because she knew darn well she wasn't ever supposed to leave evidence that she had even been in the TV Room aka Movie Star School. What sort of a Movie Star spills peanut butter and jelly even if she's suddenly snuck up on and taken by surprise?

When Maria pulled a spray can and a powdery mister from her cleaning cart, she turned to Sophia and said, "Missa, you-a say-a you-a prayer-a I getta this off-a ta sofa this!" and that's when her Mother called and Sophia was never happier to leave her Movie Star School in her whole life.

But as she walked down the path towards Mr. James in his waiting limousine and it was safe because Maria was back in the house and couldn't hear her and give her the Evil Eye, Sophia said over and over, "Missa, you-a say-a you-a prayer-a I getta this off-a ta sofa this!" Sophia was teaching herself Italian. Until she remembered where she was going and by herself, too, and that there was nothing she could do about it. And a Movie Star's face popped into her head, the one with the big face and the sad eyes and the blonde hair that sang "Vhat am Ihhh tu doooo ... khan't heellp eett?" with her deep-voiced German accent and so she switched to that song the rest of the way down the path because she was sad just like her. She was also teaching herself German. "Vhat am Ihhh tu doooo ... " And down the path Sophia sang out, wondering, wondering, wondering. She stopped when she got closer to the limousine. She didn't want Mr. James to hear her.

She also didn't want to talk to Mr. James since he was the one who found her last night. And he's the one who told her Mother. He was what they call in the movies a "dirty rat."

And she stepped into the back of the limousine.

"Good evening, Miss Sophia. The ride to Goliathon should take just under two hours."

"Yes, Mr. James." She had always been taught to say, thank you, when people do things for her but she couldn't say it. Not to him. 'Yes, Mr. James' was all he'd get out of her. He wasn't her friend anymore. She didn't care how many people and their voices he could do.

"Goliathon, here we come!" And Mr. James tipped his hat and looked at her through the rear-view mirror.

But Sophia had turned her head away from the front of the car where Mr. James was and hadn't seen him tip his hat because she wasn't looking in his direction and wasn't going to look in his direction. She knew what she was going to do on this whole trip. Slouch.

·:·٭(·:·

("Author, Lady, believe me, we wasn't quiet like Sophia and keeping everything we was thinking inside. No, we couldn't stop tawking about Goliathon. Me, you couldn't stop tawking about your favorite stores. And most of us didn't want to miss a word ya said on that subject.")

·:·)·:·

And when after a really long time, Mr. James announced that Sophia was very close to the tallest buildings and the most people she would ever see, Sophia forgot to slouch. Forgot to be mad.

·:·٭(·:·

("Lady, it's a wonder our eyes didn't burn a hole right through that window! We forgot everything we'd just been tawking about and every pair a' our eyes just about apoplexied theirselves on to that window so we could see what was about to parade in front of it!")

·:·)·:·

• • • CITY LIGHTS • • •

"Miss Sophia, we are about to get on the bridge! Actually, you won't see much until we're riding over it, but look sharp!" Mr. James said.

·:·(·:·

("Hey, Me, do you remember what Thee said when he said that?"

"I'll tell you myself," said Thee, "since what I said was so important it must be recorded accurately. I'm not sure I can trust either one of you to tell Sophia's story. From what I've been hearing so far, and I have been listening, I get the feeling her story was about to become all about shopping. Admit it, didn't you just bring up the shops you were about to see? Ms. Author, aren't you writing this story to enlighten Readers? And by the way, this story you are writing will be the only record ever made of any human child's Emissaries from the Universe. And if we are seen discussing shopping at this, Sophia's crucial, crossroads moment, what will your Readers think of us, the Emissaries from the Universe? I will not allow the only record of Sophia's to be diminished anymore by discussions about shopping and mafia movies."

"Jeez, Thee!" said Lorraine, "You make this story sound like it's vegetables for Readers!"

"What fun!" said Me, "Seriousness! Enlightenment! Without shopping! Enlighten away, Thee, we wouldn't dream of shopping … oops! … stopping you!"

"Readers, kindly ignore them," said Thee, "and hear what I said -

" 'Things are changing so fast for Sophia now and we had better pay attention. She is our responsibility and responsibilities are serious matters, after all! Fairies, we must look sharp and take care of Sophia better than we ever have. When Mr. James drops her off, she'll be all by herself for the first time ever in her whole life and by herself in a place like this! Goliathon, the biggest city in the world, filled with so many PEOPLE. And we all know how PEOPLE can be.' "

" 'Uhhh oooh, People ahead! Big whoop!' " said Lorraine.

" 'How exactly does uhhh ooh! warn or help anybody?' "

" 'Thee, you're, like, so literal. I'm, like, cracking a joke!' "

" 'Your saying 'big whoop!' indicates that you don't understand the full range of possible dangers that just might ensnare a human child when she ventures away from her home! And cracking a joke at a time like that! That just shows how you, Lorraine, aren't taking Sophia's predicament seriously! There'll be no Miss Kitty, no Father, no Mother. She's going to need us. If you hear her say anything that doesn't seem right and you know you can help, please make sure you do. We're all she's got now!' ")

·:ᗡː··

Sophia looked up when she looked sharp. She had to. Because through the Moon roof was the Moon Man, his face was glowing and seemed to be peeking through the bridge's wires and smiling at her. *'Is he happy to see me? The Moon's never looked at me like that before!'* And sure enough when she looked through the side window into the river way below, there he was again, his wobbly smile bouncing back and forth through the wavy water. *'Maybe the Moon is friendlier down here ... but is the Moon even supposed to be friendly?'*

When she looked through the front windshield, she saw something else she had never seen before either, except in the Movies. Goliathon. The city. And there was so much city to see. And as they made their way over the bridge, soon every window was full of it. Such tall buildings! And so many of them. No wonder they called it Goliathon. And because it was the nighttime, many lights were on and she could see them shining through the windows of all those buildings; so many lights, so many windows, so many buildings she would never've been able to count them all. And there were even more lights than those. Lights that came from cars, from signs; from the top of the bridge in a long string; from the boats on the water, from the docks on the river. Lights that were working very hard to illuminate every speck of Goliathon's nightness and darkness.

'These sure aren't country lights; city lights boss the dark around down here. They make nighttime daytime! They turn something into something it's not. It's not even allowed to just be itself! But even so, this city is sparklier than anyplace I've ever seen before, than even the city in my Movies. And it sure is Tall! Everything here is so big and so bright. But will there be a place for me in all this bigness? I'll never ever be as sparkly as all of this. Or maybe if this night, these lights can be something they're not, I can too? I do want to walk around inside it all. But will I be able to? Or will I feel too small?'

And making her eyes as sharp as Mr. James had told her to, she looked at that tallness, those lights, those buildings, that Moon and tried to find the city she had been dying to walk around in, the city she had seen in all her Movies but could not.

'Maybe when I get inside it it'll look like it should. Okay, no matter how scared I am, I must find out for myself what it is! Or I won't ever get to see the swell gentlemen in their top hats and the ladies in their satin evening gowns and their feathery capes.'

And because she was sure that that Moon Man was peeking down at her, she looked up again at him through that Moon roof. He wasn't smiling at her anymore, she had a distinct feeling he was laughing.

'The Moon down here sure is different than the Moon at home!'

And then she heard herself think but didn't remember coming up with the stuff inside the thought. 'And they sho' won' be able to see you either now Missy, iffn' you don' go outside 'n show'em y'r stuff too! Now won' they now won' they?'

·∴C·∴

("Lady, when Free heard that voice inside Sophia, she busted up laughing. We all looked at her. We heard the voice, too, but we didn't think it was that funny. She couldn't stop laughing long enough to explain why she was laughing. Although, not having Free explain something maybe isn't so bad. But eventually Free stopped and joined you, Thee, by the Moon roof and both of you was looking every which way just like Sophia. Neither of them, Author Lady, had ever been to Goliathon before. Thee, you says, 'Goliathon is suitably named!' and Free told me later that she had looked up at her old friend the Man in the Moon and noticed how much light there was even at night here in Goliathon and wondered if her old friend could finally take it easy and relax since he didn't have to work so hard to light this Goliathon place up.

"Lady, already we, like, loved it there. During our free time, our fly time, we planned on finally meeting up with all of our old Fairies pals who lived in the children's heads down there."

"Who we hadn't seen in, like, so forever, darling!" said Me, "It was going to be like what you humans call a Convention but filled with Fairies and like a Homecoming Weekend and a Sorority Reunion and a Sleep-over, like, rolled into one! In the Shopping Capital of, like, North America! Second only to your Paris! There goes our beauty sleep! Although no human place could ever hope to compare to our own out-of-this-world city, Fareé, the true Shopping Capital of the World!"

"That is hardly why you are here, Me!" said Thee, "Author! Readers! Now do you understand why I've presented myself! I didn't want this story to deteriorate into a Goliathon Shopping Guide!")

·∴꙾·∴

And just like that, their car was off the bridge and on a wide road with a ton of traffic coming toward them and another ton going with them.

Gone were the lights. Gone were the buildings. Now they were driving on a bendy road by the side of the river. And the road was taking them through a forest. Sophia was surprised to see such a sight here! "Are we still in Goliathon, Mr. James?" Even though Mr. James was a 'dirty rat,' she had to know if she was there yet because it sure looked like they weren't. "Yes, Miss Sophia, keep looking out the window, you'll see!" That he didn't have to tell her, she hadn't stopped looking out the window once. As they drove, there were less and less trees and more and more cars and these cars were whizzing by them, driving faster than Mr. James ever ever drove. And they kept driving along the road which got less and less bendy and more and more wide and straight and filled with many many cars. And more and more of these cars were yellow cars. And these yellow cars were driving like they were in a race; driving right beside their car one second, in front of them the next, back beside them, in front again. Behind them. In front. And then Sophia got really scared. What if they drove right over top of them and straight down their front? If Mr. James didn't beep-up his horn, they just might. Because of all her Movie watching, she knew exactly what these were. The Taxi Cabs!

"Presently, one would wish to have eyes in the back of one's head!" Mr. James said.

··*(··

("Jeeez, Lady, did we want to give Mr. James exactly what he wished for! Eyes-in-the-Back-a-the-Head-Eyes. It wouldda been, like, so easy!"

"And you knew perfectly well, Lorraine, we wouldn't dare!" said Thee, "The Fairy Dispatcher would have gotten wind of it! He has his ways and his nose and his spies and he would not have been pleased, not have been pleased at all. And then he might have even … well, he didn't because we didn't, rest assured, Readers.")

··)*··

Mr. James wasn't talking like himself. Sophia took a good long look at the back of Mr. James because that's the only part of him she could see. '*I wonder if he's feeling sick. A polite person would ask. That's what Mommy would do. Ask how Mr. James is feeling. And probably, that's what she would want me to do. But I can't do what she can do. Or sound like her when she does it …*

'*But she isn't here! I'm the only person here who can do it. I have to. Even if Mr. James is a 'dirty rat,' he shouldn't feel sick and think nobody cares. That isn't right. It's up to me now to carry on as Mommy would.*' She cleared her throat of all its lowness and deepness, and sing-ing up her voice the best she could, the best way she knew how, she said, "Mr. James, do you feel okay?"

But even as Sophia was speaking, the hugest trucks, the most towering buses, the super-widest billboards, and a million taxi cabs were whizzing by, and she couldn't stop herself from watching all of them. Suppose one of these mountainous things fell on top of them in their now suddenly very-small-seeming but formerly-very-wide and very long and very roomy limousine? And even as she had just inquired about Mr. James' health, even as she tried to sound as much like her Mother as she could, she forgot to hear if she actually did, if she actually could, do what her Mother could do. She almost didn't remember to listen to Mr. James' reply.

"Miss Sophia, I'm just chipper. It's just these frightful Taxi Cabs! But have no fear, Miss Sophia, I will maneuver our chariot through this obstacle course and we will arrive at our destination in fine form. In fine form. As we always do. Indeed, Miss Sophia!"

But he still wasn't talking like he should and she wasn't sure what her Mother would've said or done next. It was a good thing they were now in the middle of a mix and a muddle of so many cars and trucks and buses and blinking lights and flashing lights and yellow cabs and lighted billboards and piers on the river side and huge buildings on the city side that Mr. James stopped talking altogether. He had to get their car over to the turning lane and he had do some fancy-fast, over-under-around-taxi-cab maneuvering himself to get it there. She wouldn't have to worry about showing good manners right now. And when at last they were in the turning lane, their car drove off that wide road and into the city deftly and swiftly.

• • • CITY LIGHTS CITY PEOPLE • • •

But now there was something else. Car horns that weren't going beep-beep, honk-honk like they did in the Village. No! these were city horns going SHRRIIIIIIIEEEEEEKKKKK because most of these horns never even stopped once to breathe.

And she heard people, and these people were shouting and yelling and saying bad words. And she saw why when they got a lot closer.

One of those taxi cabs had hit another one of those taxi cabs and there, screaming at each other were the two taxi cab drivers, and in the back seats of both of the cabs, the passengers were screaming too, but it wasn't at all clear just who they were screaming at. And they weren't the only ones screaming; so were the people who were driving the cars that were stuck behind the cabs and couldn't move; so were the people on the sidewalk, and some of these people it turns out were lady people and they sure weren't wearing satin evening dresses; and even some people leaning out the windows of some of the buildings, as if all of this wasn't enough screaming, were screaming, too. And then just as their limousine was crawling closer to this free-for-all, up strolls a police officer who came and stood right in between the two taxi cab drivers and then he started screaming and in Sophia's whole life she never heard anyone scream as loud as him.

····(····

("Lady, as soon as the Police Officer showed up, I couldn't stands it no more, I wanted in. I flew off Sophia's ear, through Mr. James opened vent window and right over to that screaming Police Officer. I started flying in circles around his hat with my wand out but not for long because in the next second, I flew over to the screaming taxi cab drivers, where I started pummeling the air with my fists and screaming myself—"

"Ms. Author," tattled Thee, "Lorraine was screaming Fairy bad words!"

"Yeah? So what, Thee! Like, 'Wheredja elfing learn to drive, ya' big bag a' bugs?' Hey, I was there on the side of right and wrong and to aid and assist that Police Officer—"

"Which sure surprised us!" said Me.

"Lorraine, you can't be on both sides! right AND wrong!" said Thee.

"Lady, see, I wasn't usually on the side of the establishment. And then the car started moving and the Fairies started screaming at me to get back in Sophia's head before the car took off and left me behind. 'Now wouldja just tell me how I'm gonna get lost here? Jeez! Like, I KNOW this place. Like, this is where my people come from.' "

"Darling, and when you did fly back in, you were spitting fire and we were afraid to remind you that you don't come from people, that you came from Fairies, the Mafairyia to be exact, in the Enchanted Lands!")

····)····

Sophia scooted away from the car's window. She wanted to make sure that none of those screamers saw her. Not a single soul in any Movie she ever saw ever screamed anything like the souls in this Goliathon place just screamed. Those Movie screamers had nothing on these Goliathon screamers. These screamers could have been in the Olympics for screaming and won the gold medal. She was so glad she was safe in her car and Mr. James was there with her. He would protect her. Even if he was a dirty rat. Mr. James managed to drive by the commotion and pretty soon, she could barely hear the screaming, which gave her some time to think.

'What WAS that? Who ARE these people? THESE? are the people of Goliathon? The ladies are not wearing evening gowns and they definitely don't have evening-gown-mouths. Maybe they have to be wearing evening gowns to talk the way they should. But none of the men are wearing top hats either or even the other kind of hats that look like the kind of hats I see in my Movies. And every one of these people have big mouths. Even the lady people. And they sure use them.

'Does everybody in Goliathon have a big mouth?

'Maybe you have to have a big mouth to live here ...'

And then Sophia got scared all over again.

'What happens to a person in Goliathon if they just have a little mouth?

'What'll happen to me?'

⋯⋆☾⋯

("Author Lady, I have to tell ya what Free did right then when nobody was looking. She tapped her wand on her head then onto mine. Ya wanna know why? So I could hear what she was thinking. As soon as she did, I knew why. This is what I heard:

"Listen, Lorraine. My thoughts are clear, you'll hear. I wish my talk could be as clear as my thoughts, with all of the words coming out of my mouth in the right order like they do in my thoughts. Lorraine, I know just how Sophia feels. After talking all mixed up all my life, I have learned to have a little mouth, too. I don't say things right and if I use a little mouth when I speak, you and the Fairies won't hear me so well when I mess up. I know I speak funny. It's just plain terrible to have to say everything wrong you speak and to have everybody hear you mess up plain as day, day after day. But when you have a little mouth, you won't even have to hear yourself. That's why Sophia has a little mouth. But that's not all Sophia and I have in common. Just like Sophia isn't telling Mr. James what she's thinking right now, I'm not telling the Fairies what I'm thinking either. Although, I am finally telling somebody – you. But I usually keep my fears and my thoughts safe inside me just like Sophia does. You and me and all the Fairies can hear whatever Sophia is thinking and worrying about, but none of you ever thought to listen to my thoughts, because maybe you thought somebody who talked like me, had mixed-up thoughts, too. And there's something else, Lorraine. Sophia and I are really alike in another way, too. Sometimes I wish I could talk like someone else, could be somebody else, just like Sophia does."

"And Me and Thee, do you remember what Free actually said really, really loud? I sure do, 'Embarrassed me am, too, PhoSiaPho. Funny talk me, too, PhoSiaPho! Laugh them me, too at too, too!' She was really hoping Sophia would hear her.")

∴꙾∴

Sophia heard something rumbling through her but just then the car window was aglitter. Outside, were lights the size of dinosaurs! Outside, wonder shimmered everywhere.

∴☾∴

("PhoSiaPho, hear me did she? Hope me so.")

∴꙾∴

The lights are on the skyscrapers! The skyscrapers are covered with them! And the skyscrapers are everywhere. But so are the lights. Purple. Turquoise. I love turquoise. Look at that! Here they even have a huge lit up space just for my favorite color! Wow! They light up color here and make it dance and dive and speed and bounce. There's fuchsia. And lime green, too. Pink. And yellow. Orange. White. Silver. Gold. How could a purple light be the size of a whole building? But wait that purple light is turning orange.'

"Oh, Miss Sophia, I'm afraid, I've made a wrong turn! Of all places to land in! The Square that's lit up in a perpetual New Year's Eve celebration. But since we're here – By jove! Feast your eyes, Miss Sophia! It's simply mad with light and color, isn't it? Take it all in; you've never seen the likes of this before! Certainly not in the Village Van Der Speck!"

"Mr. James, look the purple is bending and flipping and rolling into orange. They're like acrobat colors!" But there was even more going on than that. There were billboards that covered almost all the buildings, and the billboards were as big as the buildings. Skyscraper-sized! There were even several enormous televisions so people could watch television in the street! And on one of those television screens Fred and Ginger were dancing! She even knew the movie. Imagine that! The people in Goliathon watched Fred and Ginger just liked she did! Nobody in her class at school in the Village even knew who Fred and Ginger were! Maybe this place wouldn't be so bad after all. Even if everybody had a big mouth. And then she saw the biggest picture of all, of a lady in pink underwear with a lacey edge all around it and the lady was so big, she was the size of a giant, and because she was so big, so was her underwear and so was its lacey edge. They didn't have pictures of Giant ladies in their Giant Underwear where she came from. Everywhere she looked there were more advertisements, almost as big as that one. But then she recognized a character from another one of her Movies, and something else besides. It was a bottle of her Mother's Giggle in the hands of an

electric King Kong who was somehow climbing up one of those giant buildings; first, he'd take a sip of the Giggle, then he'd bang his chest and then
he'd giggle; and he repeated that sequence all the way up the skyscraper!

·∴☾∴·

("Author, darling," said Me, "amusing, n'est-ce pas?"

"Now, don't even try to tell me, Lady," said Lorraine, "you humans don't
do magic! Don't know how to hypnotize! How to cast spells! I couldn't take
my peepers offa it!")

·∴☽∴·

"Mr. James, how do they do that?"

"Oh, Miss Sophia, these people who make these advertisements are
fiendishly clever."

And she was hopping over to the window on the right side, the left
side, the moon roof. She'd stick her face right up on the glass and look
up and up and up and still she couldn't see everything. The place was
practically exploding right in front of her eyes. Lights were everywhere –
a cascade of light that speckled everything up, down, to the sky, to the
ground - lights here were alive. She never saw lights do such tricks and
she knew then that this place was nothing like what she had seen in her
Movies.

·∴☾∴·

("Lady, we was smooshed up against the moon roof looking at those
lights, too. I says, 'That's gotta be Our Guys inside those lights doing
that!' But meanwhile, Lady, Free was still deep at work inside Sophia
saying over and over, 'Embarrassed me am, too, Sophia. Funny talk me,
too, PoSiaPha! Laugh them me, too at too, too!' She was pretty sure
Sophia didn't hear her and she so desperately wanted to make sure she
did.")

·∴☽∴·

And then Mr. James turned the car away from all of those lights and
drove down a street that was not at all as wide, or that had lights in any way
giant-sized. "Miss Sophia, at long last, we are on your Grandfather's street.
Pay careful attention, we must find his building."

"Mommy said he lives in a house that is on the roof way way way on the
top of a tall tall building, Mr. James."

"Yes, Miss Sophia, your Grandfather is one of the lucky few in this city
who actually live in a house. Believe me, there are very few large houses
on skyscraper's roof! I've always been so curious to see this house. A big
house tucked way far away on the tippytippytop of a skyscraper. Shakespeare

wrote, 'Blow, blow, thou winter wind! Thou are not so unkind …' I can only imagine him adding this proviso to his immortal words, 'as to blow my house away!' had this been his house."

"Mr. James, do you think Grandfather's house could blow away?" And Sophia's eyes and ears …

···⁎⟨⁎··

("Author, Lady, every other pair of eyes and ears in the back seat of that car opened wide - with the exception of Free's. Her ears were still busy listening to see if she'd gotten through to Sophia.")

··⟩⁎··

"Your Grandfather's house! Miss Sophia? Why that house wouldn't dare budge! It would be afraid to. EveryONE and everyTHING does what your Grandfather says, Sophia. Your Grandfather is a great man. A powerful man. Everybody who works in Show Business knows who your Grandfather is. In fact, everybody who lives in Goliathon knows who your Grandfather is. Make no mistake about that!"

And Sophia (and the Fairies) relaxed … a little bit.

···⁎⟨⁎··

("Author, Lady, not exactly. Not Free. She was still listening but couldn't tell if Sophia was even just a little less worried about tawking funny.")

··⟩⁎··

Sophia turned towards the window again to watch as they drove by building after building. So many buildings! And no trees! She was sure that's what her Mother would've said. Her Mother liked trees to be everywhere. Her Mother would've probably said that whoever put all those buildings here forgot to put in the trees. But they sure didn't forget the buildings! But then, Sophia thought, trees could never have grown as tall as these buildings and the poor trees probably would've died trying. She was surprised her Mother spent so much time in a place that hardly had any trees.

And finally Mr. James stopped the car. "We are here, Miss Sophia. But first, I must find out where to park, so wait here. I'll ask the doorman."

And Sophia watched to see which building Mr. James would go into. He walked up to a shiny door that had a design all over it. The design was made out of gold and was a cut-out of a tree trunk and its branches all of which formed a filigree that she could see through to the black door underneath. *So that's where they put the trees! They draw them on gold and put them on their doors!* The shining tree door opened and an immense man stepped out. This must be who Mr. James called the doorman. Did they call him a doorman because he was almost as wide as the door and almost as tall and almost as shiny? He was wearing a bright green military-type uniform with big shiny buttons and shiny gold braid and a big tall hat made of dark fur and a long red cape that went down to the ground.

'A giant! Is this city filled with them? And even when they're not real giants, they talk with such big mouths that they think they're giants! In their giant advertisements, people wear giant-sized underwear! In their giant Square, they have lights the size of skyscrapers! Giants could have a party there! Or just watch giant televisions!'

All she could do was stare when the shining Christmas Tree Man and Mr. James came towards her. The Christmas Tree Man was wheeling a cart and even THAT was gold and shining and he towered over it and everything else nearby.

'He sure makes tall Mr. James not look so tall.' The both of them reached the car and Mr. James opened her door and said, "Miss Sophia, I am delighted to introduce you to Mr. Keys, the Doorman."

"Well, hello! Miss Missy, we have been expecting you with much antici-perspirations. I, in fact, was just about to call out the search party. Welcome to this, the greatest city in the world! And I am the best Doorman in the greatest city in the world. Keys the Doorman, at your service. Remember you cannot lock your Door without the Keys. Keys." He pulled out his keys. "Door." He pointed to the door. "Man." He pointed to himself. "Got it?" And he held out his hand.

⋯∙ᗯ∙⋯

("Ms. Author," said Thee, "I will not interrupt willy nilly the way my associates do, but I saw Keys the Doorman's gesture and knew instantly what Sophia had to do. I flew into Sophia's ear and began whispering, 'Sophia, you are to shake his hand with your hand and say, "Pleased to meet you, Mr. Keys!" Oh, her Mother would've been so disappointed if she remained timid now. And, of course, it goes without saying, Great Aunt Hortense ...'"

"Author Lady, ya gotta hear what Be says to her," said Lorraine, " 'Thee, if it goes without saying, then why are you saying it? Don't bring Great Aunt Hortense up just when Sophia and all of us are finally on vacation from, as Mr. James says to himself, the old Hoot! – cause, like, I've heard him thinking!' Imagine here we all are, finally free of Great Aunt Hortense and Thee brings her up!"

"Ms. Author, here's what I said in response. 'Manners are ALWAYS important, and Great Aunt Hortense is not ALWAYS wrong, Be!' "

"And Be says back to you, Thee, 'Vacations are important, too, Thee! And Great Aunt Hortense is a pain and I don't care if she's not always wrong! She's a pain when she's right AND when she's wrong!'

"And then Thee went, 'Thcch! Thcch!' - and don't say you didn't, Thee! – and kept on whispering, 'Pleased to meet you, Mr. Keys ... Pleased to meet you.' ")

• • • CITY LIGHTS CITY PEOPLE CITY MOUTHS • • •

Sophia knew exactly what a polite young lady was supposed to do in such a circumstance. And her head was even telling her so, and in no uncertain terms either. She was to step out of the car, hold out her hand so this Keys person and she could shake each other's hands. But this Keys person was the very first person she had to talk to here in Goliathon, and she wasn't sure how she would sound when she said the very polite greeting she knew she was supposed to say. Suppose she sounded too croaky? Suppose her voice came out too little because his voice was so big? He had, after all, one of those city mouths just like that Police Officer.

("Lady, Free heard what Sophia was thinking and began to say over and over, 'Mouth kay-o little ... NO! O mouth little kay ... NO ... Talk little kay-o ... NO!!!!' And Free started crying. She couldn't get out what she needed to say so that Sophia would understand her. Free held the wand to my head again. 'How am I going to get a message to Sophia if I can't talk myself? Maybe that's why Sophia's afraid she can't talk because she hears me say things all mixed up all the time, and I make her feel like she's mixed up too. It must be hard to have to listen to me talk all the time!' ")

'Why does the first person I have to talk to in Goliathon have to have a big mouth! This would be so much easier if I could say what I had to say like a Movie Star!'
Sophia stayed right where she was, inside the car, and felt how little her own mouth was and listened to what her head was telling her. So many things. But the loudest of all was the one telling her to do the right thing ... For her Mother. For Great Aunt Hortense!

For Great Aunt Hortense!??

Why was her head saying that? And she couldn't stop it from saying it either. And even though she knew Mr. James and Keys the Doorman were waiting for her to say, 'Pleased to meet you Mr. Keys,' and could even feel both of them out there; still she didn't move. *I'm taking too long! And showing no manners!'* And the next thing she knew she was watching a scene from a Movie. She couldn't remember what it was called, she couldn't even remember the Movie Star's name but there was this Beautiful Whoever arriving in the Big City for her very first time.

'Just like me.'

And Sophia saw herself as a Movie Star stepping out of the back of her car and saying what she had to say.

Or better yet, saying it with an accent, like a French Movie Star - 'Pleaze to meeeeet you, Meessyur Keeez!'.

Or an English one – 'So pleased to make your acquaintance, Mr. Keys!'

Or an Italian, but not in Maria's choppy Italian; in the voice of a fiery Italian Movie Star - 'Please-a to meet-a you-a, Mr. Keys-a!'

'... Oh! How I wish I could ...' Then Sophia looked down at what she was wearing, *'Movie Stars wouldn't be dressed like this.'* Because it was so cold outside, Maria had made her put on her heaviest woolen jumper that fell way below her knees and underneath it her highest-necked, longest-sleeved turtleneck. "You-a freeze-a today-a, itssa so cold-a!" Maria had said. The whole way down to Goliathon, Sophia had felt as if she was being cooked AND being swallowed alive AND she was itchy. She wished she was wearing a shiny, pink satin dress and sparkly slippers. Sophia looked down at her own feet locked up in the black rubber galoshes that Maria had also made her wear and she heard all over again what Maria had said to her this afternoon when Maria practically stood on top of her to make sure that she put these clodhopping-walruses over her shoes, "If-fa snow-a you-a no-a catcha cold-a, or ruin-a you-a nice-a leath' shoe-a. You mama she-a pay-a the-a' good-a money for dis-ashoe-a. You-a leave-a on-a you-feet-a. No-you-a take-offa! No-a!" And Sophia could still see Maria wag her finger right in her face while giving her the eye. Sophia wondered if that was the Official Evil Eye. Sophia hadn't dared to even dream of taking the walruses off during the entire trip for fear that Maria would find out. *'Miss Kitty'd never've made me wear these!'*

·∴·(·∴·

("Darlings, I burst into tears!" said Me, "How did I miss those hideous things! I can't believe that someone on the outside of me was wearing something like THAT and, by default, I was actually being conveyed all around in them. I know just how Sophia felt. What an entrance to have to make in this Divine City wearing, like, a horse blanket and submarines! I told everyone that Maria must never be allowed to dress Sophia again, AND was to be banished to her broom closet forever. Miss Kitty must return! Maria obviously prefers to multiply in the uglification tables. But what is far worse and really can NOT be tolerated is - this Maria is tasteless like a - like a - discount shopper ... or I can't believe I'm even saying these words ... a thrift store shopper ...' ")

·⸰꙳)꙳·⸰

'These walruses are the first thing of mine to touch down in this city for Movie Stars! To think!' As Sophia planted those tanks on the sidewalk, she saw all the shoes she had ever seen on all the feet of all the Movie Stars in all the Movies she had ever looked at as they stepped out for a night in the big city. And her heart banged away inside her.

But ...she WAS in Goliathon! Just like all those Movie Stars. Even if she was standing there in galoshes.

'Pleased to meet you Mr. Keys.' She heard her insides say.

'I'm really in Goliathon!

'All by myself.

'And about to talk to my very first person from Goliathon!

'Who is gigantic.

'If I could just talk to him.

'The way a Movie Star talks.

'Or like every Movie Star I've ever seen talked.

'And act like every Movie Star I've ever seen act.' Sophia could feel herself shrinking onto the pavement.

'While showing my good manners.' And getting smaller.

'And making everybody proud.' And smaller.

'I can't do all that!' Sophia was overwhelmed.

·⸰꙳☾꙳·⸰

(" 'Sophia, say it like yourself ... like a ten-year-old girl with good manners. You don't have to be a Movie Star. You don't have to be any-one but yourself. Come on now! Please?' Ms. Author, it simply had to be stated."

"Lady, Free did that wand thing again, 'Thee talks so well, she'll be able to get through to Sophia. I'm not like Thee, I don't care so much about good manners. I wish that Thee would just tell Sophia it's okay to talk with a little mouth; that just because Sophia talks with a little mouth, that that should never stop her from talking. And that manners are not the most important thing.

" 'You see, Lorraine, Thee isn't saying what I would've said to Sophia. But getting Sophia to talk is the important thing, little mouth or not. Although, Lorraine, maybe I'm all wrong. Maybe what I have to say to Sophia is not as important for Sophia to hear as what Thee has to say to Sophia. And besides, I'd have such a hard time getting all the words out in order, nobody would understand me and by the time anybody did, it would be too late.' ")

⚬⚬⚬

As small as Sophia felt, she knew one thing. She was here. In Goliathon. She couldn't get over it. She may not ever have the right manners or speak with a big enough mouth or ever ever speak so perfectly or even like a Movie Star, but she made it this far, so maybe she could do what she had to do. She got her mouth ready. She got her hand ready. She would say what she had to say. She would shake Keys the Doorman's hand. She put out her hand. Her hand was all that was needed, not her head; her head didn't need to shake his hand.

But she didn't open her mouth.

⚬⚬⚬

(" 'No!!!!!' Lady that's what Free screamed. 'Thee her tell. Mouth kay-o little – fine is – fine is!' "

"Ms. Author," said Thee, "I was leaning out Sophia's ear to see just how she would do and I must admit, I wasn't paying attention to Free.")

⚬⚬⚬

And Sophia couldn't see where to put her hand because she couldn't see Keys the Doorman's hand.

⚬⚬⚬

(" 'Oh ... Sophia, Sophia, please, please just lift up your head ...' I again, Ms. Author.")

⚬⚬⚬

And Sophia panicked. Her hand had no hand to shake. Keys the Doorman hadn't given her his hand. Plus her head was down so she couldn't see where his hand was.

⚬⚬⚬

("Lady," said Lorraine, "Thee's browbeating did no good. Because Sophia's hand shook the empty air!"

" 'You have to wait for his hand!' I do admit, I did raise my voice, Ms. Author."

"Free, who by now had joined Thee and all of us on Sophia's ear, was sobbing. 'Little kay-o! Little kay-o!' But Lady, I'm sorry to have to tell you I didn't hear her, none of us did, cause not a single one of us was paying any attention to Free.")

⚬⚬⚬

"Okay, short stuff, I can see that you are giving to me the plus five. And I am giving to you the minus five!" said Keys the Doorman.

'*Oh, I look so stupid!*' Sophia pulled her hand behind her back. '*Oh! Just let me collapse into the backseat and maybe Mr. James will drive away so that I never have to see Keys the Doorman again.*'

·:·☾··

("Lady," said Lorraine, "no one like even looked up when Free flew off Sophia's ear, we was so busy watching Sophia. I did hear her say something like, 'Thee said everthing everwrong! Nervous make her. Seem right not! Help she can't. Help can I. Will do help ...' And then apparently she went back inside, packed up a few things, put them in her wing-sack, threaded her two wings through its openings, secured the sack around her and flew off, with tears streaming down her face, 'Me friend old find. Help he me. Help he she!' And out of Sophia she flew and not one of us even noticed."

So that's when Free left! Thanks, Lorraine! Can I go on now?)

··☽··

But the thought that Sophia wouldn't see any more of Goliathon seemed even more awful than having Keys the Doorman find out how embarrassed she was.

'*I can't just give up. I've made it to Goliathon. That mysterious place that I've seen so many times in my Movies. It was just a little mistake.*'

And Sophia stood there. But she still didn't lift her head to look at Keys the Doorman or Mr. James or Goliathon itself. She kept her hand behind her back and her head down - '*at least my body is here*' - and saw the pavement she was standing on. A pavement in Goliathon. '*They don't just have gray pavements here like in the Village, their pavements have sparkles all over them. They're twinkling at me. Wow - Here even the PAVEMENT sparkles. Things in Goliathon are sure different than they are in the Village.*' But as the sparkles filled her eyes, she remembered why she was staring at them. She was staring at them because she hadn't lifted her head. She hadn't lifted her head because she didn't like to make mistakes. Mistakes like not talking right the first time you arrived in the city for Movie Stars. Mistakes like talking like a scared little girl with a little mouth and not talking like a Movie Star the first time you arrived in the city for Movie Stars. The Movie Stars who she saw in her Movies who came to Goliathon didn't make mistakes the first time they had to talk to somebody. She could feel her face heating up even though this city-air was ice-box-cold.

'*Movie Stars don't get embarrassed and don't have bright-red faces!*' Now she wouldn't dare pick up her head.

'*Some entrance I've just made! Some Movie Star I'll be. I can't even shake somebody's hand and say pleased to meet you!*'

"Now as I come to reconnoiter, maybe that wasn't five, Mr. James? Cause as I gaze down yonder upon her, I can't help but notice, she's hidin' 'em. What do you think, Mr. James, you are a trustworthy and not a scalawag observatory of fact! Did she show five fingers or was she cheatin' me and only givin' me two? Ya gotta watch yourself around this town; the Goliathonians are always tryin' to chizzle you, even when they shake your hand. Mr. James, perhapst you can tell better'n me cause you are a lot closer to the ground."

And then there were two most peculiar laughs. One silk, one gravel. And Sophia imagined a rough-tough guy in a top hat, like Goliathon itself was laughing at her.

Sophia waited for them to stop; they didn't. She stood there not moving her head or her hand either; her face, still a hot red. Standing there like that, she felt odd. She had to do something. But they were still laughing. Were they laughing at her? She didn't like people to laugh at her. Maybe Mr. James was a 'dirty rat' after all. And she was mad. She put her two lips together as tightly as she could, made her maddest face, lifted that red hot face, and at last, looked up. And there way way above her was Keys the Doorman.

And he had the laughing-est face with the widest grin that spread across his whole mouth and that showed his big giant teeth.

All of that! On one face!

But there was even more! He had eyes that were the biggest and the brightest she'd ever ever ever seen. And in her whole life, she'd never seen anyone look so happy. Just looking at him, she almost forgot how mad she was. Her face was barely red hot any more. And her mouth, almost, opened all by itself and laughed right along with them. Almost. And when his shiny eye caught her eye, he put his hand down so fast and shook her hand so firmly, she could feel every bone in her own hand and every bone in his. He turned his hand up, held it flat against her hand, tapped her hand with his flat hand, and kept tapping it even as one of his fingers on his other hand kept pointing at her hand. Did he want her to slap his hand with her hand? And she did. And then he said, "Well, Mr. James, she had five all the time. She will be a good poker player after all."

·⸱·(⸱··

("Lady! 'Poker!' I says! 'Oh! My people! My people!' ")

·⸱·)⸱·⸱

"Now, short-stop, what was your name? Miss Short-phia? I understand ya' gonna be visitin' with your Grandfather. Wack-a-doo! Wack-a-doo!"

"I'm not short!" That swooped down her tongue and flew into the Goliathon air before it could be examined for sound-worthiness and there was nothing she could do about it.

·∴C·∴

("Ms. Author, that exclamation should never have been the first thing out of her mouth!"

"Thee, she couldn't very well let him get away with saying that," said Be, who had reappeared, "And besides, didn't you notice? She talked. She opened her mouth and talked! And did you ever think about this Miss Thee, what about his good manners? Is she the only one who has to have good manners? Can't you hear that he called her short stop and short stuff and Miss Short-phia? What if someone doesn't use their good manners with you? What does your rule book say about that?"

Thee tossed her head, lifted her eyes to the heavens and said, "Just because someone else isn't using their good manners with you, that doesn't mean you should stop using your good manners with them, Be! We must lead by example."

"Well, Thee, why don't you jump in one of those taxi cab driver's head and tell him that, right before he's about to slug the taxi cab driver who just slugged him. What do you think he's gonna do, Thee, pull his punch or blow you right out of his head?")

·∴Ɔ·∴

Sophia wasn't finished. She forgot to be terrified, forgot she couldn't get her mouth to say the one thing she had to say; her hand to do what it was supposed to do, and that her first entrance in Goliathon was, what people in the Movies call, a flop. And though she well knew everybody here had city mouths that were a lot bigger than hers, *He called me short stop AND Shortphia. And I'm the third tallest girl in my class!* She had no choice; she'd have to straighten this Keys the Doorman out. "I'm the third tallest girl in my class!"

"Well, whaddya know about that, you do talk! Somebody upstairs told me you didn't like to. And I made a bet with her and said you would, 'cause I'd make ya'. And just in case you have not noticed cause your eyes might be asleep cause it is nighttime and you are just a youngster after all, woudja jus' take a look at me! To me, everybody's Short-phia, so do not take it so hard. You heard the expression; it is lonely at the top? Take it from me, they weren't kiddin'! Spend some time up here where there is nobody but a bunch of pigeons and you will soon find out. At least, you got people down there with your pigeons!" And then he did the same trick, with his teeth and his mouth and his eyes.

'Who told him I don't like to talk? Somebody up there in Grandfather's house is talking about me. Who? It's a she, that I do know. Just who is this … this she?'

She couldn't quite get it out of her mouth to ask him so it stayed locked up with all the rest of her thoughts. But she wouldn't take her eyes off him, hoping that by looking at him, she could find out, and save herself from having to speak up and ask. He didn't take his eyes off her either but she still didn't find the answer to her question in his face. She did see that his face was now playing a different trick: looking like it was laughing even when it stopped.

"Okay, okay, if you do not like it I will not call you short stuff or short stop. But I can call you Miss Short-phia, Miss Short-phia?"

'No!' But she didn't say it. And it mixed up with all of her other thoughts. And some new ones too - like maybe he was just making jokes.

Which confused Sophia. Was he just making jokes? But, even so, she still didn't want to actually say out loud in her own voice for everybody, including herself - especially herself, to hear, 'I don't want you to call me 'Miss Shortphia' even if you are just making jokes!' But then he wasn't waiting for her answer, he just started laughing again. But this time he wasn't laughing with his whole mouth, just out one side of it; and then just like that, he switched to the other side, the side that looked like it was barking. And when he said, "Now, Mr. James, you can keep that junk heap here for a little while, then you better move it, or do not worry it upon yourself, one of our Goliathon tow trucks'll cheerfully move it for ya!"

And finally Sophia's ears heard what he was really doing. And then she understood. And she was delighted - by his voice and its way of saying things - and she forgot she was confused. She watched him. He laughed and then he didn't while a part of him still looked like he was. She would have to learn that trick. She would use it when she was creating a character. Watching him was really like watching a character in the Movies. He was the character who made everybody laugh. Movies always seemed to have people like Keys the Doorman in them. Even when they were sad movies. People like him made the Movie more fun.

But even if he was like a silly man who told jokes all the time she still didn't like him calling her Short-phia.

Now all she had to do was get a city-mouth and tell him.

"Mr. Keys," said Mr. James, "I assure you I'm just accompanying Miss Sophia up to her Grandfather's house and then I'll be off. Miss Sophia, shall we?"

Keys the Doorman put Sophia's suitcase on his cart and began wheeling that cart towards the shiny tree door. Mr. James and Sophia followed close behind and Sophia, from her safe spot beside Mr. James and behind Keys, examined this Goliathon in the night. This night around her Grandfather's building wasn't anyway near as lit up as the square for giants, but it was more lit up than places in the village would be. The people in Goliathon really mustn't like the dark. And Sophia thought of all the dark corridors in The Castle L'Oomla she had run through to get to her Movie Star School. Maybe it wouldn't be so bad here at night if their corridors were lit up like it was day-time. When Keys opened those shiny tree doors and they were inside at last, the dark night disappeared entirely and there was the brightest moon-white she'd ever seen and it was coming from everywhere.

• • • THE GREAT-WHITE-YELLOW-BRICK-ROAD-WAY • • •

"Of course, your Grandfather has his very own private elevator, he is a Producer after all. Wack-a-doo, wack-a-doo. And Producers get what they want. Wack-a-doo, wack-a-doo. Everybody here knows that, and you will soon find out."

Keys the Doorman turned around and gave her a look and his face did not have a single laugh in it anywhere. "His elevator is all the way down at the far faraway tippy tip end of that yonder corridor."

And Keys nosed the cart into the long bright white corridor and again Sophia and Mr. James followed close behind. Keys began whistling.

'I know that tune. It's from a cartoon. I think, it's one of the Ducks' theme music – Daffy or Donald's – or maybe it's the theme from Looney Tunes.' The cor-ridor was made from white marble that went from floor to ceiling. They had marble in The Castle L'Oomla, too. But the marble there was nothing like the marble here. This marble was so bright, it glared. Sophia wished she could reach for her sunglasses. After all, that's what a Movie Star would've done. There was white everywhere. She was walking on white. Just like in a Movie she saw.

'Like Dorothy in The Wizard of Oz and her yellow-brick-road. Except my road isn't brick and it isn't yellow and my shoes aren't ruby red, and they sure aren't slippers.'

She could hear her rubber galoshes kaflumphing and plooplinking and urpchuckiling along the white-marble-road. She tried to stop them from making noises that no respectable person should ever make but couldn't. But when she noticed that Mr. James's heels tip-tip-tapped very precisely, and Keys the Doorman whistles bounced all around the marble, and that their clicks and tweets mixed together with her umphs and plinks and urps and, altogether, it wasn't a mess, she was shocked.

'We're making music. It's not exactly like the kind of music Daddy always used to play for us at home. I wonder if he'd like this kind of music too? It's just played by different instruments. If Daddy would've heard me plooplinking in my galoshes, he probably'd say that I'm like the tuba; and that Mr. James' shoes are the drum sticks beating time; and that Keys the Doorman, whistling his cartoon, is the Giant playing a Tweedie Bird flute. As we travel down our white road way, we're making music together, too, just like Dorothy and the Scarecrow and the Tinman and the Lion. Just like in the Movie. Except Dorothy and the Scarecrow and the Tinman and the Lion all knew they were making music. But on this road, only I know, and I won't tell my two compadres either. Because Mr. James doesn't know about all the Movies I watch, and Keys the Doorman probably better not ever find out. He might tell everybody. He probably wasn't supposed to tell anybody that I don't like to talk, and he told Mr. James and me. Besides, neither one of them would understand anyway. Probably.'

Sophia began to sing but inside herself ... *'We're off to see the Wiza ... No ... the Producer ... We're off to see the Producer, the wonderful Producer of ... Oz ... No! Goliathon - too long ... Gi ... We're off to see the Producer ... the Wonderful Producer of Gi ... A Producer? Is a Producer anything like a Wizard?'*

She wanted to ask Keys the Doorman but then he would've found out she didn't know what a Producer was. She wanted to ask him why he looked at her like that when he talked about her Grandfather the Producer. But she wasn't about to speak up to ask him. And because she didn't speak up, she knew, she'd never find out.

And because she didn't speak up, she'd never know. Anything.

She kept walking on down that long long corridor and did what she always did. Listen.

Plop.

Whistle.

Click.

And the plopper plopped and the whistler whistled and the clicker clicked, and it resounded everywhere, on the ceiling, on the wall, on the floor. In the Wizard movie, Dorothy and the Tin Man and the Straw Man and the Lion had all locked their arms together and sang as they high-stepped down the yellow-brick-road. She tried to imagine what kind of music she and Mr. James and Keys the Doorman would make if they were walking on a yellow-brick-road and not a white-marble-floor. Maybe if they were all walking on brick they'd all join together just like that Wizard movie. Maybe the only reason they weren't all singing was because they were walking on the wrong kind of floor.

···C···

("Hey, can't I at least change the marble to brick?" said Lorraine.

"Oh sure, if you don't mind the Fairy Dispatcher turning you into a Meep, just because he can?' said Be.)

·:·꒰·꙳·

Oh, how Sophia wished she, and Mr. James and Keys the Doorman were on that yellow-brick-road and in that Movie, so all of them would be singing a song.

'Everything is better in the Movies.'

·:·꙳꒰·꙳·

("Oh No! Did you hear that? What's wrong with the road they're on, this white-marble road?" said Thee. "The reason they're not singing is not because they're on the wrong road. They're not singing because Sophia didn't start singing, didn't tell them what she was thinking. That's why they're not singing. Sophia could make this so much more fun for herself, for everybody if she just shared what was inside her. Keys the Doorman and Mr. James would never have been able to come up with what she just came up with. I'm sure if Sophia would open up and tell them what she was thinking, they'd all be—"

"Cracking each other up!" said Be.

"Now, Be, that's hardly how I would describe this particular situation," said Thee. "maybe Sophia would not wish to be in movies if she understood she's in something even better, her own life and she's the star of it, because everything that happens to you in life is not pretend."

"Like very very soon," said Be, "we have to like leave Sophia forever, and before we do, we've got to help her accept her voice. Because if she can, she'll share all that's going on inside her with others. And we know what's going on inside her is fascinating! Man, if she shared it, she'd sparkle like a movie star, too."

"Then, Lady, we looks at Be and Thee and our jokes just fell outta us. Soon we'd be gone outta Sophia, like, forever. She had way too much to learn before she'd, like, live happily ever after. I mean, she could just about say those few, itty, wittle things to Keys the Doorman! At the rate Sophia was going, her sparkling like a movie star seemed next to impossible."

"And then, Ms. Author, I looked at each Fairy and turned whiter than Fairy Snow."

"Lady, I didn't even notice because I was telling everybody, 'I know, let's sing along with her really loud and because we're so loud, her song'll just bust outta her and then all a' us and all a' them'll start singing like one big happy family on, like, a wacky road trip.'"

" 'Where's Free?' Is what I was thinking but didn't say, Ms. Author."

" 'Here! Here!' I said to Lorraine. I wasn't paying any attention to Thee." said Be.

"Lady, none of us was paying any attention to Thee. And then me and Be and Me joined Sophia in her silent song. We aimed our song into Sophia's throat trying to make it tickle and vibrate and open. 'We're off to see the Producer, the wonderful Producer of Gi—' "

" 'Where's Free?' But I, Ms. Author, could barely whisper it! And here I am lecturing about Sophia's not being able to talk and the same thing was happening to me! Not one of the Fairies heard me or even noticed I hadn't joined in the song and that I had sat down and that my wings were drooping and my head was low because I had a hunch that Free was far away. But then again, I couldn't have told anybody why I had this hunch either."

"And then Lady, Sophia stopped her silent song all of a sudden which made us sing it even louder. We was really hoping we could get her to sing out.")

·⁘ ⁙ꙩ⁚·

Dorothy and the Scarecrow and the Tinman and the Lion needed to see the Wizard because they wanted something from him. So why do I need to see the Wizard? Maybe I need something too. But what do I need? I don't need a heart because I can hear my heart right now and it's even louder than my kerplumps, so I'm not like the Tin Man. I don't need a brain because my brain's been talking to me so much on this whole trip telling me all sorts of things and still is; in fact, my brain never seems to stop, so I'm not anything like the Scarecrow. And I'm almost positive I'm not like the Cowardly Lion, although I'm not that positive, but I didn't shake all over like he did and cry like a baby when I got here. And, eventually, I did get out of the car. I stood tall when I had to, no matter what Keys the Doorman said. I came to Goliathon all by myself, without Miss Kitty, without Mother, without Daddy. I didn't refuse to go. But I know I need something. What could it be?' She could only wonder what it was. But nothing seemed to occur to her and so she had time to wonder about something else that was bothering her.

'What sort of place am I going to? Somebody is talking about me up there and they don't even know me. And they're telling on me too. They told Keys the Doorman that I don't like to talk! I like Keys the Doorman but I don't like him to call me Short-phia. And he even said he wants to keep calling me that too. And I don't know how to get him to stop. And besides how can I, with my little mouth, tell that great big person he has to stop? And wouldn't his feelings be hurt if I did? But what could I say to him so that his feelings wouldn't be hurt? But because I didn't tell him, now my feelings are hurt. And how will I ever find out just who up there is talking about me? How will I ever be able to ask all those questions?'

She knew she had to ask a question to get an answer; she couldn't just think a question in her mind and expect everyone to hear it; she'd have to ask it out loud - with her mouth. And she knew she hadn't done that. She didn't ask her questions to Keys the Doorman, to Mr. James, so the only thing she heard from her two companions was the sound of Mr. James' heels going click click click that mixed up with the tune piping and trilling and loop-de-looing out of Keys the Doorman tricky big mouth.

His tricky big mouth.

Big mouth.

Little mouth!

'A mouth! That's what I need. That's what I have to ask the Wizard for. That's why I'm on this white-marble-road. To get a mouth! So that I can tell Keys the Doorman not to call me Short-phia even if he's just teasing me and making jokes. A mouth! To ask and keep asking everybody I meet until I find out who's talking about me. A mouth to set that person who talked about me straight; once I find out just who that person is. A mouth to tell Maria that I don't want to wear someth ... well, maybe not Maria. And maybe a mouth so when I'm in school, I can talk loud enough, so people don't want to send me to a stupid speech therapist. That's what I need.

'But Grandfather isn't the Wizard. Although everybody sure has been telling me how great he is, how powerful he is. And isn't that what the Wizard said about himself. 'I am the Great and Powerful Oz!' Well, then maybe Grandfather would just be like the real Wizard in that Movie, a scaredy-cat old man pretending to be powerful. And the Wizard wasn't even a Wizard, he just called himself that. The Tinman got something like a heart but not a real heart. And the Scarecrow got something like a brain but not a real brain. And the Lion got a type of courage but not the kind of courage real Lions have to have when they roam around in the jungle. I can't imagine THAT Lion in the 'Jungle' jungle.

'So where am I going to get this mouth I really need?

'But didn't Keys the Doorman just say Grandfather gets what he wants? Does that mean, he would help me get what I want? And didn't Mr. James say Grandfather was the only person in this whole city who built a whole house on top of a skyscraper? And didn't Mommy say that he's a Producer — I wonder if that's the same thing as powerful? Maybe he's not like that fake Wizard after all. Maybe he is Great. Maybe he is Powerful. Maybe I will get a mouth after all.'

'Now all I have to do is ask for it.'

⋯∴C∵⋯

('And, Lady, me and Be and Me says, 'We'll help ya! Don't worry!' ')

⋯∵⊃∴⋯

'Haugh! I know what I need to ask for it.

'*A mouth!*'

And Sophia got scared all over again. She'd have to have one to ask for one.

·∴Ꮯ∴·

("But Ms. Author," said Thee, "Sophia wasn't the only one who needed to find her mouth. I did, too. I had to tell everybody that Free was missing. Gone. I was sure. Far far away.")

·∴Ꭰ∴·

• • • THE PRODUCER OF GI • • •

Even as Sophia fretted her way down that long white corridor, she couldn't help but hear - Click Clack Click Clack

Wrrrrrrrrrrr Wrrrrr Wrrrr Wha Who Whaa Whaa

Kaflouf Kaplop

The sounds they were making! That bounced, clacked, pinged, slapped and mixed up altogether and reverberated through that corridor and through her. Sounds. Round and round. Sounds. That mixed up with all her frets. Her worries. Sounds that traveled all over that white marble and down that great white way.

And then it hit Sophia. '*It's the music for this movie! The Producer of Gi! Wow! Listen to this stuff. Music in movies makes the movies sound as extraordinary as they look. The Movie Stars can't say everything they really feel, because there aren't words for everything, and the parts that there aren't words for, the music says. All the audience has to do is listen to the music to know what's going on and to feel how the Movie Stars feels. As soon as I hear the music, I understand what's going on even better than I did before. Sometimes when there's music in a part of a movie when it wasn't there before and it's louder, it's like the music reaches out from the screen and grabs me right where I'm sitting, and makes me feel whatever it wants me to feel.*'

Click. Kaflouf. Whaaa.

'*But this sure isn't the music I'd play if my character was feeling the way I feel right now. Because right now, I feel worried. And this music sounds silly. If I wanted everyone to know how I was feeling in this movie, I'd play a whole different kind of music. I mean, how's a person supposed to feel after listening to this?*'

Kaplop. Clack. Wsssssssssh.

'*Kaflouf Kaplop! That's the music for now? For this movie? For our movie?*' And then something else hit her, '*Maybe they'd all be making different sounds, if I told them how I really felt!*' And she glanced up at Mr. James and Keys the

Doorman, but they were just walking down that corridor and not paying attention to her at all. *'I don't think I can do that. And because I can't – or I won't - this'll just have to be the music for The Producer of Gi. For our walk down this great white way. That'll have to be the music of me. The music of us.'*

'Kaflouf Kaplop Wrrrrr.'

And its silliness made her itch all over and she didn't know whether to laugh or cry.

⸳∗◖⸳∗

("Lady, soon even our wings was beating its rhythm!")

⸳∗◗⸳∗

And finally she gave in, and put in extra kafloufs, and more kaplops, kaFLOUFFING on one step, KAplopping on the next as she went down that great white way. Did Mr. James peer down at her and do an extra click? Was that Keys the Doorman looking at her out of the corner of an eye and wssssssssshhhhhhhhhhing even longer? Sophia fished around inside her deep deep pool of Movie Star voices and found the voice that would've floated over the top of it all. If only she would've let it. *'We'd be making the music of us. If I'd just sing it out.'* And she almost did.

Until by and by they reached the elevator and their music came to a stop. Keys the Doorman pushed the button and the elevator door opened so quickly, so quietly, so perfectly that Sophia thought, *'This is sure not like the rickety old moaning croaking elevator in Great Aunt Hortense's house. It's awfully quiet for a machine. And it opened so fast, it must have heard us and known we were coming … or something. But elevators can't hear. Unless elevators in Goliathon can.'* Sophia and Mr. James stepped inside and Keys the Doorman wheeled the cart in behind them. Mr. James was his usual self, head neither to the right nor the left, but very discreetly observing everything he could about that Goliathon elevator. Sophia also wanted to observe everything she could about a Goliathon elevator as attentively, as discreetly as Mr. James, but this was her very first ride in an elevator that wasn't Great Aunt Hortense's, and she could only be as discreet and attentive as she could contain herself to be, and that was by looking up, down and sideways. Even by looking every which way, she couldn't tell if this big city elevator could hear but she could clearly see that there was even more shine in it than in that whole entrance-way and down that long long corridor.

For inside the cab of that elevator, lining each and every wall and the entire ceiling, were mirrors and on the edge of each mirror were lights, and the lights were in straight rows that went from floor to ceiling, and even across the ceiling too. And each and every light in each and every row was on. And oh how they shined in those mirrors. That elevator was awfully small to have so much shine in it. Sophia really wished she had some sunglasses, and this time not because she wanted everyone to think she was a Movie Star.

'These piercing gleams! It must be like the flashes from the cameras that those photographers are always pushing right into all those poor Movie Star faces! It's a wonder those flashes don't poke out their poor Movie Star eyes! These lights are needling into mine. So their eyes must positively kill them! No wonder Movie Stars are always wearing dark glasses! Those poor things! And then they have to walk through spotlights too, all while those camera flashes are flashing! Camera flashes! AND spotlights! It must feel like a firestorm has fallen over every part of them! They could never hide from it no matter how big their sunglasses are! Oh, the hard hard work that lies ahead of me!'

⸱⸱⋆☾⸱⸱

(" 'Do you hear her?' I said, darling. 'She understands what I go through! All is not lost, everyone! There is hope for a happy ending, Sophia is showing a rare insight into character, and sensitivity to the needs of others - my needs in particular!' "

" 'Oh! I think I'm going to vom—' but just then Be interrupted me, Lady! Tell her what you says."

" 'Lorraine, if you even think you're gonna do that, I'd go outside, before Thee snaps out of it and decides to join us again and gets a whiff of it with her Super-Nose and then makes us all get down on our hands and knees and scrub our Remarkably Small Place. Again!

" 'And Me, first off, you are not a Fairy Star, remember, you flunked the screen test because you are way too thin AND you have a stuck-up, Lark-Avenue voice, so the last I remember, dear Me, you are still just a flyway model; and second of all, you think everything is about you, and if all Sophia has learned after these ten years is how to make you happy, then she's in more trouble than we even realize. And so is our mission.' "

"Lady, see what I mean about Be?"

"Author, darling, here's what I said right back to Be. 'I could hardly expect you to understand the sunglasses-requirements of a highly stylish, glamorous person who is pursued relentlessly by bright lights and thrusting cameras.' And then did I give Be a look! From her stringy hair down to her black toe lacquer! Please! 'My mission is to make sure that Sophia will always know how to look fabulous in all sorts of lighting conditions. Why else would the Fairy Dispatcher have put me here?' And I made a great show of huffing over to my corner."

" 'Hah! First off, Me! There ain't a corner in here!' snapped Lorraine. Show-huff is right!"

Fairies! Enough!)

·:·**)**·:·

And while those lights shone down on them, the elevator kept going up and up for what seemed like forever. Sophia and Mr. James had by this time put their heads lower to shield their eyes. When Keys the Doorman noticed, he laughed and said, "Uh oh! I have forgotten! The lights in your Grandfather's elevator! I used to shield my eyes too but have stopped in the noticing of them. I will turn them down. Your Grandfather designed this elevator so these lights can do anything he wants! They are like a marquee in one of his theatres. And he wants everybody who ever rides up in this elevator to know and to never forget that they are about to enter HIS world - the world of ..." And Keys the Doorman put the mischief in his eye and said, "THE THEATRE!" not like himself at all but more like Mr. James. Keys turned a knob and instantly the lights dimmed. "Is that better?"

"Indeed, Mr. Keys, a much needed improvement. Better, Miss Sophia?" And Mr. James smiled at her.

Looking at Mr. James's smile reminded her he was soon to leave and the bravery drained out of her and she couldn't smile. She wanted to ask him not to leave but didn't want to be such a baby in front of Keys the Doorman, who had called her short already. She would've loved to say, 'I don't want to have to be here all by myself. With Grandfather and Grandmother, who I still can't remember. And all those other people Mommy told me lived in this house, too. And one of them is already talking about me.' But she knew Mr. James had to leave. She remembered she'd been mad at him but now she couldn't remember why. She wasn't at all mad at him now. She'd never be mad at him again.

And then Keys the Doorman stretched himself tall, made his face even taller, which he then set with the tallest mischief. She could sense what he was about to say even before he said it, "Miss Shortphia, has the weather improved way way down there?" And he didn't even try to hide his mischief when he winked at her.

'He called me that again! I wish he wouldn't! However will I get him to stop calling me that? Why he might call me that forever. Unless I tell him to stop.'

But she didn't.

'What sort of a place am I going to? Suppose everybody up there calls me that? Suppose my Grandfather does too? I'll hate it up there if they do. Will I be able to talk to Grandfather, or will I just clam up like I always do around people and just be too afraid to hear myself say even one word? But if he does call me that, I won't

like him at all and I won't want to talk to him. I hope my Grandmother'll be nice. Or maybe she'll be just like Great Aunt Hortense. Mommy said Grandfather and Grandmother came to visit me many times when I was very very little, but I don't remember them. She said they loved me.' She tried again to remember them but couldn't.

'... Auugh! we've stopped! But the elevator stopped so quietly. Just like it started. Nothing at all like Great Aunt Hortense's elevator. Everything in my Grandfather's house sure works perfectly. Or maybe that's the way everything works in Goliathon. Everything but me.'

• • • HER GRANDFATHER'S HOUSE • • •

Sophia, not wanting to miss a thing, kept her eyes and ears wide open. She watched the elevator doors, knowing they were about to open. They opened alright. On another set of doors. Those doors opened, too. And in a blink, she could see that again she was in another place like no other. And she wasn't even in it yet; she was only looking at it through a huge floor-to-ceiling, wall-of-glass because when they got off the elevator, they had stepped inside an enclosed glass pavilion. They still had another door to walk through but that door was also made entirely out of glass. Which she looked through - and there were many many twisting and bending and reaching and swaying and gesturing things that seemed to be everywhere and seemed to be like people and some of them seemed like old people who were older than old, and they might have even been people if they weren't so tall and had so many, too many, arms that came from every part of them.

And she watched as these dark things danced all about in the howling wind, even as she and Mr. James and Keys the Doorman made it through the glass door. As they stepped into the cold air, Keys said, "Now for which you are about to see, brace yourself—"

Sophia gasped. Even Mr. James gasped. And it wasn't the cold that made them gasp. Keys the Doorman couldn't stop laughing as he watched them take in the spectacle. Because there before them was the tallest blackest filigreed gate that was so high it seemed to be touching the night sky. And attached to that gate was a fence almost as tall made of lines and lines of black iron bars that stretched all around the rim of whatever was inside.

Sophia's eyes followed the bars upwards: on top of each and every one of the bars was something that sure looked like a tiny person; then downwards:

the infinite amount of holes created by the tracery in the gates filigree revealed something. And she finally understood what those things were that had been reaching and swaying and gesturing. And so did Mr. James.

"What ho! Trees, Miss Sophia!"

"Haugh! I see them too, Mr. James!"

'Whole trees up here in the sky! Hiding! There's one on one side of the gate that looks like it's shaking with laughter! And there's another on the other side that looks like it's sad and bent over and crying! But there're so many trees. They couldn't all be like these two, could they? Because those two trees are like characters in Movies! How do they make trees do that? Are there such things as actor trees?'

·∴☾∴·

(" 'Holy elfing gnome nuts!' Author, Lady, I had flown to the top of the bars and was checking out the tiny little carved metal people that stood like police guys on the top of each bar. 'Dag! This one looks just like my Uncle Benito, aka, the Finisher! He'd sure hate to find out that somebody in human land knows what he looks like. Hey, maybe these humans gotta holda the pictures from all those line-ups he always has to stand in! But how did humans get a holda a photo from a mafairyia line-up?' But then, Author Lady, because I was way up in the air, I was the first of all of them to really see the house. 'Wow, get a load a' this place! And I thought my relatives' houses was weird!' And then all of a sudden it occurred to me that I'd better find Free because I knew poor Free'd probably be scared to death a' this place. So I flies back inside but in a quick search, I couldn't find her, and so I asks, 'Hey, any a youse see Free?' ")

·∴☽∴·

Next to that gate, Keys was a horsefly. Sophia was even about to laugh - out loud! but just then Keys yanked on the gate's golden handle and it was the one that laughed out loud. Or was it bawling? How did that handle feel? She couldn't say for sure. But then the gate began to move and Sophia was afraid she'd be a hundred-years-old before it ever opened all the way. *'What kind of a Movie would a gate like that be in? And suppose it never opens! Or only opens enough so that all of us have to squeeze through and just when we're in the middle, it shuts right on us, and we're stuck! Or worse yet, crushed! Like in that Movie I once saw.'*

·∴☾∴·

("Ms. Author, Fairies, Readers, do you now understand what excessive movie watching does to a child's imagination?")

·∴☽∴·

But Mr. James had already stepped through the gate, and Sophia could clearly see that gate hadn't done anything of the kind to him, or had even tried. But Sophia sprinted through it anyway, keeping her head down. Keys, who was whistling again, neither walked nor ran but moseyed his way on in.

Now all of them were inside.

And what had been mysterious and indescribable, no longer was. Sophia hadn't even lifted her head and already she saw something. A path. And it wasn't a sensible, straight path either; it was winding and covered with some sort of pavement with the tiniest of sparkles in it. *'Another sidewalk that sparkles!'* Immediately, her head lifted up and she looked every which way for more sparkling darkness.

The sparkles were on a path that winded its way up a very slight hill.

How could there be a hill on the top of a roof?

She had no idea but the winding, sparkling path had trees on each side of it. These were the trees they had seen when they had looked through that gate. The trees were in planters that were wide and oddly shaped and were made out of a coppery-colored material that had aqua-colored splashes running down their sides or covering them entirely. The planters weren't square; weren't round, but looked like they were made out of the shells of giant nuts. And the trees in their planters really did look like characters in her Movies. How could a tree look like a character from a Movie? She'd have to study these trees just like she studied Movie Stars, so she could learn all she could about them, too. She looked hard at one of them. Slowly, her eyes moved up its trunk with its gazillion jumbling arms that were clowning all about in that wind; and when they reached the spot right before the tree trunk broke up into several trunks, she saw what sure looked like a face with eyes and a human mouth that sure looked like it could laugh if it were a mouth. But, of course, it couldn't be a mouth because it was a tree. Or was it?

"Now, Miss Sophia, we must follow Mr. Keys," said Mr. James, "we don't want to lose sight of him in this most unusual of places."

Sophia had been rooted to her spot on the sparkling path, staring without blinking at that tree with its laughing face til her eyes bulged. She didn't want to move from this him-in-a-tree. But then again, she didn't want to be left behind, if this him-in-a-tree really was a him and really did go from ready-set-go and laughed. So she hurried past. But as she made her way along that sparkly path, walking in front of Mr. James, her eyes darted to each trunk, looking for more faces. She found them. Each had a laughing face. And as she kept on walking, she noticed that none of them did laugh. They looked like they might. They looked like they could. But they didn't. But what was alive in each tree were their branches.

'Maybe these really are just trees. Trees with faces on them.'

She stared at each face. She didn't know why these trees were wearing faces. Did they grow these faces? But how could a tree grow a face? Was there a mind behind these faces, like people had minds? And she looked at each tree as if there maybe really was a mind behind them who knew she had asked a question, who knew she was wondering about them, and would answer her presently. Until, that is, she saw a tree whose face wasn't laughing at all. No, the face on this tree was not laughing. Definitely not. The face on this tree was crying. And she looked on the other side of the path and saw the exact same thing. Another tree with a crying face. And as she kept walking on and on and up that hill, each tree that she now met had a face that looked like it was crying. Laughing trees back there, crying trees up here. They didn't have such sorts of trees where she came from. She didn't remember seeing trees like this in any of her Movies, either. Trees like this would be in cartoons.

"the ArborTreeMeians ..."

'The tree trunk men in Daddy's poem! That's why Daddy wanted me to walk to school! Is this who he wanted me to get to know? But the tree trunk men I see when I walk to school aren't like these fellows! But wait ... can trees laugh and cry? The way these trees do? But then again, I haven't heard them do either ... thank goodness!

'So many peculiar things up so high in the sky! And here I am! In the middle of it all! On top of a huge tall building, walking up a hill in a place where there should be no hill, on a path that sparkles where there should be no sparkles, towards a house where there should be no house! And so far away from home!'

Even so, she kept walking along the winding path up that hill, but now there were fewer trees til the path finally stopped at a set of steps and Sophia realized, *'I'll have to climb them or I'll go no further!'* But she couldn't take the time to look up those steps to find out just where they led, because Sophia was now looking in amazement at the last two trees that stood at the end of the path on either side of it. These trees were bigger than all the rest and had many, many more branches. And since they were now at the top of the hill, there was more wind to blow their branches all about. And these branches really did look alive. Sophia examined these trees to see if they had faces on them, too. They did: a laughing face on one, a crying on the other.

But these faces seemed different than the other faces. Or was it just the wind that was making even their trunks move, which, in turn, made the faces look like they were really laughing, really crying? It had to be! *'As if those faces could really see and speak and hear and laugh or cry! Although they sure look like they could!'* The branches on the laughing tree, the funny tree, made the man in the tree look like he had a million big fat tubby elbow joints that pointed every-which-way. But the branches on the sad tree only pointed down and were so painfully thin that Sophia was afraid for them up here in all this cold and wind. She watched as they swayed so-for-ever-ly-slow, like they were even too sad to move. How they made that sad tree look even sadder! She wished she had a hat and scarf and gloves to give to each frail, little thin sticky of a branch. She remembered the weeping willow tree that grew over the lake in the village that her Mother had so often taken her to see but hadn't in such a long time.

'Weeping trees! Laughing trees! Actor Trees! What a place I've come to! Trees that can make you feel how they feel without saying a word! Trees that are quiet like me but say so much just by being quiet! Trees shouldn't be expected to talk because trees can't talk. That's just the way trees are. These trees express themselves but quietly.'

Keys, who had been waiting at the bottom of the steps for them, said, "Well, we have made it. What did you think of those trees, huh? I would wager three to one that you have never seen the likes of them before! Would I not also be correct to state that your Grandfather's place is like no other such place in the world? Are you ready to walk up these steps and face the rest of the music of it?"

Sophia's noodle had enough to ponder and she and it didn't hear a word he said. For there in front of it had just been things quiet AND expressive, how could it let anything or anyone else in that it would've had to make sense of? She only looked up when she noticed the silence outside herself. And there was Keys waiting for a response that she knew she couldn't give. But he didn't wait long; he went right back to whistling Looney Tunes.

'I, your noodle, have had enough of pondering! Outside me are - Giants that whistle cartoons! And Trees that can act! If you stay in here with me, you'll miss such wonders! By the way, aren't you, a famous scaredy-cat-little-girl! still standing! after experiencing the world's mysteries?'

And she smiled at the world, the whistling giant, and then looked over at Mr. James to see if he was smiling, too. What she saw should've surprised her but somehow it didn't. Mr. James was no longer just looking attentively with only his eyes. No, Mr. James was looking everywhere, up, down, all around; his whole head pivoting just like hers had been.

'Has Mr. James turned into me? Is it because he's walked on sparkles too? Greeted trees AND golden handles that can laugh and/or bawl? He could hardly be expected to look at things the way he usually does! He'd've never seen all the stuff up here if he

did! Why a truly attentive person would not've wanted to miss one thing about this place! Maybe Mr. James and me aren't so different after all!'

But somehow she didn't want to say anything to Mr. James about his sudden transformation. She wasn't sure if he would've liked anyone to notice. Mr. James did everything with Dignity. And telling him that he had been rubber-necking just like she had been might make him feel like he lost his Capital D. Sophia knew that Mr. James was a little like Great Aunt Hortense; just nicer.

Mr. James had now turned his attention to the steps, so she did too. The steps were attached to something else that was huge, too. That something was the house. Her Grandfather's house. It had been hiding behind all those actor trees. Keys the Doorman turned round to them and said "It is imperative that we do not keep such nabobs whom are waiting waiting. And it is important, too." He ran up the steps and disappeared.

Sophia watched Mr. James put his polished-to-a-shiny-satin shoe on the first tread of those steps; Sophia looked down at her scuffed, old, rubber galoshes and felt herself turn red even though she tried not to. She wished she too could put her own satiny-Movie-Star-slipper down right next to it. She peeked up at Mr. James. He knew what she was thinking, she could tell. Probably because they had just gone through something together. Or maybe because he saw her look first at his shiny shoes then at her old galoshes. He took her hand in his, and winked at her, and she couldn't stop herself - not from winking, because she didn't know how to wink - but from turning bright red. She wished that she could wink back but she hadn't yet mastered winking from all her Movie Star practice.

There was so much she hadn't mastered yet.

Oh, how she wished her face wasn't like cherry jello when she had to make her entrance into her Grandfather's house. Oh, how she wished she'd mastered all the other things Movie Stars know how to do. But even without being able to wink back to Mr. James, Sophia knew exactly what'd just happened between them; what'd made him wink at her in the first place. Because this moment was *'A Movie Moment! Our Movie Moment!'* But she was too shy to tell him.

'I hope there are gleams in my eyes. Because in Movie Moments, the Movie Star's eyes always gleam. A Movie Moment happens in only the most special time in the movie. Movie Moments can happen for all different reasons. And sometimes the Moments are just like this, when both characters know what each other are thinking without having to say a word! Even though nobody talks during a Movie Moment. But if we were talking, this is what we'd say -

'WHO CARES ABOUT SHOES IF I'M WITH YOU AND YOU'RE WITH ME AND WE'RE TOGETHER—

'Except there's no beautiful music playing right now.

'Oh, how I wish I could tell Mr. James about the Movie Moments I've watched that were just like this one! But then again, if I tell him that this is a Movie Moment, I'd have to talk. And a person isn't supposed to talk during a movie moment.

'But I don't even talk when a person's supposed to BE talking!

'How will I know what Mr. James is really thinking if I don't ask him?

'But isn't the whole point of a Movie Moment that each person knows what the other is thinking without either of them saying a word?'

And she looked at Mr. James and he was smiling at her and she stopped thinking and they laughed and walked up the steps, hand-in-hand, looking up, down, sideways.

Together.

Until something made them turn completely around. Could it have been the moon's brilliance that tapped them on the shoulders and lit up the very steps they were walking on?

'But how could the moon tap us on our shoulders?

'Because we're on top of tallness itself?

'Because we're closer than ever to the moon and its glow?

'That glow sure is helping us see Goliathon better.'

They gazed at what lay below. Such lights! So many colors! Such tall tall buildings! And here they were standing in the up-tall part of one of those tall tall buildings! And there, way way below, was the river!

They continued up the steps, and as they did, they noticed something else. The steps they were treading on were shaking. And there were sounds coming from the house. As they got closer, so did the sounds, until they could clearly hear, THWACK THWACK BANG.

"KICK!"

"Did somebody just say 'Kick?'"

THWACK THWACK BANG.

"Indeed, Miss Sophia, someone did!"

• • • PINK FLAMINGOS • • •

When they stepped onto the porch, it was shaking, too. It was even shaking the mighty Keys who'd been waiting there for them. And now it was shaking them, too.

And they shook and they listened.

THWICK THWACKY WHACKY, SWISH SWISH CRICK, CRACKETY SWISH, SWISHETY SWHACK

"KICK LADIETH KICK! HIGHER!"

So loud!

As if the person speaking was standing on the porch with them.

"No! You there! Itth that ath high ath you can kick? Are we wal-ruthes? Flipperths can't reach prottttthenium archeth. No! We are FLAMINGOTHS! THhocking! Pink! Flaming! THE FLAMINGOTHS OF FLAMINGERA. With long legth. KICK LADIETH! KICK! You over there, did you say your name was DARLene? Well DAAAAAARLene, could you find it in yourthelf to touch the THeiling! FRRROM THE TOP." And then total silence, the porch and steps finally still, until, "Maethtro, repetez, th'il vous plait!"

And a piano jingled a lively tune but was soon drowned out by THWACK THWACK BANG which thundered and shook - the porch AND Sophia AND Mr. James AND Keys AND their shoes with their feet in them AND the dou-ble-doored, front doors with their double windows - the way a hurricane would. Sophia didn't miss a sound of any of it.

'What a voice! It's a man's voice. Or is it? But what are those thwacky sounds?' She would've loved to have looked through the double-windows to find out; if only she dared.

What were those sounds?

She wanted to get closer. Who was making that voice, that music? But she didn't run over to the windows and look. Peeking inside someone's house was very rude. But, oh, how she wanted to. But just then Keys strode over to those shaking, wide, double-doored, front doors and without so much as a knock or a ring or a tap or anything, he opened them. Sophia, who was still hold-ing Mr. James's hand, felt his grip tighten. She looked up at him. Mr. James had turned as white and as stiff as his starched shirt collar. Mr. James always knocked on every door before he entered it. Mr. James had told her that a person should never walk in on any person unannounced. He said that it often didn't work out for either party - the tramped-in-upon or the tramper-in-ner. The tramped-in-upon might take that tramper-inner for a burglar which could be very bad for that tramper-inner. Or the tramped-in-upon might only be embarrassed which could also be very bad for that tramper-inner. Sophia could almost hear Mr. James say because he had said it to her so many times. *'Civility turns man into Man-Kind! And I didn't learn that in the Kings School of British Butlers. I learned that, Miss Sophia, when I was young like you are now. And since you are young, you must learn such lessons too.'*

'I bet Mr. James thinks Keys the Doorman never learned his door-knocking lesson. But Mr. James isn't about to teach it to a gigantic man with a gigantic mouth who lives in Goliathon!

'Mouth!!!

'I almost forgot. I'm here to get a mouth. But how will I be able to do that here? This place sounds like a hurricane. And shakes like one, too. In such a noisy place, nobody'd hear me even if I did get one and used it.'

Keys had turned around and saw that the both of them had stopped in their tracks and were standing as still as they could on a shaking porch, which wasn't very still at all. And from where he stood inside the highly-polished wooden frame of that open door; he exclaimed, louder than everything! "Oh! Did youse think such noise makers what are in your Grandfather's house at the present time would be able to hear our knockity-knock, tippy-tap-taps on yonder window pane through all that racket! Come on, do not be so shy at this time which is the very last moment!"

And as the noise and the shaking blasted them right where they stood on their spot, Sophia looked up at Mr. James and Mr. James looked down at her and their eyes held and then Mr. James whispered, "Well, Miss Sophia, as they say, when in Rome do as the Romans do; well then, when on a Roof do as the Roofians do!" and he winked at her and they proceeded across that rocking porch - THWACK WHACKY THWACK – until they reached the open front door. Mr. James pulled himself up to his full height and put his foot on the step and so did Sophia and now both of them stood with Keys the Doorman in that open doorway.

But Sophia couldn't push herself around the giant Keys or soften an edge on the T squared Mr. James, so she teensied herself as best she could and leaned along the door frame. Now she'd be able to see for herself why her Grandfather's house was shaking. But even if she had been the size of a thumbtack, she could never have missed what was now strutting before her.

Pink flamingos!

Wherever she looked throughout that entranceway - and it was a very grand and wide entranceway - there they were! DANCING PINK FLAMINGOS LADIES! So bright, they lit that dark-paneled hall into flames! And they really were dancing. And Sophia turned as white as Mr. James' shirt.

What were dancing, kicking pink flamingo ladies doing in her Grandfather's house?

The ladies were in one line that had two parts: the line coming down the stairs and the line in the entranceway. When the pink flamingo ladies reached the landing, they added themselves to the curvy line in the hallway.

So the line kept growing longer and longer as more pink flamingo ladies joined it. And both lines were dancing. Kick. Down. Swipe. Pivot. Kick. Down. Swipe. Turn. They would face first in one direction and then the next, pointing their toes straight towards the ceiling. And not one of them ever stopped.

In Movies, Sophia had seen lines of dancers but never ever, right before her eyes had there been real-live-dancing-girls that looked like Movie Stars. This was spectacular! And was far more thrilling than any old thing she had ever seen in a tiny glass box! Even Mr. James looked more Delighted than Dignified; decidedly more. There were so many pink flamingo ladies, Sophia didn't even try to count them.

"Do these feathers look like fur-rrrrh? Shu-YUUUUT the doorrhha!" A flamingo cried out from her spot in the line. Sophia couldn't believe her ears. The flamingo talked exactly like that Goliathon police officer!

Keys strode into the center of that wide entranceway and proclaimed: "Mr. Solomon Oomla's granddaughter is here for whom we have all been waiting!"

Everybody stopped, including the piano-player and a small man. And then every single flamingo and the piano player and the small man turned to the front door.

Sophia, from where she now stood in the hallway, watched as a swirl of pink feathers and long legs and sequined head-dresses swooped down and surrounded her. "Why, helloooooo SoFEEya!" "We been WAIT-TIN' for youse' all night, we was so woorried!" "Don't she have beautiful curly hair!" "Oh, she's so youngggh and so aDOORible!" Sophia looked up at the feathers that were everywhere; at the pink-lipstick on mouths that were smiling and showing the whitest teeth; at the longest of lashes on the sparkliest eyes that were looking right at her, and she had never been so dazzled so up close in all her life. She didn't even do what she usually did even if she would've remembered to do it; and that was to listen and hear the sound of them, to learn how they talked, how they breathed, how they said and did everything. She could only see their pinkness, their shining beauty and feathers and sequins and glamour. She could even smell them.

They smell like flowers. These pink flamingos are just like Movie Stars. But I can't really say they smell like them because I've never smelled a Movie Star. I can't really smell my Movie Stars through the television screen. Plus these ladies are really looking at me. My Movie Stars never do that. But then they couldn't very well look through the glass on the television screen to see me sitting on the other side looking at them. These pink flamingo ladies aren't behind glass. They are real and are stand-ing right in front of me. And look happy to see me. The Movie Stars, not even one of them, ever look happy to see me.'

The Pinknesses were smiling at her, every one of them, and suddenly she felt like a million-suns were melting something right off her and had even penetrated straight through all those layers and layers of clothing to her inside part.

But that inside deep part of Sophia was very deep. But then again the inside deep parts of all people are usually very deep. But Sophia had the ex-tra deepest kind. And I'm sure I don't have to remind you, Readers, about who occupies Sophia's deepest deepest parts.

⋯·(⋯

(Readers, before I continue, I really must say something about the Occupants of this "deepest deepest." You may have been wondering why you haven't been hearing from any of them lately. I'm sure all of you no-ticed – most of you – some of you - any of you? - that they have not been pok-ing their opinions, their by-the-ways, their chit-chat, their squabbles, their theories, tirades, preachifications, their ephemeral etcetera etcetera etcet-era into the action lately. That's because there was not one single Fairy on the premises. They were all gone. Some of you, I'm sure, even missed them and their opining. And their bickering.

Their constant bickering.

They were AWOL. Including Thee! When Lorraine noticed that Free was missing and she told the Fairies, they knew they had no choice. They had to find her no matter how much the Fairy Dispatcher had warned them they must never all be absent from Sophia at the same time and that Sophia was never to be left all alone, never ever ever. Me and Be were scouring Goliathon and Thee and Lorraine were fine-combing the Enchanted Lands. Every one of those Fairies knew quite well they were doing what the Fairy Dispatcher had forbidden them to do: leave their charge unattended, but this was the first time one of them had simply vanished without first telling anyone where she was going – although that's technically not correct: Me does it all the time.

But when they heard who it was, every one of them had screamed - "Of all Fairies! Free!" The one who didn't even know her way around the Enchanted Lands, let alone Goliathon! The one who could get lost inside Sophia. Although Thee did have the presence of mind to summon a Substitute Fairy who arrived in an instant.

But, Readers, Substitute Fairies must be approved by the Dispatcher and their stay within a child's Remarkably Small Place is to be of a very limited duration, plus there must be at least two Magical Creatures on the premises during their stay. Well, our Fairies never asked permission and there was certainly no other Magical Creature, Fairy or otherwise, on Sophia's premises. Incidentally, the Substitute told all of them what happened to Sophia when they were away and because she did, our story doesn't have any glaring holes in it. I will report more on the search for Free later, meanwhile back to the action.)

·:☽:·

'These ladies are so beautiful! So pink! I wish I looked like them!' And Sophia put her head down. *'Oh! But if I'm hiding, I won't be able to see the pink ladies.'* But her head stayed down. *'I want to be just like them when I grow up. I should be listening to them. Learning from them. Plus these ladies are talking to me. I should talk back. But what should I say to them? And I don't want to sound funny when I say it either.'*

She kept her face hidden from all those Movie Star smiles that were closer to her than such types of smiles had ever been. But she didn't say a word in answer. *'Anyway, how would I sound if I do speak?'*

She remained quiet until, finally, her head poked up, in spite of what was going on inside it. And she listened to the ladies. And watched them. As if she were at home in her Movie Star School watching a Movie. As if she wasn't right there in her Grandfather's entranceway surrounded by pink flamingos.

But her quietness didn't shut the pink flamingos up.

"Galawshes! I haven't seen them in years!"

'GaLAWshes?'

"My mothuh used to make me wear them too!"

'MoTHUH?'

"Don' you just hate havin' to wear galawshes, SoFEEya?"

'SoFEEya?'

"Didja Mothuh make you wear them, SOfeeya?"

'Didja?' Sophia heard every word they said and suddenly she was dying to laugh; and dying because she didn't dare laugh; and dying to shrink herself tiny so she could hang from the lips of those pink ladies and hear with her own ears how they made such sounds so she could practice making such sounds herself; and dying because she was keeping everything inside her; and dying to say just how she felt to somebody about the very

silly way those pink flamingo ladies said their words. But who could she say it to?

Mr. James?

Keys the Doorman?

Mr. James'd never laugh at the way these ladies were talking. Mr. James'd never laugh at a lady. Period. She even knew what he'd say if she did, 'Most inappropriate, Miss Sophia!' And come to think of it, Keys the Doorman talked funny himself. And so did that Goliathon police officer. And so did that little man. The people in Goliathon sure talked funny. Sophia looked at Keys. He was looking at the pink flamingo ladies and he was happy. These pink ladies were his friends. He'd never laugh at his friends. She'd better not even think of laughing at his friends, especially in front of him, just in case he could read minds. Sophia looked at those pink ladies.

'They are so pretty. And they are smiling so much at me, they must be so happy to see me. I should never laugh at them. Never. Ever. No matter how they talk. I would hurt their feelings. Besides, they're being nice to me. And that pink lady over there even understands that I hate galoshes and I never even told her I did. I wish I could tell those ladies it was Maria who made me wear them!'

But in spite of all she just thought about what Mr. James might say or Keys the Doorman might do if they found out what she was thinking, she still couldn't stop herself from thinking it.

And from thinking thoughts that perplexed her even more and quite considerably.

'Why can they talk and talk and not care how they sound? When I hear them, I want to laugh. Is it okay to laugh at someone? But why is it okay to laugh at them and not myself? I hear them talk and want to laugh but I hear me talk and want to cry. Why can't I just talk and talk too and not care how I sound, like they do? Because maybe it's not so bad to talk funny. Maybe I can learn how to talk just like them; it might come in handy someday.'

And then the tittering and the screechy teehees rang throughout that entranceway and filled up Sophia's ears so much, she couldn't think anymore. Which was a relief. But when a flamingo said, "Oh, don't worry about it, SoFEEya, I couldn't tawk neither when I was little, and now I can't shuyut up!" Sophia almost screeched herself.

'That same somebody who told Keys the Doorman must have told her, too!'

"Oh, she'll get over it! She's just shy!"

'How do they know that? Who told them? Somebody up here is talking about me!'

And then there was such a sound, as if the night itself had floated into that entranceway and started whispering, that all talking ceased and all heads turned, including Sophia's.

"Darrrrrlings, darrlings, darrrrrrrrrrrrlings!!"

'Maybe up here, so close to the sky, the night really can whisper! What else is going to happen in my Grandfather's house?'

Sophia couldn't see through all the flamingos who were still gathered round her, she could only hear, floating in the pink mist, even more whispers that were so low, so deep, so dark, so mystifying that Sophia almost believed that if it wasn't someone, it really might be that night-sky whispering.

• • BUT IT WASN'T THE NIGHT-SKY • • •

"Flah-MIN-go Darrrrrlings, doooo bring her over to me. I've been waiting my turn soooooo patiently here, resting and in my Sunday best. No, no, no, this is my Saturday best. No, it's more my Saturday-night best. I always did preferrrr dressing for Saaaaaaaturday night than I did dressing for Sunnnnnday mornings – although dressing for Sunnnnday was such a challenge and I really did love finding just the perfect blend of rrrreverence and chhhhic. But Saaaaturday night clothes are such wicked fun, mixing va-va-voom with no-no-nannette. But as you delightful young people say, 'Whatever'- which is so apropoooos of just about eeeeeeeeeeverything. Now haven't I been so goooood waiting here? Not saying a wwwwwwwwwword to anyone. Not even telling Serf Darrrrrrrrrrling how he shouldn't have the flamingos do sooooo many of the saaaaaaaame type of kicks. Oops! Now Serf Darrrrrrrrling don't be cross, that just ssssslipped out of me! And you surely must appreciate that was my ooooooonly piece of advice. Which makes me such a good audience."

'But it's not the night whispering. It's a lady. What a voice she has!' Even in a whisper, that voice had steamed up the entire entranceway.

"Now, it's my turn to see my Granddaughter. Keys, Flah-MIN-go Darrrrrlings, Monsieur Serf Soufflé, don't be sooooooooooooo selfish!"

'It's my Grandmother!'

Everybody formed an opening so Sophia could pass through.

Sophia was supposed to walk through that opening the pink flamingos and Mr. James and Keys and the man her Grandmother called Serf Soufflé had formed. And that at its end would be her Grandmother. But she couldn't …

'The people staring at me are strangers from a strange place because I'm in a strange place surrounded by ladies dressed up like birds and a man that doesn't talk like any man I've ever heard before and am about to meet a Grandmother who sounds like a dark cloud ...!'

... for she was nothing but a quivering wind chime. With no feet to get her to that end.

But she didn't have to see their stares to feel them. Even so, she wanted to stay there and shiver and not do what everybody was waiting for her to do - which was to put one foot in front of the other. But Mr. James reached down and gently put his hand in hers, and suddenly she wasn't shivering anymore, and she looked up and there he was winking at her, and somehow that wink made one foot move and then the other and Mr. James and the rest of her were walking through the opening the flamingos and Keys and that man called Serf Soufflé had made. She was scared. But her feet did as they should, one following the other, because her feet knew exactly where they were taking her.

Straight towards that dark cloud ...

If-the-night-could-whisper ...

That voice!

... that belonged to her Grandmother. She got closer. And closer. And now she could smell the whisper, and the whisper smelled like - *'Perfume! It smells like the one on my Mother's perfume table. The one I love the best.'* And she felt less scared. *'My Grandmother wears that perfume, too?'* And she walked a little faster. The closer she got, the more she smelled it. *'It's the one that comes from Paris - the one with the picture on the bottle of the lady with the mounds of flowing hair - Absinthe.'* And she was excited and hardly scared at all. *'Grandmother wears my favorite perfume.'*

And she got closer.

'My Grandmother smells wonderful.'

And closer still.

"Now I can see youuuuuuuuuuuu! It's been entirrrrely toooo longgg since we've last been togeeetherrrrr."

'Grandmother talks with such a voice. It really is like the night talking—

'Or maybe like where there's smoke, there's fire.'

And she was scared. But something inside her was dancing. And she lifted her head even higher. Everybody was smiling at her. The pink ladies. Keys. And even that man called Serf Soufflé. And their smiles made her smile.

That something was her hula-dancing-heart. Only her knees were a-wobble.

But she felt Mr. James' hand in hers.

She was about to meet someone who talked like the night.

And who smelled liked Paris, France.

And who might even be nice.

She couldn't wait to meet her Grandmother. She forgot to be timid. To be shy. To be scared. To put her head down and keep it there. She was excited. She was in a new place. With smiling people. Meeting her very own Grandmother. Who had a voice. Like the night sky.

Finally, Sophia reached the last of the pink ladies who stepped aside to let her pass but she didn't have to look too hard to find her Grandmother. Because there through an archway in an alcove just off the entranceway laying on some sort of something, and surrounded by blazing candles that were on short pillars, tall pillars, even taller columns, on pedestals, on candelabras placed around the floor, and even as those candles flickered, fluttered, flittered, flamed not one of them shone as much as her Grandmother did lying on that something; because her Grandmother blazed through it all. Her eyes shimmered mystery; her evening gown was a pitch-dark, star-lit playground, and Sophia wanted to see more and took a whole step closer, not even giving a half thought to being scared. And when she did, she couldn't believe her eyes.

That piece of something her Grandmother was reclining on was the same kind of furniture her Mother had in their conservatory. A recamier. That's what her Mother called that kind of sofa-chair. Sophia thought its name was as beautiful as the chair itself. And there was her Grandmother lying about on a recamier, too. Sophia loved their recamier. She especially loved saying 're-CAH-me-a.' When her Mother pronounced it and told her it was a French word and Sophia heard its name spoken so musically, and so different than their plain English words, their plain English furniture, and Sophia loved it even more. But, above all, she loved lying about in it. In the late afternoon, she would, as if in a swoon, throw herself on it, and in an instant, she was - A! Daring! Woman! with the Deepest! and Darkest! of Secrets! All because she was on such a chair! A French chair. With an exotic name.

Whenever Sophia's homework was done and the coast was clear - Miss Kitty was cooking dinner and Mr. James had chauffeured off and Maria and the staff of Polishers and Dusters and Closet Persons and Gardeners and Pruners and Rakers and Mowers and Weeders and Blossom Tenders had gone home for the day and her Father was still at work and so was her Mother, Sophia raided her Mother's closet, pulling fineries and jewels and doodads and feathers and mantillas and shawls and gowns and heels and

jewel-encrusted clutches so she could prepare her costume for her Movie
Star School. But it was there on the recamier that she did the test-runs of
these Movie Stars. She would assemble the costume and then lie-about in
that costume on that chair and see and feel if that costume and that recamier working together with what she had come up with inside would cook
her into character! A Madame of the World!

Sophia had to admit, being on a recamier in costume was sometimes
even better than being a character in her Movie Star School, because on
that recamier, she was actually herself - a fancier herself. And it was the
other magic carpet that took Sophia away from being the second shyest student in Mr. Snoggley's Fifth Grade Class. Away from being the student who
had trouble speaking up when anybody was even looking at her, let alone
looking cross-eyed at her. The only student in her class who nefarious persons aplenty were attempting to farm off to a speech therapist. The timid
Sophia. The shy Sophia. With a best school chum named Melinda, who
talked enough for two people, maybe even eleven and who often talked for
Sophia because Sophia often didn't talk.

And here was her Grandmother laying about on what Sophia loved laying about on, wearing what Sophia would've died to wear, and smelling like
her favorite perfume. Her Grandmother's eyes were smiling at her, glistening even and Sophia felt her own eyes do the same. Maybe that's why her
Grandmother shone more than the candles did, because of something in
her eyes.

The something in her Grandmother's eyes made Sophia want to edge
closer to her and when she did, she could see even more of her Grandmother.
Because there, through the glow of the candles, was her Grandmother who
had around her shoulders, a velvet dusky magenta shawl, its dark, sparkling
fringe falling around her like a long necklace. Underneath the shawl, she
was wearing a deep as the blue-night long-gown speckled all over with the
tiniest of silver stars, its long train peeking around her dark velvet, star-stud-
ded slippers. Draped around her legs just so was the deepest-ocean-blue
crocheted throw and on top of her head was a midnight blue turban and
pinned to its crown was a round diamond brooch that, set against all those
deeps, those dusks, those darks, made her Grandmother glow like the moon
itself.

Even through the flickering candles, Sophia saw that her Grandmother
was wearing much much make-up. The kind that Sophia would've loved to
paint all over her own face, if she could've ever gotten a hold of such stuff.
But her Mother's make-up room was not in the closet and too hard to get

into and Sophia was afraid she might get caught. She didn't think she'd get in too much trouble with her Mother if she got caught in her closet considering how much her Mother didn't really care for clothes. Only the Closet People, or Maria, would've been mad if they caught her in there. But getting caught in her Mother's make-up room would've been an entirely different matter, everybody would've been mad at her for that, especially her Father. And Sophia never wanted her Father to be mad at her.

Sophia knew by looking at her who her Grandmother was. She was a Movie Star. She looked like one, dressed like one, talked like one. Sophia was certain, as she gazed upon her Grandmother draped in all her dark clothes and shawls and scarves and turban, that her Grandmother would've been a very serious, maybe even a little sad, very mysterious Movie Star type person. If her Grandmother had been a real Movie Star and been in an actual Movie, she would've been in those not-so-funny kind of Movies Sophia sometimes watched. And Sophia made up her mind. The next time she was laying on her own recamier, she wouldn't be a Movie Star, she'd be her Grandmother. She'd make herself look exactly the way her Grandmother looked right now. And she'd talk exactly like her, too.

So it would be up to her to remember everything! What her Grandmother was wearing! How she was lolling about! Everything! She realized, she'd better even have candles too since they added so much to her Grandmother's sparkle. But before that thought could even sit down, she dropped it. She'd never get away with that. *'Everybody'd probably kill me dead if I lit even one of those.'*

Sophia studied her Grandmother's beaming eyes and lustrous face. *'I don't think I really need candles. The candles aren't making my Grandmother glow so much. What is it then? I'll have to figure that out for myself. Sneaking into my Mother's closet to find a turban won't be so dangerous. And I could certainly pin a diamond brooch to the center of it. And put on the perfume. Although not too much or Miss Kitty will hold her nose and fan the air and make me go wash it off.'* And her heart sank. *'If Miss Kitty is even coming back! But they would never leave me with just Maria! I'd die!'*

And Sophia looked down at her galoshes; they already had. The idea of Maria as her Nanny for the rest of her career as a child was so awful that Sophia pushed it right out of her head. *'Miss Kitty is coming back, she's got to! Maria is just a substitute Nanny!'* And soon, she was lost in the image of herself laying on her very own recamier at home just like her Grandmother was right now. And she stood there, gazing at her Grandmother, admiring her, gawping at her even, gobbling up and swallowing every single part of her, but not saying a word to her, at all.

"Well, Sopppphia, I haven't seen you since you were a baaaaby, and you reeeeally arrrrrrre just soooo lovely—"

'Above everything else in the whole entire world, I must learn how Grandmother makes her voice sound like that. All smoke. All fog. All mystery.' And she really listened.

"Taaaaaall like your Faaaather. And grrrrreen eyes and soft currrrrls like your Mother."

Now that Sophia was close to her Grandmother, she could see that her Grandmother was working very hard to say each word. Maybe that's why she could only whisper. She held onto her words so long, she seemed to cherish them. Some of the words, she didn't even seem to want to let go of at all.

"What doooooooooo youuuuuu thinnnnnnk of my candles? Don't worry, if I caaaatch on fire, my accccccomplice, Josephine, hiding in the shadows, will puuuuuut me outtttt." And what a mischievous look her Grandmother gave her, followed by the most exaggerated wink Sophia had ever seen made by anybody, even by a winking Movie Star.

And Josephine, an African-American older lady in a uniform stepped from behind the candles, and waved and smiled at Sophia and said, "Miz Sophie, I've only been hearin' bout you for a blessed eternity now. So happy to be finally meetin' you at las'. But don't you be worryin' yo' pretty little head - and tis a pretty little head - if your Grandmother do blow, I'll douse her good. And here she is, at her age, concernin' herself about how she gonna look in lights. And you'd better know this, Miz Sophie, a person can't talk a word a' sense into your Grandmother atall. Sof light. Sof light. Dat's all I hears about for the preparation for yo' visit. I say how she gonna look with her nose singed off, dat's what I say. No amount a' candles gonna make dat look good."

"Oh, now Sophia, isn't she just dreaaaaaadful?" And now her Grandmother winked the tiniest wink at her that Sophia ever saw. So tiny, she almost missed it. And Sophia vowed to pay close attention; she'd never learn how to be her Grandmother if she missed even one of her tricks.

"Josephine would have lovvvvved nothing better than to spooooo-il my enTRANCE. Josephine Darrrrrrling, don't you hear the - "Trance" in "EnTRANCE"? That's whyyyyy Mr. Weeeeebster put it therrrrrre. A tttttttrance is supposed to folloooooow every "en" as in "in" as in "enter," Josephine. Ergo, a persssson should dooooo what the word sayssssss to do, namely cause trrrances whenever they ENter. And Josephine, from the expression on Sophia's face, I'd say, we've succeeded. Why, Josephine, you could look it up yourself in Mr. Webster's Dictionnnnary and then you would see, in fact, any sennnnnsible person would clearly see, I'm just Mr. Webster's obeeedient servant."

And Sophia heard yet another trick of her Grandmother's; coating her every utterance, her whispers, her laughs in molasses until she'd let them float off slowly, darkly, sweetly, into the night.

"N' everbody know what else Mr. Webster put in his dictionary - "nonsense." And if you don't hear the "no" in front a dat "sense" I sho' do. 'N any sensible person can clealy see I'm jes da Truth's obedient servant." And tee-hees could be heard behind the candles.

"Remember if you doooooo douse me, Josephine, we'll only have to hop right back on that elevator and change my costume again."

"Hop?? ... Between my las' blink, Miz Sophie, did yo Grandmother jes' turn into de Easter Bunny? Why Mizzuz Sarah, can you even remember the last time you hopped? You haven't been seen hopping in a long time Mizzzuz Sarah. More likely, I'm the one who'll be hopping! Hop my foot!"

And her Grandmother leaned in to Sophia, as if she didn't want Josephine to hear but she didn't lower her voice a bit. "Well, now Sophia, you look so pretty in this dreamy light. And it's my fondest hope that I look pretty, too. Why look at Josephine, Sophia, doesn't she look pretty, too? In fact, we all look pretty in this light. It hides every speck of a person's orneriness."

"Uuuuh Mizzzuz Sarah ... Watch it now ... watch it."

So Sophia could observe her Grandmother's lips move as she spoke in her dramatic whisper, she had drawn even closer to her. Maybe if she really really listened to her Grandmother, she could learn how to whisper and talk and laugh and tease like the night air - just like her Grandmother did.

"Darrrrling Sophia, this dreamy light is nooooot reeeeally meant to seeeee with. It's only meant to be seen innnnnnn. So commmme even closer, deeeeear child. At my delicate age, I need to be seen in only the most flattering light, but in my delicate condition, this light is hardly enough for me to see a rhinoceros in. Not that a rhinoceros would come a' calling at suuuuch a laaaaate hour."

"N' if'n he did, she sho'd be the only person atta let him in, Miz Sophie! But only after she kep him waitin' out dere on dat cold porch while she be puttin' on her fine self de perfect-rhinoceros-howdie-do outfit for to greet him in!" And more teehees could be heard coming from behind the candles.

Sophia burst out laughing. Her Grandmother and Josephine were funny. Sophia was wrong. Her Grandmother wasn't sad at all. Then her Grandmother laughed too, like foggy smoke, and Josephine, who hadn't really stopped teeheeing, teeheed a lot louder and now all of them were laughing. Sophia happened to look down at her own hand. Mr. James's hand wasn't in it. She had let go. She was standing by herself in front of her Grandmother. And she wasn't afraid. But that wasn't the only thing Sophia noticed. Just like the Movie Stars did in the old Movies, her Grandmother called people "Darling." But even though she called people that and even though she dressed like a Movie Star, she wasn't exactly who Sophia thought she was when she first laid eyes on her.

For one thing, mysterious, foggy talking persons usually aren't laughing, silly jokers. Plus silly jokers don't lay about on recamiers. In the Movies, they don't. Recamiers are for sad people. Her Grandmother didn't look silly, and like a joker. What type of character was her Grandmother?

Was she a comedienne and, if she was, why did she dress like a sad, heartbroken Movie Star? She was dying to ask her but didn't know how.

"Now, child, darrrrrling … what is this I hear about you not liking to talk? Is that trrrrue? Is a grrrrandchild of minnnnne a shrrrrrinking viiiiio-let? How in the wwwwwworld did that ever happen? To a grandchild of mine? If my condition hadn't kept me from traveling, you would never've become that, never—"

Sophia stopped cold. She stopped laughing, listening, watching.

'My Grandmother just said I don't like to talk. The only Grandmother I have in the whole world is the one who is talking about me. She must be the one who told Keys and those pink flamingos, too. She shouldn't talk about people who she doesn't even know.' And Sophia could feel tears rolling down her cheek. *'So what that I don't talk? I know I can talk. Miss Kitty knows I can talk. Daddy knows I can talk. I just don't want to talk in school. Who would want to talk in School? School is not a Movie. It's not fun. There're just kids there. Just kids. They're not Movie Stars. They're just ordinary. Those kids don't know about my Movies. They don't even watch Movies. At least the Movies that I watch. Those kids don't have adventures. Movie Star type adventures, anyway. Besides Mr. Snoggley and those children would never understand all my different accents. All my different voices. And suppose one of my voices just slipped out. Everybody would make fun of me. The only way I would be allowed to talk in that school is like a ten-year-old kid and who wants to talk like a ten-year-old kid? With a deep voice like dirty old rocks were talking? When you can talk like a Movie Star? Why that would be a waste of perfectly good talking! Somebody's gotta understand that. Maybe my Grandmother,*

with her voice of smoky-fog, would. Oh, what am I thinking? How could I tell anybody about all this? I certainly couldn't tell my Grandmother. Would she even understand? I've never told anybody. Not even Miss Kitty. Miss Kitty only knows a little bit but she doesn't know everything. But I'm so sick and tired of people telling me I can't talk. If I don't say something, people will keep saying stuff like this to me, like Keys the Doorman did, like those pink ladies did. They'll talk about me for the rest of my life.'

And Sophia saw herself as an old old lady standing in the middle of even older old ladies, and listening to them talk about her. *'For the rest of my whole life! And it's all because Mr. Snoggley thinks I should go to a speech therapist, and somebody blabbed it to somebody else. Unless I finally finally tell somebody to stop. Why not tell her? Why not tell my Grandmother? Why not tell her right now?'*

And Sophia opened her mouth; she could feel that no one nor no thing could stop what was balling up inside her. She looked in her Grandmother's eye and saw that her Grandmother was looking at her most kindly and not like she wanted to stop her at all and Sophia felt encouraged, so in her real voice, in her own voice, in her deep voice, she said,

"I can too talk! I can talk very well. I talk when I have something to say and when I don't have anything to say, I don't talk."

And she could see that her Grandmother was still looking at her, waiting for her to say more, and Sophia knew her Grandmother was right because there was more to say because Sophia knew there was more to the story than what she had just said, so she added,

"Most of the time."

But that wasn't the whole story and she knew it and she put her head down. She didn't want to look in her Grandmother's eyes because what she was saying wasn't a story; life is not a story; stories are what people make up, like her Movies were just made up stories and that right now she was talking about her real, true, hard life. The only life she had. The only life she ever will have. And she lifted her head, looked into her Grandmother's eyes square and said,

"Okay, Grandmother, not most of the time. Some of the time. Just some."

And Sophia wasn't finished and she didn't even know why but she stood up on her ballerina toes and never took her eyes off her Grandmother who was looking at her like she was the most fascinating person she'd ever heard, ever seen, ever known and Sophia felt more than encouraged now, she felt heard, she felt understood for the simple reason that someone was actually listening to her and actually looking at her and really seeing her. And she blurted out,

"But I'm always thinking. I never stop thinking. So I'm always talking. But just inside."

And her Grandmother still said not a word which surprised Sophia a lot because her Grandmother hadn't even interrupted her once, like her Mother would've, or Melinda would've since they were such fast talkers and since neither of them seemed to like anybody to talk too slow or to take too much time to say anything or to have silence when there was supposed to be talk noise. Or maybe it was just that they liked to be the one talking. But whatever the reason, Sophia knew that whenever she was in a conversation with either one of them and it was her turn to say something and right before she was supposed to say it and she was quiet on the outside because on the inside she was coming up with what she was going to say or trying to say or thinking she might say or wondering if she should say, her Mother or Melinda would almost always talk during those quiet moments when it wasn't even their turn to talk, when it was Sophia's turn. And whenever they did, Sophia always felt a little funny, like maybe they could think faster than her or talk faster than her or think of better things to say, like talking was a competition or something, Sophia wasn't sure what. But her Grandmother hadn't said a word and didn't seem to mind that there were some spaces for quiet between sentences. Her Grandmother was waiting patiently for Sophia to say whatever she was supposed to say, whenever Sophia chose to say it. Her Grandmother didn't seem to mind quiet.

"So maybe I'm just talking to myself."

It just sprung out of her and then she twirled a full pirouette, which surprised her even more than a lot since she was in front of people she didn't know that well. Her feet landed firmly on the floor and she felt stupendous and knew that those words were just about the truth of almost everything she thought, almost everything that'd ever happened to her. Almost everything (except for the part about watching Movies in the middle of the night, and doing all the voices, especially the ones with the accents) and spoken how she really spoke, no tricks in her voice, no accents, no drama, and with no costume on for mood and effect and emphasis (not that she wasn't extremely disappointed that the most truthful, most revealing, most dramatic words she ever spoke were said while she was wearing galoshes).

And she stood there looking at her Grandmother who was looking back at her with eyes opened very wide and Sophia couldn't tell what her

Grandmother was thinking. And they both were quiet, Sophia now back to keeping her thoughts inside, as she waited to hear what her Grandmother would say. And as she waited, it occurred to her that before she'd said all that, she hadn't even known how she'd say all that, since she'd never put all of that into words before because she'd never actually spilled her beans to anyone before. But there they were. Her real beans, her true beans. In fact, she'd never been so proud of any beans she'd ever spilled before. Even when, in the middle of the night, she was a ravishingly-beautiful, soul-baring, bean-spilling, silver-throated Movie Star. But whenever she was one of those, she was all by-herself-alone when nobody could see even one of her slinky-moves or hear even one of her spilling, spinning, silvery-beans.

Sophia noticed that her Grandmother was still quiet, and she began to feel something like doubt and it must've clouded her face because it was only then that her Grandmother spoke up,

"Sophia, why you talk perrrrrfectly wellllllll! What a thinnnnnnng for sooooomeone to tell me. Josephine, darrrrling, what do you think, don't you thinnnnnnk Sophia speaks wellllll?"

"If she don't sound like she be talkin' for years, I don't know who do! Now who be tellin' you Mizzuz Sarah, Miz Sophie can't talk? ..."

Sophia looked at her Grandmother to see if she would reveal the name of the dastardly character but her Grandmother didn't say and Josephine kept right on talking.

"... A person should never put much faith in what you hear from somebody elses mouf. I always say, trust yo own ears and eyes. Yes indeed. Cause that's why the good lawd gave each 'n every one of us our own set, so everbody can hear everthing for their own selves, 'n see everthing for their own selves. Bless you chile. But tis plain, the Lord already done that."

"Here!! Here!! Josephine, welllll said! Now Sophia dearrrrrr, weeeeee alllll mussssssssssst listen to Josephine. Why Josephine is jussst about the wisest, kindest person I know who always does what the Doctor says! And who always is insisting I doooooooooo the sammmmmme! But doooo I?" And she laughed a low deep laugh.

"No truer words has ever been spoke! Amen!"

And then they all laughed. Never in her whole life had Sophia felt as good. And she pirouetted again. She couldn't have stopped herself from bouncing and jumping and laughing if she tried, no matter how much like a child, how un-Movie-Star a thing it was to do. Her Grandmother's and Josephine's eyes widened. But Sophia didn't care, she was so relieved. And now that the pink flamingos were back to rehearsing again, she wanted to kick up her legs and dance all around the entranceway with them. And sing, too, using her real voice, and not a Movie Star Voice, and even if everybody heard her sound like a ten-year-old child and not in her oh-so-many-voices of melodious-mystery. She wanted to kiss everybody. Hug everybody. Mr. James. Keys the Doorman. Even Serf Soufflé, that little man who talked so big and who didn't talk like such a man either. Her Grandmother had just told her she talked perfectly well. And she just DID talk perfectly well. She didn't stumble or stutter or mumble or sound to herself like her voice was too deep. She sounded just right. And she hadn't even done a thing, not a single thing, to her voice.

"Now, Mizzuz Sarah, it's time for yo medicine. I need to be gettin' you back up dat elevator. Miz Sophie, yo Grandmother has to take her medicine or that Doctor be callin' me up and givin' me the dickens' again!"

"Sophia darrrrrrrrling, I'll see you at breakfast." And her Grandmother's eyes beamed as they gazed into Sophia's. But in about three seconds, she cried out, "HAUGH!!!! OH JOSEPHINE! We almost forgotttttt!" Abruptly, the light went out in her Grandmother's eyes, her voice changed and she was whispering so low that Sophia had to move closer to hear her. "Sophia darrrrrling, your Grannnnndfather will be coming home at his usual time this evening. Which is after his last show ends. But that shouldn't really concern you because you should be safe and sound ... I mean ... sound asleep in your bed then. Your Grandfather will be most happy to meet you at dinner tomorrow. Dinner time is really the beeeeeest part of the day for him. Everything before or after that is just so ..." and her Grandmother's eyes locked onto Josephine's and said, "if-y? ... wouldn't you say Josephine?"

And Josephine rolled hers, "If-y? Now Mizzuz Sarah, I myself be callin' it somethin' else entirely. Oh! yes, I would. Try Grouchy Grumpy and Cranky, Miz Sophie!"

"Sophia, darrlllling, breakfast is a delightful part of our day here in our house in the sky. We will be all together and finally yyyyyyyyou will be there with us. Darrrrling, do make sure you go to bed when Antoinette Fifi tells you its time for bed and that you stay asleep in your bedroom. His shows are doing too well and that can put him in such a mood!"

'Boy! She sure sounds different! I can barely hear her. Could my Grandmother be nervous? Her, of all people? And she sounded that way as soon as she started talking about Grandfather. I wonder why?'

And Sophia began to feel a little nervous herself.

She wasn't surprised. Strong emotions always affected her. Ever since she had been sneaking into the television room to scrutinize Movies and Movie Stars, she had become quite an expert on Movie Stars and how they expressed themselves. And she had concluded that expressing feelings was what Movie Stars did magnificently. But she also knew that Movie Stars had voices and accents; she had known that forever. But what she could never finally conclude, once and for all …

• • • WHAT WAS MORE IMPORTANT? • • •

Expressing feelings.

Or having a voice and an accent.

That was what confused Sophia. What she had observed contradicted what she had always believed for so many years - that a voice and an accent were everything.

But when a Movie Star expressed themselves with true deep feeling, she couldn't take her eyes off them. That was really when her heart would melt; and it wasn't their voice or accent that had melted it at all.

But voices and accents were everything.

Weren't they?

Lately, very lately, she had even wondered, could she be wrong? Because as she stood glued to the television in her Movie Star School, Sophia found herself paying more attention to what that Movie Star's emotion was.

As if how they sounded didn't even matter.

And, oh, what a terrible time she sometimes had in her Movie Star School, considering that the Movie wasn't stopping for her to learn the lines, let alone anything else. Anyone else would have given up. She would often only get one or two lines or maybe three out of a Movie Star's big speech. And with those three lines, she could never just do the voice and the accent. Because a line spoken with just a voice and accent never would've made an audience feel anything. No! To make her audience feel, it was up to her to get the feeling the Movie Star was expressing in those lines. And when she got the emotion, there was still the movement, the accent, the sound that she had to learn; and when she nailed all that – if she could nail all that - was when she got the character.

The cold hard fact was that emotions and faces and eyes and clothes were very very important too, as were voices and accents. And the scientist, the teacher, knew it. And that all these things together were what made Actresses convincing. And should just be The Law of her Movie Star School.

If she could just admit it.

But no matter how confused she was, that didn't stop her from keeping up her demanding performance schedule. She had so much to learn, after all. And so many characters to do.

For her audience of no one.

But when she could forget about her confusion and put it all together, for a fleeting but unforgettable moment, she was the Actress she was dying to be.

Who no one ever saw. Except Miss Kitty once every blue moon.

• • • HER GRANDMOTHER IS NERVOUS • • •

But about her Grandmother, she was not confused. After all, Sophia was a scientific observer, and she could certainly tell that her Grandmother had just delivered those lines very differently than all the other ones she had spoken. Her Grandmother was nervous when she talked about her Grandfather. Why?

"Anytime except dinner time … well … it's just so … you just never know with him. He's so unpredictable. So just be surrrrrrrrrre to be in bed befoooooore your Grandfather gets hommmmmmme."

"Now, Miz Sophie, be listenin' to yo' Grandmother on dat point! Do you hear chile? We don't want to deal with yo Grandfather's fussin'. No one in this household wants to do dat, I can tell you!"

"I'll send Antoinette Fifi down and shhhhhhe'll taaaaake you to your bedroommmm, after she gives you some lovely dinner made just for you. And wait til you see how we fixed up your room." And both of them hooted with delight. "We did it especially for you - especcially! I hooooope you liiiiike it! Good night my lovely Granddauuuuughter who talks."

Josephine, in a rubber-soled-sneak, had slipped a wheelchair from the shadows and crept alongside her Grandmother; Sophia hadn't a moment to sort out all her thoughts. Keys and Mr. James had already tip-toed over to her Grandmother's side so they could assist. And now the three of them surrounded her Grandmother and were doing what had to be done to get her off that recamier and into that wheelchair. Sophia could no longer see her Grandmother or even what they were up to because they had blocked her view. Down low they bent, back and forth they moved. She wished all of them would go away so she and her Grandmother could continue their talk. But they didn't. Those people hadn't heard her wishes. But she hadn't told them what her wishes were either. Finally, they straightened up and stepped away.

And there was her Grandmother - that beautiful madame in the dramatic clothes and glamorous make-up and with the voice of the midnight hour - in a wheelchair. Her Grandmother was sitting slightly slumped in it too. And now that she was out of that soft, candlelight that had glowed all round her, and in the harsh, overhead light of the hallway which was x-raying through her, Sophia could clearly see poking through the drapery of her Grandmother's long sleeves, the outline of bones. Bones that were like the painfully thin limbs on that sad tree outside, the one that needed a coat. Her Grandmother was as thin as that, almost. Maybe that's why she had to take medicine.

And Sophia felt worried. Maybe her Grandmother was sick. And she hoped and prayed to ALL the Saints, not just Miss Kitty's Saints, that it wasn't true and that her Grandmother wasn't sick. She needed her Grandmother to be strong. To be well. Because her Grandmother listened to her. Her Grandmother didn't mind when she was quiet, and didn't interrupt her when she talked. Her Grandmother may have been old but she wasn't at all like Great Aunt Hortense. Her Grandmother was funny. Her Grandmother was nice. Her Grandmother wore beautiful clothes. Glamorous clothes. Not stiffed nor starched nor creased. And lots and lots of make-up. And her Grandmother had a deep, foggy voice. Like hers.

'I just don't have the fog. Although maybe what I always thought was a frog in my throat was all the time really just fog in my throat!'

Her Grandmother talked like a Movie Star and looked like a Movie Star. Just like she always wanted to. So what if her Grandmother only looked like a Movie Star in candlelight? And looked like a sick person in real light? Sophia couldn't believe how lucky she was, *'I have for my very own a Grandmother who's almost really like a Movie Star. Oh Saints! please! If you can hear me - I only have one Grandmother! She's the only one I'll ever have. She shouldn't be sick, okay?'*

Sophia watched Josephine wheel her Grandmother away - away from her Grandmother's very own private stage. Sophia stared at that riderless recamier, its Movie Star vanished; it seemed so lonely without her, *'Does the recamier miss her, too?'* But Josephine and her Grandmother just kept rolling away, oblivious to Sophia and her wonderings. Sophia hoped at least one of them would turn around and wave good-bye to her or say something but they didn't. And even though they didn't seem to notice her, Sophia was now dying to jump in front of the wheelchair and say a very dramatic good-night to her new friends, in the style of one of her Movie Stars, something she never ever would have dreamed of doing for any living person before.

But just as she was about to, she saw that her Grandmother's head had fallen very slightly to the side.

If Miss Kitty had been standing alongside of her right now and had even an inkling of what she had been dreaming of doing, she imagined what Miss Kitty would've said to her. *'Josephine has enough t' worry about, making sure y'r Grandmother is not fallin' out o' her chair! Neither one o' tem will be tinkin' about ye at tis particular moment.'* Because Miss Kitty knew Sophia's deep-down-real secret, and Sophia knew she did: that Sophia would've loved to have people pay attention to her and didn't like it when they didn't. Miss Kitty, after all, had caught her in the television room, center-stage and acting the grand lady two too many times. Miss Kitty had even said to her, "Shrinking Violet! Hah! Sophia, you are all Violet, and no shrink! Violet - hah! VIOLETTE, more like it! In fact, I tink you is just about dying t' be te center o' attention."

Sophia did not jump in front of her Grandmother and act and dance and sing. *'Miss Kitty would never want me to bother a person who might be sick. I can just hear her, 'Tis is hardly t' time t' be doin' y'r fancy characters!'*

Readers, Sophia was certain Miss Kitty didn't think much of her acting and voice-doing but then she'd never come right out and asked her either. And she was dead wrong. She had no idea how dead wrong she was. Why Miss Kitty would've been doing the jig that Sophia actually wanted to and was even dying to perform for her Grandmother. Why Miss Kitty would've even died to see Sophia jump in front of her Grandmother and been nudging her to do that very thing.

Sophia must've gotten her Miss Kitty confused with her Mr. Snoggley or her Great Aunt Hortense. After all, Miss Kitty was the one who was always asking Sophia, "Miss Sophia, why for t' love of all tat's good 'n holy in te world, are you prancin' all around like a circus poodle 'n acting up a t'understorm 'n a famine or two but ten, as soon as ye walk out a' tis room, out a' tis house, 'n into y'r schoolroom, ye barely say peep t' a livin' breathin' soul? Tis not makin' a bit a sense t' me sensible self. 'N I'm from te ole-country where I just about seen 'n heard it-all!" Whenever Miss Kitty would ask that question, Sophia never even tried to answer her as she didn't know why herself.

Miss Kitty could hardly answer the question either, try as she might, even after she wracked her "seen-it-all self" trying to. But she just couldn't stop wondering, *'How could somebody be so shy, so shrinking, so downright rabbity in one place 'n so bold, so nervy, 'n such a sauce-pot in another?'*

Dear Readers, Miss Kitty, well aware what Sophia's Father did for a living, was dying to ask him her question. He'd have the answer. But she didn't dare as she didn't want to get anyone into trouble. Most of all herself, for failing to disclose beforehand what his daughter was up to in the middle of the night.

Sophia watched her Grandmother's body drift lower and lower in the chair. *'Besides, if I did one of my characters, Grandmother'll never be able to see me, or even hear me, her head has fallen down so!'*

Sophia watched Josephine stop the wheelchair and adjust her Grandmother to a slightly more upright position. She was dying to say something to her brand new friends but did not. Sophia had surprised herself that she, so famous for only talking to a few people and not talking to just about everybody else, wanted to talk to people she hardly knew, and was even sad, so sad, that she couldn't. And not only wanted to talk but to pour her heart out to. And to even dance and sing for them too. Like the way she did when she was all by herself in her Movie Star School.

Her Grandmother was almost out of the hallway and she still hadn't waved to Sophia. Could her Grandmother have forgotten she was even there? *'No.'* Sophia thought, *'It's probably just because Grandmother is not feeling 100% right now. I hope that's what it is. And it's not because she's really sick. But Grandmother couldn't really be that sick because Grandmother has such a voice! Like the stars in the night sky! And she looks like such a Movie Star! And she wears such clothes! Sick people don't wear clothes like that and look like Movie Stars!'* But her thoughts were not comforting her.

Mr. James turned towards her and must've seen how forlorn she was because he bent down and gave her a gentle pat on her shoulder and said, "Well, Miss Sophia, aren't you proud that that smart, funny, glamorous lady is your Grandmother? You are in the best of hands, so don't worry in the slightest, you're going to have a jolly time here. But I must be off or my good man Keys here will personally see to it that a bobby gives the Oomsmobile a thousand-dollar parking ticket!"

"Which, Mr. James, would relief no dyspepsia nor yield no enjoyment." And Keys winked at Sophia.

"Right ho, my good man. I do wish I believed you. And speaking of no enjoyment, I must be off!" And Mr. James winked at Sophia. And even if Sophia could've winked, she wouldn't've because she didn't feel the thing inside her that would've made her want to wink. She didn't feel light-hearted or silly or whatever it was that made people wink.

And it hit her.

She was on her own! No Mr. James, No Miss Kitty, No Father, No Mother. Really on her own, for the first time in her whole life. And even her new friend, her Grandmother wasn't here now. She didn't want Mr. James to go, to leave her alone in this big house sitting way way high in the sky - so high that it was even close to the moon because she could see the Man in the Moon staring at her through these rocket-high windows! How could she be in immensity by herself? And she melted to a heap of miniscule-ity on the floor, even though she was her same size and clearly still standing there.

"What an interesting adventure you're about to have, Miss Sophia! Why with the characters you've already met," and Mr. James bowed to Keys the Doorman and Keys bowed back, "and are about to meet in this house, I assure you, Miss Sophia, your Mother was correct! Never a dull moment. Will you have stories to tell your school mates!" Sophia knew he was right about meeting characters. All the people she met so far were like characters in Movies. But somehow the thought of actually meeting people who were like characters from her Movies didn't seem so great if she wasn't safe in her own house when she met them. But he was wrong about her school mates. She couldn't imagine telling them anything about this adventure.

And for the first time ever she felt odd thinking that. And wrong. Because this adventure, she wanted to talk about. To someone.

But Mr. James by now was no longer looking at her and was all by-jove joviality and cheerio cheerio-ness, waving at the pink flamingos and Serf Soufflé and smiling at Keys and wasn't paying attention to the expression on her face. And then he shook her hand without really looking at her, started off towards the door with Keys the Doorman by his side but then quickly turned round.

"Gadzooks, I almost forgot! What would the Immortal Bard say? 'A plentiful lack of ...' gray matter, no doubt! Here is a cell phone from your Mother. You are, according to her strict instructions, to keep this on you at all times! Your Mother will be calling you regularly." Mr. James still hadn't notice she didn't look at all cheerio, but then the moon's light hadn't reached the dark spot she was in. And Sophia would've been far too embarrassed to tell him or anyone her childish feelings.

Mr. James and Keys waved and smiled and went out the door. And Sophia stood there by herself. Now no one talking to her. They were both gone. And so too were her Grandmother and Josephine. And even though

Sophia was standing in the grand entranceway surrounded by dancing pink flamingos, she felt so all alone, she couldn't ever remember feeling this alone before.

But though there may have been no one talking to her, there were creatures talking about her. Actually there were several creatures talking about her but I'll just discuss the human ones now. There were two of those. And they were about to get into an elevator.

"Josephine, darrrling, we forgot to tell our dear Sophia … oh! Josephine … isn't she lovvvvvvvvely? I'm so happy she's herrrre with us, it'll be so much fun. But we forgot to tell her not to eeeeevvvver-neeeeeever talk about moooooovies to her Grannnnnndfather. He surrrrely must be the only living breathing Producer of Theatricals still walking the face of the earth who speaks of movies and the movie business and movie stars with such imprecations and contumely! And oh! his indelicacy! Why to think of the imaginative language he comes up with when describing it, it's a shame not a worrrrrrd of it can be spoken in polite soooooooociety. Oh! Josephine, when he goes on and onnnnn about Movies, I would never let him know this, but he's actually quite hilarious. To him "The Theeeeeatre" is THEEEEEE art form of show business. The ONLY art form. And he is its last living protector and defender. But wwwwwwwwhat are we to do? He is so stubborn! There's not a soul among his theatrical producing colleagues alive anymore who agrees with him. Everyone who thought that way died off years ago with the diiiiiinosaurs. It must be very looooonely for him. But then again, Josephine, I can't imagine why we would have to wooooorry. Whhhy everrrrrrrrr would a ten-year-old girl from the country eeeeever talk about the moooooovies? And knowing my sonnnnnnn, Sigmund, I'm sure he's never even taken her to see a single movie considering just how much he loves music and literature and believes that THEY are the only forms of art a person could ever need. My son and my husband! Such lovers of art, aren't they devinnnnnnnne, Josephine?"

"Oh, now Mizzus Sarah, you're problee right. Prob-lee. Though little girls now a days sho' loves the mooovies. My sisters grandkids, why every one of them loves the mooovies and are peskerin' me or some me to take 'em there. But Sophia now, she is from the co'ntry … and isn't she jes' like the fresh air itself, Mizzuz Sarah … well, how could such a sweet young co'ntry thing ever know anything about dat ole devil mooovie bi'ness? So we don' have to worry our fine selves abou' dat. And speakin' of dat ole devil, it's time to put some medicine in you, so you get rid a' yours and give everbody some peace for a change!" And Josephine began to hum as she pushed her Grandmother's wheelchair into the waiting elevator. Her Grandmother's head was bowed low again and she didn't say another word.

Sophia was, as always, trying to do the impossible: shrink into a spot in that hallway and grow wide-wishing-well eyes so she could stare at the pink flamingos whirling by, winking at her.

She smiled back but that's absolutely all she was brave enough to do, even though she would've loved to have lifted off and whirl away with them. Serf Soufflé, in between his "Flamingos, I want thtrrrut and thnap! I want legthhh! Not flapthth! Kick! Are your girdleth too tight? Oh! Give me thtrrength," snuck a wink in, too.

And then a Frenchy cat began pawing her ears.

• • • IN VOICE HEAVEN • • •

Who was that?

Because into the same hallway that her Grandmother had just been wheeled out of came a song sung in an accent that Sophia recognized from its first note as French. Now Frenchiness was tickling her through and through.

'A Frenchie? juke-box? hot-box? is blowing smoke rings all over me and the flamingos and the 'thnaping thillineth' and the plink-plank-plunk piano!

'Could there really be someone else to hear here!'

She couldn't believe her luck and suddenly she had no difficulty lifting herself off her spot. *'Grandmother's house is Voice Heaven. I'M in Voice Heaven. How many voices have I heard since I've been here? And now I'm about to add ANOTHER one, a French one, to my treasure chest? Let me count them all—'*

But she had no time because she could see that a girl, older than a teenager but younger than a woman, was headed straight towards her. Frenchie-hot was dressed in the most beautiful black and white maid's uniform Sophia had ever seen. Maria's uniforms were black and white too but they never looked like this. This wasn't baggy and it sure wasn't saggy. It was sleek in places, and in other places, like a frilly petal. And such lace! With its open work and tiny threads that were so delicate, so fine, so intricate.

'Why a person could hardly ever clean in such a uniform! They'd certainly get it dirty! Oh! I want a uniform exactly like it so I can wear it and not my uniform to school every day. And then for the rest of my entire life!'

The BonBon was getting even closer and Sophia could see that its merry eyes were sparkling and swaying as if they were doing the singing. And then in a rustle of lace, the confection stood before Sophia. She had stopped singing, and was batting her long long eyelashes (covered in mascara) and shaking her ringlet curls, when out of her mouth rolled such words "Enchanté, Mademoiselle SoFeeYa!" that Sophia had to check to make sure she hadn't started singing again. And the pussycat smiled and so did her eyes, her nose, her cheeks even and then she laughed a laugh that was much more spice than sugar, that even Sophia, who just moments ago had been shrinking (or trying to) laughed right out loud with her.

And Sophia's heart melted. Yet again.

Here was a she-bebe wearing lots of make-up, just like her Grandmother; smelling delectable, just like her Grandmother. And just like the pink flamingos, too. And talking in a French accent. Just like she dreamed of doing herself. Sophia would've loved nothing better then to spend an entire day talking to everybody she met, including all her classmates and Mr. Snoggley too, and even Great Aunt Hortense - well maybe not Great Aunt Hortense - in a French accent just like this.

'Because I was right! Voices and accents ARE everything! And she proves it. And now I'll be able to learn a French accent from a French person who isn't in a Movie but is alive and real and right in front of me. I might even be able to practi—'

But le-bebe-chat was speaking again and Sophia stopped her scheming at once and listened, "Moi, je m'appelle Antoinette Fifi Merree. Et toi, tu es Mademoiselle SoFeeYa?" And as Antoinette's eyelashes fluttered, she held out her hand, "Enchanté Mademoiselle SoFeeYa! Oh pardonnez … ME!! NO! Anglais, Antoinette Fifi!! Par … don … me, I mean to say." And laughs from the Land of the CanCan and more ringlet shakes. "But excusez-moi, ze peoples call me Antoinette Fifi for ze short. We go togezair to ze keetchen to get ze dinnair and zen would you like when we are feenished zat we are going up to your room to play ze "dress-up?" You like to play ze dress-up SoFeeYa? I love to play ze dress-up!" And Antoinette Fifi winked at Sophia and waited for her answer.

"I play dress up all the time, Antoinette Fifi!"

Just like that! her secret had rolled off her tongue, out of her mouth and into the ears of a stranger. But a stranger in France-y-prance clothes who talked more like cat than person.

But a stranger nonetheless!! *I've never told that secret to a soul! So what that this stranger is everything I want to be - why in the movies, I bet they'd call this person a minx-box or a kitty-hotty or a co … co … copette or something. But oooh … with an accent. A French accent … ooh! But … but … just because I love how she talks and*

I love her outside that doesn't mean my secret will be safe with her! Forever and ever? I mean … How do I know if her inside is as good as her outside? Because sometimes in the Movies, people look nice but they turn out to be dirty rats. And how do I even know that she won't turn around and tell … like … like … Great Aunt Hortense or Maria or Melinda or Mr. Snoggley or all the stupid people in my class or Daddy or Mother or … or … Grandmother.'

But it was too late now to pluck her precious secret out of Antoinette Fifi's ears and stuff it back inside her where it had been buried for so long and been so very very safe.

'Since when did I get such a big mouth? And why would I suddenly open it and tell her that?' And Sophia coyote-eyed Antoinette Fifi Merree to see if she could catch the dirty rat that surely lurked underneath all that lace, those frills.

"Wondearfull!! You like ze dress up too! I 'oope soooo … I am, you know, l'apprentice costume deesignair."

'WonDEARfull? She doesn't look shocked at all! She looks happy.' And Sophia could relax. Her deep dark secret was safe.

"Sometimes I am heelping your Grand-pere on his zeatricals sewing up le costumes and sometimes I am heelping your belle-mere here chez-cha-teau-roof with le cleaning and sometimes with her clothes - oooh, but not so much le cleaning." And Antoinette Fifi made a wrinkly face then she tossed her curls and shook the parts of her made for shaking and when those parts were still, she whispered in Sophia's ear. "Your Belle-Mere … ooooh lah lah … she loves le costumes!"

And now they were laughing as they walked along the very same hallway that her Grandmother had just been wheeled out of! What a difference a minute could make! How alone she had just felt in that hallway as she watched them wheel her Grandmother away. But now Antoinette Fifi was blowing on Sophia's cold hands and then bubbling over with all she had to tell her. Surely her Grandmother sent this swizzle-stick to her. And as Sophia listened to her, she knew a golden opportunity had just come her way in more ways than one. Because here she was walking beside a real live French person who probably knew the Eiffel Tower and, to top it off, was not a confection behind glass on a television screen.

'I must listen to Antoinette Fifi's every word and try to figure out how exactly she makes each word sound so French; like what she's doing with her mouth and maybe her tongue even. After all, if I watch and listen, I could learn to speak French. Because voices and accents really are everything! I have work to do. Important work!'

"We have up ze stairs in your special rrroomm a tresor chest full of le dresses, le skirts made of such materiel! I don't know ze English word … le soie … ooh … ooh … chiffon and tulle evening dresses and scarfs and perfume and beaucoup of zis and zat's and … so beaucoup much … but zen your Grandmozair, she asked for me to have ze chest full to ze brimming up over to ze tippy top with such la girl, la jeune fille, la femininities." And Antoinette Fifi laughed. And oh! was Sophia happy she had come to her Grandmother's house. She had met a person who talked like a French Foreign Pastry. Sophia really couldn't believe her luck. Not only had she entered Voice Heaven, she was about to enter Costume Heaven, too. *'I wish Daddy were here. I bet he'd love all these voices too.'* But then again, maybe it wasn't so bad he wasn't here. She wasn't so sure how he'd feel about seeing her in costumes.

But just as they'd reached the end of the hallway, a pink flamingo came racing over to her.

"Miss Sophia … Miss Sophia … my Aunt told me tat I was to be wishing a cheery hello to you now."

She would've recognized that accent anywhere. Miss Kitty's! Sophia looked up and there beaming through a pink-plumed, black-beaked, head-dress, was a very pretty smile.

"My aunt is your Nanny. I'm Margaret Finnegan, Miss Kitty's niece. Aunt Kitty just talks about you all the time, she misses you so!"

'Miss Kitty's niece! A pink flamingo? Oh! Miss Kitty!' Her very own Miss Kitty. Who could keep a secret. Who understood her. Who was always there. And now who suddenly wasn't. And without warning, tears filled her eyes and rolled down her face, and she couldn't stop them. *'I hope nobody is looking at me. Little girl's cry! But not when they're with big girls!'*

"Oooh … now don't cry Miss Sophia. Miss Kitty misses you too. I can't wait to tell her I saw you. Good-night then Miss Sophia!!" And Margaret Finnegan smiled at Sophia.

Sophia's smile may've been watery but it was a smile. And then Margaret Finnegan dashed back to the pink flamingos. And Sophia and Fifi set off again but now Sophia was practically skipping as they headed towards the "keetchen" so Sophia could eat her "dinnair." Antoinette Fifi took a plate with a tall domed cover out of the warming oven and pulled off its cover. Sophia gasped. *'Their food is just like their buildings.'* Sophia had never seen or eaten tall food before. *'Food probably has to be tall here, too. It must be a rule or something. Maybe if you eat tall food, you feel tall and you act tall.'* And she zipped over and started eating it.

"Oooh ZoFEEya, I see zat - how you are saying - you are turneeng ze mountain into ze molehill! Well, as we say - Bon appetit!"

'No, Antoinette Fifi, what I'm really doing is turning a molehill into a mountain!' But Sophia kept that inside. *'Antoinette Fifi probably wouldn't understand.'*

But Antoinette Fifi didn't even notice Sophia hadn't smiled at her joke or said a word to her; she just kept purring on about "your rrooommmm ... ooh ZoFEEya, wait til you see your ooh-la-la-rrroooomm," or grinning mischievously, and then more "rrroommm zis" and "rrroommm zat" and grinning even more from ear to ear even as she placed Sophia's dessert in front of her. And since dessert was now before her, it was Sophia who wasn't noticing anything except it. Dessert was a tall piece of cake (wedding cake tall but without the usual suspects on top because in their place was just a single tiny occupant - a princess doll in a dress covered with the celestial sky - tiny stars, tiny moon, tiny planets) and very delectable and soon only the tiny doll remained. Which Antoinette Fifi scooped up, handed to Sophia even as she was springing out of her chair. "Keeeep zis doll, ZoFEEya, I made her dress and all ovair it are zee stars and zee moon. Ooh-ooh ZoFEEya, let's to gooooo now! You must to zee what wee did to your rrroooommmm! Your doll wiilll look zo prettee in your rrroommm and she wiilll keep you company zere. Ooh-la-la!"

And what Sophia had only half-way heard, hit her now; something wonderful was waiting for her. And she sprang up from her chair and they dashed out of the "keetchen." *'What will this room be like?'* Sophia wondered as she placed herself directly behind Antoinette Fifi. But just a footstep later, she was wondering something else entirely, *'How she walks! So ... slinky!'* She'd become hypnotized.

But even if she could've figured it out, even if she'd got it down perfectly, Sophia knew one thing. She'd never get her own wiggle to wiggle like that. And a song from an old movie whirled around her head, 'It must be jelly 'cause jam don't shake like that.' And she finally understood what that funny old man had meant when he sang it. *'I know what he'd say about her. Antoinette Fifi is jelly. And I bet I know what he'd say about me. That I'm not jelly. I'm not even jam. That's what a walk like that needs. But I'll practice anyway, with what I do have. My sticks. But not here. In front of Antoinette Fifi ...*

'actually, I'm behind her. I'd get away with it. She wouldn't even see me.'

But she was too afraid to try. *'I'll joost have to prackteece by zinking my zhoughts in my new accent - while keeping my eyes on 'zis Frrrrench slinkee toy - Whatevair I figure oouuut now I'll prackteece when I'm allll by myself. But now I'll joost concentrrrate on moi Frrrrench. Vhat vill zis rrroommmm be liiike?'* not daring to say it out loud. *'If I zay it out loud, Antoinette Fifi might zink I'm making ze fun of her. And not realize 'ow much I'm trying to be her and turn moiself into ZoFeeya Fifi!'*

They reached the front hallway but the pink flamingos were no longer dancing and now stood gathered round Serf Soufflé as he pecked away on them. "Previewth thtart in two weekth, go home, go to bed, go thtraight to bed, abtholutely no late night romping, cavorting and/or frithking! And don't let that very important preview date danth out of your little headth!" But as Sophia and Antoinette Fifi darted by, the group turned and alley-catted a "Goo'NIYITTTTTTT SoPHIYAH." Margaret Finnegan smiled at Sophia. And Sophia, who had filled up again with shyness at the sight of everybody, lifted her head to smile at Margaret Finnegan and then put it right down again.

Antoinette Fifi skipped up the stairs and so too did Sophia. Sophia stopped when they got to the second floor but Antoinette Fifi said, "Ooh-non-non-Mademoiselle, we 'ave ze manee stairs to climb!"

Sophia practiced, *'Ooh-non-non-Mademoiselle, we 'ave ze manee stairs to climb!'*

They climbed up the second flight of stairs to the third floor. When they reached the third floor Sophia stopped but Fifi shook her head again. And up to the fourth floor they clambered. And then they had to stop because there were no more steps. Sophia looked at Antoinette Fifi who said, "Ooh-non-Mademoiselle, we 'ave even more steps!"

• • • A PUSHY MOON • • •

Antoinette Fifi led the way down a long hallway that was glowing end to end in moonlight. Yet there was only one teeny-tiny, lonely-little-petunia window at its way, faraway end for all that moonlight to squeeze through. And Sophia was mystified. How could moonlight stream through such a puny porthole and souse a long long hallway everywhere with moonglow? Yet it could. *What kind of moon is in this place? A pushy moon? But why does the moon want to get in here so bad? Or is the moon gigantic here too?'* Sophia felt her feet drag her over to the window, like the moon itself was pulling them there, and she had no choice but to examine it.

'What big eyes that moon has!—

'What big eyes it has? ... Does the moon really have eyes here?' But just looking at that moon made another song pop into her head, a song she must've heard in another movie, a song that was always sung in a Maria accent. She sang it inside her head, *'When da Moon hits yourra eye-a like a bigga pizza pie-a—'*

And just like that, she stopped her song and switched to her new Antoinette Fifi accent. It was her more glamorous accent, and was the better one to use when describing a moon such as this, ' *'e seems even biggair 'ere zen 'e does back home. 'e seems to fillll oop zee entire window, zee entire sky, zee entire citee. I wondair, ees 'e watcheeng what I am doeeng? Zis moon ees veree different 'ere. Maybe 'e 'as to be much biggair 'ere een zis big citee. Much brightair because no one would see heem eef 'e wasn't. Where arrre my moonglasseez? Zhat's what zee Frrrrench Moooveee Star would zay eeef she 'ad to walk 'srough zis 'allway.'*

Oh! how she wished she could've said out loud what she just thought inside! She was dying to share her joke with Antoinette Fifi, dying for her to hear her French accent, for her to hear her talk just like her! But she knew she wouldn't. She would just have to imagine she had.

And suddenly, the light was too bright and she couldn't imagine anything at all.

Or was all that light making her see the botherations and perplexities that were lurking about in her mind?

Botherations and perplexities? She didn't like to think about such things. She would've much preferred thinking about French Movie Stars.

But she couldn't because all she could think now was -

'Why do I have to talk with an accent?

'Why do I have to be a Movie Star? Why can't I just talk? Why can't I just be myself?'

She usually didn't wonder such things; she liked to feel good, not bad. But now perplexities were suddenly all lit up as if that moonlight was trying to flood into her mind, and not just the hallway. As if her favorite things: her imaginings, her fantasies, her movies, her acting were in her darkest place and needed to be lit up.

'Is this moon trying to light up every last one of my secrets on purpose? Why?

'How does that moon know what's inside me?

'And now that they are all lit up, will I open up my mouth and talk about them? Out loud? To Antoinette Fifi?'

And oh! Were things speaking up now that they could be seen and thought they might be heard!

Except, they didn't speak up outside; they spoke up inside.

'Telling Antoinette Fifi about my accents! I can't imagine telling anyone about the persons I can do. At all! Period! My Movie Stars are my own private deep down secret. I could never tell, like, the people in my class. Never … if they ever found out, I'd just die …

'… Antoinette Fifi does seem nicer than them …

'Even so, I just don't believe she'd understand ... and if she wouldn't understand, they'd never understand. Probably. They all think of me as 'Sophia Oomla, that timid girl' – I've heard some of those school people even call me 'scaredy-cat girl' because I can really really hear! 'Movie Star!' they'd say, 'Scaredy-cat girl must want to be important!' And even if some of the nicer people didn't laugh, even they'd probably never understand just how much I really can be a Movie Star. Nobody'd take me seriously. I've been too quiet for too long. They'd never accept the fact that I-me, shy-me, can't-open-my-mouth-me, could be a Movie Star. With an Accent. They'd never believe that. And they'd think it's stupid, dumb and dopey for a person who can't even talk when she's called on in class to even try to do any such thing. And then they'd probably ... might even – no WOULD get a great big, laughing-out-loud, falling-on-the-floor-yuk-yuk-hah-hah-festival out of imagining me trying to be such an exotic creature as a Movie Star with an Accent. NO!! It's my secret and it's going to stay that way.'

Again, Sophia had fallen so low inside the deep well of herself, she couldn't see. Until she felt eyes on her that weren't the moon's eyes. *'Antoinette Fifi must've been staring at me the whole time!'* And Sophia shot out of herself and stuck herself to the floor. But her eyes weren't stuck and, with the brilliant moon-light shining in through the tiny window, she took a good look at Antoinette Fifi, expecting to find that she had lost patience with her the way Great Aunt Hortense or Maria would whenever Sophia was supposed to be doing what they said but was instead frozen in place, dreaming. Why even Miss Kitty would lose patience with her for doing the same thing. But Antoinette Fifi had such kind eyes; a person behind such eyes would never laugh at her and Sophia knew that as soon as she looked into them. And she wasn't at all stuck.

And it hit her.

She was wrong about Antoinette Fifi. She may not be wrong about everybody else, like her classmates and Mr. Snoggley, but she was wrong about her. She would've been able to talk, to sing, in her accent, to tell her jokes and secrets to Antoinette Fifi; she would've listened and appreciated every word, every accented note.

But her-self-absorbed-self was now lit by a pushy moon and Sophia had no choice but to see her feet walking her towards Antoinette Fifi. When she finally reached her side, a Movie Star smile spilled out of her which she aimed, very shyly, very self-consciously, and very quickly at Antoinette Fifi. But then just as quickly, she took it away and looked away; she and her smile had spilled back inside herself. So she didn't see Antoinette Fifi's shy smile that she had aimed at Sophia and that the moonglow was illuminating.

But the moon did not give up; it was also illuminating a door along the corridor and Sophia snapped out of it.

• • • THE DOOR • • •

The door was dark and wooden and different than the other doors along that corridor. The others were plain; this one was carved.

'Whatever is on this door?'

Sophia, of course, didn't say, even after all she had just understood about Antoinette Fifi; it stayed where her thoughts usually did. What she did do was draw closer to the door so she could see it better. The largest of the carvings was towards the top of the door and was of a round head. Above and down each side of the head was another carving but this was of a streamer that had words running along its entire length.

'What sort of face does this head have and what do the words say?'

And she got even closer.

'It's the Man in the Moon. And he looks like he's laughing … no … what is his mouth doing? Is he singing? Well, whatever he's doing, he's looking right at me!'

And she looked back at him. *'He's such a happy moon.'* She felt happy just looking at him. Like singing even. And then the oddest thing happened. She read the words on the streamer - Out Loud - the words just burst out of her. She couldn't have kept them in, even if she tried.

"The night walked down the sky with the moon in her hand." At the end of the words was a name. "Frederic Lawrence Knowles."

There was another streamer that ran along the lower part of the door that had words on it too; but this streamer had many words. How easily those words flew out of her mouth, too! "This here MY Room Mister Knowles … Ooobie Doobie Oh Yeah … Ms. Night no be walkin' in here, Mr. Knowles, Ooobie Doobie Oh Yeah … Ms. Night be dancin', Ms. Night be singin', up down that sky with me … Ooobie Doobie Oh Yeah!" There was no name after those words, just two words, "The Man."

She couldn't stop those words if she tried. But she didn't try. In fact, she was about to say them all over again and even louder, using some sort of an accent (she wasn't sure which one, she'd have to see what came out of her mouth) but Antoinette Fifi began talking. And even though Sophia was now talking with ease, she'd forgotten to ask her why this door was different than all the other doors in the house.

"Oh, ZoFEEya. Zis is your rroooommm." Antoinette Fifi didn't sound like herself. She was speaking so low it was hard to hear her. Sophia, who had been examining the door, quickly examined her.

'Antoinette Fifi has her head down now! She's doing what I do! But why?' And Sophia really studied her.

"Zis rrooommm ees zee most beaUTifuulll in zee whole hooouse. But no one haz been uzing eet for zo long. Zo wee feex eet for you - specialitay." She kept speaking in a voice that was a whisp-of-a-whisper, the pussycat now hiding in her eyes imploring Sophia to hear what she was saying. "Wee 'ope you likkke eet."

'She sounds like me now. She's talking like a scaredy cat!' Anyone else might not have even noticed that she sounded different but Sophia, from all her years of studying and listening and hearing people, noticed it immediately, so she aimed her practiced eye at her to see if she could figure out what was wrong. 'She even looks scaredy cat. I'm usually the one who looks scaredy cat and feels scaredy cat.'

And, like a doctor with a patient, she examined Antoinette Fifi.

'But maybe she's not really scaredy cat. Maybe she's just worried. Her voice would be much more shaky if she was scaredy cat. Her head is down but only slightly so and her voice isn't a pussycat's anymore. It's not as teasy. It's much more whispered. Sometimes I whisper and it's usually because I'm not so sure about stuff. And if she's not so sure about stuff, she's probably worried, too. Well, if I'm to be the World's Greatest Actress, I'll have to know the answer to that question. I must understand what's going on inside a person so when I have to play that person I can bring their insides to their outsides! So why why why is she so worried?'

When Sophia was eight and three-quarters, she had decided that one day she would be the World's Greatest Actress. 'It won't be easy and I'll have to know a great deal, so I will watch Movie Stars use their voice and their body! From their screeching-iest shouts to the slip-sliding-est swoons to the tinsiest-up-tick, down-tick of their eye-brows, eye-lashes, mouths, noses, nostrils, ears, heads, shoulders and every movement, every word spoken or unspoken in between – I will watch them! To become the World's Greatest Actress will require so much knowledge! Acting like another person is serious business.

'But I can't just know what their outsides are doing, what costume I'll wear, what voice I'll use! Even if that is really hard for a Voice Fiend such as myself to admit!

'An actress has to understand what's inside each character's heart first. And then she has to make what's inside show through that character's eyes. Which are really my eyes. But I have even more work to do than that. I have to figure out what I, as the World's Greatest Actress, will do to express those feelings. And that's when the real work begins. An actress can't just know what she'll do to play the character. An actress has to figure out WHAT makes the character do what they do; the actress must know the character's MOTIVATION.'

Sophia had heard all about this MOTIVATION because one time she had watched a director on a television program about Acting talking about

MOTIVATION. This director had said that every actor had to know the MOTIVATION of a character before the actor could even begin to create a character. Right before each actor (that director called even the actresses actors) even started to act in his scene, the director would ask, "What's your character's motivation?" As she watched the program, she realized if she knew this MOTIVATION she would know the secret of acting.

Of course, Sophia was only eight and three-quarters at the time and couldn't figure out for the life of her what this MOTIVATION word meant from what that director was saying. But she knew where to go to find out. A stand in her Father's library, for there towered a Webster's Dictionary. Her Father had told her that if a person looked up all the words they didn't know in the dictionary, and then learned the meaning of these words, that that person would be able to read all sorts of book with all sorts of hard words in them and that eventually, after reading all those books, that person might even become a smart person, though he did say there were no guarantees about that. Sophia knew quite well he never said knowing what was in the dictionary would turn a smart person into the World's Greatest Actress but Sophia figured that if it just made her the World's Smartest Actress, she would do the rest. She didn't know how to spell MOTIVATION, so she pointy-fingered her way through the "M"s, down one column, then down the next, inspecting each micro-teensie printed word, one after the other and after searching for a while, she finally found it.

'Motivation – Something that causes a person to act.'

When she read the word and what it meant, she practically passed out. And she fell in love - with a word – because it was a word that knew all about her. What a word! And she'd say it to herself many many times a day. Something that causes a person to Act! To ACT! She knew why she Acted. She knew what HER motivation was. To speak. To sing. To turn words into music. Or thunder.

Or crescendos of caterwauling cacophony … those words she heard too but not on that program; in a Movie, and she really liked them, too, even though she didn't know what they meant either. The best she could figure was that it had something to do with screechinating cats. Or raucous, rumbling trucks that hauled walloping hugenesses and their bull-sized and bully-mouthed drivers. Or maybe it meant really, awful un-musical, ugliness. Or maybe all three put together but was never able to confirm it because she was never able to find even one of those words in her Father's dictionary.

But she knew making all sorts of sounds was something the World's Greatest Actress would be called upon to do, since she would be required to play all sorts of people, some of them probably not such sweet-talkers …

And she must express feelings without even having to say a word, with just her face. Or her whole self. From her head to her toes. And, oh yes, to look like a Movie Star. To look unforgettable. To be unforgettable. To not ever disappear or ever ever ever be invisible. To talk and talk and talk. And to say something that mattered. To say something important. To be important. And above all, to be heard. By everybody. By the whole entire world.

And when she figured all that out, out she would step on to her stage in the television room, in front of her audience of zero, ready to begin. Audience of zero wasn't exactly accurate because somehow or another she was simultaneously listening and watching herself to see how she was doing. And if she didn't like what she saw and/or heard, she'd stop and start over again. Sophia had to get it right and there were many stops and starts. Good thing for the audience there was no audience.

'So why is Antoinette Fifi so worried? Well, because of all my years studying Movie Stars, I've become very good at understanding normal people. It's easy for me to study people because I'm usually the one who's not talking, I'm the one listening. Some listeners appear to be listening but are not really listening at all; not paying attention when someone is talking to them; don't really hear what is being said to them; don't really watch the talker talking to them to see the expression on the talker's face; to see the position the talker's body is in. I know, because I've even had the opportunity to talk to several people who are just like that. People who don't really listen. But I've learned from them and I'm not like them, I listen when a person talks to me! I really really really listen. And watch. And study. All of that. And even more!

Sophia knew that if she had to play Antoinette Fifi right now, it would be her duty as the World's Greatest Actress to understand first and foremost what was causing Antoinette Fifi to act the way she was - what her MOTIVATION was, and, next, how she really felt and why she felt that way, and, lastly, what she, the World's Greatest Actress, must do to show all of that even before she figured out what clothes to pinch from her Mother's closet to play her in.

'Why IS she so worried?'

But she didn't have the nerve to come out and simply ask her why, even though she knew that's exactly what she ought to do.

Antoinette Fifi started to turn the doorknob on the Man in the Moon door but as she did, Sophia noticed that now Antoinette Fifi was the one who was smiling shyly. And Sophia found herself filling up with shyness too, as much as she was trying not to. But even if her smile was shy, she smiled it anyway.

And then the door opened and there was yet another staircase.

"ZoFEEya we are almost zere, just zees steps to go. Togezzair, let's go, shall we?"

Sophia followed Antoinette Fifi, not noticing a speckle of the resplendent light that made that dark-wooded-stairwell glow because as she climbed further and further up those stairs, she was descending deeper and deeper into thoughts, notions, thinks and surmises.

'There's so much mystery in a person. You have to figure them out just like you have to figure mystery stories out - like a Nancy Drew mystery story. You have to look very carefully at what the person says and does or doesn't say or doesn't do. Nancy Drew calls all that stuff clues. If you really want to figure people out, you have to look at their clues because very few people ever tell you what they really think, and who they really are. Like me - I don't tell people what I really think and who I really really am, either, do I? People would never know that I can speak in so many foreign accents because they think I'm quiet. And they're right, I don't really talk so much. So what clues has Antoinette Fifi left for me so that I could figure out why she sounds different right now? So shy, so worried?

'Okay, what do I know about Antoinette Fifi so far? She kept teasing me about how much I'd love this room that's to be my room. Maybe she's just worried that I won't like the room she spent so much time fixing up just for me. And she was only teasing me to make a game out of it, to make it fun because she thought if she made my room sound like fun, I'd like my room. And now she's just a little worried I won't. That's it. I think.

'I don't really know though do I? Because I haven't asked her!'

Sophia made up her mind that no matter what she thought of the room when she finally saw it, she would act like she loved it. But she knew, Sophia Oomla, the clammed-up, buttoned-up, zipped-up ten-year-old would never be able to do that. She'd need to be the Actress. And she mentally prepared herself. And a vision of herself floated into her head -

- she was speaking earnestly, sincerely, with her whole heart, not the slightest hint of hesitation in her voice, nor a speck of shyness showing anywhere when she'd at last tell Antoinette Fifi how much she loved her room. And, yes, she would use her real voice – not a trace of an accent and as deep as her Grandmother's! Antoinette Fifi must not ever worry; she was so nice and so happy with such a voice, such a pussycat voice, with a French accent, a foreign accent and thereby so extraordinarily and extra specially wonderful.

But there was quiet everywhere.

Antoinette Fifi must have stopped her "zis's and zat's." And Sophia, whose eyes were open, finally looked through them.

• • • THE ROOM • • •

And there was the moon. Looking at her.

Looking at her? Through a window? No, not one window. Many windows. And she looked back at the moon and the moon looked back at her. She had never been so close to it before because she had never been so high in the sky before and she could see that there really was a Man in the Moon. She could barely tear her eyes away from him who seemed not to be able to tear his eyes away from her either, but somehow she did. For there was so much to see.

'Haughh! I'm actually in the room now!'

Windows! Why, the room was filled with them.

And then she forgot she was supposed to tell Antoinette Fifi a thing because all she could do was stare with eyes wide, mouth wider. Such long windows! That went from floor to ceiling. And every one of those windows were doors that opened onto a terrace. And these door-windows went all around the room. And round the room was right because the room was a circle and not a square, or a rectangle either. And then Sophia's eyes were pulled up because there was a skylight and it was round too. Yet there again was that Man in the Moon looking at her through that skylight, too.

"Oh ZoFEEya, I zee you are lookeeng out all zeze windows. Can you please to look at zee specialitay bed coVAIRS and cuSHUNS and curTANS we have zewed just for you?"

But now Sophia couldn't tear her eyes from the eyes of the Man in the Moon who couldn't be but seemed to be looking at her through every window she looked out of. When she was able to, she saw that there was furniture in the room. And that there was a four-poster-bed that glowed in the light of the moon.

'I'm going to sleep there?!'

On the top of each of the posts was a different carved figure – a maiden in a long flowing dress; a lion; a half/horse-half/man who held a bow and arrow; and a bull. Attached to each post were midnight-blue filmy curtains which cascaded all around the bed, surrounding it in clouds of indigo.

'My bed is floating on the night sky!'

So many stars and planets with rings and comets with tails and moons that were crescent or full or half or gibbous were sewn all over the curtains in mother of pearl thread with flourishes of silvery bangles and crystal beads and opalescent seed pearls and diamond sequins and sapphire jewels. And those bangles and beads and sequins and jewels caught the moon's light, danced with it, and then threw it around the room, giving that bed, that entire room and everything in it - the walls, the ceiling, the floor - a luster.

But Sophia found that her eyes were being pulled up, to the source of the light - the moon.

'Is that moon-man really looking in on me?'

And she felt so peaceful and not so all alone with just her thoughts anymore because the light the moon-man was shining on her was so bright and penetrating, she was sure he could see straight through to her insides, straight through to what she was thinking even. And he would even find what she was thinking very interesting.

'Surely he was looking at me in that hallway, but here, too? Ever since I've got to this city, everything is just like they say in the movies so 'marvelous,' so 'swell' but it sure is odd, too. And now here I am in a room up in the sky with a bed made out of clouds and the moon for a roommate and—'

And she was overcome.

She felt sleepy, weary almost, and was aching to get off her feet, to sit down because in a chair she might still have the strength to think about all she'd seen. Or better yet, to lie down in her bed-in-the-night-clouds and think about it all from there. If she didn't fall fast asleep first. Sophia tore her eyes away from the dazzling bed that was made just for her to find a place to sit. She saw a chair like an evening slipper filled with pouf cushions and knew such a chair would be the place to think thoughts that would certainly turn to dreams and into its wispy softness she sank, already forgetting her promise …

… to speak earnestly, sincerely, with her whole heart, not the slightest hint of hesitation in her voice, nor a speck of shyness showing anywhere. Forgetting she had promised to tell Antoinette Fifi how much she loved this room. Forgetting she had promised to use her real voice - not a trace of an accent and as deep as her Grandmother's! Because Antoinette Fifi must not ever worry, she was so nice and so happy with such a voice, such a pussycat voice, with such an accent that was so French, and so foreign and thereby so extraordinarily and extra specially wonderful.

As if all of that was nothing but vapor in her head and not promises she meant to keep so that her brand new friend would feel better. Oh yes! There she was up to her old tricks; and in a wink of an eye and a nod of her head, there she was down in her chair, lost in thought, again, per usual. Sophia even forgot to look at Antoinette Fifi.

'Everything really is just so different here, so different than home. Especially here in my Grandfather and my Grandmother's house. Why they have their very own

dancing pink-flamingos! And all those voices! Different than the ones I hear at home. Everybody talks so this, so that, just like in the Movies. Keys the Doorman talks just like one of those tough guys who knows he must turn himself into a gentleman and talk politely and show everybody what good manners he has. And Grandmother, like midnight would if it could talk! And Josephine, like one of those sassy, smart-mouth ladies from the Movies who don't let nobody get away with nothing! And Antoinette Fifi with the accent of the French-Foreign-Legion. And now here I am, farther up in the sky than I've ever been, in the place for flying saucers and it looks like I have a new friend, the Man in the Moon.'

"ZoFEEya, you are not lookeeng at all ze ozair seengs in zis rrroom!"

Sophia was wandering, lost in her head again but through her half shut ears and eyes, she heard that Antoinette Fifi sounded impatient and she knew she'd better pay attention. Up snapped her head. And there was Antoinette looking at her. And she looked cross. Not Great Aunt Hortense cross. But cross enough. *'I have to talk. I have to leave the world of me now! But what should I say? I'll have to apologize. Probably.'* But a miracle happened. When their eyes met, Antoinette Fifi's cross look just melted away and she looked happy again and began jabbering again. And Sophia was relieved. *'All I'll have to do is listen. I won't have to leave the world of me!'* She wouldn't have to talk to Antoinette Fifi. She could just listen to her and continue talking away to herself. Like she always did.

"Zere ees ze whole sky painted on ze walls too and ze ceiling wiz all zee celestial bodies in it. Zese paintings 'ave been in zis rrroom for zo long. Your Grandfazair 'e loves ze stars. And not just ze actress stars – ooh lah lah and does 'e love zee actress stars!"

When Sophia heard those very last words, she jumped in her chair, *'My grandfather loves actresses? Actresses! My Grandfather is like me. Then maybe he will like me ... and maybe I could tell him my secret ... if I ever would decide to tell anybody my secret. Since I have been telling people secrets lately; practically, almost, anyway.'*

" 'E likes to zee ze stars by day and when 'e's home, 'e comes up here in ze nighttime to zee zem too. At least 'e used to. But 'e remember zis room and when 'e 'ears you are comeeng to viseet, 'e got all 'iz stage designairs and 'iz set designairs to make zis room especially beautiful for a ten-year-old lovelee jeune fille, as if 'e was designing a set for one of 'iz extravaganzas on zee stage. And zay made zis bed and retouched over ze figures zat were painted on ze walls zo many years ago, because all of zese designs were fadeeng and peeleeng and 'e ask moi to design ze curTANS and ze cuSHUNS and ze piLLOWS. And all ze ladies sew zem. Do you like zem, ZoFEEya?"

And Sophia looked around the room and took in each of the things she had never quite seen the likes of before, even in a movie - its long French door-windows and every one of them looking out onto the terrace which surrounded the entire room; its moonroof where the Man in the Moon was; its bed; its bedcurtains; its walls and its ceiling painted all over with celestial figures; the chair she was sitting in. She looked even deeper into the room and discovered even more furniture painted or carved with more characters that inhabit the nighttime sky; and every last bit of everything gleaming with a pearly luster.

"ZoFEEya, you look zo tired ... it is time to go to bed. Tomorrow we do ze dressup. I show you to your special basroom and I draw for you ze warm bas filled with ze tres aromatique Lavendair Provence." And there behind a wall that Sophia hadn't noticed was the bathroom, a room within a room.

And soon Sophia was lying in her bed of clouds and stars, smelling her lavender-ed self, ready and willing and able only to dream, and in between yawn after yawn after yawn, she heard Antoinette Fifi talk so accented-ly, so French-ly, she forgot she wasn't dreaming already. Which was easy to do as she was half in dreamland and half in the land of the-heres-and-the-nows and she could barely focus to see where she was. But wherever she was, she was trying very hard to hold onto every last French-foreign syllable she could.

She began to sing a song inside herself, one that she heard in a movie, *'My lullaby ... My lullaby from old ... Voice Land.'*

Antoinette Fifi placed the tiny doll in the celestial clothing in Sophia's fingers and then bent over and whispered, "Do I kees to you ze goodnight, ZoFEEya?"

Surrounded by the night sky, underneath the coverlet glittering with stars, with her head on the soft silken pillow and the celestial doll in her fingertips and as the Man in the Moon peeped through the windows, Sophia fell fast asleep. Anyone who might have wandered into that room and looked up through that moonroof would've surely thought that old Man in the Moon was standing guard.

• • • THE FAIRIES FIND FREE • • •

"Author Lady," said Lorraine, "it's time we filled our Readers in on us. Because without us, this story ... well ... it's like a movie without bodies lying around writhing in agony ... I mean, who cares?"

"Ms. Author, Readers," said Thee, "I assure you, no one will be doing any such thing in this story. Honestly, Lorraine!"

"Hey, Thee, keep your wings on! I'm trying to mix it up here! Okay, okay, so here's the deal, and I bet youse out there in Reader-Land won't be surprised - I was the first to get the skinny on Free. And I absolutely had to find Thee and rub it in … no … inform you … okay, okay … I get it, Thee. Readers, so this is how it went down: …

'Guess who I just so happen to run into when I was casing the hoods here in Goliathon? And now I know where Free went. But I still can't believe Free would just up and run off like this and not tell nobody. She's never done nothing like that in, like, the whole ten years we been here. Okay, give up, Thee? The Fairy Dew Dew Daffidew! You know her, she's a friend of Free's. So Dew Dew was doing her usual flybys and she ran into Free. And ran into Free was right because Free wasn't looking where she was going and they collided. And she couldn't help but notice that Free took off again so fast, without barely saying she was sorry, which is so unlike Free. AND, she went up and not down, like she was heading toward the high parts of the sky, like where the stuff is … you know, the stuff … which ya gotta admit, is an unusual thing to do. AND that she was flying pretty fast, like she was on a mission or something. So Dew Dew, real fast herself, caught up to her so she could ask her why she was flying so fast and where she was going. And she said that Free told her, 'I have to see an old old old very old friend and I don't have any time to talk right now because it'll take me 3 hours to get there and back and I'm missing from my post already and if the Dispatcher finds out, I'll be in a whole lot of trouble.' But what blew Dew Dew's mind the most was, Free didn't hesitate, didn't stutter or mumble or mix up her words or nothing. And then Free twisted into a coil … which is what we Fairies do, Readers, when we want to fly fast … and she blasted up and away like she was a Fairy-Manned-Rocket-Ship.'

'That is excellent work, Lorraine. So you just said you know where she went. Where did she go?'

'Thee, you are, like, so dense. She went Up!'

'Up! Up? But did she come down?'

'What difference does it make! We know she's comin' back in three hours! Free told Dew Dew she'd be back in three hours because she didn't want to get in trouble with the Dispatcher. If we just turn around right now and head back to Sophia and wait there, she's bound to show up. And as far as I can figure, it's been about three hours now.'

'But Lorraine, everyone knows Dew Dew loves to tell tales, how do we know Dew Dew told you the truth?'

'Thee, Dew Dew is a Fairy. And that's what Fairies do. They tell tales. And tales to Fairies are the truth.'

'Lorraine, I agree with you, that tales are Fairy truths. And unlike personages, we fairysonages know Fairy Tales to be nothing but the truth in narrative form. I, like most of our Fairy sisters, tell Fairy Tales. But that one, Lorraine, that Dew Dew tells Tall Tales. Suppose Dew Dew was just telling you another one of her Tall Tales?'

'Lorraine, would you just consider this –

'Were you really listening to the truth in narrative form?

'Didn't you just tell me Dew Dew described Free as going Up? Let's examine that, shall we? Couldn't Up be construed as just another way of saying Tall?'

'Well, would you listen to Miss FairySNOTage herself! Thee, you're being overly ana-criti-balistic and just too elfing fussy!'

'Lorraine! No elfspheming! And the word - correction - words you have mish-mashed so unfortunately are analytical, critical and ballistic respectively. Analytical and critical! Thank you! I accept your compliment! But when applied to me, ballistic is unkind! And one should simply never be unkind, Lorraine.'

'Hey, you're welcome! And unkind! Well, that goes for you, too! And I bet if you ever would be ballistic, the Fairy World would pay top dollar to see it. Promise me if you ever feel an urge of the ballistic variety coming on ya, you'll tip me off in time so I can sell tickets. I'd clean up. Hah! Hah! Okay, okay. But look Thee, this is the only lead we got. I say we just go with what Dew Dew says and head back to Sophia. We've covered every last elfi … excuse me … Fairyhood in Goliathon, and that's the skinny. By the way, Miss Sainty Dainty, when you was out and about making your rounds, what scoop dju get? Hah? Hah? Nada! Zilch! Noopzednick! So let's just take what we got and go with it.'

'Lorraine, we'll wait for a half an hour on Sophia's ear. And if Free doesn't show up, then back on our search we go.' …

"So, Ms. Author, we flew off. In less than a minute we had reached Sophia because we knew exactly where to find her. Which, I'm sure, you think is pretty surprising because when we left her last she was nowhere near where she was now. But we Fairies have special senses - extra-sensory senses - in our eyes, noses and ears. We know many things that you humans could never know just by smelling the scents in the air (scents that even animal noses couldn't have detected) and by looking at the patterns in dust-parti-cles and by listening for something as barely audible as a breath. Remember to a Fairy, the invisible is visible, the impossible, possible. We could look and know which way the air had just moved; we can sniff and know exactly who had moved it; we could listen and hear who was breathing, from as far away as a field. And then off to the target we go. We Fairies know a great deal, like Indians know how to read a forest, like elephants know where to run when a tsunami is coming."

(Author's note: something to be thankful for. Do you remember when Lorraine described Free as twisting herself into a coil and then flying as fast as a Fairy-Manned-Rocket-Ship? Well, some of you might be wondering now that you've just read about Fairies extraordinary powers, what would hap-pen if actual Fairies did man rocket ships, cars, buses and the like. Might that put an end to the Energy Crisis and Global Warming? Would a transfer from a Dependence on Foreign Oil to a Dependence on Fairy Coils do the trick? What do you think? Hah hah is right! Because after just one excru-ciatingly long week of this Fairy-Propulsion, Fairies would've been given the old 'heave-ho' from all engines and the Energy Crisis and Global Warming would've been hastily reinstated.)

"And, so, Ms. Author, Readers, as we rounded the poufs of indigo, we saw our Free sitting on Sophia's ear; her fairydress caked all over with phos-phorescent tufts of grit, her gossamer wings ripped and torn all around the edges and splattered with spots that glowed luminously; every hair on her head mucilaged into a single wave that stuck out behind her like the tail on a comet; her face colored so red that in the entire history of the color, it had never been as red as it was that moment on Free's face. And she was breath-ing hard and fast."

'Whems were you? Whems too is the others? Be and Be ... No! Me and Me ... No! Oh! Dispatcher mad be iffens he out fiends we all been gone together with just a toot-toot-stubby watchin' the watchin'.'

"And then," said Thee, "with a rocket's-red-glare and a 'hee-haw hee-haw,' she keeled over and disappeared into the vast thicket of Sophia's hair.

"We dove in, too," said Lorraine, "and found Free already sound asleep way way down, in the lower depths. We still had to find our missing mates, and we quarreled about whether we should, like, wake Free and take her with us; leave her lying there by herself; or put her back safe inside our very cozy and warm Remarkably Small Place. The Place none of us should've ever left in the first place and that none of us had stepped foot or winged wing in for several hours. The Place that so far tonight the Dispatcher hadn't entered for one of his surprise inspections. Although, tonight was far from over."

'Lorraine, we shouldn't really leave her lying here. We really ought to take her with us when we go out looking for Be and Me. But I just hate to wake her. Maybe we really should put her back inside. Sophia has been left alone for hours now, even though the substitute has been there. But leaving Sophia alone, even with a substitute, is something that's never supposed to happen.'

'Thee, look at her, Free's dead tired, I betcha she could sleep for, like, a thousand years. It'd be a crime to wake her. She ain't going nowhere! Besides, the Dispatcher hasn't been by in weeks on an inspection. We're safe, I just feel it.'

"Ms. Author, I didn't feel "it" at all. As we flew up and away and left Free asleep deep in the thicket of Sophia's tumbled tresses, I knew then that we were outside of our Remarkably Small Place, our safe haven and the post assigned to us by the Sacred and Benevolent Rite of the United Fairies Association ("UFA"), and all I could feel was my heart sinking. And Decree Number One kept playing over and over in my head the whole time Lorraine and I were scouring the Enchanted Lands for Be and Me, 'At Least Two Fairies Must Be Present In Your Subject's Remarkably Small Place At All Times! And Substitutes are no substitute!' "

• • • A MIDNIGHT, MOONLIT STROLL • • •

Sophia woke up. She felt odd. Like she never felt before. And she was breathing most peculiarly. *'I can't breathe. My ribs are a jail! My lungs are the prisoners! I feel light-headed. And so all alone! I don't even have a headache, so why does my head ache? But it doesn't exactly hurt either. It just feels empty. Like something is missing.'* She put her hand up to her head to make sure everything was there. She tapped all around her ears. Still there. Nose. There. Forehead. There. Hair. There. But something was missing. And then she remembered.

'I'm in a new place. That must be why I feel so odd! It's because this place isn't my home! It's because my home is missing!' But that didn't make the emptiness go away; or the ache either.

Readers, we know why she felt this way. She was all alone. There was not a single Fairy in her head because substitutes don't count. And Free, remember, was outside her head, lost in the thickets of Sophia's tumbling tresses. Since Sophia'd been born, she had had five constant companions and never knew it. Although she should've known it by the feeling she had that she wasn't really alone even when she was; as if there really was some-body inside tugging on her actual heartstrings making sure she knew that somebody cared for her and worried about her; that to somebody, she came first. {Okay, maybe not to Me.} That if she was crying, somebody was crying with her. That even when there wasn't a soul around, that somebody was looking out for her. That somebody was listening to her. {Okay, Me wasn't listening all that much either.}

·⁖☾·⁖

("Oh yes, I was, Author darling! May I remind you who told you this story!")

·⁖☽⁖·

Rooting for her even. And that no matter how silent she was, or timid she was, or how much sneaking around she did in the middle of the night or how much she wasn't like all the other schoolchildren because they weren't up all hours of the night attending a Movie Star School –

… by the way, Readers, if somebody besides Fairies could've read Sophia's mind they would've heard what she really thought about school-children: *'Because the idea'd never even occur to them! Because they're a bunch of goodie-goodies who not only HAVE to but actually WANT to be ready for boring elementary school the very next morning!'* …

… that no matter what she thought, or what she did or didn't do or how she behaved, that somebody was there for her anyway. Without even know-ing she felt that way, that's how she felt. Without being able to put a word of it into words. It was just so deep down, she could never've reached the spot where those feelings were even if she'd tried. But without ever knowing she knew it, she knew it. Nobody ever asks water to put into words how it feels and what it knows. Water couldn't do it. And Sophia couldn't do it either.

Actually part of that deep-down-something did have a tongue – tongues to be exact and they were chatterboxes. As she went here, there and every-where, they babbled, they bubbled, they rooted, they tooted away at her. And what opinionated or helpful or contrary or curious or argumentative or thoughtful companions they were! They enjoyed nothing better than squeezing or poking or even going right ahead and pounding their par-ticular point of view into Sophia whenever they had a mind to. No won-der she felt less alone. But she would never've even wondered who kept saying such stuff to her, or even where they came from because why ever would she think for even one second that what was bubbling away inside her wasn't her?

Now, Readers, remember who told me this story. Fairies. So I can't tell you for certain who actually made her feel that way, whether it really was the

Fairies, or some other mysterious force that was in her. But the Fairies sure wanted me, as the writer of this story, to believe it was them.

Sophia didn't feel right and was sleepy to boot; even so, she laid her tired eyes on what was outside her windows. Every place that moon-man wasn't, the night-man had wrapped in its black cape. *'Please, if you are hiding terrifying mysteries under that cape, don't show them to me now, for I am up here in this sky all by myself!'* If she could've actually found a way to cement herself on to that shiny-faced-moon-man, she would've but somehow his glow made her feel a little less frightened, a little less alone. And pretty soon she was thinking about all the people she'd met since she'd arrived in this place, their voices playing over and over in her head. Her Grandmother's, Josephine's, Keys the Doorman's. Until she heard Antoinette Fifi's. And Sophia shot up out of her bed like a scarecrow in a wind squall; she remembered what she hadn't done -

To speak earnestly, sincerely, with her whole heart, not the slightest hint of hesitation in her voice, nor a speck of shyness showing anywhere. She remembered her promise to tell Antoinette Fifi how much she loved the room she had created for her. She remembered her promise to use her real voice – not a trace of an accent and as deep as her Grandmother's! Because Antoinette Fifi must not ever worry, she was so nice and so happy with such a voice, such a pussycat voice, with such an accent that was so French, and so foreign and thereby so extraordinarily and extra specially wonderful—

'I never did what I said I'd do. I never said a word to Antoinette Fifi. I never said how much I loved this room. I was shy and I didn't talk. Didn't talk again! Thinking and not talking again! The thing that keeps getting me into trouble! And now Antoinette Fifi must be worried that I didn't like her room because I didn't even say peep. After all the work she did! Because I don't talk, I hurt her feelings!'

··⋆☾·⋆·

("Ms. Author," said Thee, "Sophia's coverlet had slumped in a silken heap to the floor, and Free tumbled out of Sophia's hair like the dust and magic she was. Down down down she floated, until she landed on top of the bed. But she was worn to such a frazzle, she never even woke up. Now she was just sound asleep on Sophia's bed as if nothing had even happened and she hadn't fallen at all. But when Sophia picked up the slippery coverlet and returned it to the top of the bed, she'd placed it on top of Free. And now Free was underneath the coverlet. Way underneath the coverlet. So way underneath, she was buried, dear Readers!")

··⋆☽⋆··

Sophia knew what she must do - tell Antoinette Fife how much she liked her room. And she couldn't wait til morning either. It hardly mattered it was nighttime. And mysterious and terrifying outside. And mysterious and terrifying inside her Grandfather's house.

'I'm used to being up in the nighttime, aren't I? And French grown-ups like Antoinette Fifi, at least, according to all the Movies I see that have French people in them, are up in the nighttime getting ready to go to cafés so they can do the can-can. French people never go to bed early! Antoinette Fifi, being such a French grown-up person, will be up somewhere in the house getting ready to go out and be French.'

Then Sophia would be able to come right back to her bed of clouds and stars and finally fall asleep because she had done the right thing and made Antoinette Fifi happy. After all, that was the least she could do for someone who had made her so happy.

But first, she had to find her.

Sophia felt so cold as she ran to the staircase that she ran right back and put on her bathrobe and slippers. *'I'm warmer … a … .little … bit!'*

But a pearly moonlight flooding through the moonroof and the windows was making every thing glitter and seemed to be lighting her way, inviting her places, begging her to have an adventure.

··*.*(··

("Buried under the coverlet! Our Free! And separated from Sophia! Again! Ms. Author! Readers!")

··*.*)·*.*·

As Sophia walked down each step, she shivered. *'But I won't stop because I'm cold! I'm on a mission!'* She opened the wooden door, stepped into the hallway, not even glancing at that carved Man in the Moon's many fascinations because the real Man in the Moon was pouring his own fascinations through the window. Moon-snow. Or so it seemed. And it was covering the floors, the walls, the ceiling and making everything look so irresistible, she couldn't wait to walk through it.

'Could the Man in the Moon be making it look like that on purpose?

'That's nonsensical! And besides! Man in the Moon! Moon-snow! That's stupendously nonsensical! There's no such person and no such thing!'

She knew she was right because pouring, too, through that same window was so much cold-air that if the moon-man was out there making moon-snow, there would've been an ole-man-winter out there making the air so cold. And that was just more nonsense. But knowing neither one of them didn't exist didn't make her feel any better. For even if that air wasn't coming from some mean-winter-man, it sure was trying to stop her in her tracks. *'That wind that's blowing in through that window and then blowing all around me is the same wind that's blowing all around a skyscraper! Will it blow us all away, like Mr. James said?'*

But way way up high in her Grandfather's house that sat on the tippy top of a tall tall building, Sophia stood her ground and faced that air. She felt terribly cold but brave, too, that she, a mere ten-year-old girl from the country, on her first visit to the city, was up so high in the sky and facing the cold-cruel-world itself. Even so, she wrapped her bathrobe around her tighter. But in the very next second, the cold bit through to her toes and her fingers and she forgot about her adventures in the high sky entirely and wished she would've thought to bring her coverlet with her so she could wrap that around her, too. Sophia remembered where it was. On top of her bed. And she turned and ran to the moon-door, towards warmth and safety.

But just as quickly, she turned and ran back. *'Antoinette Fifi! My mission! I won't go back and get it, no matter how cold I am. I can handle this. I've faced the elements before!'*

And she walked swiftly down the corridor and the staircase.

But oh! as she did, how she wished she was in her warm cozy bed with that coverlet over her head. She even imagined she heard it call her, as if it actually missed her, needed her, and wanted her back. But even as she heard it, she made herself listen really hard for Antoinette Fifi's voice or for any sound of French music or any noise that a person would make if she were doing the can-can. But she didn't hear any such sounds. At least along this corridor. She would have to go down one more flight of stairs and listen on that floor. Antoinette Fifi would surely be there. Sophia speeded over to the staircase and raced down it. When she reached the landing she cocked her ear down one of the corridors, then down the other but heard nothing. So she walked down to the next landing and did the same thing but didn't hear anything there either. She kept that up, until she got to the top of the very last staircase she could walk down, the one that would lead to the first floor, the very same staircase that the pink flamingos had danced down. But who certainly weren't dancing down that staircase now.

"&¢@^^^^!"

"That's not a French accent!" Sophia spoke that out loud; she couldn't have kept it inside if she tried. "And it's not music! Or somebody dancing the can-can either. No! Somebody talked! In the 'language of sailors!' That's sure what Mr. James would call those words!"

Readers, the words in symbols will not be spelled out here. This, after all, is family entertainment.

• • • 'THAT BAD-WORD TALKER IS TALKING TO ME!' • • •

"I sure don't hear words like that where I live!" She imagined her Father or her Mother or Mr. James ever saying such words.

Or Great Aunt Hortense.

"Why Great Aunt Hortense must starch and press every word before she'd let them go anywhere!"

And Sophia was so tickled by her joke, which she'd said OUT LOUD, she began to giggle, OUT LOUD.

In spite of the fact it was the middle of the night! and she was all by her-self alone! on that staircase! in a house she'd never been to before! Which wasn't like any other house she'd ever seen even in a Movie! because it was a house that sat on top of a skyscraper that was surrounded on all sides by the biggest city she'd ever actually been in! A city filled everywhere she looked with nothing but skyscrapers! and she just 54 inches high! who always had had the big idea she was from this city after watching all of those Movies! but now knew definitely she was not!

Or maybe she didn't know anything of the kind because somehow she was on that staircase, in this house on top of a skyscraper, surrounded on all sides by gigantic-ness, and she, a famous shrinking violet who didn't always like to talk even as she was famously shrinking, and though she was very much still all of the above, here she was in this gigantic city forgetting to be terrified, forgetting even to shrink even though she just heard something that sure sounded like she should do at least one of the above because it certainly was sailor-language that was definitely coming from somewhere below where she, all 54 inches of her, was standing on that staircase alone.

But there she stood anyway. Alone in the middle of the night … far away from her coverlet … from her bed … making her own private jokes … in her own private world.

"Miss Kitty is the only one who might say those words!" Sophia spoke that out, too.

… but the only difference was … now she was laughing out loud at her jokes … her shoulders shaking.

"Who in the #@((is that?"

And it hit her. *'Somebody heard me! There's somebody down there! The person that used those words. Of course! That bad word was said by a real somebody! What was I thinking? I'm not alone! That bad-word talker is talking to me! And I'm talk-ing and laughing out loud! I know better than to make noise when I'm on a mission. I should've run right back as soon as I heard him!'*

"Is that a &@^^^^ mouse in my house? Hmmmmm ... now think about that Solomon ... here you've got a mouse that can laugh in your very own house! I want to meet such a mouse. Why such a mouse is a talented mouse. Come out now ... don't be afraid ... I'll make you a star. You'll have your own show on the Great White Way! I'll make you famous. No! I'll make you FaMOUSE, the Laughing Mouse."

And then a raspy cough with a gargle in it, then a low laugh that turned into a wheeze, like he would never be able to laugh again but he soon did ... "Well, Mr. Mouse, or is it Ms. Mouse? Or Missus Mouse? Or Mickey Mouse? Or City Mouse? Or Country Mouse?"

Then a hack hack hacking cough. And then in a wheeze, he said, "Don't you want to come out, so I can see you? Don't you want to be FaMOUSE? Hah! Hah!" Wheeze ... rasp ... deep deep breath ... then a long cough ... "Now I'm laughing, but none too good. So come on out and show yourself, you varmint before I take my last breath and your chances of meeting your Producer turn to zip!" And then Sophia heard breaths, in-out, in-out, and when he breathed in, there was a high-pitched rattle, and when he breathed out, a wheeze.

'What a voice!' Sophia had dropped into the shadows at the top of the stairs where she now stood frozen, making up her mind whether to run back to her room where she'd be safe or to go down the steps and find out just who this was who could talk like that. But her mind didn't make up her mind because she already had a foot on the top step, then her other foot on the step below and then her other foot on the one below that. Something inside her had to see for herself just who was using such words. Just who was talking to her like that. Just who had such a raspy, crotchety, old-ruckus of a voice? It hadn't really sunk into her that by going down those steps, she just might have to talk herself and use her own voice. She just might have to answer his question. But then she wasn't really thinking like herself at all.

"There's a mouse in me house. A mouse in me house ... Oh Yo! Oh Yo! A flea in me scalp. A flea in me scalp. Oh Yo! Oh Yo! ... What ho?"

The voice was singing in such a pitch: up high on some notes, down low on others. And then it howled until it whistled, and said, "Would you take a look at that moon! No wonder the meeces are laughing." And down a sliding board it went, then up, from high to low and everywhere in between.

When she turned round the bend in the stairs, she saw him. There sitting just above the first floor, on about the third step and leaning against the banister was the man who'd been howling. Who'd been singing the mouse song. Who'd asked a question. Who'd used the sailor language. And she barely blinked or breathed as she took a long look at him even though the man was making so much noise, she was sure he'd never hear her. The brilliant moon light had blazed his howling mouth, his pointing, waving fingers into a shining glory. He reminded her of her Father who also conducted imaginary orchestras.

He had a full head of silvery white hair: most of those hairs were laying exactly where they should but the rest pointed either one way quite definitely or the exact opposite way and just as definitely. Sitting as he was, with arrows for hair, and fingers going every which way and he himself leaning first one way and then the other, he could've been the Signpost to Everywhere. But then those pointing hairs and waving fingers were the only thing about him out of place, as the rest of him was perfect. His coat looked like the newest coat she'd ever seen. And here it was at the end of the day and he didn't have spill marks on his clothes the way her Mother's clothes would've had. And he wasn't all rumpled up the way her Father usually looked at the end of the day either. His shoes shined as much as Mr. James's shoes did. His buttonhole had a flower in it. He looked like a man in a Movie, like a very very old Cary Grant but without the Movie Star smile because, no doubt about it, he was scowling. But no doubt about it either, smile or no smile, he was very elegant.

She knew who this was.

Her Grandfather!!

Howling away. At the moon.

At the moon?

And her feet dragged her down those steps even though her mind hadn't at all concurred that was the direction they should be heading in; until she and her feet stood just two steps above him.

She stared down at him.

He stopped howling ...

'Did he hear me?'

... Only to start back singing again. "Oh yo ... Oh yo ... there's a mouse in me house ... A flea in me scalp ..." And his arms waved all about.

'I guess not.'

But suddenly Sophia's nose started to twitch, maybe because he was riling up the air with his arms so much, and she felt a sneeze coming on she couldn't hold in and out it came and her Grandfather's head pivoted around and suddenly those silver arrows were aimed right at her. And the next thing out of his mouth was definitely not a song,

"Who the #@((are you?"

Sophia couldn't believe what he just said to her and she slumped down hard on the step, only to shoot up like a bullet. She knew when even she must speak up. No one had ever said such a word to her in her whole life. And, in spite of never usually talking to people she wasn't acquainted with, and, for that matter, to people she was acquainted with, she said,

"You're not supposed to talk like that to a little girl!"

"And you're not supposed to be wandering around … Hack!! Hack!!! … my house in the middle of the night sneaking … wheeze … up on an old man with breathing problems! Okay okay okay ya' got me! I'm not supposed to talk to a little girl like that. Now wait a &@^^^^ minute … Hah! Ha … hack … hack … wheeze … Now as I was saying …wait a &@^^^^ minute … I know who you are! Wheeze … You're my grand … wheeze … daughter! I thought they said … Hack! Wheeze! you couldn't … ta … Hack … tatatalk."

"I can too talk. And if you ask me, you can't talk none too good either." Because he had been snippy with her, she was snippy with him. Snippy was a first for her. But she couldn't listen to another one of these Goliathon people saying such a thing about her, especially somebody who was talking the way he was. And now that she said it and said it snippy too, she felt wonderful. Like a new person. And she had more to say to him, too. And she would say it. And she would say it like a Movie Star in a scene from a Movie. What she had to say demanded nothing less. Why this Grandfather of hers was a very dramatic person, with his singing and his coughing and his howling and his scowling and his bad words. And a person should never speak to a dramatic person sounding like a mouse. She knew that from her years of watching Movies. Now it was finally time to unmask herself and be who she truly was. The Queen of England! Full of dignity, majesty even! And with her Mr. James accent and Great Aunt Hortense words, she spoke,

"Imagine you saying such a thing about me! I don't talk. The very idea! Why you don't even know me!"

"And … hack … hack … wheeze … wheeze … didn't you just say I can't talk none too good … why imagine you saying such a thing about … hack … hack … hack … me and you don't even know me either! And you sure are right I … hack … don't even know you because why do you have an … hack … hack … hack … English … acc … wheeze … accent and you're from the &@^^^^ country?"

And here was Sophia finally showing her stuff and there was he, still being difficult and not bowing down to her, the Queen! But she couldn't say that because her voice failed her, she could only whisper, in her real voice,

"Well ... I'm very sorry ... but ..." Hearing her words spoken so without distinction, and she opened her eyes as wide as she could, pulled herself up, looked at her Grandfather and with just the right touch of what she was certain was Queenly hauteur said, "Sometimes I have an English accent because certain situations demand I do! And who told you I couldn't talk anyway?"

"My wife Sarah that's who! I can't talk! Nobody's ever said that to me in my life. So you like accents, do you? Well, I've never met an actor who doesn't. So you must be an actor. Hah!

"And what does my son think of that! Serves him right that his only child wants to be actor! That's what he gets for refusing to learn the family business! He only has to deal with the crazy ones during the day! Now he'll have his very own prima donna to deal with day and night! I've had to deal with prima donnas for years! Although, let me ask you, have you ever met a sane actor? But then, how would you know? You're one of them! Hah!

"And let me tell you something about talking and me ... there's a lot of people in this city would get down on their knees and thank the Impresario Above if the Impresario Below, Solomon Oomla, stopped talking. But I'd never give them the ... wheeze ... satisfaction.

"Oh, alright, alright, I admit that sometimes during the day, I may not talk but sometimes that's just part of being a good negotiator. Keep's people wondering what I'm gonna do next. Most of the times they think I'm gonna do something I'm not. Which works to my advantage. Nine times out of ten. Eight times out of ten. And okay okay, I don't always reveal every little thing on my mind. And sometimes I don't have a &@^^^^ thing on my mind. But the other side can't know that. But let me tell you, when I finally talk, people want to hear every word out of my mouth. Which is just the way I like it. And just the way they don't. They even listen when my words are pounding them like a hammer. And besides if I woke up one day and found I couldn't talk, I'd chew up and swallow the best voice actor money could buy and he'd do my talking for me!"

Sophia'd been listening to every word her Grandfather said. And they were puzzling her deeply. What was he talking about? What was he saying about her Father? And actors? But when he said - Chew up and swallow the best voice actor money could buy and he'd do my talking for me! - all of those questions dropped away. And only one question remained, *'Would my Grandfather do that? I'm a Voice Actress! Would he chew up and swallow me?'*

But she couldn't have even used her pretend voice to ask her Grandfather her question. Why the very thought of saying anything to a person who said they would do such a thing - chew up and swallow the best voice actor, scared her through and through.

Her Grandfather didn't notice that Sophia had shrunk back from him because he was still talking away. "Okay, okay, you got me … I may not talk sometimes, but you better believe I … hack hack … can talk when I have too. I'm just having a momentary … hack … hack … wheeze … cough … problem right now cause I've been doing things I shouldn't. And by the way, don't tell your Grandmother I've been cussin' either or coughing either … or I'll be in trouble. Again!" And then he whistled and wheezed, and whistled again.

'He's waiting for me to tell him I won't tell on him! To tell him I'm no squealer! I shouldn't keep anybody waiting who says he would eat a Voice Actor!' She was trying to make sense of everything he said. *'Okay, he said he'd eat Voice Actors, which isn't good, but he just said he may not talk sometimes … so sometimes he doesn't talk too … and that is OKAY … when HE does it? And look … he's still able to be so … so … '* Sophia wasn't sure what her Grandfather was. She studied him: he seemed fine, he even seemed important, *'Could he be like me … a person who sometimes doesn't talk too … but I'd never chew up and swallow anybody so I could talk … let alone an actor of all people!*

'… Not so fast, Sophia! You do that all the time! When you turn yourself into a Movie Star!' And she went from shrinking to collapsing on her step.

But with an iron will, she kicked such a terrible, spiteful, mean thought out! of! her! head! and made herself imagine her Grandfather doing what he said – chewing up and swallowing somebody instead. Imagining him doing it was better than imagining herself, such a decent, innocent, well-meaning person, ever doing such a thing.

But it wouldn't go away. It bounded right back. *'YOU SWALLOW UP MOVIE STARS WHOLE AND SPIT THEM OUT OF YOURSELF TOO! YOU DO! YOU DO!'*

'I DO NOT!' Such a thought must be banished. Such a thought should never be allowed to enter her head! She was a nice person, and nice persons don't chew up and swallow anybody. And with a mighty push, and with a great good riddance, she vanished it forever.

And then she was able to look at him, this man in his Movie Star clothes who was waving his fingers conducting an imaginary orchestra just the way her Father did, who sang about mice, who, though he didn't have a trace of a smile on his face, she still couldn't imagine him really chewing up and swallowing anybody.

'He's joking!'

And she felt better. Because if he couldn't do it, neither could she! She wasn't eating up and spitting out other people. Of course, she wasn't. Of course.

But she'd better tell him quick she was no squealer. She'd been keeping him waiting long enough. Because somebody who said they'd eat people just so they could get their mouth, might not really be able to do that but they might be able to do it another way, like by doing all the talking with their own mouth and not letting somebody else talk with theirs. She knew all about that. Besides she had enough problems with her mouth, let alone having somebody not let her use her mouth when she was ready to and really really wanted to and even could.

"Okay! I won't tell." That, she said loud and clear, in her real voice.

But as soon as she heard herself, she wished she would've said her words in one of her Movie Star voices. And she got herself ready. Her next answer would be delivered that way. But then all of a sudden she remembered something else he said. He said she couldn't talk. That's what Keys the Doorman said. And her Grandmother. And the flamingos had said it, too. And she remembered what she hadn't found out yet. Who told her Grandmother? She'd never come right out and asked anyone yet, even though the question had been right on the tip of her tongue so many times. Her Grandfather had asked if there was a mouse in his house. There was a mouse in the house. It was her. And she had had enough. Enough of being a mouse. She looked again at her Grandfather. But this time she looked at him with eyes opened wide.

The man who said he could eat a Voice Actor.

The man who used bad words.

The elegant man who talked like a Tough Guy. At least that's what they called persons like that in all the Movies she'd ever seen.

And she looked at this elegant Tough Guy, this Grandfather of hers leaning back on the stairs, whistling away, wheezing away, coughing away, conducting his invisible orchestra, and something occurred to her - maybe he just talked tough, just like she liked to talk tough. When she was alone. When she was a Movie Star. Maybe he was a little bit like her after all, except he liked to talk like he was tough - when he was with people! But maybe he was just pretending too.

She realized now she WOULD be able to find out who told her Grandmother she couldn't talk. Now nothing was going to stop her, not a scary Grandfather who said words he shouldn't and who pretended he could eat people when anybody with any sense would know he couldn't. She knew what she had to do.

She resumed her Queenly hauteur and said, "And who told her that I can't talk?"

Hack. Hack. "I ..." Wheeze. Wheeze. "don't know ..." Hack! Hack! "you'll have to ..." Wheeze. Wheeze. "ask ..." Wheeze. "her!" Wheeze. Gasp.

"Are you sick?"

"NO!"

And Sophia listened for him to say something else but he didn't. And it got very quiet. *'Nobody is saying nothing!'*

And she heard the silence because she wasn't even talking inside. But in a blink, she was back to her old ways.

Though not exactly.

The thoughts she was thinking this time weren't her usual ones:

'I don't want to sit here thinking. I don't want to sit here not talking. I want to talk. And to keep talking. I've had had enough of quiet. I'm sick and tired of quiet. My mouth is already open, so why not talk? Things are practically jumping inside me now anyway, all I have to do is let them out.'

She forgot to be a Movie Star, to be a Queen, she just opened her mouth and out popped the first thing she could think of - what Antoinette Fifi had told her about her Grandfather.

"So you love Movies and Movie Stars, too, just like I do?"

But what Sophia really should have said was, "So you love Actresses?" Because that's what Antoinette Fifi had said about her Grandfather. But that isn't what Sophia remembered. Sophia remembered two things that Antoinette Fifi had said about her Grandfather. The first was that her Grandfather loving acting or ... something about acting. And the second was not what Antoinette Fifi had said, at all. What she remembered was her own conclusion about what a love of acting meant - that because her Grandfather loved acting, he must be just like her. Which, of course, must mean he loved Movies. And Movie Stars. Just like she did.

But there was another reason she shouldn't have said that. She forgot what her Mother had told her. That the people who lived in this house didn't like Movies. But saying that the people who lived in this house didn't like Movies was like a mountain saying it wasn't a mountain. Why this whole huge house-in-the-sky, and all the people in it, with their midnight voices, their flamingo costumes, their silvery arrow hair was a Movie and she was in it. So, of course, her Mother's warning would've laid abandoned somewhere inside her. Her head right now could only entertain its sensible visitors.

"I HATE Movies and Movie Stars are a pain in the @$$! ... Who told you ... hack ... hack ... wheeze ... gasp ... that?"

Sophia was crushed. And though she hadn't moved, her insides had shrunk right back into the tongue-tied-rag-tattered-nobody she feared she really really was. *'I'm never talking again. I say one thing and I'm wrong AND I'm in trouble!'*

Sophia didn't notice the Man in the Moon's glittering moonlight streaming in through the window in the stairway landing and splashing all over her. But Sophia couldn't feel that light; couldn't see what the moonlight was doing; couldn't see how his glitters were dancing, silvering her and her Grandfather and those dark stairs. Because Sophia had put her head down. Had shut her mouth tight.

'Thinking doesn't get me into trouble. Talking does. I bet Grandfather is glaring at me just like Great Aunt Hortense would. Probably. He's old too, just like her. I bet he's giving me the eye just the way she would. And scowling at me with his face that's almost like hers. I know he's waiting for me to answer his question. My mouth really does belong on a mouse. I was talking so good and now I'm right back where I started. It's like I'm sailing along in Cinderella's coach and the next thing I know I'm a smushed-up old pumpkin. I better just admit it, I should keep my mouth shut. But even if I could talk right now, I'm no squealer. I won't ever tell him that Antoinette Fifi told me that ... but then why would my Grandfather hate the Movies? And hate Movie Stars, too? Doesn't he work in Show Business? That's just plain wrong for a person who works in Show Business to hate Movie Stars and Movies, too. And what WAS he saying about my Father, too? And didn't he just call Actors crazy? Everybody knows what the Old Chief said, that you don't get people better by insulting them. Why he should be ashamed of himself working in the exact same business that Movie Stars work in and hating the very people who work right alongside him. Why is my Grandfather so mean? Why would he, my very own Grandfather, the only Grandfather I have, who should love me, his Granddaughter, be so mean to the people I love?'

She knew the answer to that question, and her heart sank. *'He doesn't know how much I love them. Nobody knows. Because I've never told anybody.'* And then Ginger Rogers' and Fred Astaire's and Katherine Hepburn's and Audrey Hepburn's and Cary Grant's and Edward G. Robinson's and the Marx Brothers' and so many faces passed before her eyes, she couldn't even name them all. But when she heard their distinguished, unique voices, too, that's when she knew she had to do something.

'They're not even here to defend themselves; there's nobody here to defend them. Except me and, look at me, I'm too chicken! But if I don't defend them, who will? If I was in my Movie Star School right now, and I had to play a character that had to tell her Grandfather how wrong he was to feel the way he did about something - about not liking Movie Stars - about calling actors crazy - that character would speak up and set her Grandfather straight.'

Sophia picked up her head and looked at her Grandfather. He was looking at her. But he wasn't exactly looking at her the way Great Aunt Hortense would. But he was looking at her just the same. He looked … well … Sophia couldn't figure out how he looked exactly. He didn't look happy, he certainly wasn't smiling; he looked grouchy as a matter of fact, but however he looked, she knew if she was going to do this, she'd better get busy and do it.

But she didn't, her mouth wouldn't open and she sat there disgusted with herself.

'I'm sick of being scared. If I have to do this, I'll just have to pretend and not do it as me and do it as one of my Movie Stars and just act my part. Even if I'm wrong and Grandfather is not acting like a tough guy and he really is a tough guy, he still needs to know that I love these people. And that he should love them too, because of all the interesting voices they bring into the world. Why they could teach people how to talk … how to talk better.'

And with her heart beating so loud that she couldn't hear a word she was saying, her mouth opened, and she forgot to speak in any voice but her own,

"Grandfafafathether! I'm sursurprised at yayayou hatatating Mo … Mo … vies and Movie Ssss … stars. Why no … no … no … one should hahahate Movies and no one should ha … ha … hate Mo … vie Sssstars! That's just wr … wro … ng, Grandfafatherer."

Her words were breaking into bits like straws of uncooked spaghetti, but she wasn't listening to them, she didn't hear them splinter. Maybe if she could've heard how unlike a Movie Star she sounded - that at that very moment, she was spunk-less, tongued-tied, the un-Ginger, a tizzy with a bad case of the shakes; maybe if she could've taken a long look into her Grandfather's eyes that were freezing to ice cubes on every one of those words she was saying, she might've stopped cold. But she couldn't hear and she didn't look. This time, she only cared about what she said; and wasn't giving a thought about how she said it.

"Why Momovies and Movie Stars give people something to dddream about … something to look up to … because people in Movies usually sos- ooner or later do do the right thing …"

She finally knew what it felt like to say exactly what she wanted to say to somebody who needed to hear her every word. And that somebody was alive and not on a television screen. And she felt stronger, til her words were hardly breaking at all.

"And Movie Stars speak smart words and have such vovoices when they speak those words ... they are the most interesting persons in the whole world to listen to! Why Grandfather, could you tell Katherine Hepburn to her face you hated Movie Stars? Could you tell Audrey Hepburn that? Could you, now?"

And she looked him dead in the cold of his eye. And she felt the chill, but it didn't stop her. In fact, him looking like that only made her realize how much she still had to explain to him so that he would understand, so that she could help him, so that she could save him. She had so many things to tell him; things she'd never told anybody in her whole life; things he really needed to hear. She could see by that look in his eyes, she had much work to do. So he'd hear her better, she even leaned in closer to his scowly face.

"Most people in real life don't have voices like their voices ... like Movie Star voices. Most people don't really talk the way the people talk in Movies, Grandfather. In the Movies, you can really hear voices, all sorts of voices and not just smart voices like I just described or pretty voices, you can hear funny voices, deep voices, odd voices that sound like ... like ... like ... an old mud bucket is talking.

"And, too, in the Movies, there is beautiful music playing when things happen. Why Grandfather, Miss Kitty is always saying 'Bring out te violins' when somebody in our house is sad. But in Movies, they really do bring out the violins and play them when somebody is sad. You don't actually see them playing the violins, but you hear them. And they put that kind of music in just when you need to hear it. But they don't just play sad music either. If people are happy in the Movies or if something scary is about to happen, they have music for all that, too.

"They think of everything in Movies.

"Like what is the music playing now for us, Grandfather? But if you and me were in a Movie right now, we would know, because there would be music playing, special music, which would be the perfect thing to hear for what is happening right now between us.

'And colors are so much more color-y in the Movies. And Movie Stars wear such clothes. And they have such adventures. They go such places. And when somebody says what's on their mind, they say it with so much oomph, there is no mistaking it, you really know how that person feels. And you see so many types of people. And Movie Stars have faces. Oh! Such faces. And eyes too, I almost forgot - how could I forget about them - such eyes, you can't stop looking at them or into them, why you can't take your own eyes off their eyes, Grandfather. A person should never think they don't like Movie Stars, Grandfather. Because they'd be wrong, because it would be like saying you don't like people.

"You like people, don't you Grandfather?"

'In the whole entire world history of me, I've never said to anybody what I've just said to Grandfather. I had important work to do and I did it. Why! I saved my Grandfather's life!'

"People? Hah! Not all of them, make no mistake about that. And voices! You want to hear voices? I'm taking you to the Theatre first thing in the morning. That's where the voices are, Miss Voices! The Theatre!"

And he lifted the finger he'd been using to conduct the imaginary orchestra and waved it –towards the ceiling -then down -then about her as if she were the imaginary orchestra.

She couldn't tell what he was thinking. He wasn't smiling, his eyes were the same, nothing seemed to have changed. Sophia wasn't sure if she'd saved him after all.

'And I just gave my first big speech! To him! And that's how he's acting! It's like what I said didn't even matter!'

"Forget the Movies. In the movies, a voice can only do one-hundredth of what it can!"

'Forget the Movies? I could never forget the Movies! Movies are my whole life! Didn't he hear me? Why doesn't he understand?'

But she wasn't opening her mouth.

'What will he say if I say what I'm thinking this time?'

He waved his arms all about again conducting his imaginary orchestra, "And what do you think I'm doing ... hack ... hack ... right now? I'm conducting music ... I hear music all the time. Why do you have to have music playing anyway to hear music for &*%$ sakes? If music is playing, you can't hear the music that's already playing. Like the music from windows and traffic and wind and rooftops. What is my foolish son teaching you up there in leaf land? Of course, if my son and I were better acquainted, you and I wouldda been better acquainted and then you'd be whistling a different tune. But we're not, and we probably won't be since he is so &@^^^^ stubborn. And another thing I want to know ... hack ... hack ... hack ... how does a ten-year-old girl know so much about Movies? And Movie Stars?

That's what … wheeze … wheeze … I want to know! And the Hepburns! why those two are dead and buried! Aren't you a little young to have heard of them? And, by the way, you're a chip off the old block! You are definitely my son's daughter. Another one who loves voices and music.

"And you two sure love to keep people waiting while you think!!!"

"And come to think of it, that Mother of yours has a voice from days gone by too, back when men were men and women were dollfaces! And speaking of Movie Stars, she sure talks like a tickly, soft few of them. And speaking of talking, she sure never stops." And he laughed until he wheezed.

"And by the way, what's a ten-year-old girl doing up so … hack … hack … &@^^^^ late anyway? Shouldn't you be in bed? How're you ever going to get up in the morning and be ready in time so we can get to the Theatre so you can hear the real voices? Movie Voices! Hah! Wait til you hear Theatre Voices - the only voices worth listening to! Voices that have been trained to project so that a houseful of a thousand people and every last one of those people, even the ones sitting in the last row, can hear every syllable. Movie voices! Why an airy, breathy movie voice could never do that. You ain't heard nothing yet. You don't know what you're talking about!"

"I do too!" Before she had time to decide if she should say it, out it came.

"Oh, you think so do you!"

And her Grandfather gave her such a crabby look, and then said, "After a day spent at my theatres listening to Theatre Voices, we'll see how you feel. I tell you, you'll be whistling a different tune. And now I'm taking you back to your room, little Miss Movie Voice, so you can give your ears some rest and get them ready for what awaits! Why the first thing I'm going to ask my son, the next time I see him is, if I ever do see him again … just exactly what he's been teaching his daughter up there in that &@^^^^ country ?" And he attempted to get up but couldn't until he anchored his arms on the step above to lift himself off. "My &@^^^^ back! Hip! Knee! One of those things is not working right! Or maybe it's all of them! Oh, $#(+! I'm not supposed to cuss! Oh, $#(+, I cussed! Oh! … I give up. Now, keep quiet or your Grandmother will hear us!"

"I'm not the one making noise, Grandfather."

And in a raspy whisper, out came, "Okay! Okay! Miss Movie Voice! I get it … as I was saying about your Grandmother … if she hears me, I won't be alive to take you to the Theatre! I'm bringing you back to that room of yours that, when I heard you were coming, I had no one less than a stage designer, and his crew, and the stage hands, build a real stage set. They did a great job considering they had such short notice. Do you like it Miss Movie Voice or would you rather've had it designed by a Hollywood Set

Desi ... Hack ... Hack ... Hack ... Wheeze ... Wheeze ... Cough ... Cough ... Cough ... Cough ... Wheeze ... Wheeze ... Wheeze ... Solomon, what are you thinking even saying the word Hollyw ... hack ... hack ... wheeze ... wheeze ... cough cough ... I'm making myself ... hack ... hack ..."

The moon shining in through the window lit up the scowl on her Grandfather's face so much that he could've been the actual ole-man-winter. But even so, Sophia smiled at her Grandfather. Her Grandfather knew about voices!

Her Grandfather certainly didn't smile back, he just continued talking, "That room! It's like the moon is in there with you!" He did hook out his arm and Sophia locked hers inside and together they walked up the staircase. The moon seemed to be throwing his spotlight on them as they passed each and every window. But neither of them noticed.

Sophia kept sneaking peeks up at her Grandfather. Just who was this man who seemed to know so much about voices? Just who was this man who didn't like Movie voices? Just who was this man who said things about her Father? Did something happen between her Father and him? What?

And her Grandfather kept sneaking peeks at her. Just who was this little girl who knew about Katherine Hepburn? Audrey Hepburn? How could a ten-year-old girl know about those actresses from so many years ago? Didn't the kids nowadays only know about their own actors? What sort of a ten-year-old was she anyway? Did she have the curse of the Oomla ears too? Like he did? And his only son?

But even as the moon radiated on them and through them, neither of them asked each other their questions. They just made their way up the stairs and kept their thoughts to themselves.

• • • THE FAIRIES RETURN • • •

"Ms. Author, Lorraine, Me, Be and I had just squeezed through the USE and the USA border on our race back to Sophia's Remarkably Small Place."

Readers, some history: Remember, USE as in United States of Enchantica? Well, as these, after all, are the Enchanted Lands in the United States, and, as such, couldn't be anything less than a democracy; and certainly couldn't be anything like the Royatocracy that's in the United Kingdom's Lands. However, speaking strictly, loosely, or any way you please, the USE is not a democracy. The citizens of USE are magical creatures, and as notorious schemers, they had recognized certain traits in certain of their inhabitants - their Fairies, in particular - which might make a true democracy based on equality for all less than ideal for a nation filled to brimming with so many vain, elite tricksters. So when they crafted the government for their Fairies, they borrowed a little something from both to form a Fairyocracy. In a Royatocracy, there is one Queen; in a Fairyocracy, there is no Queen and every Fairy is equal to every other Fairy, but there is royalty and equality nonetheless; as every Fairy is, of course, not a Queen but a Princess.

"As we plunged through the freezing night air racing back to Sophia," continued Thee, "Me was just about suicidal as she looked at herself. She was a disheveled mess of dress tatters and wiry hair that the moon and stars above and the city lights below seemed to be gleefully illuminating. But when she glanced over at us and saw that we looked even worse, she screamed out -

" 'Gargoyles!' "

" 'Yeah! like, what an insult, Me, I'm cryin'!' "

" 'I can't believe I have to be seen with them!' "

"She didn't give an elf's toot who heard her." said Lorraine.

"Lorraine, our Readers!"

" 'Thee? Look at us! You're, like, ruining our hair! If we can't slow down, I'm warning you, first thing in the morning, I'll have no choice but to book makeovers for all of us, no matter what we have to do tomorrow. And if the rest of you won't join me, then that's where I'll be no matter what the stupid rule is! I mean it, Thee! Look at this hair!' "

"Lady, I hate to admit this but I kinda agreed with her," said Lorraine, "but not about how we looked - because she should watch her big fat mouth! - but about the racing part, 'Me is right, Thee! What's the rush? This is elfing stupid, Free is sound asleep. And the Dispatcher? There's, like, no way he's coming here tonight. You're scared for no reason. And you're scaring us, too. Or trying to scare us because I for one ain't scared. The Dispatcher hasn't been here in, like, forever. We have nothing to worry about. You're acting like the worst is about to happen. Free and Sophia are both sound asleep by now. We all found each other. We're going home. Could ya just relax, Thee? Can't we all just relax now?' "

"But Ms. Author, I kept on through that frigid night air. Although, I knew I'd better show them I had, at least, registered their complaints, or I'd never hear the end of it ..."

"Yeah! She, like, flipped round and gave each of us a look that only her face, outta all the faces in the Fairy AND the human solar system, couldda made. And we, like, shut our yaps!"

"Ms. Author, at last we reached the front door of Sophia's Grandfather's house. We flew under it—"

"And we, like, crash landed, and then each of us stood there, like, panting, gulping for air, and purple. You know, I'm no spring itchken!"

"Lorraine, here it's chickens."

"Yeah, okay, sorry! I was bent over double, belching cold air when I wasn't elfspheming ..."

"Profusely, Lorraine. She was, Ms. Author, profusely! You are lucky you weren't there to hear her! Until every one of us stopped suddenly. There were odd patterns in the air dust. There was a mushroomy aroma we hadn't smelled in a good long time wafting down the staircase. The Dispatcher! He was here!"

"Lady, we was done for. Thee was right all along. And not only that, we'd have to listen to her 'I-told-you-so's' for, like, ever!"

"But, Lorraine, that's not the point. You'd be listening to me forever for a very good reason. Because you were wrong about something that really was serious. Without saying a word, I flew up those staircases and so, too, did they. Each of us was as pale as a ghost fairy. Me, even paler, so afraid that the Dispatcher would sense immediately that she'd been places she shouldn't. Our noses led us right to the Man in the Moon door. And under the door, our noses, with us attached to them, flew. We were up the stairs in a flash. We smelled Sophia and we smelled sleep; then we smelled Free and the Dispatcher and knew they were inside Sophia's Remarkably Small Place. When we spotted Sophia, we flew inside!"

"Lady, we was scared. But we, like, didn't share our feelings about what might happen with the Dispatcher. Hah! Come to think of it, all of us should tawk about Sophia not sharing her feelings! We wouldn't even, like, look at each other. We keep our fears to ourselves!"

"Ms. Author, Fairies are a proud lot. We proclaim loudly how invincible we are, but know deep down we're not. 'Will he listen to reason?' That's what I wondered."

" 'Will that son-of-a-witch take away my pension?' Lady, that's what I was thinking. Me was, like, 'Will I ever be allowed to shop in Faree again?' And Be, 'Good cat bad cat like what kind of a cat is this cat?' "

"Ms. Author, Readers, I said, 'In all the jobs we had ever done, in all the Remarkably Small Places we had ever been in, over all these many many years, none of us have ever ever done anything so wrong!' "

" 'Yeah! And been caught so red-handed when we done it. Hey, Thee! Boys'll be boys and Fairies'll be Fairies!' "

" 'Speak for yourself! We broke the rule, Lorraine!' "

" 'Yeah! And what's he gonna do about it?' I says real tough, lady, but I really wasn't.

• • • THURSDAY, FEBRUARY 5, BREAKFAST • • •

'It must be daytime, light this warm couldn't be coming from the moon. That old-man-moon must be long gone by now. And so is my Grandfather.' Sophia would miss that elegant but scowly man who knew about voices. And she'd miss that funny old moon face that seemed to be watching over her. If only he'd always really and truly watch over her.

She opened her eyes and there, through the many windows all around her, was the light of a new day. And there too were lacy, fluffy, dainty clouds drifting across a blue sky and she was astounded. *'What are those measly wimps doing in a place like this? They're country clouds. What are COUNTRY clouds doing in the CITY? If the sky were my own Movie Screen and the clouds were the Movie Stars, I'd turn those clouds into clouds that should live here. I'd turn them into hundreds and hundreds of giant taxi cabs clouds colliding with each other while tons and tons of sky-scraper clouds tower over top of them, even as a King Kong cloud, a super-cloud, keeps growing larger and larger and ape-ier and ape-ier until it overshadows them all. There was a King Kong in that square last night. Well, I'd put him up here, too.'*

But then all she'd actually seen since she'd been here flashed before her. The shocking pink of the flamingos; those rocketing, racing, exploding, billboards that pounded out mile high colors, and all those masses and masses of mountainous buildings and so so so many people in so much of the same kind of grayish clothing.

And then all that she had heard squawked up too; all those accents! those voices! - the policeman's, the taxi cab driver's, the pink flamingos', Grandmother's, Antoinette Fifi's, Josephine's, Keys the Doorman; and then the millions and millions of all mixed up honks and roars and hums; and all those screaming arguments between the policeman and the taxi cab drivers, and the policeman and the people in the street, and the taxi cab drivers with everybody. And didn't her Grandfather say last night that music is everywhere! Would her Grandfather have called all of that music? Were screechiness, and arguments and bad words even allowed in music? She was sure they weren't. And she lay in her bed comparing all of that to what she heard in the Movies.

'Well, whatever it was, it sure boomed and razzed and tingled my ears up more than any Movie music I'd ever heard. Things here sure are not like what I'd thought they'd be. I never thought I'd say this but I think this place might be even wilder than a Movie!'

And then she reexamined those clouds. *'There's nothing wrong with those dainty clouds. There's enough drama here already! To think clouds can float by peacefully when they live on top of all that! Wow! Even dainty things can live here!'*

And she gazed with new appreciation at the tame and tranquil clouds.

Very soon, there was a soft knock on the door and a spring up the steps as soft as a cat's tail. And there stood Antoinette Fifi, looking so gorgeous and so beautifully dressed in an entirely different type uniform - with a face full of make-up that made her glow like a Movie Star on a Movie screen - that Sophia said a silent prayer to Miss Kitty's Irish Saints that her school would change their uniform to a uniform just like that and that she would be allowed to wear make-up to school, too. Sophia knew not even Miss Kitty's loosey-goosey Irish Saints would answer a prayer like that, but she prayed it anyway.

Antoinette Fifi slinked into the room, opened her mouth and out spilled a mixed-up bouquet of laughs, songs, whispers, "Ooh, ZoFEEya, Good Morning! Did you sleeeep well? Were you comforTAbull? Zis morning, you are going to meeeet ze everybodee! Ooh la lah! Zere is quite ze crazee crowd here every morning for ze Oomla breakfast! Your Grandmere is almost fineeshed dresseeng and we mustn't keep her waiting. She has planned quite ze day for you. And we must be fineeshed ze breakfast and away from ze tabull before your Grandfazere gets there. He likes all ze wild ones to be gone so he can have ze serene breakfast before his hectick day begins. You will meet him much later today but not at ze breakfast ..."

Sophia lay in her bed and let the Frenchness twirl round her. *'Oh! To sound like that!'* Until, that is, Antoinette Fifi began talking about her Grandfather. Then Sophia raised her head up, placed it on her elbow, opened her mouth all set to tell Antoinette Fifi she'd already met her Grandfather. Until something told her not to.

"Mais non, at ze breakfast, ZoFeeYa ... but your Grandfazere ... well ... it is just as well, he is too grouchee in ze morning!" And Antoinette shuddered, made a face and burst out laughing. "Zere is your Grandfazere in ze morning," And Antoinette Fifi shuddered again. "And your Grandfazere in ze evening, ooh la lah!" And she laughed. "Two different Grandfazeres, Sophia!"

'Antoinette Fifi can't be right. Grandfather is pretty grouchy in the evening, too.' Sophia recalled his sourpusses. *'So technically speaking, then, the Evening*

Grandfather's not even supposed to be grouchy. Unless … could she mean … he's even grouchier during the day?'

Antoinette Fifi bent over the bed and whispered in Sophia's ear, "We all prefer ze evening Grandfazere!" And in an arpeggio of ooh-la-lahs and giggles, she ducked over to the closet where Sophia's clothes had been unpacked and were now hanging.

'I'd better never tell Antoinette Fifi I met Grandfather already. And where I met him and when either. Sounds like I wasn't supposed to even meet him yet. Sounds like they want to introduce me to him, as Mr. James would say, formally. When he isn't so grouchy. Formally, like the way I have to meet Great Aunt Hortense every time she comes over. But that never stops her from being grouchy.'

While Antoinette Fifi examined the contents of her closet, Sophia wondered, *'What would Antoinette Fifi think of me if she found out what I'd been up to in the middle of the night? Surely she wouldn't like to hear that I was roaming the corridors and the staircases all by myself at nighttime, especially after she put me to bed! Even if I was just looking for her. Grown-ups never like to know that children got out of their bed in the night by themselves and walk about unsupervised. Even if they are French grown-ups.'*

And as if cold water had been thrown on her, Sophia jumped out of bed. Antoinette Fifi was by now taking each and every one of those sacks Maria had packed, examining them, shaking her head, wrinkling up her face, saying "non-non," "non-non" and putting them right back into the closet. Sophia looked in despair at those baggy, woolen lumps congealed onto their hangers. She would have to walk around in of all places! this city! the city that Sophia had been dreaming about ever since she saw it in the Movies, looking like a puffy farm animal. Miss Kitty would never've brought clothes like that for her to wear here because in this glamorous city Miss Kitty knew Sophia wanted to flounce and flit and float like a Movie Star. Miss Kitty would've understood how important clothes would've been to Sophia at a time like this. *Finally, here I am in my dream city and I'll be in sheep's clothing! Mope! That's how I'll walk here!'*

("Lady, when Sophia jumped outta bed, it was, like, a jolt, but we, like, woke up!")

• • • AFTER THE DISPATCHER WAS THROUGH WITH US! • • •

"Five guilty consciences woke us up, Ms. Author, Readers. Sophia's five companions were where we should be: up and attentive to the ensuing

Sophia/Fifi action. And not a word of protest. AND no whining. AND no bickering. But then after the Dispatcher was through with us! it really was not at all surprising. And no, Lorraine did not lose her pension."

"Yeah, Lady, Thee found out the Dispatcher would listen to reason; yeah! Like, after Thee debated every point he made with a well-aimed counter-punch—"

"Lorraine, with a well-reasoned counter-point!"

"Yeah, yeah, Thee, but none of that persuaded him until ya finally busted out crying, which you had never done in front of the Dispatcher before so that even he was shocked! He gave in, although he, like, really didn't want to. But Author Lady, it was, like, the shock of seeing her of all a' us in such a state!

"Then Be says, 'I watched Thee and the Dispatcher go at it and thought he really was a bad cat; until the very end when he gave in; so I had to give in, too.'

"Although," said Lorraine, "that instigator, Free, and that Dispatcher would NOT tell us what Free actually did do when she did explain this mission of hers to him - and only to him! - like, where she'd been and, like, why."

"That is, Ms. Author, when somehow Free managed to get the whole story out and the Dispatcher got a grasp of the gist of the essence of the substantives in the elocution of her circumlocutions and what it meant, or possibly meant, he forgave her at once!"

"Lady, he was just relieved she shut up!"

"Ms. Author, I'm afraid though, our Me was the only one who didn't fare so well. And it turns out, it wasn't for this transgression. It seemed it was for another one entirely that, somehow, he'd found out about. Although he wasn't saying how he found out or what it was and she certainly wasn't either. And whether she'd ever shop in Faree again, he was yet to decide. He'd announced his verdict the next time he returned. And since no one ever knew when that would be, Me had to do her utmost at all times. She, of course, was miserable. But when the day-of-reckoning came, her approach to this 'utmost thing' for handling her Duties and Responsibilities would impress the Dispatcher; if that failed—"

"There was always tears, Lady! Tears had worked for Thee, they certainly would work for Me. Me could outcry anybody any day!"

"And I would do it with such style! But, about the tears, I'd need time to rehearse. And by the way, tears that pour out of me, from all those health substances I consume, would be as pure as rainwater, as morning dew as … as … what am I thinking … distilled water for perfume from France … or …

baby tears … Oh … whichever is purer! I'd, of course, have to work on my presentation and its accompanying monologue and block the whole thing as if I were performing on a professional stage, just like an actress would, hands here, feet there, head down, but eyes completely visible at all times. Oh! I'd be ready for him. Make no mistake about it!"

• • • GOOD MOONING • • •

"Ooh Zofeeya, none of zese will do for your day in ze city. We go to ze costume shop and I whip somezing togezair for you. Come, put on your bazrobe, we go. We do not 'ave ze much time."

"Oh Antoinette Fifi, can I wear what you have on?" Sophia called out as she put a foot into a slipper but Antoinette Fifi was half way down the stairs and must not've heard her. By the time Sophia was on the staircase, Antoinette Fifi was off it already. Sophia could hear her calling, "Come on ZoFEEya." Sophia raced down the steps, *'Oh! Suppose I get to wear something like that!'*

The Man in the Moon door was open wide and Sophia had to fly past, not even peeking at him, she was so afraid she'd lose Antoinette Fifi.

When she got to the hallway, Sophia could hear all sorts of noise: women's voices, men's voices, some singing songs or musical scales when they weren't shouting or laughing, all of which seemed to be coming from the rooms along the hallway and drifting up from the staircase below. The place was abuzz.

Antoinette Fifi called out again from down below and Sophia flew down the second staircase where several people joined her also on their way down. Who were all these people? Why were they singing scales? But they all knew who she was because they all greeted her.

"Good Morning, Sophia! Will you be joining us for breakfast?"

Now that she was on her way to her own adventure in this city from the Movies, now that she was alongside so many people who sang in the morning when they walked down the stairs - her ears heard another song on another staircase from so so many mornings ago.

The song her Father used to sing when she walked down the stairs with him, before their house got too big.

But that didn't make her less cheerful as she walked down the stairs. She, after all, was on her way to becoming French, to becoming Antoinette Fifi. And as soon as she had the clothes on, she would certainly talk with her French accent.

Sophia forgot to be timid, smiled at everyone and would've answered all if she wasn't on such a desperate search for Antoinette Fifi.

Antoinette Fifi was waiting on the next landing. She beckoned for Sophia to follow her, then ran down the corridor to a door and opened it. Again, she beckoned for Sophia, who was almost half-way there, just before she passed through the doorway. Sophia flew the rest of the way, and soon she had passed through the doorway, too. Antoinette Fifi was nowhere to be found but a vast room was visible.

All around the edge of the room were racks, each filled from end to end with clothes. And in the center of the room were several long, long tables. Dressmaker dummies were dotted around the room, some on the tables, some were even men dummies. And all of them dressed in clothes that didn't look like normal clothes that people would wear nowadays. Most of the clothes looked like things people wore a long time ago. But not all. Even though she knew she was supposed to be looking for Antoinette Fifi, Sophia just had to stop in front of each costume and imagine what her life would be like if she were wearing it.

·:·(··

(" 'Duds on dummies!' We was cracking ourselves up, Lady!")

·:)··

There were so many! A hula dancer. And was that a giant flower petal or a gown for dancing with the prince at the ball? These must be the costumes the actors wore that were in her Grandfather's shows. And there she stood, frozen on her spot, looking at the clothes of her dreams, making up a Movie for each costume. She knew she shouldn't be late but she couldn't stop; her Grandmother was waiting; her Grandfather was grouchy; Antoinette Fifi needed her this very second; time couldn't wouldn't wait for her; it wouldn't, it couldn't.

But somehow the thought of disappointing all those people seeped in and she tore herself away and went in search of Antoinette Fifi.

After much highing and lowing, she found her in the far corner of the room. Antoinette Fifi had already laid out several complete outfits on the table in front of her. Just glancing at them and Sophia felt something inside flounce and flit and float. *'I get to wear one of those?'* She didn't have anything in her entire wardrobe that was as cool as any of those.

·:·(··

("Darlings, actually, I was the cause of that tiny quake inside Sophia. Finally, my charge, my Sophia was about to wear something hip, something chic, something that I myself would've been caught dead in if I were a human child!"

"I hoped she, like, picked that leatha numba! That was goraahJIIS! Remember?"

"Lorraine, don't you dare say another word. And that's what I told you then, too, remember? This was, like, my forte, my raison d'être, Author darling. Plus if the Dispatcher just happens to appear, I'll be doing my job! And, most importantly, Be seen BY HIM doing my job correctly."

"Yeah, Me, I remember, you smiled the way a cat smiles, which is, like, hardly at all, and then you flew to Sophia's heart. Me, like, knew the rules, even if she didn't follow them; no hanging out on the client's ear and actually looking at the clothes and then whispering her 'suggestions' into the client's ear. Which, admit it, you'd been doing for years! Me was gonna follow Rule No #52 from the Emissary / Client Rules of Engagement to the T. Thee, tell everybody what that rule is. You're so good at Rules!"

"Thank you, Lorraine. 'Whenever your client must decide between things, sit not on your client's ear; stand, instead, by your client's heart.' The Emissary who stands by the client's heart has no ability to actually see the things that are being decided between thereby eliminating any temptation for the Emissary to pick out what itself would prefer.

"Blah blah blah, darlings. I also knew the Rules. Sophia would be choosing her own outfit. And whatever Sophia selected, even if Sophia ended up looking like a meatball, Sophia's decision would be supported by moi! And would be a decision that I had not influenced in any way! This time I would do it right. Not how I'd done it before. With her Mother. How did the Dispatcher ever find out? I wasn't inside her Mother's head all that much. I mean a year, on and off, isn't really such a long time, is it? Or was it two years? Or was it longer? None of you had ever found out. You had no idea where I was whenever I was missing. How DID that Dispatcher find out? Who's the spy? I knew it wasn't any of you. None of you could keep a secret for two minutes. Except for you, Thee, and you don't have it in you to be a spy. You are, after all, our very own Ms. Rules and Regulations. If you'd ever found out what I was up to, you would've straightened me out in a wing flap. You take your role as 'The Keeper of The Rules of Engagement' very seriously. As if they were your very own, as if they were named after you. Thee couldn't have any of her Fairies breaking The Rules of Engagement on her watch. So it definitely wasn't any of you!"

"Thank you, Me, for such a compliment! I'm truly flattered."

"Thee, I wasn't complimenting you. Following rules is stifling! You don't get to think for yourself! And express yourself either.")

·∙:)∙·

Antoinette Fifi looked at Sophia, then at the four outfits on the table; Sophia looked at Antoinette Fifi, waiting for her to pick which of the four outfits she wanted her to wear.

"Ooh ZoFEEya, which do you like the best?"

'I can pick?' And she was free and she was scared and pick she couldn't. She might pick the wrong thing. She examined each outfit. She tried talking herself into one. And she got lost in thought, *'It's not like I don't have a lot of experience picking clothes. Whenever I'm performing in my Movie Star School, I pick out the best things I can find in my Mother's heaps of clothes that would be just right for the Movie Star I have to be that day. I've done this before so why is picking so hard right now? But nobody ever gets to see me in those get-ups. Because that's what they really are - they're get-ups because, I hate to say this, those clothes don't really fit me. This time, everybody's going to see me in what I pick. A roomful of everybodies. And it'd better be perfect! And it'd better be me! So who am I?'*

Just for a second, Sophia's eyes lifted off the outfits and on to Antoinette Fifi who was smiling at her so merrily that Sophia felt merry too and like she could do this after all. And she stopped thinking and the next thing she knew her heart had found its outfit, and in a few minutes, she was in it and they were on their way downstairs.

And Sophia pranced down those steps even as more and more people were on those steps with her. Who were all saying Good Morning. To her. Whose eyes, their eyes, were on her. And she felt their eyes. Felt their smiles.

And she smiled back.

She was in the clothes that the best dressed girls at school wore whenever they didn't have to wear their uniforms.

And she wondered. How did she look in these clothes?

And she worried.

And her prance stooped. She stopped smiling at the Good Morning people, didn't look at them but only at the mini-skirt and the patterned-tights and the knee-high boots and the jewel-colored tops layered one over top the other with their bands of colors peeking out at their necklines, their hemlines; and the tiny-knot, tiny-string, tiny-bead necklace and the other beaded necklace and the rows of knotted string bracelets. *'Suppose Great Aunt Hortense shows up mysteriously at breakfast and catches me in this get-up?'* But even she knew that was impossible, so she stopped worrying that.

Only to worry something else entirely.

'I'm not Antoinette Fifi. I haven't turned into her. I'm just myself. Myself in spiffy clothes. And now I'll have to talk to all these people at the breakfast table! Everybody'll be looking at me, just me! I'll have to like just being me! I'll have to like not being Antoinette Fifi! Like not having a pussycat voice! Like speaking in my own voice! Because I'll be sitting down and eating my breakfast with all these people who know my name, who'll be staring at me in my spiffy clothes as I eat! Including my Grandmother! My spiffy clothes won't be able to talk for me. I'll have to talk. I'll have to be the spiffy one. I'll have to have something to say. And it'd better be spiffy too. Movie Stars always have something to say. And they say it with a VOICE!'

The perfume of hot cinnamon toast burned through the fog that'd descended only on her and she was shocked. She'd reached the first floor. She slipped behind Antoinette Fifi who was gabbing away to somebody who was gabbing right back at her. Her legs sped her towards that toast; all legs were speeding there too; the legs that belonged on the people who she finally looked up at saw and who were actually walking right beside her. The people she'd stopped looking at. She kept her head up this time but something inside her was wishing mightily she could shrink herself smaller and smaller so these people wouldn't see her. But she kept walking alongside everybody, heading towards that toast, too. Soon she'd have to be sitting down among these people, eating that toast and talking to them, too. Eating and talking. Eating and talking.

The people streamed through the wide doorway to the room that smelled delicious. Sophia, stuck to Antoinette Fifi, could only stumble through that doorway but stopped abruptly.

Was she in a castle?

Was this a banquet hall where Knights in armor and Damsels in tall, pointy hats would eat feasts? Sophia, though stuck again, was transfixed, as she imagined them sitting there in long gowns and shiny suits. Until Antoinette Fifi whispered, "Come now ZoFEEya, I'm zo hungree, aren't you?"

And Sophia saw what really filled that room: along one of its wall, there was a sideboard set with many silver chafing dishes; in its center, was a table that was the longest table Sophia had ever seen. And all those people that'd been streaming through its doorway were now in a line waiting to get at those chafing dishes where all that cinnamon and maple syrup and toast perfume was coming from.

"ZoFEEya, the room ees grand, yes? And the food smells merveilleux! Yes?"

Sophia said not a word in response but as Antoinette Fifi had already started chatting with the cheerful people in the line who were all chatting about the food, she hadn't noticed. No one even glanced at Sophia and she was relieved.

Soon Antoinette Fifi and she were finished filling up their plates. Antoinette called from over her shoulder, "ZoFEEya, we go to sit at ze far end of ze table where your Grandmere always sits. And we wait for her zere. Your Grandmere, she is not yet here. Believe me, you will know when she is."

Sophia gladly obeyed. She didn't look at a single soul as she gripped her plate that she'd very deliberately, and for a sensible reason, piled sky-high with food. She'd figured that as soon as she sat down, she'd have something to hide behind. Nobody'd ever be able to peek around the edge of all of that to try to talk to her. And besides, they wouldn't. They'd know she had to eat all that food because it was breakfast and growing children are supposed to eat their breakfast. Everybody knew that. She'd have to chew all that food, but very very slowly; and she would chew and chew, then chew some more and anybody who was still trying to talk to her would plainly see that her mouth was already busy and they wouldn't try anymore. And then she wouldn't have to talk to anybody at all.

Sophia steadfastly steered that plate and that food, and wended her way behind Antoinette Fifi, even as the load pitched one way and then the other. She would just set it to rights again and keep going. She finally reached her seat at the long table, plopped the plate down, collapsed into her chair and tucked in, though the muscles in her arms were positively stinging from carrying such a heavy load.

·∴∙C·∙·

("Lady, I had had it, I says, 'Holy efing gnome skull! Sophia's losing her mind! Again! But this time, I don't know about youse, but I'm doing the right thing. I've had it with this chick's crazy schemes. Remember her other scheme, the one with old Aunt crabapple, well that last one was a flop! And this one's gonna be too! But this time she's gonna fail on her own, 'cause I ain't helpin' her. Like she's gonna be able to hide behind all that food! Did ya see what everybody else is eating, like a spoonful of yogurt and a raspberry they cut in half; the other half of which, they probably are saving for recess. Next week's recess. These are people-canaries. If these skeletons ain't dancers or actors or something, then my name ain't Lorraine. Sophia's plate sticks out like a sore bum!' "

" 'Lorraine!' "

" 'Thumb, Thee, thumb, my tongue slipped!' "

" 'My eye! it slipped! But Lorraine, I must admit, is correct. We simply have to do this the right way. Let's all join Me at Sophia's heart and stay put. We will provide support for her and whisper kind things to her no matter what she chooses. It's the safest place for us. And if the Dispatcher drops in, he will see for himself that we do our duty.' "

"Free says, 'Worry we not should. Okay soon be Sophia. See you, you-you.' "

"Lady, that was, like, the fourth time Free said that since she'd come back!"

"Oh! Ms. Author, Readers! I was remiss, I should have asked her what she meant.")

··:)··

Sophia looked up at the mound of food: it was so high, she'd need a step ladder to get to it. And how could she be invisible on a step ladder? But just as she thought maybe she made a mistake, there was a commotion at the doorway and everybody who was sitting stood up. "Madame Oomla, as usual, so glamorous!" "Ah, the lady must be beautiful!" "Just stepped off the Champs Elysees, by chance?"

··(··

(" 'Ooh, like, I gotta go up there just to see what's she's wearin'!' "

" 'Lorraine, don't you dare. If Me can stay put when there's a costume to inspect, so can you!' ")

··:)··

"Good morrrrrrning all! Stepppppp off a Parisian Boulevard? I wish! Wheeled! Caned! Walkered-off is more likely darrrrrlings. Thank you so much for your kind words. Those who are kind are the truly beautiful! Welcome to my table. Eat up! You have much to accomplish today!"

As her Grandmother's words swooped through that vast banquet hall, Sophia wondered, how could her Grandmother sound like midnight AND sunlight? And laughing AND talking? All at the same time? And, oh! her lucky Grandmother got everyone's attention. And didn't her Grandfather tell her that an invisible orchestra was always playing somewhere if she would only listen for it? Well, when her Grandmother spoke, Sophia certainly heard it and now even she felt sunnier. And then Sophia remembered where she was – Voice Heaven - and forgot everything else and she just let that voice wrap her and that vast hall in its fanciful mystery.

Talking and laughing with whoever talked to them, her Grandmother and Josephine made their way down the table. But they weren't even half way there when her Grandmother whispered, "And where is my grand-daughter? Is she here yet?"

"Oooh Madame, she ees down here avec moi! And is dressed and readee for her adventure du jour!"

"Thank you Antoinette Fifi! Have all of you met my granddaughter Sophia?"

And Antoinette Fifi called out, as she waved and giggled, "Ooh, here she is!"

Sophia, who hadn't been hiding, who had even completely forgotten her scheme, suddenly jumped, knocking at least a pound of food from her teetering, cockeyed, rhomboid of waffles and flapjacks – plop plop – onto the floor. She prayed that all those people, especially her Grandmother, heard only Antoinette Fifi and not those plops, and that they didn't notice the slipping, sloping, soppy mess that was left on her plate.

Her Grandmother, who couldn't even see Sophia yet, spoke to her as if she could, "Good Morning, Sophia, darrrrrrling. Excuse my shouting, but I can harrrrdly wait to hearrr. What diiiiid you think of your rooooooom?"

Sophia could feel every eye on her and on her pile of food and she quickly slid into her chair.

⋅⋅⋅(⋅⋅⋅

("Ms. Author, Sophia's heart beat so fast we had to keep flying out of its way."

"It was, like, smacking us upside our heads!"

"Ms. Author, we chanted, 'Just smile and say I loved it!' ")

⋅⋅⋅)⋅⋅⋅

"Why Good Morning, Miz So ... now, would you look at that! Miz Sarah, wait til you see what's piled on Sophia's plate. Food! As I live and breathe! That sho is something' we don' ever see 'round here what with all these skinny-minnie, boney-maroneys."

⋅⋅⋅(⋅⋅⋅

("Elfing gnat noogies! Here it comes. We should never've let her do that to her plate!"

"Lorraine ... NO elfspheming! And if you remember correctly, all of us are finally doing our job the right way. No interfering. And if we had been sitting on her ear, that's what some of us might have been tempted to do. Fairies, we simply cannot forget any longer - our time inside Sophia is drawing to end. From now on, we have to do things the right way. And by being here, close to her heart, whispering our thoughts to it, we are in the exact spot we should be in. That's what we should've been doing all along. We should've always used her heart as the base for our operations, instead of her ear, as if we were hanging out on some street corner. What was I thinking? What were any of us thinking? Sophia will be turning eleven-years-old soon, and the second she does, we must be out of here!"

" 'Out of HER!' said Be.

"Lady, I, like, poked Be in the side and high-fived her."

" 'This is no joke!' snapped Thee. 'We don't have much time left!' ")

⋯☽⋯

Sophia was pink and sorrowful and queasy and she wasn't sure she wanted to see her Grandmother. Or anybody else, either. And she ducked even lower behind her wobbling fortress. But rolling throughout the breakfast room, getting closer and closer, was that unmistakable, irresistible throaty-voiced laugh and she had to peek. Every pair of eyes she spied were doing the same thing hers were: trying to get a glimpse of her Grandmother. And finally there she was, her Grandmother, as plain as day. Although as plain as day was not how anyone would've described her Grandmother. Sophia didn't notice even one bone sticking out of her, let alone an entire rib cage, like she had last night. This morning her Grandmother didn't look bony at all, she looked svelte as a dancer. And she glowed like a sparkler on snow as the sun poured in from the windows and danced all over the tiny-crystal-beaded-necklaces that flowed down her wintry white sweater.

And Sophia was dazzled but only momentarily because something else had caught her eye. What everybody else had on their plates. *'Oh no! These people eat like gerbils!'* And Sophia wanted to die and she put her head down only to pick it up again because she couldn't see her Grandmother, and she didn't want to miss a trick. Her Grandmother was looking at her. And then she watched her Grandmother see the tower of food on her plate, lean in so she could see it better, open her eyes wide, wider, blink, then look at Josephine, at the people standing at their plates, at what was on their plates, and then back at Sophia's plate.

And her Grandmother burst out laughing.

"Oh, my friends! I propose a toast. Let's forget about our sticks of dry toast and slivers of grapefruit! Today, let's pile our plates high with palaces of French Toast and pancakes and waffles! Oh! To be young again and to eat anything we please. Take your seats everyone and enjoy!"

Throughout that hall, there were shouts of, "Here here, Sophia!" "You lucky stiff Sophia!"

⋯☾⋯

("Lady, I thought I was, like, gonna have a heart attack! Can Fairies even have heart attacks, Thee? Ten year olds might, but Fairies? Anyways, I couldda swore—"

"Lorraine!"

"I couldda but I didn't … okay Thee! … as I was sayin' … I thought she was in for it, didn't all a youse?")

·⟨)⟩·

The people sat down and soon the sound of forks scraping on plates and laughter and buzzing conversation filled the banquet hall. But there wasn't a soul who went back to the sideboard and filled up their plates.

Sophia was stunned. *'Grandmother may be old but she's nothing like Great Aunt Hortense!'*

"Oooh, Sophia, I used ta eat like that too when I was youra age, ooh my gawd! Youra' so lucky! It looks delicious!"

'That sounds like a pink flamingo!' Sophia turned and there was the flamingo smiling at her. And she smiled back! And not shyly either! She even knew what she was going to say – I don't always eat so much, I usually eat just like you, I was just extra hungry today – and she opened her mouth and out came,

"Ahhh … ahhha … I … ya … ya … dadadon't … alwa … all … lays ways … WAYS … ea … eattt tta … eat … soo mooch … maamuch … MUCH …" She stopped.

·⟨C⟩·

("Lady, we all thought the same thing! 'Elfing snatch coocheries! She sounds like Free! Where is Free? She didn't fly off again and get stuck in Sophia's mouth did she?' "

"'M'ims here is … m'ims … but worry you don't. Sophia m'im's soon be kay-dokay.'")

·⟨)⟩·

And back down went Sophia's head. *'What's happening to me? I'm stuttering. I don't usually stutter when I have to talk. Why when I finally want to enter the world of talking, and I want to talk, can't I? That isn't fair. Maybe that stupid old Mr. Snoggley is right! Maybe I do need a speech therapist, after all. I can't even talk when I want to talk, when I have something to say!'*

And Sophia turned away from the pink flamingo lady and began stabbing at what was left of the mountain of food on her plate. She could eat, she was hungry, after all. At least she had something to do as there was nobody to talk to since she wasn't talking to the pink flamingo anymore and everybody around her was by now talking to somebody else because they probably all heard her and figured out that she couldn't talk. As she chewed away, she listened to all of the conversations. The pink flamingo was now talking to the person on her other side. Antoinette, to a person across the table from her. Her Grandmother, to Josephine.

'I'm talking too but inside and to myself. Which is all I ever do!'

"Good Morning, everytwo! Ooh! What a bountiful day thus is. So cold but so deblightful!"

Sophia picked up her head. *'Who is that? What did she say?'*

"Good Morning, Marielaina! I'm so happy you could make it. Sophia, meet your Great Aunt Marielaina."

'Great Aunt?!'

But she must never disappoint her Grandmother. And dutifully her eyes met the eyes of Great Aunt Marielaina. Who was very old. Even older than Great Aunt Hortense but she sure could smile. In fact, she was smiling so much Sophia was surprised that a person as old as her could be as happy as a kid at Christmas. And plus, she held her head so high, like she was a prancing show-horse.

"Ooh, Sophia! I've heard so much about you and am so pleased I'm acquaintincing your ship."

Sophia saw that her Grandmother was smiling, then nodding at her and then smiling at the smiling lady. She knew what her Grandmother expected her to do. And she did it. For her Grandmother she'd talk, even if she stuttered on every word.

"Good mooning!"

'MOONing? MOONing! Listen to me. Mr. Snoggley is right, I really can't talk!'

"Oh, yes, Sophia, it certainly was a good mooning last night, wasn't it? The moon was simply extrapolatious in the skymament! Sarah, did you see it? But then how could anythree miss it?

·:•(:·•·

(" 'Free, where are you? Are you telling the truth? You haven't snuck off? Come on now, you can tell us, you didn't just fly into that lady's head too, did you? If you ask me, it sure is suspicious; first, Sophia is stuttering, something she doesn't usually do and now this lady? Come clean Free!' "

" 'Be, m'ims is here. Moved haven't.' And Free waved. 'M'ims no go. Hee Tee … Lady talks funnies.' "

"Ms. Author, I said, 'I don't believe it, just what Sophia needs, having to listen to somebody like that when she's having a case of the stutters. Why that individual gets me confused, and I can talk!' ")

·:•):·•·

"Sophia, tell me what you think of our boptopolis?"

'Boptopolis?'

Sophia did open her mouth but shut it. She knew what would happen to the answer on the tip of her tongue: even though it lay there perfectly, it wouldn't get out of her mouth sounding anything like that! And she didn't want to hear one more mangled word come out of her mouth. And she and her answer sat there.

Her Grandmother must have noticed Sophia struggling and said to her, "Our city, Sophia, what do you think of our city?"

"It's very insteresting!"

Which hit her hard, *'INSteresting! INSteresting?! Listen to me. That's it! I'm not saying another word! But look at the smile on that lady's face. I don't even think she heard that I said the word wrong. And why does somebody who talk funny look so happy? She doesn't exactly talk right either but she doesn't behave like I behave. It doesn't seem to bother her at all that she doesn't say some of her words the way they should be said. Her face isn't red like a boiling lobster. I don't see her hiding her head away when she makes a mistake; her head is high, like everybody thinks very highly of her. And like she thinks very highly of herself.'*

Sophia noticed that it had gotten quiet. She saw that the lady was smiling at her so sweetly and looking at her like she was waiting for her. *'Is she waiting for me to say something?'* But then in the very next second, the lady bent down very low, leaned into Sophia and whispered to her so that no one but Sophia would hear,

"Ooh, Sophia, the word is interesting. In-te-res-ting. Interesting! Just want to make sure you pronounce your words correctly. I can't tell you how important the proNOUNciation of words is! Why sometwo might think you had a speech impediment, and I wouldn't want anyone to think that of such a lovely person as yourself." And then she winked a tiny wink like what she just said was their secret.

⋅∴ℂ∵⋅

("Ms. Author, as you can well imagine, I was not amused! 'The nerve of her! SHE JUST SAID proNOUNciation! Instead of proNUNciation. Doesn't she hear herself? The lady who needs a lesson herself is giving our Sophia a lesson about how to pronounce words! The pot is calling the kettle black.' "

"Lady, the rest of us couldn't stop snickering, 'Would you listen to Thee! I didn't think Thee had it in her!' And then we gave you the Wings-Up, Thee. But Thee, you, who never miss a trick, didn't even notice, you was fuming so much!")

⋅∴꙱∵⋅

Sophia was positively horrified. And without a thought about what to say or how to say it, she blurted out, "I how now to say interesting. And I wouldn't ever want to ever have a peech imspediment or for that matter for somebumbody to think I had one either!"

What she said hung in the air but a second. Sophia knew those words were her words. She couldn't run from them, hide from them, disown them. There was no escape from them. She had said them. No! She had blurted them. And then … wait … did all conversations just cease in that banquet hall? Sophia was now quadruply horrified.

Everybody in that hall must have heard her words, too!

She looked round expecting to see every eye on her. Her Grandmother's. Antoinette Fifi's. The pink flamingo lady who had just talked to her. They must have just heard her.

But no one was looking at her.

And that lady wasn't standing over top of her anymore but was walking towards an empty chair.

And then Sophia heard it - the sound of swift, sharp footsteps - what all those eyes must really be staring at.

'They're looking at the person who's making those footsteps.' Sophia was re-lieved. *'At least, they're not paying attention to me, and those words I said. Those words that truly mean I have a speech problem. That really and truly mean I need a speech therapist. Now I understand. Mr. Snoggley was right. Maybe that speech therapist could save me!'*

Everyone in that hall was looking in the direction of footsteps. Sophia could feel that something had changed drastically in that hall. And it was all because of those footsteps. Sophia couldn't see who was making those footsteps, so she stopped looking and just studied the faces of the people instead. She knew faces. She had watched so many of them in so many Movies; she knew how faces looked when they showed feelings. And these faces sure looked different than they looked just a few seconds ago. Just seconds ago, the people wearing those faces were having fun. They weren't now. If she would've been watching a Movie that had those faces in it, she would've bet they just saw something that made them nervous, maybe even a little spooked. Who could make people who were so cheery just a minute ago, look like they just saw a spook? And what was a spook doing walking around in broad daylight in her Grandmother's house?

"WHERE'S MY GRANDDAUGHTER?" Demanded a voice ready to pul-verize any eardrum in its path. *'It's Grandfather! What a voice! But that's no mere frog in his throat. The animal in that throat might not even be an animal, at all, but a beast. And a very bossy one at that.*

'That's who everybody is staring at. It's him! And he sounds ferocious. That's why everybody's so quiet. And he's looking for me! Me! Why me? Why would he need me?'

She was so rattled by her morning—

'So many voices!

'Too too many faces in-my-face!

'Wearing such clothes on a school day!

'Talking-screwy in the talking-world.

'Mr. Snoggley! Is! Right! I need a speech therapist'

... she had completely forgotten what her Grandfather had said last night about where he wanted to take her today. For Sophia was so busy riding today's up-I-go, down-I-fall-roller-coaster, how could she ride yesterday's too?

Every eye in that vast hall was now aimed at her. Again. Every eye. And she felt every last eye on her. Again. Back down went her head. She didn't want to see all those eyes stare at her. Again. She knew she should answer him, but she hid there, feeling like she'd never lift her head again, even as she tried to figure out why her Grandfather would need her. The only thing that came to mind was what Antoinette Fifi had told her this morning. That her Grandfather ate his breakfast alone. But now he was here with everybody. And even though he was way on the other side of the hall, she could feel something. Like he was tugging on her. And from inside something began to tug on her too.

And then she remembered. What he'd said last night.

• • • THEATRE VOICES • • •

He wanted her to hear Voices! That's what was tugging on her. That's why he was here. That's why he wanted to see her. To hear Theatre Voices. Somebody wanted to take her to hear Voices! *'If I wasn't such a chicken, I'd've answered him then run right over to him. He's only here to find me. He's here because I'm here.'* She was disgusted with herself. No more hiding. It wasn't right. All she had to do was tell him where she was. That was easy. She could do that. So what if she messed up her words? So what if everybody in the whole world heard her? Back up went her head. And even though she knew what she was about to say would come out of her all mix-matched and funny-sounding, she opened her mouth and spoke,

"Grandfather! Here I am. I'm over here! Good morning to you!"

But every word did not come out all mix-matched and funny-sounding. Every word came out like the English word it was; whole; and with not even a single part of another word stuck in the middle or at the end or at the beginning of a single other word. Out those syllables came, one after the other, in order. And not only that, she spoke loud and clear. Her words resounded throughout that vast banquet hall, landing in each and every ear, one after the other, like eleven basketballs slamdunked through a hoop.

·∴(·∴

("And the Fairies went wild, Lady!")

·∴)∴·

All eyes were on her but were his? On tiptoes and with a craned neck, she peered over heads so he would see her.

"Now where is my wife, Sarah?" he bellowed. There was silence in the hall; everyone knew only one person better answer that question. "Why, Solomon, I'm herrrrre where I always am. Good morning is how one usually begins all forms of communication in the morning. So good morning to you darrrrrling and why are yoooou calling out for your graaaanddaughter? You haven't yet been introduuuced."

As her Grandmother spoke, that cheery blue sky with its dainty clouds came rolling through that vast banquet hall covering everyone with daintiness, especially her Grandfather; because when he spoke again, he sounded a little less bossy.

"Now, Sarah, Sophia is coming with me today. I have much to show her. And I must teach her all I can about the family business. And I don't have much time ... we don't have much time ..."

As her Grandfather spoke, Sophia wondered, 'Could the sound of Grandmother make even him feel different?' And she listened to see if she was right and not really to what he was saying.

"Today might even be the day she'll have to be shipped back to that Siberian outpost my son calls home ..."

But Sophia was hardly noticing the plans he was making for her. Instead, she was remembering what he said last night, about the music in everything. He was right; his sound was his kind of music.

"During my discussion with her last night, she displayed quite an aptitude for our line of work, Sarah."

"Last night, Solomon? Discussion, Solomon? Aptitude, Solomon? Sophia?"

"Last night. Last night on the stairs!"

Sophia did understand those words. But she didn't have time to wonder what her Grandmother thought of her being on the stairs in the middle of the night because that bossiness was creeping back in to her Grandfather's voice and she didn't want to miss a note of it. In fact, as he continued to speak, his bossiness ratcheted up a notch on each word he said so that by the time he finished, it was right back to where it was when he entered that vast hall – at a 21-gun-salute.

"Sarah, we will talk later. I am starting much earlier than usual because I want Sophia to see much, to learn much today, to experience the world of Show Business from a front row seat. From a Producer's point of view. The best view point there is. I have set up quite an agenda for Sophia. If we don't leave in approximately five minutes, we will miss our first appointment. Sophia, please get your coat. It's cold outside!"

Her Grandfather bent down and kissed her Grandmother on the lips and then sped out of the hall. But her Grandmother wasn't even looking at him; she only had eyes for Sophia now, as if Sophia was the most intriguing person in the whole world. Sophia could tell her Grandmother was dying to find out what happened on the stairs last night though she didn't ask her. Antoinette Fifi looked the same way her Grandmother did but didn't say a word either. She just sprang out of her chair, headed towards Sophia, grabbed her hand then off they took, chasing after her Grandfather. Sophia's eyes held onto her Grandmother's, even as Antoinette Fifi held on to Sophia and moved her so fast that Sophia's mouth wouldn't even open so she could've told the both of them exactly what did happen.

Antoinette Fifi and Sophia reached the entranceway and only stopped when they got to the front door. "ZoFEEya, your old coat is in ze closet, but I 'ave for you anozair coat. Eet will go bettair viz your outfit but I must get eet before your Grandfazair returns." Antoinette Fifi ran off but got back just as the sound of sharp footsteps could be heard coming down the stairs. Antoinette Fifi was out of breath and her hair was flying here and there, but she carried with her a coat, hat, scarf and gloves. And in a few beats, Sophia was in them, even as the footsteps were now not only echoing throughout that entranceway but inside every nook and cranny of Sophia's and Antoinette Fifi's ribcages. But somehow Antoinette Fifi winked a shaky wink at Sophia and whispered, "Ooh, SoFEEya, you look wondearful!"

·⟡·

("Darlings, do you remember what I said? 'I can't believe I'm missing this! Could this, like, French Fifi Maid slash Costume Designer really know about fashion? I mean fashion is usually not created by ... like ... Costume Designers! Costume Designers exaggerate every single thing they design! Understating is the essence of fashi ... oh ... what's the use! Why should I expect simple Fairies to know the secrets of elegance? And here is my

Sophia, finally stepping out in THE city, in clothes that, even if they were styled by a Costume Designer, fit her! And I'm missing it!' "

" 'Me, you're doing so well,' said Be, 'don't mess it up now!' ")

·:)·∵·

Sophia looked at herself. She was in beautiful clothes. That weren't big. That she wasn't tripping over like the clothes she took from her Mother's closet! And, even better, that weren't anything at all like those baggy lumps Great Aunt Hortense'd been buying for her now that her Mother was too busy to buy her clothes.

What a sight her Grandfather was as he strode towards them. He towered over them like Goliathon itself; the only thing boyish about him was his hair, though it was silvery white; his overcoat long; his scarf buttery; his two shoes gleaming like mirrors; his wide-brimmed derby in his hand. Sophia's eyes popped.

She peeked at herself then at him. *'My clothes are wonderful too.'* He finally reached them but instead of smiling at them, barked, "Mademoiselle, does my granddaughter have everything she needs?" Antoinette Fifi and Sophia jumped.

And Sophia wasn't quite so dazzled anymore.

'That voice! Grandfather's so bossy! He sounds so much different than last night.'

"Sophia, are you ready?"

'He means business!' Sophia was not listening to what he said: all she could hear was how he said it. She couldn't even feel his stare because the sound of him was mixing up with her thoughts. But staring at her he was, as she stood there thinking.

'I know exactly what this voice is. It's a Great Aunt Hortense, Mr. Snoggley voice. I know Bosses alright. But how very confusing! For last night he was singing about the mouse in his house and waving his arms like he was conducting an invisible orchestra. Last night he was much more silly than bossy.'

She examined him examining her: What an expression on his face! Not like last night's expression! *'He's not silly now. How was I able to talk to him and say all that I said to him last night? About Movies and Movie Stars and Movie Voices. But he didn't sound so ... look so ... so like this.'*

Antoinette Fifi had waited for Sophia to answer but when she didn't, Antoinette Fifi quickly filled in for her, "Oui, Monsieur Oooomla. Ooh ... sorree ..."

'Now even Antoinette Fifi sounds different. Like an obedient pussycat, something pussycats are not!'

"J'ai oublie … uuuoh … I forgot to speak English … SoFEEya is readee, Mistair Oomla."

'She must sound like that because Grandfather is the boss of her!' Sophia looked at Antoinette Fifi: she wasn't smiling.

'That's why! He's her boss. Is Grandfather going to be the boss of me, too? All day? Will going out with him be like going out with Great Aunt Hortense?'

"Well, Sophia … Are you ready? Or are you going to stand there dreaming …" Her Grandfather leaned over and said, "… like you have a head full of Fairies?"

("Haaauuuuuuuuuuuuugh!" said Me.

"Holy elf toots!"

"How does he know? In all of my tenures, I've never heard one single human ever say that before!" said Thee.

"That ole cat works in Show Business." said Be. "I've heard it said that a very very select few of the people that work in Show Business still have Fairies in their heads, and those few are, like, grown-up people. People who haven't been ten years old for, like, years and years and years. Women AND EVEN MEN! How it works is, the Fairies keep sneaking back into their heads, the Dispatcher finds out, they get busted only to go sneaking right back in again at the first opportunity! And the reason they give is usually something like they've never had so much fun at work before. You know … all that applause and star treatment and gift bags … It's a real problem for the Dispatcher."

"M'ims goes out to see if hims can hims me see!"

"Free, stay right where you are! That's all we need! The Dispatcher to spot us outside Sophia."

"By the grandhimhim or by silverherehim, Thee?"

"Pray the grandhimhim, Mr. Higgs Boson, is no where near here! And make no mistake about it, Free, no human has ever seen us while we're working. Ever! Impossible!")

Sophia blushed, *'Dreaming! But I wasn't dreaming, I was thinking deeply! There's a difference between dreaming and thinking!'*

"Well, Sophia, are you ready?"

Her Grandfather and Sophia studied each other again.

When her Grandfather had her full attention, he locked his eyes on hers and spoke very, very flintily but not exactly unkindly either, "You really do remind me of my son! Your Father. He'd stand there just like you are now. Not talking, looking like he was a million miles away. As if the whole world should stand still just so he could dream. But now is not the time for dreaming. Now is the time for action. Don't you want to hear those voices I told you about? Those theatre voices?"

Two words got through. *'Theatre Voices!'*

'I'm going to hear Theatre Voices. I! Have a date! To hear! Voices!'

Then more got through, *'My Father didn't talk either? And he liked to dream too? If my Father could do it, why can't I? Miss Kitty says the same thing about me, about how I need the whole world to stand still while I think. But they don't understand, the world goes too fast and I have to slow it all down so I can figure it all out. That way my ears can listen, my head can surmise. And I need time to do that. Why is that so wrong?'*

"Dreaming is for nighttime. I need to know, are you with me, or do you want to stay here and dream?"

Though Sophia's eyes were as wide as they could be, her ears were back to catching the sound of what he said and not so much his words.

"Well, Sophia, you didn't answer me, are you ready for action?"

They stared at each other. Sophia didn't want such a bossy boss to know that her insides were by now so filled up with all she had just thought because all she'd just thought had caused her to think some more, and she wasn't ready for a new question. She was still stuck in her very private thoughts that wanted to stay private. And double besides: she couldn't imagine actually sharing her thinking experiences with a real person right now. Like she did last night when she actually told him that he might know about voices! his type of voices! these Theatre Voices! but that she knew about voices too! her kind of voices! her Movie Star Voices! including the voices she heard around her, like his and all the others? Oh! How ever did she tell such a bossy boss all of what she did tell him last night? But even last night, when he was speaking to her in his sillier voice, she hadn't really told him she actually did their voices. He was a grown-up person, after all. Grown-ups couldn't possibly understand about pretending.

When she didn't say anything, her Grandfather, without taking his eyes off her, spoke again, "Now is the time to learn something new, see different sights" and he bent down, caught her eye, held it and said, "and hear voices like you've never heard before." And then he whispered, "I've been looking at you, and I can't say for sure that you've been with me, even though you're standing there. And even though you haven't told me you were dreaming, you haven't denied it either. But I believe you were, and by that look in your eye, you just might again. Another thing: I'm not sure you've been really listening to me either. I think you may've just been listening to what's going on inside yourself. You might be remembering things that happened yesterday, or the day before or even the day before that. But this is today and you're going out with me today, and what I need you to do today is be here and to really see and to really hear what I'm taking you to see and to hear. I want you to learn something. Remember you've never heard theatre voices. You've only heard your movie voices …"

'Movie Voices … he said Movie Voices! … would he understand? …'

"… And I want you to hear my theatre voices. Really hear them. And to do all that, you've got to open up every part of you – which means Sophia, your eyes will have to see what's right in front of them and your ears will have to hear the sounds that are happening right then and there. Sophia, you have to be here. And if you're dreaming, you'll miss it all."

And then he stood up and said firmly, "Well, Sophia, are you ready?"

'Did he just see inside me?' This time, she heard his every word. And was startled. She could even feel that her blush completely covered her face and reached even to her toes and her hair roots.

'How does he know that I'm always listening to what's going on inside myself? Does that mean he knows I do Movie Voices, too? Last night, he did say that I was an actor. But I don't understand - how could such a bossy boss be nice?'

But even as she wondered if he knew her whole secret, she knew he was right about her dreaming. And she liked that he was right. And she really liked that he, the bossy boss, figured out what she really really was up to. If only she could stop blushing.

"Yes or no? Will you talk to me and tell me your answer?"

'Of course I will! Come on mouth say it. I can pay attention. I can stop dreaming. I can stop thinking deep thoughts. He's taking me to hear voices! No one's ever taken me just to hear voices. Great Aunt Hortense'd never do that—'

"YeeeSSsss, granDfaTHER! I'm reaDY!"

In a mixed up hush/bark, she spoke. And it might have been a blurt, a blat, a scratch, a noise. And it wasn't music. It was hardly spoken by a Movie Star either. But she didn't care. Those were her words. And she was amazed at how good she felt when she said them.

"Then we're off! Stay with me now!"

She waved good-bye to Antoinette Fifi.

He opened the door and her two feet glided onto the porch but her Grandfather's pounced and then took off as if jet propelled.

She'd have to run to ever keep up with him.

• • • REALLY HERE • • •

As she ran across that porch, out of the corner of her eye, she caught a glimpse of the city way below; she stopped in her tracks and peeked. It was vast. Even from way up here, it didn't look like the city she had seen in any of her Movies.

'That's because it's real.' And then something else occurred to her. *'I'm real too! And I'm really here. And I'll be the one walking through the city this time, not a Movie Star. I won't be watching a Movie Star. I won't be watching anyone. Today, I'll be walking through it myself. I'll be the one having the adventure.*

'But who will be watching me?' And she imagined strolling on a crowded city street. Just as she was. Herself. And no one really seeing her.

But that city was slam-banging her eyes, her ears, her everything, and a corner of her eye would never help her understand all that lay beneath her. Oh, how she wished her head could pivot all the way around to take in all those many, many buildings of so many different styles and sizes, with their slanted roofs and flat roofs and crowns and turrets, stretching everywhere! This place was bigger than she ever imagined it to be.

'How will they even see me?'

And then she remembered, *'Grandfather!'* She dared not lose him but didn't find him anywhere near where she was so she ran even faster. Soon she was beside those funny-shaped trees. Still no Grandfather and she could only hear the city; it was singing to her.

'Is that a trumpet? A trumpet? It's like the old funny jazz horn music my Father used to play for us when we lived in our little house and danced at night. But who ever could be playing the trumpet way up here?'

As she ran, Sophia looked all around but could only see trees. No one was up here. And she gave up trying to find the trumpet player. But the trumpet wasn't the only sound she heard: there were beeps, deep low booms, crashes echoing; some of the sounds were harsh and loud, some were almost sweet, some funny sounding, some even thundering but whatever sound it was, it would fade even as whole other sounds started up. And together they mixed up and hummed; up high, way down low and everywhere in between.

'Music is everywhere if you just listen for it! That's what Grandfather says. Yes, there's a trumpet playing and it's playing melody and the beeps are the bass and that hum is the harmony and those crashes are the cymbals!' And all of it all together made her feel giddy, like dancing, like singing, like talking, like being a Movie Star, like putting on a show just like she did at night when no one was looking. And she ran and wondered - who could she be? Audrey Hepburn? Katherine Hepburn? Ginger Rogers? But she didn't have time to imagine, or she'd never find her Grandfather so she just kept running, running through that forest on that roof so she would find him.

·∴☾∴·

("Do hear you? Do hear you?" said Free.

"Free, what? The city noise? The hums? That trumpet sound?" said Thee.

"Means me that trumpet, YES, Thee! That trumpet! That no sound, Thee! Friend that."

Thee said, "Free, whatever do you mean?" but then turned to speak to Be.)

·∴☽∴·

Sophia knew this day would be like no other and didn't want to miss it. She was on an adventure. This roof. These trees. This garden. The city below. They were all a part of it. AND she had to spend the whole day with her Grandfather, a bossy boss - BUT a bossy boss with x-ray eyes who'd seen inside her but who was kind about what he saw in there. AND on top of all that, she was about to spend an entire day listening to Voices! What perfection! For her! AND her ears! And she smiled.

Had she'd been close enough to see her Grandfather, she would've seen that he wasn't smiling at all. He was waiting at the large gate that led to the elevator, looking at his watch. And no! He wasn't smiling at all.

• • • SWEET REVA SWEET • • •

"Sophia, do you know who Robinson Crusoe and his Man Friday are?"

Not only wasn't he smiling, he wasn't waiting for her answer either—

"Well, today, I'm Robinson Crusoe and you're my Girl Friday. They stuck together, and so will we. So Girl Friday, I've planned a big day for you filled with much to see and hear. Your job is to listen and to learn what I've brought you to hear and to experience. So the first thing you must do is walk a whole lot faster than that so you can keep up with me. Which means you need to be right by my side so I can point things out to you. And Friday! I intend my experiment to succeed."

… or even a nod from her head …

"And Friday, I don't like my time wasted, so walk fast and pay attention!"

Sophia, who had been feeling so understood just moments ago, was nervous all over again. Who was THIS Grandfather? He didn't sound the way he sounded when he had seen inside her. That man was gone. And so was the one who had waved his fingers all about conducting an invisible orchestra. Who sang about a mouse in his house. He was long gone. That man liked to play. But this man was Very Serious. This man was Bossy Boss. That's what had a grip on him now. And that's what had a grip on her now, too.

But then his phone rang and, as he raced to the waiting elevator, one hand held his phone to his ear as the other chopped the air impatiently for her to follow him. And she did. And during the entire elevator ride, he barked into his phone, "10% percent of the gross from the first dollar! Is she crazy? This is theatre! Not those flim-flam-film-shops with their black-clad hipsters!," "NO!," or "box-office receipts." But mostly, it was "box-office" this, "box-office" that.

'Box-office? What is box-office? It must be life or death to him!'

When the elevator stopped and the door opened, Sophia saw a young man who was slouched against the wall light up like an electric scoreboard. Until he took one look at her Grandfather, bowed his head and whispered as if in church, "Good Morning, Mr. Oomla! Miss Oomla! The car is waiting, sir. Here is your schedule, sir!" Sophia, with her considerable experience studying Movie characters, heard right off the bat that the young man had a very sporty voice that he was doing his utmost to disguise. He was even twinkling his eyes cherubically and then floating them up and onto her Grandfather's. *'Well, his eyes may be holy angels but the rest of him is a hot dog and no matter how hard he tries, he'd never pass for even an Irish Saint.'*

Her Grandfather snatched the schedule from the young man's outstretched hand, even as he barked more mumbo-box-office-jumbo into his phone. Though her Grandfather now had the schedule in his hand, he didn't read it; he didn't even look at it, he just folded it carefully only to then absentmindedly scrunch it up and roll it into the pocket of his overcoat. And then he took off down that white marble corridor, still barking into his phone. His Girl Friday dared not lose him; she took off too.

But she was still behind. The young man fell in beside Sophia lessening his stride to stay with her and as they ran, he spoke so that only she could hear, "Hey, Sophia, welcome to Show Business! I'm Bart Barone, a wolf from your Grandfather's pack of personal assistants. I'd like to tell you that I'm the Alpha Wolf but I cannot tell a lie because, let me tell you, entre nous, everybody in our pack thinks they're the Alpha Wolf. Til your Grandfather shows up. He's not only The Man, but he's an 800 pound gorilla besides, Sophia. We wolves have planned quite a day for you. Your Grandfather wants you to hear theatrical voices. Well, guess what you'll be hearing to-day? And if you said theatrical voices, you'd be correct! Our first stop will be a rehearsal at the Sarah Bernhardt Theatre, one of your Grandfather's Theatres—"

Bart Barone shut his mouth fast; her Grandfather had disappeared. As they were about to run through the lobby door, Sophia took one last look at the white marble road and thought about the night before. *'So much has happened to me since I walked up that hall! Who would've thought that the next time I'd be walking down it, I'd be on my way to hear Voices?'*

Sophia and Bart watched her Grandfather step up into the back seat of a high black car whose windows were as black as the car itself. Sophia never saw black windows before; she couldn't see her Grandfather though she knew he was inside. *'How will I ever be able to see my city looking out black windows?'* Hovering by the open back door were two doormen, neither of whom were Keys the Doorman, and who were murmuring "Certainly, Mr. Oomla!" "My pleasure, Mr. Oomla!"

'They sure are making a fuss over my Grandfather.' The doormen turned to Sophia, one of them reached out his hand to assist Sophia into the back of the car but Bart winked at Sophia and, like a white knight, made a great show of giving Sophia his arm. The doorman parted to let them pass. *'Everybody's looking at me!'* And she stepped up and into the back of the car. *'I'm like a Movie Star. Look at me!'* Then from her seat behind her Grandfather, she watched Bart turn to the doormen and hand each of them a crisp five dol-lar bill and with a toss of his head, "Gentlemen, thank you!" snapped he, "Thank you, sir!" snapped they, and Bart whammed into the seat beside Sophia. The doormen shut the doors soundlessly and the car drove off.

"Your Grandfather is their recess-money!" Fred leaned into Sophia and whispered.

But he mustn't have whispered low enough because her Grandfather turned full round in his seat, looked Bart square in the face, stopped bark-ing into his phone and barked instead at Bart, "No, Bart, I'm not their recess money, my shows are their recess money. In fact, they're your recess money too. Mine too! Today! But if I flop, Bart, that could change on a dime. On a dime and never forget it! Y'a ever hear that song, Bart, 'Brother Can You Spare a Dime?' Well listen to it sometime." And before he had even turned back round his seat, he was barking into his phone.

As her Grandfather spoke, Sophia had been listening and watching. Even bouncy Bart was less so as he spoke; though not entirely because Sophia could see his feet tapping away noiselessly on the car's floor. Sophia certainly knew what flop meant and hoped her Grandfather didn't ever flop. But she didn't want to think about flopping now that she knew what it was like not to flop like she did at school; now that she had had all eyes on her as she slid into the back of a big dark car like a real Movie Star. She turned away from both of them and saw with great relief that she would be able to see out these black windows after all. *'Nobody can see inside. So … wait a minute … that means nobody can see me being a Movie Star.'* Was she disappointed.

But shouts, laughter, horns, roaring motors, shrieking teenagers, car radios, arguments in those taxidriver's accent, voices that didn't at all come from anywhere-near-heaven, bus roars, sirens, police radios; all of it fading in, blaring out; loud, soft, faraway, gone for good; then something entirely new would blare and fade all over again and she forgot her disappointment.

'Driving through the village never sounds like this.' She scooched over to the window and pressed her forehead against the dark glass so she wouldn't miss a thing. These morning people were just like those night people she saw yesterday when she first drove through the city with Mr. James; they certainly weren't anything like the people from her old Movies. Where were the gangster suits? The wide-brimmed hats? The top-hats? The plumed-hats? The veils? What were these people wearing? Where were the men in tails and the ladies in satin capes? These ladies hairstyles were nothing like what she saw in the old Movies either. These people were ordinary people, like the people from the village. Except there were so many of them. *'It's a wonder they don't knock each other over.'* Sophia kept her eyes peeled to see if anybody would.

The car stopped at a curb and, in an instant, a swarm of people attached themselves to it; one of them opened her Grandfather's door. Her Grandfather, who was still barking on his phone, sprang out of the car and started barking at these people. Bart sprang out, too, and was already at Sophia's door opening it. Sophia stepped out and, wonder of wonders, the people that were surrounding her Grandfather turned to look at her. And it happened again, that feeling of being seen, really seen, looked at, stared at, appreciated, admired. Several people smiled at her. Sophia stopped dead in her tracks, oblivious to everything around her, and smiled back at these wonderful, friendly, nice, kind people who seemed to really like her and wanted to be her friend because they were giving her such understanding looks and warm smiles probably because she was so dazzling like a Movie Star in her gorgeous clothes.

·∴(·∴

("Uh oh!" said Be.

"Well, wouldja just listen to her!" said Lorraine.

"Duh Fairies! That is, like, how I feel all the time. But then I'm not so sure any of you would understand." Me then winked a wicked wicked wink which they ignored.

"She'ms feel even better soons! She'ms will."

"Thee, hey, can't we just zip out and poke around?" said Lorraine. "We could check on Sophia, then take a quick look-see around the Theatre. I've always wanted to check out a human Theatre. Even you gotta admit, Thee, their movies are something else. So maybe their Theatres are, ya know, like action-packed, too."

"Lorraine! We are staying put. And Fairies? Weren't you listening to what Sophia just thought? Confident is the way we want Sophia to feel, especially now that we are reaching the end of our journey with her; but super confident presents a whole other predicament. Why Sophia seems more confident than I've ever known her to feel and I don't like it. For one thing, how does she know what kind of people those people are? Just because they're smiling at her, that doesn't mean they're nice. This is the big city after all, run by humans, I might add!"

"For once, can't you just let her enjoy this feeling, Thee?' said Be. "How many times has she ever felt like this? The only time I ever remember her feeling this way is when she's surrounded by a party of no one in front of her television set acting like a character she isn't, in clothes that are several sizes too big for her. Right now, she's just being herself, not a character, and she's in cool clothes that fit her and she feels good. Let her enjoy the feeling."

"Be's right, Thee. Relax.")

·∴)·∴·

"Sophia, your Grandfather's almost inside!" said Bart, "and we're supposed to be right beside him. We can't be late for the rehearsal. And it's my job to get you there. He'll kill me if you're late. You don't want to see a future Hollywood agent dead before he ever wraps his first three-picture-deal."

Even though she heard every word Bart said, Sophia reluctantly stepped out of her dream cloud to find herself standing on a pavement outside a

Theatre with a marquis over her head. And there was Bart who was bright red and, even though it was such a cold day, sweating. Bart turned to her and said on the down-low and hush-hush, "Hey Sophia, can you keep a secret? Remember I just described myself as a future Hollywood agent? Could you not tell your Grandfather I said that. Your Grandfather is not a big fan of Hollywood. So, whatdaya think, ya gonna turn me in?" He started to run, and she ran right after him and whispered on the down-low and hush-hush right back at him, "No, Bart. I'm no squealer." Sophia remembered that line from a movie. She just wished she could add the other part ... about not being a stool pigeon. But she wasn't sure what a stool pigeon was. She'd never looked up those words in her Father's dictionary. But suddenly, she didn't care and said it anyway because the line wasn't right without it, "I'm no stool pigeon, neitha!"

Out of the corner of his mouth, Bart spat, "Say kid, I could tell when I first laid eyes on ya, ya wuz OK. And no stool pigeon neitha. Any joe couldda seen dat." Then Bart winked at her.

Sophia was dumbfounded. Bart had a gutter-rat-voice, too. Bart did voices. And not only that, he saw the exact same movie. And remembered the lines from it, too. Word for word. Just like she had. And it was an old Movie, too. The kids at school would never've been able to do that; they didn't know the old Movies.

"Yeah, Sophia, don't look so surprised, I love that movie, *Rats in the Gutter*. I see you're an old Movie aficionado also. The lines from that Movie have served me and my wolf colleagues very well. Especially working in your Grandfather's office. And in this city. AND in this business. Three cheers for the Movies from the Golden Years!!"

Was Bart like her? The idea just about bowled her over. Was Bart someone who might really and truly and finally understand her? Did Bart have his own Movie Star School too? She felt her mouth opening, ready to ask him, knowing full well that if she did, she'd be revealing her deep secret to a stranger. But they'd just reached the lobby and there was her Grandfather laying down the law to even more people and now was hardly the time.

"Mr. Tiglione, for this rehearsal, use the alternate lighting design. I want to see what effect that one has."

"Yes, Mr. Oomla."

"Mr. DeBeauvancamp, there are too many chairs on the set! I can't have a $25,000 a week star tripping and falling on her hindermost on a set of mine."

"Yes, Mr. Oomla."

Round and round, he went, to each person, each of them answering him very quickly and so respectfully. Sophia began to count up all the people she'd seen her Grandfather give orders to today. *'Not counting my Grandmother because she sassed him back; Antoinette Fifi, the doormen, Bart, and from the way he's been talking to me lately, me too, and now all of these people. At least twelve.'*

Her Grandfather was the Boss of Everybody.

Bart was beckoning her to follow him. He opened a set of doors and she walked through not knowing what she'd find on the other side. But there it was! A theatre! With a million seats, all empty, not a soul in them. And then she saw what every seat was facing.

The stage! With not a person on it.

And a thousand souls rose up within her ready to fill up that wide open space. Oh, how she was dying to swoop onto that stage and let them fly.

·∴᛭∵·

("Can't we go? Can't we go? I wanna see. C'mon. It won't take a second. I'll run like a Vamoose." said Lorraine.

"Think of the Dispatcher, Lorraine. We're right where we should be. By her heart. Fairies, no one ever said our job would be easy." said Thee.)

·∴☽∵·

And jump and race and shout and scream and cry and faint and collapse and float and tramp and vamp and flirt. Oh! How she wanted to be on that stage doing all of that and so much more. Had she'd been all by herself, no Bart, no Grandfather, she would've gunned down the aisle, shot up those steps and splattered herself all over that stage. But just then her Grandfather walked in with several people following him close behind and she forced that itching, aching, pining longing out of her. But it wouldn't leave; it walked with her when Bart led her to one of the rows of seats; when she sat, it sat. The feeling. Such a feeling. And it wasn't a funny feeling; no, this feeling was serious; yet she felt giddy, like she had been hit by a train but she wasn't hurt. She felt flipped and spun and wheeled and looped and light-headed. Better than she ever felt before. And she knew exactly what was making her feel this way. The stage. All she had to do was look at it, and she was up there on it, doing a thousand, no a million, different things.

·∴᛭∵·

("Titania! Ruler of us all! Fairies, look at her heart!" said Thee.

"Holy elfing—!"

They stood in awe.

"And here we are! Fairies! who are used to the odd, the spectacle, the curious happenstance. Is Sophia's heart doing—"

"the, like, charleston? … the fandango?" said Lorraine.

"Or is it just beating like it never beat before? Can a heart even dance?"

They were captivated, utterly and stayed right where they were and didn't even think of leaving.

"Theatre! Who needs theatre when we're already watching the impossible, a heart doing the—"

"The hootchie-cootchie! The rhumba!")

····)····

Sophia was horrified when people, actual people, not phantom Sophias, not dolled-up Sophias, not wildest-dream-Sophias, not elephants-fly Sophias, but real people walked onto her stage. And in the very next second, her Grandfather barked again and she almost jumped out of her seat, he was that close. She turned to see exactly where he was. Right next to her! And she hadn't even noticed.

"Well Sophia, are you ready to hear?"

"Oh, yes, Grandfather, I am." Her dancing heart wasn't waiting around for her to get up the nerve to speak. It spoke for her.

Talk was coming from all over the stage that was now crawling with stage-hands moving furniture, a piano, all sorts of stuff onto it. Then lights were beamed down - one light then another, then more, then less, then none; then lights that made circles that would move up, down and sideways on the stage. Then shouts to move the furniture here, there, no back to here, try there. Back and forth. And Sophia watched as if it was the most interesting thing she'd seen in her entire life.

And then the stagehands exited. And the lights went off on the stage and in the theatre. And she couldn't see anything. Everything was black, everyone still. Even her Grandfather. And from the stage, she heard - Foot. Steps. That were slow, so slow, so meandering, so this way, then that. Each step echoing throughout the theatre as if they were prancing on a gigantic drum. High heels. Sophia's ears felt tingly. No doubt about it, those heel clicks were coming from A. Woman. *Footsteps just footsteps are filling up this whole place. How could that be?'* And as they sat in the pitch black, suddenly a single light went on that was as bright as the sun. And in the exact center of that sunbeam was a woman. And she was facing them.

Sophia examined every inch of her: there were those high-heels and not a drum in sight. They were just ordinary high-heels. How did such small things make a sound big enough to fill up a place as huge as this? Then she looked at the rest of the footsteps-woman. No doubt about it, she was not anywhere as pretty as Audrey Hepburn, who was her favorite. Today. She wasn't anywhere as pretty as most Movie Stars Sophia could think of.

'Grandfather is not as right as he thinks he is about these types of actresses!'

Sophia turned to glare at him as if to tell him so but he wasn't paying any attention to her and she turned back to take in more of this type of actress. But just at that moment this type of actress opened her mouth.

"George ... well ... he's so ... so—"

And suddenly there was a lot more than just tickling inside Sophia.

"It's just ... I thought ... but ... he—"

'How can she sound that way? She's only talking.'

"He wasn't anythere ... Where! ... No! Oh!"

'Oh ... the poor thing is blushing because she said a word wrong. I do that too sometimes. Oh, look she's about to cry. But she's trying not to. Oh, listen to her voice now that she's trying not to cry. Would I ever be able to sound like that if I were trying not to cry? How does she get ... oh look her eyes are sparkling. Or are they just tears shining them up so?'

This poor sad soul in such high heels who couldn't possibly be acting kept talking about someone named George. And this George she was talking about didn't seem to ever talk about her, because that's what she said. And then this enchanting sad soul in such high heels laughed. Until she stopped. And she looked out into the theatre and Sophia was absolutely certain, right at her where she sat in the sunless, pitch-black theatre. And then this enchanting sad soul cried a river at her. And Sophia smiled a rainbow back, hoping that for now it would cheer up that lovely sad creature in such high heels and with that captivating voice. And for the rest of her life. But oh how the sad creature still ached about George, this oh so pretty-voiced-lady in such high heels, the sound of her rising way up high then crashing way down low as she breathed and talked and sighed and laughed laughs low and long and tried so so hard not to cry anymore that the slam of it all skimmed and bounced then vibrated til it penetrated straight through Sophia, shaking her up so. And from what was raining and storming down from that stage, Sophia was certain, the theatre's very walls and seats must be soaked and shaking, too. She peeked at Bart. And her Grandfather's people. All of them, the same. Watching, listening. And oh how sad they all looked. Even her Grandfather. *'What sort of person could this George be? How could he be so mean to such a creature?'* But then a piano began to play and then this angel-sad began to sing.

⋯⋆☾⋯

("Thee was the first one out, Lady!"

"And Lorraine, in the swish of a unicorn's tale, the rest of you followed. But Ms. Author, we simply couldn't believe our ears as we perched on the edge of the back of the seat in front of Sophia and listened to the sad human lady who could sing like one of our siren relatives.")

⋯☽⋆⋯

And Sophia wondered no more. *'George, that he-devil! Must be deaf, dumb and blind for the beauty of the lady can be seen and heard by everybody here!'*

Just like that everything was black again but that didn't stop this swan and her song from flying around that theatre or her high heels from brushing its beat gently along the stageboards. Sophia felt like she was flying, too, as she hung on to every note even as they grew fainter and fainter until they stopped altogether. But her Grandfather barked and then like a whack, the lights came on. Sophia, who had been heartaching and bellyaching and nearly toothaching for the sad beautiful lady, almost slid to the floor.

⋯⋆☾⋯

("Ms. Author, each and every one of us were in tears and couldn't move from our edge on the top of the seatback. We had lost our senses. Really lost our senses for we didn't even notice that we had a visitor, I'm deeply ashamed to report!")

⋯☽⋆⋯

"Now, Sophia, off to the back row. We'll listen to the next set there.

⋯⋆☾⋯

("Ms. Author, this is difficult to confess but we didn't even notice that Sophia and her Grandfather had gotten up and moved away." said Thee. "The only thing our eyes had eyes for was sweet Reva Sweet on that stage.")

⋯☽⋆⋯

"I want you to hear how every word a well-trained theatre actor utters on that stage - from a whisper to a shout - can be heard and not just heard but understood clearly, with ease, without a single audience member, especially those in the back, straining forward in their seat trying to hear. Any good theatre actor worth his salt must be able to do that. But that isn't the only thing he must be able to do. In fact, that's just the beginning. Think back on the performance you just saw. How did you feel as Reva Sweet told us her story?"

Sophia was about to say 'Ooh, so sad' but her Grandfather didn't wait for an answer.

"How did you feel when she sang her song?"

And again Sophia's answer was all ready, "Ooh—" but again her Grandfather didn't wait for an answer. Even Sophia recognized how strange this was. *Imagine me! Dying to answer a grown-up's question! Dying to talk! And imagine an adult talking to me officially about acting. I've never had an adult talk to me officially about acting before. I mean, I've talked to Miss Kitty about it - sort of – in fact, she is the only person I've ever talked to about acting, but Miss Kitty is really just listening to me talk about it—'*

And suddenly Sophia missed Miss Kitty. Miss Kitty listened to her. More than her Grandfather was doing right now. She couldn't wait to see Miss Kitty again. Although, she had to admit, as much as she loved Miss Kitty, there was a big difference between Miss Kitty and her Grandfather. *'Miss Kitty doesn't work with actors every day of her life the way Grandfather does and Miss Kitty doesn't know what Grandfather knows about actors. So I've never had an opportunity like this before! To talk to a grown-up about my favorite subject, my best subject, when that person knows as much as I do ... But he's not letting me talk!'*

"Sophia, I do believe I know what you felt."

"But Gra—'

"I believe that however you felt when you sat down in your seat before Ms Sweet's performance began—"

'He still won't let me talk! Finally somebody is talking to me about acting but that somebody doesn't want to hear what I have to say! When will it be my turn to talk? Somebody is always jumping onto the stage before I ever even have a chance to get there! It may never be my turn.'

She could feel her tears begin to gush. But she couldn't let that happen in front of her Grandfather. After all, she was trying to be grown up on her first trip by herself to the city. A glamorous Movie Star wouldn't cry on her first trip to the city. But as hard as she tried, she couldn't stop the tears from welling up in eyes. The least she could do was will them not to roll down her face. She could even feel what she wanted to say try to push itself out of her, but she was far too polite to let it.

"In fact, how did you feel when you sat down in your seat, Sophia?"

And again her Grandfather didn't wait for her to answer. He didn't even notice that her eyes were now floating in a lake. He was making his point and was not about to pay attention to anyone or anything else.

"I'll imagine what you felt. Here you are a ten-year-old girl: one day you're in school, the next, you find yourself not even in your tiny village but being driven through this larger than life city, my city, staring out the window of the back seat of a car at all of the different sights, the fantastic next to the unheard of and just ten feet away from an alley of ashcans and all of that just six feet away from a marquee that glitters. And the people! Beauties, troglodytes, bums, thugs, punks, homeboys, billionaires, fashionistas, and all of them sticking out like sore thumbs from the rest of the 99.9 percent of the people who dress in colorless clothes that hang on them like recycled cardboard. And watch as 99.8 of them look the other way when they pass a homeless person in tatters - just watch - but that's a whole other story. And the sound of it all - as George Gershwin's song says, is a Fascinatin' Rhythm, whose music I always hear playing in my head when I'm roving through the city, even when it's not playing.

"Now, Sophia that's what you watched from your seat in the car, and as you did, I bet you must have felt happy, excited, interested. There are different sights here than in your village, aren't there? And I'm sure you must have felt delighted to be on such an unexpected adventure. And then wonders of wonders, you are escorted into a theatre, and this theatre you are escorted into belongs to your Grandfather, the paterfamilias, a theatre where people get to tell their stories on a stage. So there you are, this happy, excited, interested person, and the lights in the theatre are turned off and you are sitting in the dark, not knowing what to expect when suddenly you're listening to one of those characters from the streets tell her story - and it's a sad one - then sing a song - and it's a sad one - and then the next thing you know, you, Sophia, the happy, excited, interested person are sad, too. You're full of sorrow. I bet you even wanted to cry. All because Reva Sweet, an actor, was doing her job. The song required her to be sad, and she was. She genuinely acted sad and she genuinely sang sad, she made sure you could clearly see every expression on her face and clearly hear every note, every sound, every word that came out of her, even from where you were sitting, am I not correct? And it wasn't just that you could understand what she said. You also could feel how she felt. Any person sitting in that audience had to be moved listening to her, if that person had a heart.

"And now my young miss, you try to do that from a stage! You try to make sure that every word you say, whether spoken with great feeling and strong emotions or said simply and plainly, is understood and experienced by every member of your audience - who happens to be far away from you. That is the task of the stage actor! Imagine Sophia if that was your task ..."

And Sophia, who had, at first, tried desperately not to listen to this man who had just barreled over her, had gradually become less and less tearful and more and more spellbound as her Grandfather spoke. *'He knows so much and he talks so good! He's like an expert, an expert who can talk. I may know stuff about acting too, but I can't exactly hold forth about it the way he can!'* He had overpowered her and she surrendered. He knew more than she did. But when he reached the part about her trying to do that from a stage, she knew one thing he didn't know. That she could over-power him, overpower everyone, if only she could get up on that stage. And that she didn't require even a speck of imagination to see herself up there on that stage doing that very thing, doing all that he'd just said. She could do it too. And so much more. Naturally. Longing-ly. Ecstatically.

"... that all of what you say and do and feel up there on that stage must be understood by every member of the audience. But then you couldn't possibly know how difficult that is to do because I know you are not a Stage Actor—"

'He knows I'm not a Stage Actor!' Sophia almost screamed. *'He knows I'm not a Stage Actor because I haven't told him who I am. I may not be a Stage Actor yet but I bet I could do what Reva Sweet did, if somebody'd just let me! And I certainly am a Movie Star ... or at least I could be ... And someday I will be! I have to tell him. I must tell him. And I will.'*

And she opened her mouth to do just that but her mouth, the guardian of her locked up and hidden away secret, must've either have felt too scared to show its all too apparent lack of practice in Speaking Spunk in the Real World because maybe it knew if you spoke spunk you'd have to act spunk or maybe it wanted no part of the risky scheme to expose her True Self and Deep Secret that she'd kept hidden away for so many years to a stranger even if he was talking to her like an expert about the very thing she believed she was an expert on too - because her mouth, that no-nonsense gatekeeper, that take-no-prisoners-but-one - wouldn't open.

"... And incidentally, when an actor does that from a stage, that's called projection. Sophia, you try to feel all of that and say all of that and sing all of that and then have to project it out into a vast space, a space as large as this space. Well, Sophia, now tell me, was I right, is that how you felt, did you feel sad and sorrowful? Or am I wrong?" And at long last he looked at her with searching eyes and said not a word but waited for her answer.

Which tsunamied out of her. "I bet a Movie Star could do that too!"

It wasn't what she hoped to say. But she did speak it without stammer-ing or stuttering a word of it, which should've pleased her more than it did. Because, oh, how she would've loved to tell him the real truth. *'I could do everything you're talking about - this projection thing - even though I've never done it before - why couldn't I do it? - I'm an actress, after all.'* Again she was dying to tell somebody about her Movie Star School. *'But how could Grandfather ever understand about a Movie Star School? Since he's so wrong about Movie Stars anyway. Although he sure seems to know a lot about acting!'*

But she couldn't pull it out of her to tell him. *'So what does it matter?*

'When elephants fly!' That's what that kid in school said would happen when she finally did talk. But now she understood something else entirely about elephants and herself. *'If I tell him all that I'm thinking, an elephant just might fly. And so would I.'*

She could feel every word the elephant was longing to say. *'Yes, Grandfather, I did feel sad, you're right about that. But you are not at all right about me. I AM an Actress – even though you call everybody Actors. Actors! Why do you call Actresses Actors? How could any man actor ever be Audrey Hepburn or Sophia Loren or Marilyn Monroe or Ginger Rogers? Why if somebody called Ginger Rogers a boy, she'd knock him down. And by the way, I have my very own Movie Star School and I act in that school every chance I get. Being a Movie Star is my life! Is WHAT I LOVE. I am the Midnight Movie Star! And when I'm not the Midnight Movie Star, I'm dreaming about BEING the Midnight Movie Star. Even when I'm just walking down the steps, when I'm brushing my hair, my teeth; when I'm doing anything, I'm doing it the way a Movie Star would. And incidentally, why couldn't a Movie Star do all that up there on that stage and make a person feel sad too? Why if you'd give me a chance, I could show you because I know I could do just that!'*

And the elephant did fly, "I bet a Movie Star could do that too!" Her Grandfather looked as if an elephant had just punched him in the nose. And he punched him right back.

"Young lady, I heard you the first time! I really must set you straight about Movie Stars. Movie Stars simply can't project! Because Movie Stars rely on their faces to express how they feel.

"Oh, don't get me wrong, Movie Stars can certainly express themselves with their voices, too. They might have tricky voices, sultry voices, distinctive voices, any number of alluring, even arresting voices; but on a stage, those very qualities, can't usually be projected by that Movie Star beyond the tenth row. On a stage when it's time to talk, a Movie Star better know how to make their special, tricky voice heard throughout the entire house or what they're trying to do with that voice will be lost after the tenth row.

"Yes, it's true, just like in the Movies, up there on a stage, an actor can just express themselves with their face, too. But young lady, I want you to look at that stage and look at where we are way back here in the last row.

Tell me, Sophia, from where we are, how much of a person's face do you think we can really see? I can tell you not enough to know how they are really feeling. And that's why, young lady, a stage actor must have a voice, too!"

As if on cue several actors walked on the stage and Sophia's blushing face turned to look at them. Her Grandfather turned, too. And then he called out to the actors. But this time each of his words had a salute at the end of it and Sophia, who made a point of never missing any unusual voice or accent just had to turn and watch her Grandfather speak. She could hear every word he was saying to those actors clearly as if he was shouting at them. Which he wasn't. And Sophia who was so used to studying every part of a Movie Star, could clearly see that the middle part of her Grandfather was moving, the middle part where his belly would be. If he would've had a belly. Which he didn't. Then from the stage, one of the actors answered him. And she could hear every word that actor was saying too, even though he was far away. Projection. That must be what that actor was doing. And that must be what her Grandfather was doing too. Her Grandfather spoke again and this time Sophia watched his middle part where his belly would be – if he would've had one – go up and down. Tonight she would practice making her belly go up and down when she talked just like her Grandfather was doing now. She'd practice this projection. But then the lights went off everywhere in the theatre except on the stage and the actors began the scene.

·⁖·**(**·⁖·

("Oh, Ms. Author, out of the corner of my eye and through a tempest of tears, I must admit that I noticed something unusual - an unfamiliar dark color." said Thee. "I pride myself on always being able to remember what each Fairy is wearing each day. Could Me have slipped away and changed? Could I, who really do pride myself on not missing a trick, just've missed a trick? 'No!' I thought. 'But why would she have changed? Unless she wanted to wear a darker, more dramatic outfit, one that would be more in tune with the singer's sad song? Or maybe she thought the singer's outfit chic-er than her own?' And then Ms. Author, the lights went off again, I couldn't see an inch in front of me again, but I didn't want to use my Fairy power to see. This mysterious, theatrical, human experience was magic enough. But I had to confess, something didn't seem right about my surmises. For one thing, Me never thought anybody was ever dressed better than her, especially a human who, according to Me, could never've even dreamed of dressing better than even the worst-dressed Fairy. I tried again to discern just who or what was in that dark color beside me because now there was a very small amount of light coming from the stage but my vision was still blurry from all those tears and I couldn't make out a thing!")

·⋅⋅⁾⋅⋅·

The scene ended, the lights went back on, and her Grandfather stood up and said, "Come Sophia, we must run. We're late. We're off to another theatre to see the rehearsal of my latest project. Now, I have just one question to ask you? Could you hear every word those stage actors were saying?" But he turned and talked to the group of people who were standing at the end of their row and didn't wait for her reply.

And in a flurry of people and fast walks and ringing, snapping, flashing phones, Sophia found herself sitting next to Bart in the back seat again. As her Grandfather barked, Bart leaned down and whispered in her ear, "Well, Sophia, whadja think?"

And Sophia whispered back, "I loved it, Bart, with my whole heart and my whole soul."

And Bart whispered back, "Yeah, I know. There's no business like Show Business, kid. I feel the exact same way every time I walk into a theatre. Don't tell the Wolves I said so because we make it our business to be cool. 'Image' is, like, everything to the Wolves. Hey, now listen to that - that is my second secret. Pretty soon you'll know all my secrets."

"I'm no squealer, Bart."

"Yeah, I could tell when I first laid eyes on ya' kid!"

But then the true meaning of those *Rat in the Gutter* words hit her. *'I'm no squealer alright. I wouldn't even squeal on myself when I had a chance to. Bart told me his secret. So why couldn't I tell Bart mine? Bart's the one person who'd appreciate it. All I have to do is to ask him to be quiet and listen to me! I might not even have to ask him to be quiet, because he'd want to hear what I have to say! Will I be like this forever? Will I only ever speak up when there's no one around to hear me? When will I let the world know who I am? That I am the Founder AND the Principal AND the Star Pupil of my very own Midnight Movie Star School. AND real Movie Stars are my Teachers. And that one day, someday, I myself will be a real live Movie Star.'*

And now all she could do was sit there imagining what might've happened if she had. It would've been like she herself was in a Movie. Now nobody knew who she really was.

And her whole entire morning ran through her head. She'd had an adventure but only a part of an adventure because she hadn't put her real self in it. She'd only been listening and not talking, not revealing what she was thinking, not acting.

'Oh! Acting!'

And then she imagined herself up on that stage. She didn't know how she'd do it but she would act on that stage. She would. She would.

• • • SOPHIA PROJECTS • • •

Soon Sophia and Bart were walking down the aisle of another theatre. The stage of this theatre was choc-a-bloc not with actors or stagehands but dancing dancers. Bart guided Sophia to a seat and then sat down beside her. And they watched the dancers stretch their arms out wide til their fingertips almost touched those of the dancers next to them. And then their fingers began to move.

"Look, Bart, their fingers are dancing!" Sophia spoke up.

"Would the dancerrthh on THHtage-Left thtay together ppleathhh!" Even without their s's, the words snaked all about.

'He sounds like a nincompoop! But that doesn't stop him from talking out loud!'

"Sophia, I am your handler, and you are my charge! And since you are now in the theatre and at your second real live rehearsal, you need to learn the lingo. Didja hear that guy say Stage Left?" Bart said, "Well, Stage Left means, if you were on the stage facing the audience, that's what you'd call your left side. And that guy who said it, who's talking to the dancers right now, that's the Choreographer. A Choreographer is the person who makes up the dance the dancers dance. So what's Stage Right?" And he looked at her. With no hesitation, Sophia spoke up, "If I was on the stage facing the audience, that's what I'd call my right side!"

Bart winked at her.

"Dancerthhh, downthtage!" said the Choreographer.

And all the dancers shuffled towards the front of the stage.

"From the top!"

"Downstage, Sophia, is if you were on the part of the stage closest to the audience then you'd say you were Downstage. And if you were at the back of the stage, you'd say you were Upstage. Got it?"

Sophia nodded and so did her heart, she could feel it inside her. She was learning the Lingo. The Lingo of the Stage. Bart was right. She really would need to know the Lingo since any day now she too would be performing on the stage, just like Reva Sweet. After, that is, she was a Movie Star in a Movie. First things first. Could Bart have guessed her secret? Is that why he was teaching her the Lingo? She snuck a sideways glance at him. But he looked right back at her and didn't wink. He hadn't guessed.

The Choreographer called out another series of steps and the dancers did those too. And very precisely, Sophia thought. But apparently not precisely enough for the Choreographer. "Together … you call that together … I call that Depart! Which is what thome of you may have to do if you don't get yourthelveth together."

'That's no nincompoop! That's Therf Thoufflé! Could those weary dancers be the pink flamingos?' Sophia looked them over. Their hair was pinned up severely, their faces were sweaty and flushed, none of them were smiling, a few of them even looked like they might pass out. But even without their make-up and their smiles, she remembered those faces. They were the pink flamingos! But they weren't glamour girls anymore! No! They were working girls, hardworking girls. Ordinary girls. She knew they hadn't noticed her, or anyone else in the audience, because they hadn't dared taken their eyes off Serf.

Sophia could hear whispers coming from all around her; who else was filling up the - as Bart called it - 'House' with such noise? There were people holding hushed conversations all about that House. Sophia couldn't help but notice, too, that there was even a group of boys and girls sitting together who looked to be about her age. What were they doing here? But then there were all sorts of people in the House. At the back were workmen on ladders wiping the lamps on the walls; at the front, uniformed maids were silently polishing the grill work on the railing that rimmed the orchestra pit.

In the last row of seats but in the aisle furthest away from Sophia was a group of ladies who were attaching long plumed pink feathers to what had to be the pink flamingo costumes. The sewing ladies were not the best whisperers because even from where Sophia was sitting way on the other side of the House, she could hear every word. One lady's voice, who was talking in scratches, was carrying over all of them. "Now, Thelma, me advice t' you is, just get on y'r hands n' knees n' pray, but when ye do, tis always best t' bypass tose Saints from te Continent n' just pray straight up t' te dear blessed Irish Saints instead; tey'll be te most forgivin', te most understandin' of tat ne'er-do-well y're praying for ten all te Saints put together."

'Miss Kitty!'

Sophia knew her ears never deceived her but she still couldn't believe them. *'Miss Kitty? Here? Just rows away from me?'* She didn't move a muscle so she could hear Miss Kitty go on and on about her favorite subject. Of course, it was Miss Kitty. Who else had a voice of scraggily broom-straws with such an accent who talked about Irish Saints? Her voice sounded like music to her, even though Sophia knew darn well that when she was home and Miss Kitty was far away, or far enough way, or not really too close, she used to mimic it, telling herself that when she was a Movie Star she'd need all sorts of accents and voices - most of them glamorous or dramatic - but some funny, for when she had to do those kind of characters. And she'd be ready: she'd speak like Miss Kitty. But that wasn't the only reason she used to mimic it.

She had to admit, she mimicked it because she was making fun of her.

And Sophia was so remorseful that she said a silent prayer to Miss Kitty's Irish Saints asking them that if Miss Kitty ever did hear her imitate her, that they'd make sure that Miss Kitty knew she never meant to hurt her feelings. She was itching to leap out of her seat and rush over to Miss Kitty but Sophia knew her Grandfather, the Expert on Acting, wouldn't be at all happy to see her go tearing through his Theatre. Her Grandfather was probably a little like Great Aunt Hortense; or even Mr. Snoggley - he had taken her here for one reason. To learn. And in order to learn, he certainly expected her to pay attention to the action on the stage. So he needed her To Listen, To Watch, and she couldn't be listening and watching very well if she was racing through his Theatre.

But something made her peek at Bart and the helpers and all the strangers in the House anyway so she could see just exactly who she'd have to walk in front of to get to Miss Kitty. And everybody she saw was looking at the stage, just like she was supposed to. She couldn't very well get up and start making beelines and then have everyone in the entire house stare at her instead of the stage. And no doubt about it, if she got up from her seat, everybody in that house would be staring at her.

And then she peeked at Serf on the stage and knew she didn't dare move. What would Serf do if she jumped out of her seat and ran clear across the theatre? He'd start hissing and trilling at her for 'dithurbing hith rehearthal!'

She wasn't even sure where her Grandfather was but she didn't dare turn around to find out. What would he think?

And that was that. She was just too perplexed to do anything, and she sat there and did what she always did. But this time as she shrunk down in her seat thinking, she felt the pins of something, the needles of something sticking straight through her in her cocoon. But that didn't stop her from doing what she did best.

But finally those pricks of feelings pushed through where she'd been hiding. Pushed through what she'd been holding up for all to see as if it

were really her. And at long last what Sophia felt flooded through every part of her.

'I'm timid. Is that who am I? I'm so far away from home. From school. From Mr. Snoggley - Yick! From my Movie Star School. From Father. From Mother. From Great Aunt Hortense - Hooray! I'm in this big city! And I'm learning.'

Even as she digested the oh so many confusions and contradictions, even as her old experiences met these new experiences and all of it together percolated away inside her same-old-same-old, brand-new self.

'Grandmother's here. Josephine's here. And so is Antoinette Fifi Merree. And Grandfather! And I'm in the city I've seen in the Movies, but it isn't really like the Movies at all. But I did learn something! I can be a Stage Actress, too.'

And she saw her Grandfather's house with its twisted old trees and its jutting into the clouds roof with its pointy turrets that could poke the moon and probably had because that's why the moon kept staring at the house and spying through its windows.

'That house is mixed-up. It probably thinks it's residing on a street when really it's way way up in the sky, on the tippy top of a tall building.

'But I'm mixed up, too. I act like what's inside me isn't inside me. I'm always wishing something. To be here when I'm there. Or there when I'm here. And here I am wishing again. This isn't my home. This isn't where my Father or my Mother live or where Miss Kitty and Mr. James live, even though Miss Kitty is here too but that's only temporary because she'll be going back home soon, just like I'll be. And, on top of that, it's not where my Movie Star School is either. It isn't even where Mr. Snoggley and each and every one of my fifth grade schoolmates live.

'Mr. Snoggley? Why am I thinking about Mr. Snoggley? Do I miss Mr. Snoggley?'

The thought that finally shocked her awake.

'WHAT AM I DOING?

'I'm sitting here THINKING! I bet I'd rather think the whole entire encyclopedia before I'd ever do anything! I'm not ACTING at all! I should be ashamed of myself. Miss Kitty is here! and I haven't even gotten out of my seat to say hello! It's like I'm sitting here out in the open for all to see but who they're seeing is not me because who I really am and what I want, I'm only thinking about. It's like the real me is hiding inside the fake me. I have to bring the real me to the outside. Before it's too late. And besides, what has all this thinking ever done for me? It hasn't gotten me any closer to Miss Kitty. A Movie Star slash Stage Actress would never just stay in her seat and do nothing. No wonder I like Movie Stars so much. The second they would've heard Miss Kitty, they'd've made bee-lines towards her. But look at me, I haven't budged, and because I haven't, I haven't found Miss Kitty. Miss Kitty doesn't even know I'm

here. Miss Kitty might even get up and leave, and then what'll I do? I'd never find her in this gigantic city.'

Sophia leaped out of her seat. She WOULD find Miss Kitty. The quickest way to reach the sewing ladies was to pick a row that nobody was sitting in then run through the space between the rows. She raced up the aisle and there, in the dark part of the House, she found one. She began to run through that row but it was so dark, she couldn't see that some seats were not pushed into their upright position, and she cracked her knee and tripped on about every other step she took. And to make matters worse, as she pushed those seats upright, quite a few of them squeaked. And, with the way she heard things, every squeak sounded as if it'd been pumped into a public address system then broadcasted throughout the whole entire theatre!

'Everybody gotta be staring at me!' Though she didn't dare lift her head to find out. *'I bet I know what they're thinking. Who's making that irritating noise? Look at her! Who's that skinny kid? She sure isn't any Movie Star! Well! I'm not going to watch them think that. And besides, if I catch somebody's eye, that person might stop me. Or even if nobody stops me somebody might ask me what I'm up to, and I'd never be able to get my mouth to work to explain as perfectly as I know I should, exactly what that was. And besides, what I'm doing is plenty enough for me to handle.'*

And she was handling it. Suddenly she felt proud. And she kept going.

And then the oddest thing occurred to her. *'This is my Movie, and I'm the Star! ... I'm the Squeaky Movie Star!'*

After what felt like a hundred, long years, she reached the ladies. In a blink she saw Miss Kitty, though Miss Kitty didn't see her because she was busy as she herself would've said "gasin' " to the lady next to her.

"Miss Kitty!" Sophia didn't mean to say it so loud. And it was loud because every sound in that entire House and on that stage ceased. She could hear heads turn as if they were on rusty swivels and knew now what she had only believed before. That every eye in every head was looking at her. But this time Sophia didn't hide. This time she didn't keep her head down, didn't look at anyone; this time she picked her head up, turned it round and saw that every flamingo, every workman, every cleaner, every audience member, every Grandfather-helpers' eyes were on her. As were Bart's and Serf's and her Grandfather's, too. But when Miss Kitty said, "Sophia! Tanks be t' me blessed Irish Saints. Telma, woudja jus look what tose Saints brought t' me - me girl! Which just proves what I' been tellin' ye' all along about Irish Saints!"

It was as if Sophia had just stepped off the freezing cold Arctic tundra and was handed a soft blanket, steamy hot chocolate and warm, buttered bread. She turned away from all those eyes, and with sore eyes that now felt all better, watched Miss Kitty, with her bright eyes, her flushed face, her hair poking out from her skewered hat, jump up from her seat, step over the sewing ladies, reach the aisle, all while screeching, "Tanks be t' tem! Me girl. Me best girl! I'm so happy t' see ye! I missed ye someting terr'ble." And while the entire house looked on, Miss Kitty and Sophia hugged each other.

And then everybody in that theatre applauded. But not mild applause. Wild applause. There were cheers. "Here! Here!" "Yo!" "Bravo!" "Daaag!" "Hip! Hip! Hooray!" The theatre was no where near capacity, the people were just scattershot all about it, but no one would've known by the roar those people were making. Sophia was positively shocked. Nothing like that had ever happened to her before in her whole life. And yet it was vaguely familiar. As if it had. Though she knew for a fact it hadn't because something like that a person would've never forgot. She could feel her heart race. Beat. Spin. Her head get light. She felt like laughing. Crying. Running away. Taking a bow. Kissing everybody in the room. Then something made Sophia go up on her tippy toes and kiss Miss Kitty. And everybody whooped it up again. But not only that, they stood up from their seats as they did. Sophia wasn't at all surprised. She couldn't've said for sure that she kissed Miss Kitty because people were looking at her. Yet she also knew she should've kissed Miss Kitty, because she missed Miss Kitty and she loved Miss Kitty and Miss Kitty was kind and Miss Kitty needed a kiss. And she also knew that the crowd expected it and would love it when she did.

And then one sewing lady said to another, "Don't you just love a happy ending, Mavis?"

"Oh! Rose. It warms the heart."

And then her Grandfather was standing beside them, smiling. Sophia, who only a few seconds ago had stopped caring what everyone thought about her; who just had gotten the kind of attention she'd didn't even know she craved; who at last had received a standing ovation, the first ever in her whole life, had completely lost track of his whereabouts. She hadn't even heard him coming. It hadn't even occurred to her that she just brought his entire rehearsal to a standstill and that not one person was cleaning or sewing or dancing or fixing or polishing or choreographing or barking into a phone or doing what he was paying them to do, which was what they were supposed to be doing. The only thing she was aware of was that everybody in that entire Theatre had stopped everything to look at her.

Sophia sparkled a Movie Star smile at him. Which we all know, Readers, was extraordinary for her. Solomon Oomla sparkled one right back at her. Which was extraordinary for him, too, Readers. Sophia, however, had no idea how extraordinary it was for him to be smiling - which he was - between the hours of 9 AM and 7:15 PM. So, of course, she certainly didn't notice how rapidly his smile was darkening.

"Well, now, I haven't had the pleasure of meeting you. New here, aren't you? Tell me, Madam, what is your name? And how do you know my granddaughter?"

"Oh, Mr. Oomla, sir, I'm jus' delighted t' be makin' y'r acquaintance. I'm Katherine Devine, Margaret Finnegan's Aunt. Ye know Margaret Finnegan, surely te sweetest, prettiest dancer in te whole wide world who is right now up on y'r stage pouring her heart n' soul into her role as a dancing flamingo who sings. 'N who acts! Which by te way, Mr. Oomla, ye really ought t' know tat too 'cause she acts someting devine. 'N I'm not just sayin' tat cause I'm her aunt 'n me name's Devine."

Miss Kitty tee heed. So did the sewing ladies. Solomon Oomla did not.

'He isn't teeheeing. He's barely smiling.' Now that she'd had her first lesson with a real live audience, she'd already figured out how to read an audience. And at that moment, she began to understand that when she was on a stage, she'd always need to know second to second just how her audience was reacting to whatever she was doing. So not only did she notice he wasn't teeheeing, she noticed no one else was either. And she fell off the cloud she'd been floating on and really examined her Grandfather. His smile wasn't at all like Miss Kitty's, on the silly side of kind. There was nothing in the slightest bit silly about him, not like there was last night. But Miss Kitty was talking on and on and in a rush even as her Grandfather was smiling back at her with what Sophia knew was not a real smile and she didn't know what to make of it and who to pay attention to. So she looked first at one, then the other.

"Not tat ye'r askin' I know, but I really did tink ye oughta know tat 'n oh … I know, ye'r waitin' t' find out how I know y'r lovely granddaughter. Well, I'm only here on but te briefist of temporary employment wit' ye fine company, as I was saying, for but a few days because I will be returnin' any day … any minute … I'm sure … I'll be called back any moment … I ho … ope …" And her voice broke.

'Is Miss Kitty going to cry? Something isn't right. Miss Kitty's talking to Grandfather like everything's alright but she doesn't sound like everything's alright and she doesn't really sound cheerful either even though she sure is trying to.' And

Sophia took a good long look at Miss Kitty. *'She doesn't look cheerful either.'* Sophia kept her eyes on Miss Kitty. Miss Kitty didn't cry but smiled. *'But that's not a real smile because she just stuck it on top of how she really feels and now it can only wobble around on the outside of her.'* And still Miss Kitty didn't cry but just went on talking the same odd way.

"With certainty ... some certainty ... t' me other ... ah ... more ... perma ... permanent employment, te best job in te whole wide world ..."

'Why is Miss Kitty talking like that? Like she may not be coming back to my house. Something is wrong. Something's been wrong since I left my house. Maybe even before I left. What is Miss Kitty doing here sewing feathers on flamingo costumes instead of being at home where she should be? What was it that Mr. James told me about Miss Kitty? What did Mother tell me? What is going on? Why isn't Miss Kitty where she's supposed to be? At my house, cooking for everybody and being my Nanny?'

"... as te Nanny t' ye dear, sweet, granddaughter, Sophia." And Miss Kitty squeezed Sophia to her side, while Sophia puzzled over this sudden mystery she found herself in. "And as I was sayin', I'm just here to help out ye Wardrobe Mistress, Madame Fleurette. Today we're embellishin' te flamingo costumes with te long curly' plumes."

"Well, well, we're always in need of competent seamstresses. Now would my dear granddaughter, Miss Oomla and our temporary Costume Embellisher, Miss Devi—"

From the stage came a pizzicato of coughs. Every head turned to see Serf toss his hairdo, scrutinize his watch, sigh dramatically, impatiently, wearily, then roll his eyes, touch his head with his palm, pirouetting his toe-shoe-fingers about until down down down they flew and then swiftly, gracefully those daggers knifed the air as they reknotted the sweater tied about his waist. And when that bit of business was finished, he tapped his foot on the stage's wooden boards, stared out at the pit and grew his dudgeon majestically. And when it had reached its zenith, he spat out, "ThcccCH!!!!!!!!!!! Mithter Oomla, the clock ITH ticking and my dancerthhh are paid by the hour. HelLO? And I have a luncheon engagement which I am loathe to mittttttttttttttth."

'Now that was a hissy fit! Better than even a Movie Star's.' Sophia, of course, knew hissy fits. Who didn't who loved Movie Stars and Movies? And had a friend like Melinda. She had almost cracked up a few times during his performance but knew she didn't dare. But she hadn't missed a trick of it. She had watched every bit, heard every word, and listened to each syllable that had spun out of his mouth because she intended to do it all later. Knowing how to do that might come in handy one day.

"Most everybody in the house is paid by the hour, Serf." And now it was her Grandfather's turn to glance at his watch, turn around and speak in that special voice Sophia had heard him use in the other Theatre when she was sitting next to him, "Ladies and Gentlemen, Sophia, my granddaughter and her Nanny are at last reunited. Now we all know the show must go on; however, if the rehearsal doesn't go on, the show never will. Sophia, if you please. Miss Devine, a pleasure."

And then Sophia watched his smile-that-wasn't-a-smile that had been hovering on his lips as if it were, vanish, leaving only what was left. And what was left had nothing whatsoever to do with what puts a smile on a face and more to do with what makes a grizzly bear so scary.

'Can Miss Scaredy Cat tell Mr. Scary Bear that she's staying by Miss Kitty's side? Because if I walk away from Miss Kitty, I'll never find out why she almost cried just now when she talked about being my Nanny. I'll never know why Miss Kitty is here in this big city sewing plumes on flamingo costumes and not back home in my house. I'll never know if Mr. James had something to do with it. Miss Kitty is my friend; she's the only person in the whole wide world who knows my secret.'

And there was Miss Scaredy about to tell Mr. Scary that she was staying right by Miss Kitty's side, no matter how much he might not like it.

Sophia looked squarely at her Grandfather who was looking squarely at the stage. He began to dash down the aisle towards it and even though he hadn't said so, Sophia knew he expected her to dash right behind him. And that she wasn't going to. Her Grandfather was now many rows away and Sophia knew she'd have to speak up loud and do it fast or otherwise he wouldn't hear her. *'I can do that. I must, even if every person in this whole entire theatre hears me talk all wrong!'* That thought didn't rattle her as she threw her voice not-too-much-but-just-enough into the big house to get his attention, though he was halfway down the aisle.

Which, Readers, is really quite remarkable since Sophia was famous for mostly not being heard.

"Grandfather, I'm going to stay here with Miss Kitty. I haven't seen her since forever."

Sophia was sure every eye was really scrutinizing her now, even if they had only just been looking at her before. But she stayed strong and so did her voice. "So I'm going to watch the rehearsal sitting here right next to her. I promise I'll pay attention and listen to the actors when they're talki—"

'Hauggh!

"When they're projecting ... like you wanted me to."

'Projecting's why he brought me here! But did he notice how quickly I said the right word? Grandfather's too far down the aisle and I can't really see if he's giving me the eye. He couldn't possibly know how incredible it is for me to keep talking after I make a mistake. He probably thinks I talk up loud and clear all the time. But then he doesn't know how I really talk. But I know how I talk. And this time I kept talking, in spite of that mistake. That mistake didn't clodhopper through me like the mistakes I've made when an entire roomful of my classmates AND Mr. Snoggley were staring at me OR ESPECIALLY WHEN GREAT AUNT HORTENSE was staring at me. Because I didn't blow the rest of what I had to say. And I know exactly how I did it. I didn't feel bad when I said the wrong word so I didn't get nervous. When I get nervous, I can never say anything right afterwards.'

Calmly, she stood there watching her Grandfather turn around, walk back up the aisle and face her. And now Sophia could see that he was more than just watching her; he was examining her and her feet that were planted firmly on the floor. She didn't budge or flinch but stayed right where she was, holding Miss Kitty's hand and gazing right back at him. She wasn't anywhere near as intimidated of him as she had been, even if he was the boss of everybody. For one thing, his whole entire face didn't look like a grizzly's kisser. She could see that his eyes were really alive and his face was expressing many things one after another, and from what Sophia could decipher, not one of them was cold or scary. He only looked slightly ticked-off. But slightly might have been an exaggeration because maybe it was only a tiny bit. And a tiny bit was nothing to be afraid of in a grown-up. Even if those tiny bits could have also been seen on a Great Aunt Hortense type person.

"Very well, young lady! Just be ready when it's time to leave. And remember, you're here to hear! PROoooJECCTionnNN!"

The way he said it – projection went up! down! over there! through her! on top of her! underneath her! and all at the same time! sounding out through the house!!! tingling her frontways, sideways and everyways in-between til all of a sudden, it stopped. And when it did, her Grandfather continued on but in his normal voice.

"Any moment the actors will begin their rehearsal; so pay attention. Watch, and above all, listen to them practice their scene and see if you can understand every word they say from the seat you're sitting in."

And he sprinted down the aisle, calling out over his shoulder, "And by the way, young lady, I did notice how quickly you corrected yourself just now. You showed you understand that there is a difference between mere talking and PRoJecting."

Then Serf called out steps; dancers danced; workmen worked; cleaners cleaned; audience members turned back round and regarded the stage with the same attention they'd just paid to Sophia, Miss Kitty and her Grandfather. Miss Kitty pointed to the row in front of the sewing ladies and they sat down side by side. Miss Kitty winked at Sophia, leaned towards her and did her very best to whisper, and on or about every eleventh word, she actually succeeded, "Well now, Miss Sophia, look at ye, speaking up like tat t' such an important man, just like a big girl would. I'm awful proud o' ye!"

Sophia felt herself beaming and knew she was blushing, which made her blush even more. Miss Kitty witnessed her finest hour; she saw and heard her speak up.

At the same time she was very aware that Miss Kitty's whisper had to be carrying. Plus she had this feeling Miss Kitty wasn't finished saying what she had to say and just might say something Sophia wouldn't want any but her own ears to hear. But she willed herself to be a big girl and stop blushing but couldn't no matter how hard she tried.

"Miss Sophia, ye seem different all of a sudden! Ye spoke up 'n, I hope ye don't mind me saying so, tat's not a-taaall like you. I mean ye n' me n' not another soul walkin' te face of tis good earth knows just how ye can talk so fancy n' with so many accents n' voices when ye're by y'rself watching yer Movies but ye 'n me both know tat tat's only when ye're by yerself 'n not with other people who just so happen t' be te people ye really need t' speak up t', like yer teacher in yer school 'n yer schoolmates!"

'Everybody now knows my deepest secret!' Sophia's blush had been growing deeper on every word Miss Kitty was divulging. She wished that Miss Kitty could whisper better and that the sewing ladies weren't sitting directly behind them. Sophia made up her mind that when they were finally safe back at home, she'd teach Miss Kitty how to whisper. She could only hope the sewing ladies weren't really paying attention to Miss Kitty as she spilled Sophia's most classified, most confidential beans out into this wide open space packed with so many ears. And yet in spite of her fears and worries, she was just so happy to be sitting alongside her old pal, whom she had missed so desperately, that she wouldn't have shushed her for all the Tea in China. All the Stars in the Sky. Or in the Movies, either.

But finally Miss Kitty aimed herself right at Sophia's ear and this time she did manage to whisper every word and Sophia felt herself relaxing, "N, if you don't mind me puttin' in me two cents, tat's why ye have t' go t' tat speech therapist, young lady. I know ye wouldn't have t' atall, if only ye could do what ye do with ease when ye'r in front of te television set!"

And then Miss Kitty went to whispering every fourth word, which wasn't as bad as before, "Why, Miss Sophia, bein' here seems to be doin' ye a world of good! 'N by te way, I'm so happy tat tat's what ye told him. I'dda been scared meself t' but it was exactly what I would've liked t' tell him. I can't tell ye how much I didn't want ye t' walk away just now. I've missed ye n' te house n' me kitchen n' sweet Dr. Oomla, sometin' terrible. Now I can't say te same ting about tat Grand one, yer Great Aunt Hortense. 'N Mr. James, well tat's another story entirely! 'N yer Mother is sweet but … I hardly ever see her, except maybe late in te afternoon when she's not too tired or maybe early in te morning when I'm too tired 'n can barely see a ting anyway."

"Ssssssshhhhhhhhsssh! Now Kitty Devine, if you keep up your chit chat, it'll be your fault all of us are escorted out of here. And then we'll never get invited to do our sewing at a live rehearsal again."

Miss Kitty turned around and aimed her haughtiest look at her sewing colleague and, just in case that hadn't hit home, her dirtiest one too. And not even pretending to whisper, she snapped, "Now, Mindy Loomis, I haven't seen me Miss Sophia, for a long lonely eternity, 'n ye should be ashamed t' say someting like tat t' me at a time like tis! How do ye expect me t' talk - like a mouse in a church?" And then a hissing sort of steam rose up from the stage. But it was only Serf, "Ladittth! Laditttth! Laditttth! DO you mind? We can hardly hear ourthelfes danth!"

Which finally clammed Miss Kitty up but as the rehearsal went on, she opened her purse, noiselessly this time, took out a rolled up piece of paper and a stump of a pencil, and as quietly as she could, she unrolled the paper, smoothed away its creases and then wrote something on it very painstakingly. When she finished, she examined what she wrote line for line and when satisfied every letter was correct, she handed it to Sophia. And in her best whisper yet, a real whisper, she said, "I'm staying with me niece Margaret Finnegan. Tis is her address 'n phone number. Call me after 5 o'clock 'n we'll talk 'n I'll tell ye all about everyting tat happened t' me since I twas seein' ye last."

Sophia took the scrap of paper and began to search through her new Antoinette Fifi clothes for a safe spot to put it in. She felt a zipper inside one of her coat pockets, a hidden pocket; she unzipped it and tucked the paper inside. And then Miss Kitty and her settled back in their seats and watched the dancers.

Soon the dancers left the stage and a group of actors entered who were talking. *Wait, I think they're acting because they seem to be right in the middle of something that sounds like a scene.'* Sophia listened to make sure she could understand every word they said from where she sat. Her Grandfather was right. She could understand every single word they said. And every word they said was fascinating and so was their story and, as she watched them, she laughed, cried and wondered about life and had many, many interesting thoughts and feelings about living with people on the earth. Until she sat up arrow straight because she felt such an urge. She wanted to run down to that stage, spring up the steps and jump into their scene. *'I could do that too. And I don't want to wait anymore!'*

But a great big hand pushed her back in her seat. Or she felt like one did. She couldn't do that with her Grandfather sitting right there. He would see her. What was she thinking? Jumping up on the stage and acting in front of her Grandfather! She wouldn't dare. *'Someday I will. Some day soon!'*

Just then, the rehearsal stopped, the actors left the stage and the children who had been sitting in the audience, ran down the aisle, sprang up the steps on the side of the stage and jumped onto the stage.

'They're doing what I just dreamed about doing! That's not fair!'

And now that very same hand that had pushed her back in her seat, grabbed hold of her and was pushing her to that seat's slippery edge. And there she hung, with her eyes just about popping out of her head, staring at those children strut about the stage –

HER STAGE!

- laughing and looking so happy!

'Why aren't these children in school? They look to be about my age. What are children my age doing on the stage? Or children of any age for that matter! On MY stage? The stage I'm dying to be on? Is this like a Movie Star School and all these children are in it? Why can't I be in it too? Except – wait - that couldn't be a Movie Star School because this isn't the Movies!'

She got her answer quickly because a woman rushed down the aisle, stopped at the first row and sharply called out the children's names. And when each of them had answered "Present!" she said "Places!" and instantly they moved to a spot on the stage. Then she said, "Scene!" and they began acting in what Sophia was sure was a rehearsal.

'They're having a rehearsal! THEM! That's not fair! Oh! The indignity! I need my fainting couch!' But there was no fainting couch and she watched every move they made and listened to every word they spoke. *'Wait a minute! They're not doing what I do! They're not pretending to be a grown-up! They're acting like children! Like kids!'* And Sophia was overwhelmed with contradictions

and confusions. *'Before this, I was so happy and now I feel like I might even cry. All I ever want to be is a grown-up when I act. I never even thought about just being a child - somebody just like myself. Why act at all if you're just yourself? Where's the challenge in that?'*

And then Bart was leaning over and whispering a whisper that would surely've won a gold medal in the Whispering Olympics, but Sophia didn't even notice, "Please pardon my intrusion but I'm afraid I must pull your charge away, Miss Devine, because Sophia and I have to be off again. We're on a very tight schedule and now it's time for lunch. We gotta heave ho Sophia! Enjoy the rest of the show, Miss Devine."

Sophia unrolled her hat and scarf and purse and gloves, but she couldn't unroll the lump inside her. To have to leave Miss Kitty after just finding her made her feel so sad, but on the other hand, having to walk out of the rehearsal now that those! children! were on her! stage! didn't make her feel sad at all. Miss Kitty also looked sad when she said, not even trying to whisper, " 'N for Heaven sakes, Miss Sophia, call me! 'N be sure to pull tat scarf round you. O'! Te wind in tis city cuts right trough t' yer bones!"

'That's not the only thing that cuts right trough t' yer bones Miss Kitty! But that thought is staying where all the rest of my deep dark thoughts stay. In my own personal bat cave. It's filled to the brim with them.

Sophia did manage to whisper back, but then that's all her insides could have mustered out anyway, "Don't worry, I'll call you, Miss Kitty. Your phone number is safe inside my zippered pocket!" As her smile teeter-tottered, she got on wiggly legs, gave Miss Kitty's hand a pat then scrambled over her and wobbled up the aisle beside Bart, trying with all her might to block out the sound of all those children and all their "PROJECTIONS." But they were doing exactly what her Grandfather told her these big city stage actor people do; project their emotions, their words, their voices, their personalities, their perfect-little-actor-selves round that theatre. And straight into her ears. And no matter how hard she tried to shut her ears, her ears just wouldn't shut. In fact, the harder she tried to shut them, the more they tried to hear. *'I'm the only person alive who has ears with a mind of their own!'* She would've laughed if she didn't feel like crying. But then she shouldn't've been surprised; Sophia was used to her ears.

'It's just not fair that CHILDREN get to do that and I don't. But I wouldn't want to do what they're doing anyway ... be with a bunch of babies on a stage! So what—'

And then the blazing light of day struck her almost blind as she emerged from that black hole of a theatre. And she was glad. At least she didn't have to hear THEM. Or see THEM either. And there she stood on the sidewalk, with eyes that were tearing and even burning, but she was filled with relief anyway.

• • • SOPHIA HOLDS FORTH • • •

"Now for the next part of your excellent adventure, we're off to have lunch at La Terre. Your Grandfather will meet us there. Well, Sophia, this is where everyone who is anyone in Show Business gets to eat shrubbery for lunch and pay top-dollar for the privilege."

Sophia gladly jumped into the back of the waiting vehicle as Bart hopped in behind her. "Scoochest thyself, fair Sophia. We dars't not be late." And the driver revved and roared their vehicle right into the line of traffic that instantly screeched and shrieked its welcome; then more of those bad words poured down upon them. But those street words hardly seemed bad to Sophia. The only words that Sophia thought were bad were the ones coming out of the mouths of those children actors that were on the stage back there in that theatre. Her theatre. Her stage. Sophia was at least comforted that she didn't have to hear them and their words anymore, and she sat back in her seat ready for whatever was next. As long as it didn't have any child actors in it.

"Well, Sophia, Show Business! You've just seen the Show, now it's time for the Business. But first off, let me give you the skinny about this establishment we're about to dine in. First off, only a tourist would call it La Terre. Anyone who's in the know calls it something else; most of those names not fit for your ears. Or for mine either. Although if we keep driving around here, you'll be sure to hear them all and a few new ones. But here're two that are fit for both of our ears:

"Food Terrible refers to the food and is used mostly by hungry people.

"And then there's Enfant Terrible, and refers, of course, to the customers and is used by the poor soul who has to take the reservations of those customers; and, coincidentally, is also used by those same customers to describe not only that reservationist but the wait-staff too.

"So most everybody who has to deal with the customers AND the restaurant staff AND the food uses one name or the other. And since you don't look like the food police, I can confess to you that I am a hungry person and an avowed non-foodie, and when I eat in there, I gag. I mean you really might as well be eating a hedge, Sophia! Arugula and fiddlehead fern tips washed down with beet juice! So, Sophia, make no mistake about it, I use both names with pride! But then I, of course, would since I'm on a first name basis with the personal assistants of those customers and have heard such stories about them! All of them, Do-You-Know-Who-I-Am-Napoleons!

"But alas, Sophia, these customers are the Makers of Deals and Dolls and Dollars throughout Goliathon. These customers decide who gets to Prance, Dance, and De-Pants on the stages here; these customers are the very Keepers of nothing less than the World's Theatrical Treasures, including the plays, the actors, the very theaters themselves - well, guess who actually get the tables at this establishment? These Customers! That's who. In short, ordinary civilians, like you or I, cannot get a table there. Only people like your Grandfather can. Or people who know your Grandfather. Ergo our seats.

"Well, what people really do there besides dine, is pitch and catch and throw and score. And by the way, your Enfant-Terrible-Grandfather sure is nice to you. Since I've been working for him, I've never actually seen him smile when he does his rounds in the morning. Of course, what really makes him 'terrible' is when he's talking about the movie business."

The more Bart talked, the more those child actors' voices stopped echoing in Sophia's ears, and the more she could relax. She even laughed along with Bart's story. She knew funny when she heard it. Bart, she was sure, was a joker sort of a fellow. And she even mostly understood what he was saying. Mostly. Though, she had to admit, sometimes not at all. But even so she'd pretend she did. And she nodded and smiled right along with him, which encouraged him to continue. His story was a million times better than having to listen to a bunch of children doing what she should be doing - that is - what her whole entire Star of Screen Self, which included her Body, her Soul, her Heart, her Mind, her Sparkling Eyes, her Dazzling Smile - in short, every gleaming ounce of her, ought to be doing. She understood almost all of the English words he was saying, but none of the French ones - which she knew were French by the sound of them. But when he said the words about pitching, it was time to stop pretending.

She'd just have to ask him, "Why do such important people have to play baseball? In a restaurant? With food and water glasses and starchy tablecloths everywhere! My Great Aunt Hortense would have a heart attack!" And she burst out laughing. It may be bad to get away from some people, like Miss Kitty, but it sure was wonderful to get away - far away - from other people, like the child actor-tresses. And Great Aunt Hortense.

"Baseball! I can see you catch on quick. This is a sport alright except there's no real ball but there's a ball all right! The ball is an idea. And that imaginary idea is what they're pitching. It could be for a show or a play or a movie. They throw that ball to somebody like your Grandfather hoping like crazy that your Grandfather might be interested enough in their ball, their idea, to pick up his whopper of a bat and bat it out of the park and make a home run for everybody. Sophia, do you know that your Grandfather has the means to turn that pitcher's ideas into a show, a play, an extravaganza? But not their movie idea, because nobody is dumb enough to pitch a movie idea to your Grandfather."

The car stopped and a gigantic scarlet coat opened its door.

Bart jumped onto the sidewalk and held out his arm to Sophia, who grabbed it then climbed out of the back seat, all the while eyeing that giant coat.

"Bienvenue chez La Terre! Good afternoon, Miss Oomla. And Mr. Barone. We've been expecting you."

'It looks like the coat is talking! Hah! But that's not the coat talking, that's the giant inside it. And listen to that voice! There goes another giant voice in this city of giant everything and everybody. His voice is as big as his coat. As big as the city! And what a costume!'

Sophia was almost laughing out loud as she walked besides Bart and this scarlet-coat, realizing with every step, just how easily that thought, her thought, her private thought had almost burst out of her mouth and would've been heard by one and all! if she hadn't bitten her lip! Why Bart! The Scarlet Coat! Everybody! just like that – boom! - would've known what she was thinking! *'Wow!'* She thought, *'What's happening to me? The bats are flying out of the cave! Since when did I ever have to stop myself from blurting?'* And in a blink, she knew the answer. *'Since I've been here! That's when!'* And Sophia walked into the restaurant, and she felt like singing the song Fred sang. Fred of Fred and-Ginger. *'I'm fancy free and free for anything fancy.'* She would've danced, too, but didn't. *'Child Actors! Who cares?'* But, finally and at long last, what flew out of her mouth was something she'd always heard people in the movies say, "I feel like a million bucks!"

When they were inside, Bart in his whisper-of-champion's voice said, "Unlike the rest of us diners, you, Sophia, have nothing to worry about. So don't worry. Show Business folks know how to treat children. You won't have to eat a hedge, a shrub or even a single blade of grass. You'll get to choose from the children's menu and you'll be the secret envy of us all. You'll get to eat milkshakes and French fries and hot dogs and grilled cheese and hot fudge sundaes. You lucky dog! But don't worry. I'll protect every last French fry on your plate. I won't let one of these Caesars cease a dog-gone thing. Or a hot-doggone thing either. In particular, you'll have to watch out for two of 'em - your Grandfather and that wily old character, Hamlet Bonofsky, aka Ham Bone the Super-Agent. Especially that one! Not only would that one take candy from a baby, he'd give it right back. Giving candy to a baby! Pshaw! Although, to be safe - we'll really need to keep our eyes on all of Show Business's finest – slippery scheming devils, every last one of them."

Sophia sat down. And she finally felt how starving she really was. For food. For conversation. She was dying to tell somebody what was dying to come out of her - what she'd seen and heard and learned today. But she knew she didn't have to die because she knew what was inside her was about to pour out of her and she couldn't believe how lucky she was. For today, at this lunch, with these people, she was about to have a conversation about her favorite subject in the whole world – Actresses - and she couldn't wait. Her Grandfather sat beside her and this time he wasn't barking into his cellphone, he was smiling, smiling like that silly guy again. Then a pink-sweatered gentleman came over. Her Grandfather introduced him. It was Hamlet Bonofsky aka Ham Bone, who then sat on her other side. Bart, who was sitting across from her, caught her eye, winked at her slyly then surrep-titiously made a quick motion covering his plate with his hands and then sticking out his elbows.

"Well, well, well, what did you think about those actors you saw this morning, Sophia? Now do you understand what I was talking about?" said her Grandfather.

And because the answer to his question required her to dip down into her cave, and because she had not opened that cave for anybody else before, and that cave was by now so deep with so many thoughts, opinions and theo-ries about this, her favorite subject, everything raced out of her just like she thought they would - like a bat out of the bad-place.

And her Grandfather and Ham Bone and Bart listened to her every word. And so too did she, even as she was speaking those words. *'Why! What I'm saying is so intelligent. It's exactly what I should say! Yes! That's what I think! That's what I know! That's what I feel!'* Everything she experienced this morning, minus how she felt about the child actors, she explained just right. And when she'd exhausted herself and couldn't say another word, then all of them started talking at once about what she said. And then she and all of them all together laughed and joked and teased and were even deathly serious, even it seemed about the very same ideas, as all of them, as Miss Kitty would've said 'gassed,' on and on and on about "songs sung in theatres by actresses!" and "What about that projection," "What about that Serf," "those dancers," even while they ate. All of them now yakking at her and her yakking right back. Them saying what they thought about what she said. And she saying what she thought about what they said. Back and forth. Back and forth. And everything they talked about was about nothing but "Show Business."

Sophia had never been so happy. She was talking about what she loved. Even she knew just how unusual this was. *'Why I've never talked like this in my whole life. Imagine me talking to grown-ups about Show Business! I wish Miss Kitty or Daddy or Mother or Great Aunt Hortense or Mr. Snoggley could see me.'* Anyone looking at her now would never have suspected that just days ago she'd been sentenced to a speech therapist for non-communication. Because there she was joking and teasing and laughing and chattering right along with these people - people she barely knew. Sophia could just imagine what Great Aunt Hortense would've said. 'Sophia! Chattering away to people she barely knows! Sophia, in the talking world! What's gotten into her? And pray tell me, is our shrinking violet talking about! Show! Business!' And Sophia was happy all over again to be far away from home. Far far away.

Bart, true to his word, earned a title - Sir Bart, Friend of the French Fried. He kept his eye on every last one on her plate. And because of finagling fingers and skirmishes springing up everywhere, Sophia suffered losses, in spite of Bart's sharp elbows. With the final score: Ham Bone, three. Solomon Oomla, two. Sophia, thirteen.

But that still left six unaccounted for French fries. So they had to do a recount - Ham Bone, three. Solomon Oomla, two. Sophia, thirteen. And Bart, six.

Nobody had been watching Bart. In fact, nobody had even seen him score. Finagling fingers was right! But Bart owned up like a true Knight would, and they took a vote and Bart was allowed to keep his title anyway.

Then lunch was over, and it was time for her afternoon adventures. And Bart was correct. The morning, may have all about been about Show but the afternoon was all about Business. Period. The 'Business' part didn't really interest her, but she didn't mind hearing about it. As long as she wasn't watching children perform in a show that she wasn't in, she was fine. And as far as having to listen to the 'Business,' she wouldn't've dreamed of complaining, even if she had been a complainer.

But Sophia did notice something curious.

Unlike the morning, her Grandfather insisted she stay right by his side the whole, entire time. And not only that, he seemed to want to make sure she watched and heard him do everything he said and did in every appointment he had. And when each appointment was finished, he would explain in detail every single thing he'd just said and done. Almost as if he was trying to teach her. And she made sure he saw that she was listening and watching because her Grandfather really seemed to want her to understand what he was doing and she wanted to make him happy, since he'd made her so happy by taking her to watch actresses and talking about them with her and listening to what she had to say. And it was easy. Sophia was a great listener. Sophia was really used to listening. In fact, if Bart could have won the Championship of Whispering, Sophia could have won the Championship of Listening. After all, listening is what she did all day long in school. And all night long in her Movie Star School. But the best part about the whole afternoon was she hadn't met or saw or heard another single child actor even once.

• • • GOOD BEHAVIOR • • •

"Ms. Author, as we were sitting on the back of those seats, we heard the unmistakable voice of … I'm ashamed to say—"

"Lady, I got no problems laying it out for the Readers. This is what went down:"

"Well, would you look at the bunch of you! And don't even try telling me my eyes are deceiving me! Every single one of you out of Sophia at the same time! You've abandoned your child! Your responsibility! Leaving your human all alone with not even one of you on the premises! That is a clear violation of Code # 62. Do I have to remind you what Code # 62 is – The human child must be creatured at all time! Which means! NEVER LEAVE YOUR HUMAN UNFAIRYED! I can't have all of you in violation of Code # 62. Not Code # 62! Every last one of you must receive a punishment! With no exceptions!"

"Ya got any guesses as to who that was, Lady? Readers?"

"And the punishment was swift, Ms. Author."

"Swift! Ya gotta be kiddin' me, Thee! We're dealing with Fairies here! Because in this case, the only thing that was swift was the hemming and hawing. Any magical creature apprehending any other magical creature has been a problem for months and months and months of Sundays, Moondays, Stardays and any days in betwixt, even if one of the magical creatures is the

Dispatcher! Hah hah! Netting up squirrelly, squirmy, squeally, scheming AWOL Fairies! Just what everyone needs."

"Oh, Ms. Author, our Unfortunate Dispatcher, Mr. Higgs Boson, found himself in quite the pickle after rounding us up! And Unfortunate Dispatcher is right, Ms. Author. A sensible person undoubtedly would have believed the Fairies were the less fortunate ones, because sensible persons everywhere would always conclude that anyone caught-red-handed, including Fairies, would ergo be the less fortunate ones."

"But not, I bet, our Readers, Lady! They've spent time with us Fairies. And by now, there ain't a sensible one left!"

"Ms. Author, the Dispatcher had just opened his mouth for the second time when …"

"ALL #@((BROKE LOOSE!"

"Lorraine! Please! I'll explain it to our Readers in appropriate language. The moaning, the tears, the prostrations, the hyperventilating, the bellyaching, the elf-sailor and even the human-sailor-language that scorched up all about him would have been enough for anyone to run for cover, let alone Mr. Boson, a gentlemanly, law-abiding Dispatcher who was just doing his job! He pronounced Me's sentence with dignity, not dithering at all, as any citizen who had to assume the duties of a judge would. He said, 'Me, your ten year assignment with Sophia Oomla is soon to be over, but because of your continued non-compliance with the Rules of Engagement (specifically Code # 454, # 652, # 2216 AND Code # 62) when in a Human's Remarkably Small Place (namely a certain Miss Sophia Oomla) you will forfeit your one year vacation and serve a one year punishment of my choosing. The day after your ten-year assignment ends, you will report immediately to my office where I will then place you on an assignment to aid and assist the underprivile—' "

"Darlings, I cried, 'One year! The UNDERpriVILEged! OH! MY! GODDESS! Not … A MALL! You would sentence me to a MALL! NOT THAT! Anything but THAT … I can't take all those like Mall bRats dressed in bomber jackets, with their panty lines showing through their Walmart jeans and wearing … Beatle caps! ICK! Oh, the humiliation! Those prêt-a-porter porpoises. My mother will disown me. Please don't make me live in a mall for a year!'"

"Yeah, and he says right back to you:"

"Who said anything about a mall? Who is underprivileged in a mall? I was thinking more like a stint with the inhabitants of DarFairy!"

"And then with a feint of faint, a soupcon of stupor, I crumpled to the floor, my fairy skirt flumphing about what surely appeared to be my fading ghost. And how its tussore framed my evanescence, even as my fairy wings beat ever-so-gossamery but oh-so-gracefully! Think Dying Swan. No! Dead Swan! But think nothing less than a Prima Ballerina. Such was the effect of my tableau!"

"Ms. Author, after that a sane Dispatcher might not have gone on. But not our Mr. Boson!"

"Yeah, Lady, he did firm as Me did apoplectic there on the floor."

"Firm, darlings? Actually, I heard something jingle jangling, and from my unique vantage point there on the floor, I quickly spotted his wavering limbs and negotiated that sentence down in no time to no stint anywhere except where I was planning to go anyway when my assignment inside Sophia was over! And to just six visits to Faree for that year!"

"Lady, considering her 52 Farisian visits a year, the sentence was nothing less than a soul-crushing deprivation for Me."

"As for the rest of us sorry lot, since none of us had what it took to be either dramatic dramati or persecuted personae, our sentences, of course, were tougher. As a credit to the Dispatcher, he did hem, he did haw as he figured out exactly what our punishment would be.

"But, Lady, after a few looks at my sorry mug, he whiffled it down to cutting our one year vacation in half. However he dithered again about whether he would let us take our six month vacation before or after we served our six month punishment. Lady, undithering was how I delivered my opinion. I was clearly in favor of taking our vacation before. And what really sold my argument was the clever use of both species of sailor language already described earlier - elf words for the gist and human ones to punch it all up a nice notch or two. And wonder of wonders, he caved and decided in favor of us four taking our six-month vacations, six months before our punishment!"

"And then, Ms. Author, guaranteeing he wouldn't hear another blessed word from any of us, or unblessed either, or see another dramatically reenacted death scene, he decided to make use of some old fashioned Enchanted Land magic and POOF! he disappeared. Such a display, he knew would've been frowned on by the Executive Committee, and was probably breaking at least six different Codes from the 'Rules of Engagement.' And was particularly hypocritical since it had taken place in front of us. And he certainly had been trying so hard to set a good example by really following the

'Rules for Visits to the Non-Enchanted Lands: Rights, Responsibilities and Restrictions.' But, I'm sure, he had to get away that instant or he feared he might commute our sentences even further."

"Yeah! We watched until the last of his poof-vapors evaporated. And then I says, 'Why doesn't somebody just shoot me?' "

" 'Shoot you, Lorraine! Shoot moi! Imagine Me! Mimi Meselk only being allowed to go to Faree just six times a year. 'Poor! Little! Me!' Haven't you heard humans saying that? They must have known what was about to become of me and named an expression just for me and this occasion, which is so totally extrasensory of our human companions and so very tres sympathetique to me and this dreadful situation I'm in. Oh! I might as well be dead!' "

"I said, 'Like, let it go, everybody. It's not like it's really happening yet! He's just saying it will happen! And that doesn't really mean it will. We might, like, be able to get it down for, like, good behavior or something.' "

" 'Be is right. If we do something really wonderful and something really useful and something that really helps Sophia. Like getting Sophia to talk up in school or something like that, the Dispatcher might forget all about our sentences.' "

" 'I me'ms ... oooh ... do ... good ... happen ... I ... soon ... you see ... Oooh ShoeT'"

" 'Sorry Free, didn't catch that but don't worry. We understand what you're trying to say. You're just agreeing with us, right?' "

But then, Lady, Free did that wand thing again and I heard what she was thinking, 'They probably don't want to watch me struggle anymore. They gave me a chance to say something and I couldn't. And because I can't talk good they have no idea that I've already developed a plan to help Sophia. And it's all because I can't talk when I get nervous. I'm just like Sophia. Maybe that same plan can help me too, because I need help! I think perfectly! My thoughts are clear! The words roll out in the order they should be in and as they should be said. If only I could talk as good as I think! Maybe when my Sophia plan finally starts, I should ask the man behind the plan to help me too, so that I can talk just like I think.'

"And Lady, for the first time, Free felt encouraged. And not just about Sophia—

"I know! Did I even think to ask Free what her plan was? I could kick myself! But at least I heard her out! The rest of them sure didn't!"

"Ms. Author, that, unfortunately, is true. We just kept talking and paying her no mind ...

" 'Everybody, it's so easy. All we have to do is get Sophia to talk up. Really talk up. But it's gotta be in school.' said Be. 'She can't really talk up to Great Aunt Hortense. Nobody talks up to her. And she sort of already, talks up at home, mostly, especially when Great Aunt Hortense isn't around. But if we could get her to talk up in school … The way she does in her Movie Star School … That's where it would really matter.' "

" 'Yeah … just a little magic … and it's a done deal!' "

" 'NO MAGIC LORRAINE. Haven't you noticed? We're in enough trouble!'"

" 'And how are we gonna do that without magic? Besides, didn't we all just witness the Dispatcher himself use magic?' "

" 'Hey, hey, hey! What's the hurry everybody? We, like, have time to plan.' Said Be. 'We're, like, here in Goliathon and not anywhere near the village and her school. She won't be going back there for days, at least!' "

" 'Oh! No! We've lost track! Look at us!' Thee said. 'We're in the dark. Where are we again? I've been so upset by receiving my very first punishment in my whole entire life, I'm not thinking like myself, which isn't at all like me. How could I forget? Of course, of course, we're in that theatre! We were listening to that singer! Well, I don't hear that singer anymore! Does anybody? And where is Sophia? We gotta get back to Sophia immediately … where could she be? But if she were here, surely, our noses would've smelled her by now!' "

" 'We rose up from the floor and flew around the darkened theatre but the only humans we saw were work persons.' "

" 'Like, why knock our noses out … haven't we had, like, enough stress today?' Be said. 'Let's just go back to Granpops-pad and hang out there til Sophia gets back. We can hook up with her then. Hey! the Dispatcher already busted us. I think we'll be safe at least for today. I mean we do have an excuse – there's no city in the world that is filled with as much scents as this place. Why it's enough to bewilder even our noses.' "

" 'I can't believe I was agreeing with Be, Ms. Author, but she was right. So I said …

" 'Let's just all go back and wait there. Maybe a plan will come to us if we just sit and relax.'"

" 'Relax? Wow, would you listen to Thee!' "

"And then Free says, Lady, 'Plan … mim's is plan … happen … soon … even. Soon. Oooh ShoeT!' "

"And then off we all flew!"

• • • THE MAN • • •

'I can't believe it! The moon light is even brighter in here than it was last night. And it was bright last night! Now it's like it's in here with me.' She watched its light blaze up her room, her canopy, her silky coverlet, her fingers into a beautiful, shining phosphorus.

The hour was very late and Sophia should've been sound asleep and not paying a bit of attention to any sleepwalking light, especially after the day she'd just had. But though she was beat, she couldn't fall asleep. She was filled top to bottom, side to side with worry.

Except her worry was being tickled by a light. A lightning-fast-hockey-puck of a light. That mustn't want her to sleep. Did it want to play? But how could a light want to play? And she gave up wondering and just lay in her bed worrying. And sparkling.

'Maybe if my day had ended after I had returned here to Grandfather's house when I was so happy, so excited, so filled up with such adventures, adventures like I've only ever had before alone in my Movie Star School; or in my dreams when I'm a real Movie Star and like not ever before in my real life! Because there I was with my favorite people, real live Actresses and Actors and Dancers and even a Choreographer! And not only was I with them, I was at their Rehearsals! Listening to them PROJECTING! to them singing! to their accents! to all their different Voices! SOOOO many different type of sounds! And there I was! when-elephants-fly-Sophia, in-need-of-a-speech-therapist-Sophia, Yes! That Sophia - actually talking about the No-Business-Like-Show-Business – and it was just like what that song said because there is No Business Like Show Business – imagine that! a grown-up person being paid to teach people how to dance like Pink Flamingos! - maybe there is a future after all for a person like myself who lives only to wear a costume! – and I talked! and talked! and talked! about this No-Business with all the Grown-Ups listening to My Every Word, and me listening to Their Every Word …

'But no! My day didn't ended there—

'No! My day didn't end when I walked in the door of the house on the roof in the sky.'

All the way home in the car, Sophia had been fingering the piece of paper that was snug and safe in her zippered pocket. *'The second I walked in, I asked Antoinette Fifi what time it was so I could keep my promise to call Miss Kitty right on the dot of 5.'* And when the time came, Sophia called Miss Kitty.

And that is when her happy day changed instantly. Because Miss Kitty had told her first thing that she had been suspended from being her Nanny by Mr. James.

"Mr. James?"

"Mr. James!"

Sophia could hear Miss Kitty's tears through the phone because they were splashing. Sophia knew all about this 'suspending' thing because Mr. Snoggley had suspended Transton Biglotte for doing something to somebody in the cloakroom. Sophia had never gotten the whole story because she was not in the circles where she heard the juiciest, thoroughly reliable and most fact-checkable gossip. And this time, even Yak-Yak-Melinda was keeping it a secret because even she wouldn't repeat what she'd heard. She just shook her head when Sophia asked and changed the subject faster than Sophia ever remembered Melinda changing a subject before. And Sophia knew it must have been a bad thing, a very bad thing, Big Ton did. That's what they called him. Because he was a Big Ton of Trouble, and everybody knew it.

But Miss Kitty was no Big Ton! How could anybody suspend her? And Mr. James, he was a nice man, wasn't he? Or was he? But surely suspension was a very bad thing to happen to her Nanny. And then Miss Kitty had told her why. That he, Mr. James, and they, Mrs. Oomla and Great Aunt Hortense, didn't believe what she, Miss Kitty, told them about the missed appointment. And that he, Mr. James, believed that watching movies at midnight on school nights made Sophia, her charge, tired and might be why her charge, her responsibility, who she was being paid to mind, was required to seek the services of a speech therapist. After that, Sophia was too afraid to ask if Miss Kitty had let things slip about her Movie Star School.

And now Sophia lay there wondering who was the bad one? Mr. James? Miss Kitty? Or her very own secret-keeping-self? Sophia was pretty sure she knew the answer. But how could she live without her Movie Star School? And if all that wasn't enough for Sophia to digest, now Miss Kitty expected her, Miss Meep Mouth, to get Miss Kitty unsuspended. And she lay in bed filled with dread, *I have to speak up to Mr. James. And probably Great Aunt Hortense and Mother and Father, too. And I'll have to speak up good, like I speak up every night in my Movie Star School, so Miss Kitty'll come back and be my Nanny. And I'll have to do it as my real actual self.*

'How could I speak up as my real live actual self? When I'm my real live actual self in school, when all those people are looking at me, I could never speak up. The only way I could do that is if I were a Movie Star. Then I could tell all those people. If I were a fancy Movie Star, then I could tell all of them … including Mother and Great Aunt Hortense, that I need Miss Kitty to be my Nanny.

'Miss Kitty is almost like my Mother. Because that's really what Miss Kitty is, almost, isn't she? Maybe Mother is good at doing important things in the great big city because isn't that what she does all day? Walks and talks importantly. Plus, didn't she invent the drink that EVERYBODY drinks? So wouldn't that make her some sort of magician? Because what she sells, everybody buys? When she talks, everybody listens? But Miss Kitty is more like a plain old reliable mother-type person.

'But how could I tell my Mother that Miss Kitty is the plain old reliable mother-type person and she, my Mother, isn't? And what would Great Aunt Hortense have to say when she heard me say that?

'But if I don't say it, I won't get to keep Miss Kitty anymore!'

She could very well imagine what Great Aunt Hortense would have to say when she said it. If she ever could say it. Just the thought of even getting ready to, and Sophia, even as she lay under a heap of warm blankets, was afraid she might freeze stiff. And remembering that she was in Goliathon and that it was February in the deep-dark-night ... which surely it had to be even though it was so very bright in here at this particular second ... didn't help her condition.

She knew her Mother would not like her Movie Star School, especially the late hour of it. And especially her sneakiness about it. But she wouldn't be anywhere near as mad about it as Great Aunt Hortense would be.

'No doubt about it, Great Aunt Hortense'll hate my Movie Star School. She'll be furious about it. And she'll do her sharp, shrill best to convince Mother to be mad about it, too. And if she doesn't at first, she will eventually because she'll keep at it til she beats her down. And that's how she'll put an end to it entirely.

'But Daddy'll be heartbroken if he ever finds out that I want to be an actress! Because of the sad, sad Artistes! And about my sneakiness - he'll not like that one bit, either!'

How could she defend what she did to each of them? And say the perfect thing so that Miss Kitty could stay and be her Nanny?

And that's when her head had heard enough and set her straight: "DIDN'T YOU HOLD COURT AND GAS AWAY WITH ACTUAL, REAL, LIVE SHOW BUSINESS PROFESSIONALS DURING TODAY'S SUNLIT HOURS? SO WHY WOULDN'T YOU BE ABLE TO DO IT AGAIN?"

But then her head did an about-face, 'Whatever turned you in to the magician today and let you oompah-pah like that, would never be countenanced by Great Aunt Hortense. And besides, that magic has vanished to never return to you again!'

Even so, she'd have to say something. She'd have to speak up. Because if she didn't, Great Aunt Hortense might pick out her next Nanny because her Mother and her Father were just too busy nowadays. Great Aunt Hortense'd surely pick out somebody just like her own self. Somebody Sophia wouldn't like at all. And that'd be the end of Sophia. Her Movie Star School. And Miss Kitty too.

The very thought of which turned her flesh cold and goosey and her teeth wouldn't stop chattering.

What would life be like without Miss Kitty? Funny old Miss Kitty?

It seemed the whole entire world needed her Mother. But Sophia needed Miss Kitty. Miss Kitty was just nice. But her Mother was nice, too. And she had such pretty voice. Miss Kitty's voice wasn't anywhere near as pretty as her Mother's was. But then nobody in the whole world had a voice as pretty as that but then nobody in the whole world was like Miss Kitty either. Even if her voice was like a scratchy old bar of flea soap.

'Miss Kitty is nice on the inside. Even if her outsides aren't like a Movie Star's. Miss Kitty is good enough for me!'

And Sophia lay there remembering the rest of that call. Miss Kitty, trying to tell her what else had transpired until she stopped talking entirely because all she could do was cry. And it had something to do with Mr. James. And now Sophia had to wonder about him, too. He had such good manners. He was so perfect. But that was on the outside. What was he like on the inside? Maybe his inside and his outside didn't match at all! Could that be? Because how could such perfection do that to her Miss Kitty? It was so hard to understand grown-ups.

And now one of her favorite grown-ups was in tears. And to Sophia, a grown-up in tears was a very serious matter. She had never had a grown-up cry in her ear before. She certainly had cried on a grown-up shoulders but a grown-up crying on hers was a whole different matter entirely.

But then just like that the moonlight sat down in the chair beside her bed. Sophia studied that light in that chair but that light must not have wanted to be studied because it skipped over to the walls, the bed canopy, a long windowed door, then the next, the next, til it completed the full circle of windowed doors like it was chasing its tail. Or playing possum with her. Or the windows. Or something. Or somebody. Sophia didn't know what, but it sure was wonderful to watch. And Sophia gave up worrying and just let her eyes follow that dippy-loopy-light.

And then Louis Armstrong started singing. Her ears could never deceive her. He was outside one of the windowed doors that was now all lit up like a Mardi Gras float. She knew his voice from his Movies where he sounded like the sun itself was singing, if the sun could sing.

'Which it can't!'

And now that rainbow-light was swaggering, front and center, all about the door to keep time with the beat. Sophia couldn't be in bed with sorrow another second. Nobody could. Nobody but a mean person. And Great Aunt Hortense.

And she jumped up, opened that door then flew through it to the balcony outside sure she would see somebody in one of the buildings across the way playing music way loud, the way her Father used to. But scouring every rooftop of every one of those buildings, she didn't spy a single solitary soul playing anything at all. In fact, everywhere she looked, the only thing she saw was moon light, bright moon light.

But Louis Armstrong was singing somewhere.

Where? Who was playing the Louis Armstrong music?

Now that she was outside in the night and the light and filled up to the top of her with Louis Armstrong, his song didn't sound like a CD or a record or the radio or the television at all. It sounded like he was singing. And he was there.

But that was impossible.

But it didn't sound impossible. Because she was listening to it.

It?

Him!

And he was singing to her.

And that's when she knew she'd have to search, all over again, every rooftop of every one of those buildings looking for where the man singing Louis Armstrong was standing. But this time, it appeared, she had gotten some help. Or so it seemed because the brilliant moonlight itself was providing her with more than just light; it was scanning those rooftops right along with her, like a search light would.

Like a searchlight?

As if the moonlight itself was looking for the culprit, too.

Looking, too?

And she examined every single rooftop and peered into every window she could!

And so, too, did the moonlight.

The MOONLIGHT?

But even with such distinguished help she still couldn't see anybody at all.

She finally gave up her search. And just listened. To the way he said his words. To the way he sang his song. *'He sounds like a big-fat-bowl-of-wobbly. Like a Santa-Claus-dog! Which is probably like a St. Bernard but one who can really sing. Well, if there ever really was a Santa Claus Dog, he'd sing like that. How could anybody do that to their voice? To each and every note? Well, if he can do it, I can do it too! Although I probably won't be able to do it right away. First, I'll have to learn. But learning is what I do about this time anyway. After all, isn't this the time I'm usually in Movie Star School anyway? And wasn't I supposed to practice this projection thing? So why not have my Movie Star School right here, right now? Especially after the day I've had around all those Show Business professionals. People like that must have to know how to do all sorts of people and their voices, too. And they must have to practice first before they can. And since I'm going to be a Show Business professional, too, just like them, I better know how to do all sorts of people and their voices. Well, tonight I'm learning Louis Armstrong! All I have to do is figure out how to make my notes laugh. And then project it out so a whole theatre could hear me. Boy! If I can figure out how to do all that, when the time comes for somebody to be Louis Armstrong, I'll get the job.'*

And she listened.

To the melody, to the words. And that licorice voice. She heard how low his voice was. She'd have to get her voice down that low, too. She opened her mouth, even as she pushed up from down in her belly, just like she watched her Grandfather do this morning when he was projecting. And she started singing the words he was singing, just a beat behind him, and as loud and as deep as she could. Who could've heard her anyway way up here? Besides, how could anybody hear over the Louis Armstrong who was actually singing? He was singing bigger than the moon itself! But as her words came out, she noticed how far off she was from his sound, and she stopped and listened again but much more closely this time. His voice had a growly, wobbly shake AND a laugh, too, and sometimes he hissed out his 'sss's. She got the low part, she was pretty sure; she certainly had the deep part; that wasn't that hard for her since her voice was low and deep anyway. All she had to do was jigger it up to a wobble and a growl and then mix them both together. She tried. Her wobble, growl part was just okay. But sticking a laugh on top of it all and then getting every part of it to fit together as one voice was pretty tricky … nigh impossible and for the life of her, she couldn't figure it out.

····C··

("Lady, Free's Fairy heart had been beating faster and faster and louder and louder, so loud that Free could hear it even over all the Sophia and Louis Armstrong noise. But she couldn't have been more excited. Her plan had worked! Just as she'd hoped it would! Just as she'd dreamed it would! And her heart was not slowing down any time soon. Now all she needed to do was wake up the rest of us so we could see what she did and hear what she did in its full, Never-Before-Seen Spectacle. She couldn't believe we was sleeping through the light and music and magic show she had been responsible for. She flew back into Sophia's Remarkably Small Place ready to rouse us herself, since this miracle hadn't been able to. But, Lady, we was awake. If sitting up in our beds bolt straight, with the same stupefied look on our faces counted as being awake. And not a one of us saying a word! Which was yet another miracle. When our eyes finally could focus, we aimed that same look at Free. And for the sake of Fairy Solidarity, Free put the same look on her face too, only to start, three seconds later, flying all around, whooping it up, beating her wings and yelling at the top of her lungs, "Up! Up! Up!" Which was exactly what she wanted to say, and was yet another miracle and which finally made us snap out of it. Thee was the first to actually get her mouth to work. This is how it went down, Lady—"

"Ma … aa … ggi … ggicc? Issss tha … thatttt magic out there? Free, tell me, you didn't just do magic, did you? After the Dispatcher told us not to, did you? Tell me you didn't. Tell all of us you didn't."

"Did did did I. Lis-lis-see … lis-lis-hear! Lis-lis-ten!"

"Is that who I think it is, Free?" continued Thee.

But Free was up in the air, flipping this way and that as if she was swinging about on a flying trapeze, and giggling so much she didn't even try to answer.

Thee went on, "Free, before you did this magic, you fixed it so that everybody in the Enchanted Lands, especially the dispatcher, wouldn't hear it or see it too, right?"

Free flapped yes.

"And tell me, too, Free, before you did it, you also remembered to turn on the other part so that everybody in the Human Lands wouldn't witness it, too - except for the person the magic was intended for - which would be Sophia herself? Tell me that? Oh, please please please tell me that!"

Free stopped cold, and so did her wings, and she wouldn't move, nor would her wings, and soon she fell down with a thud because even Fairies must use their wings to stay up.

"You didn't! Oh no! Did you hear that Fairies? She didn't! She didn't. What will all these humans think when they hear this and see such a sight up in their sky in the middle of the night?"

And that same stupefied look returned to the Fairies' faces. But not Free's. Free just picked herself up from the floor and went right back to flying. She refused to worry about a thing now that her plan had worked.)

∙∙:)∙∙∙

But then Louis Armstrong stopped singing and - no mistake about it - a man was laughing. No! A man was cracking up!

'And I know why. That person must've heard my Louis Armstrong.' Sophia could feel her face ignite. *'I've been caught. Caught doing a character! Nobody ever catches me when I'm in my Movie Star School, except Miss Kitty and Miss Kitty doesn't count because no matter how mad Miss Kitty acts whenever she catches me, I know for a fact Miss Kitty likes watching me play all my different characters. I see the look on her face. And besides, Miss Kitty would never laugh at me like this person is doing. The only reason Miss Kitty acts mad at me whenever she catches me up late is because I have to go to school the next morning. She's really just afraid that somebody like Mr. James or my Father or even Great Aunt Hortense might find out what I do at night. But this time I will not melt away like I would've if I'd been in Mr. Snoggley's class if somebody started laughing at me.'*

And now whoever it was, was howling. In fact, he was howling so much he was probably bent over double. Who was it? Who was listening to her? *'Maybe I can't see him because he's bent over. Well … he'll have to stand up eventually.'* She had already walked the entire length of the balcony, looking on every rooftop for whoever was playing the Louis Armstrong music. Now she'd have to retrace her steps and search for this howling-man. But this time, she wouldn't give up til she found him. She set off but by her third step it was very apparent that the moonlight had set off, too. And it was lighting up the exact same area she was looking in.

'When I look there, the moonlight's there and when I look over there, the moonlight's there. Is that moonlight looking, too?' And she looked in another spot to see if she was right. *'Definitely! That moonlight is shining up the exact same spot I'm looking in. The moonlight is looking for this laugher guy, too! Why? That's ridiculous! The moonlight is just lighting my way so I can see better … but how would moonlight know to do that? That's impossible! Maybe this just happens to anybody when they're in the big city standing on the very top of a tall building, because whoever is up here is just so much closer to the moon and its light.'*

And the guy was still laughing!

On every step she took! And she'd even stopped doing her Louis Armstrong! She listened. He had a good-sport type of laugh. *'Maybe I did sound pretty funny! Maybe he's just like me. Maybe he likes to listen to how people talk and how things sound in the middle of the night, too. I bet if I had to listen to me just now doing Louis Armstrong, I wouldda thought it was pretty funny, too.'* And then she cracked up. And now both of them were cracking up. Who was this person? Where was this person? *'Why can I hear him like he's right next to me and not see him no matter how hard I look?'*

'Next to me?' That wasn't where that sound was coming from. Her ears knew where it was coming from.

And she looked up.

"Welllll, well, well, howww do you doooo, oh yeah? 'Here's looking at you, kid!' That's what my old friend Humphrey Bogart liked to say. As I'm no kid, you can't say that back to me! You is the only kid pressssent – Oh, yeah!" And he laughed, and Sophia, wonderstruck and mystified, watched as his cheeks puffed up. And then her lower jaw dropped so far it might have touched her knees.

Or the sidewalk 57 stories below.

And her heart raced and stopped and raced again. Louis Armstrong IS the Man in the Moon.

"Ole Satchmo hisself, 'n it's a pleasure to meet you. I can't tell you how patiently I've been waitin' up here hopin' you'd look up so I could introduce myself, MizzzzZooooophia! And pardon me but I do know your name. When you're sittin' in on the Man in the Moon's gig, you sure get to know a lot of people. Tho' I do admit, I don't know anyone or anything near as much as that cat. Except maybe a thing or two about blowin' the bee'zzz honey out of a brass trumpetttt and singing the bippity into a song or two.

"But this evening The Man was real particular about having me, Mister Louis Armstrong, sit in on his gig. And it had to be TONIGHT. He told me to make sure I sing somethin' niiiiccce, and to aim it right down here.

"From time to time he does ask us Show Business folks to sit in for him. Why just last month James Cagney was here. Make no mistake about it, the Show Business folks love to sit in on this gig, 'cause we sho' 'nough love to dazzle – now tell me what dazzles more than the moon as it glides across the midnight curtain - ain't dat da truth now?"

And he laughed and Sophia watched his cheeks that were made out of moon, puff out again.

"But make no mistake about it, that Man knows not to ask us Show Business folks unless he's a full-stage, because he really doessssss know ussssss – we ain't gonna sssssit on no quarter stage or half stage, it's gotta be the whole stage, the full stage or nothing atall! Now me, I don't mind being here when it's even a quarter, because my cheeks puff it out til it comes up full anyways."

And he laughed and laughed ballooning the moon to two times its size.

"So I was wondering when you might be findin' the time to look my way. Now I couldn't help but overhear … you was doin' me … right? Now that's nice of you. I'm flattered that such a sweet young lady like yourself would deign to do my gruff-old-hooch of a voice. Not many young people now-a-days bother with us old timers any more. Imitatin' how I sing, why that is music to my ears. You sounded real good. Real good."

Sophia had been listening to his every word, too shocked to speak, or even think of a question to ask him, like how could he be up in the moon in the first place. The only sense she could make out of it was that it made no sense for a living person to witness such a thing and that realizing that didn't make it – or him - go away or stop it from happening and happening right in front of her eyes. Now that he had stopped talking and was smiling at her, she didn't know what to say to him. All she could do was stare back at this Louis-Armstrong-Man-in-the-Moon-Man.

She could feel herself breathing. In out. In out. She knew her mouth was wide open. She shut it, but it opened right up again. But she wasn't scared. She knew she should've been scared. She wasn't. The only thought that was getting through to her was that this Louis-Armstrong-Man-in-the-Moon-Man just said she sounded good. Louis! Armstrong! Said! She! Sounded! Good! The very person who she was imitating, that very same person, thought she sounded good. That had never happened to her before. That the very person she was imitating heard her imitation. What a wonderful world! Why that was the best compliment she'd ever received. And it danced all about inside her.

Deep down she'd always wondered what the person she was imitating would think of her imitation. And now she'd just received feedback straight from the horse's mouth - the person himself - a real Show Business profes-sional! A professional! Why he was more than just a professional. He was Show Business! And even if she could've thought of a question to ask him - like how he could be up in the sky in the first place – just didn't seem im-portant enough to ask - even if she could've gotten her mouth to work to ask it. Louis Armstrong said she sounded good! She felt as if she'd gotten an A+ in a very hard test. And the dance that had been cooped up inside her finally stepped outside and now she, too, stood on that roof smiling and glowing, just like him in the sky, just without the puffy cheeks.

'BUT DON'T YOU REMEMBER! HE LAUGHED! YOU HEARD HIM! IF YOU'RE REALLY SO GOOD, WHY WAS HE LAUGHING? WHY?' Her head screamed.

Its arrow had pierced her heart. Her smile vanished and she felt faint. The old Sophia had stomped right back inside and the dance had fallen right off her face. But the old Sophia wasn't finished. She yelled more. But not on the outside. On the inside. Sophia hadn't said a peep out loud yet. And it was so loud, nothing could dance through that. Nothing. And now there was just a whole lot of yelling going on inside. And a whole lot of quiet on the outside.

To anyone looking at her outsides, it was cat-got-your-tongue-land. And that Louis Armstrong-Man-in-the-Moon-Man sure was looking at her outsides because he had suddenly pulled himself a lot closer to that roof so he could. But Sophia could only listen to her insides:

'HE'S JUST LYING TO YOU TO BE NICE. BECAUSE HE'S LOUIS ARMSTRONG AND EVERYBODY IN THE WHOLE WORLD KNOWS LOUIS ARMSTRONG'S NICE. BUT HE REALLY THINKS YOU'RE GULLIBLE AND STUPID BECAUSE YOU BELIEVE HIM. EVERYBODY KNOWS, ESPECIALLY HIM, YOU'RE JUST A KID WHO'S TRYING TO SING AND TRYING TO TALK LIKE LOUIS ARMSTRONG JUST BECAUSE YOU THINK YOU CAN BUT YOU CAN'T. YOU HEARD YOURSELF. YOU HADN'T EVEN BEEN ABLE TO GET THE LAUGH PART OF HIS VOICE INTO YOUR IMITATION YET. ALL YOU GOT WAS THE GROWLY LOW PART BECAUSE THAT'S HOW YOU ALWAYS SING AND ALWAYS TALK AND ALWAYS SOUND ALL BY YOURSELF ANYWAY WITHOUT EVEN TRYING.'

And Sophia's head dropped. The yeller was right. Of course! Her voice was low and deep all by itself, she didn't have to make it that way. And then she remembered all those years ago about how she didn't want it to be. What was she thinking? Imitating somebody who talked low and deep just like she did. Of all things in the whole wide world for her to choose to do! Why that was the very last thing she ought to be doing! She didn't want to talk low and deep. And then it all came back to her! When she was little. How she didn't like to listen to herself talk. How she sometimes hated the sound of her voice. How when she really really heard her voice, she used to hide so nobody else would hear it. And sometimes how she wouldn't even talk in the talking world. And Oh! How she used to wish she had a Fairy's voice. Another voice. And how and how and how—

·⁖☾⁖·

("Ms. Author, I must tell you, even as we were down and out and under our covers so afraid to rise up and see for ourselves what Free had wrought upon the human world, we could still hear Sophia. And we were listening.

And we couldn't help but fill up with pride. The first voice Sophia had just wished for was a Fairy's. And not her Mother's! After all these years, maybe we had done some good. We didn't ever remember her wanting to talk like a Fairy. And now here she was wishing she could talk like one of us! Maybe she'd heard our echoes. Maybe we had some influence on her after all. And our heads popped up one by one from underneath our covers. Maybe this wasn't such a bad thing Free had done after all.")

Oh! My wish-voices. How I used to wish I could talk and sing just like my Mother. I forgot! how I felt! when I was a little girl! Now I remember. But nothing's really changed since then. I still wish about my voice. In fact, I'm always wishing about my voice. I've never really stopped. But when I got older, I did something even better than just wishing about my voice. I made my voice into the voice of a Movie Star. I've taught myself how to do that! But I'm so confused. That was a good thing to do - wasn't it? I did something about what I was always wishing for? So why do I feel so sad?

'I'm not just a little girl anymore wishing to be something I'm not – or am I? Why am I still so sad?

'Why? I've changed my voice! I have! I have! I have!'

But memories from long ago, and wishes from then and now; and things she couldn't do and wished she could; hopes, feelings, fears, boiled up inside her; and like a strawberry beat to a pulp; like a topsy in a turvy; a turvy in a topsy, she tossed about - high, deep and wide, and she didn't even know it, her face was nothing but a waterfall of tears.

"Now MizzzzZooooophia, what IS inside you? One minute you is as bright and shiny as me and the next you is bent down as low as a weepin' willow and your smile done jumped off your face n' on to the floor where I can see it trying to smile all by itself but it's not doing such a good job without you to wear it."

'I forgot about him. He's still there!' And she peeped-a-watery-up and he smiled-a-shimmerey-down. He'd never left. He'd been watching her the whole time. He was real after all. He hadn't gone away. He stayed by her side, no matter what. That's what friends do. Could he be her friend? She had to talk to him. Her friend. "Excuse me, Mr. Armstrong, but I'm not feeling too good!"

"Well, well, well, you talked! Now I'm happy! And in your own voice! I wasn't sure if you was just about the youngest, prettiest, daintiest Louis Armstrong I ever did see in the whole wide world! And by the way, I've been waiting up here very, very patiently for you to talk to me. And now that you have, would you mind telling old Satchmo what seems to be the trouble. I pay you a compliment, and right after I do, you look too sad even to march in a New Orleans funeral parade! Now, MizzzzZooooophia, I gotta get you cheered up 'nough 'cause right now my brothers and sisters mummers wouldn't let you even dance your handkerchief behind them! You too gloomy! And I'll let you in on a Big Easy secret, even sad music cheers up when they playin' it down there. So if you getting' ready to march with us, you gotta let go of dat gloom. And by the way, since you gotta go, and you sure look like you gettin' ready to, the New Orleans way is the only way TO go."

On every word he spoke, Sophia was getting more and more worried. *'Do I look that bad?'* She knew what funerals were. She knew that people died. And that funerals were very extremely serious, and sometimes calamitous matters filled with sad people and one very dead person who was gone forever and who would never ever come back, no matter what. It would never do for him to think that that was what had just happened, or was about to happen, to her. She'd have to straighten him out immediately. No more not-talking. And this time every ounce of her would speak up. That's why she had a mouth; that's why all people had mouths, after all.

"Mr. Armstrong, I'm not going to a funeral. Nobody died."

"Oh! I'm glad! Well then, maybe you'd care to enlighten me - was it anything old Louissssss said? Was it my compliment? Don't you want to sing like Mr. Louis Armstrong? Because you sure fooled me! When I heard you do me, I thought you was having a whole lot of fun. And, you know, you sounded just about pitch perfect to me. And when old Louisssss talks pitch perfect, that is somethin' he know a little somethin' about. But wait now, I also just gotta say, it's not every day dat a lovely young chile such as yourself can nail me. I have to admit, it's pretty funny to see and hear someone so young, singing out with a voice like mine. Why, they ought to put you in da Movies! I believe you are a comedienne. A born performer! And make no mistake about it - that is a very special gift! Making people laugh. Don't know no one down there, or up here either, who don't need some extra help from time to time having a good laugh. I'll let you in on another little secret, I didn't really have to puff out my cheeks so much, but for my audience, it was a fascination and a kick, too."

He twinkled his eyes and hooted up and down the scale until his cheeks ballooned, his mouth opened and his pearly-whites flashed as if they were the keys on a player piano. And the moon, with him in it, was singing. And then he stopped and went on right where he left off, "You know, I heard all sorts of Louis Armstrong imitators but I can't say I ever seen or heard the likes of you. And since I've been up here, I've heard even more. Why the sound of people doing Louisssss travels to wherever I am, even when I'm scattin' with the Seraphim. I wouldn't miss those imitators for the world. And let me tell you, you is the best of the dainty-iest, I ever heard. No doubt about it."

As each of his words and their meanings fell on her very attentive ears, she knew that nothing less than her whole entire life, and every little thing she loved and cared about, depended on hearing every last thing he had to say. Of course it did, he was talking about the most sacred thing in the world to her - her performance as a Movie Star, her performance as Louis Armstrong. She had never heard anybody talk about a performance of hers as a Movie Star before. Other than Miss Kitty. And he was saying such things to her about it! Things that she must hang on to! And he was making so much sense. By the time he finished, her smile was back and dancing. And her smile looked up and found his smile. It had finally found a partner to dance with. But smiling wasn't ever going to be enough now. She wanted to talk. She knew she could talk to this man. She wanted to tell him not just thank you for saying such things to her – but to tell him the real truth about herself. About her deep voice, her performances, her Movie Star School. She was dying to tell him. But could she - her smile faded. Could she? Could she tell somebody what she really thought, what she cared about, what she loved the most - Pretending! - and what she didn't like so much – being a plain, messy, bony kid with a deep froggy voice! And she put her head down as she tried to solve this cryptogram. Could she tell him how she had taught herself not to be so young, so froggy-voiced, unless, of course, the character she wanted to be was froggy-voiced? Could she? Could she tell anyone what she'd done?

What she was so afraid of?

Would she? Could she?

"Oops - for a little while there, I was afraid your smile was about to jump on that old dusty floor again ... Aren't you going to tell your friend Louissssss what you're thinking ... pretteeee pleassssssssse."

"Uuh ... I'm sorry" Sophia peeked up at him. His eyes were still dancing. What was she so afraid of? She could feel the step-heel-step in her heart.

"No yes uuh yes I will not ... will will will tell you what I'm thinking. Bubububut—

'Listen to me!! This is terrible ... '

"Ththa … thank you sososo much, Mr. Armstrong. You said the nininic-est thing to me that you could have said—"

'So now keep talking, keep talking and so what that you're stuttering … so what!'

"And I WAS doing you and I wanted to do you but then I heard my deep voice—"

'Listen, I stopped stuttering, I can do this! I can!'

"… You see, Mr. Armstrong, I'm really like you, you know. I have a deep voice, too. But I'm a girl and maybe a girl shouldn't have such a big-toe for a voice. And I wasn't at all sad that you complimented me. I was really happy you did. Really I was. But all of a sudden, I just got really sad. You don't understand. I just can hear everyone and everything. Ever since I was little, I've been listening to all sorts of things. To just about everything. And everybody. I guess I just can't help it. But sometimes when I'd hear myself and then I'd hear somebody else, I didn't always think I sounded as good as I could, or as good as they did … or—"

"As good as who? Just who was you listenin' to?"

"Well, as good as … as … some people!" She was saying what she really thought! Almost. She hadn't ever said what she was saying to a soul before. And she was talking! She could do this.

"First off, let Louisssss tell you something about us Musicians. And I said us. I said us 'cause you're just about pitch-perfect and if you're just about pitch-perfect than you swingin' in the same jungle with us. Do you know there are many Musicians who don't even have perfect pitch and only wished they had? And let me tell you something important about hearin' and something about listenin'. Listenin' is only tunin' up your ears and getting them ready to hear. And I can be straight with you, there are some Musician Cats and Catessas who do listen but can't hear. Now let's take your case. Not only did you listen to old Louissss, you heard him, too. But that wasn't enough for you. You took it one step further than that even. Cause then you did what only the rarest Cats and Catessas can do - you did me. But you did me just right. With the beat and the bop and the boodiddily, too. You didn't miss a trick o' me. Bravo! Catessa! Bravo! Now why ever would a Catessa like yourself be sad? You got the chops, Catessa! Chops! I'd take my hat off to you, if I wouldn't scratch up the sky!"

"I do?"

"Voodoo, you do!"

"Do you ever hear things, Mr. Armstrong?"

"Hear things? I been hearing things ever since I can remember. And by the way, how'd you think I heard you from way up here? I got some ears, some ears, let me tell you!"

"Is chops good? Does my Mother have chops too? Did you ever hear my Mother?"

"Chops IS good. Chops means everything is working just right. Chops is - your mouth, your hum, your soul, your skididdlee that mixes all together so it can take a ride, up on the melody, round on the harmony and down on the beat. Your chops can fly wherever the music flies ... Now ... does your Mother live here with you in this tall building, too?"

"No, she doesn't live here. And I'm only staying here for a little while. I have to go back soon. I live up river in the country with my Mother. Although my Mother works here during the day. Maybe you heard her when she's here?"

"Does she sing like Louissss, too?"

"I don't think so. I never heard her sing one of your songs ... well ... she may have sung one of your songs but she doesn't sing it like you. She sings it like herself. She sings and talks like an angel – that's what people say anyway – she sings like nobody I ever heard before. I can't sing like that or talk like her either."

"Hmmmm ... who said?"

"Nobody ever said. I just can't. I talk too deep and she talks just right."

"Now ole Louissss sees ... Like an angel you say ... Hmmm ... Now you say she doesn'ttttt live around here and livessss up river in the country. Well Louisssss' ears are always open for a treat. I do recall when I was workin' this same moon gig several years ago hearing a lovely-voiced song or two coming from up-river. I thought one of them Seraphims done fell off their cloud again. Now I'm wonderin' if the up-river country you is talkin' about is the same up-river country where I heard this voice comin' from. Is that the country with that big ole ramshackle place on the hill? That place where some of my happy and not-so-happy Show Business friends and associates end up? I wonder now if that couldda been your Mother I heard?"

"It was my Mother. It was my Mother for sure. She sings like an angel, you know ... up high ... like a—"

"Soprano? Old Louisssss knew what you was gonna say even before you said it. Now I have to ask you the sixty-four-dollar question. And the sixty-four-dollar question is the most important question of all, so make sure you do more than just listen to it, make sure you hear it. But then why am I worried about that, since I'm talking to the Catessa who can hear as good as me. Are you ready? What do you think of Altos? Second Sopranos? Contraltos? Basses? Bass-baritones? Basso-buffos? Are they angels too? And me and my big-fat-sugar-daddy voice? Am I an angel? Or are only Sopranos' angels? Tell ole Louissss thattttt pleassssse."

Of course, he was an angel. He was Louis Armstrong. And all of those other type voices ... why they were angels, too. All of them ... even the altos ... but ... wait ... does that mean ...

"An angel too! Excuse me for interrupin' your thoughts which Louissss knows are very very private but I could tell what you was thinkin' just by looking at how all of a sudden you was lookin'. Yessssssss! You isssss an angel too! And so is ole Louissss ... Now would you excuse me for one sweet second ..."

And then he called out such names - "Gabriel! Charmeine! Israfel! Ambriel! Trgiaob! Zuriel!" ... unearthly names ... each name stranger than the last. Which didn't stop him from having fun blowing such oddities throughout that night sky ... like jazz was teaching thunder a lesson. But then, after all, he was Louis Armstrong. And, oh, did those names rumble the sky.

And then he talked but to whom, Sophia couldn't for the life of her see. But even as he talked he kept laughing as if he were being tickled, "This is Louissss ... Dolls and Brothers Mine ... It's so nice to be back where I belong ... It's almost as nice up Moon here as down N'Orleans there."

Sophia scrutinized that opaque sky and finally saw something shining through but what was it? Stars? No! Stars weren't shaped like that. There was definitely something shining through that dark curtain. Bodies with wings? But how could it be bodies with wings? But whatever it was, it was twinkling specks of silver and gold and ivory and Mother-of-Pearl ... And now those specks were growing larger ... And much more distinct.

"ANGELS!" There were men angels and women angels gleaming through the midnight sky and they were beautiful. She shouted and jumped up and down and ran around in a circle. She had to tell somebody now that she was telling everybody everything. She couldn't keep this to herself. And she shouted out even though the only person to tell already knew, "Look! Look! Up in the sky! Real live angels!" And Louis Armstrong had himself another laugh.

And Sophia watched as the light radiating from the tops of the angels' heads reached just about every spot she ran to on that dark roof, just about everywhere she looked throughout that dark sky, as if the angels' halos were shooting ray-guns.

"Are they real HALOS, Mr. Armstrong?" Sophia shouted.

"They angels! What? You expect pitchforks?" Louis Armstrong laughed even louder. "MizzzzZooooophia, I have a halo too, I just didn't put mine on tonight, considering who I'm impersonatin'. I didn't want to shine so much that I'd blind my new friend MizzzzZooooophia!" And he laughed some more.

"Real live angels in the sky," she whispered to her doubting encyclopedia inside, trying to convince it that what her eyes were looking at was real and sensible and possible and plausible.

The silver and white and gold and mother-of-pearl she'd spotted were really the color of their robes and wings and halos and even their musical instruments. But these angels weren't dressed like the pictures of every day angels Sophia had seen in Miss Kitty's holy books. These angels, at least from what Sophia could figure from all of her years of watching Movies, were dressed like they were stepping out to a nightclub. But then it was the nighttime and this was the night sky, maybe this was evening attire for angels.

"Angels, say hello to my friend MizzzzZooooophia! MizzzzZooooophia is an Earth Angel."

"Hello, Earth Angel, MizzzzZooooophia!"

"So that's what the Voice of an Angel really sounds like!" And Sophia was all a-tingle and filled with awe and the finest of feelings that such a sound had fallen on the ears of her, a true Connoisseur of Sound.

"I called you down here, Angels, 'cause I want you to sing a medley for our MizzzzZooooophia! And only heavenly voices will do. But tonight it's different than other nights. Tonight, I only need a few of your voices. Only some of my friends. My low, my deep, my alto, my bass friends. So you high voices, sit this one out for ole Louissss. Tonight the altos, the basses, my deep voice compadres, be doing it all; the melody and the harmony. So, my down-in-the-dumps friends, you can do that, can't ya now, can't ya? And you, my Trumpet-Blowing-Cousin, Gabriel, since I didn't pack my horn tonight, if you wouldn't mind weaving a melody through their melody with yo' sweet trumpet, 'cause if I can't play, I guess, you'll jus' has to do." And Louis Armstrong laughed so much he just about dislocated himself off the moon. Just to bug him, Angel Gabriel blew his trumpet like a New Years Eve horn.

The Angels were all abuzz, "Basses! Altos! Did you hear that? We're about to be the pretty ones! It's about time, Brother Armstrong! I've been waiting a long time for a moment like this. Let's show those Sopranos and this Earth Angel, we can sing the melody, too. Everybody already knows we can harmonize. But now it's our turn to sing the lead. Just say the word and we'll grumble!"

"Let's do some jazz, some scat, even some Puccini. As long as it's deep and low. Okay, let's start with something easy. Why don't we do some of my songs ... Now I'd say let's do 'Sittin in the Sun' but that wouldn't be quite true anymore now would it? So howsa bout we switch it to 'Sittin' in the Moon' ... then we jump into 'Keepin' out of Mischief Now' ... you with me?"

Louis Armstrong began with a low note and one by one the angels joined in, each in their own uniquely deep voice, blending their voices til they got the sound just so. Then they swung the arc of that melody down low, then down even lower, sometimes with a pow, sometimes with a bam boom bam, but sometimes with just a swish like a Zorro cape. Up quick, down again, over there! Kapow on the roof tops! Kaboom through that night sky! Like fast tapping feet pouncing down that staircase from heaven, scuffling, shuffling and stepping low and straight into her open ears, and she was riveted. She had never heard singing quite like this before. Downbeat, then upbeat but never too high for too long. And the odd thing to Sophia was that when they weren't singing the words of the melody, they were singing the melody with words that sounded like words but weren't. And even those sounds were coming from down-in-the-cellar. Sophia hung on to every single syllable. Ba beee; boop bee booh; bing bah bah booooooo; bing bang boottoey; boo bee. And those were just their 'b' sounds. They were making sounds that came from every letter of the alphabet. But what shocked her more than anything was how deep-and-low voices sounded so mysterious! And striking! And unusual! And unforgettable. And funny! But not mean funny because deep-and-low voices were ridiculous; good funny because deep-and-low voices made sounds that tickled a person.

'This is so neat. It's almost as good as me being a Star in a Movie where I get to play the Princess who wears beautiful dresses, and triumphs over much adversity and sad sad sorrows, and helps all the little people get better and prosper, and then, at the very end, I dance with a kind, handsome prince who lives in a castle—

'It doesn't even have to be that ... it's like I finally spoke up in school. NO! Not just spoke up! I finally did all my voices and my characters and spoke them up loud and clear in school for everybody to hear just like they're doing now and because I was so good, I don't have to go to speech therapy anymore. That would be just as wonderful, too. No! That would be more than that. That would be an answer to prayers.'

And the angels sang and Louis sang and Gabriel blew his trumpet and she was standing on the roof yet gliding through the sky. And she made up her mind; she would learn how to sing just like them. She'd have to practice but she'd be able to do it. All she'd have to do was use a low voice, a deep voice on the melody parts. She wanted to sail on and on and on. *'Listen, listen, listen to them doing the melody parts just as beautifully as the high voices would.'* And it dawned on Sophia. *'Deep voices are just as enchanting, just as captivating as any high voice ever could be. When deep voices sing the melody, it lingers in the air because it's heavier. And because its heavy, it can't move as fast, so it has time to haunt whoever's listening. It's so strong it's like its gripping me right where I'm standing. It's stronger than a light, high airy voice could ever be! Low voices are something! Something to hear! They're making my insides jounce all around and shake! It's not really like that other singing. It's not like anything I've ever heard before!'*

But then there was an odd sound, like the sound a siren would make. And then there were more sounds like that. They were coming from far away but they were getting closer. Were they real sirens or were the angels playing tricks and making sirens sound, too? Sophia examined the angels but they weren't doing anything different. They were still singing the same song and making the same type of sounds they had been making all along. And so was Louis.

But just as she was looking at the angels, they stopped singing, and every single angel looked down below. Not at her on the roof but way down into the city itself. And then every single angel vanished from the sky, taking their song with them, leaving just Louis Armstrong in the moon and her on the roof and the sounds of sirens coming from way below that were getting louder and louder and closer and closer. Closer to her. Closer to Mr. Louis Armstrong. As if those sirens were coming to get her in this very building and get him, Mr. Louis Armstrong, in the Moon, too.

"Now MizzzzZooooophia, I can't stay here no more." The sirens were growing really loud. "But tell me, did you like our down-low-in-the-subway tunes? We have fun, don't we now, us Whooping Cranes, us Cats of Scat? Now tell me MizzzzZooooophia, from now on, promise brother Louisss you'll do the same and have fun with the voice you was born with, just like your deep-voiced angel brothers and angel sisters do?"

The shrieks of the sirens were getting even closer. Sophia knew those sirens had driven the angels away, and were about to drive her brand new friend, Mr. Louis Armstrong, away too. And, oh, how she wished he wouldn't leave.

"Now I didn't hear your answer. Aren't you gonna promise me that?"

'I haven't answered my wonderful friend! I must speak up to him!' And she burst out, but the sirens were so loud, the loudest they'd ever been, she was afraid he wouldn't hear her, "Oh, yes! Mr. Armstrong! Yes!" And then

whatever was making those sirens, Sophia was sure, was surrounding their building. *Could they be coming here because they heard Louis Armstrong and the Angels sing? Is that why they're so close to Grandfather's building?'*

"Now MizzzzZooooophia, I see your lips move but I can't hear your answer though I'm hoping and betting you said Yes to your brother Louissss. So tell me, how did it make you feel to hear all your deep-voiced brothers and sisters have so much fun?"

He waited for her to speak. And she opened her mouth to tell him; that it made her feel like a Princess in a Movie or even better, like she had spoken up in school for all to hear but the sirens were smashing through the night sky now and the words came out but they were being smothered to death by screeching sirens.

"Do you think your deep-voiced brothers and sisters can make music, too, or can only our airy-voiced friends make music?" And then he winked at her. "Now Louisssss knows you know that answer. Always remember - you is one of us. One of the lucky ones who can hear all the music whether its way up high or way down low and everywhere in between that's rollin' all throughout the wonderful world waitin' for wonderful you to hear!"

And he drove the moon closer to where she was on the roof and looked her straight in the eye and smiled his best Louis Armstrong smile, and she smiled back at him knowing he was about to say something that was meant only for her ears and that was very special.

"And don't ever forget MizzzzZooooophia, there never'll be another sound like the sound of you. So let dat you outta you. We all up here, and down there, too, are waitin' to hear dat you in you! Don't be a—"

But then the sirens became so loud they pierced Sophia's eardrums and they must have pierced Louis Armstrong's, too, because he didn't finish what he was about to say. And Louis Armstrong, the Man in the Moon, drove this time even higher in the sky, and she could barely hear his rumbly laugh over the howling sirens. And she felt so alone on that balcony. She lost a real friend, a wise friend, like he was her own private advisor.

There never'll be another sound like the sound of you. Let dat you outta you. Don't be a? Don't be a ... what?' What was her wise friend about to tell her? Something important, she was certain. Something she really needed to know. Something, she was sure, that might've really helped her.

She could see him up there in the sky and wondered if he would hear her if she asked him to finish what he was saying. But she knew this was too important not to try, and so over that shrieking ruckus that was now fully surrounding her building, she spoke up as loud as she could, "Don't be a what,

Mr. Armstrong?" He looked at her and she could see that he was smiling but then something began to happen to that smile. To that face. Rapidly his face began to melt away. There went his Louis Armstrong nose! His Louis Armstrong cheeks! His Louis Armstrong forehead! His Louis Armstrong mouth! Til there was nothing left. He was gone! There was nobody to ask anything to now. There was just the moon. The plain old moon. He was gone. Her friend was gone. She hadn't told him what she'd've loved to've told him. Or asked him any questions. Like did he mean what he said? Did he really really think she really and truly might be a person like him? She'd've loved to've told him about all the voices she could do besides his. Maybe she might've even done a voice or two for him … something she never did for anybody. Except Miss Kitty. She'd've told him about how she was always listening to everything and everyone there was to hear. Did he do the same thing too? She hadn't even gotten to tell him that she intended to practice so she could sing just like he sang tonight … and the angels sang, too! The angels! The angels! She couldn't forget the angels.

And now she'd never know the important thing he'd tried to tell her.

• • • PUT UP A FIGHT • • •

"Lady, we was crying our eyes out as we hung from that, you know, thingy that was all around what Sophia was standing on."

Balustrade, Lorraine.

"Ms. Author, first myself, then Lorraine and Me and then Be had finally risen up from our beds and joined Free out there as soon as we heard Mr. Louis Armstrong. And when Mr. Louis Armstrong, that delightful entertainer, that kindest of gentleman, from the land of the humans, vanished from the moon, we didn't have to be inside Sophia to know how sad she was. All we had to do was look at her."

"Jeez, Be, what was Louis Armstrong gonna tell her? Whadju think it was, since you seem to be the one wid all the answers."

"I'm working on it, Lorraine. When I get it, I'll share."

"Hey! When you do get it, Be, tell us and then we could you know, maybe-hah-hah, whisper the answer inside Sophia."

"Lorraine, get that right out of your head. NO MORE MAGIC!"

"Hey, Thee, didn't I just say maybe-hah-hah, so you're tawkin' to the wrong Fairy. You need to tawk to Free! And if Free wouldda turned on the part of the charm where nobody in human land but Sophia couldda witnessed the results of her enchantment, maybe those city sirens wouldna be going off right now and maybe Sophia wouldda heard what she was supposed to hear. So whadja think about that ... huh?"

The Fairies cast their eyes on Free, who peeked back at theirs through huge tears, forlornly, but very peacefully for somebody who was in so much hot water. She tried to speak but could only gulp.

"Free, Lorraine, does have a point. We all know you were really trying to help Sophia but what will happen when the Dispatcher finds out about this? And you know he will find out. Our Fairy colleagues on other assignments here also - who may be our colleagues but remember Free, all of them are not our friends - are going to—"

"SQUEAL!! BIG TIME!"

"Yes, Free, I'm afraid Lorraine is right. Squeal, as Lorraine so aptly phrases it, is what they'll do."

Free, still peaceful, now added gasps to her gulping, not saying a word.

"Look, everybody," said Be, "Free did this and she can't undo it! She'll face whatever music she has to when it's time."

"Well, Be darling, you're right, Free did do this and I didn't and I am simply beside myself that I didn't!"

"Me! This is not about you!"

"Listen everybody!" Be continued, "Tell me what you think. Free really did help Sophia. She got Louis Armstrong, the human singer with the unforgettable deep voice, to sing and to talk to her. Now even if Sophia didn't hear that final word or final words – I'm like still not sure what the final words are - she sure heard a lot. She heard him sing in all those deep voices. You heard him, too! He made deep voices sound like the only kind of voice to have. And we know when Sophia hears her deep voice how much of an obstacle that is for her."

"Be, I think you're right. Listen," said Thee, "I'm going to repeat back word for word what he said - 'And don't ever forget MizzzzZooooophia, there never'll be another sound like the sound of you. So let dat you outta you. We all up here, and down there, too, are waitin' to hear dat you in you! Don't be a ...' No human ever said that to her before!"

"So maybe, like, the Dispatcher won't be that mad at Free." Said Lorraine. "Because Free can argue—"

"Free? can argue? Good luck with that, darling!"

"Me, that wasn't ni—" Thee knew Me was right and stopped. All the Fairies looked at Free who looked back at them, now smiling between her gasps and gulps.

"Come on, everybody, we're in this together." Be went on, "If Free can't argue, then maybe Lorraine can on her behalf, or, like, Thee for that matter. Well, whoever ends up doing it could tell him that Free finally figured out how to help Sophia with her biggest problem. I mean, they put us here to, like, help these humans. If they don't really intend to let us help these humans, I mean, like, daddy-o, they should never've put a bunch of Fairies in here in the first place. They ought to have known we were, from time to time, going to perform magic. I mean, it's pretty ridiculous to put a bunch of Fairies in a person and not expect them to perform magic. I mean, we should really put up a fight about this. I mean, I would, if I was the type who put up fights. Lorraine, like, this is a job for you."

"If Lorraine could use the Queen's English. And watch her temper!" said Me.

"I'm, like, insulted. I elfin' can do this job, I'd be elfin' great at it!"

"Maybe I should do it!"

"We, like, think you should too, Thee!"

Free had stopped gasping and gulping and was smiling serenely. Lorraine was too busy turning the color of exploding dynamite.

• • • SEARCHLIGHTS • • •

Finally, the sirens stopped. From where Sophia was standing way up high, she could only hear the faintest sound of voices coming from way below. Whoever was speaking was far away from her, and she relaxed. But then, from the distance, she heard a helicopter getting closer and closer until it was almost at her balcony. And then she realized. She might be in trouble. Of course, she might be. They heard all the singing and saw Louis Armstrong and the angels, too. Of course, they did. If she could see them and hear them, so could other people. And Sophia got scared. The helicopter had turned a big searchlight on and was aiming its beam on the roof of the building across the way from her. It was looking for Louis Armstrong and the angels. And for her, too! And with that she hurtled herself to the open door, slid inside, dashed to her bed, dove in and pulled the covers up over her head. And waited. For what, or who, she didn't know. And with what sounded like an earthquake and ear-cracking thunder, the helicopter circled her building. Somebody was looking for her. And as that helicopter circled her roof, her balcony, her room, she watched its wind turn her silky coverlet into a moiling sea. And she lay beneath it, shaking.

·∴ᙅ·∴

("And we lay shaking inside her, Ms. Author!")

·∴꙰·∴

But the ruckus and wind grew fainter and weaker.

She waited. And waited. And waited.

But somebody was coming. They had to be. But she didn't hear anyone. She listened even more intently. That helicopter must have really flown away. But somebody was coming. Definitely. She waited. And waited. Somebody was coming. Somebody. Was.

Til she fell into a deep sleep.

• • • FRIDAY, FEBRUARY 6, 5:45 AM • • •

"Good morning, Meez Zofeeya!! How are you? Deed you sleep ze good over all ze excitement last night? Deed you hear eet?"

Sophia shot up in her bed. Was it time to get up? Sophia looked outside; there was just a bit of light in the sky.

And nobody came to get her! Antoinette Fifi wasn't coming to get her. She was just waking her up. She looked at Antoinette Fifi and wondered how ever would she answer Antoinette Fifi's question? She'd never've wanted to lie to her, her brand new friend.

Happily Antoinette Fifi didn't wait for Sophia's answer, she just continued talking, and Sophia felt relieved and not at all annoyed for once that somebody was doing all the talking, '*Whatever could I say about last night? About Louis Armstrong and the angels and me?*'

"Last night, somebody was playing such wonderful musique so loud and now all ze televeesion news trucks are on ze street down ze stairs outside our building. Zhey zhink your Grandfazair waz doing some promotionalitay tricks and projecting them up in ze sky creating zis 'sneak peek" and zis, how zhey say, "le buzz" - for his next show. Some people are even saying zat he used zome special cameras to project ze angels up in ze sky and ze Louis Armstrong onto ze moon and some special sound effects machine to make eet sound like zay were singing. Your Grandfazair is denying eet, of course. He is zo clevair. And right now he iz not happee cause zhey woke him too early. Nobodee should wake up your Grandfazair too earlee. But zhey couldn't find heem last night anywhere. He got home very late and snuck in ze back way when he saw all ze police cars and zhen he just went to bed. Wheech zhey believe waz all part of hiz plan. Ooh lah lah, eet is so much excitement. Wait til you go down to zee eet.

"Deed you hear eet??"

Sophia said not a word.

"And zhen as eef we didn't have enough excitement here but your Mozair called at Five O' Clock zis morning and you have to go home immediatement! Because your school is starting back zis morning! I am zo sad. Zhey caught all ze run-away patients. Ooh zo much ees going on. I have to pack you up and get you readee for school. I'm goin' to miss you, my new friend. I brought you some beautiful new clothes and I will put zem in your suitcase. Zay will be a surprize for you when you get home. When you zee zhem, you will think of moi. Oh and Zofeeya! I zhink I zhrew away all zose ozair clothes you brought. Ooh! Zofeeya zhey were so baggeee!! I wouldn't even use zhem for ze rags!"

Chatter. Chatter. Chatter. And as Sophia dressed and packed, Antoinette never stopped. Even all the way down the stairs. And Sophia could've kissed her. She wouldn't have to explain what anybody in their right mind would've known in the light of day was unexplainable. And impossible. Or worse yet, tell Antoinette a lie - that she didn't hear a thing.

They reached the first floor's entranceway but there was not a single person anywhere. Not an actor or a dancer. Nobody. "Ooh! Look Zofeeya, everybodee must be downstairs lookin' at all ze television trucks. Zees people who stay here, zay are actors and dancers, after all, and ooh la lah - do zay love ze camera!" Then out the front door to the porch, down the steps, onto the pathway that wound through the laughing/crying trees, Antoinette never letting up for air for a minute. She didn't even all the way down on the elevator, which they had to operate themselves because Keys and all the doormen were outside, as Antoinette said 'controlling ze crowd!' Sophia didn't have to talk at all. It hadn't even occurred to Antoinette that Sophia had a thing to do with, or even heard, the Louis Armstrong incident. Sophia realized how fortunate it could be to have a reputation as a shy person, reticent to talk.

As the elevator began to approach the first floor, Sophia could hear a roar. And when the elevator stopped and the doors opened, she saw what Antoinette was talking about. There were so many people, Sophia didn't think Antoinette and her would even be able to get out the elevator door and fit into the lobby, let alone walk through it. But Antoinette put Sophia in front of her and began to cheerily call out, smiling and laughing and winking, "Let us zhrough, pleaze. Mr. Oomla's granddaughtair has to go to school. Merci! Merci! Merci!" And with those words, that throng of people parted as if Antoinette Fifi had performed magic. But what really struck Sophia even more, was that when she began to make her way inch by inch through the crowd, everybody was staring at her. Even people who were standing in the back, craned their necks so they'd get a good look at her. In her entire life, she'd never had so many people staring at her the way these people were staring at her. Her classmates didn't stare at her like this. These people were studying her up and down - her hair, her clothes … her shoes even? And the strangest thing was Sophia, who had a hard time even answering a question when she was in school, didn't feel scared. But she also knew why they were staring at her.

It was because Antoinette had said 'Mr. Oomla's granddaughtair.' Sophia knew now like she'd never known before, her Grandfather really was a Somebody in this town. And as she kept walking, and more and more people stared at her, she realized how much of a Somebody he was. A feeling began to creep inside her, that as much as she liked being looked at, she wasn't sure, she liked being stared at. *'Looking is just a glance but staring means their eyes stay on you no matter what - I wish they'd just've been looking at me because I was a Somebody in this town, too. And not because I was my Grandfather's granddaughter. AND I wish they wouldn't stare. Although how will I ever get to be a Somebody if I don't talk? Somebodies talk!'*

They made it out of the lobby, through the front door and then! just like that! Sophia never saw so many things happening in one space in her life! Bim-ditty-bam-ditty-boom! Now what she had always daydreamed - what she always night-dreamed - what certainly her dreams dreamed, was happening right there before her eyes! And her heart sang just like Louis Armstrong!

Because in front of her Grandfather's building were crews aiming their lights and cameras at reporters who were under those lights and facing those cameras and were talking into microphones. And there she was right in the middle of it.

'In! In! In! Huh … huh … huh … How do you breathe? Out-in … OUT-IN!'

When those lights were on, Sophia knew from her television watching experience, that those reporters were talking live on television. Live on television! Right in front of her eyes. Antoinette Fifi was right. This was so exciting. This was where the action was. Imagine that! Sophia! In a place where there was Live Television! She might even be on Live Television! Sophia! On Live Television!

And she felt even her clothes blush!

No wonder all the actors and dancers had come downstairs to gape. Or to get on television themselves. Sophia was awe struck, dumb struck and bowled over. Live! Action! And she was in the middle of it. She had only ever seen anything like this in the movies. But this was nothing like the movies. This was a million times better and a million times more exciting. For the first time in her life, she was right there. She was where the action was. This was nothing like watching a Movie in her Movie Star School, because no matter how much she pretended when she was acting a part in her Movie Star School, she knew she was only pretending; she knew she was really in the television room in her parents' house acting like she was somebody else and someplace else.

Antoinette Fifi was looking everywhere and was positively giddy and as struck as Sophia. Neither Antoinette Fifi nor Sophia would budge from their spot though they were supposed to be looking for Mr. James who was supposed to be meeting them there. Their eyes were roaming but weren't searching for him; their eyes only had room for the reporters, the cameras, the crews. The glamour! And then suddenly a reporter and her camera crew moved right in front of them. Sophia and Antoinette Fifi couldn't believe their luck.

"Ooh lah lah!" Antoinette Fifi poked Sophia and they began jumping up and down. Now they, too, were just inches away from the action. Sophia could actually see just how much make-up that reporter had on. Now she knew, she'd have to put on a lot more make-up when she was a reporter. One of the crew members pointed his camera at the reporter, another turned on a very bright spotlight, and within seconds, the reporter began to speak into a microphone. THE REPORTER WAS BROADCASTING! AND THEY WERE STANDING RIGHT BEHIND THE REPORTER! THEY WERE ON TELEVISION! Suddenly, Sophia felt so shy and so aware she was shy and so embarrassed she was shy, that she turned herself into a perfect statue. A statue can't talk, can't show feeling and can't turn pink when it's on television. But then whoever was watching her on television would probably think she wasn't even a real person. And she was pretty sure that wasn't so good either.

"This is Cynthia Gordon, live for Channel Six, City News. I'm here in front of the building where that world famous Producer and Impresario lives, Mr. Solomon Oomla. Certainly everybody here and throughout the world knows Solomon Oomla. Solomon Oomla has produced for the theatre some of the greatest hits of our times. From serious dramas to campy revues to Shakespeare to farces and even the ancient Greeks; when it's a

Solomon Oomla production, it will usually be lauded by the critics and attended by the multitudes. His original shows, like his revue, *'Bats,'* his drama, *'UpTownDown,'* and his musical *'Marilyn Elvis Blues,'* were completely sold-out runs, almost impossible to get tickets for. Certainly some of the greatest actors of our times have appeared in his productions over the years.

"Before I tell the viewers what happened last night, I would like them to understand why everybody thinks Solomon Oomla had something to do with it. Last night's events share some things in common with a Solomon Oomla production. Solomon Oomla productions are often controversial, some might even say, way-out, AND are famous for their voices, their out-of-this-world voices. Every one of his productions had some of our country's most legendary thespians and singers in them. Voices are the true signature of a Solomon Oomla show. Critics often have described the voices in his shows as out-of-this-world.

"Well, last night, out-of-this-world and way-out are exactly what people might have said if they would've been there to hear those voices and see that night sky. That's the impression I've gotten from everybody who I spoke with who did witness the events of last night. Because last night, out-of-this-world voices, way-up-in-the-sky-voices are what everybody in the immediate vicinity of Solomon Oomla's building reported hearing. In particular, a very unmistakable voice could be heard by those lucky few. And when I heard whose voice it was, I have to admit I was disappointed I wasn't one of the lucky ones.

"Last night several people who live in or close by this building reported that they heard and saw something that everyone is describing as a spectacular vision complete with sound and costumes. And these same people aren't at all surprised that it was happening in the sky above the building where Solomon Oomla has his production company and lives, because it was suspiciously on the level of a Solomon Oomla production.

"Although some are refusing to call it a vision and are simply calling it a tease or a promotion for a possible new show – and this vision, or promotion, if you will, was like something they've never heard or seen before. Now it is interesting that every person I talked to this morning who did witness this event is describing it as one of the most thoroughly entertaining, swinging, upbeat like-a-sunny-day (even though it was happening at the midnight-hour) shows they ever saw. Every person who I spoke with believes Mr. Oomla had something to do with this - for want of a better word - spectacle.

"So now let me tell the viewers what the eyewitnesses did see, and mind you, this is coming from every single eyewitness I spoke to this morning, and I do not exaggerate, because what you are about to hear, some may find hard to believe. And I am quoting … 'That suddenly the moon turned into Louis Armstrong and this Louis Armstrong moon seemed to be talking to somebody on the roof of one of the buildings' - though, viewers, nobody I talked to could figure out who or which roof, though they believed it might be Mr. Oomla's roof.

"And another eyewitness said, 'and then this Louis Armstrong moon was joined by several angels and a trumpet player who all began floating through the sky around the Louis Armstrong moon and then the Louis Armstrong moon started singing and the angels started singing and the trumpeter started trumpeting and that soon all of them were scatting and singing jazz tunes while the trumpeter blew his trumpet.'

"Now, viewers what I would like to stress is whoever heard it, said that this Louis Armstrong moon sounded exactly like the real Louis Armstrong. And I want to remind our viewers that the exact replication of a voice and sound is the signature of a Solomon Oomla pro—"

Sophia had been growing weaker and weaker on the reporter's every word. And the reporter was still talking. Sophia willed herself to stop listening but her ears, those ever-merry, ever-tuned-in, thrill-seekers, simply would not be co-operate.

'The reason why all these people are here is because of what happened to me last night.'

Her stomach began pitching itself towards her throat. Was she going to throw up? What an embarrassing thing to do the first time she was ever on television! No, she couldn't let herself do that; although she just might fall down. How she didn't, she had no idea.

Of course, Antoinette Fifi had told her what was going on even before she came downstairs but it didn't really occur to her that a reporter was going to tell her story to everybody in the whole wide world.

'What happened to me last night is now on television! And the whole wide world is hearing it! In fact, what happened to me last night is why all these television reporters and cameras and people are all here in the first place. All I have to do is tap the reporter on the shoulder - she's just inches away - and tell her that that really was Louis Armstrong, and that last night Louis Armstrong was the Man in the Moon, and that the person he was talking to was me, and that he sang for me and that he told me special things.

'But should I tell her that? If I do, then I'll have to tell her the special things he said to me. But those things weren't meant for anybody else's ears but mine. I don't want everybody in the whole wide world to know those things because then they'll know

I don't always like my own voice. And that I don't talk too good in school. And that when I'm there, I don't always even talk. If I told them all that, they'd think I can't talk. But I can too talk; I can even do other people's voices. Plus if I tell them that, I'll have to explain to them about my Movie Star School. And that real school would be so much easier if every time a teacher asked me a question, I could answer in my Movie Star voices, because that's what I'm good at. But that I'm just not so good at my own voice. And that's why Louis Armstrong was up in that sky talking to me last night because he wants me to like my own voice. How ever ever ever could I ever ever ever tell them all of that?'

The reporter was still broadcasting ...

"... just how did he project those images into the sky? What techniques did this producer use, who is famous for shunning anything which has anything to do with the movies - like special effects, for example—"

'Maybe I should say something after all!

'BUT WAIT!! That's the exact opposite of what I just thought. No, I shouldn't!'
But then every thought, every feeling that followed each other contradicted her last feeling or her last thought, exactly. She was sinking and swimming in the mighty ocean of doubt and it was bouncing her this way than that. And she didn't know what to do.

'Yeah! If I'd just jump in front of that camera and start tauking to that lady reporter, I could set her straight! I could set everybody out there in TV land straight!

'Oh, how good I would look in front of that camera, in my best Movie Star voice – maybe Katherine Hepburn - and in these great clothes Antoinette Fifi gave me to wear, so I really really should tell them about what happened to me. After all, these people are here because of what happened to me! They should really get to know me and see me in these great clothes and listen to me talk like a Movie Star!

'And if I do that, then I can't keep a secret. Even though Mr. Louis Armstrong didn't tell me to keep it a secret, I'm sure he'd prefer that I did. Mr. Armstrong may not like it if he would hear me tattle. And I don't like it either because I would be telling on myself. And my Grandmother probably wouldn't like it either. If she's anything like Great Aunt Hortense ... oh, she's probably nothing like her, but I bet she still wouldn't like it, because old people like things just so. And I am a guest in my Grandmother's house and tattling and bragging and showing off is certainly not just so, after all. And probably my Grandfather wouldn't like it either. Although I'm not so sure if that's true, either.

'Besides, do I really want to jump in front of a camera and become famous for this, when someday I could become famous for something I do all by myself?

'Oooh ... inside is side-in and side-good simetomes ... oooh ... which for should I do?'

·∴🌙∴·

("Lady, by the time, Sophia had finished, our eyes was almost out of our sockets and our jaws was wide open. I, of course, was the first who was, like, able to speak. I'll take you there:

"She just said what I was thinking. And I performed NO MAGIC to get her to do that! Youse people may have been performing magic because it sure sounded like the rest a youse when I heard what else she was thinking but when she said what I was thinking, I was NOT using magic. And everybody, make no mistake - she thought word for word what I was thinking! I mean I was just thinking she should jump in front of the reporter and that's what she thought. I can't believe it! I swear I didn't do any magic to get her to think that! Youse just better believe me! Especially with this strict magic ban goin' on around here!"

"And neither did I, darlings! I wouldn't do magic right now if anybody's life depended on it. Except mine, of course."

"Ms. Author, I most certainly didn't do magic!"

"Me neither!"

"Ne meither!"

"This is a mystery!" said Be. "We didn't do any magic and she took the words right out our heads! How did she do that? Or how did we do that? But it's a wonderful mystery. We have an effect on her after all. We weren't just wasting our time here. She's thinking the way we think.")

·∴☽∴·

' *"Let dat you outta you!" that's what he said. But if I really let me out of me, I'd be too shy to talk. How can I talk to her or to anybody, if I'm too shy to talk? Letting you out of you doesn't mean letting a Movie Star out of you. Because a Movie Star's somebody else. So if I want to do what Mr. Louis Armstrong wants me to do, let me out of me, if I talk to the reporter like myself, I can't use a Movie Star voice to do it. I have to use my own voice. I have to use my own words. And for that matter, I can't use memorized words from a movie script either. I'll have to use my own words.*

'What would I say?'

You'd say the truth. She knew what the answer to that question was.

She knew exactly what to do. She looked up at Antoinette, she turned towards the reporter ...

"... we've been told that a spokesman for Solomon Oomla we'll be down within minutes to read a statement and to take our questions ..."

Sophia stood up as tall as she could. She would do what Mr. Louis Armstrong said. She would 'let the you out of you.' She looked at the reporter and again at Antoinette. She would stand here beside Antoinette and be the shy person she was and not say a word. That's who she'd be. That's what she'd do. 'Let the you of you.' She was letting the you of you. The you inside her was a shy person. And shy persons don't always talk.

···✳☾···

(" 'Do you believe her? After all the advice I gave her! She couldda gotten on television! Elfin' patungees! She couldda been famous!! Used that yapper she's always shooting off when nobody can hear her and finally used it in front of a live television audience! Shown everybody out there in TV Land what she can do! She didn't really listen to me, at all!

"We got very quiet and stayed that way for, like, a long time. Til Be spoke up about a half hour later. Tell everybody what you said."

"For what it's worth, everybody, she didn't do what any one of us was thinking. So we shouldn't feel so disappointed. Maybe human beings are supposed to just be their real selves and not do whatever Fairies want them to do. Maybe Louis Armstrong was right. She did let her 'you out of you.' The you in Sophia is a shy person. So she didn't do what we think she should do. We're us and she's her. We're always letting our you's out of ourselves and now finally she let her you out of herself. She's gotta learn to be her real self and quick and not some fake movie star or, for that matter, us either!"

"But Ms. Author, we were still disappointed in spite of what Be said and we stayed that way all the way home to the village.")

···☽···

Sophia, however, was anything but disappointed. As they traveled back to the village, Sophia felt so many things:

Sad that she was leaving the city and Antoinette Fifi! Her Grandmother and Josephine! And Bart Barone! And Keys! And her Grandfather!

And Louis Armstrong!

'Look at where I've been! Look at all the people I met. Look at all I've gone through. Look at what I've learned.'

Proud was she as she rode in the back seat of the car. She could only give a passing thought to her troubles. Her Miss Kitty troubles; her Mr. James troubles; her speech therapist troubles; her classroom troubles; her Great Aunt Hortense troubles. And that she hadn't heard the last thing Mr. Louis Armstrong had said to her. She wasn't really giving a serious thought to where she was going. She really only wanted to remember where she'd just been. And what she'd heard. What she'd actually heard.

●
●
●

Boom
Boom
Boom

●
●
●

• • • 9:00 AM • • •

The Institute for the Compassionate Care of the Extraordinary and the Always Interesting, such as it was, was about to be no more. That big-fat-kiss of a name was about to become, at least to Dr. Oomla, a big-fat-lie. The Institute for Efficiently Applied Science. And he was bereft.

The programs for self-expression of the old Chief, Dr. Edwig G. Knittsplitter III, were to be replaced with the kind of procedures that insurance corporations could approve of, such as the cornucopia of teeny tiny little pills offered by other corporations - pharmaceutical corporations.

Pharmaceutical corporations preferred to get sick people better with what they claimed were scientific remedies. It didn't matter one twit to them that just too many of their scientific remedies were funded by their own research and any results their research dug up that didn't support their foregone conclusions never saw the light of day. And their foregone conclusion was: Mental patients needed to buy their drugs to get better.

Insurance corporations, like pharmaceutical corporations, also preferred to get sick people better by ignoring evidence. They, too, didn't care that the Old Chief's tried and true practices worked. They dismissed his remedies, saying that they were nothing but what 'a long dead, eccentric made up out of whole cloth! And we will not pay for such practices! We will only pay for those teeny tiny little pills! Read this research! Pills work! By golly, they work!'

Incidentally, said the insurance corporations, those mental patients are not to be called Artistes any more. Nowhere in the nomenclature for the mentally ill does such a name appear. And we will pay no claim if the mental patient is described thusly.

There was to be one last meeting at the Institute for the Compassionate Care of the Extraordinary and the Always Interesting so the changes could be announced officially to the staff and the mayor of the Village and representatives from the mental health community. No Artistes were invited; nor were members of the entertainment business. And for the first time in its history, a Knitsplitter was not its chair.

But IV was no fool; he certainly wasn't about to chair the meeting whose primary purpose was to announce that what the Institute and its staff had stood for, was all over. His staff certainly no longer trusted him and would have no problems openly showing they didn't. They'd probably have a hard time even looking at him. They'd never let him hide behind the venerated name of Knitsplitter anymore. He was sure if he even opened his mouth, they'd jeer. And if it were up to the Artistes, they'd tar and feather him, if people even tarred and feathered people anymore; his staff may not, the villagers may not, but those Artistes, the genuine practitioners of all things dramatic, and horror movie-ish, just might, especially after what he had just done to them.

IV had lost all authority and he knew it. Only a higher authority could chair this meeting. And he had found that authority. None other than the Chairman of their Great State's Health and Human Services Committee. That's who would announce the changes at the Institute: its new name and what that new name stood for. He had come down from no less than their Great State's Governor's office and was sitting there in the chair's seat ready to begin.

Very early that morning, when the Chairman and the Committee members' car drove through the streets of the village, escorted by a truckload of the National Guard, the last of those runaway Artistes had come out of hiding and limped, crawled or shuffled back to the Institute and surrendered.

But the staff didn't have to be told what that name stood for. The Institute for Efficiently Applied Science stood for ripping down everything that IV's own Father had built so carefully and so well over so many years, and that the staff, and even IV himself, had held in place with such pride and care for all these many years. IV was certainly going to need a higher authority to describe that to the staff, since he no longer had the authority of his Father's traditions and practices to hide behind.

The Chairman of their Great State's Health and Human Services Committee and the several members of his Committee he had brought with him now sat eyeballing the staff. And the staff eyeballed them right back. IV sat beside the Chairman in the meeting, but did not say a word. The staff said later that IV, for once, was too afraid to speak. IV didn't look himself.

IV seemed to have lost stature. Or starch. Or maybe his head was just down. Whatever it was, IV seemed to have shrunk to a One. But apparently he was not too afraid to be the Chief of this new Institute, for the Chairman announced that IV was still to be the Chief of this Institute. The Institute for Efficiently Applied Science.

Thus spoke the Chairman of their Great State's Health and Human Services Committee.

The Institute was to continue taking care of psychiatric patients but the Institute would no longer be a private institution. The Institute was to be a public institution and would be accepting patients from every profession. Not just Show Business anymore. Private institutions could determine who its clientele were, but since the new Institute would no longer be supported by private funds and endowments and charitable donations and rich donors and rich patients but will rely instead on traditional sources for its funds, it will no longer be choosing its clientele. There will be no discrimination whatsoever at The Institute for Efficiently Applied Science. And that is the law.

So said the Chairman of their Great State's Health and Human Services Committee.

HMO's, private insurance, Medicare, Medicaid, community aid and out-of-our-patients-pockets, even if the pennies we pick from those pockets are covered with lint – that is where our funding must come from. And healthcare organizations do not pay for the kind of theatrical programs that the Institute runs. So The Institute for Efficiently Applied Science would not have such programs. In fact, there were to be no more daily programs of the theatrical kind for any patients. Such programs cost money and require specially trained staff. And if the insurance organizations aren't going to pay for such theatrical programs, and the Institute has no more charitable donations, who will? And certainly the Artistes - patients in treatments themselves, even if they are skilled in their crafts - do not count as specially trained staff. And to set the record straight, the preferred patient, of course, would have insurance and not be indigent but The Institute would, of course, make every effort to accept the indigent patient. Etcetera. Etcetera. Of course. The patients that were already here in the old Institute could stay in the new Institute; provided, of course, they had insurance or could pay. And if they couldn't pay or didn't have insurance, The Institute would make every effort ... etcetera ... of course ... of course. The Institute ... blah ... blah ... blah. And incidentally, the staff of The Institute for Efficiently Applied Science was to be cut.

• • • 10:30 AM • • •

"Class, open your Readers to page 275. Let's see … I would like … hm-mmm … Sophia Oomla to read our story to the class this morning. Sophia, would you please go to the lectern in the front of the room and begin …"

What was wrong with Mr. Snoggley?

Calling on Sophia Oomla to read aloud to the class! What a morning this had been, this first day back to class since the incident at the Institute.

What was wrong with Mr. Snoggley?

First off, he wasn't talking like himself. He sounded like he was coming from the bottom of a tiny tin can when he wasn't wheezing and roupy coughing and it was hard to understand a word he was saying. But for some reason, when he asked Sophia to read, those words shot out of him loud and clear, leaving the class doubly astonished. But then again they shouldn't have been because he'd been doing strange things all morning. He had not roamed around the classroom because his foot was in cast. As soon as he walked in that morning, he had sat at his desk and hoisted his leg with that foot in its cast and plopped it on the top of one of the neat stacks on his carefully arranged desk. And there were Mr. Snoggley's bare naked toes sticking right up out of that cast! For all to behold. Which was an improvement over staring at him or having him stare at them. His crutches were leaning against the blackboard directly behind him and the students were expecting him at any moment to leap up and hobble over and turn some poor soul into a wretch and an outcast. The usual.

But nothing was usual today.

And when they'd been able to take a peep at him behind his toes, he looked even more crabby than usual. And they didn't know how that was even possible. And then during the math lesson, he had actually lifted that foot from off his desk, rose up from his chair, higgled onto his crutches, then wobbled to the blackboard and began writing the problems on the blackboard, hobbling back on forth on his crutches. But then when he had finished writing the problems, he hadn't called on a single student to come up to the blackboard and solve those problems but instead wrote the solutions on the board himself. Then, at recess time, he had left the entire class outside in the freezing cold for a full 13 minutes after the bell rang. And if that wasn't enough, he had been calling on the wrong students to answer questions or do things all morning. The students who had demonstrated time and time again they had not and probably never would know the answer to his questions were the ones he kept calling on to answer his questions.

What was wrong with Mr. Snoggley?

Calling on Sophia Oomla, who had such a hard time being heard and even getting a sentence out of her mouth! to read! The student to ask to read in Mr. Snoggley's class was C. Biggleton Jr. That's who Mr. Snoggley usually called on to do the story reading. C. Biggleton Jr. was the best reader in the class. Stories came alive when he read them. When C. Biggleton Jr. read a story, he did each and every character in the story in a unique voice which suited the character perfectly. He could do girl voices, too. And even when he got to the part of the story that didn't have talking and was filled with just description, the part that was usually read by most other readers in an expressionless voice, he read with conviction and attitude and energy so even that came alive. When C. Biggleton Jr. was standing at that lectern reading, every student in the class was paying attention, not a one of them asleep or slipping notes to each other or even goofing off. He was that good. Coming from C. Biggleton Jr.'s mouth, stories were nothing less than sword-fights on precipices and far faraways and everything wondrous and terrifying under the sun. Everybody loved when C. Biggleton, Jr. read aloud. Even Mr. Snoggley. The class wouldn't even tease him and call him by his nickname, C Big Jerk, for at least three hours or sometimes even until the next day.

But Sophia reading the story!

Pitiful. What a day this was turning out to be. The very first day they were back to school after the incident at the Institute, and here Mr. Snoggley was behaving like one of the escapees. Students were openly looking at the classroom clock. Four and half hours to go before they could leave Mr. Snoggley's booby hatch.

After Mr. Snoggley had called on Sophia, no one said a word, til finally someone sniggered, then so did a few more, then people in the back of the room began poking each other. Til somebody whispered very low, "Wow! Snoggley's brain musta cracked in half, too!"

Like everyone else, Sophia had heard Mr. Snoggley, her classmates' sniggers; after all, she was in the classroom, too. Her heart had sunk, she couldn't breathe; what always happened to her, happened to her again. She should've been used to this. She wasn't. As she picked up her book and got up from her chair, her arms jittered, her book almost slipped away, her knees almost buckled and she was so sure she could feel her classmates' cold big fisheyes on her, that she felt every single nerve she owned roller-coaster up and down on her body. And to top it off, she was blushing so much that she was certain she must have turned into one of those red corpuscles she'd seen in her Father's medical books. And there she was, the only one stand-ing in the entire room, and she, a giant red corpuscle! If she wasn't the bull's eye for all those fisheyes to gape at, who was?

Their target! Again!

And she knew it. She couldn't just stand there and have everyone see her be so unMovie-Star-like! She had to move. And she lurched forward.

'Why me? I hate school. I want to go back to my Grandfather's house.' And Sophia lurched forward again until suddenly the angels were singing and she stopped in her tracks right where she was. Which was beside Grace Botticelli's desk. But she wasn't beside Grace Botticelli's desk any more. She was back where she wanted to be. With her real friends. She was with her Grandfather. She was with Bart. Reva Sweet. And Louis Armstrong was singing, "Let dat you outta you."

'Let dat me outta me,'

Hm … Fairies … Fairies? Where are you? Don't you want to tell the Readers what you were up to?

Readers, apparently, it will be up to me to speak for the Fairies at this juncture of the story. They, like Mr. Snoggley, were having a difficult morn-ing, too. They, like Mr. Snoggley, weren't themselves either. Oh, they weren't sitting at their microteensie desks with their microteensie feet on top of them. No. They were laying in their microteensie beds, silent and sulking with their microteensie covers over their heads and had been that way ever since Sophia had so disappointed them with that reporter this morning. And now they were doing their best to push that painful memory out of their mind. But how could they? What good were they doing here on Planet Sophia anyhow? They'd been so close this morning to actually mak-ing a difference. The closest they'd ever been to making a difference since they'd been placed on this assignment - Sophia had actually thought what each of them had been thinking without any of them doing a bit of magic to get her to. And for a few sublime moments, they believed that they'd had a real and lasting influence on her. But then Sophia had gone and done something else entirely. Instead of doing what she was thinking when she was thinking like them, she had gone and "let dat you outta you." And what that really meant for Sophia was just letting the shy person out of her. And how would Sophia ever progress if that was all she ever did? But, above all else, what about their own progress? Like them having a real and a lasting influence on her?

And after all they'd done for her! She'd ended up listening to Mr. Louis Armstrong. And not to them!

Sophia hadn't jumped in front of the camera and set everybody in TV land straight the way Lorraine wanted her to do. She hadn't slinked and swanned and swanked in front of the cameras to show the world how good she looked or how she could talk like Katherine Hepburn the way Me wanted her to. She hadn't shunned the camera because she was noble and could keep a secret the way Thee wanted her to. She hadn't ignored the camera because she believed she should only become famous for doing something she had done all by herself the way Be wanted her to. She had, instead, done what Mr. Louis Armstrong wanted her to do, the man Free had found to help Sophia.

But Free lay in her bed, too, and was sad because her Fairy friends were sad. Free was just sensitive that way. And besides for the longest time, Free had been wretched and nervous and flummoxed but oh-so-inexpressively because wasn't Sophia maybe just a little - or was it oh-no-awfully! - like her in the talking department already? And Free grieved and stayed sad and in her bed, too.

So, Readers, our Sophia was facing yet another crisis in Mr. Snoggley's classroom, but this time, without her Fairies by her side. Instead of being there for her, each of those Fairies lay under their covers with not even a half an ear cocked towards the action outside. They simply couldn't muster up the energy to be there for her. But then again, in their defense, hadn't they been worrying and wondering, and wondering and worrying about her for ten long years now? Well, apparently it didn't work! So what was the use of cheering Sophia one more time? Even if it was why they were here in the first place, even if it was their job to do? And they wouldn't have budged from under their covers even if the Dispatcher would've shown up at that very moment and caught them hiding under them. What was the use? Sophia would end up doing what she wanted to anyway. She wasn't going to listen to them. This morning they'd felt for the first time that they might have some actual influence on Sophia. And then they found out they didn't. They were so close. And since they had gotten so close, they realized how desperately they wanted to have influence. Real influence. But now they knew they never would. They were sick and tired of the whole experience. They, too, just like Sophia, wished they were someplace else. Even Thee Fairy Prudence Priss Primly felt that way.

So how, Readers, will Sophia do without them?

One of her feet had stepped itself in front of the other. Sophia wasn't lurching anymore. She was walking. And as she began to move towards the lectern, she finally felt the open book in her hand. She still had her book open to page 275. The page Mr. Snoggley had told the class to open to, even with all the pitching and lurching about she had done when he called on her because somehow, without even intending to, she had kept her book open. She took a good long look at that open page. Her heart jumped. She knew this story. Of course, she did. She should've remembered when Mr. Snoggley called out the page. She'd read "The Orphan, the Spy and the Policeman" aloud so many times when she was all by herself in her room at night, she practically knew all the words. She loved this story even more than she loved her Movies. It was filled with such wonderful characters – the American Orphan Girl, the Foreign Spy Lady and the old English Policeman. She had never seen anybody do it because it wasn't a movie, it was only in her Fifth Grade Reader and there was no movie to see, no actors to imitate. She'd had to figure out how to do the characters all by herself. And she had. She had made up a voice for each of them. For the spy lady, she used an old Movie Star, glamour-girl kind of mix and match of a foreign accent, a little Parisian, a little Hungarian, a little she-didn't-know what but whatever it was it rippled up from the back of her throat and made that spy lady sound like a cherry bomb one minute and a dark cloud the next. She had to reach all the way down to her diaphragm to create the full blast of tarantaras and humphs and hurrahs she needed to create the old English Policeman; it might have been Mr. James, if Mr. James had had enough of the Queen's English and went off his bazoo. But she didn't need an accent to do the young orphan girl. She just did her in a soft voice with much cheer and spirit even though it was clear from the story and the things she said that the orphan girl had a sad sad life. Sophia knew what was really inside that orphan girl.

'Let dat you outta you. Let dat you outta you.'

Sophia had finally reached the lectern but she stood there with her back towards the classroom as she heard her friend's words over and over. 'Let dat you outta you. Let dat you outta you.'

She had such a feeling inside. Suddenly she understood a lot more about those words than what she had understood about them this morning. Those words meant many things. She listened to who was inside her. She could even feel their voices bumping up against the edge of her. She could hear the funny old English Policeman, the Foreign Spy Lady, the Orphan Girl. If she didn't speak for them, who would? If she didn't let them out, their voices would be roaming around forever inside her voiceless. If she didn't stand up at this lectern in Mr. Snoggley's classroom and open her mouth and read their story to her classmates, those characters would never have had a chance to step outside and be themselves and be heard and tell their story in this real world of her classmates and of this very moment. And they had been waiting so patiently for such a long time. They were the you inside. They were the you she had to let out. Those characters were her after all. Her friend, Louis Armstrong, was right.

'Well, Mr. Louis Armstrong, there's a lot of yous inside me!'

And then an image from the day before jumped in her head. Those children who got to act in a play on the stage of her Grandfather's theatre. And she began to fume.

And pow, she was ready. She turned around and faced the class. She stood up straight, lifted her head and made herself every inch as tall as she really was. She looked at her classmates and Mr. Snoggley. Very few of them were looking at her but those that were, their eyes were growing. She placed the open book down on the lectern. She even felt just before she said the first word, that something was being turned on inside her, like whatever the thing is that lights up a star, for a blaze had swooped inside her, and was pouring out of every part of her, especially her eyes. She could even feel them sparkle the way a Movie Star's eyes do in a close-up. But then this was her close up after all and her eyes were ready. In fact, they were Roman Candles. But then they had to be. She had a cherry bomb inside her.

She opened her mouth and began. The very first to speak was the old English Policeman. He came out of her in a rush and a roar since he was the loudest of them all and Sophia didn't stint a bit on producing his sound.

The class jumped in their seats and Mr. Snoggley's leg fell off his desk.

But that old policeman carried on …

… even as there were gasps coming from all about the class room. "What's wrong with Sophia?" was whispered by several students right before they gaped in disbelief. Holy Moly! Holy Cow! Holy Mackeral! Holy BAD WORD!!!

What was wrong with Sophia?

But nothing stopped the old policeman.

"Quiet, I can't hear the story!" Now suddenly there were factions of students; the captivated ones were shushing the crying-out-loud ones, and the laughing-out-loud ones were doing just that, laughing out loud.

The old policeman kept roaring and harrumphing.

Mr. Snoggley, the Palaverer-in-Chief of the Fifth Grade Class, could palaver no more through his twisted tongue and his bugged-out eyes.

The Spy Lady began to speak.

Then the entire class was palavering. Til even that stopped and every individual in that classroom shut up and watched and listened in mesmerized mystification as if Sophia's face was a movie screen and her voice was the soundtrack.

They knew from the words of the story it was war time but they felt how forsaken the country was from how she said each of the words. They saw the bumbling policeman. They heard his jokes. Then out slinked - or did she snake - the mysterious - or was she traitorous - spy lady, who didn't laugh no matter how many jokes he told her. Whose side was that spy lady on? The wrong side? Maybe. Then the Orphan Girl entered on a tip-toe, and they listened and heard her story. Then they began to wonder, if that Spy Lady was on the wrong side, why was she helping the Orphan Girl? Or was she helping the Orphan Girl? Or just pretending to in front of the policeman? And did the policeman know the Spy Lady was a spy? And was the Policeman really trying to help that Orphan Girl? And should that Policeman help her? Who should help her? Who would help her? Which of these characters had the right character to help her? Who should she trust? But the Policeman was the good guy and the Spy Lady was the bad guy? Right? Because policemen are on the side of what's right and never what's wrong and spies are always underhanded sneaks who betray their country? Right? That's how they were ... ON THEIR OUTSIDES ... BUT WHAT WAS INSIDE THEM? Could insides and outsides not match? And what would happen to the Orphan Girl? Then just like that, the story ended.

And there was uproar in the room.

"The Spy Lady is a spy. The Orphan Girl shouldn't trust her!"

"No, the Policeman was only pretending to be nice by telling all those jokes. And he knew she was a spy but even so, he was the one the Orphan Girl shouldn't trust!"

Back and forth they argued; Mr. Snoggley now leading the discussion. Nobody noticed Sophia prance - or did she samba (or was that the rhumba) or was she drum-majoretting - back to her seat. She listened to them go on and on and sat there glowing like incandescence itself. They were talking that way because of what she'd done and how well she'd done it. She'd told the story so dramatically and so convincingly that from the things they were saying, they seemed to have even forgotten it was a story. Of course, she would've glowed. This was the best moment in her whole entire life.

"Sophia! How did you do that?" Suddenly somebody remembered her and now everyone of her classmates and even Mr. Snoggley himself was looking at her.

'And here I am sticking up like a giraffe! How could I ever answer that question, how did I do that? And besides that, what must the class think of me? They had no idea I could even get three complete sentences out of my mouth and be heard, let alone do this!'

And it was February but she felt a tropical heat wave and she flushed pink and got queasy, and lowered those eyes of hers that just had to be shooting live sparks, and stuck her towering neck, fireplug face and burning hair between her shoulders where they would be safe from the inquisition that was about to follow. How could she explain where all of what she just did came from? How could she tell them AND Mr. Snoggley about her Movie Star School? About all the voices she practiced night after night, year after year? About how she loved listening to voices and had been doing voices by herself ever since she could remember? And by the way, just how would she've been able to do all that explaining about voices, using her very own, really real and really shy, Sophia voice? She couldn't. She wouldn't. She was just going to have to be her other self. She was shy. That's who she was right now. Her friend had said let dat you outta you. And that's who dat you outta you was - now. Besides she liked being shy. She didn't mind being quiet. When she wasn't talking, she could hear voices and sounds so much better. She dug her head down lower and waited. She would stick to her guns. She would keep her secret. They couldn't make her tell it.

But all of a sudden the class burst into applause and cheers and hip hip hoorahs. And they were all looking at her, she could feel it. What was going on?

And everybody started talking at once, "Good going, Sophia!" "Nice job!" "Pretty cool!" "I wish I could read like that!" "That was amazing!" "Hey! Sophia, that was the best reading I ever heard in my whole life!"

Sophia was shocked and now not only was she speechless outside but inside, too. She was incapable of holding even a thought in her head, their reaction had flabbergasted her so. But a thought finally arrived. She was wrong! What was in her head was wrong! Her classmates weren't going to ask her tough questions. They were happy for her. And suddenly she was thrilled and her head popped up all by itself and she smiled without even trying to do that either.

Finally, Readers, she had showed up at her own parade.

⸱⁖🝔⁖⸱

("Thanks, Lady, for telling our part, just then. Ya' gotta understand, it's hard for us to admit to, okay? Be, tell her what you said."

"Okay, Lorraine. 'Look everybody, weren't you listening? We don't have anything to worry about. Didn't you hear her? Didn't you notice what she said? Didn't you see what she did? She let all of those different voices out of her – and they're only some of the yous inside her. Well, we're inside her, aren't we? One day, she's gonna let us out of her, too, just wait and see!' "

"And I says, 'Oh! yeah, Be! Wait and see, Be? How can we? We'll be long gone and won't even hear her when she does!'

"We was hanging out on Sophia's ear and some of us was still pouting, in spite of what Be'd just said, and in spite of this being Sophia's happiest, proudest moment in her whole entire life, the moment we'd all been waiting for, hoping for, praying for. But even as Sophia had begun that Reading and it was plain to hear that she was finally doing in front of others what we knew she had done so many times by herself, we had just about dragged ourselves out of our beds with only half a heart. Me was kicking her knee-high, stiletto boots back and forth. Thee had her arms folded across her chest and her elbows were sticking out like a witch's nose. I had that Tough-Fairy, Big-City look on my face. But Free had moved closer to Be and was noddin' her head in agreement even after Be had stopped tawking.

"Then I said," Be went on, 'You know, we really ought to be proud of Sophia. I mean, look at what she just accomplished. Instead, we're all just thinking about our own selves.' "

" 'Stop trying to sell us Fairy-Dreams, Be! We want to have some influence on Sophia. Some lasting influence on her.' " That, Lady, believe it or not, came from Thee! Admit it, Thee!

"But Be wasn't lettin' up, Lady! Tell her what else you said, Be."

"Okay, 'Thee, this isn't a Fairy Dream! Haven't we always wanted Sophia to do what she just did? Well, she just did it. We should be happy for her! But instead we're pouting like a bunch of cry-babies!' "

" 'Be, I'm just worried that all our work here has been for naught. I myself want to see that she's well-mannered and speaks like a lady.' "

" 'And well-dressed in nothing but the very best! With just the right hair and thin! Very thin!' "

"And I says, 'And street-smart and no dope! And not afraid to speak her mind! Whichever or whose-ever mind it is. You know, if she has all these voices inside her, which one of them is really her? Ya know what? I don't really care, I just want her, when the time comes, to be tough and cool, like me. And I want to see it with my own eyes before I have to scram outta here for good. And anyways, if she can be all these other people, and do their voices, why can't she be us too, for elf's sakes! It's not like she doesn't have the talent!'

"Oh, yeah … Free was going on about something, 'But Moon-Strong … uh … meanme … Moon-Arm … no … UUUH! Because of Fairies … me … because … him … talk … now … she! We did dood this … Dood …AUGH!' "

" 'Free … what are you, like, trying to say?' "

" 'we … dood this … we dood … we Fairies—' "

"But just then we heard something, Lady, very close to us and looked up. Mr. Snoggley was tawking very low and our ears began to tingle with the sound of him, he was that close. We peeped and saw that he was leaning on his crutches and whispering to Sophia right in the ear we was sittin' on. And he had the strangest look on his face. He was smiling. We never remembered seeing a smile in his cemetery plot before, he didn't look himself! Yeah! I mean, it was like a clown'd just jack-in-the-boxed outta a casket.")

"Sophia, I am absolutely delighted you are seeing that speech therapist who seems to have done wonders with you already and in just one session. I always knew you were very capable, although I never quite suspected you had such a dramatic flair, which is so important when reading a story to a class full of fidgeting students. When read to in that manner, students not only never fidget but they pay close attention to the plot and the meaning of the story. Which is exactly what happened when you read just now. Look at the lively discussion the class had at the end about the character of the characters in the story. And the way you said the words of the narrative part was so distinguished. Indeed, the trickiest part for all dramatic readers is unadorned description, without any peppy dialogue to entice your listener's ear. Why, it requires nothing less than a true vocal virtuosity to carry it off. But the way you read it, with such flavor, why those students were transported right out of our classroom and into that war-torn country. And when you did the dialogue, you were that Policeman and because you were, they could hear his jokes as if he, and not you, were telling them. Then with another voice, you were that Spy Lady. With another, the Orphan Girl. Why, Sophia, your classmates were hanging on the edge of their seats. Keep up the good work with your speech therapist! I expect to be calling on you to read to the class again."

"Thank you, Mr. Snoggley!" Sophia whispered back. She was transported skywards even though she hadn't budged an inch off her chair. Even her head hadn't moved and she kept it right where it was, which was peering down in what she hoped appeared to be a scientific examination of the floor. And there she sat trying to figure out all that had just happened. Certainly the whole class had seen Mr. Snoggley stand at her desk speaking to her confidentially. Did anyone overhear what he said to her? She worried they might have and she felt so embarrassed. And yet what they would've heard if they did hear was Mr. Snoggley really appreciate what she had just done and telling her so. What was embarrassing about that? And ... Was Mr. Snoggley NICE? She still couldn't get over that! PLUS he'd said he was planning to ask her to read again! She would have to set him straight and tell him she hadn't been to the speech therapist though and she'd have to do that immediately and was just about to but he had crutched off.

·∴☾·∴

("Speech therapist! Speech therapist! We was cracking up, Lady! 'Hah! Hah! That's a good one. She saw a speech therapist alright. She saw—' ")

·∴☽∗·∴

'Louis Armstrong! Wait a minute ... I did see a speech therapist. Let dat you outta you! He was my speech therapist. Louis Armstrong is MY speech therapist!'

And just like that a note landed on Sophia's desk. It was folded sharply and on its face SOPHIA was printed boldly and underlined with a masterful upswoosh. Sophia stared at the note like it was a live-hand-grenade and with lightening speed, scooped it off her desk and jammed it inside the shelf-pocket of her desktop. She knew what was inside. Something like, 'How did YOU do that? I thought you couldn't talk!' For sure.

'Except today! I don't care what anybody says about me!'

And with the utmost nonchalance she lifted her head to check if anyone was looking at her. Mr. Snoggley had returned to the front of the room and was teaching History; the class was paying attention to him, not her and she shoved the note way to the back of her desk's undershelf. She didn't need to read an insult.

But as soon as she had, she couldn't stop wondering, *'Why would anyone write an insult in such fancy handwriting? Insult notes are usually printed jagged and scratchy.'* For the rest of the morning, she couldn't stop agonizing, what was in the note? When Mr. Snoggley announced that it was five minutes til lunchtime, she pulled the note forward so she could reexamine the handwriting. Whoever wrote it, wrote artistically, like they were writing an invitation. Could it be? And she unfolded the note and read it.

"Sophia, Congratulations on a fine Reading. I couldn't have done better myself. I've never told anybody before but I write plays. Would you be interested in doing the girl parts in the play I've just written? There are several juicy parts for girls. I've never really liked having to do the girl parts myself and after what I heard you do just now, you sure would do them a whole lot better than I would! Could you come over to my house and do a run through of my play this Saturday? I wish I would've known sooner that you could do voices. I've written so many plays and you could've done all the girl parts. Let me know. C. Bigg"

C. Biggleston Junior wanted her to be in his play! She was going to be an actress. A real actress. In a play!! A play! This was better than Movie Star School. A real live person was going to be there with her and hear her and see her do what she could do, and in broad daylight, too, and not the shadowy midnight with its prowling-pouncing-picture-people.

·∙·**(:**··

("Oh, Ms. Author, forgive my silence. All of what Lorraine just told you is true. I admit it. But at this particular moment, I, we, all of us, forgot what had made us sulk so badly before. We simply forgot everything! 'Sophia is going to act in a play! Sophia! Our very own quiet Sophia!' And sad, de-flated, prostrated us began flying all around Sophia's head."

"Yeah, Lady, we whooped it up so much, that all the other creatures in all the heads in Mr. Snoggley's Fifth Grade class came out, and whopped it up right beside us. Itssa wonder Mr. Snoggley didn't hear us and smack us all with detention.")

··**:)**:··

• • • 6:00 PM • • •

Towards the Castle L'Oomla, Dr. Oomla trudged. No, he wasn't cut. Yes, he still had a job. Though what that job would be, or whether he would even like this new job, he hadn't a clue. The weekly production of plays and musi-cals and revues for the village, the daily theatrical exercises, the singing pro-grams, the dancing exercises, the playwriting classes, the costume designing, the set designing, the evening karaoke ... all gone ... over. Never to happen again. What IV had told them in that staff meeting at the beginning of the week was a lie; the theatricals would not happen even once a year. And Dr. Oomla had had to face the patients yet again and tell them that he hadn't lied to them; that he'd been lied to. He'd prayed that they'd believe him.

Dr. Oomla had felt sick all day. He had failed. The old Chief. The Artistes. Himself. Freud!

But these events weren't what Dr. Oomla was focusing on as he trudged home. Because something else had happened at the end of these historic, awful days that was equally as historic but whether it too was awful, Dr. Oomla couldn't stop wondering. He was even holding a debate with himself about it all the way home. Because after he had sat down with each and every one of his Artistes telling them the news, trying to keep their hearts from breaking, assuring each and every one of them that he wouldn't abandon them, and when finally, finally, finally those never ending days did end, and he was ready to go home, he had dragged his weary self up from his chair, turned the light off in his office, shut his door and stumbled down the dusk-darkened corridor when somehow through the 15-watt-dimness he discerned through the cast shadows what had to be a real person coming towards him but who looked ground-down, bent-low and so askewly-slanted, that he was more worthy of the night and the squirming and an 'it' than the upright and a sapiens. Could it be yet another downtrodden, dejected, distraught Artiste? Had he, or his colleagues, missed somebody? In a few more steps, he and the 'it' came face to face. And when Dr. Oomla saw who the 'it,' he was almost grounded, too.

IV!

His face was almost unrecognizable. There was not even a ghost of a snarl or a grimace lingering on his lips. His skin was yellowed. Dr. Oomla had never in his life seen IV look this way. He was simply bones in a suit, he looked that inhuman. But flashing through the dullness was an unmistakable set of glistening eyes, the most sorrowful ones Dr. Oomla had ever seen.

Then IV spoke, his voice, in a toneless drone, so thick with phlegm, so without bounce, music, emotion, it sank and drowned on each word. A voice so unlike the voices Dr. Oomla had been listening to when each of his Artistes had used theirs so expressively to let out such a range of feelings from deep sadness to resounding fury, that he had to strain so he wouldn't miss what it and the man behind it was saying.

"Oomla you have to believe me I had no choice I could not take any more fund raising I hated it I hated begging those Show Business people for money I hate begging anybody for anything but Show Business people – I have had enough of them - I do not care if they are famous or beautiful or geniuses or legends or whoever they are - they act like they care but most of them only really care about which newspaper which journalist which TV camera is there and witnessing the great act of charity that they have done for the poor unphotogenic unconnected witless nin-compentents who are not as lucky and as Movie Star A-List and as beautiful as they are - it's all a sham a sham - besides I am not good at begging to beg you have to be humble to be nice Oomla I am not that nice I hate being nice I have never been that nice it is just not in my nature it never was - my father even knew that about me but that did not stop him from insisting that I run this place and keep it going after he died and just before he died he told me to get an MBA because that was where my talents lie and that if I got my MBA I would be able to apply sound business principles when I had to run the Institute after he was gone and I did - I went to business school I got my MBA after I become a Physician but I should have sold this place when my Father died - I do not have it in me to do this kind of work but did I listen to myself - I thought I could turn this place into a successful venture I was sure with my MBA I would be able to run it correctly - I was sure I could get this non-profit organization to not only be in the black but to make a buck and I did for a long time but Hah Hah Hah the liability insurance to run this Institute with all its ridiculous programs and live productions and that Dance-Dance ferry past Sing-Sing on the way to the White-Way every Wednesday why suppose somebody got injured suppose somebody fell off the ferry or suppose there was a fire at the Institute what then - my father never thought of any thing practical - no he was a big dreamer it was up to all the rest of us to clean up after him we could have gotten sued - we were lucky no catastrophe ever happened here every time I received one of those insurance bills I could not sleep they gave me nightmares and besides the insurance bills there were those constant fund-raisers those photo-opportunities for rich Show Business people and let me tell you rich Show Business people are not like other rich people - rich Show Business people couldn't stand me - I could feel it - I am not anything like my Father a lot of them knew my Father - my Father was good with the flash the gab the vision thing the simpatico the feel-your-pain but I am not - I am serious I am strict I am a banker-type - rich people like serious like strict like bankers- but Show Business rich people do not like strict - strict is not hot and then after awhile I just stopped being able to rake in the money from those types anymore they could not stand me but I could not stand them either and you know who else I cannot stand those publicists those pushy pushers who spend their whole lifetime making stupid people outrageous people ridiculous people look like they should be members of your own family - phonies - every last one of them, if I meet another publicist I cannot be responsible for what I will do - did I tell you how much I hated begging day after day year after year it was impossible for me to keep up my Father's dream this place is impossible so many programs and Oomla do any of these patients these Artistes ever really get better - we keep seeing the same ones coming back year after year over and over and over again - those programs just cater to those Artistes those Artistes need to escape into fantasyland - babes in Toyland well this is Artistes in Fantasyland that is what this place is. That is what I was the keeper of ... A Fantasyland. Maybe that is what my Father should have called this place ..."

And then IV rejoined the shadows and skulked away through the darkness, even as he rasped out more questions, more theories and incriminations, more nightmares and meditations that stuck to the floor and to the walls. And to Dr. Oomla.

And all the way home, they stayed stuck on Dr. Oomla and all he could do was think about IV and the Old Chief. About sons and fathers. Fathers and sons.

'IV never talked like that to me before! I didn't know any of this about him! But then I never talked to him. He always spoke so forbiddingly! But look at him now! Is it because he let his Father down? Is that why, he's acting this way? But then there he was giving the speech of his life, telling the truth for once, and every word he spoke, he spoke with not an ounce of feeling! At least the patients aren't afraid to express themselves with passion. At least the patients aren't afraid to feel and to express how they feel. So the Institute did some good after all, unlike what IV says. And the Institute is not impossible. It's not Fantasyland. It wasn't fantasy to see that after a few days at the Institute, those patients would start participating in the programs and were alive again. Where will those Artistes be without those programs? Patients whose spirits are sick, can sometimes just want to give up and not want to live anymore. But the old Chief's programs got them up and believing again. So IV is wrong. The Institute really did do a lot of good. But IV did tell his truth. And his sorrowful eyes were speaking in a way he couldn't. That's where his feelings were hiding. So maybe IV isn't so hopeless. Listen to me! As if IV was my patient. As if I could help IV!'

And suddenly he didn't feel right. But he pushed on down the path anyway, trying to think about IV and the old chief. But he couldn't. He could only think about himself. And his own Father. Solomon Oomla. He tried to push those thoughts out of his head. He didn't like thinking about himself at a time like this. *'I have to help IV. Have to help IV. Have to help. Help.*

'Help, help, help! That's what it is! It's that word! That word is the story of my life! When I was growing up, all the people that I ever knew were in Show Business and so many of them needed help. So many actors. And all of them came trooping through our house. Some of them were so funny, so good at imitating people, mimicking their voices, their way of walking, how they carried themselves, they used to crack me up. I loved them. They knew how to have fun. Anyone who didn't know better would think they were the coolest, smartest, hippest people in the room. But for some reason, I could see through them. Although there were the quiet ones, because

the acting profession can attract really quiet, shy, almost withdrawn people and they were the hardest to see through because they don't walk around saying or doing anything to see through. But a lot of those actors weren't quiet at all. They could really express themselves. But no matter what type they were, when they wanted attention and they didn't get it, watch out world and everybody in it. I used to see them monitor who was really paying attention to them. And if somebody wasn't, they would up the ante by doing or saying something even more daring or more outrageous til they scored. And if they didn't score, some of them would throw temper tantrums like spoiled brats. I used to laugh at them, even imitating them myself when I was really really young and boy did I get in trouble with Father and Mother for that. I learned never to laugh at them or anybody. And boy have I had a lot of practice since at not laughing at the ridiculous. But then, actors are not all that different from any of us. They want to be loved. The only real difference between them and other people is, some of them want to be adored. Which is a whole other issue. Even though I was the child and they were the grown-ups, they so needed my understanding, sympathy and love, they really were the children. Well, when I was little, I made up my mind that when I was a grown up, I'd be the one to help them. I'd be the one who helped everybody. Who helped Mother. She with her glamorous outside, voice and clothes and attitude, she was so confident, it was as if she was standing tall on the starboard side of a sailing ship as it ribboned through the sea but somewhere down deep inside, I knew she was scared and worried and didn't know where that ship had been, where that ship was, or even where that ship was headed. And that ship was Dad.

'Help! I even wanted to help him. Dad, who didn't believe then and doesn't believe now that he even needs help. Mother. Dad. Could be so ... what? What was it about them? And what is it about me that makes me want to help them? To help everybody? Maybe I'm just trying to right all the wrongs I see. Dad's drive for Show Business - he valued it above every business or thing or person in the world even though he knew Show Business respects only Perfection and Power and Fame and Fortune. And the Notorious, of course. That and his own unyielding, opinionated, bull-headed stubbornness. No wonder the force of him found the force of all of that. And speaking of a flair for the dramatic - it was life or death with him when he was just placing a phone call. And Mother who lived to perform and did it so well that everyone really thought she was so clever and so witty and so informed and that that was who she really was. But she hid her hurt and her fear and her loneliness away from everyone, including herself. I could always sense how she felt. She'd never have left Dad either, though she threatened to many times. But then he wouldn't have let her. He always said, she is my music. But then maybe, no matter what Dad did wrong, she loved Show Business and his power as much as he did. Or maybe it was

more complicated than that. Maybe they really do love each other. Look how long their marriage has lasted.

'*My Father wanted me to take over his business, too, but I would've hated it just as much as IV hated taking over his Father's business. Just like IV, I didn't have the personality for my Father's business, either. But the difference between IV's Father and my Father, was the old Chief insisted IV go into the Institute business but my Father backed off when he realized I didn't want to go into Show Business. But then my Father has never really forgiven me. Ever since I turned my Father down, my Father and I don't really see each other all that much. Or talk all that often. Our Fathers wanted us both to go into the family business. I never wanted to be a producer. IV never wanted to be head of the Institute. I know how IV feels. I let my Father down, too. IV and I really do have things in common. Our Fathers were very stubborn.*

'*But the old Chief may have been more stubborn than even my own Father was. I always admired the Old Chief. Looked up to him. Even maybe more than my own Father. Maybe I should start admiring my own Father a little more. At least he let me be myself. Even if he never forgave me for it.*'

And for the first time he could remember, he felt a small bit of sympathy for IV. Even as he recalled what IV had done. And undone. But he knew nothing would come of it. '*I don't get the feeling IV and I will ever sit down and have a heart to heart about all of this. IV wouldn't want to, for one thing. He's too far gone. It's funny, I always find out whether my patients had parents that put pressure on them to do something that they really didn't want to do. I seem to've forgotten that I had, still have, and may always have, the same problem. It's so hard when a Father puts intense pressure on his son to do what he wants him to do, instead of what the son wants to do himself. Especially when the Father knows it's not even in the son's nature to do what he wants him to do. Look at the consequences! The Institute. The Artistes! The Staff! This whole village is about to change. Everything is about to change! My life, too! If the old Chief would've advised IV to sell the Institute, somebody might've bought it who would've kept it the way it was. The way the old Chief had intended it to be!*'

Then something else struck him. He hadn't ever really talked to IV. What else didn't he know? Who else wasn't he talking to? Who else didn't he know?

And then he was home. He hadn't been home since all this dreadful business had begun. And he couldn't think another thought. He felt so relieved even if it was the Castle L'Oomla he was looking at. Even if it was a pile, it was the pile where his music was, his library was, and where the people he loved and who loved him, his Sophia, his Sigrid, his Miss Kitty, his Mr. James, and all of the dusters and scourers and polishers and closet queens and orchid-orphanage attendants and flower-bed gardeners and grounds-keepers were, all of whom kept that pile humming. He needed all of every-whom and all of every-what who were in that pile now more than ever. He had a family. A big family. His family wasn't going away. And he had to take care of all of them. He could because after all that'd just happened, he was still standing. And he ran up the Castle L'Oomla's long winding driveway, through the allee of wintering trees. What a past few days he'd had! The Institute was no more. His job, as he knew it, was over.

What if anything else happened?

Well, right now, he couldn't worry about that. He was to be with his Sophia, his Sigrid, his Music. And maybe he'd be lucky; maybe Great Aunt Hortense wouldn't be there.

∙
∙
∙

Boom

Ticka

Boom

Ticka

Boom

∙
∙
∙

• • • DR. OOMLA GOES … … … • • •

"Movie Star School! Sigmund. You heard that! They have both confessed. Sophia and Your Miss Kitty, Sigmund."

Dr. Oomla's ears heard 'Movie Star School.' But the actual meaning of the words didn't register, but something else sure did. *'That voice! Great Aunt Hortense! The sound, the screech, the screed of her! That's what I have to listen to! After the week I just had! But then what should I expect? Exactly who I did not want to see, is exactly who I do see! Am I to be sucked forever into the Cave of Trophonius? I leave it only to walk right back in it! Well! I'd rather disappear into even that gloomy abode than listen to Great Aunt Hortense!'*

And in a blink, he entered that ancient dark place of sorrow though he was standing in the Orchid Orphanage. But his ears couldn't escape; they were still listening to that voice that was in His Castle! Her! Cacophony! Was! Echoing! Throughout! His! Blossom! Filled! Sanctuary! Was his Castle to be the polar opposite of what he'd so craved all these wearying days? And he had no choice but to open his eyes.

And there she was, shrieking up the place.

And that was it. He willed his ears to hear not a word more, and he withdrew again, *'Why couldn't I meet some other more melodious member of my household? And why has she taken it upon herself to surround-sound me with her deluvian elocution! Whatever she's talking about, as far as I'm concerned, is more vociferations of her high-toned flapdoodle which I have no intention of even trying to understand!'*

Every ounce of the compassionate healer had been bled out of him. And he didn't give a hoot. He'd had enough of caring, of compassion, of healing in the past few days. All he could muster now was pity for himself as Great Aunt Hortense kept filling up his ears, his soul, his space, his consecrated sanctotum, with her braying, blaring blather.

And she went on though Dr. Oomla heard not a word of her.

"Your Miss Kitty! Your Miss Kitty, Mr. James! Your Miss Kitty indeed! Sophia, of course, is a child and can't be expected to behave like a responsible adult. But Your Miss Kitty is another story. She was the one who was supposed to take care of Sophia. Well, Your Miss Kitty never cared to inform you, Sophia's parent, that her charge, her responsibility, Sophia, was up at midnight on a regular basis conducting her very own Movie Star School. And Miss Kitty knew all about it AND was the person entrusted with Sophia's care. Care indeed! What else will happen to your daughter, with our Sophia, under your Miss Kitty's care? Will she discover the village's street corners? She already needs a speech therapist! What else might she require? What else?"

She might as well have been saying, "NYAH NYAH NYAH!" for all he cared. The hairs on his skin were already standing up all by themselves. And he told himself over and over, *'In the past few days, I've showed more than enough understanding to people and their problems to fill up two lifetimes of understanding.'* And just in case he might suffer a relapse and be tempted to feel understanding and/or compassion towards the Deluded Deluvian - because he very well knew what his weakness was, and that was - he had too much 'feel-your-pain-compassion' and too little 'how-dare-you-temper' - he didn't let himself glance even once near, let alone, into her eyes.

Not only wouldn't he look into her eyes, he stayed firm and did not take in her words. Nor did he articulate even one of his own, though he was thinking a multitude, *'Great Aunt Hortense! Who else would have greeted me after the awful week I just had? A chorus of pearly-voiced, flaxen-haired Venuses? Of course not!'* And without even a twinge of guilt, and with abandon, glee even, like one of his Artistes, he gave himself full permission to continue – not to 'act-out,' he was a mental health professional, after all, but to surrender to his version of it, which was, in his case, a no-holds-barred, full-fledged 'think-out' - *'Yes! Nothing less than a womping, Wagner-screeching, horn-helmeted, glass-shattering, Teutonic-Brunhilda would be waiting for me to complete this week's awful perfection! And there she stands. Great Aunt Hortense.'*

He was delighted with himself. He, too, could think dramatically. Just like his Artistes! Wickedly, devil-may-care even. But wait! He hadn't gone far enough. What an opportunity he'd missed. And his thoughts fandangoed this way and that, every which way without meeting a single speed bump. But even that wasn't enough. Now he wanted to burst out in an uproarious stage-laugh and proclaim his thoughts, those very thoughts, out loud for her to hear, in fact, for the entire Orchid collection to hear. And in the blink of an eye, a laugh, a real laugh, an actual laugh, ripped out of him.

But freezing, cold air whipped into the Orchid Orphanage from the bitter February that was just outside, and round and round on that draft his laugh rode, sailing round him, ringing his ears, and the ears of the Orchids, too - the Orchids in their Orphanage where he and they and Great Aunt Hortense were standing.

Which was only just a glasshouse.

And the icy shock of that laugh! to those ears, his ears! reverberating through him and echoing throughout that Orphanage for Orchids and their blossoms, and that House made of Glass, was too much for those ears, his ears! to swallow! *'Here I am letting my brain, that holds in its memory the Hippocratic Oath, the words from the great Works of Freud and the pamphlets of the Old Chief, even think such thoughts!'* And he disowned himself in the instant and felt the hot flames of liquid guilt erupt inside him, squelching once and for all every last possibility of his ever dabbling in the devilishness of the near-hot-head again.

And then a new thought brought him right back to where he was actually standing, which was right next to Great Aunt Hortense.

If Great Aunt Hortense was now in charge here in his home, things at the Castle L'Oomla must have gotten awful here, too. Just like they had at that other Castle. The Castle Gloomla. How had that happened?

But the better question was, and he knew it, how had he let that happened?

It was time to find out.

And he would. He would.

In a minute.

'When I finally stumbled through the Castle L'Oomla's door, I was so happy just to be here, even if the Castle L'Oomla is a pile of elephantiasis, it's my pile of elephantiasis, with sincere apologies to the elephants. There are no rules here, no treachery here. And there is no boss here either. I couldn't wait to be seated at my table, surrounded by my family and finally in the company of those who love me and those who I love. But when I arrived, it was only a little after six and there wasn't a light on anywhere and, it was surely time for dinner and yet there was no aroma coming from the kitchen. I didn't see even one of the scrubbers or cleaners or polishers who are usually getting ready to go home at that time. Where was Mr. James? Miss Kitty? Sigrid? Sophia? Where WAS everybody?

'I hiked through each dark room. I turned on every light I came upon but I didn't find anyone. And then I heard what might have been a muffled cough coming from the Orchid Orphanage and I ran that way. But when I shot through the entranceway of the Orchid Orphanage, I found a human there alright. Great Aunt Hortense!

'Who was very anxious to tell me something ...

'which I was even more anxious not to hear.

'But she didn't even notice and she plowed on with her jeremiad til she reached the final syllable. I bet she thought I was, and am, and will continue to be, hanging on to her every word!'

Wait! Was it silent in the Orphanage? Had Great Aunt Hortense just finished and had his ears just caught up with the blessing? Whatever that wham of a mounting crescendo she had just deposited in his ears meant, he still didn't have a clue but at least it was over. What a relief.

Until he and those ears were interrupted by that same muffled cough that he'd heard before.

His eyes pierced the shadows and he couldn't believe his eyes, and his ears, for there was Sigrid. Right next to her was Mr. James. Was that Sophia sitting there too? 'Everybody is here and I didn't even know it.' He began to feel very odd. 'Has all that has been happening to me at the Institute overwhelmed me so much that I am barely conscious? What did Great Aunt Hortense just say? I don't even know. I don't know because I tuned her out. And not only did I tune her out, I don't even know when the people I love are right next to me. Did Great Aunt Hortense say something about a Movie Star School? Movie Star School? What could she've been talking about? There is only one person in this room young enough to attend school. She had to've been talking about Sophia!'

And he felt his head grow hot again that Great Aunt Hortense had been talking about Sophia in that snotty, haughty, hauteur of a voice, even though he didn't have a clue what she'd actually said. It didn't matter. 'Sophia surely heard what she said. She was right there listening to her every word, to her every snob-bily spoken word.' But in the next second, he realized something else entirely. 'But listen to me! Here I am calling Great Aunt Hortense a snob and I'm silently mocking her diction just like a snob would, and because I'm doing that, I didn't pay a bit of attention to what she was actually saying. I should've been listening to what she said, not how she said it. And I think she's a snob! I'm no better. Although I have to admit, even though I don't know what she said, I know she went too far.'

And he turned the fury on himself this time.

'It's my ears. My ears didn't care to listen to her and now I don't really know how far she did go! I am ruled by these ears! These sensitive, discriminat-ing, dictatorial, over-orchestrating, over-reverberating, overbearing ears! My ears turned up their nose at what they were listening to and shut off. These ears - my ears – are not Carnegie Hall – they are not just the passage-way for pure-as-a-bell decibels; they are the place where all sounds, whether I care for those sounds or not, must come in. Those ears which I always thought heard so well have just *failed me. They haven't heard what they needed to hear. I let them tune out. My ears have a nose which they like to turn up! It's true! And I don't even have the sense to realize it. I think just because I am a psychoanalyst that I have insight! Well, then, shouldn't I have insight into why I do things, too? And I call Great Aunt Hortense deluded! What about me? If I don't have insight into myself, but I think I do, I'm deluded, too. Well, Dr. Oomla, here's the sixty-four dollar question, why didn't those fancy, hi-fi sound systems you call your ears let you know when something was wrong in your own house?'*

Just then there were more muffled sounds. He looked even more closely through the dusk that had by now enveloped the room. But he didn't need light to know that they weren't muffled coughs after all. They were muffled tears. Sigrid was crying.

'And, of course! What am I doing? I'm standing here thinking. Everyone here must believe I really have turned into The Thinker for all the good I'm doing them! Enough thinking! It's time to take care of my family. Sigrid, first!'

"Sigrid, why are you crying?"

• • • MRS. OOMLA GOES … … … • • •

Sigrid had been watching him as he stood there during Great Aunt Hortense's stinging rebuke not even looking stung; not looking at anyone, not saying anything. She wondered if he'd even noticed them at all. Even when Great Aunt Hortense had finished and they'd been waiting for him to say something, anything, he didn't. Was he building castles? Listening to imaginary symphonies? At a time like this? Whatever he was doing, he'd separated himself from them. And she! a parched flower about to wilt. Would SHE have to speak up to Great Aunt Hortense? Would SHE have to handle this problem? And she was mad. Hurt. And mixed up between the two. But now that he had finally opened up his mouth and he had spoken so kindly, Sigrid really did almost wilt. She couldn't muffle her tears anymore. She started sobbing, her chest and shoulders heaving. She tried to tell him what she was thinking …

"Whyyaagh wereyou so ough ough momomotion …"

But it blubbered out. She, the one who talked, the Oomla spokesperson, the polished-professional, was incoherent. She tried to compose herself but couldn't and sat there gasping for air and listening to herself think what she was trying to say to him …

'motionless and quiet the entire time Great Aunt Hortense was delivering that rebuke of you and Sophia and Miss Kitty?'

… but couldn't say because she was leaking and heaving and spewing and couldn't stop.

And as she did, she realized so many more things. Things that she wouldn't dream of saying to him, but that she couldn't stop herself from thinking anyway.

'They are right, he really does look like The Thinker on two feet. He really is oblivious to everybody around him while he thinks his great thoughts just as that statue would be if it were there in his place. And speaking of rebuke! Great Aunt Hortense was rebuking me, too! Even though she didn't actually say a word about me, she might as well have. After all, I am Sophia's Mother!'

… and she felt ten times worse …

… which only made her cry more. And her shoulders lurched and she was burping and dripping a Galapagos Island of snot.

'Listen to me! Look at me! I'm a mucus mess! Inelegance itself. And they call me The Voice! Hah! I don't dare stick this voice around what I have to say to him. Him! Of all people. Him! With his ears!'

Dr. Oomla stroked her hair, then he reached into his jacket pocket, pulled out a handkerchief and handed it to her.

Which made her hiccups ruckle and fortissimo til she belched and burped and wanted to die from mortification. And still she couldn't stop thinking.

'Why didn't he silence Great Aunt Hortense right on the spot? Why didn't he defend his daughter and Miss Kitty and me? Why? I don't want to be the one to have to say anything to Great Aunt Hortense. Especially after the past few days I've just had! I couldn't talk tough to another person for all the orchids in Madagascar. He's quiet because he's waiting for me to do the talking, to be the one to say something to Great Aunt Hortense, the way I always do. After all, I'm used to always being the one to speak up for him when he's faraway in the land of The Thinker Statues. In fact, in this household, between Mr. Thinker and Sophia, the quiet one, I'm always the one who talks. But, today, I just can't do that. Maybe that's why I can't talk. Especially after the week I just had, I can't say another tough word, even if it would be to defend my family. And I know a Mother is supposed to defend her family but today, this minute, I just can't. I need help.'

And to see if she was wrong, she opened her mouth …

"Whyyyaa didn't yououggh helllyelp me?"

She shut her mouth. *'Listen to my voice. My voice has changed so much. That kitten-whisper is gone. I really sound tough. Because of what I have to do every day. Because I've become tough. I sound like a stevedore! Some Voice! I'm croaking and dripping on every word.'* And still she couldn't stop thinking.

'Yes, of course, there's truth in what Great Aunt Hortense said. Sophia having her own Movie Star School … and Miss Kitty not telling us … well … I'm not sure what I think about all of that. But I know this, after the days I've just spent, I refuse to think another thing because somebody tells me I must. And besides, today of all days, I've never seen Sophia look so happy. But even if Great Aunt Hortense is right about all of this, why is any of this Great Aunt Hortense's business? This is our business. Not Great Aunt Hortense's. And he should've told Great Aunt Hortense that. Because I just can't. Even though I am tough. And am even tougher after just spending the last few days with the Giggle board! But right now, I can't say one more tough word. I just can't.'

But something made her try again to see if The Voice had returned, "Whyyya didididdn't youyouggh hellhellyelp me?"

Her words were rattling because her mouth was rattling. And she could hear how loud, how tough she was! How very, very tough. He must hear it, too!

'And as far as I'm concerned that board is just a roomful of Great Aunt Hortenses!'

"Thaat'sssWHYYAHamcryinnnng!"

A volcanic eruption! Echoing throughout her Orchid-ed universe. Coming from her. But as soon as her racket lost its echo, she realized what she'd just said was dead wrong! She hadn't told him or anybody why she was crying because she hadn't told him or anybody what she was feeling, what she was thinking. She hadn't said much of anything at all. Except a mash of wails and gobbles. Some tough person she was! And she was humiliated. And her shoulders heaved more. And all she could do was sit there listening to all that she wished she could say but couldn't.

'Because if I do, what would he think of my Voice now? And what will he do when he finds out how tough I am. Even though I can't seem to be tough now. But I do know one thing. I have had enough of the Great Aunt Hortenses of the world. I can't humor another one again. No matter how right they are. Or they think they are. I've just had to face a roomful of them. And lost. At least, for now. But I! Have! Made! Up! My! Mind! I refuse to have my ear chewed on by an even broader assortment of Great Aunt Hortenses from a wide variety of countries in several different languages. I'm about to become the boss of my corporation! Giggle Inc. is NOT to become a multinational. And Giggle Inc. will NOT exploit foreign factory workers. Not after all that I, the founder and CEO, and the Voice of Giggle, have been reading. And anyone who tries to convince me otherwise, will have their ear chewed on by me. I AM tough. And, another thing! My voice and I are not going to say anything we don't agree with! We've had enough of that too!

'As soon as Great Aunt Hortense began injecting me and every one of us with her righteous words, I knew right then and there I had enough. Here I am the inventor of a national sensation, and a woman who has become a role model to women everywhere, and I'm letting a board push me and my voice around! Well, finally this role model is going to put her foot down. And open her mouth, and if what comes out of it is not polished and is nothing but spit and nails, as long as it hits the bull right in its eye, that's all that matters. Who would consider me a role model if I don't? I can hear the back-room buzz already - Couldn't stand up for herself. Let a board run all over her! Wasn't smart enough, tough enough. See, what did I tell you! only a certain type of women in the world can really do that kind of work after all. But Sigrid Oomla, with her flower-petal voice, isn't one of them.

'But what will Great Aunt Hortense think?'

And her face burned and her throat was sore and in a spot deeper than deep she ached. How could she ever explain all of this to Great Aunt Hortense? And to him, especially in this voice? She couldn't even explain why, if she was so tough, she couldn't speak. Maybe it was because she was so tough that she couldn't speak. And she was tough. And would stay tough. She had to. Because the world could be so tough. But she knew, too, how alone she felt though her family was right there beside her.

"I'm here now. Please tell me why you are crying! Whatever is wrong, whatever has happened, please tell me, Sigrid."

But Sigrid still couldn't get a word out. She would look up at her husband and heave and sob all over again. Til out came in a sharp voice, bitter words but spoken on such a huge wave of snot and saliva and so slightly that even Sigrid had a hard time hearing them and recognizing them as her own,

"Oh, Sigmund, they're using me for my voice!"

But not a soul heard her.

And she was relieved for how could she, her voice, The Voice, own up to such acrimony, just like that? And like an evildoer, she cast the orphan - her ache, her hurt, her truth - out in to the storm. Which only made her sob more.

There was a long huff and a deep sigh and a short sniff, and Great Aunt Hortense spoke again, "I have been most patiently waiting for one of you to comment about my discoveries. But you, Sigmund, as usual, are speechless. And Sigrid, even you are too? Please understand, I do so sympathize with you, Sigrid. Dear Sigrid, I can see by your tears, that you have taken my admonitions to heart. But Sigmund, when you walked in, you wouldn't even look at me. It was as if you were ignoring me. You didn't even say a proper greeting. Is that how you treat guests in your home? And when I was giving you my report, I kept looking at your face to see what your reaction would be, but it wasn't even clear to me that you understood a word I said. Or that you were even paying attention to me. But it did occur to me that you may be adopting, even with me, and even in a discussion about your own daughter, that neutral visage that psychoanalysts are known for when listening to their patients, even though what I was saying may really have alarmed and upset you. But no matter what your own personal reactions are to what I said may or may not be, I stand very firmly by them. Please understand, I am only trying to help your daughter who so desperately needs your attention."

·:·*(:·:·

("Elfin' bag a' wind! Listen to her! I wish somebody'd just shut her up!"

"Oh, Lorraine, if only we could perform some kind of very precise Fairy magic that would go undetected by the Dispatcher and would make her go away!"

"That would be way cool, Thee!"

"Of course, if I was Sophia, I'd be able to shut Great Aunt Hortense up!" said Me.

"Me miims think could she could! Me you we magic her up? Trouble big though! Big trouble! Big fun! Before the slammer hit we.")

·:·:)·:·

• • • SOPHIA GOES BOOM TICKA BOOM TICKA BOOM • • •

"Great Aunt Hortense! Don't worry, I heard every word you said. Don't forget, I'm sitting right here …"

·:·*(:·:·

("Ms. Author, before our wings even touched, Sophia spoke up!"

"I says, 'Did youse do anything? Did any of youse do anything?' "

" 'NO!!!!!' "

"And ten, nine, eight, like ground control to a rocket-ship, except faster because on seven, we was already perched on Sophia's ear. Lady! There was no doubt about it, Sophia was speaking up to Great Aunt Hortense and we hadn't performed a bit of magic to get her to! We listened to Sophia's deep voice, her confident voice, the voice we knew was her very own, that wasn't borrowed from a Movie Star's, but was her 'Let dat you outta you' voice,' the voice that Louis Armstrong had told her was inside her. But that wasn't even the real wonder. The real wonder was that Sophia wasn't using that voice on any elfin' bag of wind. She was using that voice on THE elfin' bag of wind. Great Aunt Hortense!")

·:·:)·:·

"... And my Father and my Mother and Mr. James probably heard you, too. Even though they're not talking right now. And the reason they're probably not talking is because sometimes people just can't talk ... I know all about that. Because sometimes people tried to get me to say things, like in school and I just couldn't. And the other thing I want to say is, I love Miss Kitty. And you're wrong. Miss Kitty takes very good care of me ..."

⋅⋅⋅☾⋅⋅

("Ms. Author, Readers, we Fairies were listening, raptly, eagerly, acutely to Sophia. We were all ears. And all eyes, too, because Sophia wasn't just talking, she was doing something she had done with her Grandfather when they were having their Show Business lunch together: Sophia was holding forth. And we sat still, in gazingstock attention, our ears boggling or popping or widening, because this holding forth was something to hear and Sophia was someone to see.")

⋅⋅☽⋅⋅

And because Sophia's deep, alto, confident voice had carried to the room that adjoined the Orchid Orphanage where Miss Kitty had been waiting to find out her fate – whether she was to keep her position as Nanny to Miss Sophia and cook to the Oomla household - Miss Kitty had crept in and she, too, was listening. Miss Kitty wouldn't miss this even if every one of her Irish Saints had winged down and barred the door.

"And she is a good person. She prays every day. Everybody knows only people who are trying to be good pray! And besides that, you were also talking about my Movie Star School! Great Aunt Hortense, my Movie Star School is the most important thing in my whole entire life and I will not stop going to Movie Star School. I love my Movie Star School. I have learned so much ..."

As Sophia talked, she'd find herself glancing away from Great Aunt Hortense's eyes, those eyes, and down at her own arms and legs wondering where were her costumes? All she saw was her boring old uniform. But somehow catching sight of her dinky old school uniform, which was no Movie Star costume, and her loud and strong didn't turn into wobbly and shaky. And she talked and kept talking without so much as a pause. Not a word she uttered was shaky. If, as she was talking, she caught sight of her clothes, she wouldn't have cared if all she was wearing was just a fig and a leaf. She knew that even if she'd been wearing the costume of a Queen, it would not've made what she had to say any more important. All she had to do was what her secret speech therapist wanted her to do. What he knew she could do. What she should do. "Let dat you outta you!" It was so easy. Even if she wasn't in a fancy costume and that Those Eyes! were glaring down at her. Nothing was going to stop her. Nothing!

"... why just today in school, Mr. Snoggley called on me to read, and I read the story like it was really happening! I did each of the characters voices. That whole classroom was my audience! I could do that because of what I taught myself to do in my Movie Star School. Because of my Movie Star School, I knew how to read that story, Great Aunt Hortense!"

Though Sophia's Father was statue-still and didn't appear to be blinking or even there, Sophia's Mother was certainly breathing normally again. And Mr. James, though his at-attention posture remained at-attention, he aimed it a few degrees forward in his chair and set the dial on his face from gravely serious to seriously attentive.

And as Miss Kitty listened to Sophia talk about her so kindly, it was as if Sophia had by some unexplainable mystery joined a chorus of harp plucking angels. But when Sophia began to tell Great Aunt Hortense about how she'd read a story out loud to her classmates using her character voices and it was all because of her Movie Star School, Miss Kitty recognized how right she was. It was all because of her Movie Star School. And not a speech therapist. And then Miss Kitty was certain that that harp wasn't just any harp but an Irish Harp and a lucky one at that. Miss Kitty always knew Sophia to be a good little Actress. Now her classmates and her parents and Mr. James and even Great Aunt Hortense were finally finding out. And, too, maybe the Oomlas and Great Aunt Hortense and Mr. James would come to see that Sophia was fine without having to see a speech therapist. And maybe then they'd see that Sophia's Movie Star School wasn't such a bad thing after all. And Miss Kitty'd get to keep her blessed position in the Oomla household.

"... and if I am to be able to continue to read stories to m—"

"Oh Sophia, you read aloud in school today!" Suddenly Mrs. Oomla found she couldn't contain herself another second. She'd been filling up with wishes and wisdoms and wonderings that were now about to brim over her, and she simply had to let them out. Though Sophia was still talking and clearly hadn't finished all she had to say; her Mother just knew everyone would want to hear from her now.

"I can't tell you how happy I am to hear this news about what you did in school today. Your Father and I—"

• • • "YOU INTERRUPTED HER!!!" • • •

Shouted Sophia's Father
and Great Aunt Hortense
and Mr. James
and Miss Kitty
and the Fairies.

(Readers, one of the Fairies did inform me that she did not actually say the same thing. But since it registered on the Richter scale - its Fairy equivalent, actually - it won't be printed here. You might wonder why not, since the exclamation only registered on the Richter's Fairy equivalent. But this book has certain standards and I, as its Author, refuse to lower those standards, even if it would be just to divulge what exactly registers on the Fairy Richter.)

Such words spoken to her! Of all people! And how swiftly! How vehemently they'd said them. Even Great Aunt Hortense had weighed in! And Mrs. Oomla was crushed.

'Sophia is talking out loud for all to hear and speaking up so well! And here I am interrupting her! Interrupting my Sophia who needs to see a speech therapist because she has trouble speaking up and being heard in school, and all of a sudden she is speaking up and being heard just fine without even seeing a speech therapist - and there I go and interrupt her! And not only that, she was doing good deeds, trying to help Sigmund and me by talking about Great Aunt Hortense's issues with Great Aunt Hortense directly; and speaking up for herself, too, because we obviously weren't. And she was trying to help Miss Kitty, too, because obviously we couldn't seem to do that either. I don't remember her ever doing anything like this before, especially with Great Aunt Hortense, and I go and interrupt her!'

"YES! THEY'RE RIGHT! YOU INTERRUPTED ME AND YOU TALKED ABOUT ME TO MY GRANDMOTHER! YOU TOLD HER I COULDN'T TALK!!!"

And finally Sophia understood Ginger Rogers and spunk.

Until she blushed purple then shut her mouth, and couldn't say another word. Think, however, she could, *'What did I just say to my Mother? I've been talking too much. Mother is the one who talks.'*

Sigrid looked over at her daughter and saw that they were both the same burning color. And Sigrid cringed again. Her daughter must feel as crushed as she did! Crushed by something she did! But what Sophia said was true! She had told Sigmund's Mother about Sophia's talking problem; she felt her blush go from crimson to purple.

But Sigrid had to admit something else. Something that humiliated her. And that was, she was a little surprised by everyone's outcry. And unprepared for their reaction. For the first time in a long time, people, other than the board, and Goliathonians, wanted HER to stop talking. Including her husband. And there was something else she was unprepared for, that Sophia should be the one who did the rescuing and the expressive, persuasive talking. Sophia wasn't the one who did that. She was!

'Well, Sigrid, it's somebody else's turn now!'

That back-talker again! Her guilty conscience! And it wouldn't stop – 'Shame on you. That's your own daughter you're talking about. The daughter you need to raise so she can succeed. And weren't you just grumbling to yourself the other minute about always having to be the one who has to do all the talking in the Oomla household! That you were always the spokesperson! always interceding on behalf of the Thinker Statue and the quiet one! And now finally an Oomla stops thinking, stops being quiet and steps forward and takes charge, and does talk, and you're not so sure how you feel about it! Oh, and by the way, look who's the Thinker Statue now! The quiet one! You! And, by the way, did you really notice that your daughter, whose teacher told you needs a speech therapist, was speaking up with the passion of a ten-year-old Sarah Bernhardt and she hasn't even seen the speech therapist! And by the way Ms. Role Model to Women Everywhere, your very own daughter just spoke up like a Ms. Chip-off-the-Old-Ms.-Block! So why aren't you telling her how proud you are of her? Why?'

Everyone was staring at her and they weren't smiling and she was so ashamed and so thankful no one could see into her mind and know what she'd just been thinking; she was triply ashamed she'd even thought it. She knew what she must do.

And that's when those orphaned words tore up out of her and pounded her, pounded everyone, hard,

"They're using me for my voice!"

Dr. Oomla jumped. From those few words, he understood so much. He didn't even have to ask who was using her. He took hold of her hand, saying, "That's what happens to beauty. But I can stop them, Sigrid!"

But now her back-talker was pounding her, too, 'Everyone was paying attention to your daughter and you couldn't take it, could you? So, you, Princess Charming grabbed the attention back to yourself! You needed sympathy! But so does your daughter! As if you didn't know Giggle is using you for your voice! As if you weren't using them to become a billionaire! Stop bellyaching and pay attention to your daughter!'

And finally the pounding stopped. And she understood so much. She looked up at her husband, "Oh, no! Sigmund! It is I who must stop them and I will!"

And she rushed over to Sophia and knelt down before her, "Oh! Sophia! I'm sooooo sorry. Don't worry about me. I'll take care of them, I'm a big girl, but you're my little girl! Who'll take care of you? You hadn't finished talking. I really do want to hear what you have to say! Everybody wants to hear what you have to say! You saw what everybody did just now when I interrupted you. They bit my head off! They sure didn't want to hear my voice! They wanted to hear yours! And yes, I did tell your Grandmother you might need a little help in the talking department, but nobody sitting in this room right now would ever think that about you now. Oh! Sophia, I'm just so used to being the chatterbox! We want to hear every word you have to say! Look around, can't you see, everybody is hanging on your every word."

Sophia could clearly see sorrow on her Mother's face, and that she wanted her to keep talking. But Sophia could only think. *'All the strange things that've been happening ever since we all sat down in the Orchid Orphanage! By some miracle, I turned into my Mother and became the talker and Mommy turned into me and became the quiet one. And when Mommy talked again, she said the oddest thing and was sad when she said it! 'They're using me for my voice.' But Mommy has the best voice! How could someone who sounds like her ever be sad?'*

But now that she was the quiet one again, she didn't dare ask. Besides, everybody was back to staring at her. She would feel funny talking now; she, after all, was the quiet one. And she didn't want to talk just to talk. Like her Mother sometimes did. And hadn't she said everything she had to say?

But she knew, in her heart of hearts, she hadn't. That she wasn't finished. That there still was something else she had to say. And it was the hardest thing to say.

And it had to do with her Movie Star School. She needed to know if they'd let her go to her Movie Star School now that they'd found out about it. She had to tell them how important it was to her. Just in case they didn't understand from all that she'd said to Great Aunt Hortense just now about how much it meant to her. How absolutely life or death it was to her. And how she simply must continue. Even if her Movie Star School was in the middle of the night. That was the part they weren't going to like. But she'd have to tell them it had to be in the middle of the night because that was what she was used to. She knew that this would be a problem. Great Aunt Hortense already told her so!

Nobody else'd said anything yet about her being up so late, but she knew that any moment somebody would. Miss Kitty sure didn't like her being up in the middle of the night! So she would have to straighten them all out. Because if she didn't, who would? She'd already gotten this far and she hadn't died, she'd just have to continue. Because if they wouldn't let her go to her Movie Star School, she just might die. No! she would die! Definitely.

But just as Sophia was shaking the first syllable loose, the self-appointed, Great Interlocutor with no reluctance and with great certainty, loosed hers easily and firmly, "Silence and incoherence and outbursts will not get us any closer to the solution to this problem. I can't tell you how tedious this has been for me to sit through. I have had to bite my tongue so that I wouldn't ask when any of you were planning to come to. And because of that silence, that incoherence, that outburst, I still don't know what you are planning to do about your daughter's problem. While both of you have been busy dealing with the pressing crises in each of your careers – and I do understand that these past few days have been quite trying for both of you and you've not been able to turn your full attention to the home front - I came here out of concern for your daughter's well-being and was able to find out exactly what she and her Nanny have been up to in the middle of the night, and am greeted with NO REACTION when what I should have heard is a serious discussion leading to the swift resolution of this looming problem that I have presented to you—"

And Dr. Oomla jumped again.

'Looming! Hah!'

He'd been trying to piece together exactly what Great Aunt Hortense's problem with Sophia was from all that he had actually heard. He ticked off what he had. It wasn't much. And he was deeply ashamed:

There was his wife's muddle; that hadn't registered with him, but her final coda had.

And then there was Sophia's eloquence; but even her words hadn't actually and really and truly registered with him he was mortified to admit; it was only her speaking up without a speech therapist that had.

And he was furious with himself! He! the good doctor! whose profession required nothing less than precise listening, hadn't been listening!

But what had really entered his cerebrum was Great Aunt Hortense's high-horsed disdain, before it had roiled and moiled and boiled over. However, of this he was certain: what he did hear was the axis of the problem.

Movie Star School.

But what rotated around this axis?

Though he did agree with Great Aunt Hortense about one thing. Anything which involved a Movie Star School and any living creature walking the Face of the Earth was a problem.

But if that living creature was his daughter and she had anything whatsoever to do with a Movie Star School! Why that would be nothing less than a catastrophe!

Especially after all that he had observed from the hours and hours he spent returning to sanity the misguided creatures such a school intended to educate. Creatures who might, after receiving such an education, be specifically encouraged to believe they are and should be the dazzling centers of not only Earth but the Megacosm. And he knew beyond a shadow of a doubt that anyone in the Movie Star profession who really and truly believed that would need to pay several visits to a person in his profession. In fact, when it finally dawned on him how 'Movie Star School' was the only thing he'd clearly heard of Great Aunt Hortense's reprimand, he felt a lancinating pain. He'd heard of a lot of schools but had he ever heard of a Movie Star School? Not only shouldn't he have ignored the words that followed Movie Star School but he should've paid the closest attention to find out what else would be said about such an odd concept. Why had he stopped paying attention when he heard those words? He knew the answer. He didn't like listening to the sound of Great Aunt Hortense. Sound again! His sensitive, snobby ears! And now he had to waste time, when he could be using that time to take care of his daughter.

However, when Great Aunt Hortense said 'looming' one part of his perplexifications ceased entirely. *'Looming in L'Oomla! Great Aunt Hortense is! And that shouldn't be. The Castle L'Oomla is my castle. My home. And My daughter is My problem! Not Great Aunt Hortense's. I must speak up, even though I will be the one who's interrupting now. I can't let her go on.'*

"... sometimes when both parents work it is oft—"

"Great Aunt Hortense, now I must interrupt you! And please do accept my sincere apology for it. And also for not greeting you a few moments ago. I've had a most trying past few days, and my patience when I finally returned home from the Institute had evaporated. And I'm ashamed to say, when you began talking, I just couldn't even listen to or certainly comprehend another problem as that's all I've been doing for the past few days. Now, from what I've pieced together, Sophia's been attending a Movie Star School and that you have some pressing concerns about this Movie Star School. Great Aunt Hortense, I assure you that I, of all people, have some very real concerns about an institution of learning that intends to train Movie Stars, as well! And I do intend to find out exactly what a Movie Star School is, why Sophia has enrolled in it, and why, above all, she didn't tell us about it. But Great Aunt Hortense, it's time now for the Oomla family to take over this problem. Which, after all, is our problem."

"I will be blunt, Dr. Oomla. And to make sure that both of you understand me, let me use a term I have never used before, and hope to have no occasion to ever use again. A term from the world of sports. Both of you have dropped the ball. Because of your careers, you and Sigrid for months haven't really been home in the true meaning of the word. Please do note, I said months and I do mean months. And if I haven't made myself perfectly clear, I will now. I'm not just referring to your most recent work troubles that have beset both of you in the past few days and kept both of you out of your home.

"Dr. Oomla, you weren't even paying attention now at this very moment when your own daughter was speaking. I know that because I was watching you. I hope I have your full attention now. For months and months, Sophia has been involved in a Movie Star School. In fact, I'm quite sure it coincides with the exact same time both of you stopped being available for your daughter.

"Did any of you know anything about this Movie Star School?

"You did not. I will repeat again what I said to you when you first walked in here this evening, Sigmund, because it is apparent you didn't hear me the first time. What I have found out from your Miss Kitty who has just revealed to Sigrid, Mr. James and myself what she knows, is this - that your daughter was up late at night on school nights acting along to the Movies that she played on your DVD player. And that she was teaching herself how to talk and walk and dress like each Movie Star, and when it came to the costumes for these spectacles, she was stealing clothes from your closet, Sigrid. That's what she calls her Movie Star School. She was the sole student and whichever Movie Star she was watching was the teacher. I can see that both of you didn't know. Mr. James certainly didn't. But your Miss Kitty knew! Your Miss Kitty! And, of course, you didn't know because you were relying on your Miss Kitty to tell you. But also, you didn't know because at an early hour in the evening both of you, from what I've been able to ascertain from my various sources, would excuse yourself for the night. Sigmund, to shut yourself up in your library, and Sigrid, to retire to bed, if you were even home.

"I do not fault either one of you. You have careers that are distinguished and important and wearying. And if that is what you must do in the evening to revitalize yourself and recuperate, than that is what you must do.

"Sigrid, you are a role model to women everywhere; and Sigmund, you are helping the wretched, lost souls of the world. And illustrious careers such as yours must flourish. And it is my intention to help you do that.

"The real problem is this: both of you have been relying on help that is unobservant and irresponsible. If either Mr. James or Miss Kitty had spoken up about this, you would have put an end to such nonsense immediately. You need to have help that will observe like a scrutineer exactly what is going on and report to you like a secret agent what they have observed. And if I was placed in charge of the help, I would be that scrutineer, because that is exactly what I would do."

Great Aunt Hortense spoke smugly, righteously as her audience hung on her every word. Some felt like they really were hanging. From a rope that was tightening around their necks. Sigrid and Sigmund and Mr. James. But there were seven who were not hanging like there were ropes around their necks; they were imagining there was only one rope and it was around Great Aunt Hortense's neck. Some of them imagined tying the rope and pulling it. Some of the Fairies. And Miss Kitty. Sophia would've been happy just to pinch her.

Sigrid could feel her face color and whiten then color again. Great Aunt Hortense was right.

Yet Sigrid couldn't have put why Great Aunt Hortense was wrong into words, but she was wrong. Even though Sigrid knew by the sickening feeling inside her that what Great Aunt Hortense had just said really was factual. But it wasn't her facts that were wrong. It had something to do with the glee the Immaculate have in telling the Wormy-Earthed-Others everything they were doing was wrong. But this time somebody else had to speak first and tell her; even if that somebody may have preferred to know what it all meant before he actually did speak, even if he had to puzzle it all out fragment by fragment as he was speaking. Somebody had to stop Great Aunt Hortense. And this time that somebody wouldn't be her. Now it was time for the Thinker-on-Two-Feet to show that he could think and talk and mix it all up together while standing on those same two feet.

Mr. James kept growing more and more uncomfortable as Great Aunt Hortense talked. *'Great Hecksniffery drummed those things out of me promising discretion, and now she's broadcasting what I told her worldwide! How dishonest! How untrustworthy! And she no doubt thinks herself a lady! And what did Old Hob-Nob-Olis mean when she said you need to have help that will observe what is going on! ... Why that was a direct reference to me!'*

His posture that had been merely straight, ramrod-ed. *'Great House of Horror! in charge! In charge of me! The major-domo! In my domo! Why I won't stand for it! Even if it is insubordinate of me to speak up. Even if I'm now too old to secure another position. Even if I lose my only American recommendation. And my pension. Lady Horde Penny couldn't affect my pension. Or could she? Well … There maybe things that are more important than money … but a pension!'*

And Mr. James could feel that ramrod sway. But on he raged, *'Just who exactly were Great Horb-globulus's 'various sources'? Miss Kitty would never tattle on the Oomla's to HRH Oilyship. So who else could they be? All the help leaves 6 Thirtyish. There were no various sources! Unless she had spies in the mouse and spider kingdom. She herself is the spy! Great Snoopvorious! Various sources! Hah! The Old Bird is bluffing.'* He just might say something after all.

Sophia felt all of what she still needed to say tower up inside her.

Miss Kitty had heard enough. She'd lost her position, her recommendation and her pension; Great Aunt Hortense would certainly see to that. What else could she do to her? Why she'd speak up even if Great Aunt Hortense herself marched her off to the poor house. Although, maybe the United States of America didn't even have a poor house.

And just at the moment Sigmund's, Sophia's and Mr. James' mouths opened, there was one mouth that opened a millisecond sooner.

"Now, I have something t' say. N' 'tis very important tat all of ye heed me words. Because o' Miss Sophia's Movie Star School, our Miss Sophia, didn't have t' go t' see tat speech terapist. Didn't all o' ye just hear how well she spoke up just now? Didn't all of ye understand as plain as day what she had t' say? Ye did, says I! Tank you very much! Ten tank ye very much is what all of ye should say t' tat Movie Star School. 'N I can tell ye why because I know a lot about tat Movie Star School, because I'm te only one amongst ye who actually saw her in it! I did. Indeed, I did. T'weren't for tat Movie Star School, Miss Sophia certainly wouldn't've spoken up so well here just now 'n, as she just told us herself, in her classroom tis morning where she read a story aloud t' her school chums using some o' her voices. Miss Sophia had such a grand time acting along with te Movie Stars, utterin', pronouncin', emotin', elocutin', with her entire heart n' soul ter immortal words, practicing til she nailed right on te dot ter voices, ter airs, ter poses. Even when te minor characters spoke, she'd act along with tem too 'n do ter voices, 'n ter airs 'n poses. She could do all sorts o' voices. 'N accents. Old people, young people. She even did te men parts. Why Miss Sophia has quite te ear for voices. In fact, she had such an ear, I never understood why for te life of me, she'd such a hard time speakin' up in school. N' why somebody with her abilities wouldda ever need t've t' see a speech terapist, I could never understand. It makes no sense atall. I used t' wonder what a professional such as y'rself, Dr. Oomla, wouldda tought about tat. It seemed t' me like a riddlin' mystification."

Every person in that room was hanging on to Miss Kitty every word. Sophia was doing character voices, Movie Star voices, men's voices!?? Quiet Sophia, who had a hard time being heard in school!! That Sophia?

In particular, Great Aunt Hortense was paying very close attention. Miss Kitty revealing these details now! Where were this information when she had demanded Miss Kitty tell her everything she knew during her own investigation a short time ago? Obviously Miss Kitty had omitted these details! And Great Aunt Hortense grew even more indignant.

'Quite te ear for voices' does she?' and suddenly Dr. Oomla understood. But not everything. He had questions to ask and ideas to discuss and things to get to the bottom of. He must not waste time. He had wasted enough. Miss Kitty first, "Why didn't you ask me Miss Kitty? I would've loved to've known about this so both of us could've discussed it."

"You see what I mean, Sigmund and Sigrid. Here is an example of your employee withholding information from her employer and from ..."

"Now, Great Aunt Hortense! You've had your turn. And now it's Miss Kitty's turn to explain to us what she knows," said Mrs. Oomla.

"Are we all interrupting each other? Please do remember Sigrid, you are taking the word of an untrustwor—"

"Interrupting! Great Aunt Hortense, you don't have the floor anymore! That's why I'm interrupting! Enough, now!" said Mrs. Oomla.

"Why! The audacity! The impertinence! Giving the floor to a—"

"Great Aunt Hortense, please! Remember you are a guest in our home!" growled Mrs. Oomla.

"A guest! A guest! A guest in the home that I have been making sure runs! I am much more than a guest, I assure you!"

"ENOUGH! GREAT AUNT HORTENSE, IT IS MISS KITTY'S TURN! Please abide by the rules in MY HOUSEHOLD!" No one had ever heard Dr. Oomla say words with such force, such anger, especially to Great Aunt Hortense, and everyone gasped.

·∴☾∴·

("Lady, WE was not gasping. We was goin' wild!")

·∴☽∴·

And like a high, haughty horse, Great Aunt Hortense rose up. Was she actually going to walk out? She pointed herself towards the door, and took several steps. They couldn't believe what they were witnessing. Great Aunt Hortense, giving up? Great Aunt Hortense never gave up! Or did she? They didn't have to wait long to find out. She halted, stood right where she was, and like that same high, haughty horse, returned to her chair, opened her purse, withdrew a starchy handkerchief, sniffed into it, then, in their general direction, nodded that haughted head lower by a measurable milliliter, shook her gloved hand towards Dr. Oomla, and signaled him to proceed.

"Miss Kitty, please continue." The kindness had returned to Dr. Oomla's voice.

"Well, Dr. Oomla, I, of all people know tat Miss Sophia was not havin' a grand time speakin' up in school. I guess we all know tat. Why without tat Movie Star School, she wouldn't've any way t' express herself atall! 'N t' prove what I'm saying, look at how she just spoke up without her ever having t' go near a speech terapist."

"Thank you so much, Miss Kitty."

And then Dr. Oomla turned to Sophia and said, "Now all of us want to hear what you have to say about this. You've heard what Miss Kitty and Great Aunt Hortense have said. What can you tell us about your Movie Star School?"

At long last, it was her turn! Everything that she'd wanted to say as she'd listened to them talk about her and her Movie Star School, and her and her reading in school, and hadn't yet said because it hadn't been her turn yet, had by now grown and grown until she could feel it just about beanstalk through the top of her. No more not-talking for her! Or being shy! Even if Great Aunt Hortense was listening. 'Let dat you outta you!' is what she had to do. She had so much to choose from of what she could say, she didn't know where to begin and without thinking what was the right thing to say, the thing that could be explained and was provable, the thing that made sense here on this earth, in this room, among these people – every last one of them from the Reality Based World – the Ms. CEO Songbird; the Proper-English, Logical, Punctilio-ed Gentleman Butler; the True Believer in the Saints Above and the Doomed Below; the Queen of Correctitude, the Squelcher of the Fantastical, the Madame Nuncio of the Cold, Hard, Indisputable Fact – Great Aunt Hortense herself! PLUS a PSYCHOANALYST! Because in front of those very people, out she blurted, "But I did see a speech therapist! A secret speech therapist. And he did help me!" Because 'Let dat you outta you!' was what she was thinking of, not of her audience at all.

• • • A CRIME AGAINST ALL EARED-HUMANITY • • •

Now every head whirled towards Sophia.

("Lady, we was gasping now!"

Readers, what they said won't be repeated here, even their less purple invectives. Hopefully, none of it will be repeated anywhere. Even if they are just Fairy words. No use tempting you, my Readers, to add blasphemies from the Land of the Fairies to your blasphcabulary. Thee and Free were, of course, not the blasphpetrators.)

"You did? A secret speech therapist, Sophia? Who is this person? And why is he a secret speech therapist?" her Father said rapidly, even as he was turning pale and looking very odd, more odd than anyone in the room; even Sophia, who was looking noticeably odd herself.

Sophia could feel her insides spin then she watched everything and everybody turn to gray, as she realized - Her new mouth was a BIG MOUTH! And she'd never be able to take back what it had just let fly. *'Some secret!!'* She examined the air around her, as if that's where her secret now was. *'I'm just like Melinda. I can't keep a secret either! Maybe that's what happens once you start saying whatever you want.'* She'd have to show her big-mouthed friend more respect, some sympathy, since obviously that was the direction she was headed in herself. She slumped low in her chair. And with that, Sophia left the Talking World. It was safer that way. But that wasn't the only thing she did - she started thinking again. Deeply.

'Why did I say that? As if I could explain to Great Aunt Hortense, to Mr. James, to Mother, to Daddy, to Miss Kitty even, that my secret speech therapist is the Man in the Moon who is Louis Armstrong! Everybody knows Louis Armstrong is dead. The only reason he visited me was to help me. I have no idea how he got up in the sky and turned into the moon but he did. And besides they won't believe me if I tell them about him no matter what I say. But Louis Armstrong is my friend and I'm lucky to have such a friend because he is a deep-voiced-talker, just like me. And he's a funny moon-cat of a man who sings in bounces and beeps his bop and smiles like the sun in the dark, night sky. Hah hah hah! Imagine him telling me and imagine me hah hah! telling them hah hah! 'Let dat you outta you!' As if! It's preposterous. Impossible. Nobody would understand. Nobody!'*

Sophia kept her head down and sat with her oldest friend - Thinking. She was safe. Plus she didn't have to practice to know how to do it. Thinking had always been with her. Thinking really was her oldest friend.

But her oldest friend was pushing her like it had never pushed her before. *'This time I can't clam up. This time I have to speak up. I just can't sit here thinking while everybody is looking at me. I can't do that anymore. Besides, I can't disappoint my true friend, Louis Armstrong. I don't think he would like it. And even if I don't know how to tell a living breathing soul about my true friend, I certainly could make up something that is 'sorta' correct about him. I'm going to have to, to get out of this. People lie all the time. I know that. I watch Movies. I go to school! I've been around! I'm ten years old! I've even been to the Big City!'*

And she waited to hear the 'sorta' her oldest friend would come up with. And she waited.

But Prince Thinking didn't come charging in on a Little White Lie and deliver a thing. Not a thing. She wasn't rescued by anybody. It was quiet inside. And hushed in the glass house where Sophia could feel without even having to look that her Father and Mother and Great Aunt Hortense and Mr. James and Miss Kitty were waiting to hear from her.

·∴·**(**··

("Lady, it was anything but hushed-up inside. We'd all flown back and'd been yelling til we was hoarse, 'Say he's just one of your Grandfather's friends. That's all ya gotta say!' We was, for once, in agreement. But what we was saying – yelling, actually - didn't seem to be registering with Sophia because Sophia hadn't thought of it yet, and we couldn't understand why not!"

"Ms. Author, what we were doing wasn't magic. It was logic. And we kept it up. We would just take a breath and start all over again!")

·∴**)**··

"Where did you meet this speech therapist, Sophia?" said Dr. Oomla.

Sophia picked up her head; that, at least, she could do. And when she did, the first person she saw was her Mother, who hadn't left Sophia's side, and had pulled up a chair so close to Sophia that their chairs were touching. Their eyes met and when they did, Sophia felt her Mother's hand squeeze her hand, as if her Mother was trying to pass something on to Sophia. And a something must have come through because Sophia did feel a little better. At least now with her head up, she was able to actually see Mr. James look at her. And Miss Kitty. And her Father. She even saw Great Aunt Hortense look at her and she didn't let herself, even for one second, get sucked into Those Eyes. From face to face and Those Eyes, her eyes flitted. And as she did, she could feel something bubble inside her. It was the beginnings of a plan because something was dawning on her. Only two of them had been in Goliathon with her - Miss Kitty and Mr. James; but both of them had only been with her for a few minutes. Most of the time, she'd been there by herself! It was not going to be as hard as she feared to tell a story about this, after all. First, she had to answer her Father's question. And she wouldn't be telling a story when she did. Yet.

"In Goliathon, Daddy!"

"Where in Goliathon?"

"In Grandfather and Grandmother's house. He was visiting.

···☾··

("Lady, we collapsed in a puddle of sweat and tears!")

··☽··

"And he is a real speech therapist, Sophia?"

"Well, I don't know because he just said things and as soon as he said them, I wasn't afraid to hear myself talk so much anymore."

"Afraid to hear yourself talk? Were you afraid to hear yourself talk? Is that why you didn't talk in school?"

"Sorta of. But now not so much anymore."

"And it's all because this man, as you yourself just said, 'just said things' to you? What did this man 'just say'?"

Sophia hated having to repeat Louis Armstrong's words in a room where Great Aunt Hortense was. But she knew that Great Aunt Hortense and everybody else would never figure out who told her those words, just from the words themselves. Nobody would be able to guess that those words were Louis Armstrong's words. Because Louis Armstrong was a dead man. And dead men don't talk. And neither do moons. And the Man in the Moon wasn't Louis Armstrong. That's what they would say to her. Except the Man in the Moon was Louis Armstrong. And Sophia had to guard that secret carefully. Because she knew that people would say that anyone who said that Louis Armstrong was the Man in the Moon, was crazy. And she was not crazy. So to be very safe, she would whisper his words very low. "He said 'Let dat you outta you!' "

"That's what he said?" Her Father returned her whisper.

"Oh, but he also sang songs in a deep voice. And he made his voice funny and fun. He has a deep voice too, like me. I liked him! And he liked me."

"So why is this man a secret then?"

Sophia was stumped. What should she say? There was no doubt about it, she'd have to lie to answer that question. All of a sudden it didn't seem so easy.

She put her head down but still could feel everyone's eyes on her; she didn't care one bit. This time she would keep quiet. She would. And there was a good hour of silence and Sophia didn't care.

"Now Sigmund, this is most interesting, fascinating even. Why can't she tell us the name of this secret speech therapist man? And did her Grandmother and her Grandfather find this speech therapist for her? Don't you believe we need to know this? I do," said Great Aunt Hortense, this time gilding her sanctimony with compassion.

Mrs. Oomla, also, wanted desperately to know the answer to Great Aunt Hortense's question but knew better than to ask anybody any question using a tone like Great Aunt Hortense's. As soon as Great Aunt Hortense had spoken, she felt Sophia squeeze her hand even more tightly: Sophia didn't like it either. Sigrid Oomla had heard enough from Great Aunt Hortense. It was time that Ms. Oomla was back in charge. Besides, Sigmund had done his part, he had spoken up; even though he hadn't silenced Great Aunt Hortense and now he was the one who was silent – when, at this juncture, he should've made sure the exact opposite was happening! But then Mrs. Oomla wasn't surprised, she knew her husband. He was just being a good psychoanalyst and giving Sophia some time for his question to grab through to her inner self – her soul even – so that when at last she answered, she would be revealing her deepest thoughts and feelings that had risen up to show themselves to her, if any would or did or could. Because that's what good psychoanalysts do. He had done his part, Sigrid was satisfied; now it was her turn.

But there had been too much silence when no one had come to Sophia's defense against Great Aunt Hortense and now every person (that wasn't Sophia or Great Aunt Hortense) and Fairy (including Thee and Free) was thinking the same thing. That it was their sacred duty to come to Sophia's rescue. Pension be damned! And so too the Dispatcher!

And Mr. James, Miss Kitty, Dr. Oomla and Mrs. Oomla (and the Fairies) spoke out at once.

"Now, ma'am, a Sisela Bok said, 'All secrecy is not meant to deceive.' I read those words in my constant companion, Simpson's Contemporary Quotations." Mr. James began.

·∴·𝕮·∴·

("Ms. Author, I said to my companions, 'Sophia has got to keep this secret. They'll think she's got—' "

" 'A head full of Fairies!' I nailed that, didn't I, Lady?")

·∴·𝕯·∴·

"Haven't all o' ye been listenin'? Our Miss Sophia has been talking just grand just now! 'N anybody who gets her t' talk tis good, can stay a secret if ye ask te likes o—" Miss Kitty shouted.

"Great Aunt Hortense, we have a right to privacy. Let's respect Soph—" Not only did Dr. Oomla shout over Miss Kitty, he interrupted her as well.

"Great Aunt Hortense, Sigmund is ri—" Not only did Mrs. Oomla shout over Dr. Oomla, she interrupted him as well.

"Right to privacy! You want to give a ten-year-old a rig—" As did Great Aunt Hortense.

"Every person is entitled to—" Dr. Oomla.

·∴ℂ··

("Lady, Free was saying, and she was the only one who wasn't shouting but I heard her, 'Out find … they couldn't … us about … could they?' ")

··ː)ː··

"But a child? A CHILD! A secret man who is a secret speech therapist?! That is outrageous! We must find out who is he! Sigmund, we must call your Father and your Mot—"

"Great Aunt Hortense, we, Sophia's parents will decide just who calls who—"

"Well, let's hope that both of you are not, as you usually are, detained at work in any emergencies and you have time to actually act as her parents and place that call. Something as impor—"

·∴ℂ··

("Ms. Author, I did say to my companions, 'You've got to admit, Great Aunt Hortense has a point. You've got to—' "

"Lady, I says right back to Thee, 'Great Aunt Hortense is never right. Even when she's right. Just because she's—' ")

··ː)ː··

"Great Aunt Hortense, I do insist that we must respect Sophia's priv—" roared Dr. Oomla.

"Te secret is not what's important here! What's important is tat our Miss Sophia spoke up in school 'n spoke up just now so well. I'm beginnin' t' tink tat ye weren't listenin' t' Miss Sophia atall because ye'd all be a lot happier if—"

"Haven't you, Sigrid, and you, Sigmund, noticed that I am hearing from ALL persons present and not just you, the family, about a matter that I believe is not within the staff's domain to discuss. That would never have happened in the old days. But in this free-for-all of a household, the things that are allowed to pass as—"

·∴ℂ··

(" 'Wow, ja hear that? Great Aunt Hortense, thinks she's a Queen! The Emissaries in her head when she was little musta come from that AshQueenasi Tribe!' ")

··ː)ː··

"The Oomla residence is hardly a free-for-all household, I assure—" Mr. James snapped.

It was wild in that Glass House. The windows were rattling. The orchid blossoms were shivering. Sophia's ears were tingling and alive and open for business. And she was lock stock in the middle of it all! Everybody was interrupting everybody, and each interrupter was speaking louder than each interruptee so that the noise level kept rising incrementally on each interruption. And because of the interruptions, nobody was letting anybody finish and anyone who was speaking had to speak fast before somebody cut them off. And since it was all about her secret and about her, she wished she would've been able to hear more than just the beginnings of what they were saying. Then she would've known what was about to happen to her. Because surely something was. And speaking of the tingle in her ears, Sophia, who spent her entire life listening to the sounds of voices, and these voices in particular, had noticed immediately that nobody was talking like they'd ever talked before.

Mr. James had lost his dignified hush and was almost loud-mouthed.

Miss Kitty was Miss Catty.

And Great Aunt Hortense was souring up all her high notes, either on purpose or because she didn't know she was; and it was a crime against all-eared-humanity.

Plus her Father had really and truly screamed!

And her Mother, the Voice herself, was yoicking and ripping like one of those street toughies she had heard only yesterday.

What a soundtrack! In her whole life in Movie Land she'd never experienced one like this. And all of it was landing right in her ears. Before she'd met her grandfather and her secret speech therapist, she would've never even believed that this was music at all. But thanks to them, it was a symphony.

Mr. James was a New Year's Eve horn.

Miss Kitty was the cat-gut part of the violin.

Great Aunt Hortense was a little too uppity and singing way too sharp and she'd better watch out she didn't propel herself through the glass ceiling.

Her Father - her stringbean Father! - was a stringbean no more but the big-fat punch of a tuba.

And, for the first time that Sophia ever remembered, her songbird Mother had turned into a full-throated, shrilly-something that was blustering awfully brassy sometimes.

Sophia was so entertained, she almost forgot she was in trouble.

• • • SIGMUND OOMLA, HIPPOCRATIUS HYPOCRITIUM • • •

Dr. Oomla was not at all entertained, and would've liked to have put an end to the uproar, but just as he was about to, he was overcome with shadowy thoughts that locked up his mind with him lost inside wandering from shadow to shadow to shadow. What did all of this mean? Sophia had her very own Movie Star School! Why, of all the professions that Sophia could aspire to, did she, his daughter, his only child, want to be a Movie Star? Why would she pick that profession? That was the profession of the Artistes! His patients!

'Those Artistes are patients because of that profession!'

Dr. Oomla knew very well that thought didn't belong up there where the Hippocratic-Oath also lived, but he knew why he'd let it in. There was a part of him that really believed what he'd just thought. He even knew what believing something like meant. It meant that he was a hypocrite and not a follower of Hippocrates at all. How could he, Sigmund Oomla, be a Hippocratius Hypocritium? Did that mean that deep down, he didn't really respect his own patients? The Psychoanalyst Doctor, of all the Hippocratic-Oath-taking Doctors, must really and truly respect humanity, particularly his own patients. Because the Psychoanalyst Doctor's main concern was the patient's soul. In fact, the Psychoanalyst must do everything he can to heal that patient's soul. He knew that. For how could a patient's soul get better if the patient finds out his own Doctor doesn't respect what he does for a living?

But how could his only daughter want to do the exact same thing those crazy Artistes did for a living?

Even knowing he was a hypocrite to think it, wasn't stopping him from thinking it.

'Those Artistes who prize their outsides so much as if their outsides were who they really were and the only thing they really were and the best thing about them. Why some of those Artistes would do anything to become famous. Or even notorious, for some of them do outrageous, dangerous and sometimes illegal things just to keep their names in the paper. And household names they do become. And soon making a visit or three to The Institute for the Compassionate Care of the Extraordinary and the Always Interesting.

'Is that what would happen to my daughter? If she did what they did, would she become like them? Sophia? My little girl? My flesh and blood! Dreaming of that business – Show Business! It's one thing for people who aren't members of my family to work in that profession. But my own daughter! My own daughter wanting to be

in the same profession of the patients at the Institute! Look where all of them end up! A lunatic asylum!

'And now my very own wife is being used for her voice! Well, something like that can't happen to my little girl! I won't let anyone use my little girl! I have to protect her!'

What had he done wrong?

'Wait ... wait a minute ... wait ...'

It hit him! Hard. Because sometimes he'd forget, that Show Business was in his family already. Show Business was the profession of his Father. His Father! Oh, how his Father, Solomon Oomla, had pleaded with him to take over his Show Business Empire – Oom-Lah-Lah Productions. But no! Sigmund Oomla would have none of that. When he was a child and met all those actors and actresses - some of them such desperate creatures who were always hanging around his Father - wanting, needing, pleading, show-ing off; some histrionic - hysterically so or pathetically so - that he made up his mind, he would spend his life figuring out what made them tick, so that he could help them not be so desperate. He would not put them to work on a stage as his Father did; he would take care of them when they were off that stage. Because that's when they were the most vulnerable. But when he'd told his Father he wasn't going to take over Oom-Lah-Lah, his Father'd never really forgiven him.

All so so long ago.

And just who was this secret speech therapist of Sophia's? She said she met him in his Father's house ... I wonder where ...

And then he remembered ... and right where he was, still locked up in-side, a brilliant light that had been turned off suddenly was illuminating his every shadow ... he remembered ... a long time ago ... when he was little ... being sent to that wonderful round room at the top of the house ... with the Man in the Moon carved on the door ... and all those windows that looked out on the night sky and the stars and the moon - the Man in the Moon - was that where she slept? And then he knew. He knew why it was a secret. For him, the Man in the Moon had been Sigmund Freud. It had only happened once. But that was all he needed for Dr. Freud to tell him what he needed to know. To follow his heart ... his passion ... no matter where it would lead ... to be strong ... to do what he wanted to do ... what suited him and not what suited his Father and that he was not his Father and could never be his Father but could only ever be himself ... and that it was okay to be Sigmund Oomla and not Solomon Oomla ... and he would and could and should help others because that was truly and really in his own heart ... How could he've forgotten! Oh! There was so much he'd forgotten! So much!

He knew what he had to do. He came to. Everybody was wailing away at each but not yet whaling away on each other. And up he sprang and in a voice, part pied-piper, part wolf-whistle, "Let's solve our problems peacefully. Let's stop hurting each other's ears. And feelings. Miss Kitty, we need to get something to eat. If there's no dinner prepared, maybe Mr. James will drive into town and get us some pizzas. We'll sort this out, but this time over something hot and delicious."

And as if by magic, his voice had mobilized them, because every head swiveled towards Dr. Oomla, and soon the occupants, without exception, were gazing at him serenely and looking very, very relieved. And the casus belli that had taken hold of the human (and the Fairy) occupants in the Orchid Orphanage was no more.

Miss Kitty jumped up ready to do a jig, "O', Dr. Oomla, y'r wise words, like tat old Irish blessing says, 'ave finally warmed us on tis cold evening, like a full moon on a dark, dark night!"

'A Sigmund Freud moon! If they only knew! And if I told anybody, they'd tell me to see one of my colleagues!'

'A Louis Armstrong Moon, Miss Kitty! But I don't ever dare tell her – or anybody – who would ever believe me?'

"I'll set te table, 'n make us a Shamrock Salad to go with tat pizza. A Shamrock Salad is greener tan any salad in te whole wide world, 'n tis lucky too, so te doctor should never earn a penny out o' us!"

• • • OUT OF THE GLASS HOUSE • • •

Miss Kitty, forgetting her aching hips, flounced out of the Orchid Orphanage, not even glancing in Great Aunt Hortense's direction. *'Maybe te're not going t' fire me after all! Tanks be t' me Irish Saints who're always watchin' over me! Oh! merciful tanks!'*

Mr. James was counting his blessings, too. "Back directly!" he cheerio-ed as he dashed down the footpath. *'Here I am in America, having just had words with the Mistress of the house's Great Aunt - Old Horse-a-sauris herself - and I'm still employed. Now if only the Oomla's would corral Horse-Top-o-lis to gambol here just once a week, things'd be more than suitable in America. But then things really are suitable! Not only wasn't I dismissed, no one even reprimanded me for my spirited display of feeling which might even be considered an infraction itself. Like Miss Kitty's infraction. Now what was it she did exactly? And if*

Hound-of-the-Baskervilles would forget, then so could I! I feel jolly good. Jolly good. There may be something to say for these Americans after all! They really might be slightly more democratic with their speak-up, talk-back households than the house-holds of England where my Butler counter-parts must button-up and carry-on and do their duty. And since speaking-up seems to be the order of the day, then I must find an occasion to speak-up to Miss Sophia, to tell her that if she wants to be on the stage, or in the Movies for that matter, then she'll need some real training, of the Thespian variety. She can't just be strutting around like an overdressed peacock and think that an actress doth make. She'll have to have vocal training. After that, she'll need to read the great plays written by the great playwrights. She'll have to understand what those great words mean that've been spoken so eloquently from the stage for centuries past. Ah! What a noble calling acting is! To spend your life saying the wisest words that've ever been written about life. And proclaiming them for all to hear. Maybe she could even start writing her own plays, filling them with her own wise words. She can't just go around spouting words she's memorized. Why couldn't she write her own plays? I don't see why not! All of us have some wisdom in us. And some poetry. And some drama. Certainly a ten-year-old does. I wish I would've done that when I was ten. At ten, that's when it's all just begin-ning. What could be better than creating even more wise words for the world to live by? Wise words are what this world needs more of. Wise words lead to wise actions. Speaking of wise actions, I wonder if Hot-Too-Mahto will actually eat pizza!'

Mrs. Oomla stood up from her chair but felt like she was floating now that all the racket had stopped. Having to listen to her corporate voice, her power voice here in her sanctuary for orchids must've been a terrible shock to their soft petal ears. But if it was shock to theirs, she could only imagine what it must've been to Sigmund's. *'Whatever does he make of my new voice? Surely, the connoisseur thinks me unmusical. A real she-man! Although, surely, the psychoanalyst deems it a breakthrough and very therapeutic that we've at last aired our feelings. But for my husband to've had to actually listen to his favorite voice … or what's left of his favorite voice … and for that matter, to all of our voices speaking up like they've never spoken up before, and sometimes all at once, after the days he just had at the Institute, has to've been giving him a pounding headache. It has to, because I'm getting one; I have sensitive ears, too.'*

Mrs. Oomla saw that Sigmund had taken Sophia's hand so she made her way out of the glass house with Great Aunt Hortense by her side. But this time she wanted to be the one lost in thought the way her husband always was; she needed time to understand what it all meant and reflect about it privately, the way he did. But then she remembered who she was walking beside: Great Aunt Hortense would insist that she smooth everything over in a conversation that didn't dare speak yet another note of discord but was only talk about trivialities and niceties. Such a conversation would've had nothing whatsoever to do with what they'd just been saying, and would never've referred to how they'd just been anything but pleasant to one another.

'When I was a little girl, Great Aunt Hortense always insisted that I do just that after we'd had a tiff. No wonder I talk the way I do! Great Aunt Hortense only ever wanted to hear me sing but never to hear me cry! Hah! Etiquettely correct she wanted me to be but seldom, if ever, emotionally correct.'

Mrs. Oomla eyed Great Aunt Hortense wondering how she'd taken all of this spontaneous expression of feeling. But Great Aunt Hortense only nodded back at her solemnly and then turned her head in the direction they were heading. She was wrong: Great Aunt Hortense was not about to discuss pleasantries. She stole another look at Great Aunt Hortense; this time she saw a porcelain statue, a fragile, perfect figurine that had stepped down from a Victorian mantelpiece, so valuable and so like a precious person from a whole different day and time – long long ago. *'That must be how I've always seen Great Aunt Hortense! Why I've always felt I have to protect her. When I was small, I was so afraid that if I said anything to her that wasn't good-girl-nice or was sassy, she'd shatter into a thousand pieces. No wonder I talked like an angel. If I didn't, I might not've had anybody anymore. I must've known deep down that Great Aunt Hortense was only doing her duty when she stepped into raise me, and that she'd never love me the way they did.'*

And Mrs. Oomla stared again at Great Aunt Hortense. Great Aunt Hortense was a real live flesh and blood human who had an opinion about everything and couldn't wait to tell you what her opinion was, and sometimes they were not just opinions, they were orders. *'Why sometimes, on the exact same matter! Great Aunt Hortense'd have one opinion, one day, and a totally contradictory one the next. She may not go around screaming 'Off with her head!' but she really is a little too much like that Red Queen who does. She rules and that's what matters to her. And not only that, she may require me to be harmonious but she doesn't require herself to be!'* She'd been wrong all these years, Great Aunt Hortense was not about to break.

And then Mrs. Oomla had had enough of thinking about Great Aunt Hortense and put her out of mind; but Great Aunt Hortense's words, those denunciators, refused to leave.

"BOTH OF YOU HAVE DROPPED THE BALL!"

'Great Aunt Hortense is right: I don't even know what my own daughter is up to. A Movie Star School! I go to bed too early. But I always thought Sophia was in good

hands with Miss Kitty and Mr. James. I always thought they were the best employees I ever hired. Although Great Aunt Hortense did find them. And she had her doubts about Miss Kitty, but I didn't. Great Aunt Hortense really is right, I am just so tired at night. But so many people depend upon me. I've a corporation to run. And a family. And a staff. And a house—'

'Congratulations! You put the corporation first! Finally, you put something ahead of yourself!'

Private Enemy No. 1 was back.

'Isn't that great! Great Aunt Hortense in my head AND you! Arrived just in time to tell me what I'm doing wrong?'

'C'mon, now, admit it, haven't you always thought you come first?'

'Alright! I do think that! But for so many years, I did! And by the way, can't you see that I work harder than anybody? When I was young, I loved plants and orchids and botany and spent so many years going to school and learning everything about them, what was I supposed to do with all those years and years of study and training and practice when I got married to my Sigmund and had my sweet Sophia? How could I just up and abandon my plants and been content to only be a housewife and Mother? I went to school and learned complicated things because that's what smart women do nowadays! Don't you understand? Women are on nothing less than a great mission, just like men are. We, too, must save the world. We must develop our talents and burnish them so that we can perform on the world stage, just like men do!'

'And loving somebody and being loved by somebody is not considered enough for a woman nowadays, right? And I guess it's not enough for you!'

'How dare you put that thought into my head! Suppose someone heard you?

'And about me thinking that I come first, is it my fault that people've always made such a fuss about my voice? For so long, everybody stopped whatever they were doing to hear me talk … well … here in the Village Van Der Speck they still do. It's no wonder I always thought I was It! Suppose everybody hung on your every word, you Pestilence, wouldn't you believe that they loved everything about you, and that you're the star?

'And you know what else I always thought? That I was taking care of my family.'

'If you didn't know that your own daughter was up at night going to a Movie Star School, you weren't.'

'What kind of a Mother am I? Is that what you're thinking?'

'You wanna know what else I'm thinking? I live inside you, I know you better than you know yourself. You think you'll be able to put somebody else first just like that?'

'I'll not let my child come second ever again. She comes before my profession or anything or anybody. I don't come first anymore! Okay? The corporation doesn't come first either!

'Although, you try being the woman CEO of a corporation who tells her board that she can't attend a billion-dollar-merger-meeting because she has to take her daughter to her speech therapy appointment, and then watch the board roll their eyes at their good-little-Mother slash CEO! A man could do it, but I could not, make no mistake about that. But no wonder my family's in trouble! I didn't even know that Great Aunt Hortense was taking over my own house.

'Anyway, you listen to me! I must work, because I have a talent. I don't care what you think about that! In fact, I truly and really believe every person is given a unique talent that must be nurtured—'

'Nurture? Who were you supposed to be nurturing, your talents or your child's?'

'The modern woman believes women can nurture their own talent and their child's. And I've already admitted that it's hard for me to place myself second when I've always been first. And besides, every good Mother knows that a child must be loved and supported and taken care of but eventually taught to take care of themselves. And once that child learns that and grows up, the Mother's most important work is finished. Can't you see that I have a real talent that must be developed and exercised and used for the benefit of the world? Having a child is not really a talent. Should I be hanging around my child for the rest of her life because I have nothing better to do with my own?"

'Hanging around a child for the rest of her life! You haven't been hanging around that child all that much for the beginning of her life! You've farmed that job out to others!'

'I've farmed that job out to the right people! Mr. James and Miss Kitty really love Sophia and've been there for her. Lately, even more than Sigmund and I've been! And since you claim to know so much about me, why don't you know this? Sigmund is great at everything but making money, and I am! And I admit, shame on me and I know my husband doesn't like this about me at all, but I like money. I was, after all, raised by Great Aunt Hortense, and fortune is her favorite word.'

'Fortune's also the favorite word in Faaairrry! Taaaaaales!' No. 1 spit out those words as if the words and what they stood for were distasteful to it.

⋯⋆C⋆⋯

("That Mind-Worm!" said Lorraine.)

⋯꙰⋯

'Whatever is wrong with Fairy Tales? Fairy Tales show children the world's mystery and magic, its sorrows and dangers. Suppose a child's kind-mother and

good-father are so blinded by the perfect beauty of a rose-covered-cottage that they drive right over the mountain that cottage is sitting on leaving that child alone forever. Because of Fairy Tales, that orphan has learned that if she's hard-working and clever, she might be alright. Or even suppose that that child should happen to be a candy-tongued-weed who happens to cross the path of a fire-tongued-dragon. Because of Fairy Tales, that child has learned that if she uses her best asset, her candy-tongue, she might, in her own way, defeat that dragon. Fairy Tales have taught her that one day, if she's been good, she, too, will, 'Go and seek her fortune!' just like all those storybook heroes have done before her.

'Although, sometimes I wonder if a vast fortune can put people under a spell. Sometimes I wonder if I'm under its spell. But if I am, we know who put me under it: Great Aunt Hortense. She certainly loves vast fortunes. But then it seems to me the whole world and everybody in it loves vast fortunes, and Great Aunt Hortense could NOT've put ALL of them under a spell. So nobody would really fault me for being under that spell. Well, okay, maybe Sigmund would. And you.

'But be clever, work hard and get a fortune. Well, isn't that exactly what I did? And isn't that exactly what I got? A vast fortune. That, after all, is what we-the-clever and we-the-hard-working are entitled to. That's what's supposed to happen. That's our just reward. Isn't it?'

'And what's happened to you and your husband ever since you got your just reward?'

The Pest's question stung Mrs. Oomla's eyes and ears and conscience and she wanted to run far away rather than answer it but knew it'd keep asking her over and over until she did. Her eyes filled as she walked beside the silent, solemn fortress that contained Great Aunt Hortense. Mrs. Oomla glanced at her but Great Aunt Hortense seemed oblivious to her and her tears; she just continued walking very slowly and very deliberately and very straight ahead.

'Will nobody ever protect me from that Pest?'

And the answer shot through her like a torpedo.

'My husband's holed himself up in his study every night. He's withdrawn from me. He avoids me. But I've been avoiding him, too. Because I might've been tempted to tell him, once and for all, that no matter what he imagines, daffeine is harmless! And then his kind eyes would've looked into my eyes like they've never looked into them before, like I was a traitor. Which would've made me so upset, I might've even ended up using the voice he so admires to scream at him - "No! I haven't given the pill-popping-generation another pill to pop!" - and that, I assure you, is something my voice has never done to him. But since I've already lost it, what's to stop me from telling him that I actually like daffeine? That I like my vast fortune?

'And then something I don't want to come out would finally come out: and that is what I've been made to do down in that big city to make that vast fortune! And then the whole dam would've just burst. I'd have to tell him how I really feel. And who I've become. And what's really happened to his delight ... my voice. That it's turned me into the sock-puppet of corporate masters. They tell it what to say and it then spins their message into something that captivates consumers. When it talks, consumers buy. Which pleases my corporate masters no end but which really means – "Your voice is our voice! Your voice is Giggle! Say this, not that!"

'Don't you understand, you Pest, if I would've talked to him, he might've found out what my voice actually does down in the big city! And what would he think of his perfect angel then?

'And you know what else'd come out, that my vast fortune has caused me to meet people who do nothing but dream up a 1001 new tricks to grow a vast fortune into an even vaster fortune. And some of those tricks I know for a fact are dirty tricks. And yet, I perform their tricks. And if he asked my why, and I know he would, I'd have to tell him I don't know why. No wonder I've been avoiding him.

'I can't stand my corporate masters. The only thing they delight in is keeping their vast fortunes all to themselves, making sure that they never have to share it with anyone else. They're nothing like my husband, my good-deed-doer.'

'Yeah! They're more like you! The evil-deed-doer. The CEO!'

'Why are you're always needling me? You try to make me feel bad because I'm not an old-fashioned Mother. Because I like money. Because I don't confide in my husband. Because I don't rebel against my corporate masters. But if I did stay home with my daughter, I bet you'd make me feel bad that I wasn't out like all the rest of the women making my fortune in the workplace.

'When will you stop stalking me? When I'm perfect? Which means, that you'll never leave me alone. It's like you've got me under your spell, too. "Be perfect, or else!" Okay, so you'll only be happy if I'm perfect! And since I'll never be, I'll never get out from under your spell. Are you happy now?

'Well, here's something else that should make you very happy! I'm under even another spell. For the longest time I haven't felt like myself,'

And Mrs. Oomla stared long and hard at the power suit she was wearing. And then she glanced over at Great Aunt Hortense's clothes; at least, her packaging described its contents; but her own, she prayed, did not.

·∴C·∴

("Author darling, Reader darlings, Fairy darlings!" said Me, "First off, I had nothing to do with that Pest! He is not one of us and I haven't a clue where he came from. I never ran across him even once when I was trekking about Mrs. Oomla and I did look for him, believe me. He's the one been

putting her under that 'be-perfect-or-else spell'! My featherweight suggestions about clothes could only flit about that mind of hers. Mrs. Oomla
has, as she just admitted, a very intimate knowledge of our 'once upon a
time' historical records which've obviously taught her these very important
lessons about a human's right to a vast fortune. When I was at-play-in-the-
fields-of-her, I clearly saw that our records already had a very tight grasp on
her mind. And that so, too, did her Great Aunt Hortense. All I had to do
was fan those influences a tad, and voila! Certainly I could never've produced the spells that she's under."

"Me, you big fat phony!" said Lorraine. "You gonna give us Fairies a bad
rap! Your 'featherweight suggestions' put a tree-hugger in a power suit!
And you say that the Pest is the perfect-or-else guy? You're the one who's
image obsessed! You're the one who kept trying to turn nature-girl into a
CEO-It-Ms.! And about that vast fortune! It wasn't just Great Aunt Hortense
so don't even try it! And did you just say when you was 'AT PLAY???!!!' Try
when you was 'up-to-no-good! Hey, ja ever think about fanning our records
that go into the gory details about what happens to like greedy people? Ja
ever consider that?")

·⋆⋅⋗⋆⋅·

'But Miss Kitty is still going to be Sophia's Nanny. Sophia loves Miss Kitty.
Everybody loves Miss Kitty. Except Great Aunt Hortense. And I may be the only
person in the whole world who loves Great Aunt Hortense. Sophia can express herself
with Miss Kitty. Sometimes, I think, better even than she expresses herself with me.'

'Especially since you interrupt Sophia!' said the Enemy.

'I must stop doing that! But Miss Kitty isn't going anywhere. No matter how
much Great Aunt Hortense insists. And Great Aunt Hortense isn't going anywhere
either. Great Aunt Hortense has nobody. I'm her own family. Miss Kitty is good for
Sophia. And we're good for Great Aunt Hortense, though I'm sure she doesn't know
it. Great Aunt Hortense must learn that sometimes employees make mistakes. I make
mistakes, too. And we have to be forgiven. I just must tell Great Aunt Hortense to
stop being so bossy. I just have to get up my nerve. She won't break. She's no statue.
If Great Aunt Hortense was a statue, she would've broken a long time ago. My telling
her now to stop being so bossy isn't going to break her.'

"Yeah! Good luck with that!" No. 1 got one last dig in before, at long
last, Mrs. Oomla and Great Aunt Hortense reached the kitchen.

As they crossed the kitchen's threshold, Mrs. Oomla peeked at her companion. Her face was as long and stiff as her collar. 'She's been heading backwards on every step! But so have I! And right after our breakthrough in the glass
house! Room after room after room we've walked, locking thought after thought after

thought away! I was arguing with my invisible pest when I could've been talking to her.' And she peeked again at Great Aunt Hortense: her jaw looked more like a projectile than like features on any porcelain statue she'd ever seen. *'What, pray tell, is she thinking? She's surely plotting the takeover of my house. Maybe it's not so bad that Great Aunt Hortense kept her thoughts to herself! Because when she lets them out, and she will, it's watch out everybody!'*

Miss Kitty was humming away and setting the table but abruptly stopped humming when Great Aunt Hortense entered the kitchen. Mrs. Oomla watched as Miss Kitty ducked her head but continued on with the table, and then as Great Aunt Hortense squared her shoulders, arched her brows and, like a general in a grandstand reviewing a parade of alfalfa-haired-oafs, cast a critical eye on Miss Kitty's placement of the water goblets. Mrs. Oomla squared her own shoulders, *'Well, she may be a general. But so am I. And she is reviewing this parade from my grandstand.'*

Dr. Oomla and Sophia didn't say a word to each other either as they made their way towards the kitchen. Dr. Oomla was dying to ask her about that Movie Star School of hers but whenever he'd gaze down at her she did not gaze up at him. She didn't even seem to notice him. She was in her own world.

And he smiled, in spite of himself. They really were made from the same mold.

But when he took a longer look at her, he noticed her smile was a secret smile. She was thinking about some special-secret-something that was hers alone. Her Movie Star School!

And he seethed. Silently. And the Thinkers walked on, one wondering, one worrying.

'How could a daughter of mine want to train for that line of work? A Movie Star! The world treats them like they're Gods and half of them come to believe they are, the other half already believed they were in the first place, and the other half never'd believe that about themselves no matter what they did or who they are, and the other half – wait – just thinking about it burns me up so much, I can't do simple arithmetic!'

And he pulled himself up straight as he walked hand in hand with Sophia, but his mind didn't come with him. His rational mind had burst into flames. And he let it.

'And the problems all that causes for Movie Stars and for everybody who has to deal with them. Always worrying about how they look. Or worse yet, changing their look and then asking, 'Do you like me better the other way?' One person having a hundred looks! One person shouldn't have a hundred looks. One person should have one look. Their own. And worse even then all that! Having to worry what somebody

else thinks about that look! What a thing to have to worry about! It's one thing for my patients but MY SOPHIA? For anyone, let alone my daughter, to have to base everything, their actual in-the-here-and-now well-being, and their employability, on what the world thinks about how They look! They talk! Their outsides! Their face! Their body! Their walk! Their type! Their weight!

'Their voice!

'Hah! And there's my wife, her own Mother, in tears because those corporate clones are using her for her voice! My wife has a beautiful one and the goons are exploiting it. Sophia has got to be made to see how that makes her Mother feel. But if Sophia only values Movie Stars, she may not've even noticed. Because if that's who she values, that'd mean she really and truly values a face, a body, a walk, a voice and a charisma over her own real and vulnerable and very human, flawed and imperfect self.

'A dazzling outside is what a Movie Star values. Is what they think defines them. My little girl must not grow up to value only her outsides. Why if a Movie Star were a whiz at math, or an angel of mercy to the infirmed, or a writer of a heartfelt thank you note, or a crackerjack car mechanic and some so-and-so told them they were, they'd thank that so-and-so, but'd be secretly surprised that anyone would prize such a thing at all. A Movie Star wouldn't really prize that about themselves. To them, the only talent worth having and worth developing are those that can make them a Star. Because those're the talents that make them the fairest in the land. I know because that's what some of my patients really want to be and believe they are – the fairest in the land. Which is why they are my patients. And anyone who's ever read a Fairy Tale knows what happens when a person believes that. But then Movie Stars mustn't remember their Fairy Tales! Because some of my patients sure don't!'

····ᐰ····

("Ms. Author, Readers All," said Thee, "notice that Dr. Oomla understands that Fairy Tales do not just teach greed as Me would have you believe!")

····ᐰ····

'But will my Sophia remember her Fairy Tales?'

Again he gazed down at his Sophia; again he saw that secret smile on her face and the fire blazed higher.

'And then they end up in my office! A Movie Star walks into a room and thinks everyone should drop everything, stop talking about whatever they're talking about and hang onto her every word. Because that's what a Movie Star is used to! Because our whole entire culture idolizes them.

'But then, even I have to admit, there can be something about a Movie Star's eyes and smile when they sparkle down so brilliantly from a 20 foot movie screen. And they

really can be beautiful. But still the public is duped. And so now is my own daughter. My little Sophia!

'But doesn't Sophia understand what I do for a living? Who my patients are? Didn't I ever really tell her? That I've spent my lifetime treating Movie Stars because of these exact same ridiculousnesses. And I'm just getting started. Those are minor in comparison to all of the problems I've had to treat over the years. Sophia wanting to be one of them! My little girl! What've I done wrong? I can't let this happen to her. I can't. I can't.'

Somehow he hadn't exploded; Sophia and he were even still holding hands. She must not've felt the fire raging through his hand or fingers. He cautiously looked again at Sophia, and this time she did feel his gaze and she did look up at him. Her face was a field of smile-flowers; he never remembered seeing her so happy.

How could he interrupt her serenity with his fears and laments and … and … prejudices? He hated to apply such a word to himself but he'd heard what'd just ripped through him, he was a psychoanalyst after all. How could he do that to her? She was lost and happy in a star-filled dreamland. He knew that look. He'd seen it on a million faces. But knowing that only made his anxieties crash and burn all the more.

'But how would she feel when she auditioned for a part and didn't get it? Or worse yet, got a starring part, and then never got another role like that ever again! Like that poor middle-aged Artiste of mine who when she was ten-years-old, got a starring role in a musical then performed in that show for two years, but after that she auditioned for role after role after role and never got another starring part again. How could I forget what that Artiste said to me? "I was so special then and now I'm nobody." Special. Performing in front of audience after audience who do nothing else but watch your every move! That's how it makes all of those actors feel! Special. All those people paying attention just to them. All that applause just for them! But who else has a job where there's a room full of people adoring their every move? I don't have a job like that. Who does? It really does make them feel - Special! And when the applause is over, when the audience is gone, when there is no one watching their every move, they feel like they're a nobody.'

Sophia pulled on his hand and began tugging then swaying their arms together til soon their arms were swinging back and forth as they walked. She burst out laughing and in spite of himself, he did, too. And she kept swinging their arms back and forth on every step they took. She wanted to play. She was so carefree. How could he tell her any of his fears - because he knew enough to know that that's what he was feeling - when she was so happy? If she told her his fears, they might become her fears. And then he might destroy her happiness. Destroy her dream. He could never destroy a dream. That was against everything he stood for. Though he kept laughing along with her, though he tried to stop his mind from flaring up again, he couldn't. But then he didn't try very hard.

'I, of all people, can understand why Sophia wants to turn herself into a Movie Star. Those're the people I work with. They can have such silver-tongues and gorgeous-faces which makes you want to hear everything they say, and sometimes even I can't take my ears and eyes off them. But that very thing about them is a false front and very deceptive, for the simple reason that their outsides are so beautiful. Sophia probably thinks that because Movie Stars' outsides are so beautiful, that their insides are too. But no one could possibly have a character to match outsides like that. That kind of beauty can be nothing less than false advertising!

'My daughter must learn what really makes a person beautiful because outside beauty often doesn't do it at all. How devastated she'd be to find out that her favorite Movie Star has a vicious temper; or can't be trusted with a secret; or after push came to shove, really does believe she should come first because, after all, she is the Movie Star, the important one, the famous one, the beautiful one. What would she think if a Movie Star abandoned her child or hit a person with their car then drove off? And then what would she think of a plainer person, an ordinary person who adopted that abandoned child or who took that bleeding victim to the hospital – who'd she think was beautiful then? Would she still think that Movie Star beautiful when she found out what that Movie Star did? I hope not! I can understand why a shy child like Sophia who's had such difficulties expressing herself in school'd be impressed by a Movie Star who can be so compelling and commanding and bespeak her thoughts and feelings with such panache.

'Sophia is an introverted child, whose talk and thoughts and feelings are all there, too, but just not on her outside stage where that Movie Star's are, where that extrovert's are, but hidden away and safe on her inside stage where they've already been talking away but nobody but Sophia can hear them. Those feelings and thoughts know that nobody heard them. And that's why there're all lined up and ready, dying even, to leap and strut out of her, just like that Movie Star's do.

'Of course, Sophia would want to be a Movie Star. For my shy, introverted daughter to let her noisy feelings out, she'd've had to pretend to be another person, to be a Movie Star. Because only then can she do what they do, what Movie Stars do, what extroverts do, which is express her thoughts and feelings the second she feels them.

'I'm a psychoanalyst, and I'm surprised at this?

'I'm a psychoanalyst and I should know better! That can't be the only reason she had a secret Movie Star School!

'Is it really just because she's an introvert?'

And the fire in him died, and there he was, shut off in his library at night, not communicating anything to anyone, including his own daughter.

'Or is it because she wasn't really being listened to?

'Was I listening to her?

'Abandon a child! I should talk about a Movie Star abandoning a child! And I'm wondering why she doesn't know who my patients are and what I really do for a living. I never really told her about my patients and what they do and how all of their problems are complicated so much more by that profession. And now look at what's happened. She wants to become a Movie Star!

'I could've prevented this!

'The acting profession is one of the hardest, and sometimes the most ridiculous, in the entire world. And filled with unscrupulous people. Unstable people, who show themselves off for a living. Impossibly high standards for looks and weight and perfection and if I warn her about it, I will save her from so much disappointment and psychological stress. But then again, why'd I ever tell her about all the problems my patients, the Artistes, have had with that profession! I'd worry her! Frighten her even. And I must never forget what Sophia just did. My shy Sophia figured out her own way to become less shy by teaching herself how to become an expressive Movie Star. I'm ashamed to admit, I wasn't the one who helped her overcome her shyness. I should be proud that she found her own way to open her mouth and be heard! Maybe that's all this is. Just a way to express herself. Maybe, she really doesn't want to act for a living, and be a Movie Star."

As they reached the kitchen, their arms swung back and forth, and he, too, swung back and forth. 'Should I tell her what I know? Or should I keep it to myself?

'Should my little girl do what she wants to do? Or should my little girl do what I want her to do?

'Should a daughter pick her own profession? Or should the Father pick it for her?'

• • • WHO CALLS THE SHOTS • • •

His wife and Great Aunt Hortense were seated at the kitchen table as Miss Kitty set that table the way a table should be set: silverware, lined-up; plates, just-so; goblets filled not-too-high, not-too-low; and napkins folded á la Lady Windermere. In spite of the questions that were now dueling it out inside him, Dr. Oomla had to smile: Miss Kitty must believe that Great Aunt Hortense would only show mercy to perfect cooks who knew the Butlers Guild's way around a table. Thankfully, his wife was talking away; even more thankfully, Great Aunt Hortense was listening. Sophia ran to her chair and sat in it but he, smile fading, stood by his, pondering his dilemma.

But the music of his wife was resonating throughout the entire kitchen. And him. And he pondered that instead. How much that music had changed since he'd first met her. She'd been a songbird on a delicate tree branch; now she was the orchestra of the deep forest, more darkening cello and dusky woodwinds then silvery flute ... or wait, was that note there ... could that be a brassy horn? From his songbird? Did the hair on his arms just stand up?

She was certainly lively but gone was the playfulness, gone was that breathy, soft voice from a different time that had drawn him to her and haunted him ever since. She still had a melody, but a different melody. This voice belonged to A Person. A Person who had to be reckoned with. And he knew why. She needed a voice like that. She was the leader of a corporation. She couldn't play with her words now. Now every word she spoke had to be correct. And make sense. No! not just sense - Perfect Sense!

His heart which he wore in his ears listened. That old melody really was gone. Was it gone forever? And was the person who made that melody gone, too?

If he remembered her from the past, and he surely did, now she was definitely not saying everything that came into her head. Though he had never visited her in her corporation, this must be how she talked there. In the old days, round the cottage, she used to actually sing and, to his ears, sing her talk. He shut his eyes. He could still hear that Sigrid. But he hadn't really heard her do that kind of singing ... maybe just on a Sunday and maybe just sometimes ... in a long time. She was always so tired when she came home; and she left for the city so early every morning, many times, even on weekend mornings, too.

He listened. This city-talking of hers was now her.

Could he learn to like the melody of A Person Who Had To Be Reckoned With?

There wasn't a day that had gone by that he hadn't hated being in the Castle L'Oomla. But then the Castle L'Oomla hadn't been filled with her music for so long now.

And then he noticed Sophia.

She looked different. *Is Sophia really listening to her Mother, too? What a look on her face! So respectful, reverent even. Like she's under a spell. Could Sophia, my own daughter, be listening to the sound of her, too. Could she be under her spell, the way I, too, have been?*

'*Spell?*'

And like a tree going down, he toppled into his chair.

'*Is the great psychoanalyst under a spell, too? Spell! That word should not even be in my vocabulary. But how else can I describe it? I mean it's perfectly understandable that an enchanting voice would keep me under a spell! But for the love of Freud! What else is keeping me under its spell? Could my mind have a mind of its own? After all the work I've done on it! I mean, I've only been over its inner working a million times! Well, I'd better go over it again for whatever's in there is causing me to neglect my own daughter!*

'*I defied my Father. I became a psychoanalyst. I followed my dream. And shattered my Father's dream in the process. I abandoned him. And then he abandoned me. I know my Father is furious that I didn't do what he wanted me to do and I haven't seen him in a very, very, long time because of it.*

'*I may not have seen my actual Father in a long time but he's still with me. Our real parents may be long gone but the ones inside us are still in there, even though we've left our childhood homes and they haven't been in charge of us for years. If we listen, we can even hear their voices telling us all sorts of stuff: what to eat, how to vote, where we should live. They're still trying to be our parents! No doubt, they have opinions about everything we do, or don't do. Of all people, shouldn't I realize that a Father can still have a hold on his grown son. Did I think that because I'm a psychoanalyst that my Father would never be able to take over my mind because I would know right away when he did?*

'*Okay, so what about him, the Father-who's-always-with-me, the one inside, how does he feel? Could he be there in my deepest mind, that mysterious continent, venting away because I talk to a dead man night after night? A dead man who is not—*'

He spoke to his Father ... '*You! And I talk to that old dead Chief as if he's my Father and you're not! Are you hurt that I'm not talking to you? Mad?*'

No answer.

'*Am I walking around with a furious man inside me? And wouldn't such a man be against me? So how does a person carry on if there's somebody against him who also just so happens to be inside him? Am I in the backseat of a car being driven all around by such a man? At this ripe old age? Am I really in control like I believe I am? Or is he?*'

Sure that his Father would answer ... '*Do you think I've abandoned you? Abandoned you! But I'm an adult! Wasn't I supposed to leave you and stand on my own two feet? I isolate myself from everybody; lock myself up in my study night after night after night, apparently with you inside me. And you're angry. Are you in their wreaking havoc because I didn't do what you wanted me to do? Have you turned me into a Father who would abandon his own daughter the way you abandoned me?*'

Still, no answer.

'Hah! Dr. Oomla, the great psychoanalyst! doesn't know who's inside him! Am I no different than my patients? Is lurking within me the very thing that could destroy me, too? But could it really be my Father?

'Are you the reason I isolate myself and am so distracted? Well then, if that's true, now hear this! I! am! Not! Like! IV! I took control of my own destiny. And you, inside and/or actual, may never forgive me for that.

'But will I ever forgive myself?

'How could a psychoanalyst not realize when there's someone ... or is it something, an idea, a thought, a pig-headed prejudice ... inside him calling the shots? Well, if it is him - I may never get his approval – the real one's or the inside one's. But the work I have to do stays here, right in front of me. I have a daughter to raise and Artistes to save!'

It must have been those last words for now there was a voice inside mocking him ...

'There you are, Oomla, over-dwelling and over-knowing and talking to somebody who may-be-there/may-not-be-there! Again! And now you're even trying to figure out this spell. It doesn't matter! You'll never be Dr. Freud. You'll never understand yourself perfectly!'

'Aren't I lucky? My mind not only has a mind of its own but a mouth of its own.'

'That's right and it's telling you the truth. You'll never be able to enter that no-man's-land inside you to find out what really goes on in there! Forces could have invaded that very vulnerable psyche of yours that come from anywhere, anyone, anything. Like, for example, who am I? So how could you ever really know why you missed what your daughter was up to?'

'But what would Dr. Freud say?'

'You'll never know, will you? And you'll never know what the old dead chief would have to say either. Stop worrying about the perfect Dr. Freud. And the old dead chief. And your Father. Did you notice, your Father did not answer you.'

'Wait ... I'm laughing at Miss Kitty trying to be perfect but aren't I always trying to be perfect, too? The perfect psychoanalyst. As if that will save me! More likely ruin me! Day in, day out, I'm too busy spending my time analyzing everything and everyone! Because that's what the perfect psychoanalyst must do, right? But look what's happened: I missed what was going on with my only daughter. Why do I need to be perfect? Why am I scared to be human? And what good did trying to be perfect do for me? Nothing! For after all that, this psychoanalyst still doesn't and probably never will understand all that goes on in his mind. Do I really think understanding

it will allow me to control it? As if! Whatever or whoever is in there, is in there for good, whether it's understood or not! Can I live with that?

'There is only one thing I must do now. Be here. Be here for my own daughter. My little girl. No matter what's in my mind. And no matter if I understand what's in it either. My little girl needs her Father. I must love her and be here for her, even if she doesn't do what I want her to do. I can't do to her what my Father did to me. When I didn't do what my Father wanted me to do, he stopped being there for me.'

And he opened his ears and his eyes, sat up straight in his chair and looked and listened to his little girl.

'Sophia seems even ... could she be sad? ... what could this be ... could she be ... yes she could ... I should know after seeing that look on so many patients' faces ... envious?'

"Great Aunt Hortense, I know what you must think, but nothing like this will ever hap—"

"But Mommy, when I read the story in school today, you should've heard how good I can sound, too." Dr. Oomla's ears picked up. He heard how loudly, proudly, boastfully even, Sophia spoke; how again she wasn't in the least bit shy.

"Sophia, you interrupted me and I haven't quite finished speaking to Great Aunt Hortense." He saw how quizzically Mrs. Oomla looked at Sophia. Was she thinking what he'd just been thinking: that their shrinking violet was now a Johnny-Jump-Up? But his wife turned back to Great Aunt Hortense so quickly, he couldn't figure out what was on her mind. It was as if she couldn't really see, nor had time for, anyone else in the room but Great Aunt Hortense, "I assure you, Great Aunt Hortense ..."

And then what Sophia said really hit him. 'how good I can sound TOO!'

• • • WILL HER HIGH HOLY HORNET'S NEST NOT BE REQUIRING PIZZA AFTER ALL? • • •

'There it is! She said 'TOO!' She believes she sounded as good as her Mother when she read in school today. Has she been comparing herself to her Mother? Could that be the reason there was envy on her face? Is that why she has a Movie Star School because she wants to dazzle too? The way her Mother always has and always will? Has my little girl noticed just how much I've always been so transported by her Mother's voice? Is that why Sophia wants to be a Movie Star? So that I'll be dazzled by her too?

'But now finally Sophia is interrupting! Now she's asserting who she is into the conversation. Something my shy Sophia would never've done. She can't hold herself back; she's showing her stuff to everybody present, including her Mother!'

He studied her face. The sadness had vanished, and so had the envy.

"I will make sure that it doesn't, Great Aunt Hortense. Miss Kitty, tell me, tell Great Aunt Hortense, that you'll let us know from now on what Sophia is up to. And that you'll never let her stay up so late at night for any such reason as a Movie Star School, or any other such reason that she may dream up in the future."

Dr. Oomla heard how Mrs. Oomla's voice was growing more forceful on each word.

"Oh, Mrs. Oomla, as sure as me name is Kitty Devine, I'll never allow anyting like tis t'happen ever again!"

"Sigrid, this is certainly neither the time nor the place to be discussing such things! This is a private matter, and such things are never meant to be aired so freely and openly!"

"Great Aunt Hortense, if you mean that this matter is not to be discussed in front of Miss Kitty, which is I'm sure what you've just implied, I do not agree—"

'Miss Kitty's, in church; Great Aunt Hortense, the bully in its pulpit, and Sigrid is stomping up its aisle.'

And Mrs. Oomla stomped on, "... Mr. James asked Miss Kitty to leave our employ for a few days and because of that she's had to lose several days' pay. And I've decided that that is all Miss Kitty'll have to suffer, Great Aunt Horten—"

"Miss Kitty will suffer?! Miss Kitty? Sophia was the one who was suffering! Sophia was the one who was up all hours of the night in this so-called Movie Star School and therefore not getting enough sleep. Because of Miss Kitty's negligence, Sophia was never awake and alert enough to pay attention and answer questions and recite her lessons in school the next day! Why, pray tell me, shouldn't Miss Kitty suffer?"

'Listen to them both! I've never heard Sigrid speak to Great Aunt Hortense like this before! Sigrid has always spoken so ladies-luncheon proper to her Great Aunt Hortense, even when Great Aunt Hortense is bossy, and Great Aunt Hortense is almost always bossy. In fact, I've never heard Sigrid speak in a tone like this to anybody! especially Great Aunt Hortense. No, she always seems to humor her and lets her have her way. I'd hate to have to admit this to Sigrid, or for Sigrid to even know what I'm thinking, but Great Aunt Hortense is even a little bit right this time,

at least about Sophia staying up late for her Movie Star School, but Sigrid won't even give her that.'

"Great Aunt Hortense, Miss Kitty has suffered a consequence for not telling us about Sophia's Movie Star School - a financial penalty and that's all she'll suffer—"

'... And I don't dare intervene. This is between the two of them. What else I hate to admit and, above all! to hear, is that Sigrid is beginning to sound like her Great Aunt Hortense. I never thought the day'd come that my poor ears'd have to witness that!'

But then listening to them try to out-starch, out-rule and out-edict each other and he almost burst out laughing, but knew he didn't dare. *'Sigrid wants to win. And she's learned how. My wife, my sweet wife, my music, has become a tough cookie. It has to be that city, that corporation that's taught her how to stomp down so.'* And Dr. Oomla didn't know whether to laugh or cry.

"I've just taken Miss Kitty's word and that satisfies me." Finally, his wife and Great Aunt Hortense stood bull to bull in the pulpit.

"Well, Sigrid, since you are speaking so freely in front of a servant—"

"Great Aunt Hortense, Miss Kitty is not a servant!! She is so much more than that. And you should know by now after living in this country for as long as you have, that servant is not a term we use here."

'Sigrid is not giving in. Now she's attacking Great Aunt Hortense's snobbiness!'

But Great Aunt Hortense was not giving in either, "Well, then I will speak directly, too! If Miss Kitty were on my staff, and Miss Kitty did—"

"Great Aunt Hortense, I need you to remember something very important. Miss Kitty is not on your staff, she's on—"

"BUT GREAT AUNT HORTENSE, YOU SAID I WAS SUFFERING AND I WASN'T SUFFERING! My Movie Star School is a real school and I was learning a lot of things! And I'm going to continue in my Movie Star School, even if it is late at night on a school night! AND MISS KITTY IS NOT A SERVANT. SHE LOVES ME."

Sophia's words ripped right through Dr. Oomla. He saw that they ripped through everybody.

'Leave it to a child to talk about the only thing that matters – who loves her! And if I hadn't been locked up night after night trying to understand myself perfectly, she'd've known that I love her, too! And imagine that! The person who everybody thinks needs a speech therapist, it turns out, can use her mouth quite effectively. She can even get herself into trouble with it. Is this my little girl?'

But his mind struck again.

'I've forgotten that the very persons we're arguing about are right here listening to every word we just said!' Even Sigrid and Great Aunt Hortense must've

understood because he saw them look at Sophia and at Miss Kitty: one penitently, the other hazed with just a tinge of regret.

And he filled with regret. He, too, had forgotten Sophia and Miss Kitty were there because of his ears! His Poor Ears! Having to listen to his wife speak so uncharacteristically! To Great Aunt Hortense carrying on so! All parties talking so unamiably and unaffectionately! His Poor Ears had to listen to people being snappish and sharpish and downright shrewish to each other!

Enough!

'How ridiculous I am! Me and my sensitive delicate ears. As my ears were doing its discriminatory thing, I forgot who else was listening. And some psychoanalyst training I'm exhibiting! I didn't even think to do what I do every day of my life at the Institute when my patients are arguing! which is mediate their argument and not take either one of their sides but to remain neutral, so they could talk through their issues, so they could live together peaceably again. These sensitive ears of mine are ruling me, and it's becoming a very bad habit! Because of these ears, I let Sophia down. Again! Of course, I should've intervened. Now, because I hadn't, I wonder, how must Miss Kitty and Sophia feel having to listen to Great Aunt Hortense go on and on about them?'

There was Miss Kitty, with a wilting bouquet of napkins in her hand, collapsed into a kitchen chair. But, on closer look, not half as upset as he thought she'd be. Sophia was a sparking fireplug, not upset at all. Or even shy. Just the sight of her, and Dr. Oomla had to smile.

'Thinker Statue, start your engine!' It again!

And, at long last, he did, "Sophia and Miss Kitty, all of us really do love and appreciate both of you very much. Sophia, we are relieved that you're finally being open with all of us and telling us how you feel and what you want ..." And then the thought ... *'If I correct my bashful Sophia will that make her go right back to being bashful again?'* ... stopped him just as he was about to continue. But three words, Movie Star School, chased that thought right out of him and on he went. "But make no mistake about it, Sophia, taking part in activities on school nights, must come to an end! Taking part in activities, openly, during the day, is another matter and a subject for future discussions.

"Miss Kitty, I just heard, and I know you just heard how strongly Sophia's Mother and her Great Aunt Hortense feel about Sophia's late night activities. They take those activities very seriously. And I do, too. We all do. But I hope you can forgive them for getting carried away and talking about you and your role in those activities as if you couldn't hear! Please tell us how you feel about that, Miss Kitty?"

Miss Kitty had pulled herself up from her collapse, "Oh, Dr. Oomla, but now I know where I stand wit' everybody. It'weren't so bad, really, t' listen. 'N again, I can't tell ye enough how awful sorry I am about Sophia's late nights. I hope all o' ye believe me when I say I won't ever let it happen again!"

"Sigrid and Great Aunt Hortense, both of you heard what Miss Kitty just said. I believe her. Do you believe her, Sigrid?"

"I do. It's Great Aunt Hortense that doesn't, with all due respect to you, Great Aunt Hortense. But Sigmund, you must understand that it really doesn't matter if Great Aunt Hortense doesn't believe Miss Kitty, again with all due respect to you, Great Aunt Hortense, but Miss Kitty is our employee, Sigmund—"

If his wife would've told Great Aunt Hortense a hundred more times about the respect due her, Dr. Oomla would not've been fooled. He heard something in his wife's voice he hadn't heard before; or maybe he had only finally heard it. He heard the music, but he heard something else. Something he wasn't sure a voice could even have, the upper hand. He wondered who else heard it. He peeped at Sophia who was examining her Mother with very big eyes. And he knew, with even bigger ears. Did that music, that upper hand make Sophia feel like she had the lower hand? Could that be why she didn't always speak up? What effect did her Mother have on Sophia? He saw the effect she was having on even the high-hat, high-minded, high-handed, Madame herself because something surely was cracking through even her visage.

"... Sigmund, this is really between you and me. If we believe Miss Kitty, that's enough. Sophia's our child and it's up to us to say who'll watch her!"

But the crack had become a fissure and the personage inside the monument began talking, and everybody had to look twice to make sure that personage was Great Aunt Hortense because she wasn't stiff or starchy or sharp. She was talking in a wobble and softly and they had a hard time hearing her.

"I have been very kind to both of you over the years. When you were too busy with your careers to take care of your household and your domestic staff and your daughter, it was I who was here making sure all of that ran smoothly for you. Over the past few years, that sometimes even included Saturdays and Sundays. I would drive by even when it was an inconvenience to me, making sure that everything was in order. Now I'm just sorry I didn't drive by at midnight on school nights also, because apparently when all of you were at home, you still weren't aware of what your own daughter, Sigrid and Dr. Oomla, and what your charge, Miss Kitty, who you were being paid to mind, was up to. You ask me if I believe Miss Kitty. Why should I? Why do the two of you? I have always understood how important your careers are and have respected that. Sigrid, you are one of the few woman in the world who not only has invented a successful product, but then started her own corporation to manufacture and sell that product, and are about to grow that corporation into a multinational, which would be an enormous accomplishment for anybody, and a particular one for a woman. And, of course, Dr. Oomla, your work with patients at the Institute is crucial to their well-being. And because of these important careers - incidentally, both of you really do important work - you have trusted your staff to oversee your daughter's education and upbringing. Well, look at what's happened because you did. So I really do believe it is I who should be placed in charge of your household staff. Not Mr. James. And not Miss Kitty. If you insist on keeping Miss Kitty, then it is I who should supervise her."

But Dr. Oomla needn't worry about Great Aunt Hortense. He could still hear the old Great Aunt Hortense loud and clear, no matter how much her words were wobbling. The Great Aunt Hortense who always knew what she wanted. 'It is I who should be placed in charge of your household staff!' The Great Aunt Hortense who always knew what was wrong, because all of them had missed Sophia sneaking out of her room in the wee hours and holding this Movie Star School of hers. Great Aunt Hortense may be fragile, she may be cracking, she may have spoken atonally, but she knew what she wanted and what was right and what was wrong, and she wasn't afraid to say so.

Great Aunt Hortense had spoken softly, but it hadn't been soft enough, because he could see that everybody - Miss Kitty had collapsed back into her chair and Sophia was just a pale thing now and Mrs. Oomla's mouth was open but she was speechless - had heard every word she said. But he couldn't have stopped Great Aunt Hortense using his mediator skills. Because a mediator had to be neutral and he was far from neutral. How could he be neutral on the subject of raising his own daughter? Anyone who was trying to be mediator wouldn't dare think what he was thinking, let alone say it out loud. A mediator! Hah! Great Aunt Hortense had just disparaged Sophia's Mother's skill as an attentive, caregiving parent. And his, too. And that no Mother would tolerate. Or Father. Besides a husband's duty was to root for his wife. But something else was sticking him in his side, and he would've rather died than let his wife hear what it was. Great Aunt Hortense was actually more than just a little bit right. Both of them really had missed Sophia's sneaking around. And he didn't want his wife to know he thought that. No, he couldn't play the mediator for this argument like he did at the Institute. How could he be neutral when he agreed with one side, and the next second, he agreed with the other? And how would his wife feel if she even suspected he was rooting for Great Aunt Hortense a little bit?

But Dr. Oomla knew Great Aunt Hortense was waiting for an answer and one look at his wife and he saw that she was not ready to give her that answer. What should he do? What should he say? After all, he was the only one in the room trained to handle emotional situations like this. Exactly what approach should he take?

Then he knew. He shouldn't be the one to answer Great Aunt Hortense at all; he remembered that tone in his wife's voice. He knew what that tone meant because he knew what this was. A battle. But not his. It was his wife's. And Great Aunt Hortense's. If he'd say the wrong thing, he'd certainly offend his wife. Or Great Aunt Hortense. Or he might very well offend them both! Great Aunt Hortense was his wife's only living relative! His wife might have his head if he hurt Great Aunt Hortense's feelings.

But then again, his wife might have his head if he didn't speak up to Great Aunt Hortense.

His wife had told him so many times to overlook Great Aunt Hortense's faults because she was all alone in the world and that she and he and Sophia were all Great Aunt Hortense had. He also knew that though his wife had never said so, the reason Great Aunt Hortense was always welcome in their house, no matter how snobby and bossy and critical she was, was that Great Aunt Hortense connected her to her long lost Mother and Father. And she was the only person in the whole world who did and ever would. That's why he had always let Great Aunt Hortense be.

But then no one was saying anything; everybody looked uncomfortable. Somebody better say something.

He didn't even know where to begin, but he began. And as he spoke, he kept an eye on his wife. "Great Aunt Hortense, thank you so—"

And his wife jumped down his throat. His ears. His heart.

"No! No! No! Sigmund, I can handle this by myself!" She had never spoken in such a fury to him before, so sharply and so crossly, and now it was Dr. Oomla's turn to wince.

"I don't need your help, Sigmund. I've been fighting my own battles for quite some time now, and I can fight this one. Great Aunt Hortense, I can hear that you're hurt, but I'm hurt, too. We are all hurt. Me. Miss Kitty. Sophia. Sophia's Father. Sometimes people do the wrong thing. We did the wrong thing. We didn't know that our own daughter was up in the middle of the night watching movies. We were wrong not to know that. We wish we had known. But we didn't. And you know something, Great Aunt Hortense, I don't believe for one minute, as you do, that Miss Kitty was letting Sophia stay up late to watch movies. If she had known, she wouldn't have allowed it. Miss Kitty didn't know either. And when she did find out, I'm certain she tried to stop her but couldn't. Sophia's a child, after all. And children do sneaky things. But it also seems to me that Sophia may've been teaching herself something in that Movie Star School that she needed to learn. And I believe I know what that was. She was practicing over and over again how to express herself. Something she was having a hard time doing in her real school. And with us. So maybe that Movie Star School wasn't such a bad thing after all!

"And there's something else you really must know Great Aunt Hortense. In fact, all of you should know. Every night, I am so tired. And we know how out of character that is for me because I have so much energy. But by the time it's 6 o'clock, I'm dead tired. I can't keep my head up, I'm so exhausted. 7 o'clock is too early for a grown-up to have to go to bed, if I'm even lucky enough to get to bed at 7 because there're so many nights when I have to stay in the city to entertain and wine and dine potential new clients because the board insists I do. No wonder I didn't know what my own daughter was up to. I need to pay better attention to my family. And I will, I assure you, Sophia, and you, Sigmund!

"I've been sitting here listening to you, Great Aunt Hortense, but I've also been listening to me. So now about my career. I have to make some changes in that, too. I love to dig in the earth. I like to grow things. I like to get my hands dirty. And my clothes dirty. Having to dress up every day is just not in my nature. And you know what; I'm not going to do something that's not in my nature anymore. And corporate life is not in my nature. With its team-player, brain-washed, employees! And all those cheerleading board members! Hah! they don't fool me! Nothing but Napoleons in Business Casual clothing.

"And skyscrapers!

"The interiors of those shafts stretch upwards ad-nauseam and downwards straight to #@((!"

That word! From his songbird? His ears were right; they had heard brass. Dr. Oomla was shocked; his ears, appalled.

Sigrid noticed his reaction immediately and since she'd never seen its like aimed at her before, she said penitently, "Oh! do forgive me, but I'm describing where my employees have to work each and every day of the week. And it's just so soul-crushing. The interior of my skyscraper stretches with lines and lines of identical cubes as far as the eye can see, and though those cubes are measured in mere inches, each of them are stuffed with exactly one full-sized-human. I'm lucky, as the CEO, I've never had to sit in a cube but the rest of Giggle's rank and file are not so lucky. Though a cube may not be a prison cell, they have no bars and have low walls after all, but they sure look like a punishment to me. It's a wonder anyone gets any work done at all. One day, I found a note on my chair, 'Please, ma'am, may we have some walls?' I showed it to the officers in Well-Being, asking that we, at least, put up walls and give them some privacy. You know what they told me I was to say, 'We are fostering an environment that promotes 'and encourages communication among team members. Now, Mrs. Oomla, that should remind them of our higher purpose!' they said. 'But what you must know as our CEO is that Giggle's employees gave up their rights to privacy when they took employment here! Giggle tells our employees where to sit and what to say! Our employees say what Giggle wants them to say, or they won't be our employees anymore! But because we-the-corporation, we-the-Giggle are the kinder-gentler-dictator, they never even know it.' But then when I walked out the door and they thought their CEO couldn't hear them, they said, 'Hah! doesn't she understand the entertainment value we provide to us and our employees! For as the clock ticks relentlessly on, that employee's head pokes out from that cube as it sneezes and sprays its drips; masticates its meatball heroes; pitches its business; spies on its neighbors; tattles on its co-workers; slurps its pea soup; and slobbers over its bosses for all those other poking-heads viewing and listening pleasure! What a show! Plus, by setting up the work environment this way, we've turned our employees into spies. They've nowhere to hide! We hear their personal phone calls! And they hear their neighbor's. We see them read news on the internet! And they see their neighbor doing it, too. No walls keep them honest. Just think, our employees get to work in a funhouse, a courthouse, a workhouse and a jailhouse! With all that, shall we say, congeniality everywhere they turn, why! they'll be so stewed, all they'll want to do when they go home is escape to TV-land where we, and all the other corporations, can bombard them with our useful, calming, restorative messages! And last but not least, tell me, has our CEO not figured out that walls cost money? Shouldn't she be savvy enough to know the little secret? That we spend money to benefit shareholders and some employees - wink-wink – the 1 percent - but certainly not those cube-dwelling 99 percenters!'

"Now, I ask you, Great Aunt Hortense, how would you feel if you had to use your golden voice to repeat anything people like that want you to say?

"So, because I couldn't help, that poor employee's head has to come face to face all day long, day in, day out, with all those other heads inside all those other cubes. And that poor head must obey his overlords, or else; and must witness all those other heads obeying their overlords, or else, too. They all must feel as if they, like their jailbird counterparts, have been sentenced for life and must obey, or else, too. Just thinking of all those compliant souls gives me hives. And here I am, the CEO, and I couldn't even rescue my own employees because I am ruled by overlords and I, too, must be a compliant soul or else! You know, there really are such things as monstrosities - like those fire-breathing dragons in Fairy Tales - that crush our souls and keep us obedient and in line!

"But don't worry, some day, I'll start a new venture, a vertical farm, which may be a tall building but it won't crush souls because I won't let it. What it will do is grow fruits and vegetables and flowers. I'll show them I can grow what Giggle needs in my vertical farm right there in the city. And then Giggle will no longer exploit the third-world. Wait til I tell that to the board. Everybody has always admired my voice. Well, wait to they hear it now!

"I am lucky. Lucky to have a daughter. And a husband. And a Great Aunt. And a Miss Kitty. And a Mr. James. The other day, I was flying over that city and imagining that I could green up that concrete and turn it into the country. A vertical farm may be in a skyscraper but a vertical farm is as close as I'll ever get to turning that city into the country. I can't turn the city into the country and I'll no longer turn myself into something I'm not either. I'll have to abide by the laws of the universe like everyone else. And after I finally do the right thing in that corporation of mine, I'll be back digging and planting and growing, I'll feel more like myself again. I haven't felt like myself in years. And then I—"

"You are WHAT!!!?" Great Aunt Hortense rasped and rattled from what was surely her death-bed.

Mrs. Oomla's spellbound husband and listeners now gaped at Great Aunt Hortense who was faint and sick and pale. But as this was Great Aunt Hortense, her command returned on her command and in full snob and trumpeting staccato, she sniffed and snorted, "You intend to one day resign your position as CEO of your very own corporation? Have you taken leave of your senses, Sigrid? You are going to walk away from that? You are one of the few women CEOs in the world! What woman would turn her back on a leadership role like that? And, I hasten to add, a billionaire! You can stride through life doing whatever you want, getting whatever you want, going wherever you want, influencing whoever you want, because you are Mrs. Oomla, the billionaire! Haven't you noticed that whenever the media describes one of your ilk, it is always, Mr. Such and Such, the billionaire Mayor? Or Mr. Such and Such, the youngest billionaire? Or Mr. Such and Such, the billionaire philanthropist? Well, you are a woman and you have that affixed to your name! You are nothing less than the wonder and the envy and the ruler of the modern world! And with that magnificent voice of yours, there's nothing you can't do!"

Though his wife hadn't answered Great Aunt Hortense, Dr. Oomla knew what her answer would be. And now, he was much more than shocked and spellbound; he was struck by lightening, even as he was still and quiet in his chair. In fact, he was a gamboling, opera-shrieking, blossom-sniffing, ceiling-bouncing cartoon. Maybe his life wouldn't be so bad after all, even if the Institute did collapse.

'My wife, my music, will someday not work at the don't-worry-be-happy-industrial-complex - Giggle! That corporation! Daffeine! That artificial junk! That Disneyland for happy-talkers!'

Despised! Yes! Despised! He could finally say it, even if it just was to himself!

And then right out loud and very rudely, he chortled.

He snorted.

He yoicked.

Until he caught wind of himself and was terrified!

What was he doing! Was he about to reveal to his wife what he really thought? He hadn't been doing that for months. No. For years.

What had he done?

He had just broken the Oomla's unspoken rule. By snorting and yoicking and chortling, hadn't he completely Mach-4ed through their sound barrier?

'Giggle? the Disneyland of happy-talk? What about our own Disneyland of happy-talk!! Isn't that where we've all been dwelling for far too many years? Isn't that our very own personal Siberia?

'Could that be our one true problem? Our only problem?'

Everyone had taken their eyes off his wife and were now staring bug-eyed at him, including his wife. He couldn't care less. He was even about to tell her, to tell everybody, that the truth had crashed landed onto his private planet but Sigrid gave him such a forbidding look, he knew now was definitely not the time. For she, he now knew, was a tough cookie and was not about to be thrown off her primary target by his odd behavior. And he was not her primary target.

"But Great Aunt Hortense, you've wanted me to be someone I'm not ever since I was a little girl. I remember when I was ten how you kept trying to get me to stop planting seeds like a farmer and join that club that I hated, that ridiculous Entrepreneurs Club! Well, I joined it. But I knew what I wanted to do, and it wasn't to be an Entrepreneur! But I did it to make you happy. And look at what happened; you got your way, an Entrepreneur is exactly what I became! And I did succeed, so you should be proud of me! And proud of yourself. Great Aunt Hortense, I know you meant well, but I've had enough! Now it's time for me! Great Aunt Hortense, I know you were stuck having to raise me. But there's something I really believe and that is a parent, and let's face it, you really were my parent, shouldn't pick out their child's profession for them. Especially when a child displays a talent and a passion for something the way I did. And you know what, even if a child doesn't display a talent or a passion, what somebody does with their own life should be up to them!"

"Oh! Well those are fine, noble sentiments, but your family has to eat, and just where do you think your money will come from, now that the Institute is collapsing and you, on a whim of free expression, will one day dispose of the source of your family's income, your corporation and take up a dubious new venture. If vertical farms would put an end to exploiting the farmers of the third-world, why aren't there any in Goliathon already? And besides, do you know what kind of money you will need to build one of those? And do you truly understand what the water and light and carbon dioxide requirements would be to make a vertical farm viable? Where are you going to get those commodities? In that city? With its huge population that is already straining the water supply? And won't that farm need more light than the sun can give? Which means you'd have to run lights during the nighttime, too. Won't that create light pollution? And pray tell me, will you really be manufacturing carbon dioxide, which plants need to live, and which everyone knows is the cause of global warming? How do you think the people in that city will feel when they find out you're making the root cause of global warming right in their back yard? And speaking of resources, I really must inquire, are you fully cognizant of how expensive this cottage and your lifestyle, is to maint ..."

Great Aunt Hortense continued piling on but suddenly Dr. Oomla understood like he never understood before. And it was all in what his wife just said, "A parent shouldn't pick out their child's profession for them."

'I'm about to discourage Sophia from her Movie Star School! And my own Father all but forbid me to become a psychoanalyst and was so indignant when I didn't take over his company and become a producer! And there was Great Aunt Hortense insisting that Sigrid become an entrepreneur! And old Knitsplitter himself, the old Chief - the man who I so respect and emulate, the man whose approval I always thought I wanted, even more than my own Father's – demanding IV take over the Institute. And look at what happened at the Institute!

'Are all of us under a spell cast by our parents?

'Because look what happened to me. I followed my heart and yet I lock myself up at night. I might as well be in a jail cell just like those employees in their cubes. My Father thinks I committed a crime and he isn't even here to punish me for it. And now I'm punishing myself. Although maybe the one punishing me is not me at all but the one buried away deep down inside - maybe he's become spiteful - maybe he's even been the one yanking the happiness right out of me. Is it all because I didn't do what my Father wanted me to do? Well, disciple of Freud, you only see this day after day in your patients, and you didn't even know when it was happening to you. Because, of course, a brilliant psychoanalyst such as yourself would've already broken the spell cast by his Father! And a good, kind, wise, thoughtful, loving man such as yourself couldn't possibly be fueled by dark energy! But the spells cast by parents are powerful ones and hard to break, maybe the hardest spells of all to break. Because, first off, you don't even know when they've cast their spells because your parents are nothing like those storybook wizards or witches. They don't wear long capes and have daggered-shaped fingernails and chant mumbo-jumbo and drone on malevolently. And they, unlike those wizards and witches, don't cast their spells just once. No, they cast it many times: they may be weaving it about you day after day after day, even when you're just sitting there innocently eating your breakfast. I should have known that.

'Because you, after all, must know everything perfectly.

'No! More! Spell! And! No! More! Overknow! I must forgive myself for doing what I want! And for being a psychoanalyst who can't analyze himself! And remember! I! Did! What! I! Wanted! To! Do! I've become a psychoanalyst. And if my wife wants to be a farmer, that's fine with me. And if my daughter wants to be a Movie Star ... well ... I can help her become a sane, intelligent Actor! Even if it's killing me to say that ... a sane, intelligent, wise Actor! Surely they exist somewhere! I will not do the same thing to my daughter as my Father did to me. Sophia shall have her Movie St ... NO! Acting School! Just not in the middle of the night.'

Then the universe struck him again, though he still hadn't budged from his chair and Great Aunt Hortense was still prattling on ... "And let's say you still manage to have sufficient money, what about the incredible influence you have among women around the world? Do you want to lose that?"

'Acting School ... *The Castle L'Oomla ... The Castle Gloomla ... The Institute for the Compassionate Care of the Extraordinary and the Always Interesting ... the Artistes ... the Insurance Companies ... the Pharmaceutical Industry'* He could do this. He could.

He didn't even notice Great Aunt Hortense get up from her seat as she swatted her snoot with her handkerchief and then high-horsed herself towards the door. He didn't even smell the pizza when it arrived a milli-second before Great Aunt Hortense had exited. He didn't even hear Mr. James let loose with a, "Will Her High Holy Hornet's Nest not be requiring pizza after all?" He didn't even register the snickering in the kitchen. He didn't see that Mr. James face had turned brighter than said pizza and stayed that way for days. He didn't notice that Sophia was smiling one second and frowning the next. All he was aware of was that his mind was back doing what it loved and, apparently, couldn't stop it from doing - turning his idea in to stacks and stacks of possibilities.

• • • TELL ME WHO YOU ARE! • • •

"Ms. Author," said Thee, "I spoke first:

"Where is Me? She was here, but she's disappeared! I can't believe I still need to keep tabs on her. She's already in so much trouble. If the Dispatcher would show up now and not find her here, he'd have her head when he did find her. This is exactly what he told her not to do, and, of course, that's exactly what she does. And why would she disappear now of all times, when it's gotten so interesting around here. Be, Free, Lorraine, you heard what's going on! Miss Kitty keeping her job; Mrs. Oomla paying tribute to our folk tales AND someday quitting the corporation; Great Aunt Hortense walking off in a tiff. I have to admit, it's hard to tell what's going on with Dr. Oomla, but all of you had to notice that look that's been on his face for such a while did seem to melt away. And were any of you worried how Sophia was taking it when Great Aunt Hortense was going on and on about her and Miss Kitty? Well, I kept flying inside to see for myself. Oh, she was listening to Great Aunt Hortense alright but the most upset she ever got was when Great Aunt Hortense said she wanted to take over the staff. In fact, a lot of the time she was in there daydreaming about her upcoming

Play Reading with that C Big guy from school. This has to be the first time that I can remember Great Aunt Hortense wasn't really getting to her all that much. Even listening to her Mother wasn't getting to her either. That Reading, I believe, has changed her life. Now Me's missed all of this and Sophia is her charge, too! She was placed here just as we all were to watch over Sophia. I hate to keep harping but I believe Me's not interested in anyone but herself! Sophia is her responsibility, too! Not just ours. I almost wish that Dispatcher would come here right now, so he could see how irresponsible and selfish she really is."

" 'Thee, tell me you're kidding?!" said Lorraine, "Ya just noticed that Me is interested in no one but herself! Thee, why do ya think they call her Mimi Meselk? Me will never change. It doesn't matter what anybody says. Even the Dispatcher. You think that Dispatcher can control her? I've worked with her on other jobs before. She's a trip! You'll see, even if he finds out, he'll talk a good game—"

Be interrupted, "Me's in the back. I watched her conjure a fainting coach—"

"Like, she needs a test drive? on one a' those?" snapped Lorraine. "That's preferred seating for her!"

"This is no test drive, Lorraine!" Be went on. "She ain't kidding. You can't miss her. You'll see a feathery confection with droopy wings and ringlet curls dangling over its precipice but oh! so mop-top-ily!"

"Well, this time it will be different!" said Thee, "because now I'm on her team, and I believe that rules must be followed. When did she disappear? And why didn't you tell me?"

"I know exactly when it was. As soon as Mrs. Oomla started talking about digging in dirt." And then Be mimicked Mrs. Oomla …

" 'I love to dig in the earth. I like to grow things. I like to get my hands dirty. And my clothes dirty. Having to dress up every day is just not in my nature. And you know what, I'm not going to do something that is not in my nature anymore. And corporate life is not in my nature.' And then there was a piteous moan, and Me, in an instant, was a roué-ette of high-fashion dishevelment and gaunt-angular-despair!"

Me cried out, "Mrs. Oomla is a hopeless idiot. After all I did for her! I mean dressing children is so boring. Where's the challenge in that! Please tell me Great Aunt Hortense won this ridiculous argument! I can't bear it. Great Aunt Hortense is wealthy, Mrs. Oomla should show Great Aunt Hortense some respect. It's easy to buy anything you want when you're wealthy. But do you know how impossible it is to put it together just-so, creating that illusive "it" if you're not. And that is what Mrs. Oomla had; at least, when we could keep the dirt off her. And with our head-to-toe approach, she really could be something. And that voice didn't hurt either. Now nobody will look at her twice. All our work for nothing!"

"We? We?" said Thee. "What do you mean WE!? What do you mean 'our' head-to-toe approach? Who is 'our?' "

"Oh, Thee, you really should wake up and smell the magic!" Me cried out. "That's how things work in the Fairy world. We, as in Mrs. Oomla's stylist, that I suggested strongly Mrs. Oomla hire when I was inside Mrs. Oomla, putting all sorts of, shall I say, bees in her bonnet about all sorts of delicious things. Like that amazing, worthy of an architectural prize closet. What person of fashion wouldn't die to own one just like it?"

"That is outrageous!" said Thee, "You went into Mrs. Oomla's head! We are forbidden to do that. I have no choice but to tell the Dispatcher. We've been placed here to watch over Sophia. And to take care of her. You weren't placed in Mrs. Oomla's head. You were placed in Sophia's. You would never've been placed in Mrs. Oomla's head. Mrs. Oomla is a grown up. There are not supposed to be Fairies in a grown-up's head. Me! You've done wrong. And you've not done your duty. You've made us Fairies look undisciplined and untrustworthy. You've done the Fairy Kingdom an injustice. We are here to help the humans. Which means we have to do right by them. And you didn't do right by Mrs. Oomla. You didn't really help Mrs. Oomla. You may've even hurt her. And I must do the right thing for Sophia. We all must do the right thing for Sophia. And for the Fairy Kingdom. Be, Lorraine, Free, you tell her too! And I will inform the Fairy Dispatcher. It is my duty!"

"Oh! You will, will you? Betray one of your sisters? Don't you understand what a Fairy is? What a Fairy has been put on this earth to do? Fairies are here to do magic. I don't care what they told you. How do you think we could be in here in the first place? If it weren't for magic, how could we make ourselves so invisibly teensie to fit in here? Fairies do magic. And that's what I do! And that's what the Fairy Dispatcher does too! I don't care what that Fairy Dispatcher told you. I am a Fairy and I believe in magic. And you are a Fairy, too, Thee! What do you believe in? Rules? Given to you by the Fairy Dispatcher? Who isn't following them himself?"

"But Me! you agreed to follow the Rules. I heard you make your promise."

"Fairies are Magical Creatures. Not Angels who follow Rules! What do you think, Be, Lorraine, Free? Are you a Magical Creature, or a Rule following Angel?"

"Lady," said Lorraine, "Be, Free and I didn't feel right. We may bicker but we never fight like that. And we hated being pulled into the middle, first by Thee and then by Me. So Lady, we just lifted our wings to shroud our heads. Maybe if we waited long enough, both of them would, like, come to their senses and stop!"

"Darling, Author, I told them, 'Oh, do you think you can hide from the truth? We know who we are! Magical Fairies! Free is! Look what you did, Free. If you hadn't gotten your friend the Man in the Moon to help Sophia, do you think Sophia would've been able to read that story aloud in school so brilliantly? I don't think so. It was all because of what you did that she could, Free. What you did was magic wasn't it, Free? Well, Free, are you a Fairy from the Enchanted Lands who believes in practicing magic, or a Goody-Two-Wings from Heaven who follows the Rules? Free, before you answer me, remember how you helped Sophia. If you would've followed the rules would Sophia've been invited to play a character in C Bigg's new play?' "

"And I said then and I say now!" said Thee, 'Me, what you did hurt Mrs. Oomla! Fairies, don't listen to her! By going into Mrs. Oomla's head, she hurt her. And she took the same pledge we did, and she didn't keep her word.' "

"And I snapped right back, 'But look how much Free helped Sophia by not following the Dispatcher's Rules. What do you say, Free? Lorraine? Be? Who are we? We're Fairies! We do magic! We're not Angels who follow Rules! Tell me who you are! And speak up! Because you're proud! So be proud of who you are!' "

"But Lady," said Lorraine, "nobody said nothing. Nobody wanted to pick a side."

"But Darlings, I didn't give up, 'Free, Lorraine, Be, if you followed the Rules every second of every minute of every day while you were doing this job, do you really think you could really help these humans? If Sophia hadn't met the Man in the Moon, where would she be today? If the Fairies couldn't do magic to help these humans, humans would be totally out of luck."

"Ms. Author, I said, 'That's why their humans. Humans can't rely on luck to get them by. And humans don't have magic. They have intelligence."

"Darlings,' I said, 'Oh! Please, let's do debate the merits of magic over intelligence!'"

"I said right back, 'Me, no side has ever won that debate. And you are changing the subject! Fairies, the subject is: Is it right to leave Sophia and go into somebody else's head! Free was not obeying the rules but at least she helped Sophia! But Me, you weren't helping Sophia when you used your magic. You were only helping yourself because you were bored. So you convinced yourself that if you helped Ms. Disheveled become Ms. Sheveled you would help Mrs. Oomla. But you weren't helping. Mrs. Oomla likes being disheveled. Plus you went into her head! And Mrs. Oomla is a grown-up! And if you still don't get it, Me - Free helped Sophia but you didn't help Mrs. Oomla!' "

"Darlings, I said, 'No, Thee, the subject is; the debate is, Fairies - what kind of Fairy are each of you – a Magic Fairy or an Angel Fairy? Answer me, every one of you. Come on, now, tell the truth, do you want to be a Magic Fairy or an Angel Fairy? Remember what you did, Free? Where would Sophia be today if you didn't do that? Where would she be without your magic, Free? Didn't you help Sophia? Who are you, Free, Be, Lorraine? Who are you? It doesn't matter if you speak up now, the Dispatcher can't hear you. Say it out loud and stop hiding, do you believe in magic or not? And remember what Mrs. Oomla just said about her nature. Well, magic is in a Fairies' nature. Magic is our nature!' "

"I said, Ms. Author, 'But Me, if you had stayed out of Mrs. Oomla's head, she wouldn't be worrying right now about what was or was not in her nature!' "

"And I said, darling, 'Thee, the Dispatcher knew that magic was in my nature and still he put me here! He put us all here, and we're all Fairies, we're all magical creatures. Including you, Thee! What were they thinking telling a bunch of Fairies that we couldn't perform magic! Well, magic is a Fairy's nature. And, in fact, it's cruel to put a Fairy somewhere and demand that they not perform magic! So, what do you think, Be, Lorraine, Free, stop hiding behind one of the very things that make you great, your wings, and use them for what they were made for! Fly Fairies! And speak loud and clear, and tell me, tell Thee, tell everybody, who you are!' "

"Lady, we just had to remember our Sophia. And what she had done. Something that she had never been able to do before. And Me was right! It was all because of Free! And magic! And, like, we hated to admit this, if Free hadn't done what she did, Sophia'd never've read like that in school. But we didn't want to answer Me and we cried when we looked at Thee. Even Be cried, who prided herself on never crying, but, Lady, we did answer Me. Out we said, 'No! I am a Fairy. And I believe in Magic!' But out of respect for Thee, Lady, we wouldn't fly.

"Lady," said Lorraine, "I'm not ashamed to say that tears was falling from my face."

" 'Your magic hurt Mrs. Oomla!' said Thee. 'Magic shouldn't hurt people. Magic shouldn't hurt!' "

"Darlings, do you remember what I said? 'Would you listen to her! Since when do beautiful clothes and beautiful things hurt anybody? Nobody agrees with you! Nobody! Well, Miss Prudence Priss Primly, are you still gonna squeal on me now? You'll be all by yourself if you do!' "

"Ms. Author, they had all abandoned me. But I knew what I had to do. And I would do it."

• • • "THE UNIVERSE IS TRYING TO TELL ME SOMETHING!" • • •

"But C Bigg, I could do zat part too. I can too do ze French accent! I can't believe you would even worree about zat. Have I evair let you down? I don't 'ave to just read ze Irish girl and ze Tough Cookee. I spent ze time wiz a real French girl and I was paying attention to howl she said every word plus howl she moved her fannee – ooh la lah. You must know because you do ze accents too, zat when you do ze French accent, when you do ze anee accent, you start wiz howl shut or open you keep your mouz and howl much you keep your lips togezair and where you place your tongue inside your mouz, and howl you let ze air travel zrough all zose parts ... I mean, you must have figured zat out too, Meesyur C Bigg, considering all ze voices you do, too. My speech terapeast and I talk about zis all ze time when I am finished my lesSAUN. I can do ze Fifi wiz my eyes closed."

Sophia had ducked down low, in her seat, in her voice, so Mr. Snoggley or her classmates wouldn't see or hear her as she auditioned her Fifi for C Bigg who was across the aisle.

C Bigg sighed with defeat, "Okay, okay Sophia! You can have that part, too! But I have to admit, I kind of miss doing the girl's parts. They have such an extra entertainment value coming from me. That one, in particular, done by me with a French accent would've been a hoot and so amusing for our audience. It would've really packed a wallop. But you may be right. I do want my play to be taken seriously. And an Author must do what is right for his characters. But don't even think of trying to take any of my parts, no matter how much I know you can do the men's parts, and I don't even care how good you'd do them either!"

"Would Master Biggleton and Miss Oomla care to explain what they are whispering about in the middle of the History lesson?" Mr. Snoggley harrumphed. "This wouldn't have anything to do with the reading of

C Biggleton's new play tomorrow, would it? But tomorrow is Creative Expression. Today is History. Since both of you weren't paying attention to the history lesson, you need to know we were discussing what it takes to be an explorer like Magellan. Perhaps Miss Oomla, you'd take the time from your busy schedule and tell us, what quality you have that might make you an explorer?"

Sophia, though she felt her face boil, her eyes steam, her nostrils drip, even as her toes and fingers turned to ice, though she put her head down even as she was standing up, though her voice had a shake she couldn't shake, she could hear what she wanted to say standing up strong and firm within her and say it she would, "Mr. Snoggley, I knknow that I could keep my wwwits about me even if the o ocean was wobbling and shshaking me and my boat all over the pupuplace." And as she crashed back down in her seat, she thought, *'Only five words of it stammered! I bet my speech therapist would call that 'progress.' But wait til everybody hears me doing C Bigg's new play tomorrow! On my birthday! Then I'll show them what I really can do!'*

"Interesting, Miss Oomla. I agree with you that an explorer needs wits. But how does one develop wits? By learning. But where does one learn, Miss Oomla? And if you'd say, from everywhere and everything and everybody, I would agree with you. But that would include school, wouldn't it? So in order for you to develop the wits you'd need to circumnavigate your boat across rough seas, you might have to pay attention to many things, including what is being taught in school?"

"Yes, Mr. Snoggley, I'm ssosorry. I'll pay attention. I just got cacarried away about tomorrow." Sophia listened to her words ring throughout the room, only two words stammered this time. She wished her speech therapist could've heard her.

'Now even Mr. Snoggley is talking like my Father. Now even he is telling me to learn as much as I can. Ever since my Father found out about my Movie Star School that day in the Orchid Orphanage, every time he sees me, all he does is talk to me, and boy! does he want me to talk back and I do and we're always talking. About! So! Many! Things! About my Movie Star School. Which he will only call Acting School. I told him everything. And he loved hearing what I have to say about it. But, of course, that was only after he told me that I shouldn't've been sneaking around and I shouldn't've stayed up so late on a school night. But now every day we talk talk talk about so many things. And he told me that my Acting School is just wonderful because I'm learning in there too. Because he wants me to learn learn learn so I can think think think, so I'll be smart smart smart. And as long as he sees me really learn learn learn, I could keep having my Acting School. Of course, I could have my Acting

School! Of course! As long as I hold it on weekends, and I do my homework every night, and I read one extra non-school book a week, and I participate in one extracurricular school activity a week besides the Drama Club.'

Which she had been drafted into by the President of the Drama Club when word got around school about her Reading. She still hadn't chosen the extracurricular activity yet. And that's when Mr. James started in on her too, because ever since Mr. James'd heard that she had to choose another extracurricular activity, now every time he saw her, he couldn't stop pitching the Debating Team to her. He said that's really where she'd learn how to think on her feet, and talk at the same time; but not just any talk, talk about important matters, matters that affected the whole world, that might even lead to saving the planet.

And now here was Mr. Snoggley saying the exact same thing.

Her Father said everything he was asking her to do would definitely make her a smarter person, and a smarter actor too. He never would say Movie Star. Or actress. Just actor. But that was okay with her. She was keeping her part of the bargain, and so was he. She was learn, learn, learning, and think, think, thinking, so she got to have her Acting School. If only she could find the time for it. Between her C Bigg play rehearsals and her Drama Club meetings ...

At the end of the school day, when Sophia was on her way to meet Miss Kitty so they could walk home together, her ears got all tickly. "Sssssophia!"

Were catty-little-catty-cats serenading her? She turned round - and there were Marilyn and Melinda. And this time Melinda, all blush and tied-tongue, said not a word and it was Marilyn, little-voiced and flirty, who sighed, "Sophia, where did you get that Paku Piku back pack! That's like their latest. It's perfect! I've been begging my Mother to get one for me!"

And suddenly Sophia felt odd: her tongue was where it should never be. She knew it! That was the first sign that old-faithful was about to blow her up again! "Oh! Ma ... ma ... rilyn, I'm gogot it from my Mo ... Mo ... ther's stylist, Claude."

Sophia was crisp and clear on the inside, *'MISS DESIGNER CLOTHES IS TALKING TO ME?'*

"Your Mother has a Stylist! That is so cool!"

"Well ... she used to. He used to he ... help her with her clothes but now he's helping my Ffafather ..." *'SHE'S TALKING ABOUT CLOTHES! YOU LOVE CLOTHES. YOU FINALLY MIGHT HAVE SOMEBODY TO TALK TO ABOUT CLOTHES! AND YOU'RE NERVOUS! SOPHIA, YOU IDIOT!'* "... and sometimes he sssshops for me in the city … because he and me oh! do we love clclothes!"

"I die for clothes, too! That back pack is, like, so expensive!"

"Claude keeps telling me that when I bubuy something, I should only buy the bbest!" *I DIE FOR CLOTHES, TOO!'*

"Oh, I wish Claude could meet my Mother so he could tell her that too!"

"See you tomorrow, Sophia!" And before scampering off, those kitty-cats smiled at her like she was adorable too.

And Sophia relaxed and her tongue returned and she breathed again.

·∴(··

("Darling, Author," said Me, "I reminded them, 'I did not get Claude to come up here! I had absolutely nothing to do with that! Do all of you really think I have any control over him?' "

"Lady, we all shouted, 'Yeah! we do!' "

" 'Well, I don't. So all of you can just stop looking at me like that! I haven't done any magic or anything. I've just been sitting in here doing what I'm supposed to do! This just shows what an eye for beauty Sophia has! You should be proud of Sophia! I am!' "

"Lady, Be, Free and myself was sitting right next to Thee to show her our support. Ever since the argument, we stuck to Thee's side though it was Me we had agreed with. Now the four of us sat across from Me and stared at her.

"And, by the way, Lady, didja pick up on what I picked up on? Did our Readers? Well, listen to what I says next, 'Fairies, ja get that? Sophia's wishing to tell somebody, 'I die for clothes,' out loud! Isn't this just swell! The Fairy Sophia's gonna end up being the most like is Me! Kinda makes ya wonder, don't it?' "

"Darlings, I shot right back, 'Well, it's out in the open! You're just jealous!' ")

·∴)∵·

Just as Sophia was about to turn the corner, she heard her name but said on such shivering air she almost missed it.

"so … soo … so fee eya!" She knew that voice anywhere! It was Milford Squeemllee's.

"Oh! Hi Milford!"

Milford studied his shoes very grimly and said to them, "I can't wait to hear you read tomorrow!" and that took talent because his mouth was scrunched shut and so were his eyes. And then he sped away as fast as skin and bones could carry him and before she could even say thank you, though she called it out anyway.

Sophia made a mental note as she turned the corner, *'I'll have to tell C Bigg what Milford just did. Maybe he'd write a character who could do just that in his next play. Not everybody can talk with their mouth closed and see with their eyes shut. I bet Milford doesn't even know how talented he is! I'll have to tell him. Us shy people have to stick together. But I'll have to clear it with Milford first because I don't want to hurt his feelings. He might let C Bigg do it, if he felt it was okay to laugh at himself. But then, on second thought, maybe Milford isn't ready to laugh at himself and if I say something, I might really hurt his feelings. Because, you know what, it's okay to talk like he talks, it's just another way of talking, that's all. So maybe I shouldn't say anything to either one of them after all!'*

Then she smiled. She had friends to take care of.

Mr. James was waiting for her. "Sophia, Miss Kitty, is absolutely exhausted and that's why she couldn't be here. 38 Artistes came to Dr. Oomla's program today. Which means Miss Kitty had to prepare lunch for 38 people plus staff! Today is Dr. Oomla's biggest crowd yet from the Institute. Word has spread among the Artistes and that is most encouraging, isn't it? Next week, 53 people have signed up for his programs. Of course, we do have to see if they actually show up. I've never seen him quite like this. He is thrilled! Now, Sophia, before we have to wade through all that hustle and bustle that's going on at home, I've been wondering, have you made up your mind yet about that extracurricular activity yet? Let me stop beating around the bush! Have you decided to join the Debating Society? It would be such an opportunity for you to express yourself."

'Is everybody giving me advice?' And Sophia said warily, "Well, I'm still thinking about it."

"You know both your Mother and Great Aunt Hortense would prefer you do a sport because of its physical challenge. They do have a point! However, I like the Debates. But then I have always opted for a mental challenge. In a debate, you never know what issues you might discuss. But make no mistake about it, Miss Sophia, debates are very much like Cinema. Because in a debate, you'd get to talk about the very things that really need to be talked about, just like they do in your Movies. You've seen the part in the Movie when the hero stands up and says what he really believes. Well, that's exactly what you would be doing. Except this time, you, Sophia Oomla, would be the hero. There are so many issues to debate. Why you might debate world shattering issues like how to end a war; or you might debate more elementary local issues, like how to make your school a better place. Let's say, for argument sake, you debate how to make your school a better place. There would be you and the person you're debating because each debate has two debaters, two sides. You might take the Affirmative position, which means you are 'for' the idea that would make your school better, and your debating partner, who would really be your opponent, would take the Negative position which means he would be opposed or 'against' your idea for making the school better. So the debate begins: off you'd go, each of you stating your position when it's your turn. And believe me when it is your turn, you'd better make sure your argument is well-reasoned and supports your position. Remember what I said about thinking on your feet? Your opponent, I assure you, will be doing the exact same thing, saying how your idea is poppycock and would not make the school better at all, blah, blah, blah."

"Would I get to wear a costume?"

"A costume? You'll need more than a shining exterior to convince those hair-splitting-judges your argument is sound. Remember this: your outside is not where your heart and your mind and your soul are, Miss Sophia. Listen to what Shakespeare said about a character who worshiped his tailor and his haberdasher above all others:

" 'There can be no kernel in this light nut; the soul of this man is in his clothes.'

"You're no light nut, Miss Sophia; you're a nut with a kernel; though one can't crack your shell to find it! It's there in your invisible parts, where your soul and your wits are, and it's chock-ful. And in a debate, those invisible parts could come out for all to hear! Miss Sophia, this would be your big chance to hold forth, your clothes could never do that for you. Why standing there and just looking dapper, being a mere ornament, your audience'd never know all that there is to know about you, like how much you care about your school and what you would do to save it. So, no, thankfully, for all concerned, you'd be yourself."

'I'd be myself!' And Sophia was filled with terror. She would never be able to do that. Never. Be herself in front of a whole roomful of people! No matter how much they needed to hear what she had to say. *Didn't my Grandmother sit there and look pretty? If she can do it, why can't I? Besides, I'm only just now learning how to do my characters in front of everybody. But myself! In front of so many people! That's the most terrifying thing I've ever heard! He must think because he can be himself in front of people, everybody can be their selves. He'd never understand!'*

So she didn't say another word but when they'd reached the driveway, Sophia could see that Mr. James was studying her through the rearview mirror.

"Miss Sophia, please do pardon me but I can't help but notice the look on your face. I'm sure it's because of what I said. I believe it's when I mentioned you'd get to be yourself. Might I be permitted to say one more thing in favor of that very point and the Debating Society, and then I do promise I will leave you alone and let you make up your own mind?"

"You can say it, Mr. James. That's okay."

"Well, Miss Sophia, in a sense, we are in a debate right now. I am "for" you joining the Debating Society, and from the look on your countenance, I can tell you are "against" you joining the Debating Society. Well, okay, here is what I have to say in support of the affirmative position. Let me open, Miss Oomla, by telling you what a fine complement the Debating Society would be to your other dramatic pursuits. You'd still be appearing before a group, but this time, not as a character, but as yourself. You'd get to use your own voice. You'd not need a foreign accent. You could just be you, Sophia Oomla. In addition, you wouldn't be saying what anyone else wrote for you to say; in a debate, you would be saying what you yourself think. In a debate, what you think is what you say. You would finally, in front of a group, an audience, say what you believe, in your own voice and in your own words. In conclusion, Miss Oomla, you would be letting the you out of you!"

"Haugh! That's what Louis Armstrong said to me, too!"

'I CAN'T BELIEVE I JUST SAID THAT! OUT LOUD!'

And there was no place to hide! She couldn't just pouff herself away in the wide, open spaces with Mr. James staring right at her!

'WHERE'S OLD FAITHFUL WHEN I NEED HIM? WHY COULD I GET THAT OUT LOUD AND CLEAR AND HAVE SO MUCH TROUBLE GETTING THE EASY STUFF OUT? HOW EVER WILL I EXPLAIN MR. LOUIS ARMSTRONG TO MR. JAMES? Oh, Mr. James, the Man in the Moon is Louis Armstrong and he talks to me! Haugh! This is my secret. I can't tell ANYBODY! What ever will I say?'

"Well, isn't that clever of me! Saying the very same thing as Mr. Louis Armstrong!"

"Oh! I ... I ... heard ... him ... you know ... in a Movie. And he says many smart things and sometimes I used to pretend he was saying them to me."

····C··

("I was screaming, 'Groooovy!' said Be. "I mean those were my exact words! That's what I wanted her to say." I began flying all around! 'She heard me! She's gonna be like me, too!' "

Thee said, "Interesting! And we know for a fact you hadn't been doing magic!"

Me snapped right back, "Oh! I was doing magic but Be wasn't! Hah!")

···)···

"I see, Miss Oomla. It would be quite agreeable to have a man like Louis Armstrong to talk to. I imagine it would be like talking to the sun itself."

'*More like the moon!*' Thankfully, that remark stayed where it should.

Finally, they arrived home and Sophia cut and ran. '*Away from all grown-ups, even nice ones, who want to give me advice! Me and my own mind'll figure out what I do! And nobody else!*'

···☾···

("Darlings, did you hear her? Me and my own mind???"

"Yeah, Me! Even folks from Mafairyia know a figure a speech when we hear one, so don't even think of taking credit for that!")

···☽···

Sophia did call over her shoulder, "Thank you, Mr. James, for the ride!" She was certainly not about to thank him for the advice, but since he was a nice advice-giver, she wanted to thank him for something. When, at last, she was on her own and safe on the path, she couldn't stop marveling, '*How close he got to my secret! Of all things he could've said to me, why that? Can he see inside me?*'

"Let dat you outta you."

There it was again. But Mr. James wasn't there. She looked around. No one was there.

'*Am I hearing things?*'

Again she heard it. Through the fresh-air. "Let dat you outta you."

'*Could air be talking to me? If the moon could talk, maybe air can too!*'

She inspected the air and saw nothing but still she heard it.

"Let dat you outta you!"

'*Is the fresh-air trying to tell me something? Maybe the Man in the Moon told the fresh-air to talk to me? Could he do that?*'

She looked everywhere. Up the long pathway, through the bushes, the tree branches and the sky above.

But this time! There really were Bark-Beard ArborTreeMeians!

Haired-over, scraggly eyes in the bushes!

Laughing, toothy mouths on the daffodils!

And the entire Supreme Court in the clouds!

And they were swaggering. And shouting! At her!

"Let dat you outta you."

They were in on it, too!

'*But why would a daffodil grow teeth and try to scare me? But maybe it isn't trying to scare me. Maybe it's only trying to help me. It's like the universe is trying to tell me something, like Louis Armstrong was and Mr. James was and ... maybe even ... Mr. Snoggley was. But help is not supposed to be scary.*'

"Let dat you outta you!"

'This is scary.

'But the Man in the Moon wasn't scary!

'It's scary for daffodils to have teeth and talk to me!

'And it's scary just to be me!'

"Don't you understand, daffodils, it's scary to be just me!"

"Let dat you outta you!" Was their answer.

'Could the whole entire universe be in on it, too?'

"Let dat you outta you."

'But teeth aren't inside a daffodil! And eyes aren't on a bush! And an entire court does not sit on a cloud! This is not sensible! I'll have to start seeing a Doctor like my Father if this keeps up ... first the Man in the Moon ... and now this! But are they trying to say ... a foreigner shouldn't be inside Sophia! ... A Sophia is inside a Sophia ... That a person with an accent isn't inside Sophia ... a Movie Star isn't inside Sophia ... a Sophia is inside Sophia ... Is that what it is? ... Let the Sophia out of Sophia? But I like all the voices inside me. I have to tell those daffodils that. And to tell them that I have something like a great big ear inside me that's like a sponge that soaks up voices and sounds and music and accents and all sorts of noises. Or maybe it's like a mockingbird or something ... I can't help it! That is who's inside me!'

Sophia shouted back, "Daffodils! Clouds! ArborTreeMeians! Bushes! Listen to me! There are voices inside me ... lots of them! There's lots of mes!"

·∗☾·∗

("Ms. Author," said Thee, "I was shouting, too. 'Does anyone have any idea why the universe is trying to scare Sophia? Of course, my companions would not answer me. Well, I don't care if we are leaving tonight at the stroke of midnight, and our time to help Sophia is almost over, you should never have allowed the elements to scare Sophia into accepting her stammering wobbling self! Putting teeth in daffodils! Alright, who did it?' But not one of them would admit it!")

·∗☽·∗

"... There's foreigners and others too. And I like them to be there ..." Sophia went on. "But I promise I'll let the me out of me ... No matter how scared I am when I do."

·∗☾·∗

(" 'Holy smoking elfs!' said Lorraine, 'There's foreigners and others too!' - That's what I was just thinking! This is elfing unbelievable! She heard me! Ya know, somebody may've kind of, ya know, like, tawked to the elements, like, a little bit and they might or might not've been, like, ya know, doing magic of the Mafairyia kind BUT I wasn't doing any kind of magic right this very instant to make her say that about foreigners! So, like, Me is right, she wasn't doing magic just then, Be wasn't doing magic and, like, neither was I! Although I was, like, a little teensie while ago!' ")

Though Sophia had said what the daffodil people and bush mouths and tree trunk men and Supreme Court clouds wanted to hear and was sure she had appeased these creatures of the universe so the universe would never bother her again, deep down she knew that the 'me out of me' was sometimes a foreigner and sometimes a mockingbird and sometimes a stammering-scaredy-cat. That's just who she was. Nevertheless, she was very relieved to reach the steps to the wraparound terrace and get off that pathway. She zoomed up the stone steps like she was strapped to a rocket pack.

When she reached the top step, she gunned it across the terrace too, but stopped short when she saw that her Father's sign still had no words on it. He hadn't thought of a name for his brand new Institute today either.

And then she heard voices, but these weren't cloud voices, these were people voices and they were coming from the east balcony. She knew who they belonged to. Her Father's patients. The Artistes. The Actors and the Movie Stars who had troubles. They were rehearsing for their Saturday night play. She was dying to peek, but knew she wasn't allowed.

And knew she would anyway. She had to! They were doing something like her Movie Star School. This was the first time she had actually heard them. And now she would finally be able to see for herself what that something was.

She had found out two months ago – actually, the day after Great Aunt Hortense had walked out - that the Artistes would be coming to her house. That was when her Father had sat the both of them down and asked them, "Sigrid, Sophia, how would the both of you feel if I turned our home into an Institute?"

• • • TWO MONTHS AGO • • •

What an odd thing to ask them! Whatever'd made him think of it? Had he been drinking Giggle? But he would never drink that! Or would he? Because where was the seriousness on his face? When Great Aunt Hortense had walked out of the glasshouse, it mystifyingly disappeared. Now this! What was he about to tell them? Maybe all those problems at the Institute were too much for even him and he had become like the word no one in the village was allowed to say! And Sigrid and Sophia eyeballed him.

"Now, let me explain. Our home would be a little like your Movie St ... your Acting School, Sophia! In fact, I got the idea from you. When I found out about your Acting School, I knew how to save the programs and help the Artistes."

"From me, Daddy?" Sophia leaned in so close, she could count his whiskers.

"Now before both of you jump all over me, please listen. You already know that when the Artistes had found out that IV was threatening their Theatrical Programs, they were inconsolable. They loved their Theatrical Programs. But some of them were a lot more than inconsolable; they were hysterical and caused a riot at the Institute and then escaped to rove the village, and the villagers were afraid they might cause a riot there, too. That's why the Principal closed the school and you had to go to Goliathon to stay with your Grandparents, Sophia.

"But the Artistes' behavior is understandable: those Insurance carriers demanded that IV drop their Theatrical Programs or else – no benefits for the Artistes.

"Well, I may have come up with a solution; a way for the Artistes to keep their Theatrical Programs. But it all depends on what the two of you think of my solution. Let me explain.

"Just like you love your Acting School, Sophia, the Artistes love their Theatrical Programs. And I want to save those Programs. But that isn't the only reason I want to save them. Those programs really help the Artistes cope with all the hard times they've had. Talking with a psychoanalyst about the problems that brought them to the Institute helps them, but nothing seems to work as well as those Programs the old Chief came up with many years ago. I think they're the single best practice I've ever used on my patients.

"Let me explain one of the great benefits that those Programs have on Show Business patients. Those programs enable our particular kind of patient to produce one play every week. That our villagers line up to see. Do you understand what that means? It means that our Institute and our Artistes have the support of our villagers. That's something that no other such Institute has going for it. The villagers love our weekly theatricals. They pack the house every Saturday night. Do both of you understand how unusual it is for people with problems like theirs to have support from their community? People with these kind of problems are usually shunned by their communities!

"Sigrid knows but I want to remind Sophia that our Artistes all used to work, and some still do when they get better, in dramatic enterprises – in Show Business like your Grandfather, who you just spent time with down in the city. Many of them know your Grandfather. Some even work in the part of the business you like so much - the Movie Business. So believe me when I tell you the one thing our Artistes can keep front and center in their minds is that a live audience will be coming to see the play that they're in, so it'd better'd be good. Everybody loves getting attention, but our Artistes love getting attention ten times more than all those other everybodies. And when they do their Saturday night play they get attention for a worthy reason, for what they do best – performing, or writing, or directing, or designing. And the whole world knows, the Show Must Go On! And, believe me, our Artistes do too.

"But that's not the best thing about those Programs! What those Programs really do for the Artistes is allow them to finally hear again that special something that's still there inside them.

"When the patients first check into the Institute, so many of them seem lost and down low and set hard with troubles. So when the old Chief insisted everybody call those sad, spiritless, deeply stressed and unresponsive smash-ups, Artistes, everybody thought he had become that word he wouldn't let us say. But he was actually making sense because he understood our patients. They are creators. They are Artistes. They've just forgotten they are, because they can't do what they used to do. They no longer hear the thing inside them that made them Artistes in the first place because it's lost its way down deep inside them. The only thing they can hear is their trouble, which is speaking so loudly, they can no longer hear anything else.

"There's a lady named Miss Emily Dickinson who wrote a poem about that very thing:

'Hope is the thing with feathers
that perches in the soul
that sings the song without the words
and never stops at all.'

"Now Miss Dickinson called that something inside hope, but the old Chief didn't call it that, he called it the Artiste. He thought the Artiste was the part inside each person that could turn what was buried away inside them – their trouble, their sorrow, their pain – into a spark, a song, a story - so that their feathery fellow could fly up and out and back into the world again and paint its picture, sing its song, tell its story. Which is what our patients used to be able to do before they landed at the Institute. And those Theatrical Programs seem to be the thing that lets them hear their feathery fellows again. Now what actually gets them to hear its song, I can't say for sure. But I know it has something to do with those Programs.

"Maybe I'm wrong, maybe the only thing they care about is that an audience will be there paying attention to them. Or maybe the old Chief was right. Whatever it is, those programs let the Artistes get back in touch with their feathery fellows who can then sing their truths in songs that come from every part of them, and maybe whether somebody hears their song or not doesn't really matter. Because what really does matter is that spiritless people are singing again."

"Daddy, does that mean when they hear that feathery fellow, they start singing in their perfect voices?"

"Perfect?" Dr. Oomla winced. "Not at all, Sophia! Why if those Artistes thought they had to sing that song perfectly too, they might never open their mouths again. Remember what I said, they're just singing their made up song in a voice that comes from every part of them. I bet they're so happy to finally hear their feathery fellow again, they wouldn't give a hoot how they sound when they finally start singing again. That's where I come in; I help them appreciate that song so that they know it comes from no one else in the whole world but them, it comes from their very own soul."

Sophia heard herself just about raise the roof, "I KNOW EXACTLY WHAT YOU MEAN!" but she didn't even think to lower her voice, "A FRIEND TOLD ME! HE SAID, 'LET DAT YOU OUTTA YOU!' THAT'S THE SAME THING AS THE FEATHERY FELLOW, ISN'T IT, DADDY?"

And then she felt her blush turn a deep dark red when she realized just how jarringly loud she'd been and, worse yet, that she'd almost given away her secret. And she scoured her Father's face to see if he was looking at her funny but he was regarding her no differently than before and she wasn't sure if he'd really heard her.

"Sophia, what a wonderful friend you have! Yes, the you outta you is that feathery fellow! It's just another way to talk about him. I wish the old Chief could've heard what your friend said. I bet he would've liked it, too!

"I wish I could tell the both of you exactly what it was these Programs did. The old Chief cooked up something wonderful when he masterminded these Programs. The old Chief even understood the importance of a name. He changed the Institute's name which had been an insult to its occupants and picked a name that respected them. Our patients hold their heads up higher when they walk through the gate and read those words on the old Chief's sign, because now they know who they are.

"There is no doubt about it, everybody in our village and our staff and the patients and the visitors and even his own son, thought the old Chief was a bully. And being a bully is definitely not a good thing to be. Just ask his son IV. Ask me too because my Father tried to bully me to do something I didn't want to do. And Sigrid, how do you feel now that Great Aunt Hortense is insisting you run your corporation though all of us heard quite clearly that someday you intend to take up a new endeavor. Do you feel like you're being bullied?"

Sigrid could only smile sadly.

"But the old Chief's bullying was not always such a bad thing. Because every patient knew the old Chief's rule: that if they checked into the old Chief's Institute, every one of them had to participate in the old Chief's programs or they couldn't stay. Nowadays patients with mental health problems checking into any other such Institute - if Institute's like the Chief's even exist anymore – don't have to do anything if they don't want to, which doesn't help those kind of patients at all. Any other type of patient, a heart patient, or a patient that breaks his leg, is prescribed many things to do by their Doctors to get their hearts better and their legs better. But nowadays, these kinds of patients, whose hearts and bones aren't broken but whose spirit and souls are, may only be prescribed a little, tiny pill for their great big problem, which may or may not fix something in their brains but never manages to get down into their souls and fix what's broken there. Nowadays, insurance companies can even say that some mental patients need to take those pills or they might refuse to pay for that patient's treatments.

"It even seems to me, nowadays, that I, as a mental health professional, am not the last word on a patient's treatment but insurance companies are. Patients buy the insurance those insurance companies are selling sure that when they eventually get sick, that insurance company will allow them to get the services of a smart, caring doctor who will be in charge of their health and well-being. But those poor patients are being bamboozled because it's the insurance companies that're really in charge. Because they, and not the doctors, are the ones who really determine how to use that patient's money and what treatments they will or will not pay for. And remember, it's the insurance companies that pay the doctor and the Institute. And doctors can't work for nothing and Institutes can't run on air. So if an insurance company decides they won't pay for a certain kind of treatment, what's the likelihood that patient will receive that treatment?

"But the good news is, insurance companies still covers a patient's sessions with a doctor such as me, so our patients do get to talk about their troubles to mental health professionals. But it's not like it used to be in the good-ole-days, when a patient would get a full 45 minutes every week. Now the insurance companies will only cover a few short minutes out of that patient's long, long months of hundreds and hundreds of minutes, which is hardly enough time for them to express their thousands and thousands of sorrows, let alone learn how to listen for their souls singing away inside them.

"No! Those remedies, pills and talk-therapy-once-in-a-blue-moon, never seem to get even close to the thing that would really make them feel better. And that's what I've been talking about: the thing in Miss Dickinson's poem, what the old Chief called their Artiste, and what she called the feathery fellow inside; what you, Sophia, call letting the you out of you. Because when they can hear that fellow again, they really begin to feel better. The old Chief's programs are the thing that lets them hear it again. These programs get them to express themselves again, get them up and doing things again, get them to hear their 'thing with feathers.'

"But the interesting thing is nothing really has changed for the Artistes. They still have their same problems. Only now they can do something.

"As soon as I found out that those programs were to be no more, every second of every minute in my day I've been dreaming about how to get those programs back. But exactly how I would didn't occur to me right away. It was only when I began to think about Sophia and her Acting School that it hit me. And then I knew what I would do. My plan is very simple. I'd hold the Theatrical Programs in our house during the day. In The Castle L'Oomla. I'd do in our Castle what the old Chief did in his Institute. So that the Artistes would still have their Theatricals and the old Chief's tradition could live on."

And then he looked at them with a formality that wasn't there before and he became his old self, his serious self again. "If, of course, it's alright with the both of you? And the Artistes, of course!

"What would you think, Sigrid, if your home was used to help the Artistes? Remember, you'll be losing a part of your house and many strangers will be in it on a daily basis!" And then he turned to Sophia, "Suppose somebody told you that you couldn't have your Acting School anymore? How would you feel? Now think about those Artistes and how they must've felt when they found out their Theatrical Programs were gone."

Sophia didn't even have to think, "They must feel terrible! Those poor Artistes!" and she said yes immediately.

But so too did her Mother, and just as instantly. And then what gushed up and out of her Mother, Sophia would never forget. Her Father, she saw, was just as astonished.

"Oh, Sigmund, I've always suspected you never much cared for this House That Daffeine Built. And for all the money I make that built it. And that, though you never said it, I know you can't stand Giggle. And that has something to do with Giggle being a little too much like one of those teeny tiny pills you don't like giving your patients. But remember, no one's ever found a thing wrong with Giggle, Sigmund, and it is not like those teeny tiny pills!"

"Sigrid, I don't like a 'thing' to control a mind - a drug, a drink, a pill. But, you're right, I never came out and told you that. I didn't want you to think I was standing in the way of your career."

"Sigmund, if only we would've talked about this before! But from now on, let's talk. Even if we are not making music for each other's ears. So if you could find a use for this House That Daffeine Built that would help the Artistes and be a home to your brand new Institute, then maybe I haven't made such a mistake building it after all. If that's what would make you smile again - because I have to admit ever since we've started living in this huge house, you haven't been smiling all that often - then please please do it. There's room for a hundred Artistes in this house! I don't know what got into my head when I did it."

·⁎C·⁎·

("Lady, I yells," said Lorraine, 'Elfing balls of fire! I bet I do! ME?? The Castle Oomla too?'"

"I sniffled, darlings, then said, 'Lorraine, you and Thee, really need to relax. Why can't you act more like our Laissez-Fairy colleagues and just let me do what I want like they do? Stop behaving like one of those annoying Dwarftectives who are always snooping around, trying to find out what's what!' I lifted my head from my Enchantian Cotton but I certainly wasn't budging from my bed, even if it had gotten so suddenly melodramatic in Oomla-land.")

·⁎)⁎·

"But now our house would finally be filled with people involved in activities that might help them hear their feathery fellows again, as you said so perfectly just now. And I meant every word I said, after I make things right there, I do intend to step down from my corporation, no matter how Great

Aunt Hortense feels about it. But, even so, we will still be able to afford to make our house your brand new Institute. I know you've never approved of CEOs and their ridiculous salaries. But I am a billionaire!"

·∴(·∴

("Lady," said Lorraine, "at that, Me crie—"

"Lorraine," said Me, "why ever would YOU be talking for ME? And then I cried so outrageously, so wretchedly and with such abandon, that the Fairies feared if I kept it up, chic that I am, angular that I am, fashionable that I always always am, I really—"

"… Was just a boney waif draped in fufu," said Lorraine, "and might break up into bits, and we found ourselves feeling sorry for you though we didn't have to be dwarftectives to know that this house—"

"Outrageous! Ms. Author" said Thee, "that the Castle L'Oomla had been yet another one of her illegal, banned, clandestine activities. And I told her in no uncertain terms, no matter how sorry I felt for you … her!"

"Thee, clandestine?" said Me, "Hah! try clan-destiny!")

·∴꒰·∴

"And finally we'll be able to use these thorns that have been sticking in our sides for such a long time - our huge home and our much too much money - to help someone - the Artistes!"

"Sigrid, I will not and cannot accept your money—"

·∴(·∴

("Lady! Suddenly Me sat up in her bed and flew to Sophia's ear, it was like a miracle or something!")

·∴꒰·∴

"Giggle is your invention and Giggle, Inc. your corporation. And besides, I can't fund my Institute with money earned from a substance that I don't approve of. The whole point of my Institute is that I won't be prescribing teeny tiny pills to make my patients feel better!"

His ears began to howl, as if his words had cracked into a million pieces and, shard by shard, were crashing into them. And he looked at his wife: he could see they were crashing into hers as well.

'I just displayed a total lack of understanding of how my new Institute will work. I can't leave those words out there; I have to say something which shows I do understand.'

"The awful truth is the Artistes who'll be coming to my program will be patients from the old Institute and the old Institute is now prescribing pills; so the patients who come to my program will already be on pills. I understand that. But even if the Artistes coming to my program aren't pill-free, they'll be welcome at my Institute. I can work with Artistes, no matter what's inside them."

It didn't help. He looked again at his wife: her straight back was now stooped, she seemed to be searching for something faraway from him.

And then what he said deliberately crashed into his ears again, 'Sigrid, I will not and cannot accept your money. Giggle is your invention and Giggle, Inc. your corporation. And besides, I can't fund my Institute with money earned from a substance that I don't approve of. The whole point of my Institute is that I won't be prescribing teeny tiny pills to make my patients feel better!'

HE! was what was ridiculous.

How he wanted to suck his words from out his wife's and daughter's ears and spit them out the window, but he could not; they had stuck all over him and all over them.

"I sounded like a prig just now. I was disparaging your corporation, your money and your invention – your daffeine. As if you are the maker of harmful substances! As if money made the way you make money is bad money! As if I'm the purest in the land! And you're not! Because everything must be perfect for me or I won't play. Oh! Sophia, I bet I'm why you worship Movie Stars! Because they're so perfect! And perfect is what your Father adores!"

Though he could feel all eyes just about ransacking him, he couldn't meet those eyes. And though he spoke aloud, he spoke to himself, "Could I really think like that? Or is it my Ideals that like to take over and think for me? That like to keep me locked up, alone, every night, with them?"

And then his eyes met his wife and daughter's astonished eyes. "Ideals are my companions. Not you, Sigrid! Or you Sophia. And my Ideals are cruel companions. They're task-masters that like to hammer away at me. Pills! Daffeine! Show Business! Fathers! Old Chief! New Chief! Those are its nails. As if I, and I alone, could and must solve each and every one of these problems all by myself."

And though he could clearly see his wife's and daughter's expression, he went right back to speaking out loud but still to himself. "But I've gone over these problems in therapy so many times; I understand them and I still haven't been able to rise above them. Because no matter what I do or think, they refuse to leave. A bona fide psychoanalyst can't get over his problems! Imagine that! If he can't, who can? Is that why I sit alone night after night, because the great psychoanalyst is afraid to admit to himself and to anyone else that he's human?"

And finally, his eyes welcomed their wondering-eyes and then he threw his arms around the both of them, "Forgive me! Sigrid, you are so very kind to offer me your money. I … well … I don't quite know what to do or what to say. But you must know my feelings about pills but I should never've put your daffeine in the same category as them. No one has ever proven that daffeine does anything wrong to anyone. And I just made it sound like it does."

"Oh! Sigmund!I'm!so! relieved!to finally!hear you! say!that!I've always known! you couldn't stand!daffeine! even though you'd! never come out! and say so!" Gone was the weary, worried woman; never had she spoken faster.

And never had he, "Well, you're right!I couldn't stand it!But I love you!And that is all that matters to me!Sigrid, maybe now that we're!finally opening up!to each other, I can share my plans with you!I'm ashamed!that I'm only telling them to you now!I must save!the programs. And get the money!that'll be needed to save them! Because, believe me, it'll cost a lot of money!I intend to start fund-raising like IV used to do, even though I've never been an action-figure!in my life!"

But those bold words had a peculiar effect on his heart: it raced, rose and sank over and over again, as if it wanted him to stop talking; as if it recognized what his mouth was up to; as if it knew that it was his Ideals that were dancing around on his tongue showing off just then and not the-tried-him, the-true-him. Because maybe his heart was a realist that knew how impossible it would be to turn him into an Action Figure. And he fell back in his chair and waited for his heart to slow down and his Ideals to go away. Sigrid and Sophia soon realized their Thinker Statue was back, just when he was getting interesting, so they leaned back, too, and waited for the statue to go away.

And he waited, too, but not for more. Because more from him might just be more Ideals! And Ideals had no business describing anything like this.

His deepest part carried on for him; it spoke aloud but deliberately and very determinedly, as if how he said each word was his way of convincing himself he could do it, he could make it happen, he could obtain the unobtainable, he could do the impossible, he could be Ideal. "I may even reapply to the Insurance companies. But before they'll ever pay benefits, I'll have to prove our programs work. They'll need to see clinically measured studies, and I'll do them. And then I'll write very detailed reports that cite case after case showing what the patients are really getting out of the programs. The old chief never did that, but I will. I'll really have to demonstrate to those

Insurance companies that our programs help people before they'll give us a dime. And—"

"Sigmund, I like money and you don't! —"

'Another confession? This is like the part in the movie where the people are finally telling the truth!' thought Sophia. The spotlight had shifted to her Mother and now Sophia's head pivoted towards her.

Dr. Oomla was shocked into silence. *'Not money! Not now! We never talk about that! That's taboo ... to us! To me!'*

" ... I always suspected, though you never said this either, that you thought I made way too much of it. Well ... I believe that money is not my money, that money belongs to many people! ..."

The power-broker had returned. As she spoke, Readers, our ears may not have picked up what those two, Dr. Oomla and Sophia, with their ears, picked up – jangling-grating-metal and yowling-rolling-thunder and mighty-winds-that-could-level-trees – but their ears sure did. The Thinker's ears and his heart and his Ideals braced themselves for they knew not what. Of course, he and Sophia heard the startling thing she'd just said but what struck them first about it was what their ears noticed: where was her honey-tongue when she said it? And they silently wondered, would it ever come back? But after the shock of how she said it had registered, Dr. Oomla was back paying sharp attention to her words and their intent.

" ... You think I make more than my corporate colleagues. I agree. Let me tell you, receiving that much money made me feel very guilty. I invented Giggle. Nobody in that corporation could have done what I did, yet my colleagues do so many things that I never would've thought of, or even dreamed of, to market Giggle and make it so consistently good, and they needed to be rewarded, too. So I tried to be a do-gooder, too, Sigmund, like you; I proposed in the executive compensation meeting that I cut my own CEO pay in half and distribute it to all Giggle employees thereby putting an end to this unfair practice. But they looked at me not as a savior but as the living representative of the word no one in our village dares say. And did they inch away from me. But all I had to do was look around that meeting and see all those distressed faces to know why.

"Every person there was afraid that I intended to hurt the sacred idol of Corporate executives everywhere - the CEO's paycheck.

"Corporate executives everywhere must be dreaming of the day they'll receive that sacred idol themselves. A CEO's paycheck is to the Corporate executive what 'the thing with feathers' is to Miss Dickinson or what the 'Artiste' was to the old Chief or what saving the Institute is to you, Sigmund or what a Movie Star School is to you, Sophia. How dare I kill their dream? Ever since that day, I really believed those Giggle executives thought I was the enemy and had really become like that word. Because I knew their secret; the King is not dead! And neither is Versailles! They just have different names. The King is now a CEO, and Versailles, a skyscraper. Long ago, the King, and everyone else, knew that the King took it all, and that his clothes and his palace must drip with splendor so his entire world would reflect his magnificence. Minions, dungeons full of them, embroidered his many robes which overflowed with arabesques and blossoms and fruited-trees. His wigs were jam-packed with curls. His Versailles was over-the-top with lavish, gilded or-nament. But a CEO looks like one of us; it's only in subtle ways that he resembles a King. He may wear the same boxy suit that his employees do; but the employees' suits are assembled by third-world-workers whereas his is stitched with fine fabric by a first-rate-tailor.

"Oh, Sigmund, like mine are!

"With my stylist, and that closet of mine, which I know you hate, I'm sure you think I'm like a King. And there's another way I bet you think I'm like a King. His skyscraper is not gilded or flowery or lavish because nowadays, everyone knows that CEOs are not Kings. But his skyscraper is audaciously tall. Watch-me-scrape-the-sky tall. I heard you say that corporations that occupy skyscrapers can't hear the cries of the insignificant-little-ants that pass below their high-and-mighty-windows but the ants that pass below those windows can sure hear the song of that skyscraper - and that's exactly why corporations put themselves there - We-will!-We-will!-Crush-you!

"Well, my corporation is in a building like that. And my skyscraper sings that song, and the executives are awfully glad it does. They even want my, as they say, charming voice to sing it for them, Sigmund. And, I'm afraid, sometimes I did, Sigmund. But always remember this about me; I tried to do something about my stratospheric paydays.

"Now about CEOs: they don't think they're anything like Kings. They don't believe that as the winner they should take it all like that King believed! Of course, they can't countenance that nowadays, in our current environ-ment, in which a rich man gets one vote and so, too, does a poor man. But they do believe in never making poor men rich or rich men poor. Watch those $19,000-an-hour CEOs do everything they can to block their $7.25-an-hour employees from making any more than $7.25 - our state's minimum-wage. They're terrified that if they give their minimum-wage-workers even

$12 an hour, let alone $15, their companies would go under. And then watch those same CEOs never block their boards from raising them to $20,000 an hour. After all, there's no maximum-wage-law! The sky's the limit for them. Well, I never believed that, Sigmund! I wanted to give a significant portion of my salary and spread it out evenly to our lowest paid workers. I didn't want to be a wage thief!

"But to those executives, those CEOs, I was a traitor in their midst! A CEO wanting to share the booty! No wonder they gave me such a hard time! I was trying to take away their 'thing with feathers!'

"Of course, I didn't succeed.

"And, what's worse, I've kept all of this inside me. I didn't tell you. But I felt so out of place here with you, the do-gooder! And there, with those Kings in their we-the-people-clothing! And in the village, with those caring souls who work for peanuts at that noble Institute! And with those poor Artistes who have been so spoiled and so corrupted by Show Business!"

·∴C·∵

("Darlings," said Me, "I refused to listen to another word, and flew under my silken coverlet.")

·∴)·∵

Dr. Oomla's ears had long since stopped quantifying the honey in her riff because now it was just him and his mind who were in charge and who were listening to her. They heard her perplexity, her sorrow, her disappointment, her humanity and were thoroughly transfixed. She was afraid to talk to him. About her corporation! About her closet! About her money! But his heart just about stopped when he remembered at the beginning of her soliloquy that he had missed her honey-tongue, and he wanted to die of shame. Is that why his wife kept things to herself? Because to talk to him, that's! what she needed. Because to talk to him! she shouldn't work in an evil corporation! Make money! Wear fancy clothes! Were his sensitive, discriminatory, judgmental, connoisseur ears to blame? And his Ideals?

Oh Lord! He really was a prig!

Sigrid and Sophia waited for the Thinker to speak. At last, he could, "And you never told me any of this because you believe you must be perfect, and sound like music to talk to me? Because maybe you thought I thought you were perfect? And you know that you're not? Oh, Sigrid, for thinking that, and I know I did, I apologize. Incidentally, I am far from the do-gooder you believe I am. Because if I had been such a do-gooder, maybe I could have done-good and saved the Institute! Maybe I would've known that my daughter was up at midnight watching movies. And that my wife didn't confide in me because she didn't think she was pure enough. And speaking of perfect, I see your Ideals've been bossing you around, too, Sigrid! You've been living with them the way I've been! But they're impossible companions! We've a lot more in common than I realized. There's something buried so deep in us that we don't even know it's there but whatever it is, it's inside calling the shots. It expects us to be perfect. And there you were, feeling like a failure, all because perfect-you couldn't stop corporate suits from coveting the CEO's paycheck!"

"Oh, Sigmund, but that is exactly what I expected I could do. I'm ridiculous, too. And you know what else is ridiculous, I thought I was perfect. You made me feel that way."

"Sigrid, I am profoundly sorry for that! Thinking someone is perfect puts far too much pressure on them."

"Well, when I started working down there, I got over that, believe me. I didn't tell you what I was going through because I didn't want you to hate the thing I did for a living even more than you already did! And besides, there's a part of me that didn't want to stop doing what I was doing, in spite of the bad parts. My talent has given me power and money and fame and I like that."

"Well, I always told myself that you loved money because you spent your formative years with Aunt Hortense, Sigrid."

"And every one knows fortune is her favorite word, Sigmund."

"So, I'm right, that is why you like money! It is because you learned it from Aunt Hortense!"

"I don't know, Sigmund. I can't figure out if it's the Aunt Hortense inside me or if it's the me inside me—

·⋆☾·

("Hah, Lady!" said Lorraine, "Or the Me inside her!")

·☽⋆·

"I can't tell who's in control the way you can; after all, you're the psychoanalyst, you have radar for that sort of thing. I don't know where Aunt Hortense's influence ends and I begin. It always feels to me like I'm being myself. But does it really matter if it's her or if it's me? I know I like money a whole lot more than you do. But will you still like me if I do?"

What should he say? He saw her look at him; he'd better answer fast. He knew what he was supposed to say but couldn't say it. He even heard how he really felt speaking up loud and clear inside him; and if he said it he'd be in trouble. But just as he was about to say something, anything, a word that she just said stopped him cold.

'Radar!

'She thinks I have radar, then why don't I know where my Father ends and I begin? Or the old Chief? Or Sigmund Freud? Or when the Prig has taken over? Or my deep-dreaded fears? Or what happens to me when I hear music? Or remember my Mother's voice? How do any of us know who or what is really in control of us? I, the learned psychoanalyst, obviously, don't know and neither does she. So it's alright if I believe it's her Aunt Hortense that makes her like money. Or that big-city. Or some nefarious unknowable.'

⸱⸱⸱☾⸱⸱⸱

("Hah! Or some MeFarious knowable! Ya hear that Me, he found you out!" Lorraine gloated.)

⸱⸱⸱☽⸱⸱⸱

'I don't have to believe that it's really her that does! So I won't believe it!'

He was armed now and ready. "I love you, but I don't love money and I certainly don't like fame. But, Sigrid, about money, I make very little of that and, I guess, to you, I'm not a catch. And conversely, if you make way too much, to me and my druthers, you're not such a catch either. So, we're opposites. Except maybe not so much; you've been living alone with your ideals and so have I. Because maybe it's easier to live with the ideals in your head then to live in the real world with your real self where you see how hard it is to make even the smallest thing happen, let alone a big thing like that; how hard it is for everybody and that nobody and nothing is ideal, including me and you, and you, too, Sophia; and that everyone and everything is flawed, including each of us. "I'll end corporate greed!" "I'll make the Artistes pill-free!" "I'll be a Movie Star!" Now just try to do that in the real world. Ideals are cruel companions. They tower over us like so many colossi and make us feel like specks."

"Oh! Sigmund! They nag at a person, overbear on a person, obtrude in a person, get up into-your-face, in-your-ear—"

⸱⸱⸱☾⸱⸱⸱

("Uh! Oh! Lady!")

⸱⸱⸱☽⸱⸱⸱

" ... in-your-head, and never-leave-you-alone, chase-you-around-the-block, and are right there waiting for you when you first open your eyes in the morning. That's what kind of companions Ideals are, Sigmund! And you can't disown them."

"Sigrid, I would've loved to have known what you were going through down there. I would've understood so much more. I always thought you were doing exactly what you wanted to do. And I didn't dare interfere. We really do have to talk more. And that means all of us. Speaking of Movie Stars, Sophia?"

He turned to Sophia, who'd been following their conversation closer even than any Movie she'd ever studied. She was stunned to hear that her Father and Mother were more like her than she ever dreamed: they hadn't shared what they were up to either. It was like all of them had top-secret Midnight Movie Star Schools! And her smile hopped and her eyes sparkled so much, all she needed was Fred's top hat and Ginger's feathery gown. She knew what she was ready for.

"When did each of us turn into Greta Garbo?" Dr. Oomla went on, "When did we begin to shut each other out? Hey, Sophia, I bet you could say what she said a whole lot better than I could—"

At last it was time for her close-up. And she was ready. Now finally and forever she could show them what she'd taught herself at midnight and without their help: she lost her smile, threw back her head, got a remote, unapproachable look in her eyes and then sat silently until out on a single breath came ... "I vont to be let alone." Sophia had done that character in her Movie Star School so many times but never for a real, live audience before.

"Sophia, you sounded just like her!" And her Father and Mother applauded.

Ms. Garbo melted into a toothy, pink, bashful ten-year-old.

Dr. Oomla, too, was melting, *'What an ear for voices and accents she has! My child, my ears! With her Mother's vocal talent!'* until reality bit the preening parent yet again, *'And I never noticed? But of all things for a ten-year-old to say! And to say with such conviction! Especially words with a message like that! Is this what I taught her?'* He never wanted to hear those words coming from an Oomla again.

"It's okay to pretend to be Greta Garbo, but let's not really be her! Because look at what happens when we were her. We all withdrew. We all wanted to be alone; you, Sophia, sneaking into that television room so late at night to go to your Mov ... Acting School; you, Sigrid, taking to your bed so early every night to stress about your job; me, holed up in my library, fretting about how to save the Institute. We made ourselves invisible to each other.

"But we became invisible to ourselves also.

"Specks. We are the specks in the Village Van Der Speck. There we were, isolated, all alone, surrounded by the thick walls of The Castle L'Oomla and our thick skins, all of us too afraid to drop in and tell each other what we were doing and thinking and what was going on in our lives or how we really felt about things. Because maybe our fears were either so Goliathon-big we felt crushed by them or so speck-little we didn't even know they were in there and what they were doing to us. But, whatever, we were under their spells.

✦

("Uh! Oh! Lady!")

☽

"How many spells was I under? Having to live up to the Old Chief was one. And never being able to forgive myself for letting my Father down was another. I kept wishing to do what the Old Chief did but never could. Was I too guilty to try because wouldn't I have disappointed my Father yet again if I did the Old Chief's work and not his?

"And you, Sigrid, under the spell of your Great Aunt Hortense. Because maybe you were trying to become something you weren't to please her. Or trying to do something to please yourself which you knew would never please me?

"And you, Sophia, under the spell of a dazzling Movie Star, so you could dazzle, too."

✦

("Author, darling," said Me, "spells again! But don't blame me for these spells! And by the way, Author darling, didn't you say in the beginning of this novel that you humans can't be put under spells? You heard Dr. Oomla! If he says all of them were under spells, and he's a psychoanalyst … well … the defense rests!"

"Me," said Lorraine, "Not so fast! Because ya sure put old muddy-apron under your spell! But, remember this, ya didn't do such a good job!")

☽

"But that is about to change, Oomlagators! Let's break our spells! From now on, let's make a promise to talk to each other. To put windows and doors into ourselves, so we can look inside each other and step inside and stop for a while, for a nice long while, and visit. What do you say?"

"Okay, Daddy!"

"Oh, Sigmund. I really should've told you. I wish I had. But I had to appear like I was so on top of things, after all, there're not that many women in charge of their own corporation. I have an image to maintain. But I guess I didn't have to maintain my image with the both of you."

"Sigrid, I think I know why you did! Both Sophia and I've always been quite taken with your effervescence, your voice, your charming repartee. You must've known that. Maybe you were afraid to use that voice and to just be a vulnerable, scared, insecure, at-a-loss-for-words, regulation-sized human.

"And there we all were, pleasing and maybe obeying those invisible others in our heads! Our parents or some impossible dream!"

⋯⁜❨⋯

("Uh! Oh! Lady!")

⋯❩⁜⋯

"I, of all people, never really understood how much I, the great psycho-analyst, was under the mercy of what was in my head."

⋯⁜❨⋯

("Uh! Oh! Lady!")

⋯❩⁜⋯

"And Sophia, you, too, wanting to sound perfect and look perfect like you must believe Movie Stars are! No wonder you have such a hard time talking! Me and my love of music! Music is an impossible perfection for us ordinary-wonderfilled-humdrums! Which is who all of us really are, Sophia! But then there's Sigrid who puts the lie to what I just said. All I could hear was your near perfect voice! And maybe all Sophia could too? How you affected both of us, Sigrid! Because certainly Sophia and I were under your spell! You, Sophia, maybe more than I realized! What do you say?"

But Sophia couldn't talk just then.

"Hah! Perfect voice! Not anymore! My voice has changed. That city put it through the ringer. I was so afraid you wouldn't like it anymore, Sigmund!" And she choked but kept talking "It had to be so tough! And I did too!

"One minute there was just me and Mrs. Oomla's Giggle Pop and a few helpers and the next, Mrs. Oomla's Giggle Pop had generated over a billion dollars in sales and then it wasn't just me and a few helpers, it was me and tens-of-thousands and Giggle Inc.; and I'm sitting in my own giant boardroom in my very own skyscraper while all these corporate types are discussing "the product." And all those Corporate Executives around that giant conference table in that giant boardroom had formal business training, like MBAs and they were speaking their own special language that I never heard before. Corporate-speak. I didn't know what they were talking about, I am just an inventor, after all. You should've heard them. They said things like 'revenue durability' and 'risk diversification' and 'earnings stability' and 'product innovation' and 'second quarter diluted earnings per share.' They were using such scientific constructs to talk about a product called Giggle. If I hadn't been scared to death, I would've been hysterical. I was still tripping over the first words they said while they were twenty words ahead of me. My voice didn't help me there!

"But I was their CEO, I had to appear like I did know that language, like I did understand what they were talking about; because I was sure as their CEO, I had to have the upper hand. The way Great Aunt Hortense always has. I think you're right about me being under her spell. Because whenever I thought it made sense to, I would interject my opinion to make it appear like I did have the upper hand. But whenever I did do just that, it seemed, I wasn't talking like myself. But I realized a little too late who I was talking like.

"I chose Great Aunt Hortense probably because she is the strongest person I know. Some part of me must have figured that I'd better be like her. It's no wonder those corporate people didn't like me. You can't really blame them. They didn't know who I was. They didn't know I wasn't an upper-hand-taker. But I am not Great Aunt Hortense. I am not a prissy, haughty, snobby henpecker. That isn't me. But I should never've walked around that corporation talking like her. People in corporations have their own ways, but they certainly don't walk around henpecking each other the way Great Aunt Hortense likes to do.

"But even when I began to just talk like myself apparently they don't talk like me either. Both of you know the real me! I tend to talk a lot. And sometimes I break out into song. And you know something I found out, apparently, from time to time … well … I interrupt people when they're talking! And you know somebody told me in a performance review that I can sometimes even be a little overbearing—"

"Sigrid, I believe both Sophia and I could attest to that! What do you say, Sophia?"

Sophia could clearly hear she had an answer to his question but it wouldn't come out, it stayed inside. She knew she'd never be able to answer his question. But the odd thing was that's where she wanted it to stay. But what was even odder, she wanted to do just two things, listen to her Mother talk, and to herself think.

"Oh! Sophia, I'm so sorry—"

Her Mother really was sorry! She could hear it in her voice. But then her Mother started crying. And talking. But! Her! Tears! Didn't! Stop! Her! From! Talking! And as she talked and cried and talked, Sophia wondered, how come her Mother could cry and talk, and Sophia could only just cry and think? *'I keep what happens to me on my inside stage, but what happens to Mommy, she doesn't hide at all, she sticks it right up on her outside stage. Is that what I'm doing in my Movie Star School? When will I be able to do that in real life?'*

But on and on her Mother talked, oblivious to Sophia and her thoughts. And soon Sophia just surrendered and joined her Father who was listening to the tale.

"But don't worry, Sophia … They didn't like it either! I learned my lesson. I tend to talk about anything that pops into my head. I am an inventor, after all. So then I started talking inventively. But people in corporations don't talk all the time and they certainly don't talk inventively about anything that pops in their heads, and they sure don't like it when they're interrupted. Even if it is the CEO who's interrupting them. They speak corporate speak and they expect their CEO to speak it too. And I didn't know the language. But believe me, I learned it faster than I learned anything. And boy did I learn to think before I said anything. Which may be one of the best things I ever learned. I bet both of you will agree with that!" And Mrs. Oomla wiped her leaky nose on her sleeve, and on she went, full snot ahead.

·∴·(··∴·

("Darlings, she didn't use a handkerchief?!?" cried Me.

"Snot is on her sleeve, Me!" said Lorraine, "Snot on the Dior! Ya know, whatever ya did, Me, it sure didn't have a lasting effect on this one! So I wouldn't be so cocky, if I was you!")

·∴·)··∴·

"But I was just figuring out how to be a CEO. I started off as me-in-henpecker's-clothing. I was never comfortable in me-in-CEO-clothing. I used to wonder when was I ever going to be me-in-my-own-clothing? The clothes I used to wear were always covered in bark juice and green glop.

"Where were those clothes? I missed them. People in corporations certainly don't walk around covered in tree sap! And then I finally figured out, that if I couldn't be covered in tree sap, I couldn't be happy."

·∴·(··∴·

("Me," said Thee, "I hope you can hear what she's saying buried as you are under all those covers? Are you satisfied? Meddling in a grown-up-human's life. Look at what happens!"

"Thee, weren't you listening to how she just described Great Aunt Hortense? Do you want to be known as a MePecker? Don't you know what a dreadfully unattractive trait that is? Thee, I don't think you appreciate how much imagination it takes to do what I did. Because if it's not written down in the Dispatcher's Rule Book, you wouldn't dare do it. If I hadn't pushed Mrs. Oomla, the Oomlas might not even have had all this money to throw away on their Charity-for-Has-Beens? Or this Castle to run it in! So please! They should thank me! All of you should thank me. The Artistes should thank me. It's creatures like me who make life so interesting. And your life interesting, too. Without me, your life would be deadly dull!"

"I don't care what you say, Me. You're just pretending to be so sure of yourself! Besides I have great faith in Dr. Oomla. He'll get the money. You heard him. We all heard him. He's writing a scientific report so he'll get help from the insurance companies! And his report will be a good report that states precisely what it should!! He'll save the Artistes! You'll see!"

"Hah! There you go again, Thee, believing in the power of whatever is written down in a book! You really believe a scientific report is going to persuade a greedy, human, in-humane insurance company to part with their money to take care of crazy Artistes, after they've already turned those Artistes down! That's like saying there is a Santa Claus. We know there're Fairies but sensible beings everywhere know there's absolutely no Santa Claus!"

"Me, Dr. Oomla is very smart and his report will be very good. And besides, I don't care what you say, it was wrong of you to meddle in a grown-up's head. Look at how unhappy poor Mrs. Oomla was! And it was all because of you. That was wrong! Just plain wrong!"

"Well, Thee, like all true henpeckers, you really don't give up do you? So why don't I go over this again for you, Thee, and put it in no uncertain terms, the way books do, the way you like things to be. It was my meddling that made her so rich, so I don't believe I was wrong at all. And now that you fully comprehend that money is about to save those Artistes, maybe you should just give in and say sometimes two wrongs do make a right, Thee!"

"Wrong is wrong is wrong is wrong, Me."

"I much prefer to think of it my way … right is truly boring but right that is wrong and wrong that is right is delicious delicious delicious!")

·٠꠆٠··

"Oh! Sigmund, sometimes when I'd hear myself talk, I didn't recognize myself. I scared myself. My voice! scaring anybody? I used to receive so many compliments on it! You both would've hated listening to me!"

And now Dr. Oomla couldn't talk.

"But I was really trying desperately hard not to appear vulnerable. I guess I didn't even realize it but I must've been bringing that toughness, that same invulnerability home with me. I've always known that a person has to say what they really believe. But it seemed to me, when I did that, I had a hard time. I did keep trying though, but I was asking for it whenever I did. I already told you what happened to me after I offered to cut my salary.

"But there is something else I learned. There's an art to doing everything. To being a CEO; to being an inventor. I know the art of one by heart but I don't believe I've learned the art of the other. Though I tried. And now I know I don't want to learn. I love being who I am.

"But I really should've told you what a difficult time I was having. But I couldn't because my voice would've had to speak the ugly truth! Some great communicator I am! Hah! I couldn't use that voice to tell you what was really going on! And to tell my colleagues what was right and what was wrong!

"Is a voice still beautiful if it doesn't speak the truth?

"No! It's not! But it's about to fight back. I may've missed many opportunities before, but I don't want to miss any more now.

"This corporation hasn't really been so bad, if you think what we've received from it. Look at what we could do with this money! We could use it to benefit not just me, not just us, but many people! We could, by financing your new Institute, finally be spreading that money around to help many people. The Artistes need it more than anybody! And what a wonderful use for Giggle, my invention! But this time, Giggle would be making people do a lot more than just giggle. Remember what you just said, Sigmund, sometimes bullying is not so bad! And if I have to, I will bully you. Sigmund, that money is the money you will use to fund your brand new Institute. End of discussion."

"Sigrid, I— "

"End of discussion! Sigmund Oomla!!"

Abruptly he got up, said, "Sigrid, temporarily this discussion is over but …!" and then he began dancing around the room, stomping round and round, all jumbling-jacket, hip-hop-shoes, herky-jerky-tie and coin-toss pockets, as he made up another one of his poems – except, to Sophia's ears, this was more like what she heard when she, Bart and her Grandfather were driving about that big-bad-city – this was like that swagger-smack, trash-talk that came boom-boom-booming from the mouths of so many arm-swaying, strut-walking, pants-drooping, street-toughs – BUT this time it was coming from her! Father's! mouth!

"Pur-i-TAY? Per-FECT?

"Take this! Old Chief!

"And that! Dr. Freud!

"Mo-NEEEEY! from Daf-FEINE? Bang! Bang!

"To run MY?Programs?

"But before my?ARTISTES!

"even get to MY?Programs?

"They be filled from they-tips to they-tops with Pills! ...

"Ka-Boom!

"that they be gettin' from IV's Institute!

"So when they be comin' to MY Institute

"that -

"CROSS BONES SKULLS! AND HEAVEN FORBIDS!

"Prescribes!No!Pills!

"Pills already be in'ims!

"Whether I likes it or not!

"Ka-bing-bang-boom!

"That be all mix-up! Freudy Bones! Bones! Bones!

"But since whether I wants it or Not! Not! Not!

"My Institute will be run!ON and BY and WITH

"Daf-ffffffffffffeine!Mo-nnnnnnney!

"Then! Hey! Then! Hi! Then! Ho!

"The Artistes can pill-pop with IV

"and show-up chez-moi pure-moi.

"And I can fail and still do-good!

"And Sigrid can like mo-nnnnney!

"And be a Wife-Charming!

"And Sophia, a Greta Garbo impersonator!

"Who needs a speech therapist!

"Because we all mix-up, Dr. Dr.

"We be who we not. Do what we can't.

"Every-thing-every-one-all mix-up. Bing! Bang! Boom!

"Cause Perfect is the who who will never show-up.

"Can you?get by?with that?Old Chief?

"But, can I? can I? can I?

"Me? Mr. Puri-TAY-Preach, Dr. Think-i-TAY-Thunk?

"And you, you Billion-Dollar-Bewitchy-Bird?

"And you, you Little Miss Movie Shy?

"Cause Perfect is the who who will never show-up.

"Never show-up! Never show-up!

"Batta-Boom! Batta-Bing! Batta-Bang! Bang! Bang!"

Such names he called them! Mother and daughter turned shocking ever deepening shades. And soon felt dizzy from the precipitous blood flow, and since they already were that way from watching and listening to him, it was not surprising, when he danced them around the room, that they all lost their balance and crashed onto the floor. And then she and she and even he were giggling.

"Oh Sigmund, I can't tell you how long I've been trying to make you giggle!"

And her Mother couldn't say another word.

And then he let loose in yet another voice, with his plans, and now it was him and not his wife that spoke sweet and low, in bass drums and piccolos, and couldn't stop. And the serious look on his face that was usually there was completely gone.

"The programs wouldn't really be like your Acting School but would be just like the programs at the old Institute; the Artistes would write, direct, act and costume plays; decorate their sets; run the house; sell the tickets; and then we on the staff will monitor how the Artistes feel as they perform each of those activities. Exactly what the Artistes had done in the old Institute, we'd be doing here, in my new Institute.

"The Artistes would still go back to the old Institute to live and to sleep and for all their medical care and most of their meals but they'd come to The Castle L'Oomla during the day for what the Old Chief called Performance Therapy but what I'll call Limelight Therapy. And since you've agreed to my plan, I'll ask the same specially trained people who ran those programs at the old Institute but who were laid off to come and work for me in my brand new Institute.

"If you both hadn't agreed, those poor Artistes would just be sitting around the live long day at the Institute with absolutely nothing to do! With no way to express themselves! And they would certainly forget all about their feathery fellows singing away inside them because there was no Limelight Therapy to let them hear what was singing away inside them, and pretty soon our Artistes, who were so troubled, so worried, would become even more troubled, more worried."

But then he stopped his big rush of talk and suddenly his old look returned and he said very gravely, "Of course, all of this depends on whether I can get the Artistes to come to my Institute."

But the Artistes didn't come to her Father's brand new Institute. Every day her Father sent a shuttle bus to the Institute and sometimes only two or, at the most, three Artistes would get on it. And that went on for weeks and weeks. Her Father had become serious again and very, very dejected. But one Monday morning, about a week ago, eight Artistes got on the bus. The next day, one more. And the day after that, one more than that. Today, Mr. James had said that thirty eight Artistes had taken the shuttle.

And now that she was on the terrace and so close to those Artistes, those maybe Movie Stars, she couldn't help remembering - Her! Movie! Star! School! was helping them!

• • • THE GGGGIRL IN THE BUSH • • •

Because of her! those Artistes were on her terrace listening to their feathery-fellows.

And pow! Just like that she understood! There was something deep down inside her, too, that made her feel better. It was her feathery fellow. And her feathery fellow could hear! Hear voices and accents of all sorts of people. Hear the music of here. The music of everywhere. Of everything. Of bossy daffodils, of screaming-yelling-taxi-cab-drivers, of whiskey-voiced-moons and whispering-trees. And foreigners. And Movie Stars. And down-there, too, way on the tippy top of all of that, was a thinker! Who was going to stay down-there. And as for her up-there parts, her tongue mostly, sometimes a hesitating-stammerer liked to drive her tongue all around and get into all sorts of traffic jams and pile-ups. And that was okay, too! Because all of that put together was her! And it was music. Just like Louis Armstrong said it was.

And then she really and truly got it. Like she hadn't gotten it before. She got what the daffodils were trying to tell her. What the ArborTreeMeians were trying to tell her. What the Man in the Moon had said. She had to let the real Sophia out, too. Her shaky, scaredy-cat, stammerer had to come out, too; not just the chichi Sophia! Because the jimjams Sophia was somebody, too. There was much, much music in that Sophia. Why Louis Armstrong himself would've probably said to her right then and there, "There's jazz-singers, and jazz-scatters and when God heard you, he said to hisself 'I just made me a scat-talker.' "

'He would too say that!' She knew it and kept walking, and then she knew something else, something that was the most important thing she'd ever realized about her and her Movie Stars, *'I may not sputter when I'm them, but*

I sputter when I'm me, and that's okay. Maybe now I can even stop counting my sputters.'

And she proclaimed to everyone everywhere, "I get it! I get it! I finally get it!"

She'd promised her Father she would never spy on the Artistes in their Limelight Therapy. But this was the first time since the Artistes had been in their house that she actually heard them. Every time she'd come home from school, the doors were always closed, so she never heard them actually do their Movie Star School thing or saw it either. What good luck! Why these very people might be Real Movie Stars!

She crept back down the steps, slipped behind the boxwood hedge, got down on her hands and knees and crawled between the hedge and the terrace. Her ears, about to be full with the voices-of-Movie-Stars! her nose, popping with the bracing scent of boxwood! what a wonderful world this was! And then she saw—

The! Dirt! On! Her! Beautiful! New! Backpack!

·∴(·∴

("Now you see!" said Me, "She doesn't take after her Mother! So don't even try to tell me I haven't done some good after all!"

"Me," said Lorraine, "we're absolutely elfing thrilled for ya! Now, how long is it until midnight when we won't have to listen to ya anymore?"

Readers, apparently, on this their last day inside Sophia, it had come down to Me against Them. Every Fairy was heartbroken they had to leave Sophia … but not one of them was even a little bit sad about leaving Me. Me, of course, was making a point of showing how much she didn't care.)

·:)∴·

As Sophia got closer to the east terrace, she could really hear the Artistes, but as soon as she could see them through the balustrade, she stopped. Six of them were standing. There were others, but they were seated in chairs facing the six. One of the standing people was talking. He seemed frail and nervous and confused. When he finished talking, one of the ladies, who was also standing, spoke kindly to him, but funny like. Then another lady who looked like a beaky-bird said something cackly, caw-y; then the people who were sitting down burst out laughing but the standing people didn't seem to notice; then Sophia understood. This was a scene! A real scene, from a play. Sophia studied these talking people to see if they were Movie Stars. But they weren't. They were nothing like Movie Stars. They were ordinary people and not at all like the people she had seen in Movies. And they didn't seem to be acting at all. They were just talking the way people talk! The way funny people talked.

And then she stepped on a branch and it snapped in two with a shattering crash and the actors stopped their rehearsal and the nervous, jittery one cried out, "What in the #@((was that?"

Sophia was already half way to the terrace steps when she heard,

"I don't have the slightest idea, but it's coming from down therrrRRRre."

'The beaky-bird and she's close!' She didn't think she'd ever be able to slide across the terrace so she thought she'd go the opposite way. At last, Sophia reached the steps and, doing her best snake, slithered down them.

When she had gotten as far as the next to the last step, she saw shoes.

"It's just a girl! She must've been hiding in the hedges!"

Sophia's mouth dropped. She could hear each of her breaths, each beat of her heart, so her ears were working. Her legs picked her up, so she could stand; and she ran down the last step keeping her head low so she wouldn't have to look at anybody.

But then she heard one of the actors say, "Girl In The Bush, jusst let us know yoyou're in ththere next time." It was the jittery man. "We don't mmmind having an audience when we're rehearsing here at Nuthouse Playhouse! But next time, just tetell us where you are, soso you don't saahscSCcare us half to death. Believe me, you don't want to sasccare us half way to anything, in our conditions. Look up in the tree! See him? Ththaat's Man In The Tree up there, he's watching our rehearsal too! But we don't mind because we know he's in there. You coulddddda just bbbeen, you know, GGGirl In The Bush."

'He talks like I talk, and he's an actor!' She stopped and turned round so she could take a good, hard look at the jittery actor man. His top lip and his bottom lip bumped together to make a smile that he shook right at her as he pointed to a man waving frantically at them from a low branch. And Sophia waved back. She felt so good all of a sudden. She wasn't so alone. There was another wobbly talker in the world who also was an actor. And everybody on the east terrace looked at her and she felt shy but knew she couldn't stand there not talking. *'They like what I like! And they are so nice! We could be friends.'*

"I'm sssorry."

And now everybody was smiling and before she could even think, out came, "Can I really come back?" *'I said it! I asked for what I wanted!'*

But before they could answer her, the front door opened and out came her Father.

"Hello, Dr. Oomla! Are you coming to our rehearsal, too?"

'*Oh! No! He's going to kill me! I promised!*'

"How's the rehearsal going everyone?"

"Great! Dr. Oomla. Is ththis your daughter? Shshshhe was watching our rehearsal from down in the bushes. She can watch our rehearsal anytime she wants. She doesn't have to hihihide in the bushes."

"I'm sorry everybody! She's not really supposed to do that." And Dr. Oomla cast his eyes on Sophia. Sophia saw the disappointed look on his face and burned up. She had let her Father down. '*Daddy trusted me. He won't like me anymore!*' And Sophia turned cold then shivered.

"Oh, we don't mind! She's wwwelcome any time."

"Thank you and sorry for disturbing you. Shall we go Sophia so they can finish their rehearsal?"

He held out his hand and Sophia put her aching, stinging hand in his and then they walked across the terrace towards the front door, she in slow motion and him so so fast.

·∴C·∴·

("Lady, I says, 'There's never a dull elfing moment around here! On our last day, the day we have to scram, Sophia's about to get it, and we won't be here to buck her up after it's over.' Okay, okay, everybody, I started blubbering. I admit it!"

Be said, "In, like, our entire ten-year history together, Lady-o, we the Fairies had never heard little-miss-toughie, our sister Lorraine carry on like this. All of us joined her, and soon there was like this microscopic house a' blues wailing and sorrowing away somewhere on the tip of Sophia's left ear!")

·∴)·∴·

Dr. Oomla and Sophia reached the front door. Dr. Oomla opened it, ushered Sophia inside, and shut the door behind him. He stayed right where he was, locked his arms across his chest and looked Sophia squarely in the eye.

"Sophia, you gave me your promise! I trusted you to keep it!"

"I'm sorry, Daddy! I know I'm not supposed …" but then Sophia saw that the sad look had returned to her Father's face and she was the one who put it there and she burst out crying. And then she put her head down on her shaking shoulders … but her Father was staring at her, she could feel his eyes … so she kept talking … "to spspy …" But her words were covered in hot lava and her shoulders shook even more. And now her nose was dripping and she had an ache in her throat, and her arms felt funny but she must, she must, she must explain herself no matter what! No matter how hard this was for her! She couldn't break her Father's heart … "Spy. But these are real actors, in MY house. They could've even been real Mo … Moo … Moo …!" And her voice cracked! But she couldn't stop now! "Movie STARS! I had to see them. I had to …" and now wet stuff was just pouring from her nose. She was just like that song, all shook up, but she wasn't funny, she was pitiful. "And I need to lear … learrrr … learn so much if I'm ever going to be a Movie Star!"

"Sophia, do you remember how we promised to not keep secrets anymore. To not be 'I vont to be alones' anymore. To tell each other what we were up to. And then do you remember how you used to sneak down in the middle of the night and not tell anybody what you were up to. Well, Sophia, you're still Greta Garbo! You're still sneaking around and not telling us what you're up to! Did it ever occur to you to ask me? All you would've had to say is - Daddy, can I see a rehearsal? I would've taken your request very seriously. I would've asked the Artistes if they'd allow you to watch one of their rehearsals!"

"You would've! You don't mind that I want to be a Movie Star, Daddy? In spite of your sad Artistes, really?"

And just like that her Father sat smack down on the floor, as if lightning had found him in that hallway and, for a while, he didn't say a word.

Sophia knew then what his answer was: he did mind; he minded a lot. But this time, she couldn't just give up because a big, smart grown-up believed what she wanted was bad for her. She knew for a fact what she wanted was good for her and she'd have to tell him even if when she did tell him, it wobbled out of her.

"Sophia, what I want you to do and what you want you to do may be two different things, but what I've learned is that each person must follow their own heart no matter what their Father wants them to do or their Mother or their Great Aunt Hortense. And I just hope that my little girl will listen to her own heart and have the courage to follow what it's telling her! And not follow what my heart is telling her! Because you see, Sophia, what really takes the most courage is to know that you can't follow what's inside somebody else's heart, no matter how much you know the person may want you to, and even if you see that when you do follow your own heart you may break theirs. That's really what takes courage!"

"Does that mean, Daddy, if I become a Movie Star, I'll break your heart?"

"All I know is that I want my little girl to be happy! And that's all I'll say about that!"

"But Daddy, I'm happy when I'm a Movie Star, because I'm a MOVIE STAR and I can talk good and I have an accent and everything else. But when I'm just me, I stay me on the outside AND I'm only talking good on the inside but no one but me can hear me."

"Just me? Just me, you say? There's no such person as 'just me!' There is You and You are Sophia Oomla, my favorite little girl in the whole world. I'll take Sophia Oomla over any old Movie Star in the whole, entire world. AND, talking good on the inside is very important, because that means you get to think about something before you say it. PLUS when you think, you are putting your intelligence to work on whatever you're thinking about so that when you do finally say what you've been thinking about, you usually've figured out the smartest thing to say."

"That's what I do! That's what you do too! But I don't think Mommy thinks first!"

"You know, Sophia, there are two kinds of people in the world. There are people who talk a lot and there are people who think a lot. You and me are people who think a lot. Your Mother is from the other kind of people, the people who talk a lot. That's all. It's as simple as that. It's wonderful to be like us, people who think a lot. But there is one thing about us thinkers, we tend to be a little quiet. If your Mother didn't talk a lot, it would be awfully quiet around here, wouldn't it?"

"Yeah, it would be quiet, wouldn't it?" And then Sophia burst out laughing, and said, "Sometimes I'm like a mouse driving around in my very own space capsule!" And suddenly she got very serious, "But Daddy, do people who think a lot ever talk?"

"Well, I think a lot and I talk, and you're talking now, so you talk, too. So thinkers talk, but they probably talk only when they really really have something important to say. Whereas talkers talk when they don't have something important to say, they talk about anything, any little thing, and everything too, whether it's important or not. As soon as they think something, they say it. Whereas we think something and keep it inside ourselves for a while; in fact, we may even decide to keep it in there for even longer, we may even decide to never let it out."

"But, Daddy, everybody listens to talkers. Everybody listens to Mommy. But nobody listens to thinkers. Nobody listens to me."

"Your Mother liked to do all the talking, right?"

"Yes, and in my Movie Star School, I do all the talking."

"That's about to change. Your Mother is going to stop talking and listen to what you have to say and you're going to start talking and to make sure she's listening to what you have to say. That's called give and take. That's what we Oomlas are about to practice. All of us, including me. I've already started; I'm listening to you, right now."

"But what about if I don't want to talk and just want to think?"

"Well, from now on, you're going to have to figure out when it's okay to just think and when it's not. Whenever you begin to feel something burning up inside you then you must be brave and let it out. That's when you must talk. All people, including thinkers, must open up to the people who are close to them—"

'Hah! Some example I've set—'

"You had a Movie Star School in the first place because you wanted to be heard. But the problem is, you were all by yourself when you were in that Movie Star School and nobody could hear you. But I bet you think if anyone would hear you when you're a Movie Star, they'd sure listen to you then!"

"Oh, they would Daddy! They would! And you should hear my accents! I love accents, Daddy!"

"But, Sophia, when will you get to talk in your own voice?"

Sophia knew what the answer was, but she couldn't get it out of her, because it wouldn't budge. Because if it budged, a real live person would hear how she really really felt.

Her Father looked at her, and waited and then he waited some more.

And then he smiled. And he waited some more. And he smiled some more.

'I can tell him. I can be brave just like he wants me to be! It's just Daddy, and he's nice.'

"When I like my own voice! When I like my own voice, Daddy!"

"For heaven's sake, Sophia, why don't you like your own voice?"

"But I hear things Daddy, I hear so many things. I hear everyone and everything and anything. And then I hear me. And I like everyone and everything else better than me. When will I love hearing just me?"

"You know, Sophia, I'm about to bet again, even though I've been doing a lot of betting. It's a good thing you're not insisting I bet you real money, but here I go again, I bet when you feel that way, it must be coming from an inside part of you that's a little mean. And I can tell you for a fact that isn't the part of you that has the ears, because I can hear things and everyone, too, and that part of me is happy when it hears ANYONE—"

That's not really true, is it? Who has she seen melting whenever her Mother used to speak? Who has she watched over and over craving music dazzlements? Of course, she wants to dazzle herself. I'm the one who taught her to die to be a Movie Star. I made her believe that beauty, that artifice was all you needed! But, I'm my Father's son! She must understand what we Oomlas are up against.'

"Sophia, you're my daughter, you've inherited my ears, like I inherited my ears from my Father. And we have a unique sense of hearing. We three live in our very own Sound World. And that world is full of all-kinds-of-performances that play out on our private-sound-stages. So I can tell you - even if you don't know it today, someday soon you will - your ear part is happy, too. But about that mean part, that part is like Great Aunt Hortense ... everybody knows she can be a little mean sometimes, so let's call that inside meanie, your very own inside Great Aunt Hortense."

·:·☽·:·

(" 'Excuuuuse me, Dr. Oomla!' said Lorraine, 'Great Aunt Hortense ain't in here! Believe me, we'd know, because we wouldda moved out as soon as she got here no matter how much the Dispatcher ordered us to stay!' Lady, it was like Dr. Oomla poured scorchin' hot water all over us!"

" 'Lorraine, darling!' said Me, 'our very own Great Aunt Hortense has been inside with us the whole time!' I glared at Thee.")

·:·☾·:·

"And maybe when you start criticizing yourself, it's only your inside meanie! Now all you have to do is tell that inside meanie to stop being so mean! And then you and your ears can start having fun. And pretty soon, you'll hear everything and everyone like the music it is. Including you!"

Sophia looked at her Father. "All I have to do is tell that meanie to stop? That's all?"

"Yep! Just tell that meanie to stop, and see what happens!"

"That seems too easy. But I'll try it. But, Daddy, before I forget, can the rest of me be happy too?"

"Explain yourself, I don't understand."

"Well, can I get to see the Artistes' rehearsal? Because that would make all of me happy! Plus the Artistes already said I could."

"Now, Sophia, what else could they say with you standing there? I must ask them properly! And speaking of properly, tomorrow is your birthday. And there's going to be a big celebration, bigger than you even dreamed about and 'properly' herself will be here ... Great Aunt Hortense! She has forgiven your Mother for not being an example to women everywhere and for starting a Vertical Farm and for someday maybe selling Giggle Inc. and for throwing her money away and now both of them are speaking again."

And then her Father bent down and whispered, "What do you think, Sophia, how soon will Great Aunt Hortense let your Mother forget just how disappointed she is in her, though?" He winked and they burst out laughing.

"But 'properly' is not the only surprise guest who wants to be here to celebrate your birthday. Your Grandfather and I have been talking lately, and you know, we haven't for a while, and I think it had to do with what I was just talking to you about. About me following my own heart. You see, Sophia, when I was growing up, my Father wanted me to do something I didn't want to do and I didn't do it and I think I broke his heart, and that broke my heart … but now we're talking again, and I think it may very well be because he got to know you that time because he sure is interested in you and he seems to know all about your love of voices, and he can't stop talking about that … but you know time has passed. And he told me that he was wiser now and I told him that so was I and it's just wonderful because I can't tell you how much I missed the old coot—"

Now he had to stop.

"When he heard it was your birthday, he, and even your Grandmother, my Mother, my dramatic, Madame-Mother-Diva – that's what I used to call her – by the way, isn't she something Sophia? – well Madame-Mother-Diva who doesn't feel so hot nowadays, and your Grandfather - want to come to your birthday party. In fact, they demanded to come! And Josephine will be here and so will Antoinette Fifi Merree and Keys the Doorman and Bart Barone and Miss Kitty's niece, Margaret Finnegan and the pink flamingos AND your whole entire Fifth Grade class, including Mr. Snoggley. Sophia, it's going to be a huge party!"

And then his cell phone rang.

"Hello! Yep! Tell them to hold, I'll be right there!"

"Sophia, I gotta run! They need me in the office. An insurance company is calling and I gotta take that call! They won't even talk to me without knowing what Institute I'm affiliated with. So between here and my office phone, I have to come up with a name for it. Now hop along beside me and tell me what you think of my castle building."

Sophia ran beside him; they hadn't gotten very far when he stopped completely and asked her, "What about The Institute for Applied Creativity? Nah! Don't even bother telling me what you think of that one, that's no fun at all! I have to come up with a name like the old Chief came up with - The Institute for the Compassionate Care of the Extraordinary and the Always Interesting. Now THAT's a name! If only I could conjure up something like that. Oh, and by the way, Sophia, about this Movie Star dream of yours, promise me that you will let me tell you a few things I've learned. All you have to do is listen, and you can make up your own mind about what I say, because it's my job as your Father to make sure that I give you as much information as I can so you are a smart dream-and-heart follower. And the real trick to being a smart dream-and-heart follower is to learn as much as you can and to ask yourself tough questions. Deal?"

"Deal! But after I listen, and I learn and I ask questions, will I still get to follow what's in my own heart, Daddy?"

"Hah! A hard bargainer! Yes, you will! Because what stays in your heart, even after you ask yourself the tough questions, is there because it has to be. When your heart can survive the tough questions, you know you're right, Mademoiselle Diva Daughter! Okay, now what do you think—"

And then the front door opened and two bushy, blooming plants walked in, singing and talking.

"♪ Blue Skies ... nothing but blue skies will I see ..."

"Now here you are, at last, in the house! Have either of you ever been in a glasshouse before? Because you're going to live in the Oomla's glass-house! When you pick up your faces and look through all that glass, you'll see the sun and the sky. You'll meet your brothers and sisters from the or-chid branch of your family, the cymbidiums and the phalaenopsis and the oncidiums. Have you ever met orchids before? No, you say! Well, they'll be so very happy to make the acquaintance of such handsome creatures."

It was her gritted-over and soil-dipped Mother talking to and singing for the plants she was carrying. Talking and singing a mile a minute. In her mellifluous-voice. Sophia listened. *Her voice really is beautiful. I love it. I love hearing everything. And everyone. And my own voice too. My Mother has a high voice and I have a low voice. I have a voice like Madame-Grandmother-Diva. I have a distinct, dramatic voice. PLUS I can do accents!*

'The meanie is dead!'

Her Father was right! And then she realized something else he was right about. Her Mother! Her Mother really was just like he said. Her Mother really did talk just to talk. Because her Mother was singing and talking to her! plants! Talking. Singing. On and on. Non-stop. Back and forth. TO PLANTS! As if the plants could really understand her and were only quiet because they were waiting politely to answer her. Her Mother couldn't help herself; she had to talk even if the person she was talking to was just a thing and couldn't even answer her back.

'She even has to talk for people whose turn it is to talk. Like when it's my turn. But from now on, I have to make sure she lets me have my turn. Except for when I may not want to take it because I just want to stay thinking!'

And Sophia felt herself grinning from ear to ear because she knew that even if the plants could've answered her Mother, they wouldn't've been able to get a word in edgewise! Because if that's how she felt around her Mother, probably the plants would feel the same way too. If plants could feel. *'I Got it! – Talkers talk when they don't have something important to say, they talk about anything, any little thing, and everything too, whether it's important or not. As soon as they think something, they say it.'* And Sophia looked up at her Father; her Father, down at her; then together, at their Mother, and they both laughed out loud.

"Oh! Hello! Don't you like my plant song?"

"Mommy, I love your plant song, it's beautiful."

"Meet our two new houseguests who instead of carrying their bouquets are wearing them!"

"Here's one – The Castle BLOomla! Sigrid, come join us. I must come up with a name for my new Institute. An Insurance Company is on the line and before I take the call, I have to know the name of the Institute so that I can introduce myself as Dr. Oomla of The Institute BlahBlah. So fly with us and tell me what you think of that one, The Castle BLOomla? Not only do the Artistes come here to bloom, but the Institute has the extra added bonus of being surrounded by plants in bloom, thanks to my green-thumb wife. By the way, how is your experiment going, Sigrid? Have you figured out which of your fruits and vegetables would make it in a big-city vertical farm?"

"Well, so far, only a few are showing promise. It's so tricky. They would have to withstand the conditions that a vertical farm creates. So far, not so good. But I won't give up. I've been reading everything I can about it. And next week, I'm meeting with another vertical farmer, too, so I'll figure this out. Now I, of course, love the name Castle BLOomla but will an Insurance Company take it seriously, Sigmund? Nobody knows more than I do how strict these big corporations are, and Insurance Companies, don't forget, are big corporations. And a name like that sure doesn't come from their language."

"Well, I guess that would leave out The Castle-Boom-Boom? It sure has a nice ring to it, conveys the feeling of growth - the patients bursting - and it's fun!"

"I like it Daddy!"

"Sorry, everybody, Insurance Companies would never take that one seriously!"

"The Institute For Feathery Fellows? Yes! If it were a hospital for sick chickens! How did the old Chief do it?"

And he was lost again in private deliberations. Sophia didn't want to disturb him, so she didn't dare say a word. Even her Mother understood she shouldn't be talking at a time like this, so she did the same. And they fell in beside him as they made their way towards his office that had been set up in the back of the house.

They went past the room with the television in it, her Movie Star School, and there was Miss Kitty sacked out in a chair as the Irish News brogued on and on about the Emerald Isle, its inhabitants, its woes, its wonders. Sophia was just delighted because there was her Miss Kitty at home where she belonged. But then she was delighted whenever she walked by her Movie Star School. Especially with its new and improved television. And she had C Bigg to thank for that.

A few weeks ago when she was at his house rehearsing his new play, C Bigg had asked her to do some of her Movie Stars for him, and she did. But he didn't have the slightest idea who they were. She had to tell him. He hadn't heard of a single one and asked - where did she see these Movie Stars? And Sophia explained she saw most of them on her DVD player but some of them she saw on channel 15, the channel that plays the movies. And he cracked up. Those are old people movies, Sophia! Don't you have Cable TV? What's Cable TV? And boy did he give her an earful!

"WHAT'S CABLE TV?"

And he showed her. Sophia couldn't believe her eyes and knew she absolutely had to have Cable TV. And then C Bigg asked her, isn't your Mother like really rich? And your parents won't spring for Cable? There's no excuse for that! Go home and tell your Mother and Father that you have to have your Cable TV. Tell them you only know the old Movie Stars; but if you had Cable TV, you'd see the new Movie Stars, and then you could learn their voices, too. "This is about your career and your career is nothing less than life or death! You gotta stay on top of things in Show Business!"

But when she did ask her Father, he was dead set against putting Cable TV in their home. Her Father even knew what Cable TV was and he despised it.

Since even Mr. James was eager to have Cable TV, he did his very best to help her out with that negotiation. He explained to her Father that on Cable TV there really were so many new-style news shows where debates about many issues happened. And we do like our debates, Dr. Oomla. News nowadays is entertaining because news-shows are more like entertainment shows; and not only that, those news shows play all day and most of the night and not just a few times a day like the news does on regular TV. But the best thing of all about Cable TV, Mr. James explained, there are news shows that come right from my home country and from Miss Kitty's home country, too.

Her Father replied so quickly and talked so rapidly and looked so cross, his voice rising on each note, that Sophia expected that any second steam would shoot out of him.

"I've seen these debates because I've seen Cable TV. Their debaters are nothing but know-nothings masquerading as know-it-alls. And what little regard those debaters show for the classic rules of debate that you and I so respect. For one thing, they don't argue the way we argue. Their arguments are poorly reasoned; their wishes and hearsay delivered as certifiable, provable facts and are pronounced with such fury, a listener would be scared to death to point out that what the debater just said ain't so. As for debate etiquette? They don't even respect their worthy opponents because if they did, they might let them finish their sentences. And what makes that even worse, the moderators on those shows won't even care. In their debates, they'd never require that anyone finish a sentence. I bet they're sorely disappointed that their debaters can't rebut with their actual skulls rather than with what's inside them since those moderators know darn well that wit seldom resides in a numbskull. But then wit-less debaters do have the added benefit of making Cable TV moderators look wit-filled. Whatever would happen if one of those debaters turned out to be even wittier (heaven forbid!) than the moderator.

"Galoots locked forever inside a show-globe. They may be in your living room but they are not pinchable, flesh-and-blood human beings who are really and actually there breathing with you in that living room. So when you're looking at them in their globe universe, remember, they are small galoots, they measure in mere inches and are not free to throw their temper tantrums anywhere but there! But even so, they're dangerous because though they're locked inside a glass-globe, they still can somehow mysteriously slip into minds. And I don't want galoots slipping into any of our minds—

("It's too late for that, buster!" said Lorraine.)

"Mr. James, so much for debates on Cable TV!"

Sophia looked at Mr. James. A library book couldn't have been stiller. Or more hush quiet. But now she knew not to judge any book by its cover; now she, too, had attentive eyes. Mr. James, inside, was sore and disappointed. She glanced over at her Father to see if he'd noticed. But he was saying his much-too-much and though he may be looking at Mr. James, he wasn't seeing him.

"… The usurpers have taken over and the whole lot of them belong on the fighting channel where they might finally be forced to shut down their mouths, raise up their bats and take their rightful place amongst the other Punches and Judys, so that they all can lambast each other on any number of subjects. And for the good of all concerned citizens, let's hope that's where they go! Punch and Judy Land! Forever! So they might relinquish the stage to the noble and true debaters." And then very abruptly he turned and stared long and hard at Sophia.

She had seen eyes like that before. And heard language spoken uppity and bossy like he had just spoken, too. Had her nice Father turned into Great Aunt Hortense? But she had no time to ponder that catastrophe, because those eyes told her that this time he was about to say something important to her and she'd better listen. Or else.

"Ah! Yes! Cable TV! Television! The land of movies! The land of perfect people! Why do you want to live there, Sophia? Don't you understand that that isn't a welcoming land at all but an exclusive club that doesn't let just anybody in? Only certain people - the photogenic, the famous, the infamous."

And then it was as if a storm had blown in but only on him; from the look on his lips, his smile might be gone forever, and now those eyes were electric jolts ready to pierce and wound. And this time she got scared. But it was when he looked up and away and began to darken that air with his tongue, that she moved closer to Mr. James, who'd moved closer to her, too.

"Oomla, now look at what you've done! Your daughter wants to live where you, her Father, the connoisseur lives. In the land of perfection. Well, I've taught my child well all right, just like that song said. She's a veritable chip off the old block. Of course, she wants to live there, because isn't that where her Father's always wanted to live? After all, what kind of voices must I hear? What kind of ideals must I live by? What kind of television must be in my home?"

"But someday, Daddy, I'll be perfect, won't I, like Mommy and Movie Stars are?"

'I said it! Out loud! But it is what I want.' In a second, she wished she hadn't said it, because now steam really was coming from him; and in the next, he bent down and took her hand and she could see that he was trying to push that steam away, "Sophia, something must have jumped out of that show-globe and into you. So let's you and me pretend that we're not in the land where perfect lives anymore, but we're in the land where humans live."

"Can I pretend I have a shiny outside and a beautiful voice when I'm there?" She couldn't hold that in either no matter how much steam came out of him. She had to tell him what she really wanted. He was being honest, so she should be, too.

"Well, when you're in the land where humans live, you don't have to pretend anymore. We won't have to do anything fancy or special, you and me. It'll be easy. We might finally be able to relax. All the people there will be just like us, they'll be human, too. So when you hear one of them talking muddleheadedly, you'll remember that you yourself sometimes talk muddleheadedly, and you won't feel so foolish or so alone the next time you do. Being human means you have lots of friends that are just like you, Sophia. You'd also find out something else, something quite surprising, and that is this: that being human is a companion in and of itself. In fact, it's your constant companion. It's a faithful dog that'll follow you everywhere.

"Because when you're human, you always have something to ponder, like should I do this or should I do that?

"Because humans have mysteries to solve that perfect people never have: like is that person a phony or is that person a friend? A perfect person thinks they know the answer but a human wouldn't think so. Being human means you'll always have much to watch over and take care of and so so much to learn."

And he shook Mr. James' hand.

Sophia saw that Mr. James mouth was saying one thing; his eyes, something else entirely: this time, Sophia was certain her Father saw it too. *'Great Aunt Hortense'll go away and my nice Father'll come back and he'll let us have Cable TV after all!'* She could hardly wait to hear him say it.

"I have a daughter to raise who is just learning to like being a human, Mr. James. Though I know you just heard me admit that I have the same tendency my daughter has: that I like perfect, too. And that I am always trying to do the impossible - and in this case - controlling television. Which I'll never be able to control. I know that. But even so, I'm about to anyway. I want my daughter to stop comparing herself to those artificial people on television. I don't want her to think that what's inside a show-globe is life. Our Sophia thinks she must be perfect. Well, it was I who made her feel that way, and so did a certain virtuoso; Sophia compares herself to her and hopes to please me. That's what made her find that show-globe – that Movie Star School - in the first place. That's where she practiced her impossible - being perfect. I've done enough damage already. Though I know I'll never be able to control everything that surrounds her and now I'm just trying to do the impossible – again! - but I cannot allow Cable TV to perform its dirty tricks in my house. And we will all be the better for it.

"Better!? Listen to me. Didn't I just want us to be human?"

When she told all that to C Bigg, he said, "Sophia, what do you expect, your Father is a psychoanalyst, he analyzes everything! He's just like all the other people from this village. They've all worked in this Institute for years, Sophia. And we know who our patients are. Our patients are some of the sad cases from the entertainment business. So our villagers've always been just a little extra sensitive about anything having to do with that big bad entertainment business because that big bad entertainment industry had something to do with why the Artistes're here in our Institute in the first place. Why, Sophia, I bet you didn't even know for years this village voted out the cable industry. Just four years ago Cable TV finally got voted in, and that was only by the skin of their teeth, Sophia. 508 votes for and 506 votes against! I bet your Father voted no because he thinks Cable TV has hurt his sensitive Artistes. But Cable TV is ubiquitous! Sophia, do you know what ubiquitous means? To enhance my writing, I've been studying the dictionary. It means everywhere in the whole entire world, including our village. So your Father is surrounded. And you know what happens when you're surrounded, you surrender! So he'll give in one of these days, Sophia. He'll have no choice. You'll see."

And C Bigg was right, her Father had come around. But he did because of Mr. James and Miss Kitty only, and certainly not because of Sophia and her Movie Star School. He realized that the both of them, Mr. James and Miss Kitty, really really did want to watch news shows from Great Britain and Ireland; that watching those shows made both of them feel closer to their homes. And so they got Cable TV. But Sophia would only be allowed to watch it if an adult was present. But oh! C Bigg was right again! Were there movies on it! So many movies, Sophia, couldn't believe it.

As they crept passed her Movie Star School so as not to wake Miss Kitty, Sophia peeked inside. All that she had learned in there! All of the Movie Stars she had met, even if C Bigg called them old people's Movie Stars! How much she had grown up in there! How brave she'd been to even do it so late at night and all by herself! She'd be back. One of these days. But not at night anymore!

If she could find the time! No! When she could find the time!

·∴𝗖·∴

("Lady," said Lorraine, "wait til you and your Readers hear this! 'Did ja see that! I don't elfin' believe it! The old galoot himself. He's back!' ")

·∴𝗗·∴

• • • HE'S BACK! • • •

·∴𝗖·∴

("Who's, like, back, Lorraine?" said Be.

"I don't believe it! That slippery devil! I haven't seen him in years! In, like, forever!"

"Who's back?"

"The What If! He just flew into Dr. Oomla's head!"

"Uh oh! Lorraine, I, like, know why! Dr. Oomla is, like, having a dilemma and the What If couldn't resist!"

"Be! Lorraine!" said Thee, "the What If will be so disruptive! Poor Dr. Oomla! I wish there was something we could do!"

"Thee, I, like, know," said Be, "Y'all know I'm, like, no stickler for rules, but there is, like, no way we can fly into Dr. Oomla's head. We've never ever done that, and we'd better not start now! That the Dispatcher'd never allow! And we'd never be forgiven if they heard about it back home."

"Even I," said Lorraine, "wouldn't elfin' dream of doing that and I'm no lily-livered, pilly-puffer neither!"

"The only thing we can do is form our circle!" said Thee, "Maybe we can magic him away! This is too important! The What If can be such a mischief-maker!"

"Thee is right!" said Lorraine, "He can't mess with Dr. Oomla. Especially about the Institute!"

"Thee," said Be, "that's true, but not always—"

"Be," said Thee, "lower your voice, he might hear you! Don't ever give the What If encouragement!"

"But, like, lady-o," said Be, "Dr. Oomla and Sophia and Mrs. Oomla had finally reached his office and we had, like, no time to magic nothing. Sophia and Mrs. Oomla and Thee and Free and Me and Lorraine and myself could, like, only witness Dr. Oomla droop into a tortoise and drag himself over to his desk. And one look at him, and we, like, all knew that this tortoise'd never've outsmarted a hare and won a thing!")

···)···

Dr. Oomla's assistant whispered to him as she handed him the phone, "His name is Mr. Sentinelli."

Dr. Oomla turned and looked at his wife and daughter and smiled dimly, and they, hoping to reignite his confidence, smiled the noonday sun at him.

And then he put the phone to his ear, "Good Afternoon, Mr. Sentinelli, this is Dr. Oomla ... of ... This is Dr. Oomla of ... What If ... What If I You Can't ... NO! NO! What If You Don't!!! Excuse me, Mr. Sentinelli, this is Dr. Oomla of What If I Can't!!!! NO!—

"Oh! ... What If I Can! the new Institute that I have been corresponding to you about. Thank you so much for calling. In our new Institute, we stress two things to our patients, we treat, they act. We have found ... "

Later he told his wife and daughter that something inside him kept saying WHAT IF I CAN'T! WHAT IF YOU DON'T and he had a devil of a time getting his tongue around the simple word "Can!" But he did! He did! And now his patients, his Artistes would feel good about themselves when they passed his sign. Just like they did when they passed the old Chief's sign.

···C···

("Lady," said Lorraine, "we watched a very miffed What If rocket outta Dr. Oomla and then disappear in a blink. But in another blink, he joined us on our perch, making himself right at home. This is what he says, 'Well, Ladies, long time, no tease! Haha! And did ja hear? Since we last spoke, I had an Institute named after me! What do you have named after you? Oh! Diddle-y did you say? Haha! After all that time you spent toiling and troubling away in the fields of the mortals! And I'm here just a minute or two and an Institute is named after me! What if all of you considered another line of work? Well, got to run now and practice my ribbon cutting skills! Brush my top hat! Polish the "I'd like to thank all the little Fairies I met along the way!" speech. You know the drill? Catch you later!' And he was gone."

" 'I stand can't him!' "

" 'Free, nobody can stand him!' "

" 'Oh! I dig that name!' said Be, 'Thee and Free, who, like, cares what he says.'"

" 'Be,' said Thee, 'how can you say that?' "

" 'Don't you hear how positive it is, Thee?' said Be, 'It speaks directly to people who probably think they, like, can't do something and asks them a simple question - What if you can? It gets them to, like, wonder, and then, maybe, to act. Fairies don't need that but humans sure do. It's a good name! It, like, really is!' "

" 'Yeah, but even so, Be,' said Lorraine, 'the What If is right. What do we have named after us? We have to leave Sophia in a few hours FORelfin'EVER. How do we know Sophia will remember even a single thing about us?' "

" 'But Ms. Author,' said Thee, 'not one of us could answer Lorraine. And without realizing it, we moved closer together, with Me in the center of us all!' ")

As her Father talked on the phone to Mr. Sentinelli, Sophia and her Mother tiptoed out of his office. When they shut the door, her Mother informed Sophia that Claude had a surprise for her.

Even though Mrs. Oomla no longer needed Claude's services anymore since she refused to power dress, she'd grown very attached to Claude, and simply couldn't part with him. But it wasn't his styling and his grooming and his image making that had so attached her to him. It was HIM and those wild, witchy, wacky, wicked, witty things he never stopped saying. Nobody had ever talked to her like that. Mrs. Oomla couldn't care less about grooming and image making; she never did and never would. But she knew very well who would. The Artistes! So she had talked Dr. Oomla in to hiring Claude as a Costume Consultant for his new Institute. Claude was very expensive, and they could only afford him once a week. And he would not lower his price even though what he was being paid to do may have been the most noble thing he'd ever been paid to do. And his price was outrageous. But then Mrs. Oomla was a very rich woman and Dr. Oomla couldn't say a word about it. Though she know he'd like to. Dr. Oomla had had to concede that Claude was a luxury his rich wife could afford.

Mrs. Oomla had no idea when she contracted with Claude just how much someone else in her household would appreciate his special gifts. She quickly learned that Sophia cared immensely for clothes and glamour and grooming and image making and stylists. She was sure her husband would not have encouraged such a fascination. But it was keeping two people very happy. Claude and Sophia.

'Claude has a surprise! for me!' And she ran upstairs leaving her Mother a mile behind.

"Claude! I'm here!"

"Darling, so what happened with the Paku Piku Bag? Did they just DIE?"

"Marilyn, the best dressed girl in the room, told me that her Mother wouldn't even buy it for her! And then I told her my Mother's stylist got it for me, and Marilyn said your Mother has a stylist! Boy, was she impressed!"

"Oh, tell me more, this is what I live for, darling. Now wait til you see what you'll be wearing for your Birthday party. It's straight from Paris. Don't you dare tell your Father! The bill goes directly to your Mother and she won't even notice, it was just under Two."

"Two dollars?"

"Hon-eeee! Two Thousand!"

"Is that a lot?"

"Well, right now your Mother can afford it. Besides your Mother, after shopping in the city, will know she got off easy and your Father, well, he might require his own services if he should ever find out, so let's keep that under our chapeaux, n'est-ce pas? I mean with all those guests, all eyes must be on you. And by the time, I'm finished with you, they will be. And as my Birthday gift to you, I will be here tomorrow to dress you. Your hair, YOUR EVERYTHING! Down to your underthings! There is no detail that is too small. So be prepared! This is very serious. All those people! You simply must look your best!"

Her Mother walked in. Claude did his usual head-to-toe once over and blanched as he took in the grit and the outfit it decorated and then collapsed in a chair. "Oh, Sigrid! You give me pause! But I must take heart. There is one of you I can save." And his color returned and he sprang up. "So be it! Wait til you see Sophia tomorrow! And that is all I'm going to say. 3:30 Sharp, Sophia! And right to work! Sigrid, am I doing you, too?"

"Claude, I love you dearly, but I hope you never do me again!"

"Tres difficile. Give me strength. But at least, I've got one of you! Sophia has such potential. There is much to work with here! And she shows such an eagerness to learn. Now, scat, darlings, both of you! Did you hear Dr. Oomla's new idea for the Artistes? Beauty therapy? It seems Les Artistes feel instantly better when they step into this closet. Off with you, so I can complete my Mother Teresa duties. And then after that session, I must fit two plumpatoons! Oh! Listen to me referring to clients like that! Whatever am

I saying? When I turn a Blimpess to a Princess, I am patience and delicacy itself! What a world! What a world!"

• • • THE EVE OF HER ELEVENTH BIRTHDAY • • •

As Sophia lay in bed that night, the eve of her eleventh birthday, she thought of the day before her. In her whole life, she'd never had to face a day like this. A party where everybody she knew in the whole entire world would be there.

'But how will I ever be able to talk to all those people?'

And she froze up on her bed and was petrified.

'I'll just close up and think. A lot. I'm very good at that.'

She pulled her quilt around her, and was about to cover her head but stopped and instead rolled over so she could look out the window. And there was the moon. And she clapped eyes on it. And she smiled.

'Let dat you outta you.

'Okay, maybe, I won't just think and think the way Daddy does. I'll talk and talk the way my Mother does too.

'I'll let the scat talker out too. I'll let the deep voiced daughter diva out. I'll let the foreigner out. I may even let one of my Movie Stars out. I'll let whoever is inside me out. Whoever. Even if it is just me. And I will too. I will.'

And she looked at her friend.

She wouldn't let him down.

And she realized something else, too, *'There'll be other friends there too. Real friends. In fact, the party will be crawling with friends. And they'll be there to see me. I can't just close up and I can't just let me out, I'll have to let them in!*

'I'll have to let my Grandmother in. She's come all this way just to see me and she doesn't feel all that hot! And my Grandfather, too. I'll have to let him in. Of course, I do! He talks to me about acting! The way C Bigg does. And I'll have to let Josephine in! And Keys the Doorman. And the pink flamingos. And Antoinette Fifi Merree ... and ... everybody else in too. And maybe even Great Aunt Hortense! ... Well, maybe not everybody!

'It's a party. Parties are fun! And it's MY party. And I'll make sure that everybody who comes to my party HAS fun! So I will talk! I will! Plus I have to show I appreciate each and every person - which probably means Great Aunt Hortense too - for taking time from their busy day and even coming to my party. That is my responsibility, as the hostess. And if I splutter and feel shy, that'll just have to be okay. It's not a big deal! I'm tough! I've been to the big city! I've even talked to the moon. Plus

I'll be wearing the prettiest dress of everybody in the whole room, maybe even the whole village.'

Sophia fell into a deep sleep until with a jolt, she sat up in her bed. She felt awful. Sad and lost and so all alone. She must have had a nightmare, a terrible nightmare. She scratched her head because it felt so odd. She pulled at her ears, and dug inside them. But that didn't soothe the itch or get at the ache. Something was wrong. Something was missing. She glanced over at her Rapunzel alarm clock. It was exactly 12 o'clock midnight.

Readers, I'll have to tell the Fairy part this time.

The Fairies watched her from the window sill. Not one of them could fly out the window and off into the night, back to their home and country. They had done their duty. It had been hard. It had been wonderful. But they loved this little human girl.

And now they had to leave her?

And now they had to leave her.

⋯⋅C⋅⋯

("Readers, I can carry on, it's okay," said Be. "So this is what went down that night: 'Did anyone notice what she thought just before she fell asleep. It proves the What If was wrong. Sophia has a little of each of us in her. And a little of her Mother and her Father too."

"What do you mean, Be?" said Thee.

"Well, she's like her Mother because she is planning to talk and talk at her party! And she's like her Father too because she's going to think and think, too. And she's like you, Thee, because she said that it is her responsibility as the hostess to make sure her guests have a good time. Well, Thee, you are the most responsible of all of us. And Lorraine, didn't you hear her say how tough she was because she'd been to the big city? Well, Lorraine, everybody knows you come from the big city yourself and are quite proud of it, and you're the toughest of all of us. And didn't Sophia also say she loves parties? I've never heard you ever turn down a party! And Me, didn't Sophia just say something about wearing the prettiest dress at the party? And Free, you're the kindest of all of us, didn't Sophia just say she has to show her appreciation to every person who comes to her party, even Great Aunt Hortense?"

"But what about you, Be, how is she like you?" said Thee.

"Like, Be smart! Sophia smart, too! Say Sophia say, if I splutter-shy, okay I! Big deal, big no!" said Free.

"Thanks, Free. That was nice of you, as usual!" said Be.

"But, Be, come how Sophia shy splutter so? Like me is she?" said Free.

"Well, I'm not a smart enough cat to answer that question, Free. We'll have to ask the Dispatcher, Mr. Higgs Boson himself. There's probably like a million reasons. We may even know some of them. But the important thing for Sophia is that she's learned to accept that about herself. She's figured out it's okay. She's even figured out a way not to be so shy sometimes. But I can tell you one thing, we did good by her. We should be proud.")

·:)·:·

Sophia never remembered feeling so empty before. She felt like she had just lost her best friend. But she knew nothing had changed. Yet she knew something had. And she didn't know what it was. *I'm eleven years old now, is that what it is? Because I'm not a little girl anymore?'* She lay back down in her bed and wondered, *'In my Movie Star School, I never wanted to be a little girl. I always wanted to be a grown-up. But being eleven-years old doesn't really turn me into a grown up. But that's okay. I'm smarter. And I have so many ways of looking at things now.'* And she listened to all those ways chattering away inside her. She was wrong; she may be lonely, but she wasn't empty. She was brimming over with ideas and hopes and dreams and mysteries. She turned towards the window and gazed at the moon.

'And I have a magical friend!'

She wasn't so lonely, after all.

And the Fairies added their sparkles to her friend's luster and flew off into the night.

And Sophia filled with a silvery grace and soon she was sound asleep.

Midnight

Dear Readers:

Does this mean we are like belfried-houses chock full of the haunty-jauntys? So when you 'let dat you outta you,' it's not even 'you'? And worse yet, that that 'you' isn't even on your side? What're you supposed to do about that? And monkey mind? Fairy mind? Can't I have an adult mind where I control my own narrative instead of a creature-infested one that interrupts me whenever it has a 'mind' to? I do wonder what my own Emissaries were like, though. And just who was that inside my head that day who didn't want me to write! That built-in contradiction, that persona-non-grata's gotta go! But who do I evict, since whoever it is speaks in my voice. So who is really calling the shots? Where does it end and I begin? It's not my Emissaries; they should've been long gone by then! Mind-minx! I disown you! Although considering the strange-bedfellows in Sophia's Remarkably Small Place, could a mind be a contra-dictatorium? A multi-verse? But do I really have to live with those minxes even when they're giving me agita?

Speaking of contradictions, in this tale, a selfish creature did good. For the most me-first of all the Fairies talked about someone other than herself. (Could Me truly be what she said, a Fairytarian?) And here's one you may have missed – a well-meaning individual was less than ... well ... who do you think is really the revisionist historian? Me? or me? Maybe more like an unreliable source. I'm not 100% unreliable. I am 99.9% reliable. Which is still an A+. I just got carried away proving a point. As of the writing of this letter, I actually never published anything. But I needed those pests to believe I did because I wanted to tell this story my way and not theirs. You see how that went. I had no choice but to make peace with my tormentors and by my hook and their crook, you have a book in your hands. By the way, it serves Me-'you-so-looked-the-part!' right that she found the only unpublished writer in Writers Alley. Me judged a book by its cover and didn't notice on the first page of this one me pining away for a book contract

> *Sincerely,*
> *Esther Krivda*
> *(me, the author)*

P.S. In the letter which follows – surprise - Me 'j'accuse's' me! Incidentally, Me claims she was punished for her meddling, when that's not what I heard at all.

Reader darlings;

Persiflage! That's what did her in. Esther was confused as to the quantity of persiflage. Galore or not galore - that was her question. And that's what tipped us off. Could our Author not know her literary devices? So Thee did what Mary Hopping a/k/a Egleema Utrotly's said aliens do: she googled persiflage so we could find out for ourselves just how much is required in a story. And it's a good thing she did. For it turns out Esther did not know her literary devices! Persiflage should never be galore in any story. It would turn a story into 'a frivolous or flippant style of treating a subject'! Imagine Me! putting up with That!

And Esther would have us believe that humans cannot be put under spells. My foot! You met the Oomlas. Speaking of minds! You saw what was in theirs! Unobtainable ideals screaming at them night and day! Movie Stars! Parents! Old Dead Chiefs! Great Aunt Hortenses! What Ifs! Galoots! It's war in there! Parasite v. parasite! Host v. parasite! Vice v. versa! All of them trying to control the narrative! And they won't give up til one of them wins and gets you under its spell. A vicious little circle, darlings, if you ask moi!

So as if! Esther! And an As If is what I threatened to sic in Esther's Remarkably Small Place if she didn't concede the point.

And I am too a Fairytarian! I am an Emissary from the Universe here to help humans. And it isn't true what they're saying! I was punished for my meddling! I didn't receive just one day's punishment! I wasn't always allowed to go to Faree! It isn't true. Wrongdoers are punished for their wrongdoings and they are in this story, too. Why righteousness trumps all in my sanctuary of a story. I am not a revisionist historian! You can trust this teller and this tale! For I am a commendable citizen of the universe.

Sincerely,

Me the Fairy

P.S. Readers, Be insisted that we put some wise words on this novel's very next and final page so you understand why us Emissaries from the Universe are so very tres important. Sadly, these wise words were written by some Persian mystic named Rumi, and not Author Darling. Where was he when I needed him?

P.P.S. Author darling, disown, you say? Do you really think Ms. Esther, you can disown your mind-dwellers? Good luck with that!

Wise Words from Rumi
the Persian Mystic

"This being human is a guest house. Every morning is a new arrival. A joy, a depression, a meanness, some momentary awareness comes as an unexpected visitor. Welcome and entertain them all! ... treat each guest honorably. The dark thought, the shame, the malice, meet them at the door laughing, and invite them in. Be grateful for whoever comes, because each has been sent as a guide from beyond."

Mr. Rumi

Acknowledgments

I thank my lucky stars and my Louis-Armstrong-moon that Patricia Dunn from the Writing Institute at Sarah Lawrence read the first draft of this novel because she got it. She understood that to tell the story I was really telling - the story of what goes on in peoples' minds - I would need a lot of narrators. She encouraged me to refine it and keep going. She liked my fairies; she wasn't bothered that I was a character in my own novel; she didn't think five fairies were four fairies, or even five fairies, too many. So that's what I did, I kept at it even when some readers of later drafts wanted me out of the novel and the fairies gone. I'd remember what Ms. Dunn said, and I'd keep going. Thank you so much, Ms. Dunn!

Special thanks to BB, whose belief in me keeps me going; and to my family, friends and co-workers, who've been waiting patiently for me to please finish the story so that they could read it; to KR who made a very clever observation around his Great-Aunt and which he's given me his kind permission to use. And to - MF, WC, CD, WS, MH - who teach me so much when I read even one of their sentences. And, lastly, to MJK – if only you could've landed in the Institute for the Compassionate Care of the Extraordinary and the Always Interesting.

Bio

Esther Krivda lives in Spuyten Duyvil, New York. This is her first novel.

www.estherkrivda.com

www.wobblehillpress.com